MICHAEL M

The GALLERY

Macdonald

A Macdonald Book

First published in Great Britain in 1991 by
Macdonald & Co (Publishers) Ltd
London & Sydney

British Library Cataloguing in Publication Data

Molloy, Michael 1940–
The gallery.
I. Title
823.914 [F]

ISBN 0-356-19192-3

Photoset in North Wales by
Derek Doyle & Associates, Mold, Clwyd.
Printed and bound in Great Britain by
BPCC Hazell Books
Aylesbury, Bucks, England
Member of BPCC Ltd.

Macdonald & Co (Publishers) Ltd
Orbit House
1 New Fetter Lane
London EC4A 1AR
A member of Maxwell Macmillan Pergamon Publishing Corporation

The GALLERY

CHAPTER ONE

New York, spring 1933

James Gideon stood in the narrow confines of his hotel room and examined the last possessions of any worth that he owned: a pair of heavy gold cufflinks that glowed in the palm of his hand. He weighed them for a moment, as if trying to assess their value, before placing them in his waistcoat pocket. Then he crossed to the open window, where he could just see a narrow strip of 42nd Street half-framed by the entrance of the alley. Hurrying crowds of people and traffic streamed in both directions, the glittering automobiles reflecting the neon lights that shone in the gathering gloom. A gust of wind that smelt of rain blew through the alley and helped him to make up his mind; he needed better shoes and a coat; the cufflinks would have to go.

He left the room and, ignoring the elevator, walked down the two flights of stairs to the lobby. An old woman was swabbing the chipped marble floor and Gideon could feel the wet surface through the paper-thin soles of his shoes. He had almost reached the door when a voice from the reception desk called, 'Hey, buddy.' The desk clerk was waving a podgy hand at him. As Gideon approached, he held out a letter and returned to his newspaper.

The handwriting on the envelope was familiar, but not the stamps. Inside was a single sheet of hotel stationery headed 'Imperial Hotel, Rangoon' and two well-creased five-pound notes. Like all communications from his father, the message was enigmatic and slightly inaccurate.

Dear James,
I received your letter. Sorry the play closed. Money is short at the moment; life is in turmoil. This will have to do for your twenty-first

1

birthday present. Pity we did not spend it together. Your mother is in Australia.

Good luck, Frank.

Walking the short distance to the pawn-shop, Gideon considered his father's letter. It did not surprise him that he had got his age wrong; his birthday was still some months away, and Frank had always been vague about dates. But why was life in turmoil, and what was his mother doing in Australia?

He shrugged as he entered the shop, and put the mystery away. The dry little man behind the grille looked up, and Gideon held out one of the five-pound notes. 'Will you change this for me, Mr Casey?'

The pawnbroker held it up to the light briefly and said, 'I'll give you fifteen dollars for it.'

Gideon nodded, and fished in his pocket for a wad of tickets. 'I'd like to redeem my hat, my mackintosh and the black shoes.'

While he put them on, the pawnbroker said, 'Are you working again?' Gideon shook his head. Casey sighed. 'You should go into a regular business.'

'I can't do anything but act, I'm afraid,' Gideon replied, and with a quick tug adjusted the wide brim of his hat.

'Well, you certainly look like an actor,' Mr Casey said.

The doorbell tinkled behind Gideon as he stepped on to the sidewalk. The rain was now falling with tropical intensity, bouncing off the ground. He did not want to return to the depressing squalor of his hotel room. He glanced at the contents of the next-door shop window; artist's equipment was laid out in neat rows. Gideon studied the brushes and paint tubes for a moment and then pushed the door open.

The elegant premises of the Lowel Gallery, which stood on Fifth Avenue, roughly half-way between Tiffany's and St Patrick's Cathedral, drew characteristics from both its distinguished neighbours. The hushed showrooms invited visitors to gaze at the pictures on the walls with a reverence both for their quality and for the prices they commanded.

Two men stood by the wide rain-streaked window speaking softly in English. Although their accents were faultless, their conversation could just as easily have been conducted in most of the European languages. Both wore dark beautifully tailored clothes, but the

2

similarity ended there. The shorter and older of the pair was so portly that his stomach protruded like the prow of a ship. As he spoke, he would occasionally reach up and brush his spade-shaped beard with the back of his hand. The other, tall and dark, kept his hands in the pockets of his jacket, listening attentively, his head tilted so that his chin touched a wide bow tie.

The older man paused and consulted a pocket watch. 'It's almost five; they will be here soon. Whitney-Ingram is always punctual.'

'Who will be responsible for the authentication?' his companion asked.

'Sir Julian Nettlebury.'

'Julian? I didn't know he was here.'

The portly man nodded. 'He's employed for this trip by Anthony Strange. They are related in some way; when I first knew Strange in Paris, he used to mention it constantly. Now he's so successful he seems to have forgotten.' He looked up at the taller man. 'You and Strange don't get on, do you?'

'We've clashed occasionally. It's nothing serious. I do like Nettlebury, though.'

The portly man nodded again. 'Yes, he is a good man. A shame about his pictures . . . ' He spoke as sympathetically as if they were discussing an illness. 'Still, he is the definitive expert on the Flemish School.' He leaned forward and peered through the window. 'Ah, they are here.'

Across the rain-swept sidewalk a black chauffeur-driven automobile had drawn to the kerb. Three men were emerging from it. The first, a commanding figure, strode towards the entrance of the gallery, ignoring the rain. The second, slim and dark, hurried to catch him up. The third was a few steps behind.

The leading member of the group opened the door of the gallery, approached the portly man, and stood with bony knuckles resting on narrow hips. The surroundings did not intimidate Stanford Whitney-Ingram, who leaned forward and spoke in a loud rasping voice. 'So, Piet, have you got my paintings?'

Piet Liebe half-bowed and stroked his beard. 'All ready, Stanford. May I introduce Laszlo Vasilakis? He was kind enough to bring the pictures from Amsterdam.' Whitney-Ingram offered his hand briefly. It felt like bone china to Vasilakis. Liebe gestured to the other men. 'You know Laszlo.'

Both nodded, and Anthony Strange said, 'I don't think Mr Vasilakis' presence is necessary.'

Whitney-Ingram waved a hand. 'He can stay if he wants to. Let's get on with it.'

Liebe led them through the showrooms of the gallery to a small windowless room at the rear, empty except for three paintings standing on easels. All portrayed women of the sixteenth century going about their household duties.

Whitney-Ingram gave them a cursory glance and then gestured to Sir Julian Nettlebury. Attention focused on the slightly built figure while he examined the paintings. After some time he nodded. 'Lucas Van Leyden, Anthonis Mor and Jan Van Scorel.'

'There's no question?' Whitney-Ingram asked sharply.

Nettlebury slowly shook his head. 'None, although the Van Leyden has been badly restored.'

Whitney-Ingram nodded to himself. 'And you'll write the necessary essays to accompany them?'

'Of course.'

The old man turned to Liebe. 'Have them delivered to my home.' He started for the door, accompanied by Strange, and then turned to Nettlebury. 'Are you coming with us?'

'Thank you, no. I want to look at the other paintings here.'

When Whitney-Ingram and Strange reached the entrance, the old man said, 'I want you to come to dinner tonight; there's someone you should meet.' He thought for a moment and added, 'Bring Nettlebury.'

Strange said, 'I'm afraid Sir Julian has other plans this evening. He has his two young daughters with him.'

Whitney-Ingram nodded. 'Well, he must please himself.' He made for his automobile, leaving Anthony Strange in the driving rain.

Laszlo Vasilakis and Piet Liebe sat at a table near the entrance of the Hungarian Café. They were lighting cigars while a waiter cleared away the remains of their meal. When Liebe was satisfied with the way his cigar burned, he addressed his companion. 'So, has your trip been successful?'

Vasilakis shrugged. 'I sold the five pictures I brought over.'

Liebe took the cigar from his mouth. 'And you don't mind taking this back for me?' He patted a large parcel that was lying on the table.

Vasilakis nodded. 'I should be delighted.'

Remembering something, the portly little man reached into his pocket and produced an invitation. 'By the way, I've been meaning to give you this.' He passed the card across the table.

4

Vasilakis read the inscription. 'Mueller?' he said. 'I've not heard of him.'

Liebe drew on his cigar again before he answered. 'Very wealthy, from the middle west. He's going to London to put together an Anglo-German collection of paintings. In the interests of political unity between the two countries, or so I am told.'

Vasilakis raised his eyebrows. 'What does that mean?'

Liebe shrugged. 'You're sailing on the same ship. You'll have plenty of time to find out.'

Vasilakis put the invitation away. 'Would you care for another brandy?' he asked.

Liebe regretfully shook his head. 'I must be on my way. I have an early start in the morning,' he said, rising to his feet and picking up his raincoat from the back of a nearby chair. They embraced briefly as they said their goodbyes.

When Liebe had departed, Laszlo Vasilakis picked up a German newspaper he had left with the package. Before beginning to read, he glanced around the half-empty restaurant.

Apart from a thickset couple and their two equally stolid daughters at a table near by, who were eating their way with deliberation through a seemingly endless succession of courses, the rest of the diners crowded the far end of the café. Thick blue cigarette smoke hung in the yellow light and was reflected from the engraved glass mirrors that lined the room.

Laszlo enjoyed a sudden sense of well-being. Reaching out, he touched the thick bundle wrapped in heavy brown wrapping paper. Then he drank the rest of his brandy and gestured with the empty glass towards the elderly waiter, who wore a long snowy apron over his loose-fitting evening clothes. The man took a bottle from the copper-topped bar and shuffled across the mosaic marble floor seamed with ancient cracks. As he reached Laszlo's table, he rested one papery hand on the back of a bentwood chair and silently poured more brandy. When he moved away, another figure took his place.

Laszlo's livelihood depended to a great extent on his powers of observation. Before the newcomer spoke, he had already taken in the quality of his clothes and his well-shaped features. A lock of fair hair fell on to the slender young man's forehead; he brushed it aside with a combing gesture. Laszlo saw that he was carrying a pad of cartridge-paper.

The newcomer noticed the German newspaper Laszlo held and spoke in that language. His voice was deep, with traces of another accent. 'May I draw your portrait?' he asked without smiling.

'To what purpose?' Laszlo asked in English.

The young man smiled, and replied in the same language, 'If you like it, you can buy it from me for five dollars.' He was unmistakably British, of the type other nations imagined spent their lives on carefully tended lawns, waiting in permanent anticipation for games of tennis and cricket.

Laszlo considered the youth's proposal briefly, and his good mood prevailed. 'Five dollars if I like the drawing.' He took another swallow from his brandy and settled back in his chair.

The young man sat down and produced a crayon from his pocket. He held it in his left hand and began to sketch with swift assurance.

'Is this the only work you do?' Laszlo asked after a few minutes.

The young man smiled again without taking his eyes from the drawing. 'The play I was in closed two months ago,' he said drily.

'You're an actor?' Laszlo said with some surprise.

The youth nodded. Laszlo felt a slight sense of disappointment. He had begun his task with such confidence that Laszlo had thought he might be presented with a drawing that would be half-way competent. He took another sip of brandy and resigned himself to the eventual outcome.

'Almost finished,' the youth said. After a few more minutes he tore the sheet from the pad and handed it over.

Laszlo glanced down at the drawing without much interest and was astonished. The man had captured him with extraordinary accuracy. The eyes that slanted under the broad creased forehead, the thick wavy hair like black wire, his prominent bony nose, full-lipped mouth and square jawline, the slope of his shoulders under the dark double-breasted suit and the delicate, almost feminine, hands that held the brandy glass and newspaper. All were there, portrayed with masterly skill, but it did not seem possible for it to be the work of this young man. The style and execution of the drawing were unmistakably those of Toulouse-Lautrec. Laszlo studied the portrait for some time, as though trying to guess how the conjuring trick had been done.

'Is it worth five dollars?' the young man asked eventually.

Laszlo glanced up into his smiling face. He took the money from his pocket and laid it on the table. 'Certainly,' he replied. 'Would you care for a drink?' He waved to gain the attention of the waiter before the artist could answer.

'Thank you,' he replied, 'but if it's all the same to you, I'd rather have something to eat.'

'Have both,' said Laszlo. A menu was produced, and when the order was taken, he sat back and studied the drawing again.

'What's your name? And do you always draw in this style?'

'James Gideon,' he replied. 'I can draw in any style,' he said casually. 'It's just a trick.'

'How did you learn it?'

Gideon shrugged again and looked with greater interest at the plate of smoked duck the waiter was placing in front of him. 'I had a German governess who was keen on art,' he said between mouthfuls of the food. 'She had a collection of books full of drawings by famous artists. I used to copy them to make her happy.'

Laszlo watched the young man demolish his meal. 'And you say you can draw in any style?' he repeated when the duck was finished.

Gideon nodded. Without replying, he pushed away the empty plate. Then he took a fountain pen from his pocket, picked up the pad again, glanced at the family who were still engrossed in their gargantuan feast and began to draw. After a few minutes he laid the pen aside, dipped his forefinger into his glass of red wine and rubbed it over the surface of the paper. Finally he gave a frown of satisfaction and passed the pad to Laszlo. This time, instead of the bold lines of his own portrait, the group at the next table had been depicted in chiaroscuro. Gideon had used the wine to produce the effect of light and deep shadow.

'Good God! Daumier!' Laszlo said almost under his breath.

'That's right,' Gideon said cheerfully, and stood up. He pointed at the new drawing. 'You can keep that one for the dinner,' he said. 'Now I'd better try my luck elsewhere.'

Usually Laszlo was a cautious man, given to brooding before he made commitments, but he had already decided what he was going to do. 'Please, sit down. Have another drink. There's something else I want to ask you.' He felt a small surge of pleasure when Gideon took his seat again. He poured more wine from the bottle on the table and picked up his own brandy before he spoke once more. 'Why did you become an actor?'

Gideon thought for a few moments. 'My mother and father are actors. It seemed the natural thing to do.'

'Have you ever considered another profession?'

Gideon laughed. 'We're in the middle of a Depression,' he answered. 'There's rather a shortage of openings for unemployed actors!'

It was Laszlo's turn to shrug. 'Chaos brings opportunity sometimes,' he said easily. 'Take my business; things have never been better.'

'What do you do?' Gideon asked. 'Run a soup kitchen?'

As if to counterpoint his words, the door of the café opened and an unshaven, rain-soaked man stood in the entrance. The gaunt figure wore a ragged top-coat and carried a tray of apples. The other people in the restaurant turned away to banish the image from their minds, and a waiter walked forward and waved the man away.

'I buy and sell things,' Laszlo continued.

'Like him,' Gideon nodded to where the man had stood in the doorway.

Laszlo smiled sadly. 'He only has apples,' he answered. 'I sell people dreams.'

'Dreams?' Gideon repeated. 'What kinds of dreams?' When the older man sat forward in his chair, Gideon could feel his sudden intensity.

'My friend, I am called Laszlo Vasilakis. I am thirty years old and I make my living buying and selling works of art. If I teach you what I know, together we can make our fortunes.'

There was a long pause while Gideon considered his words. 'Where would we make these fortunes?'

Laszlo relaxed. He knew when a customer was interested. 'I work mostly in London,' he answered, 'but there is a great deal of travel. Would that cause you any difficulty?'

Gideon shook his head. 'No. I'm free as a bird.'

'And would your parents object if you were to give up your career on the stage?'

He laughed. 'My father is touring the British Empire with a theatrical company, playing Romeo to mining engineers and coffee planters.'

'What about your mother?' Laszlo asked.

'She was Juliet until recently,' Gideon said lightly. 'Now she appears to have gone to Australia.'

'How old are you?'

'I'm twenty.' Gideon cocked his head to one side. 'Tell me, what nationality are you?'

8

Laszlo gave a half-smile. 'See if you can guess.'

Gideon glanced around the café. 'Hungarian?' he asked eventually.

Laszlo wagged a finger. 'You are judging me by my accent,' he answered in a mock-serious voice. 'In fact, I am Irish.'

'Irish?' Gideon repeated.

'My father was Hungarian; he came to Dublin and set up as an antiquarian bookseller. Then he married my mother, whose maiden name was Flynn. After I was born they moved back to Budapest, where I went to school. They returned to Dublin after the war and I claimed my Irish nationality.' He tapped the two drawings in front of him. 'Like your pictures, I am not what I seem to be.'

Gideon thought for a moment. 'Tell me,' he said, 'why do you believe I'll be good at this work?'

Laszlo waved to the waiter to bring them more drinks before he answered. When their glasses were refilled, he gestured towards the other people in the restaurant. 'When someone is about to buy a painting, they often need reassurance. After all, what is it, really, they think. A collection of wood, canvas and pigments of colour. At that moment they need confirmation. You could give them that.'

'How do you know?'

Laszlo drank some of his brandy. 'You have a certain quality that saints and the very best confidence tricksters possess.'

'Can you describe it?' Gideon asked.

'An equal mixture of innocence and integrity.'

Gideon considered this. 'And is that enough to make me a good salesman?'

Laszlo pointed to the drawings. 'You sold me a picture you hadn't even drawn.'

'But you didn't pay for it until it was finished.'

Laszlo shook his head. 'No, I had bought it the moment you spoke to me.'

'Why?'

'You took your time before you smiled.'

As Gideon laughed, he caught sight of the apple-seller through the outside window of the restaurant. 'Excuse me for a moment,' he said, and went to the doorway.

Laszlo watched him talking to the man. 'What did you give him?' he asked when Gideon returned.

'The five dollars,' Gideon answered.

'I thought you had no money?'

9

Gideon hesitated before he spoke again. 'I don't, now. How would I get to London?'

Laszlo tapped his chest. 'I am sailing on the *Mauretania* tomorrow . . . I can afford another ticket. Are you coming with me?'

Gideon looked through the window at the torrential rain. 'Why not?' he said finally. 'It would be pleasant to get back to some English weather.'

Erich Mueller sat back, exhaled cigar smoke and looked up at the ceiling of his dressing-room in the Waldorf Astoria hotel. Distantly, in her bedroom, he could hear his daughter scolding the maid. Mueller's valet moved his head stiffly to avoid the stream of smoke and continued brushing shaving-cream on his master's ample jowls. Otto did not like him to smoke during his shave, Mueller knew, but it was only in such small matters that he could be certain of his ascendancy over the cold little man.

'It's still raining, Otto,' he said in an attempt to placate the servant. Otto said nothing. Mueller contemplated another puff on the cigar, but he knew the battle was lost. Silently he handed the cigar over. Otto placed it in the silver ashtray on the marble stand and Mueller listened to the rain as it lashed against the windows.

'Which direction are we facing?' Mueller asked.

'West,' Otto replied in a friendly enough manner. Now that victory was won, he was prepared to be magnanimous.

'It's probably coming all the way from Minnesota,' Mueller said wistfully. Despite his enormous wealth, he still felt intimidated by New York. His grandfather, in the great tradition of the American dream, had come from Germany, and during his first five years in the new country had patented an obscure piece of farming equipment that had founded the family fortune. Erich's father had further expanded their wealth in mines and railroads before founding a trust that left Erich himself rich, even in American terms, and completely without purpose or direction in life.

Even though his grandfather and father had been so powerful, both of them had remained essentially peasant farmers. Distrusting their financial peers on the east coast they had kept true to the Middle West and stayed in St Paul's, where the Mueller mansion, in all its extravagant Gothic splendour, was one of the sights of the city. Erich had grown up in the house. He missed its great gloomy rooms now. Although his home was a mansion, the Waldorf Astoria was a palace. The gilded and marbled halls, furnished with European

10

grandeur, still filled him with awe. Even though they had arrived in their own Pullman railroad car, the manager who greeted them had made him feel like a provincial oaf being put at his ease by an aristocrat.

His wife Elsa entered the room as Otto was patting bay rum into his cheeks. Her house-coat hardly covered the flimsy silk underwear she wore, so that he glanced at Otto in discomfort, but the valet continued with his duties, oblivious of Elsa, as befitted a good servant.

'You must speak to Elizabeth,' she said angrily. 'She is squabbling with the maid.'

'They're always squabbling,' he replied.

Elsa continued, 'How many times must I tell you? One does not argue with servants; one commands. If you argue, it puts them on an equal footing.'

Mueller nodded. He was as impressed by his wife as he was by the Waldorf Astoria. She had been born in Berlin and educated in Switzerland. His mother had selected her when the family had visited Germany for the purpose of finding him a bride. 'Erich shall have a thoroughbred,' she had said, and he had been delighted with the choice.

'What's the matter with Elizabeth?' he asked softly.

'She claims Renata failed to pack a particular pair of shoes. She says she can't come to dinner as her outfit will look ridiculous.'

'Can't she buy a new pair?' Erich asked plaintively. Money was his usual answer to a problem, and generally effective.

As he spoke, Elizabeth entered the room and Otto withdrew to fetch Mueller's evening clothes. His daughter seemed to Erich to be perfectly dressed in a pale grey satin evening gown that showed off her creamy shoulders. She turned to adjust her earrings in the mirror and revealed her flawless back, bare to below the waist. Her flaxen hair was plaited and piled on top of her head to accentuate her slender neck. He caught her reflection in the looking-glass, and she wrinkled her nose at him as she had when she was a little girl. Mueller loved and desired his wife, but he worshipped his daughter. It did not seem possible to him that he could have helped to create someone so exquisitely fair.

'What's all this about your shoes?' he said sternly.

She turned and lifted the hem of her dress. 'The stupid woman packed them in the other trunk,' she said. 'Why can't I have a French maid, Papa?'

'We'll see about that when we get to London,' he replied in the same voice, and Elizabeth knew that it was another problem that money would solve.

'Where did you get those earrings?' Elsa asked, noticing the diamond clasps her daughter wore.

'Papa gave them to me. Pretty, aren't they?'

'Your father is impossible!' said Elsa. 'He has the soul of a salesman.'

'But he *is* taking us to London, Mama,' Elizabeth answered mischievously.

Mueller rose from the barber's chair and began to brush his hair. 'You do want to go, don't you, my dear?' he asked, knowing the answer to his question.

'If it is a choice between London and St Paul's, London wins,' she said. 'But it is a poor third behind Berlin or Paris.'

Elizabeth examined her new earrings in the mirror again before she spoke. 'Perhaps if Papa makes a good job of London, Von Ribbentrop will make him a proper ambassador in Paris.'

Mueller stood up very straight and tightened the knot in his dressing-gown cord. 'You must not talk like that, Elizabeth,' he said. 'Always remember that we are Americans first. I happen to believe that Germany is deeply misunderstood by the rest of the world and I am prepared to do everything in my power to rectify the situation, but our first loyalties lie with the United States.'

'I must get dressed,' Elsa said in answer to her husband's little speech.

Elizabeth turned from side to side in front of the cheval mirror so that the satin dress revealed the line of her body.

'That gown really is rather shocking,' her father said. 'It looks as though you aren't wearing any underclothes.'

Elizabeth changed the subject. 'I still don't see how going to London and buying a lot of paintings is going to help Germany.'

Mueller sat down in the chair again and fiddled with the remains of his cigar. 'Germany needs the good-will of England,' he said patiently. 'Traditionally the two countries were always friends, almost the same people. During the Great War the English were persuaded by their propaganda machine that we were barbarians . . . '

'We, Papa? I thought we were Americans.'

'Don't interrupt,' he replied, while Elizabeth continued to twirl in front of the mirror. 'At the request of friends in Berlin, we are going to London to assemble a great collection of German and British art. We shall entertain on a grand scale. Our London house will be a place where the best of English society will be able to experience German civilisation and culture. This is a task of the highest responsibility.' He repeated the words like a child who had mastered a difficult poem. Now he wanted his applause.

Elizabeth, however, refused to play her allotted role. 'So we have to go to a boring dinner party with a lot of old people on our last night in New York.'

Mueller stood up and took her hands. 'Do this for me, darling,' he pleaded. 'I promise you it is important.'

She leaned down and kissed him on the forehead. 'All right, Papa. It's worth it for a French maid.'

At that moment Elsa returned, followed by Otto with Mueller's white tie and tails. 'Aren't you ready yet?' she complained, then turned to Otto. 'What have you got there?'

'Herr Mueller's evening clothes, madam,' he replied tonelessly.

'This is New York, not St James's Palace,' she said in a commanding voice. 'Bring Herr Mueller's dinner-jacket.' Then she turned to her daughter. 'And for goodness' sake go and put some underwear on, Elizabeth.'

When the yellow cab came to a halt, Anthony Strange handed the driver two dollars and then stayed, nonplussed, in the back of the cab. He had not bothered to wear a raincoat and knew from the drumming sound of the rain on the metal of the roof that by the time he had crossed the wide sidewalk and reached the shelter of Stanford Whitney-Ingram's Fifth Avenue mansion, he would be soaked to the skin. The problem was solved for him when the oak doors of the mansion slowly opened.

In the light that came from the doorway, Strange saw the imposing silhouette of Whitney-Ingram's English butler striding towards the taxi, bearing a large black umbrella aloft like the rod of Moses. He watched Grimmond approach, and composed himself. He knew that the butler did not approve of him. It was not until they entered the brightly lit hall and a maid took the dripping umbrella that Grimmond spoke.

'Mr Whitney-Ingram is waiting for you in the gallery, sir,' he said coldly. 'Please follow me.'

Strange did as he was told, walking two paces behind the stiff figure as they ascended the sweeping staircase to the first floor. The

13

atmosphere was slightly warmer when he entered the long gallery where Stanford Whitney-Ingram kept his main collection of paintings.

Although Stanford technically owned the collection, it was still thought of as the property of his late father Arthur, who had spent the last twenty-five years of his life enjoying a relentless and sometimes acrimonious series of battles with his contemporaries for possession of the fabled pictures on these silk-covered walls. There was a group of people at the far end of the long room. Strange began his journey towards them, his footsteps alternately muffled by Persian carpets or clicking on the polished walnut floor. As he drew closer, he began to make out the other guests.

Ignoring some of the most exquisite examples of European painting that had been produced over the past five hundred years, Strange picked out Whitney-Ingram and his mother Abigail, who was equally stick-like even though she had enjoyed a reputation as a famous beauty at the time of the Spanish-American war. Standing next to her was the stout figure of old Colonel Garret and his spinster sister Emily who, Strange remembered, was rather deaf. A stout, swarthy-looking man was flanked by two beautiful women, clearly mother and daughter. Both had hair the colour of wheat and pale cream-like skin. Strange sensed they were extremely wealthy; he had antennae for these things. The last member of the group was a youth with the same pale hair as Whitney-Ingram. Strange scoured his memory of the family and deduced that this was Stanford's son Charles, still a pupil at Groton. They were grouped in a semicircle. After his introduction to the Mueller family, Strange found himself between Colonel Garret and his sister. He was handed a glass of sherry; everybody was drinking it.

'Herb Pearson told me today at the Athletic Club,' Stanford said suddenly in a thin high voice. 'It's an absolute fact. J. P. Morgan did not pay one cent in income tax for the years 1931 or '32.'

There was a respectful pause as the assembled company assimilated the information that the richest man in America had contributed nothing to the national coffers for the past twenty-four months. Then Colonel Garret spoke. 'Well, bully for him.' His voice echoed the length of the gallery.

'What did you say?' his sister Emily asked irritably, but before the Colonel could repeat the phrase, Grimmond entered and announced that dinner was served.

He led them to a small dining-room where a circular table was

14

encrusted with heavy glittering silver and surmounted by a huge candelabrum lit with enough dancing flames to warm Strange's face. He knew there was another dining-room in the house where at least a hundred guests could be served, but this smaller room pleased him: the panelled walls were hung with mediocre family portraits that would not spoil his appetite. The paintings that hung in the great gallery made him feel faint with greed and there were two Tintorettos in the main dining-room that would have ruined his meal.

Grimmond showed Strange to a seat between Charles and Emily, and he relaxed. He knew that Stanford had an ulterior motive for inviting him, and it would not be revealed during dinner.

Half-way through the meal, the conversation turned in his direction. 'I see the pound has been devalued by forty per cent against the dollar,' Colonal Garret said in his booming voice. 'There must be some pretty good bargains going in the British Empire, Strange.'

'We're always keen on trade, Colonel,' Strange answered with a smile.

'What did he say?' Emily demanded.

'He said the British like to trade,' Garrett roared at his sister without embarrassment.

Emily turned to look into Strange's face. He sat impassively as she examined the long sallow face framed by a deep widow's peak and hollow cheeks. 'I thought he was a Greek,' she said finally.

A flush of colour brought two red points to Strange's cheeks. 'On the contrary, Miss Garrett,' he said tightly. 'My family came to England with William the Conqueror.' But Emily had begun to attack her food with enthusiasm. Strange turned to Charles, who sat on his left. 'What about you, young man?' he said with forced levity. 'Have you heard of the Norman Conquest?'

Charles Whitney-Ingram looked at him with pale eyes, and Strange was momentarily disconcerted by the steady gaze. 'Yes, sir,' he replied. 'It's an important part of the curriculum at my preparatory school.'

The youth's answer had been delivered in such cool tones that Strange got the unpleasant feeling that he was now being snubbed by the schoolboy.

'How's your friend Nettlebury?' the Colonel asked. 'He seemed a very decent sort. I've been thinking about buying one of his paintings.'

Strange laid down his knife and fork and sat back in his chair. 'I wouldn't advise that course of action, Colonel Garret,' he replied after a sip of his wine.

'Oh, and why not?' his host asked with sudden interest.

Now that Strange had the attention of the table, his spirits rose slightly. 'Because I would be failing in my professional duty if I were to say otherwise.' He paused. 'People in my position have responsibilities,' he said with conviction.

'Go on,' Stanford said quietly.

Strange waved a languid hand to reinforce his words. 'I'm not denying Sir Julian's scholarship,' he said carefully. 'He has no equal on the Flemish Schools of the fifteenth and sixteenth centuries, and his knowledge of British painting until the latter part of the nineteenth century is profound.' He looked at Stanford. 'Even Berenson defers to him in this area.'

Stanford nodded wisely at the name of the mighty Bernard Berenson. When American collectors had rushed to acquire Europe's masterpieces, fakes had flooded into the United States along with the torrent of genuine work. Authentication became an obsession among the collectors, who vied with each other for the most prestigious pictures. It was well known that Berenson, the leading expert on the Italian Renaissance, was paid a fortune by Duveen, the dealer, to guarantee that the works he sold had actually been painted by the masters to whom they were attributed.

'No,' Strange continued firmly. 'It is about his own painting that Sir Julian Nettlebury is unsound.'

'If he knows a good picture by somebody else, why can't he be trusted where his own work is concerned?' Abigail Whitney-Ingram asked.

Strange smiled at her with deference. 'Because of the peculiar development of British painting in the last fifty years, madam,' he said with authority. 'The British art world was torn apart by the advent of the modern French Schools. To some artists Cézanne was the signpost to the future; to others he pointed the way down a degenerate cul-de-sac.'

There was a silence, and Garret said, 'And Nettlebury thinks Cézanne was the cul-de-sac?'

Strange nodded. 'I'm afraid that he believes half the pictures in the great collections of America to be rubbish, including some of your own.'

There was a sharp intake of breath around the table at this heresy. To have opinions about pictures was one thing; to cast doubt on their value was outrageous.

'So he thinks my pictures are rubbish, does he?' Colonel Garret bristled.

'Only your Fauves,' Strange replied silkily, knowing that selections from that particular School formed the major part of the Colonel's collection. A sudden hush descended.

'Mueller here is about to begin a collection,' Stanford said into the silence. 'He's going to London to do it.'

Strange smiled at the swarthy man. 'Perhaps I may be of assistance to you. When will you be in London?'

'We sail on the *Mauretania* in the morning.'

'What a coincidence,' Strange said easily. 'So do I.'

This time Stanford smiled; he knew that Strange had not planned to leave New York for at least another week. 'Well, it will give you an opportunity to get to know each other better.' He addressed the last remark to Elizabeth, who sat beside him, but she continued to gaze with infinite boredom at one of the family portraits.

Later, when the dinner party was over, Stanford indicated that Strange should remain. When the other guests had departed, he led him back to the gallery, where Grimmond served brandy, and withdrew. Stanford came to the point immediately. 'I've decided to sell the Degas,' he said.

Strange knew that there were four paintings in the collection by the great Impressionist; three of them were ballet scenes, but the one that Stanford was referring to was the full-length portrait of a young woman known as *The Girl in the White Dress*, which hung on the far wall of the gallery in splendid isolation. Strange's eyes turned in the direction of the picture and his heart began to pound.

'What can you get for it?' his host asked casually.

'If I can take it to Europe with me, half a million dollars,' Strange said with only the slightest tremor in his voice.

Sir Julian Nettlebury sat in the automat in Times Square and studied his daughters as they ate their cheesecake. They really bore no resemblance to him at all, he thought, although they were very like each other. Anne, the eldest, had unfashionably long hair compared with other women these days, who wore theirs in a style that he thought of as permanently waved helmets. Both girls had skin in the tones that Rubens had liked to paint, fair enough to hold highlights and shadows of pink and blue. But it was their hair that pleased him most, a blending of chestnut and red-gold: autumn-coloured hair,

17

like their mother's had been. For a moment he felt the familiar melancholy; she had been dead five years now. Apart from their hair, they did not look like her at all. Where her face had been long and aquiline, they had wide high cheekbones with snub noses, full, well-formed mouths and large lustrous eyes the colour of dark honey. At seventeen, Anne was a fully grown woman; her body was strong, verging on the voluptuous. Irene, at eleven, still had a boyish figure. He decided he would paint them again when they were home in England. He liked the contrast they presented, and in a short while Irene would lose her coltish style.

They look Slavonic, he thought, whereas he considered himself very English in appearance. He was a shade below average height, and his sharp, handsome features and trim sandy moustache spoke of his nationality as clearly as his public school accent.

Irene had finished her cheesecake. 'If it's a cinema, why is it called Radio City Music Hall?' she suddenly asked.

Sir Julian shrugged, and looked to Anne to provide the answer. 'I don't know,' she replied, 'but they have dancers on the stage; perhaps that has something to do with it.'

Irene considered this solution. 'They don't have dancers on the radio,' she said scornfully.

Nettlebury stubbed out the cigarette he had been smoking. 'You know, before I had children, I used to consider myself reasonably well informed,' he said to Anne.

A middle-aged woman sitting near by had been listening to their conversation. She leaned closer. 'Are you folks from England?' she asked in a friendly voice.

When he had first come to America, Nettlebury had found it disconcerting to be addressed in terms of easy familiarity by complete strangers, but now he had grown used to the habit. 'Yes, we are,' he told her in equally friendly tones.

'I thought so. We just love your accents, don't we?' she said to the woman sitting next to her, who was also smiling with approval. 'It's like something in the movies,' she added. 'You folks wouldn't be actors, by any chance?'

Nettlebury smiled and shook his head. 'I'm afraid not.'

The two women looked disappointed.

'My daddy is a famous artist,' Irene said in an effort to cheer the woman up, more than to be boastful. 'His name is Sir Julian Nettlebury.'

The information had the desired effect. 'So you two girls are

18

called "ladies"?' the woman asked, with wonder in her voice.

'No,' Irene explained. 'My mother was Lady Nettlebury, but she's dead. So there isn't one now.'

The two women were embarrassed by this information. 'I'm very sorry to hear that, honey,' the woman said in a quieter voice as the two of them got up to leave the restaurant.

Irene waved goodbye. 'Americans are nice, aren't they, Daddy?' she said. 'I don't understand why Cousin Anthony is so unpleasant about them.'

Nettlebury decided he would answer her rhetorical question. 'I think it's because some English people, like Anthony, are envious of them, darling. America is richer and more powerful than England now and some people resent it.'

'Even with the Depression?' said Irene.

He nodded. 'Even with the Depression.'

She looked round the great cavernous room and watched the line of people taking food from the rows of little windows. 'Well, I like America,' she said. 'And I like this automat more than Lyons Corner House.'

'The United States will be glad to learn of your approval,' he said mock-seriously, and swallowed some of his coffee. In the month they had spent in New York he had gradually become accustomed to the curious liquid Americans drank in such abundance.

Anne looked at him for a few moments before she spoke. 'Do you have to be associated with Anthony Strange, Daddy?'

Nettlebury set his cup on its saucer and looked at her. 'I've explained to you, Anne, that I still have to pay for Irene's education. We have the upkeep of the house. You can't just wish bills away.'

Anne knew the cost of running the house as well as her father did. For the past year she had acted as housekeeper and managed the difficult art of scraping by on not quite enough money. They would have fewer worries when her father was paid by Strange, but the relationship brought other concerns.

'I wouldn't mind leaving school,' Irene said in a bright voice, without much hope of her father taking up the offer.

'You know what I promised,' Nettlebury said gently.

Usually the girls did not speak of their mother in front of him, knowing how painful it could be, but now the subject had been raised, Irene ventured a question. 'Mummy never came to America, did she, Daddy?'

'No, but we travelled a good deal in Europe. She spoke Italian and

19

French very well and she wanted you both to do the same.'

'It's not fair,' the little girl sighed. 'Languages are so easy for Anne. I hate irregular verbs.'

Nettlebury nodded. Although he loved his daughters deeply, he sometimes yearned for the conversation of a mature woman. Anne was undoubtedly clever, but in some ways she was as young as Irene.

'Can't you go back to teaching?' Anne persisted.

Nettlebury shook his head. 'A teacher's salary would hardly pay for my paints. When your mother was alive we had her income, but . . .' He let the sentence trail away. Suddenly he began to feel angry. Why won't my work sell again? he thought. It had once. If anything, he was a better artist now. He made the occasional sale to individuals who did not listen to the West End galleries. But the critics and dealers who controlled the art market had pronounced him passé, and it was like a professional death sentence. I'm a good artist, he told himself. Properly tutored. I have mastered the most difficult of mediums, painting in oils, and the most daunting of subject-matter, the subtle light of England. He remembered that when he was studying at the Slade School his fellow-students had collected his discarded drawings. Like the memory of his wife, he pushed the subject from his mind.

Anne could see that he had grown sad, and decided to chide him out of the melancholy mood. 'I could always model,' she said with a smile. 'You know some of your friends have asked me.'

Nettlebury glanced at Irene, who appeared preoccupied, peering around the room through an empty glass that had contained milk. 'I've told you before,' he said in a low voice. 'It is a fallacy that painters regard their models with the same detachment as they do inanimate objects.'

'Do you think they would try to seduce Anne?' Irene asked, still holding the glass to her eye.

'That is a shocking thing to say, young lady,' he said sternly, although he could not entirely suppress a smile. 'But since you ask, and I presume you understand what you have said, that is precisely what I believe.'

'Did you try to seduce Mrs Cooper?' she asked, naming the highly respectable middle-aged lady who had posed regularly for their father since before they were born.

'Certainly not,' he replied stiffly, and rose to his feet. 'Come along. It's time we returned to the hotel.'

A few minutes later, with raincoats buttoned to the throat and umbrellas opened against the storm, they battled their way towards the hotel through the driving rain. Cars swished past and the fairyland of coloured lights danced and glittered on the shiny black streets, turning their surroundings into fragments of primary colour. In the lobby, they shook themselves like wet dogs. Irene looked for the cat who prowled about the reception area, and Nettlebury collected the key to their rooms.

'I won't be on duty when you leave tomorrow, Sir Julian,' said the desk clerk. 'I hope you and your daughters have a pleasant voyage home.'

'Thank you. That's most kind,' Nettlebury replied.

'Oh, and a note was delivered by hand for you,' said the young man, handing him a stiff little envelope that had been sealed with red wax.

Nettlebury took the letter, then he removed his raincoat and handed it to Anne. 'Be a dear and put this in my room,' he said. 'I'm just going to have a nightcap in the Oak Room.'

Anne smiled. Apart from his conversion to coffee, her father had also acquired a taste for dry Martinis during the visit. He had also fallen in with a collection of cronies who drank each night in the hotel bar. Most of them were anglophiles and they had welcomed Nettlebury into their circle.

He entered the darkly panelled little bar and stood in the light of the counter to read the letter. It contained a few lines written with black ink in a bold well-formed hand:

> Dear Sir Julian,
>
> Although we only had time to form a brief acquaintance, I was impressed by your attitude to painting, and I wish to purchase one of your landscapes. I leave the choice to you, but this transaction can take place only if Mr Anthony Strange has nothing to do with the arrangement. I enclose a cheque for five thousand dollars.
>
> Yours sincerely,
> Abigail Whitney-Ingram

'Good news, I hope, Sir Julian?' said the barman.

'The best in months,' Nettlebury replied with a wide smile.

The storm had passed by the following morning, leaving a perfect spring day. Wisps of cloud trailed across the pale blue sky and the tops of the buildings lining Fifth Avenue were bathed in golden sunlight. In the shadowed canyons below, the air was cool and refreshing. Laszlo and Gideon had opened the windows of their yellow cab wide.

'What an extraordinary city,' Laszlo said to Gideon, who was exposing his face to the wind in the vain hope that the rushing air would blow away the headache that was the most troublesome part of his hangover. Laszlo inhaled deeply. 'What an extraordinary climate! This morning the weather is like Switzerland, and last night we were in a monsoon.'

Gideon turned to him. They had sat late into the night in the Hungarian Café, consuming bottle after bottle of a rich dark wine. 'What was that stuff we drank?' he asked. His voice was strained.

'Bull's Blood,' Laszlo replied, with a sympathetic smile.

'They must have left the bloody horns in it!' said Gideon. 'I've never felt as bad as this in my whole life.' Laszlo appeared to be as fresh as the rest of the morning. 'Don't you get hangovers?'

Laszlo shook his head. 'It is one of the few things I am blessed with. Besides, Bull's Blood is the drink of my nation.'

'I thought you were an Irishman?'

Laszlo smiled again. 'The two races have many similarities.'

At these words, Gideon turned his face to the cold air once more and Laszlo settled back into the upholstery. He was content. Eventually the taxi arrived at the dockside, and they collected their luggage. Laszlo had two sturdy leather cases, but Gideon's was more impressive, covered, as it was, with travel labels from every part of the globe.

'You appear to be well travelled,' Laszlo said, nodding at the bag.

Gideon smiled. 'The bag certainly is. It belonged to my father.' He glanced down at it. 'I suppose you could say it was my inheritance.'

'People have had less,' Laszlo said, not without sympathy.

'Oh, I'm not complaining,' Gideon said cheerfully. 'Possessions can tie you down.'

At that moment a young woman passed in such splendour that she put Gideon in mind of Cleopatra entering Rome. Her slender erect body was clad in an exquisitely tailored man's chalk-striped suit, silk shirt and paisley tie. Her corn-coloured hair was tucked into a silver-grey fedora pulled down to one side. One elegant hand held a cigarette to her mouth; the other was thrust into the jacket pocket. Gideon stared at her with admiration, and she gave him a cursory glance. Behind her, two porters struggled with a trolley piled with matching luggage.

Laszlo followed his gaze. 'Marlene Dietrich began the fashion,' he said. 'It suits beautiful young women, but I do hope it does not lead

22

to men wearing frocks!'

'I had to wear a frock once,' Gideon said as they set about the formalities of embarkation. Laszlo raised a quizzical eyebrow. 'It was in a production of *Charley's Aunt*.'

'Did it bother you?' Laszlo asked.

'Not in the least. But I hated having to smoke the cigar.'

Laszlo laughed as they thrust their way into the bustling crowd. He was beginning to like his new companion very much. Finally, when they had cleared customs and immigration, they climbed the gangway to board the liner.

Gideon felt suddenly elated; a new chapter was opening in his life. He enjoyed the company of Laszlo, and last night, listening to him talk about the excitement of dealing in pictures, he suddenly knew that he would come to share the older man's enthusiasm. Acting had been a pleasant enough occupation, when he actually had a part, but he knew that he did not have the commitment that others brought to the profession. In truth, he had always secretly thought there was something vaguely silly about parading around a stage wearing make-up, speaking words someone else had written. He had once, tentatively, raised the subject with his parents. But his father was so steeped in the theatre that he thought everyone in the world wished to be an actor and was only forced by cruel circumstance into other work.

Now Gideon turned to look back at New York. It appeared to be made of some precious metal, in the golden light that glittered and was reflected from the million windows set in the cliff-like skyscrapers. Tugs hooted across the great harbour, and wheeling gulls cried out in return.

Once aboard, they did not go to their cabin, as Gideon had expected. Instead, Laszlo secured a steward and gave him their cases. 'I think an early reconnoitre is called for,' he said, and with quickening steps they threaded their way through the chaotic passageways. Their progress was momentarily impeded by a porter struggling with a steamer trunk, and through the open door of a stateroom he watched an imperious blonde, dressed in mink, command a retinue of attendants.

'How can I go to a party dressed like this?' she demanded in German. 'Find the trunk immediately.'

Gideon half-expected her to add threats that they would be keel-hauled and clapped in irons. From an adjacent room somewhere in the interior, the girl in the man's suit emerged. She

23

was no longer wearing the hat and her hair swung to her shoulders. They were clearly mother and daughter. When he had first seen the girl at the dockside, he had imagined, from her confident deportment, that she was older. Now, with her hair loose, he could tell that she was not yet twenty. But despite her youth there was something else in her face when she looked at him framed in the doorway, and Gideon recognised it at once.

At the age of sixteen he had played the part of a juvenile lead in a theatre in Manchester, and on the first day of rehearsal, when he had been introduced to the rest of the cast, the leading lady had looked at him with exactly the same expression. He had imagined at the time that a woman who was at least ten years his senior would have no interest in him. Later that night, in her hotel room, she had revealed to him the secret that many men never discover: women are capable of the same sexual drive as men. Since then, he had based all his relationships with women on that fact and never confused love with simple lust. In the moment that they looked at each other, Gideon knew, even if Elizabeth Mueller did not, that it was only a matter of timing and opportunity.

The porter managed to move the trunk, and they passed further along the companionway to the room where the party was to take place. Otto, Mueller's valet, took Laszlo's invitation from him.

'Has our host arrived?' Laszlo asked, casting his eyes over the scattering of people.

'Not yet, sir,' Otto replied.

'In that case, I shall return a little later. I have a small matter to attend to.' He nodded to Gideon, and withdrew.

Gideon wandered further into the room. When he had come to America, he had booked a passage on a cargo boat, which seemed, in memory, to have been smaller than this single cabin. Lined against the far panelled wall was a long table laden with food. He had worked in a precarious profession for so long that seizing such an opportunity had become second nature. Without hesitation he strolled casually to the buffet and began to eat steadily. The trick is not to have a glass in your hand, he told himself, as he began with lobster. He chose a leg of turkey, potato salad and some ham for his next course. When this was finished, he strolled in a leisurely fashion to the other end of the table with dessert in mind.

He was studying the array of fruits and puddings when an English voice behind him said, 'Do you like cheesecake?'

He turned to look down at Irene Nettlebury. 'I can't actually remember ever trying it,' he replied.

'You should,' she said with conviction. 'It's the most delicious food in America.'

'Then I shall accept your recommendation. 'Which one is it?'

Irene pointed to what looked like a large round cake topped with glazed fruit. Gideon cut two slices and handed Irene her plate. She watched him carefully as he tasted his first mouthful.

'You're absolutely right! It is delicious,' he said.

Irene nodded happily and began to eat her own portion. After a minute of silence they were joined by Anne, who looked disapprovingly at the cheesecake and the plate in her sister's hand. 'You were told that you mustn't begin any of the food,' she said in a low voice.

'I didn't,' Irene replied indignantly. 'This gentleman had some and he invited me to join him.'

Anne turned to Gideon, and he nodded. 'I'm afraid it was my fault,' he said. 'I didn't know there was a time limit.'

Anne smiled. 'There isn't for adults, just for greedy little girls.'

Gideon looked at her. She was the same height as himself, so their eyes were level, and she was equally attractive as the girl in the suit, but in quite a different way. All he saw in Anne's face was an innocent friendliness. 'My name is James Gideon,' he said, holding out his hand.

Anne shook it. 'I'm Anne Nettlebury and this is my sister Irene . . . and our father, Sir Julian Nettlebury,' indicating Sir Julian who had come to join them.

'Mr Gideon gave me some cheesecake,' Irene said before any more accusations could be made.

'That was extremely generous of him,' Nettlebury said drily.

A waiter hovered with a tray of drinks, but Gideon shook his head. The room was more crowded now and the level of noise had begun to rise. He had the sensation that someone was watching him. He half-turned, and saw Elizabeth Mueller, whose eyes again held his for a moment and then flickered away. He was about to make his excuses and join her when Laszlo arrived.

'Hello, Julian,' he said with pleasure. 'I saw from the passenger list that you were aboard.'

'My dear Laszlo,' Nettlebury replied. 'I don't think you know my family.' The introductions were made, and Gideon was about to look for the girl again when a dark, emaciated figure confronted them, dressed immaculately in blazer and white flannels.

'Hello, Strange,' said Laszlo.

25

At first, Strange ignored the greeting. He swayed slightly from side to side and Gideon realised he was slightly drunk. 'Well, well,' he said carefully. 'Laszlo and Nettlebury together. Are you both boring each other with mutual stories of failure?'

It was an extraordinary act of brutality. Nettlebury and Laszlo were too gentlemanly to reply in the presence of the two girls, but Gideon had no such compunction. He saw the wounded look in Irene and Anne's eyes and started to step forward, but it proved unnecessary.

Irene was suddenly violently sick over Anthony Strange's white flannel trousers.

CHAPTER TWO

In the early part of the evening on the second night of the voyage, James Gideon stood at the dressing-table in the cabin he shared with Laszlo and examined the cuffs of his dinner shirt. Despite the best efforts of the ship's laundry, they remained as frayed as the edges of an old carpet.

Laszlo cast a critical eye over his ensemble, and shook his head. 'Everything else passes muster, but the shirt won't do, I'm afraid,' he said with conviction. 'Take your jacket off.'

Gideon did as instructed, while Laszlo took a pair of nail-scissors and cut the sleeves from the shirt. When he had completed the operation, he examined the remnants of material and the two heavy gold objects adorning them.

'A great pity,' he said sympathetically. 'This is a fine pair of cufflinks.'

'My father's,' Gideon said, replacing his jacket. 'The dinner clothes were in the suitcase when he gave it to me.'

'I thought the suitcase was his only bequest,' said Laszlo. 'Now I learn that valuable jewellery was included.'

'I exaggerated,' Gideon said lightly. 'There were a shaving-brush and a pair of braces as well.'

'It's a good job we're on the *Mauretania*! I hear the captain of the *Aquitania* insists that gentlemen wear white tie and tails for dinner. Whole oxen are served, and the orchestra plays Elgar. Americans are deeply intimidated.' There was a tap on the cabin door, and a steward entered. 'Ah, good,' said Laszlo, when he saw the man. 'I want you to send this cable to London,' handing him a sheet of paper. 'And will you please arrange to put this parcel in the ship's safe?'

The steward looked suddenly wary; it was clear he was not happy with the thought of this responsibility. 'I can take the cable, but I think you'll have to see the Purser about the package, sir,' he said in a voice that was both servile and defiant.

Laszlo waved aside his objections and put the brown paper parcel in the man's hands. 'I know I should, my dear fellow, but I just don't have the time. I'm sure you can manage it for me,' he said, placing a ten-dollar bill on top of the parcel.

The man's objections suddenly evaporated. He withdrew with a smile, and Laszlo put on his own jacket.

'Why did you do that?' Gideon asked as he removed the last piece of lint from the sleeve of his coat. He had begun to appreciate that his companion seemed to have a motive for even the simplest arrangements.

Laszlo made a final adjustment to his tie and gave himself a final inspection in the mirror on the dressing-table before he said, 'I want him to gossip about us,' as he opened the cabin door.

'Why?' Gideon asked as they made their way towards the smoking-lounge, where they had arranged to meet Nettlebury for a drink before dinner.

Laszlo murmured, 'Good evening,' to an elderly couple they passed. 'My dear young fellow, it is essential that we establish our credentials on this voyage. At the moment, we could give the impression of adventurers.'

'I still don't follow,' Gideon said as they entered the room, which was occupied solely by men.

Laszlo drew him to one side. 'Ships are hotbeds of information,' he said quietly. 'You are a well-educated young man with nothing but a dinner-jacket in your suitcase. I am a mysterious foreigner who tips well. We are clearly not lovers, so what is our friend the steward to think? I have to give him something he can pass on to those who will wish to know about us.'

'And who would that be?' Gideon asked.

'By tomorrow, Erich Mueller, for one,' Laszlo replied. 'Anthony Strange will warn him against us.'

'So what was in the cable?'

Laszlo smiled with satisfaction. 'I sent a message to Sir Oswald Gideon at White's Club, saying: *Venture successful. Your son returns home with me as instructed.*'

Gideon nodded. He had grasped the plot of Laszlo's charade. 'So you've converted me to a runaway son about to return to the bosom of his anxious family?'

Laszlo patted him on the shoulder. 'I think your theatrical background will prove an enormous advantage in our relationship,' he said with a smile, and they moved further into the room. They found Sir Julian Nettlebury seated in a comfortable armchair.

In his brief acquaintanceship with Nettlebury, Gideon had noticed nothing about the man's dress to indicate that he was an artist. The grey tweed suit he had worn the day before had been, if anything, like the clothes a retired colonel would have chosen for a trip to town. But now, Nettlebury was dressed in a wine-coloured velvet smoking-jacket and his large bow tie was carelessly knotted.

When they joined him, he invited them to try a dry Martini. 'It's amazing what a minute drop of vermouth and a tiny twist of lemon-peel can do to cold gin,' he said with satisfaction when the steward brought their drinks.

Gideon sipped his with caution and watched Laszlo who, while appearing to be completely relaxed, was up to something.

After a few minutes' conversation, which he carefully steered to the subject of the eighteenth century, Laszlo asked Nettlebury, 'What do you think of Watteau?'

Nettlebury sat back to consider. He had taken a pipe from his pocket, but after a pause he replaced it unlit. 'Very little. He's not really my period. And, to be frank, I've always considered his work too whimsical for my taste.'

'Not enough passion, eh, Julian?' Laszlo gave Gideon a half-smile.

'Not really. I've never cared much for Mozart, either. But I'm sure the problem lies with me, not with Mozart or Watteau. But why do you ask? Do you happen to have a Watteau, by any chance?'

'Possibly, possibly,' Laszlo said and changed the subject to Constable, whom Nettlebury did feel passionate about, until they were called to dinner.

To Gideon, the dining-room, with its carved panel walls and elaborate plaster ceiling, seemed more like an English manor house than the interior of a great ship. Then the surroundings began to sway with a new rhythm from the sea. The stewards moved with practised ease between the tables, but he was glad to find his own seat. He was surprised to find that he was not at the same table as Laszlo, who had joined Erich Mueller and his family.

Gideon had discovered that the blonde girl was Mueller's daughter, and her name was Elizabeth. He felt a moment of regret that he was not seated with the other party, but was pleased to find that he was between Nettlebury and Anne. They shared their table with a young ship's officer, who looked elegant if rather plump in his dress uniform, an Episcopalian bishop from New Hampshire, his wife and their young son, who was peering with surreptitious interest at Anne, whose splendid figure was displayed to great advantage by the old-fashioned evening dress she wore.

Gideon glanced towards Laszlo and saw that Strange was also at Mueller's table. Laszlo winked at him. Gideon raised his eyebrows. Then he turned back to Anne and asked where Irene was.

'She's not very well, I'm afraid,' she replied. 'The very act of standing on the deck of a ship seems to upset her, regardless of the motion.'

'Like Nelson, Miss Nettlebury,' the ship's officer said sympathetically. 'He was seasick even when his ship was in harbour.'

'I shall tell her that, Lieutenant Cosgrove,' Anne said with a smile. 'She is still at the age where men's exploits are more impressive than women's.'

Gideon noticed that the lieutenant was captivated by Anne as was the bishop's son, but she was blithely unaware of their attention. As casually as he could, he turned his head to look at Laszlo's table again. Elizabeth Mueller was listening with bored but polite attention to Anthony Strange. Without moving her head, her eyes came into contact with Gideon's, and at that moment the ship lurched with greater force. They both smiled, and Elizabeth touched her satin-covered stomach for a moment before she turned back to Strange. Gideon felt a stab of frustration. He had intended to dance with Elizabeth after dinner, but the increasing motion of the ship made him doubt that there would be any music that night.

'Tell me, Mr Vasilakis,' Elsa Mueller said, steadying her glass of hock with a hand that brushed against Laszlo's, 'are you disturbed by rough seas?' For some reason she chose to speak in French, so Laszlo replied in the same language.

'My life has been too stormy to be bothered by a little rough water, Mrs Mueller.'

'So we can take it that you won't be driven to an early bed?' She lowered her eyelashes and leaned a bare shoulder towards him.

'I must confess that some storms have made me take to my bed, Mrs Mueller,' he replied.

'I take it you refer to storms of the heart?' Strange said in English. It was clear that he intended to bring their little flirtation to Mueller's attention, but Laszlo was too seasoned a campaigner to be thrown by his clumsy interjection.

He looked at Erich Mueller and spoke in German. 'When I am

30

surrounded by such beautiful women, all previous storms fade into insignificance,' he said with a slight bow. Mueller was pleased by the remark; like many husbands of attractive women, he was more flattered than made jealous by an open flirtation with his wife. Lady Gresham, at his side, was also pleased by Laszlo's compliment when Mueller translated it for her.

'Did you strike any bargains in New York, Vasilakis?' Mueller asked.

'Maybe, Herr Mueller,' he replied with the caution of a fly-fisherman. 'But I shall have to wait until I return to England before I break out the champagne.'

'You don't seem very confident,' said Elsa.

Laszlo took a sip of his hock before he answered. 'In love, I believe in élan.' He shrugged and smiled. 'But art dealing is a business where reputations are easily ruined by enthusiasm.'

'So you won't take risks?' Elsa continued.

Laszlo looked down modestly at his glass of hock and shook his head, while the ship continued to pitch with increasing determination. His words lay like a fly on the water, and Strange took the hook.

'Well, you either have it or you don't,' he said impatiently. 'What's the problem?'

Laszlo did not allow his triumph to show in his face. 'Like everything in our world, Strange, authentication. I bought a manuscript in New York that is definitely in the hand of Racine.' He let the words sink in for a moment. 'The exciting thing is that there are two illustrations in it which I believe might be the work of Watteau.'

Elsa said, 'How wonderful!'

'Who's Watteau?' Lord Gresham said, bewildered. His wife gave him a withering stare that would have killed a fox at two hundred yards.

'A French painter who lived in the fifteenth century, Lord Gresham,' Elizabeth Mueller said, somewhat to Laszlo's surprise.

'And the sixteenth,' Strange added, not to be outdone.

Laszlo held up a hand. 'As I said, at the moment, I cannot be sure.'

'Who will confirm it for you?' Lady Gresham asked with genuine interest.

'The Victoria and Albert Museum,' said Laszlo. 'I think we can all trust them.'

It was too much for Strange, whose vanity began to boil like the

31

sea. 'I can authenticate anything by Watteau,' he said dismissively. 'My man Nettlebury is an expert.' He turned to Elizabeth. 'After all, if I'm keeping a dog, he might as well do the barking.'

Elsa Mueller turned to her husband. 'Darling, if it's genuine, will you buy it for me?' she asked. Like her daughter, Mrs Mueller enjoyed expensive presents. Mueller shrugged and the sea nudged the great ship from side to side.

The heaving motion had increased so much that Anne Nettlebury did not stay for the whole of the dinner. 'I'd better go and see how Irene is,' she said softly to her father.

She was not alone in abandoning the dining-room. By the time coffee was offered, Nettlebury and Gideon were the only people to have remained at their table. To a certain extent it had amused Gideon to watch the powerful and the mighty, in their fine clothes and elaborate jewellery, sway and stumble as they left the room. As an actor, he knew that dignity comes as much from bearing as from dress.

'Poor Irene,' Nettlebury said as they watched the bishop and his wife lurch out. 'I can't think why she's such a bad sailor. It doesn't seem to bother me at all.'

Gideon nodded, and glanced at his watch. 'It's a bit early to turn in. Do you fancy a drink in the smoking-room?' As he spoke, he looked across to Laszlo's table. Elizabeth was leaning forward, her back arched as she cupped her chin in her hand. Somehow he knew that she would be one of the last to leave, determined that as few people as possible should witness any moment of inelegance.

'I think I could manage a brandy,' Nettlebury replied, following Gideon's glance with a wry smile. 'Lovely, isn't she? But I fear she will cause men a great deal of trouble.'

Gideon turned back to him. 'Why? Because of her money?'

Nettlebury shook his head. 'Not entirely, although I'm sure it will be a contributing factor. I have an aunt who was as plain as cardboard, with no money at all, but there seemed to be some magnetic force in her that attracted men and disaster. The last we heard of her, she'd run off with a builder from South Norwood.'

They rose from the table and Gideon made a drinking motion to Laszlo, who nodded his understanding. They got to the smoking-room with some difficulty. Like others, they would pitch forward a few paces, then battle uphill until the motion changed and they would be thrown from side to side. There was a curious dreamlike quality to the whole episode. Because the interior of the

32

ship was so like a hotel, Gideon kept imagining they were in a building in the middle of an earthquake. Finally, when they reached their destination, they sank into club armchairs and ordered their drinks from a stoic steward.

Nettlebury produced his pipe and began to fill it from an oilskin pouch. Gideon noticed an emblem decorating the flap. Nettlebury put the pouch on the table while he searched for his matches, and Gideon leaned forward to examine the piece of brass.

'It's the cap-badge of the Grenadier Guards,' Nettlebury explained. 'I was with them in the trenches for a while.' A shadow of sadness crossed his face. 'They were very gallant men.'

'You were a war artist, weren't you?' Gideon asked.

Nettlebury nodded, but clearly did not want to continue with the line of conversation. 'So, Laszlo is going to teach you the picture-dealing business,' he said, exhaling puffs of tobacco-smoke that wreathed about him.

'You sound as if you don't approve,' Gideon answered with a smile.

'It's not for me to approve or disapprove,' he said mildly. 'I'm enough of a realist to understand that such a job is necessary.' He smiled. 'Even Michelangelo had difficulty in getting paid by the pope. Perhaps, if he had had a dealer, his life might have been easier.'

'Have they made your life easier?'

'As soon as art became big business, dealers made my life hell,' Nettlebury said without emotion.

'I don't follow,' Gideon said, gesturing to the steward to bring them another round of brandies.

When the drinks were served, Nettlebury shrugged, and continued in the same easy voice. 'Painting used to be a fairly good middle-class profession,' he said with nostalgia. 'And one where ordinary people could advance their lives. Of course it required talent, which is not always a necessary qualification in other jobs.' He paused, and puffed more smoke from the pipe.

'Why did it change?' Gideon noticed that he was drinking his brandy too fast.

'People once bought the paintings they liked for reasonable prices,' Nettlebury said with a wave. 'Galleries were more like shops then, and dealers more like shopkeepers. One saw works of genius in museums and the great houses. But then the people, who had amassed huge fortunes towards the end of the last century,

33

began to look for something new to do. A lot of them took to collecting paintings. At first it was the work of the masters but there was only a limited supply, and when that had been exhausted, the dealers began to push up the prices until they moved into the realms of fantasy. The wealthy had perfectly demonstrated the theory that supply and demand control market values.'

Gideon nodded. 'Go on.'

Nettlebury shrugged again. 'The rich always want more, so the dealers fed them the works of living artists. But they weren't content to settle for good pictures, painted by men who had mastered their craft. They wanted instant greatness. And what do you think were the qualifications for greatness that the rich could understand?'

'The highest prices,' Gideon ventured.

'And while the dealers set higher and higher prices, more and more painters were experimenting with new theories. People could no longer apply traditional values to the work they saw, so dealers were in the position to say who were the greatest artists. Subsequently some artists became very rich, some dealers became fabulously wealthy, and some of us went to the wall.'

'Was it only the dealers who were responsible? What about the critics?' Gideon asked.

Nettlebury put down his pipe and nodded to Laszlo, who had joined them. 'Laszlo, tell our young friend about the critics.' He turned to Gideon again. 'It's the one area you'll find dealers and painters agree about.'

'Which critics are we referring to?' Laszlo said, sitting down. 'The honest tyrants who denounce those whose work offends them? Or the corrupt bastards who make fortunes from pictures given to them or sold at knock-down prices?' He smiled.

'Let's begin with the honest tyrants,' Nettlebury said, but before Laszlo could begin, Anne joined them.

'I think you'd better come, Daddy. Irene is still terribly ill.'

'Of course, my dear,' Nettlebury said and looked around. 'But I was under the impression it was getting calmer.'

'Maybe a little,' Laszlo said. 'But seasickness has nothing to do with the ferocity of the storm.'

Gideon noticed that Nettlebury looked tired as he rose from the armchair. 'Can I be of any help?' he asked. 'Does she enjoy being read to?'

Anne exchanged glances with her father. 'Actually, she does,' she said. 'But all the books we brought are packed and impossible to get to

34

at the moment.'

'You go back to Irene,' said Laszlo. 'Gideon and I will find something in the ship's library.'

As they set off in search of a suitable book, Gideon asked Laszlo about Nettlebury.

'His work simply went out of style,' Laszlo replied. 'It happens with some artists.'

'He seems very bitter.'

The older man nodded. 'And understandably. Painting is as uncertain as your own last profession. Can't you think of actors who saw success followed by failure?'

'My father was a pretty good example,' Gideon replied.

On their way to the library, Laszlo stopped for a moment in one of the deserted writing-rooms and took a bottle of black ink and a fine-nibbed pen from one of the desks. 'Just a little job I have to do,' he explained vaguely. When eventually they found the children's section in the library, Laszlo steadied himself with one hand as they looked along the rows of books.

'What do you think she will enjoy?' he asked. 'Something by Louisa M. Alcott, perhaps?'

Gideon shook his head. 'See if you can find anything by Robert Louis Stevenson.' He remembered Anne's comment to Lieutenant Cosgrove about her sister's preference for boyish things.

'Ah,' Laszlo exclaimed with satisfaction. '*Kidnapped*!' He opened the book. 'And a first edition.'

'That should do it,' Gideon replied, and they began the journey to Irene's cabin. The violent pitching of the ship had definitely began to subside, as Nettlebury had observed, but the little girl was as pale as the pillow beneath her head when they entered the cabin.

'Hello, Gideon,' she said in a thin voice, trying to smile. 'Why does everyone call you Gideon instead of James?' It was clear that her illness had not reduced her curiosity.

'It's because I'm a great artist,' he said with a smile.

'Like Goya or Turner?'

'No, like Houdini,' he replied. 'You never hear anyone refer to him as Harry, do you?'

She shook her head. 'What are you going to read to me?'

Gideon sat down beside her bed, and opened the book. '*Kidnapped*. Have you read it?'

She shook her head again. 'Is it exciting?'

'I think so,' he replied, 'but you'll have to judge for yourself.' He began to read.

Laszlo listened to the pitch of his voice for a few minutes before he slipped from the room. As he walked along the passage towards his own cabin, he gave thanks that the ship was reaching calmer waters. He needed a smooth sea for the work that had to be done the following day. Then he remembered the musical quality of Gideon's voice as he read aloud to Irene. 'What a salesman that boy is going to make!' he thought with sudden satisfaction.

Elsa Mueller woke up to find the sea behaving in its usual capricious fashion. She could still feel a definite pitch, whereas she had expected the day to be calm. The ship's officer whom she had accosted at the end of dinner the night before had confidently predicted they were heading for smooth water.

'I shall complain to that young man,' she said severely to her husband, who lay beside her with his hands laced behind his head.

'Which young man, my dear?' Mueller asked with mild interest.

'Lieutenant Cosgrove, of course. He gave me an undertaking that the storm was over.'

'I don't think he was in a position to make a binding contract in the matter,' Mueller said with a rare attempt at irony. 'Perhaps you should have spoken with God?'

'Ponderous humour is the last thing I want before breakfast,' Elsa said, throwing back the bedclothes.

Mueller looked down at the swell of his stomach beneath the silk pyjamas and then at his wife's slender body, which was revealed as she briskly pulled off her nightdress. The most he could ever manage in the morning was a cup of coffee, while each day his wife would consume a substantial breakfast. It was the same at lunchtime. He would only bother with the lightest food and sometimes forgo the meal altogether, but his wife's hearty appetite was eternally renewed. Yet he had the stocky peasant's body while she remained slim and desirable. Now she threw her nightdress on the floor, knowing that it would be picked up and tidied away by other hands.

'You're still very beautiful, Elsa,' he said hopefully. But his wife recognised the tone of his voice and was ready for her bacon and eggs.

'Don't start that nonsense now,' she said firmly. 'There's a time and place for everything.'

Mueller sighed, and tried to think of a more appropriate time and place than when husband and wife were alone in their bedroom.

'How about eleven o'clock in one of the lifeboats on B deck?' he called out as she walked into the bathroom. 'We could invite Laszlo along to discuss the Racine manuscript, too.'

Elsa knew when a bargain was being struck, and she did love her husband in an exasperated way. Slowly she returned to the marital bed.

In the stateroom beyond their cabin, Otto, having overheard their conversation, replaced the silver covers on the breakfast the steward had brought. He withdrew to the far side of the room where, through a porthole, he watched the heaving seas.

Some time later, when their passion and breakfast had been consumed, Elizabeth joined her parents. After sipping at a cup of lemon tea for a few minutes she gauged, correctly, that her father was in an excellent mood. 'May I have my own automobile in England, Papa?' she asked.

'You may have one in the country, but not in town,' he answered immediately, and Elizabeth, from his lack of consultation with Elsa, knew that her parents had already discussed the subject.

'Why not in town?'

'They drive on a different side of the road in England, darling, and there is a lot of traffic in London. The city was designed for horses, not automobiles.'

'But I've never driven at home anyway, so driving on the wrong side of the road would be perfectly natural to me. And if the city was designed for horses, the traffic will be slower, not faster, than in American cities.'

Elizabeth's logic defeated her father. 'We'll see,' he said lamely, and she departed before her mother could intervene. She made for the promenade deck and was pleased to feel the cold air when she emerged into the blustery wind that whipped from the still turbulent ocean. Despite the roll of the ship, others were walking the gleaming deck, but they had taken more precautions against the weather. Elizabeth wore baggy pleated slacks and a silk blouse with a matching scarf round her throat. She glanced down and was pleased to see that the cold wind had caused her nipples to rise so that they showed through her blouse.

Although she gave most people the impression of sophistication, in many ways Elizabeth Mueller was still an immature girl. The finishing school her parents had insisted she attend in Switzerland had taught her to dress, walk and talk like a European woman of the world; she could also ride, ski, arrange flowers or a dinner party, discuss a certain amount of literature and recognise paintings by the leading artists since the Renaissance. But in the matter of romance she was as unworldly as most other girls of seventeen. The chaperon system at the finishing school had been as efficient as the discipline at a military academy. Her knowledge of sex was limited to the information contained in the books she and the other girls had smuggled into the school. To be sure, some of them had been bought in Paris, where the Olympia Press did its best to alleviate the demand for enlightenment, but, until now, her experience was limited to theory rather than practice.

'Good morning,' she heard a voice call from behind, and turned to see Sir Julian Nettlebury and his two girls. Elizabeth had met them at her father's party. She liked Sir Julian, but thought Anne stand-offish.

'Good morning,' she replied civilly. 'I was told you were not well, Irene. You look fit enough now.'

'James Gideon read to me, and I got better,' she said.

'I think it had more to do with the ship's doctor,' her father added.

'Well, I think it was Gideon,' Irene said stubbornly.

'James Gideon didn't advise you to put cotton wool in your ears,' Anne said. She had to raise her voice against the wind.

'Cotton wool?' Elizabeth asked.

'Nettlebury nodded. 'There is a theory that seasickness may have something to do with the mechanism of the inner ear. Anyway, it seems to have worked with this young lady.'

'They had reached an open stretch on the deck, and Nettlebury tugged at Irene's sleeve. 'I've had enough,' he said. 'Come on, let's leave these two together.'

The two girls walked on in awkward silence. Neither was quite sure of the causes of their antipathy; neither realised that they both held each other in a certain amount of envy and awe. Elizabeth's time at the finishing school had made her acutely aware of how provincial St Paul's, Minnesota, was to the aristocratic girls who had been her fellow-pupils; and her father's position as a Middle-Western businessman – which was how her recent companions had thought of him – had given her cause to wish he had more glamour. Anne, as the daughter of a famous artist with a title, was to be envied, and she had mistaken her shyness and English accent for disdain.

Anne, on the other hand, had looked upon Elizabeth, with her stunning wardrobe and effortless small-talk, as the epitome of worldly sophistication. Now both were trapped by a mutual regard for each other that they could not express without fearing that the other would consider the first advance a sign of weakness. Strangely it was Anne, with her greater degree of reserve, who broke the web.

'There's Gideon ahead,' she said as they caught sight of him with Laszlo, leaning against the ship's rail. Then she spoke without thinking. 'Isn't he handsome?'

Elizabeth, looking at her in astonishment, saw that a deep blush had come to Anne's usually pale features. The words had been spoken with such thoughtless honesty that she answered in kind. 'He's the best-looking boy I've ever seen,' she replied. For a moment they were united as they approached the two men.

They both smiled, but Anne noticed that something was worrying Laszlo. He was as polite as ever, but he continued to gaze out to sea after they had exchanged greetings. Gideon talked to Anne for a moment about Irene, but his gaze kept returning to Elizabeth's silk blouse.

Then, as happens at sea, a sudden calm descended on the ocean and Laszlo's disposition became as sunny as the cloudless skies. 'Please excuse us, ladies,' he said, 'but Gideon and I have work to do.' Gideon shrugged his apologies and the two men departed, leaving the girls standing at the rails.

'I think your outfit is lovely,' Anne said suddenly, looking down at her own serviceable sweater.

'I wish I had your complexion,' Elizabeth replied and touched her own flawless skin with the back of her hand. Then, after a moment's hesitation, she added, 'I have some make-up that would be perfect for you if you'd like to try it.'

Laszlo had stopped at the Purser's office to retrieve his parcel on their return journey to the cabin. When they were inside, he locked the door and turned to Gideon. 'Will you be able to draw, now that the sea is calm?' he asked anxiously. Gideon nodded.

Laszlo sighed with relief and opened the parcel. Inside was a leather binder that contained the Racine manuscript. Protecting the pages were two blank sheets of the same heavy paper. Laszlo carefully took the sheets and handed them to Gideon, then produced the ink and fine-nibbed pen he had procured from the writing-room the previous night. 'Do you think you can manage two Watteau drawings before we meet the Muellers for lunch?' he said with a dry little laugh.

Gideon questioned Laszlo for some minutes and, when he was

satisfied with the answers, sat thinking for a while longer. At last he made up his mind. 'Go to the Entertainment Officer and see if you can borrow some watercolour paints and brushes. They're bound to have some in the children's play cupboard. Then see if you can get your hands on a good magnifying-glass. They should have one in the chart-room. Oh, and a couple of saucers. White ones would be preferable.'

Laszlo set off to obtain the necessary supplies and Gideon sat down at a small table and made a few preliminary experiments on the surface of the paper. As he suspected, it was as dry as ancient bones and coated with a fine layer of gritty dust, which caused the nib of the pen to lift tufts of the textured surface. Rather like the consistency of blotting-paper, Gideon thought, and started to become intrigued by the problems he had to surmount. He put down the two sheets on the marble-topped washstand in the corner and rummaged around in a drawer until he found the remains of the two sleeves Laszlo had cut from his shirt. Then he soaked one of the sleeves in water and carefully dabbed the two precious sheets until they had flattened out on the marble. While he waited for Laszlo to return, he searched the cabin and found some pages of *The New York Times* lining the bottom of a wardrobe. When Laszlo tapped on the door a few minutes later, he was ready.

'I've got everything you asked for,' Laszlo said. 'I had to convince the officer in the chart-room that I was an expert on insects and needed to identify a rare moth we discovered this morning.'

Gideon set out the objects on the marble surface next to the dampened sheets of paper and mixed ink and watercolour paint in the saucers. He took the sable brush and made a few strokes of the mixture on the newspaper pages, then mixed again until he was completely satisfied. Laszlo was pacing nervously around the room until Gideon told him to sit down. He took a seat on the edge of his bed.

Finally Gideon turned. 'If you are comfortable,' he said with a slight bow, 'the performance will begin.' Then, with the same swift strokes Laszlo had seen him use in the Hungarian Café, he filled the first page with beautifully executed figures. Foliage was added, and quick washes of tone. It seemed only a few minutes before the first sketch was completed, and Laszlo began to rise from the bed to inspect the work.

'Not yet,' Gideon commanded, and Laszlo sank back. After a pause, Gideon flexed the muscles of his back and bent over the second sheet. A few more minutes passed and he stood up again. 'Finished,' he said.

Laszlo leaped up to examine the drawings. 'They're beautiful,' he breathed reverently.

'Just one more touch.' Gideon reached for the magnifying-glass and carefully added a few minute words and numbers, which he wove into a corner of the foliage at the foot of each page.

A thought suddenly occurred to Laszlo, and he glanced at his watch. 'My God, they're still wet, and we're due at lunch with the Muellers in half an hour!'

Gideon smiled. 'Ring for room service and say we want crêpes suzettes for two immediately.'

With the speed on which the Cunard line prided itself, a few minutes later a steward arrived at the door. When he tapped, with suitable discretion, he could hear a violent argument taking place from within the cabin as he wheeled in a spirit-stove and the ingredients for the dish.

Eventually Laszlo called over his shoulder, 'Now I, Laszlo Vasilakis, will show you how a crêpe should be properly executed, you ignorant English peasant!' He turned to the steward with a smile and handed him five dollars. 'Thank you,' he said. 'I shall prepare the dish myself.'

The man withdrew and Laszlo sought respite from his anxiety with a large glass of Grand Marnier.

Meanwhile, Gideon dried the wet sheets of paper over the flames of the stove. When he was satisfied, he threw the two drawings on the bed. 'Done to a turn, as our old cook used to say.'

Laszlo looked at the drawings again and the same question that had bothered him since he had first met Gideon entered his mind. 'Tell me why you never became a professional artist?'

Gideon, who was leaning towards the mirror to button his shirt collar, looked round and smiled. 'My family didn't think it was a proper job, old boy,' he said lightly.

'A proper job?' Laszlo repeated, puzzled.

'That's right.' Gideon began to adjust his tie. When he had his jacket arranged to his satisfaction, he lit a cigarette and leaned against the washstand. 'You see, my family were all actors. My grandfather on my mother's side of the family, and both my father's parents, were all in the theatre. As I told you before, they couldn't believe that anyone would want to do anything else. My ability to draw was considered to be about as important as being able to

41

whistle in tune or ride a bicycle. Acting was the only true art. So drawing didn't mean much to me. Maybe if I'd gone to a normal school, instead of having tutors, someone might have persuaded me differently, but by the time Ilse came into my life it was just one of those odd things I could do.' He stubbed out his cigarette. 'It was useful for making Christmas and birthday cards,' he continued, 'but no substitute for being able to remember lines or cry on demand.'

'Ilse was the governess who taught you about art?' Laszlo said.

'I suppose she was the first person who made me feel worth while. According to my family, I had very little talent as an actor.'

Laszlo covered his face with his hands for a moment, then got up and put the drawings away in the leather portfolio.

Otto was pouring champagne when they were shown into the Muellers' stateroom.

Gideon looked around, but there was no sign of Elizabeth. Anthony Strange was sitting on the long sofa next to Elsa Mueller, his white flannels restored to their former glory by the ship's laundry. Erich Mueller handed them glasses. Laszlo introduced Gideon. Strange looked at him with interest.

'Gideon . . . Gideon,' he repeated. 'Don't I know someone at White's by that name?'

'It's possible,' Gideon said noncommittally. He smiled at Elsa Mueller and sat down on the arm of the sofa next to her. It was done with such self-assurance that Strange was reluctant to pursue the question, but Laszlo caught a swift exchange of glances with Otto. It was obvious that the steward Laszlo had tipped so generously had passed on the contents of the cable.

'James has until now been, shall we say, savouring life,' Laszlo said, raising his glass to Elsa in a tiny salute, 'but his family have agreed that he shall join me in the world of art.'

'So you're going to lend Vasilakis some respectability, are you?' Strange asked. His voice seemed, to Gideon, to be on the edge of a sneer. He recognised the tone for what it was: the sound of British prejudice baying for foreign blood.

His next remark was almost predictable. 'Up to now he's had to hang around the edges of the London galleries, haven't you, old boy? Sniffing around for what he can scratch out of the cracks. I suppose with you on board, he'll be able to open his own shop.'

Elsa Mueller was in many ways a snob but she was also a lady, and this crude banter smacked of bad manners. 'Shall we have lunch?'

she said icily. Her good humour was restored when Laszlo produced the leather portfolio he had been holding behind his back. 'Oh, but first we must look at the manuscript,' she said in a girlish voice.

Laszlo laid the package down on the desk so that they could all gather round. He flipped open the leather binding and they studied the first drawing in silence. 'There is no doubt about the Racine manuscript,' he said easily. 'It was in the Scheyerman collection for years, and is accepted by the best authorities.' He shrugged. 'But are the drawings genuine?'

Strange picked them up in turn and held them up to the light.

'My dear fellow, they are not banknotes!' Laszlo protested.

Strange looked at him with contempt. Then he picked up one of the pages of manuscript, and did the same. 'I happen to be an expert on eighteenth-century handmade paper,' he said dismissively. 'There is no doubt, Elsa,' he said firmly. 'They are the work of Watteau.'

'Then I must have them,' she said.

Laszlo shook his head. 'I have no desire to challenge Mr Strange's opinion, but I really would be happier to wait until we get to London.'

'Come now, Laszlo, let them hear your real reason,' said Strange. 'You just want to make sure you're getting the right price.' He turned to Mueller, who had stayed silent. 'Let's call in Nettlebury to decide.'

'I had already thought of that,' Laszlo said in an exasperated voice. He turned to Gideon. 'Remember, I asked him last night if he was an expert on Watteau's work?'

Gideon nodded. 'He said that he wasn't sufficiently familiar with the period.'

'He will confirm my judgment if we ask him,' Strange said tightly. He turned to Mueller. 'May we send Otto to fetch him here?'

Mueller nodded, and while they all waited, the room became filled with tension. Eventually a puzzled Nettlebury joined them, and Strange took hold of his arm.

'I have assured Herr Mueller that these drawings are by Watteau,' he said. 'Will you please tell them that I am correct?'

Nettlebury gently shook his arm free and took out a pair of spectacles. 'So this is what you were getting at last night?' he said to Laszlo, who replied with a nod. He picked up the drawings and studied them briefly, then put his spectacles away.

'Well?' said Strange.

'They certainly look like his work.'

'So you are saying they *are* by Watteau?' Strange urged.

'I'm not saying that at all. As I told Laszlo, by no stretch of the

43

imagination can I be considered an expert on Watteau. In this case, my judgment is worthless.'

'Very well,' said Strange. He was fighting to control his temper. 'You have my absolute guarantee that they are genuine. When we decide on a price, I shall underwrite it. If anyone throws doubt on their veracity, I will pay the same to take them off your hands, Herr Mueller.'

It was only then that Laszlo ventured a smile.

'Pull!' Erich Mueller shouted, and two black discs were sent spinning across the calm water of the Atlantic. The twelve-bore shotgun he cradled against his shoulder barked twice, and the clay pigeons disintegrated into puffs of black dust.

'Good shot!' Gideon said with genuine admiration.

'Your turn,' said Mueller. 'Now, remember what I told you.'

Gideon stood as instructed, his weight balanced on his rear foot,. the shotgun held at waist level with his trigger-finger outside the guard.

'Ready?' Mueller asked.

'Ready.'

'Pull,' Mueller called again, and two more clay pigeons floated with deceptive speed across their line of vision.

Gideon leaned forward to transfer the weight on to his other foot, and with a smooth motion lifted the shotgun so that the polished walnut stock slammed against his right cheek. His finger curled around the first trigger, and with both eyes open he swung his body from the waist to follow the flight of the target. The first clay pigeon disintegrated, which gave him a momentary thrill of pleasure, but his second shot missed and the black disc went curving on until it dropped into the sea.

'Not bad,' Mueller said as Gideon broke open the shotgun and threw the empty cartridges over the side. 'But you stopped swinging on your second shot. It's a common fault with beginners.'

'Thank you,' Gideon called to the deck-hand who had operated the skeet-gun as they walked away from the stern. Above them, seagulls wheeled and dived.

'English birds, come out to greet us,' Mueller said, and they both felt the curious mixture of anticipation and sadness that comes at the end of any sea voyage. 'Don't forget we are all meeting in my rooms for champagne tonight before the Fancy Dress Ball,' he added. 'Oh, and I've invited a journalist I gave an interview to this morning. A man named Keswick. He's going to write a piece about my collection.'

'Have you got your costume yet?' Gideon asked.

His companion nodded. 'Elsa supervised the selection yesterday. How about you?'

'Mine is proving a little difficult,' said Gideon. 'I'm part of a double act.' Ahead he could see Irene Nettlebury, who had been watching them from a distance. 'And here's the second half.'

'You haven't told anyone what we're going as?' she asked anxiously as they reached her.

'Not even Mr Mueller,' he answered.

Mueller took the shotgun from Gideon and weighed the balance. 'I must get Otto to clean these,' he said. 'When we get to England, I'm going to order a pair of Purdeys.'

'What are Purdeys, Herr Mueller?' Irene asked politely.

'The finest shotguns in the world, young lady. You have to be fitted for them. It's rather like having a suit made in Savile Row.'

Irene watched Mueller depart before she spoke. 'Grown-ups have their toys like children, don't they, Gideon?'

'I suppose they do.' It had never occurred to him that men shooting at things they were not going to eat could be described as playing with toys.

'They told me your costume was easy,' Irene said, conducting the conversation in her normal tangential manner. 'They already had a Bonnie Prince Charlie outfit and those were just the sorts of clothes Alan Breck wore, weren't they?'

'I think Alan Breck carried more pistols than Bonnie Prince Charlie,' Gideon replied. 'But he certainly wore the same tartan trews.'

'The blood of kings flows in my veins,' Irene growled in a Scottish accent.

'What about your costume?' Gideon asked.

'They had a bit of trouble with it at first, but Lieutenant Cosgrove solved it. Mind you, it was only because Anne was with me. I think he's in love with her.'

'How did he sort your costume out?'

Irene smiled. 'Well, they didn't have a David Balfour outfit, but he's got the ship's tailor to make me one.'

Gideon was impressed. 'Lieutenant Cosgrove must be in love if he's gone to that much trouble,' he said drily as they reached the storeroom where stewards were dealing with the costumes for the ball.

Ahead of them, in the line of people waiting, they could see

45

Anthony Strange being served. It was evident, from the pitchfork he was being handed, what his choice of roles had been.

'At least he's staying in character,' Irene whispered.

Strange passed them with a barely perceptible nod, and they shuffled forward.

'Better the devil you know,' said Gideon, unable to resist it.

'Oh, we don't just *know* him. We're related. He's a second cousin of my father.'

Now it was Gideon's turn to be surprised. 'I had no idea!'

Irene nodded. 'Anthony Strange's parents were always jealous of our part of the family because they weren't as posh as us,' she said in a matter-of-fact voice. 'According to Anne, he likes to humiliate Daddy for everything they had to put up with from the Nettleburys.'

Once again Gideon wondered at the intricate web of class and snobbery that bound the English. Because of his family's calling and his erratic education, he had never fully absorbed the usual English prejudices about hierarchy. His own parents had ignored the normal boundaries of the class system; they owed their allegiance to the aristocracy that ruled the theatre.

Irene took her costume from the steward and turned to Gideon. 'I'm going to try it on,' she said in an excited voice. 'I'll see you at Herr Mueller's before the ball.'

When he reached his own cabin, Gideon found Laszlo studying two large photographic prints of the drawings they had sold to Mueller.

'I've just collected these from the ship's photographer,' he said. 'Take a look.'

He handed Gideon the magnifying-glass, and he peered at the photographs. On their way to the lunch, Laszlo had insisted that they stop to have negatives made of the drawings. The photographer had only taken a few minutes to do the job, and now the finished prints were in their hands.

'Yes, it's quite clear,' Gideon said with relief. 'When shall we show him?'

'I think Herr Mueller's party before the ball would be appropriate.' Laszlo's eyes wandered to the costume he was to wear that evening. 'I want to be dressed for the part.'

Garbed respectively as Alan Breck and Roy Rogers, Gideon and Laszlo were among the last to arrive at the party. For a while they looked around, accustomising themselves to the different personal-

ities people assumed when they wore fancy dress. Gideon spotted
Erich Mueller as a pirate captain; the heavy brocade coat and sword
belt suited his broad girth. He was deep in conversation with Sherlock
Holmes and the Devil. Elsa Mueller, exquisitely clothed in pale blue
silk and a high powdered wig, was clearly Marie Antoinette. The
Episcopalian bishop, standing arms akimbo and legs spread wide,
represented Henry VIII. His wife was more demure in a nun's habit.
Another group consisted of Sir Julian Nettlebury as Count Dracula,
Anne in the tights and cocked hat of a principal boy, with a stuffed cat
under her arm, and Lieutenant Cosgrove in Red Indian feathers and
war-paint.

Gideon felt a sudden tug on his sleeve and turned to find Irene
enchantingly garbed as David Balfour.

'Are we supposed to stay together,' she asked, 'or is it all right for
me to roam about?'

'You have to be with me only when they judge the contest,' he
assured her.

'You don't mind if I don't stay with you?' she asked, anxious not to
offend him.

'Not in the least.' His eyes sought Elizabeth Mueller, and she chose
that moment to make her entrance.

Knowing there was a certain amount of licence in what one could
wear to a costume ball, she had exercised that liberty to the extreme.
Seven wisps of floating material and a few slave bangles were all she
needed to be the perfect Salome. The effect was stunning. For a
moment all conversation died away as every head turned to look at
her. Her mother's frozen smile and fluttering fan were the only hint
of disapproval. Gideon was the first to reach her side. He was about to
speak when he heard an angry voice raised nearby.

'If you wish to speak to Herr Mueller about the drawings, I demand
to be present,' Strange was saying loudly.

'Excuse me,' Gideon said to Elizabeth. He hurried to join Laszlo,
who was holding up a hand to placate Strange's rage.

'My dear fellow, let us not spoil Herr Mueller's party,' Laszlo said
soothingly. 'It is just that I could not rest a minute longer without
telling him what I have learned.'

'Shall we go into the other room?' Mueller suggested. 'It will be
more private there.'

'I insist on accompanying you,' Strange said, 'and I want Keswick to
come too.' He indicated a figure dressed as Sherlock Holmes, whom
Gideon assumed was the journalist Mueller had invited to the party.

'I have no objections,' said Mueller. 'Do you?'

Laszlo shook his head, and they all trooped next door, leaving Elsa Mueller to entertain the other guests.

When Mueller turned to face him in the smaller room, Laszlo took a sheet of paper from his pocket. 'First, I must show you this message I received a short time ago,' he said, handing a ship's cable to Mueller, who studied the cryptic numbers it contained for a few moments.

'Well?' he asked, puzzled.

'Those are the dates of the birth and death of Watteau,' said Laszlo. Mueller nodded his understanding. 'Now look at this.' Laszlo produced a photograph and the magnifying-glass from inside his buckskin jacket. 'Just there.' He indicated the area of the print for him to examine. Mueller did as instructed, then examined the cable again. 'Well, if my calculations are correct,' Laszlo said finally, 'Watteau would have had to have done those drawings when he was seven years of age.'

To Strange's horror, he saw that Keswick had removed the large curved pipe from his mouth and produced a notebook and pen.

Later that evening Gideon finally held Salome in his arms, even though it was under the disapproving stare of Elsa Mueller, who had finally been persuaded by her husband to allow Elizabeth to attend the ball. Aware that he was envied by practically every man in the ballroom, he danced with careful gusto, making sure that he didn't tread on Elizabeth's bare toes. Nettlebury and the bishop's wife passed close to them as they circled the floor.

'I hope you and Laszlo are not afraid of curses,' he said in a jovial manner. 'The devil Strange has vowed all sorts of vengeance.'

Gideon smiled back, and Elizabeth's supple body pressed against him for a moment, making him wish he was not clad from head to foot in tartan and lace. 'Isn't it odd?' he said, looking into Elizabeth's sensual face. 'Last week I didn't have any friends or enemies.' He paused for a moment and she pressed against him again. 'Or anyone I wanted.'

At the end of their dance, there was a roll of drums and the captain announced the results of the fancy dress competition. Elizabeth won, more for the amount of her body revealed than the tiny pieces of costume, Gideon suspected.

Irene and Gideon came second. Irene was delighted with the jack-knife presented to her by the captain.

'An incomplete Salome,' Nettlebury said to Anne. 'She should have had the head of John the Baptist.'

'What does it matter, when she's got Gideon's?' Anne said softly.

CHAPTER THREE

Half-way down Curzon Street, Laszlo leaned forward in the cab and rapped on the glass partition. 'This will be fine,' he called to the driver, and the taxi pulled to the side. He gave the man half-a-crown and enjoyed the reassuring sensation of handling the heavy English coin once again.

Gideon looked up at the skyline and was suddenly cheered by the scale of the buildings. The houses that lined the street were intended to impress, but they did not intimidate him quite so much as skyscrapers; New York was a city that literally overwhelmed.

'This way. It's not far now,' said Laszlo. They carried their bags through an archway into a web of narrow cobbled streets, and the atmosphere changed from sedate respectability to one of shabby Bohemia. Gideon was reminded of an occasion when he had been watching a production from the wings of a theatre, and the actress playing Lady Macbeth swept off with regal grandeur and took a bottle of stout from her dresser who was waiting at the side of the stage.

Shops, public houses and cafés crowded close together. Bustling people spilt on to the narrow streets. Delivery-boys weaved between them, the bells jingling on their bicycles. Every few yards women, walking at a different, slower pace, muttered invitations as Laszlo and Gideon passed. Laszlo acknowleged each approach with a smile and a polite refusal, until he turned down a narrow mews. At the far end of the yard a man was grooming a bay work-horse. Laszlo took a key from his pocket and unlocked a small blue door.

The single flight of stairs was so narrow that it was difficult to manage with their cases, but at last they stood in a tiny room, so crammed with furniture that Gideon had to rest his suitcase on the arm of a velvet-covered chair. He had felt antlike on the streets of New York; now he was reminded of Gulliver among the Lilliputians.

Standing in the middle of the room was a small woman who

matched the scale of the petite décor. Laszlo threaded his way through the maze of chairs, sofas and tables, each laden with china figures, small vases and framed photographs showing various Alpine scenes.

Gideon noticed that with each tread of his foot the creaking floorboards beneath the Persian rugs sent little shock-waves through the room, so that the surfaces would tremble and the china figures jingle softly, as if affected by the tremors of an earthquake. The woman stood with her hands on her hips, as still as if she were also made of china. She made no effort to raise her face as Laszlo stooped to plant a careful kiss on her cheek.

'I am home, Sylvia. And I have brought a friend to stay,' he said in a voice Gideon had not heard before, the sort one used against a dangerous and powerful adversary.

'So I see,' she replied in an accent Gideon could not immediately place. He realised that in all the hours they had talked, Laszlo had described many aspects of his life, but had hardly mentioned anything about his wife.

Gideon studied her now, and realised how wrong he had been when he had first imagined her. Somehow he had expected an olive-skinned woman, powerful, with a dark mane of glossy hair, and jangling jewellery. The kind of gypsy wife a bad playwright would have given a Hungarian, he reflected ruefully. Instead, the unsmiling figure confronting him was as northern as a winter's day; it was as if she had been fashioned from snow and ice. He looked at the slim, well-formed figure, the pale blonde hair, and realised that the grey unblinking eyes gazing at him now were devoid of interest.

'I must go back to the shop,' she said. 'There is a telephone message for you. Make your own arrangements for your friend.' Each statement was made in a staccato fashion, without emotion, as though she were slicing sausage. They watched her go in silence, and Gideon noticed that no tremor passed through the room at her departure.

'Swiss,' Laszlo said with an apologetic shrug, when they heard the door to the street close behind her. Gideon was impressed that so much could be conveyed by one word.

Laszlo moved to a small writing-bureau and shuffled quickly through a bundle of unopened letters. 'She owns an antique shop in Burlington Arcade,' he said eventually, gesturing around the room as if to explain the presence of the clutter. Gideon noticed Laszlo's use of the word 'she'; it clearly had significance. Laszlo was always precise, unless vagueness was necessary to his plans. 'Mueller has rung,' he said in a happier voice.

When they had all parted at Southampton, Laszlo had deliberately not given one of his cards to the American, but Otto had been dispatched by Mueller to request his telephone number. Gideon already knew where they were staying. The morning after the fancy dress ball he had contrived to take Elizabeth for a long walk round the decks.

Laszlo put the unopened letters to one side, sat down in a chair by the telephone and dialled a number. After a few minutes' delay he was speaking to Erich Mueller.

'Tea at the Ritz?' he repeated, raising an eyebrow at Gideon. 'We would be delighted. Yes, until four o'clock, then. Goodbye.' He replaced the receiver and folded his arms across his chest. 'I can detect the scent of opportunity,' he said to Gideon, who had sat down in the velvet chair with his suitcase on his lap. 'Let me show you your bedroom,' he said with sudden enthusiasm and jumped to his feet. Narrowly avoiding a trembling table, he side-stepped across the room to open a door just beneath the sloping pitch of the roof. It was hardly more than a cupboard, with a small skylight window. Inside the minute space stood an iron-framed single bed, a washstand with jug and basin and a single wooden chair. Laszlo considered the closet for a moment, and looked at Gideon's suitcase. 'It's a good job you don't have many clothes!'

Later in the afternoon, before they made their way through Mayfair to the Ritz, Laszlo showed him the store-room on the ground floor of the mews house. It had once been a stable, and the whitewashed walls still had a few items of harness hanging from nails around the rafters.

'Our stock in trade,' Laszlo said grandly, indicating the few paintings that rested against the walls.

'Are they worth anything?'

Laszlo shrugged. 'One or two of the frames are not bad,' he said sadly. Then he brightened up and slapped Gideon on the shoulder. 'But who knows? Soon it could be a treasure-house.' He checked the padlock when he closed the wide doors and glanced up at the grey, hurrying sky. 'I don't think it will rain,' he said without much confidence, 'but we'd better hurry.'

After a brisk walk, they found Herr Mueller seated beneath a palm font in the lounge of the hotel, reading a newspaper. He was dressed in a grey double-breasted suit that did not flatter his bulky body. Gideon noticed that his legs were so short that only the tips of his well-polished shoes rested on the marble floor.

'Did you see the piece that fellow Keswick wrote?' he said with a quick smile. 'I don't think Strange will care for it.'

Laszlo nodded, and they sat down at the table.

Mueller was sipping a cup of China tea, surveying the remains of a substantial tea. 'My wife and daughter have already eaten,' he explained as he set the newspaper aside. 'Even now their capacity astounds me.'

'Where are the good ladies?' Laszlo asked.

Mueller nodded in a westerly direction. 'They have gone shopping. The long sea voyage has given them another appetite, as well.' He waited until the table had been reset before he began. 'I'm grateful that you could manage to come so soon,' he said as the waiter poured him a fresh cup of tea. 'The reason I asked you here is because I have a problem.'

Laszlo suppressed a smile, and Gideon noticed the new plates of cakes and sandwiches provided. A week before, he would have set about them, but regular meals aboard the *Mauretania* had diminished his appetite.

Mueller contemplated his next sentence. Finally he began again. 'Before I left the United States, I was about to enter into an arrangement with Anthony Strange to act as my agent in the purchase of paintings.'

Laszlo nodded. 'So I understand.'

'I now consider Strange unsuitable for the task, after his deplorable behaviour over the incident of your manuscript.' Mueller held up his hand before Laszlo could speak. 'Of course I hold you in no way responsible for the outcome. In fact, you behaved honourably throughout the entire affair.' Laszlo nodded gravely and sipped his tea. 'But you must realise, gentlemen, that I am now without advice.' Mueller paused again. 'I mean no disrespect to your profession when I compare myself to a sheep among wolves.'

'Surely you mean sheep-dogs, Herr Mueller?' Gideon asked innocently.

Mueller sat back, and a slight smile crossed his face. 'No, Mr Gideon, I said what I mean. When my wife and daughter are present, I may give the appearance of being a bit of a fool, but I come from generations of peasant farmers and I must tell you that my background has given me a streak of suspicion that runs through my body, as wide as a railroad track.'

Laszlo was about to speak, but Mueller held up his hand again. 'Now, I know you pulled a fast one on Anthony Strange, but if you can, others can. I don't know how you did it, but it's sufficient for me that you won. And you didn't cheat me into the bargain, which goes in your favour.' He leaned forward, clearly enjoying himself. 'So I'll tell you what I'm going to offer. You two find me the pictures that I need to buy, and I'll see that you make a good profit.'

Laszlo and Gideon exchanged glances. Laszlo steepled his fingers and brushed the point of his chin. 'Tell me more about the collection you want to put together,' he said. 'Are there any particular styles or individuals you wish to concentrate on?'

Mueller waved his hand in the air with a gentle brushing motion, and when he spoke, Gideon could hear the uncertainty in his voice. 'They must be important German or British artists.'

Laszlo nodded. 'What about periods? Do you wish to limit the collection to any particular century?'

Mueller was in difficulties now. He sat forward in his chair and puffed out his cheeks in concentration. 'I've got to be able to understand them,' he said finally. 'Nothing modern.'

Laszlo nodded again. 'By that you mean no abstract paintings, I take it? You would not object to a picture by a living artist, providing you could recognise what he had painted?'

Mueller smiled with relief. 'That's it! You've got the idea. Of course I'd like the picture to tell some kind of story – have a message.'

'A message?'

Mueller spoke with sudden confidence, as if he had remembered a previous conversation. 'Each picture must have some positive thing to say about either of the countries. I want them to stress the noble similarities.'

Gideon was reminded of an actor repeating the lines of a play he didn't fully understand, but Laszlo seemed satisfied. He reached out in absent-minded fashion and took a tiny sandwich, then noticed what he had done and placed it on his own plate uneaten.

'You do understand that there will be considerable expenses involved?'

Mueller reached for his cheque-book with relief. As always, he liked problems that could be solved with money. 'I'll make this out for a thousand pounds,' he said in a business-like voice. 'My London agents are Grant and Catton. They have offices in Gracechurch

Street. I'll arrange for a special deposit to be made at my bank, and you can present them with a monthly account.'

Laszlo took the cheque and casually slipped it into his pocket without giving it a glance. 'Excellent,' he said. 'We shall begin immediately. Now, where will you keep the collection?'

Mueller was more relaxed now; he sat back in his chair and smiled. 'We've taken a house in Belgravia. The agents say there's a ballroom that's suitable for a picture gallery. The house isn't finished yet, but you can see it tomorrow, if you like.'

Laszlo, aware of how short the attention span of the rich could be, wanted to make another point. 'One more thing,' he said firmly. Mueller sat up again at the tone of his voice. 'There is a great deal of work in acquiring a collection as important as the one you plan. We shall have to make large demands on your time. Although we shall be finding the pictures, the final selection will be down to you. Of course we shall be there to guide you, but in the end the choice must be yours.'

Mueller slowly nodded his head. 'I understand. It's really like a partnership.'

'Exactly,' Laszlo replied.

The man smiled, and held out his hand. 'In that case, gentlemen, you must call me Erich.'

Elsa Mueller and Elizabeth returned as they were shaking hands.

'You were quicker than I expected, my dear,' Erich said as they rose to greet the women.

'Elizabeth became bored. You know how disagreeable she can become when that happens,' Elsa said, removing her gloves and glancing round the table. 'Why were you shaking hands?'

'Laszlo and Gideon are going to help me build the collection. We shall be seeing a great deal more of them in the future.'

'How delightful,' Elsa said with a warm smile for Laszlo. It cooled slightly when she saw how Elizabeth was studying Gideon's profile. All her life she had known when her daughter wanted something.

Laszlo was silent when they left the hotel. They had turned into Half-Moon Street before Gideon spoke. 'How do you think he found out about the manuscript?'

Laszlo looked up; he had been deep in thought. 'He didn't. I told it all to Elsa Mueller, and she passed it on to him.' Gideon glanced at him in astonishment. Laszlo nodded. 'Women love confessions, especially women like Elsa. As soon as she knew, she was on our side. Of course I did not tell her you did the drawings. It's best she doesn't know everything.'

A flurry of rain speckled the dusty pavement ahead, causing them to increase their easy pace.

'So Herr Mueller wasn't so wise, after all,' said Gideon.

Laszlo shook his head. 'Elsa is the wise member of the family.'

'What about Elizabeth?'

Laszlo thought for a moment. 'She hasn't decided what kind of person she is going to be. It makes her erratic.'

They walked on in silence, and Gideon wondered how Laszlo could be so clever with Elsa Mueller and yet so hesitant when it came to dealing with his own wife.

The first pale light of day entered through the skylight and fell on Gideon's patchwork quilt. He had passed a surprisingly comfortable night in the claustrophobic little space. Now he awoke to the sound of someone moving about softly in the next room. The tread was too light for Laszlo; he guessed it must be his wife. Then he heard the door to the street open softly and click shut, and a few moments later Laszlo entered the room carrying a cup of coffee.

'She's gone,' he said in the tone one might use to announce the termination of an illness. 'Would you like to come out and drink this?'

Gideon did as he was invited, pausing only to put on the mackintosh that served him as a dressing-gown. Sitting on one of the tiny chairs, he sipped the coffee. It was delicious. He glanced at his watch and saw that it was still only seven-thirty, but Laszlo was already bathed and dressed.

'I didn't realise you were such an early riser,' he said. 'Do people start dealing in pictures at this time of day?'

Laszlo stood by the window that overlooked the mews, and sipped his own coffee. 'Sylvia has gone to a sale in Cheltenham. When she creeps softly about the house I find it deeply intimidating; it is as if a military band is playing in the next room.'

'So what are our plans for the rest of the morning?'

Laszlo crossed the room and picked up a pile of catalogues which were heaped on the floor by the writing-bureau. 'I want you to study these. They give the prices that pictures have fetched in sales for the last ten years. When the shops open, we shall buy you a suitable selection of clothes.'

'Are you saying I've got to get rid of my old blue suit?' said Gideon.

'Oh no,' Laszlo replied. 'There are times when an old suit is exactly the thing to wear for a particular sale.'

Gideon looked down at the catalogues Laszlo had dumped in his lap and then noticed that he was putting on his jacket. 'What are you going to do now?' he asked.

Laszlo moved towards the door as he spoke. 'I have some things to do for Sylvia at the shop. I shall be back in a few hours.'

Gideon turned his attention to the catalogues. Having studied scripts over the years, he was able to read the illustrated lists in a certain way. He found he could memorise the prices quite efficiently, and certain names began to emerge as a pattern. Some were already familiar, but others took on a new significance. He soon exhausted the pile Laszlo had given him and began to dig deeper into the heap on the floor.

When Laszlo returned, it was after ten o'clock. He found Gideon in a haze of cigarette smoke. 'I thought you had decided to burn the place down when I saw fumes creeping under the door,' he said, opening the window.

'This stuff is absolutely fascinating,' Gideon said, without looking up from the catalogue he was studying.

'Why do you say that?' Laszlo called from the kitchen, where he was filling the coffee-pot.

Gideon got up and leaned against the doorway. 'The range of prices.' He flipped through a catalogue. 'It's like some damned sports league. Somebody plays in the five-hundred-guinea division for a year and then they move up to a thousand guineas. Then, suddenly, there's a break-through and they're up there at the top.'

'The analogy with a sporting league is a good one, but there is one significant difference.' He took a bite from a croissant and held the plate up to Gideon.

Gideon shook his head. 'What significant difference?'

'Nobody's price ever goes down,' said Laszlo. 'Sometimes people vanish altogether, but they never go down.'

'There's something else,' said Gideon. 'There are no women.'

Laszlo prepared two cups of coffee and handed one to Gideon before he answered. 'Some people claim they do not have the proper temperament to be artists.'

'That's rubbish! Look at the theatre. There are magnificent actresses, and they've got the temperament to go with it. You should hear my mother when she's thwarted!'

57

'That's not quite what I mean,' Laszlo said mildly. 'Undoubtedly there are fine women painters; Gwen John and Vanessa Bell spring immediately to mind. But it is rare to find a woman who is prepared to sublimate her entire being to a single aim, and that is what every artist of any significance does. Maybe women are too practical and worldly.' He put down his empty cup and gestured in the direction of the bathroom. 'Now, get into that threadbare suit. We must go shopping. We have an appointment with Mueller to see the house after lunch, and that is an occasion when you should be dressed like the Prince of Wales.'

Ten minutes later, when Laszlo closed the door behind them, they found Anne Nettlebury standing in the mews, anxiously scanning the numbers on the doors. A look of relief came to her face when she saw them. Gideon noticed that she wore a small hat tilted to one side, and her hair was piled high on her head. She wore more make-up than usual, and her smart suit and high heels made her look older and more sophisticated. He remembered that she had spent quite a lot of time with Elizabeth Mueller on the last days of the voyage, and her influence clearly showed.

'Thank goodness I've found you, Mr Vasilakis,' she said. 'I asked a gentleman for directions in the street, and a policeman told me to move on.'

Laszlo raised his black trilby. 'Miss Nettlebury, how can I be of assistance?'

'I really wanted to ask your advice,' she said with a brief smile at Gideon. 'But if it is not convenient now, I can come back at another time.'

She began to turn away, but Laszlo caught her arm and spoke gently. 'Any time is convenient for you, Anne,' he replied. 'We are just going to buy James some new clothes. If you would care to accompany us, I am sure your counsel would be invaluable.'

'I must warn you, I like to choose my own ties,' Gideon said with a reassuring smile.

Their friendliness seemed to calm her, so she fell into step with them. 'It's my father,' she explained during the walk to Jermyn Street. 'Anthony Strange dismissed him because of the Racine manuscript.'

'But why?' Laszlo asked. 'He was completely blameless in the matter. In fact, he warned him that he couldn't help.'

'That didn't seem to matter to Anthony Strange,' she said bitterly.

58

'He waited until we got to London and then he said that my father had been of no use to him at all. And he refused to pay for any of the work he had already done.'

They walked on in silence, and Gideon could see that she was near to tears, but when she spoke again, it was in a level voice. 'You see the truth is, Mr Vasilakis . . . '

'Please call me Laszlo,' he interrupted gently.

'The truth is,' she continued, 'that my father is penniless. He sold a picture for five thousand dollars in America and he thinks that will be enough to keep us for some time, but I know it hardly covers our debts.'

Laszlo held up his hand. 'I see the problem. First we shall shop while I think, then we shall take coffee at Fortnum and Mason, and I will tell you the solution.' He spoke with such confidence that Gideon could see Anne Nettlebury respond to his mood.

Laszlo led them through various shops in Jermyn Street, and by the time they reached the Haymarket, Gideon had been transformed from pauper to prince. A trail of old clothes had been discarded with instructions for them to be forwarded, along with the other purchases, to Laszlo's mews house, so they were unencumbered when they sat down for coffee.

'I thought the motoring gloves were a bit excessive,' Gideon said when Anne admired his appearance.

'Nonsense,' Laszlo replied. 'Remember, a sense of illusion is important. Expensive motoring gloves imply an expensive motorcar outside, even if you have arrived at your destination by tram.'

Laszlo looked around the room. It was crowded with elegant women who filled the air with soft chattering voices and the chink of cup on saucer. 'How calm and pleasant it is in here,' he said in a proprietorial tone. Then he turned to Anne. 'Now, young lady, as promised, I have given your problem some thought. I am prepared to offer your father the same position with us that he held with Anthony Strange. But we, of course, will actually pay his salary. There will, however, be an additional duty to perform.' Laszlo gestured towards Gideon. 'Our friend here requires an education in the history of art and the methods and practice of oil painting. We would require Sir Julian to tutor him in these subjects.'

'How would my father's fees be paid?' Anne asked.

Laszlo looked up at the ceiling while he thought again. 'Three guineas a week for the tuition, ten guineas for the retainer and a percentage of the profit made by us on any pictures purchased that we needed him to authenticate.'

Anne gazed down at the table for a moment, and when she looked up, Gideon suddenly thought how beautiful her eyes were. Their honey colour gleamed through the veil of the hat. 'How many of the pictures will be modern schools?' she asked eventually.

Gideon did not understand the implications of the question, but Laszlo smiled. 'You are concerned that modern pictures might form the bulk of the collection, and that your father would not wish to give an opinion on them?' Anne nodded. 'You may rest easy,' he said with another smile. 'Herr Mueller wishes to collect pictures that will be approved of by the German government, who consider modern painting degenerate art.'

Anne sat back, her face much brighter. 'When can we expect you for your first lesson?' she asked Gideon.

'Any time you like,' he replied with a grin. 'I have a man who brings me coffee at seven-thirty each morning.'

'That's a bit early for us,' Anne said, missing the irony in his voice. 'Nine-thirty would be better.' She took a notebook from her handbag and wrote the address in a clear italic hand.

Laszlo peered over his shoulder. 'Kew? Where is that?' he asked.

'Near Richmond, on the Thames,' Gideon answered.

'Really?' Laszlo said, interested. 'Is that far? How will you get there?'

'Well, I go by Underground,' Anne said. 'But I dare say you could get a bus.'

Laszlo turned to Gideon and opened his arms like an impresario. 'It sounds delightful,' he said with a beaming smile. 'A trip to the country each time you go for a lesson, dear boy. It will be like having a little holiday.'

'Kew isn't in the country,' Gideon said. 'It's in the suburbs.'

Laszlo waved his hand. 'I will have to take your word for it. I often go to other cities, but never to the suburbs.'

They escorted Anne to the Underground entrance, and Laszlo shuddered when he watched her descend the stairs. 'What a brave girl,' he said with deep feeling. 'It must be like entering a grave.'

'Have you never been on the Underground?'

Laszlo shook his head. 'No, nor the Métro in Paris nor the subway in New York. I can think of nothing more horrific than being sealed in a container that is hurtling through a tunnel under the earth.'

*

60

After a pub lunch of sandwiches and pints of bitter, they caught a taxi to their next appointment. The rain had settled into a steady downpour by the time they reached Eaton Square. Gideon took extra care not to slip in his new shoes when they crossed the wide pavement to the porticoed doorway.

Otto, wearing a black linen jacket and carrying a feather duster, greeted them at the door. 'Herr Mueller apologises for his absence.' 'He said that you were to carry on with your inspection without him and he will join you later. He also said that the room to start with is the ballroom at the very top of the house.'

They entered a large hall strewn with tea-chests, scattered straw and old newspapers. Gideon carefully dried the soles of his shoes. Passing under an impressive crystal chandelier, which Laszlo noted was Venetian, they climbed the staircase to the third floor, where they encountered high, carved doors chased with brass.

'Let us see the kind of theatre Mueller has provided for our first production,' Laszlo said, and swung the doors open.

The interior was magnificent. The vast, light-filled room covered the entire top floor. The walls were panelled in pale cherry-wood and the ash floor, sprung for dancing, responded to their steps. They crossed to the centre and looked up at the glass canopy, laced with delicate ironwork, that served as the roof.

'Wonderful,' Laszlo murmured. 'And what a waste.'

'Why do you say that?' Gideon asked, and he executed a few rapid tap steps on the polished floor.

Laszlo walked to one of the walls and stroked the smooth surface with the palm of his hand. The panelling had only just been restored: there were still wood shavings on the floor and a bag of carpenter's tools leaned against one of two scruffy chairs. Gideon searched around among the boxes, jars and rags the french polishers had left and found a tin lid that had served as an ashtray. He lit a cigarette and sat down on one of the chairs.

Laszlo joined him. 'This room is superb,' he said softly. 'What a pity it will house a nonsense.'

'What do you mean?' Gideon blew a stream of smoke towards the roof.

Laszlo watched the wisps of smoke curling up to the glass dome above them. 'Mueller wants to collect only German and British paintings,' he said, almost to himself. 'One might as well form an orchestra that is composed only of brass and woodwind.' He raised his hands and slapped them down on his knees. 'It's like being able

61

to afford a great banquet and settling for a permanent diet of soup and ice cream.'

'Apart from the mixed metaphor,' Gideon said, 'does it really matter? Surely people collect just one thing? You said yourself that it's common for connoisseurs to specialise in a single subject, so why not two?'

Laszlo brushed some dust from the sleeve of his chalk-striped suit. 'That would be acceptable, certainly, but Mueller's intention is not to own paintings he loves. The theme of the collection must demonstrate that England and Germany are parts of the same civilisation. That's not collecting art; it's illustrating propaganda.'

'So you disapprove, do you?'

Laszlo smiled. 'Not passionately; only the way I do about any waste. If I had a Fabergé egg I wouldn't keep buttons in it.' He gestured around the room. 'Think what you *could* display here.'

He shrugged his shoulders. 'Still, we are but humble dealers, we shouldn't question the motives of the people who provide our living.'

'How many motives are there?' Gideon enjoyed listening to Laszlo when he was in a reflective mood.

Laszlo lowered his head so that his chin touched his bow tie. 'Greed, envy and pride are all common reasons for collecting. Inadequate people think they can achieve greatness by collecting the talent of others. Some even have a genuine love of art. Such men and women do exist, thank God.'

Then the twin doors opened and Elsa and Erich Mueller entered the great room. 'What do you think?' Mueller called out as he crossed the floor.

'It's perfect,' Laszlo replied with equal enthusiasm.

'My London lawyers found it for me. I think they did a pretty good job,' Mueller said happily.

'Won't it make a perfect setting for receptions?' said Elsa. 'It will be worth while making guests climb three floors.'

'They say they can put in a lift,' said Erich, 'but I would be sorry to alter the house too much.'

'Tell me, Elsa, will you wish to use the gallery as a ballroom from time to time?' Laszlo asked.

'Well, yes, I'm sure we would,' she replied, and looked round. 'Why, does that present any problem?'

'No, but I have an idea for which I need your approval.'

The Muellers waited while Laszlo walked to the centre of the room and spread out his arms. 'At present, the available wall space would take, oh, approximately two hundred pictures.' The Muellers nodded in agreement. 'If we were to have screens on wheels constructed in the same wood panelling as the walls, they could be moved on to the landing outside when you wished to clear the room for dancing.'

'Excellent,' said Mueller. 'And how many more pictures could we accommodate with such an arrangement?'

Laszlo thought for a moment. 'I would think another two hundred, easily. We could begin to exhibit as soon as the main walls were filled, and add the screens when necessary.'

Mueller nodded again. 'Start immediately as an absolute priority, Laszlo,' he said firmly. 'I wish to have as much of the collection as possible ready for exhibition quite soon.'

Laszlo paused before he spoke. 'Erich, I must speak frankly. Most collections take many years to acquire. It is usually a long slow process, rather like perfecting a fine garden.'

'It must be done quickly.'

Laszlo shrugged. 'It will drive up the prices; every dealer and gallery will know the sorts of pictures we want, and they will charge accordingly.'

'I don't care about the cost,' Mueller said flatly. 'Pay whatever you have to.'

'As you wish.'

Elsa turned to Gideon. 'My daughter is somewhere in the house. She asked if you would speak to her before you leave.'

Laszlo was expanding on his plans to Mueller as Gideon made his excuses and left. The house was deceptively large, and it took some time to find Elizabeth. His footsteps echoed along empty uncarpeted corridors and the musty smell that buildings acquire when they are unoccupied for some time hung in the air, but he found an open door at the far end of the house.

Elizabeth was standing by a large window that overlooked a tree-filled garden washed by the falling rain. There was a melancholy feeling about the sparse little room, and it was reflected in her mood. He edged past a small bed with a bare mattress, and crossed the dusty floorboards to stand next to her.

'Hello, Gideon,' she said without taking her eyes from the rain-streaked glass. 'I'm glad you found me.'

'It took some time. This is a big house.'

She turned to look at him, and when she spoke, her voice was

63

petulant. 'My mother says you're not suitable company for me. She's told me that I'm not permitted to mix socially with tradesmen.'

'Tradesmen?' Gideon repeated, puzzled.

'You sell pictures to us,' said Elizabeth. 'It's not quite the same as the butcher, or the boy who delivers the groceries. You'll even be invited to dinner occasionally. But I mustn't be seen alone in your company, or give anyone the idea that you are my escort. People might get the wrong impression.'

'What about funerals?' Gideon said lightly. 'Is there equality in grief?'

'You're making a joke of it,' said Elizabeth. 'She said you were presumptuous. Aren't you angry?'

'I'm angry at her decision, not her opinion of me.'

Elizabeth moved closer, and laid her head on his shoulder. It was not a passionate gesture, more that of a child wishing to be comforted. 'You're just playing with words, and I thought you would be insulted. Don't you care for me?'

Gideon folded his arms round her, and thought that it was like holding quicksilver. She was wearing a summer frock made of silk, but the room was cold; her slender body trembled against him. The scent of her hair drove the musty smell from the room. He looked through the window at the rain before he answered. 'I care for you, but I don't really feel insulted,' he said in the same light tone. 'My family are all actors; a lot of people still think of us as riff-raff, unfit for decent society. Your mother is no different from a boarding-house landlady who locks up her daughter until the actors have left town.'

Elizabeth stiffened in his arms. She did not mind her mother being considered snobbish, but she wasn't happy with the new category to which Gideon had allocated her. She drew back to look into his face. 'Do you think she is just being bourgeois?' she said, with the hint of challenge in her voice.

Gideon answered her honestly. 'When I think of some of the men I've known in the theatre, I don't think I'd take a chance with any daughter of mine if there were actors about!' Then he thought again. 'On the other hand, I'm not too happy to be thought of as a tradesman.' He had succeeded in changing her mood, but had started to alter his own.

She ran her nails across his back. 'Then you'd better not behave like a tradesman,' she said, and there was a different kind of challenge in her voice.

Gideon cupped a hand behind her head and kissed her. Shock waves passed through his body as she pressed against him and made a soft crooning noise. Suddenly she pushed away. For a moment he thought it was a rejection, but instead she unbuttoned her frock and let it fall to the ground.

'Here?' he said in a low voice.

'Yes, here,' she answered urgently and, before he had removed his jacket and tie, her underwear lay discarded with her dress on the dusty boards.

The small bedstead was covered with a mattress, but when Elizabeth threw herself on it, the springs creaked loudly. Gideon had just enough self-control left to ask her to get up while he dragged the mattress on to the floor and closed the door.

Elizabeth arched her body convulsively and gave one short gasp as he entered her. Momentarily he was aware of the coolness of her skin, and then they were both engulfed by their coupling. Like two streams meeting to form a torrent they thrust and pounded against each other. It was so utterly consuming that he could give no thought to holding back. Before he could detach any part of his mind to prolong the inevitable, it was his turn to give a juddering gasp. Elizabeth's body constricted in a spasm of tension and then she relaxed with a soft moaning sigh.

Gideon rolled on to his back and slowly became aware of his surroundings again. He felt the hard scratchy surface of the mattress beneath him and smelt the dust of the floor. Gradually, as his senses were re-attuned to external sensations, he noticed the cracks in the plaster that ran across the ceiling, and the fading striped paper that peeled in places from the walls. He could feel the old dampness of the room and the slight tickling brush of Elizabeth's hair where it touched his shoulder. Then the recklessness of what they had done came to him. He felt defiant.

There was a silence so absolute that he could hear Elizabeth's gentle breathing, and they both turned to hold each other again. Where their bodies touched there was now a comforting warmth, so that Elizabeth wriggled against him in an effort to escape the cold air. For a time, Gideon wondered if they would be discovered, but the deep silence continued and the temptation of her pressing body gradually overcame his caution. He slid his hand between them and felt her nipples both stiff and yielding, then, slowly, his hand moved down until it nestled in the dark gold tangle of her pubic hair. As he felt deeper, her body became taut again and she pushed her pelvis towards him and began to move rhythmically against his hand. She ran her own hand down his stomach and took hold of his erect penis, which she gently tugged until he raised himself on his elbows and allowed her to guide it into her. This time, he was determined to gain more control. He pushed away from the mattress with the palms of his hands so that he could look down at her face, and thrust into her with a slow steady movement. She gazed at him with half-hooded eyes and then leaned upwards suddenly to lick his chest. It was a gesture both carnal and innocent. He was overwhelmed by her loveliness again, and in a few lost moments he climaxed for the second time.

'Got you,' she said in a quick, amused voice, as if she had won points in a game they were playing. He saw her look of triumph, so he moved down to raise her legs and gently began to kiss the soft inside of her thigh. Her body grew taut again as his mouth came in contact with her wet flesh. Her hands curled into fists and she grasped the hair of his head.

When he moved his tongue rhythmically against her it was as though he were winding a spring; he could feel the tension building, but she held back, as if reluctant to allow her passions to dominate. For a time she prolonged the inevitable, but gradually she gave way until she was rocking from side to side in ecstasy, holding a fist to her mouth to stifle her own cries.

'Got you,' Gideon said softly when they held each other again. Now he studied Elizabeth's face. Her eyes were half-closed, but he could see their dilated pupils. The irises were more black than grey-blue. The slight amount of lipstick she wore had gone when they had first kissed, but arousal had made her full lips darker and brought a glowing flush to her face and body. If Elsa Mueller saw her now, she would be in no doubt which way the conversation had gone. As if reading his mind, Elizabeth began to smile.

He squeezed her, and she said, 'How do you think my mother would feel about my being deflowered by a tradesman?'

'Better that than an actor,' he said quickly. But Elizabeth's words had disquieted him. 'Was I the first?' he asked. He kissed her slender throat.

'Yes,' she replied softly. 'Couldn't you tell?'

He chose his next words carefully, knowing that the wrong phrase would hurt her. 'You seemed so natural. Some girls are like stone. Did I hurt you?'

'Only my pride,' she answered, but he could tell that she was pleased. 'So I didn't act like a virgin, Mr Gideon?' She began to knead the hard muscles of his stomach.

'Not in the least.'

'Then you can blame it all on Henry Miller,' she said. 'We had all his books during my last year at finishing school.'

'What did you learn from them?'

'This.' She leaned down to apply her mouth softly until he was as stiff again as one of the brass bed-posts above them.

This time, when he entered her, he managed to hold out until he brought them both to satisfaction. Then they lay back again, the coolness of the room forgotten, but suddenly they heard slow footsteps in the corridor outside. They waited breathlessly, until the person passed and then, with suppressed giggles, scrambled to put their clothes back on.

Elizabeth borrowed his comb when she was dressed, and she quickly ran it through her tangled hair. 'How do I look?' she asked, while he buttoned his shirt and adjusted the new tie.

'Ravished,' he answered.

'Don't you mean ravishing?'

'I know what I said,' he replied, but in truth there was now no sign of their love-making.

She leaned forward and kissed him lightly. 'You'd better wash,' she said. 'You smell of me.'

There was a small basin in the room, and the cold tap worked. Gideon found an ancient sliver of hardened soap and did as he was told, drying his hands afterwards on the new linen handkerchief in his breast pocket. After a final inspection they walked down the long corridor and descended the staircase. Laszlo and Elizabeth's parents were talking in the hall.

Elsa Mueller looked up as they joined them. 'Have you had your little talk, darling?' she asked firmly.

'Yes, Mama,' Elizabeth answered, sounding chastened.

'So we all understand each other?' Elsa continued.

'I understand perfectly, Mrs Mueller,' Gideon replied.

'Please call me Elsa,' she said. 'After all, we shall be seeing a great deal of each other and I would like to feel we are friends.'

It was then that Gideon began to feel angry. He looked at Elsa, who was standing with her head tilted back, wearing a little smile of triumph, and he felt a sudden wave of resentment that this woman should classify him as unfit to be seen with her daughter. He even doubted that she would care too much if she discovered that they had just made love; it had been a furtive backstairs affair, suitable if intercourse were going to take place between mistress and servant.

'My car will take you home,' Mueller said, and they made their farewells.

As they climbed into the Bentley, Laszlo directed the driver to take them to Bond Street. 'We'd better start shopping for Herr Mueller immediately,' he said, leaning back against the comfortable leather upholstery.

When they passed Hyde Park Corner, Gideon turned to him. 'In New York you said we could make our fortunes.' Laszlo nodded. 'How rich could we become?'

Laszlo considered the question. 'I believe we could become "comfortable". Isn't that the usual English expression?'

Gideon shook his head. 'I want more than that.'

Laszlo looked at him sympathetically. 'Elizabeth told you of her parents' intentions for her?'

'Only that I did not fit into their scheme of things.'

'Elsa wants the girl to make a dazzling match. It is a very familiar story.' Laszlo looked out at the wet street as the car turned from Piccadilly. A few yards into Bond Street, a small crowd had collected on the pavement, despite the rain, and were gathered round a window.

'That's Strange's Gallery,' said Laszlo. 'What on earth can he have that's pulling them in like that? Stop the car,' he ordered the driver, and took a large umbrella from the rear window-ledge. 'Tell Herr Mueller I shall return this,' he called out, ushering Gideon from the Bentley.

Displaying the normal English deference, the people parted at the arrival of passengers from such an impressive motorcar. Gideon and Laszlo strode forward and could see immediately what had caught their attention. Whitney-Ingram's painting of the girl in the white dress stood alone in the window, surrounded by a backcloth of black velvet.

'Magnificent,' said Laszlo. After a moment he glanced at Gideon, who had not answered. He instantly recognised the expression his companion wore. He had seen it many times before on other faces.

'Dear God,' Gideon breathed. 'I've never seen anything so beautiful!'

The portrait of the girl seemed to pulsate with life. She stood in a summer meadow with one hand to her cheek, the sun behind her, so that her features were shaded beneath a wide straw hat. Wisps of her golden hair, which the hand was brushing away, caught the light and framed her smiling, questioning face.

When Gideon moved closer, the surface of the painting dissolved into brush-strokes of pure paint. Then he stood back again, to the magic distance where they re-formed into peach-coloured flesh and dazzling white linen. In the long grass at the girl's feet, touches of vermilion, chrome yellow and azure blue suggested wild flowers, and a small posy was held carelessly in the hand by her side.

Gideon stayed transfixed, but a sudden sadness pressed against his heart. It puzzled him for a moment, then he understood. More than anything else in life, he now wanted to possess this beautiful thing. And, like Elizabeth, the price was more than he could afford.

The following morning was so bright Gideon decided he would make the journey to Kew by bus rather than Underground. He was also determined to find rooms of his own. The previous evening had been a painful experience, despite Laszlo's best efforts to bring some warmth to the occasion. Sylvia had sat with them in the tiny living-room, an untouched glass of vermouth beside her, and had listened in absolute silence to Gideon's and Laszlo's stilted attempts at conversation. Finally she stood up and announced, in lifeless tones, that she was going to bed.

Throughout the evening she had managed to convey to Gideon that he had no real existence for her. It was as though he were a ghost, visible only to her husband. Yet there was some other quality about her that Gideon found equally disturbing. Although she acted towards him with indifference, he had begun to find her attractive, and was enough of a gentleman to feel ashamed at betraying his friend, even if it were only in his imagination. He also felt disloyal to Elizabeth, but the more he tried to put the thought of Sylvia out of his mind, the more he felt his eyes drawn to her delicate little ankles and the smooth roundness where the top of her breasts just showed above the neckline of her fussily trimmed blouse. Her milky skin and pouting rosebud mouth, drawn in a line of disapproval, brought dark carnal images to him and he began to fantasise about sweating encounters in Swiss hay-lofts while lowing cows waited for the attentions of her busy hands. Now the memory of the evening faded, and he looked down from the open top of the bus on the changing streets of West London.

At Chiswick, the route crossed an unmarked boundary that

69

separated the town from the suburbs. There were more trees in the streets and the pace of movement seemed to have slowed. Gideon got off the bus on the north side of Kew Bridge and walked towards the Surrey embankment. On Kew Green the first hard buds showed on the horse-chestnuts and the grass on each side of the road was lush and sweet. He passed a young mother pushing a pram and raised his hat to wish her good morning. She responded with a smile, which cheered him further. Now a mood of contentment had replaced his worries about Sylvia.

He turned into Kew Road and strolled beside the high brick wall of the Royal Botanic Gardens. In the shade of a tree he waited until a motorcyclist rattled past, and then crossed the road. Nettlebury's house was a fine Victorian villa set back from the road, with a well-tended garden filled with shrubs and flowers. He climbed the steps and rang the doorbell.

A voice called, 'Just a moment,' from below, and he looked down to see Anne leaning from a basement window, her head wreathed in a turban made from a brightly coloured scarf. 'Oh, it's you, Gideon! I'll be with you immediately.' A moment later the door opened, and he noticed that she had removed the scarf but still wore an apron over her frock. 'Daddy is in his studio,' she said, leading him out of the hall into a long passage. It culminated at the doorway of an enormous kitchen, where a cheerful-looking fat woman kneaded dough on a table. 'This is Mrs Cooper, who helps us,' she said. 'And this is Mr Gideon.' They nodded to each other.

Anne led him out of the kitchen, along a side passage hung with ivy and into a high-walled garden filled with fruit trees. To the left of them, built against the rear of the house, stood a rambling conservatory. Grape vines grew inside against the glass wall, so that he could not see into the interior. She opened a door and said, 'James Gideon is here for his lesson, Daddy.'

In the stone-flagged room Nettlebury was sitting in an old wicker chair, wearing a leather-patched jacket and smoking a pipe. He was reading *The Times*. Initially, Gideon felt disappointed. He had half-expected to find him clad in a flowing smock, feverishly daubing paint on a canvas. He looked around, after Nettlebury's greeting, but no pictures were to be seen, and instead of chaotic jumble, all was neat and orderly. There was merely an old easel made of dark wood, with brass fittings that held a blank canvas about the size of a double page of *The Times*, and a large stained table where dozens of tubes of oil paints were carefully arranged in rows.

Big pots containing brushes stood beside bottles of turpentine and cans of varnish. The glass roof rose high above, only partly covered by the vine, but half-drawn blinds held off the heat of the sun. There was also a strong, pleasant smell that put Gideon in mind of cricket pavilions and oil-shops.

Nettlebury gestured for him to sit down in another of the wicker chairs, and chewed on his pipe for a moment before he spoke. 'So what do you want to know about painting?' he asked in a friendly voice.

Gideon shrugged. 'Everything?' he ventured.

Nettlebury gave a barking laugh. 'Then I'm afraid you've come to the wrong man, old chap. I've been studying for nearly forty years and there's still quite a bit I don't know.'

'Just tell me what you can, then.'

Nettlebury nodded. 'Fair enough.' He sat back and puffed on his pipe, then he stuffed it into his pocket. 'The first thing to remember is that painting is a craft. No matter what others may tell you, before you can produce an oil painting you've got to set about the business in a workman-like fashion or you're finished from the start. Oil paint is an unforgiving medium; you must have patience.' He gestured towards the table of equipment with his thumb. 'This stuff is a chemistry set, not the keyboard of a musical instrument. Go hammering at it in an artistic frenzy, and all you'll create is a sea of mud.' He looked up at the vine. 'Turner didn't achieve the effect of being at the centre of a storm by behaving like one and throwing himself at the canvas. To paint a thunderstorm, you've got to go about the job with the delicacy of a watchmaker.' He reached out for one of the tubes of paint. 'The Greeks and Romans used this: it was the same stuff. The theory is very simple. It's doing it that breaks your heart. They discovered that walnut or linseed oil had certain properties when you refined them. They could be mixed with the dyes we call paint and, when they dried, they left a translucent film of colour that was elastic and permanent. When one layer was dry you could add another, and so on, to build up a picture. Of course, it wasn't perfectly simple. Some colours were more powerful than others, and could show through the paint above. Others were more treacherous; they could lose their life and sink into the canvas or the wooden surface you were painting on. If the artist mixed paint and oil of the wrong consistency, the surface crazed and eventually peeled away.' He smiled. 'You can see it's a difficult game.'

A sudden thought struck Gideon. 'What about modern pictures, where the paint is thick, or the artist has stuck things to the canvas?'

71

Nettlebury smiled again. 'The truth is, that they won't last. Eventually they'll just fall apart.' He put the tube of paint back on the table. 'Oh, I suppose some smart restorer will stick them back together again, but in the end they'll just be somebody else's idea of what the original was like.'

'Doesn't that make them a rather dubious investment?'

Nettlebury shrugged. 'The idea of laying things down for future generations seems to have gone out of fashion.'

Anne came into the conservatory carrying a tray of coffee. 'How is it going?' she asked Gideon when he took the cup she offered.

'Your father is destroying my illusions about the romance of painting,' he answered with a smile.

Nettlebury took his own cup. 'Yes, I've never understood where the idea that it was a romantic business came from,' he said, sounding puzzled. 'I think it may have something to do with *La Bohème*. If so, Puccini has a lot to answer for! It's hard enough to do in relative comfort, so God knows how anyone believes you can paint well while you're starving and freezing cold.'

'What about Michelangelo?' Anne chided. 'All those years on his back painting the Sistine Chapel.'

'That was in Italy, where the climate is benign,' her father retorted. 'And I will remind you that being flat on your back is the position one adopts when taking a siesta.'

Anne prodded him. 'You always told us that the roof of the Sistine Chapel was one of the greatest feats of endurance ever undertaken by a painter.'

Nettlebury winked at Gideon. 'Some girls will believe anything you tell them.'

When they had finished their coffee, Nettlebury sent Anne off to find an old sweater. 'We can't have you spoiling that new suit,' he said to Gideon. His pupil now being suitably protected, he nodded towards the canvas. 'I've already primed this,' he said. 'Lay on some colour, so you can see for yourself how the stuff behaves.'

First they blended various tones of paint, then Gideon transferred them to the canvas. As Nettlebury had warned, it was harder than he had imagined.

'Try to look at everything you see as pure colour,' Nettlebury said, 'and do as much work as you can on your palette. If you keep mixing on the canvas, it will only lead to frustration.'

Gideon quickly became absorbed by the work. It was as though the paint had a life of its own. He began to notice how shades of pigment would alter when fresh and different applications were made beside them. Some colours, like Prussian blue and madder lake, would stain powerfully, while others seemed almost passive. Each had its own character.

Eventually, at one o'clock, the first lesson was over. Gideon thanked Nettlebury, and Anne said she would walk with him to the bus stop because she felt like the exercise.

He didn't speak at first, and finally Anne said, 'Did you enjoy it?'

Gideon smiled. 'Your father says I must try to see everything as tones of oil paint.'

'You should try a game he used to play with us when we were little,' Anne said as they crossed Kew Bridge. She glanced about her. 'I spy something the colour of madder lake merging with Prussian blue and edged with burnt sienna.'

'I give up,' he said immediately.

'The nose of this man coming towards us,' she answered.

Gideon laughed so hard that the figure ahead, holding the lead of a small dog, looked up at them suspiciously, knowing they had been talking about him. 'Tell me, where does your father keep all his paintings?' he asked, as they drew level with the man.

Anne looked out over the waters of the Thames, and when she spoke, it was sadly. 'In parts of the house that visitors don't go to. He doesn't like people to see them any more.'

'Why not?'

Anne was silent again, then she said, 'I think it's because he doesn't like to remind people of his failure. You know, it's possible to starve and be cold in a nice warm conservatory.'

Gideon could think of no words of comfort. He looked up at the clouds banked towards Middlesex. 'I spy something the colour of Chinese white, and tinged with grey and blue.'

CHAPTER FOUR

London, December 1934

After more than a year, Gideon's life had settled into different ways. He had found a flat in Shepherd Market, close to where Laszlo lived, and gradually they had evolved a sort of routine. He could not think of it as work. Three days a week he went to Kew for lessons with Sir Julian Nettlebury, who was a hard and conscientious teacher. They could now discuss with authority the work of most major painters since the Renaissance, and although Nettlebury's expertise ended, for the most part, at the beginning of the twentieth century, Laszlo guided him in the modern schools. His own taste has begun to develop, but he kept his preference for German Expressionism to himself during conversations with Nettlebury.

He accompanied Laszlo around the country, often revisiting places where he had worked as an actor, although in those days he had known the great cities only as a few streets around the theatres where he had played. Now he saw the galleries, junk-shops and great houses where they searched for their stock in trade. They visited Germany a few times, but for the most part Laszlo preferred to use contacts there to find the work they required. Gideon had become familiar with a variety of craftsmen in various parts of London: picture-framers in Clerkenwell; two brothers who prepared canvases in the King's Road; a supplier of artists' materials in Holborn; and a wide selection of antique-dealers, who ranged across the social scale from foppish aristocrats to men with discreet lock-ups in seedy streets. Laszlo introduced him to contacts in the great museums and art schools of London.

Gideon had become used to entertaining in expensive restaurants – head waiters now knew his name – and there was a constant round of parties, receptions and private views to attend. He loved it all.

74

When he looked back, acting seemed a much duller life by comparison.

The only difficult part of his existence was his affair with Elizabeth. At first they had enjoyed the clandestine meetings and the charade of being only distantly acquainted when their lives crossed on public occasions. Their mutual attraction was as strong as ever when they made love, but elsewhere the relationship grew increasingly strained. Gideon had begun to tire of her mother's intransigence, but as each month passed Elizabeth still appeared to enjoy the secrecy. She became resentful when he suggested they should have it out with Elsa, and this led to a nagging core of discontent that now affected their attitude to one another.

Gideon noticed Elizabeth slip from her seat as the music swelled to a finale and the film came to an end. He waited alone, and then stood to attention for the National Anthem. The crowd around him were cheerful as they shuffled from the cinema, but Gideon felt depressed by Elizabeth's absence, even though they had already made the arrangement for her to leave first. He crossed the street and turned up his collar against the cold. Bright lights shone from the cinema façades in Leicester Square, but an icy wind lashed through the bare trees with enough force to send a discarded newspaper whirling into a column of loose pages. In Irving Street, he stopped and glanced around before opening the nearside door of the little silver sports car parked facing towards Charing Cross Road.

Elizabeth was smoking a cigarette, which she threw from the window when he sat down beside her. The fox fur of her coat matched the metallic sheen of the motor's bodywork.

'So, what did you think of it?' she said in a brighter voice than the one she had employed earlier in the evening.

'*The Gay Divorcee*? They should make one about us called "The Miserable Mistress".'

She knew he was referring to her previous sulkiness, which had caused a muttered squabble in the cinema. As always, the subject had been her mother's disapproval. 'It's not me that's miserable now, Gideon,' she said, a note of exasperation in her voice.

'That's because you refuse to have it out with your mother.'

Elizabeth folded her arms. 'You're not being fair,' she said petulantly. 'I'm the one who has constantly to invent lies and excuses. You just come and go as you please, with no one to answer to.'

'That's the very point I'm making. Why can't you simply ask your mother if we can see each other occasionally? Then we wouldn't have to creep around London like sneak-thieves. We could still be discreet.'

His profile was caught by a line of light from a shop window and she thought, as she always did, how extraordinarily handsome he was. Then the thought continued along its usual course – oh, if only you had a position, or even money, Gideon, the world would be perfect. She reached out and held the wooden steering-wheel. 'We don't have very much time tonight. You know I'm going to the country tomorrow. Shall we go to your place?'

'I'm not in the mood for hit-and-run encounters just now.'

'As you wish,' she said flatly, touching her fingertips to her forehead.

He could tell he had hurt her, and now that his intention was fulfilled, he was sorry. He held her arm for a moment. 'Forgive me,' he said quickly. 'I'm not very good company tonight.'

She gave a quick smile. 'I'll try, Gideon. I promise, if I get the chance, I'll say we're only friends and that I would like to see you occasionally.'

He nodded. 'If it works, at least we'll be able to act naturally part of the time.'

'Do you want me to drive you home?' she asked.

Gideon shook his head. 'I think I'll walk. Give me a ring if you can.' He leaned across to kiss her, and she clung to him for a moment.

'I'll buy you something special for Christmas,' she whispered as he got out of the car.

'You know what I want,' he said through the still-open door. 'Some small dispensation from your mother.'

Despite the biting cold, there was a cheerful mood about the city, which contrasted with his own low spirits. Christmas trees and coloured lights decorated the shop windows, and a group of street entertainers sang and danced to an accordion when he re-crossed Leicester Square.

'If you haven't got a cent you'll be as rich as Rockefeller . . . ' the performers sang, and Gideon noted the irony. As Laszlo had predicted, they had become 'comfortable', but the fortune he had hoped for was proving to be elusive. Gideon wanted them to open their own gallery, but Laszlo was reluctant. The older man did not want to commit their slowly building capital, and so they were forced to share much of their profit with other dealers.

The wind was bitter, and he began to regret that he had let Elizabeth go. The thought came to him again when he passed through Piccadilly Circus and watched the street-walkers approaching their customers. Here were men prepared to pay money for company, and he had rejected someone as lovely as Elizabeth.

Hogarth would have liked the scene, he thought, when he passed four drunken young men in evening clothes who were loudly bartering for the services of a group of brightly painted girls. The previous week he had visited Sir John Soane's Museum with Nettlebury to examine the series called 'The Rake's Progress'. The faces of London had not changed much.

Half-way along Piccadilly he encountered a Salvation Army band playing Christmas carols. He put a shilling into the collection box of a girl whose smiling face beneath her bonnet was pink from the wind. 'Happy Christmas,' she called out after Gideon as he walked on.

In Bond Street, he stopped in front of the Strange Gallery. The painting was still there, bringing a moment of summer to the winter street. He gazed for some time at the portrait of the girl, and felt the same sadness of his first encounter. The painting had become one of the sights of London, and the popular newspapers still speculated as to who would be its eventual owner. He stayed there until his face felt numb and his eyes watered from the cold, and then turned away and walked on to his own rooms in Shepherd Street. His flat was over a greengrocer's shop and there, parked under the street light, was Elizabeth's silver sports car. She had her own key and must have let herself into the flat.

There were no lights on when he climbed the stairs. In the bedroom, the curtains were not drawn; by the light reflected from the street he could just make out her still shape under the bedclothes. They did not speak until he had undressed and joined her.

She turned and held him for a time. 'You've been to look at the picture,' she said softly. He did not answer. 'Do you love her more than me?'

'No. Only in a different way.'

'I hate her,' Elizabeth said quietly. She spoke as though the girl were a living being.

'Why? It's a painting, not a real woman.'

Elizabeth paused so long that he thought she wouldn't answer, but finally she said, 'If she were real, I wouldn't mind, but she will stay the same for ever and I shall get old.'

'Do you care so much about getting old?'

Elizabeth nodded her head so that her hair touched his bare arm. 'I hate the thought more than anything else in the world,' she replied, and then began to kiss him with quickening intensity. When she could tell that he was sufficiently aroused, she quickly mounted him. 'At least she can't do this,' she said, bending to kiss him again.

When they were still again, they lay in each other's arms, and Gideon looked up at the ceiling where the lights of a slowly passing car caused new patterns above them. Elizabeth held up her watch to the poor light. 'Damnation, I have to go.'

Gideon switched on the bedside lamp and glanced at the clock on the table. 'Where does she think you are?'

'At a concert with Willie Friedman,' she said, sitting down on the bed to put on her silk stockings. Friedman was a young man from the German Embassy whom her mother considered a suitable escort for Elizabeth. Elsa took every occasion she could to arrange for them to be in each other's company. But despite the sophistication that had glittered like a flame when she was in Minnesota, she had made a serious miscalcuation over the young man's intentions towards her daughter.

'And where is Willie?' Gideon asked.

'Probably out dancing with his new boyfriend.' She smoothed her petticoat in front of the dressing-table mirror. 'Do you think I'm putting on weight?'

Gideon considered her slim body. 'It's the looking-glass,' he said. 'It distorts everything.'

As Elizabeth turned, she caught sight of a picture resting against the wall by the side of the bed. It was a jagged mass of converging shapes that were predominantly Prussian blue, vermilion, lamp-black and emerald green. She could see no recognisable clue to its subject matter, except for a vague suggestion of human limbs and patches of what could have been folded material. 'Who is this by?'

Gideon leaned on one arm and looked down at the painting. 'Franz Marc. Do you like it?'

'Yes, I think I do. Is it for my father?'

Gideon laughed. 'Certainly not! Tell me why you like it.'

'That was how I felt when you left earlier,' she answered, then kissed him goodbye again, and left.

He switched off the light and listened to her footsteps on the stairs. As her car growled away, he thought of the girl in the white dress again.

Gideon stood with Nettlebury, Laszlo and a burly figure examining a huge painting leaning against the wall of a narrow passage at the rear of an antique shop in Tottenham Court Road. It depicted a group of young men dressed in late-eighteenth-century clothes posed around the plaster cast of a Greek statue, at which they were gazing in veneration. The picture was executed with astonishing skill, but he found it somehow depressing. He blew on his cupped hands; puffs of white breath came like smoke from his mouth. Nettlebury eventually nodded his head, and he and Gideon walked back into the showroom, while Laszlo remained with the owner and began to bargain. After a time he emerged from the passage looking mournful.

'You've robbed me again, Bert,' he said to the bearded thickset man, who had his hands plunged deep in the pockets of a ginger tweed suit.

'I know, Laszlo,' Bert replied in a gruff Cockney voice. 'And I'd go broke if I robbed everybody the way I do you.' He turned to Gideon. 'Would you mind getting him out of here before my wife gets back? She told me if she ever saw him in the shop again, she'd send for the police and bring charges for burglary.'

'How is Connie?' Laszlo asked.

'Still thick as thieves with your Sylvia.' Then Bert turned to Nettlebury, and his demeanour changed. 'It's been a pleasure meeting you, Sir Julian, and thank you for confirming the watercolours.'

'You're welcome, Mr Richardson,' Nettlebury replied. 'The two Crome pictures were a pleasure to look at.'

The three men stood in the cold street for a moment, and Laszlo briskly rubbed his hands together. 'Will you join us for lunch, Julian?' he asked.

Nettlebury shook his head and pulled down the brim of his tweed hat. 'No, thank you, dear boy. I must get back.' He turned to Gideon. 'See you in the morning.' With another nod, he made off towards Oxford Street.

Although Gideon could feel the wind through his scarf and overcoat, Laszlo wore only a hat and a double-breasted suit. He seemed impervious to the cold. After adjusting his bow tie, he held up his hand for a passing taxi and directed the driver to the Ivy restaurant. 'A good morning's work,' he said with satisfaction.

'Julian says it is definitely by Joseph Wright. He also told me that you identified it before he did.'

'I always get that sense of despair when I gaze on his work,' Gideon said sardonically.

'Well, you may gaze on a glass of champagne in a few minutes. That might put you in a better mood.'

'You know what will put me in a better mood.'

Laszlo sighed noisily and looked out of the window at the occupants of a bus. 'How many times must I warn you? We are not ready for our own gallery yet. Maybe another year or two.'

'Why not now?' Gideon persisted.

Laszlo shrugged. 'I presume you want us to be a large gallery?' Gideon nodded without looking at him. 'Even the big galleries are all owned by the English or the French. They would not welcome a Hungarian.'

'You're only a Hungarian when it suits you,' Gideon said with a grin. He could not be angry with the man for long. 'Besides, I'm English.'

Laszlo sighed again. 'Then I wish you would act like it occasionally.' He gestured through the window at Cambridge Circus. 'Where is the prudence and thrifty common sense that built this great Empire?'

'You're the one taking us to the Ivy,' Gideon replied, 'and we could have caught a bus!'

'Never,' Laszlo said, as they alighted at the restaurant. 'This is a necessary business expense. Suppose a client were to see us on a bus?'

They were shown to their table beneath one of the stained-glass windows and were soon sipping champagne, while Laszlo studied the menu. Gideon knew what he wanted to eat. While Laszlo considered his selection, he glanced around the room and noticed some faces familiar from his childhood visits.

'By the way, we're going to Paris next month,' Laszlo said carelessly when he closed the leather-bound wine list.

'What for?'

'To see Henri Bronstein. It has taken some time to arrange.' Laszlo looked up from the menu, and his attention was caught by a couple being shown to a table near to them.

'That's a fine-looking woman,' he said appreciatively, as he might when presented with a good picture. 'She must have been remarkably beautiful when she was young.'

Gideon turned to follow his gaze. 'Good God!' he said in astonishment. 'It's my mother and father.'

He got up and walked over to their table, and Laszlo continued studying them. Gideon looked more like his father, but his mother's eyes and mouth had given him his exceptional looks.

Laszlo was close enough to hear Gideon's mother say, 'Hello, darling,' warmly but without much surprise in her voice. Gideon held a short conference with the head waiter and they were all moved to a table big enough to accommodate them. More champagne was poured, and Laszlo was introduced to Frank and Marjorie.

'What are you doing together?' asked their son. 'I thought you were both in different parts of the world.' He had learned from a friend passing through London that the reason his mother had gone to Australia was to marry a landowner.

His mother looked sad for a moment. 'Keith died, darling, and left me the sheep station. His brother Rupert was furious. I was bored, so I went on a holiday to Singapore and bumped into Frank again at Raffles Hotel.'

'She came looking for me,' Frank said with a grin that his son had inherited. 'There were articles in all the Australian papers about my performance in *Arms and the Man*.'

Gideon turned to his father. 'What happened to Carol Blanchard?' He named the woman who had caused his mother's departure.

Marjorie answered briskly. 'She's touring Canada. We've decided to keep to our own parts of the globe.'

'So you're back with each other again?'

'And we've re-married,' Marjorie said happily. 'Such a shame you couldn't have been at the ceremony, darling. I'm sure I looked much better this time.' She covered Gideon's hand with her own. 'I wish we'd known you were in London. We leave tomorrow for Australia again.'

'Are you going to live on a sheep station for ever, Mother?'

'Oh, no,' Marjorie replied with a shake of her head. 'It's just that Keith's brother is being unpleasant, and the lawyers think it would be better if we were in Sydney for a while.' Then she looked happier. 'Now, tell me what are you up to.'

'Laszlo and I are in partnership. We're art dealers.'

'Art dealers?' His father sounded puzzled. 'What kind of art?'

Gideon laughed. 'We buy and sell paintings.'

'Do you have a shop?' Marjorie asked.

81

'A gallery,' Gideon corrected her. 'No. We don't have enough capital yet.'

'Do you mean you need money, darling?'

'Quite a lot of money,' Laszlo said with a smile. 'Your son is gifted but impetuous, Mrs Gideon. He wants to start immediately, but I think we should wait for a few years.'

'Mrs Gideon,' she repeated with satisfaction. 'Don't you think it sounds more becoming than Mrs Mulrooney? But you must call me Marjorie. Now, why do you think you should wait a few more years?'

Laszlo leaned back in his chair. 'Because money is the tool of our trade. We have to have sufficient liquid capital to buy pictures at a moment's notice. To take the lease on a gallery and hire the staff we would need to run it would soak up all the spare cash we have.'

Marjorie had been watching Lazlo with interest while he spoke, and then turned to her husband. 'What a beautiful accent! With that head and voice he could corner all the parts in the West End for Central Europeans.'

Frank nodded. 'He could probably do Ibsen as well, and the big Russian roles.'

Marjorie turned back to him. 'Yes, I can definitely see him as Uncle Vanya.'

Laszlo smiled. He had began to realise why they had never taken any interest in Gideon's ability to draw. There was an innocent quality in them both, like children who only wanted to play one game.

'So the problem *is* money,' said Marjorie. 'How much would you need?'

Laszlo shrugged. He deliberately exaggerated the sum that came to mind. 'Fifteen or twenty thousand pounds at the very least,' he said, and took another sip of champagne.

To both his and Gideon's amazement, Marjorie reached into her handbag, produced a cheque-book and pen, and wrote swiftly. Gideon read the amount she had filled in and silently handed it to Laszlo, who was equally stunned.

'You wouldn't think sheep could be quite so useful, would you?' Marjorie said with a devastating smile.

At four o'clock that afternoon, still dazed and slightly drunk on champagne, Laszlo and Gideon stood before a Bond Street building and looked up at the sign, which read: 'Premises to Let'.

'How will you feel with our names up there?' Gideon asked, nudging his companion in the ribs.

Laszlo slowly shooks his head. 'We can't use Vasilakis,' he said carefully.

'But everyone will know we're partners,' Gideon protested. 'What difference does it make?'

Laszlo smiled and tapped his nose. 'People will see your name there, and they'll be sympathetic towards me because they will think I am still the underdog. A very strategic position in which to be when you deal with the British.'

Gideon laughed. 'You are the trickiest human being I have ever encountered,' he said. 'God help the customers!'

Suddenly Laszlo reached out and seized Gideon's arm. 'Great heavens, I have just thought of something terrible!' He paused dramatically. 'For the first time in my life, I shall be working in the next street to Sylvia.'

Even though the heavy morning mist threatened to turn to fog, Gideon could not resist driving to Kew in his new motorcar. Marjorie's cheque had been so generous that he and Laszlo had walked straight from the estate agent's Berkeley Square office into a car showroom. Thirty minutes later they had driven away in a two-seater MG the colour of a fire engine. Now, clad in heavy tweed overcoat, cap, goggles and leather gauntlets, he was driving across Kew Green. It was shrouded in heavy white mist; the horse-chestnuts stood dark and brooding by the roadside. When he stopped the car, he took an oblong package wrapped in brown paper from the passenger seat.

Irene opened the Nettleburys' front door, and laughed when she saw Gideon in his bulky clothes, but her laugh turned to squeals of delight when she saw the sports car. 'Oh, Gideon, it's absolutely beautiful! Can we go for a drive?'

'Later,' he said, handing her the cap and goggles. She immediately put them on.

'We're in the kitchen having breakfast,' she said as he hung the overcoat on the clothes-stand in the hall. 'You're early.'

'Why aren't you at school?' he asked, following her into the kitchen.

'We've broken up, silly! Don't you know it's half term?'

Gideon was such a frequent visitor that he took an empty seat at the large table without formality and helped himself to coffee. Nettlebury glanced up from his newspaper, grunted a greeting and returned to the letters page.

Anne came into the room, and smiled when she saw him. 'Do you want some fresh coffee?' she asked. Then she noticed Irene, clad in the cap and goggles, hiding behind the door to surprise her. 'I'm filled with terror,' she said calmly. 'Where did you get those hideous objects?'

'Gideon has bought a new car,' she announced. 'He's going to take me for a ride.'

'When you've tidied your bedroom,' Anne said, 'and cleaned out your hamster's cage.'

Irene groaned. 'He likes the mess. Hamsters aren't human beings, you know!'

Nettlebury folded his newspaper and took a sip from his coffee. 'Mammals generally like to keep their nests clean. I make an exception for little girls who enjoy living in squalor.'

'I'm not a mammal yet,' Irene said defiantly. 'Mammals suckle their young, so Miss Edwards told us in biology.' She slapped her chest. 'I'm still flat. Anne is the mammal in the family.'

Nettlebury stood up. 'Come along, James. I think Anne may wish to chastise her sister, and I want to see what you have in that intriguing package.'

They made their way to the conservatory, where the warmth from the oil stoves was welcoming. Gideon unwrapped the parcel and inserted a painting, executed on an oblong of wood, into the easel clamps.

Nettlebury chewed on the stem of his empty pipe while he studied the work. 'Remarkable,' he said finally. 'When did you do it?'

'Last night. Do you recognise the original?'

'I think so. It's a detail from *The Annunciation* by Botticelli, if I'm not mistaken. The wing of the Archangel Gabriel.' Nettlebury put on his spectacles and examined the painting at closer quarters. 'Quite remarkable,' he said softly. 'Your technique is faultless.'

In their months together, Nettlebury had given Gideon lessons in oil painting, tempera and watercolours. As soon as Gideon had mastered a particular technique, he was able to adapt it to the style of any artist he wished to imitate, but no style of his own emerged. It was a mystery that intrigued Nettlebury.

'I'm going to use it for the sign of our gallery,' Gideon said.

Nettlebury considered the information. 'An angel's wing. You and Laszlo are going to be on the side of the angels?'

Gideon laughed. 'We hope they're going to be on ours!'

'So you have finally persuaded the reluctant Hungarian?'

84

Nettlebury said, and Gideon told him of the encounter with his parents. He got to his feet. 'Well, I'm delighted for you, dear boy. Now pull the blinds,' he ordered. 'We're going to use the epidiascope.'

When the room was sufficiently dim, they replaced the angel's wing on the easel with a large blank canvas, and Nettlebury began to project reproductions of paintings on to its surface from the large contraption which Irene referred to as the Magic Lantern. The images were cut from magazines, on postcards and occasionally from the large pile of huge books Nettlebury had piled on the paint-stained table. As each picture flooded on to the white canvas, Gideon named the artist and the period.

After some time, Anne came in with fresh coffee and stayed to listen to the litany. Gideon continued without error until Nettlebury said, 'You'll do. Let's see how much Anne can still remember.'

The images began again, and she took up the chant: 'Giotto, about 1266 to 1337, *The Flight into Egypt*. Jan Van Eyck, about 1390 to 1441, *Giovanni Arnolfini and his Bride*. Titian, about 1490 to 1576, *Portrait of Clarissa Strozzi*.'

When Nettlebury had switched off the machine and released the blinds so that light flooded into the room, he sat down again.

'You've done this as well?' Gideon said to Anne, gesturing towards the epidiascope.

'Oh, yes. When I was little. So did Irene.' She looked at her father. 'And he wasn't as patient with us!'

Gideon looked at her thoughtfully and considered her qualities. It seemed absurd to him that she was trapped in the role of housekeeper, no matter how devoted she was to her family. She spoke excellent French and Italian and had just demonstrated her encyclopaedic knowledge of the history of art. He knew what he wanted to say, but was unsure how Nettlebury would take it; nor did he want to presume too much on the kindness he had already been shown in the past months. But it was Sir Julian who solved his dilemma.

'It's ridiculous the way the girl wastes her talent,' he grumbled. 'I paid a fortune for her education, and then she spends her life cooking and cleaning this place.'

Gideon decided to take the plunge. 'Why don't you come and work with me and Laszlo? You're just the sort of person we'll need at the gallery.'

Anne looked from one to the other with such a yearning that he

85

realised how deeply the offer had affected her. But then duty called. 'What about Irene? Who will see her to school?' she said quietly.

'You wouldn't have to start until ten o'clock in the morning,' said Gideon.

'And I can collect her in the afternoon,' Nettlebury added. 'For God's sake, take the offer. It will do you good.'

Anne looked at him again, and Gideon thought that her honey-coloured eyes had grown even larger. She was half-sitting on the window-ledge, with her hands behind her and one leg in front of the other; the dress she wore clung to her full figure like the folds of material in a Greek statue. With surprise it came to him how attractive she was. For more than a year he had been captivated by Elizabeth's fragile, highly-strung beauty, and had measured other women by her slender grace. Now he had a glimpse of Anne's very different qualities.

'I would love to work at the gallery, Gideon,' she said softly.

'Well, that's settled, then,' he answered. 'I think it would . . . ' His voice trailed away as he stared at her.

The moment was broken when Irene entered the conservatory. 'The fog's clearing up. Can we go for my ride, Gideon?'

Nettlebury looked at his watch. 'In half an hour, when my tutorial is finished,' he said, and the two girls left them once again.

'Now, what was that question you put as we parted yesterday?' Nettlebury asked when they had settled back in their chairs.

'You said that you thought Constable was a true painter, and I asked you what was truth in painting.'

Nettlebury nodded. 'Well, without going into the realms of meta-physics, I think the question can be answered simply enough. When I said Constable was a true painter, I used the word in the sense of honest. He did the very best he could, as honestly as he could. But, like all painters, he used deceptions.'

'Deceptions?' Gideon asked.

'Yes. After all, any work of art is an illusion, isn't it?' He smiled. 'The real world doesn't exactly match the painter's vision. The very act of selecting subject matter and arranging it in a pleasing manner is a sort of deception. But then the real world is a deception.'

'Don't we see the real world when we look through our own eyes?'

'Of course not. You know very well that objects don't actually get smaller when they are far away from you, yet you readily accept the illusion and call it reality.'

Gideon thought for a moment. 'So, if all artists practise deception,

86

how are we to say whether a painting is good or bad?'

'By applying simple criteria,' said Nettlebury. 'Number one, does the painting the artist presents to us qualify as a work of art?'

'And how would you apply that test?'

Nettlebury shrugged. 'By asking yourself whether a civilised person would recognise it as the skilled work of a member of the human race.'

'And number two?'

Nettlebury leaned forward in his chair. 'Has the artist conveyed a mood, emotion or passion that the observer can recognise and identify with a corresponding sensation of his own?' He sat back again and opened his arms. 'It isn't enough for the artist to say, "I feel like this." He's got to say, "Have you ever felt like this as well?" so that the person looking at the picture can share the experience.' He put another match to his pipe. 'I've already said that the painter's skill is deception, but his job is to deceive the public, not himself.'

'And do you do this in your own work?' Gideon was distracted, still thinking of Anne.

Nettlebury paused. 'You'd better come and see what I'm working on at the moment; then you can judge for yourself.'

Gideon looked up in surprise. So far in their time together, he had never once talked about his own paintings.

Nettlebury led the way to the hall, and when they began to ascend the staircase Gideon realised that in all his many visits he had never been above the ground floor. They climbed to the third floor and then on into a great attic, where skylights had been cut to catch the light. Paintings lay stacked against the walls. And there, supported by three great easels, was a canvas that Gideon estimated to be at least fifty feet wide by twelve deep. At first he thought it was an abstract, as huge areas of light and dark tones gave the composition an over-whelming sense of power and simplicity. But when he walked closer, he could see the first impression of simplicity was an illusion. Each broad area of tone actually consisted of intricately related figures. He was astounded by the sheer magnitude of the work.

Some time later, when he had spent more than an hour studying the picture, he heard Irene calling his name.

'You go on,' said Nettlebury. 'I've got work to do up here.'

Gideon turned round as he opened the door and saw Nettlebury standing in front of the canvas. His hands were clasped behind his back and his head was raised to survey the gigantic work. He did not seem to notice Gideon's departure.

'Anne can sit in the front with you if I can wear the goggles,' Irene said, seating herself in the tiny bench behind the driver's seat. Anne slipped down next to Gideon and took hold of the handle attached to the dashboard in front of her.

Gideon drove them to Richmond Hill, and turned around at the Star and Garter. On the return journey, they passed Richmond station, and Irene was delighted to spot a friend on a shopping expedition with her mother. She shouted a greeting and waved in a grand manner.

When they arrived back at the house, Irene rushed inside to tell Mrs Cooper of her brief trip, but Gideon asked Anne to stay in the car with him. The mist had gone, but the sky was overcast with dull white clouds. She waited for him to speak, and eventually he said, 'Summer soon.' It was one of those remarks people use to fill silences rather than to convey any particular meaning.

Anne was puzzled by his lack of conversation, unaware that now he realised his attraction to her, it had caused a change in his attitude. Previously he had been completely at ease in her company; now he felt almost shy. It was as if he had never noticed her voice before, or the pale blue shadows underneath her high cheekbones. She unbuttoned her coat and then, as if remembering Irene's remark about mammals, she quickly drew it close about her again.

Sensing the alteration, she mistook his sudden reticence for second thoughts about the offer he had made earlier. 'If you've changed your mind about my working in the gallery, I quite understand,' she said in a low voice.

He shook his head. 'No, I mean it more now than ever. There really is a big job for you to do.'

'Is it seeing my father's work that's made you so thoughtful?' she asked. 'You don't have to say you like it to me, you know.'

He shook his head again. In truth, he did not know what to make of Nettlebury's picture, except that it had disturbed him. The images were still flickering in his mind like the memories of an unsettling dream.

Anne reached out and touched the polished dashboard of the little car. 'You and Elizabeth will have to take it in turn to drive each other now,' she said with a smile.

The remark surprised Gideon, 'Do you still keep in touch?'

She paused while a bus passed on its journey to Chessington Zoo.

Then she turned to him. 'Every now and again. She told me she was seeing you in secret.'

Gideon took the goggles Irene had returned to him and began to polish them with his handkerchief. He really wanted to change the subject from his relationship with Elizabeth, but he was slightly ashamed of his new-found attraction to Anne. He told himself that any sane man would be satisfied with what he already had, and began to wonder if he was cursed with abnormal appetites. He really wanted to stay sitting in the car with Anne, but he thought that if he remained, he might say something that would shock or offend her, and much of his new feeling was composed of tenderness. It was an impossible combination for him to deal with, and in the end his courage deserted him.

'Well, I'd better be getting back,' he said with forced cheerfulness. 'If you come to the gallery at ten o'clock on Monday morning, we can talk about everything then.'

'If you're absolutely sure,' Anne said, still sensitive to his peculiar mood.

'Absolutely,' he said, and started the engine.

Anne quickly got out of the car and watched him drive away. When she entered the house, she did not want to see the others. Instead, she went to her room and lay on the bed and thought for a long time about Gideon. Then she began to remember the details Elizabeth had told her of their lovemaking. After a time she imagined it was herself that Gideon was with, but the thought did not bring her any pleasure. Each time she visualised them together, she saw Elizabeth as well. Slowly she got up from the bed and, flushed with guilt, went down to the kitchen to help Mrs Cooper to prepare lunch.

Paris, spring 1935

When they announced themselves at the gates, Gideon and Laszlo were taken by a footman to an ante-room in the grey stone mansion where Henri Bronstein lived in the Avenue Foch. There was an oppressive church-like hush in the carpeted corridors, which were lined with display cases of Chinese porcelain, but the room they were eventually ushered into was pleasant. Thick rugs covered the dark wood floor and one long wall was entirely lined with books bound in creamy vellum. Laszlo began to inspect them with interest. Gideon peered through the window into the garden, which was being tended to geometric perfection by two grey-smocked workers.

'I liked his brass buttons,' Gideon said, referring to the dark green livery of the servant who had shown them in.

'Actually, they are gold buttons,' Laszlo said without turning from the wall of books.

'Are you sure?'

'My father told me,' said Laszlo. 'He came here in 1911 to sell Henri Bronstein these books.' He gestured at the shelves with a sweeping motion.

'And they have brought me great pleasure in the years that have passed since that occasion,' a quiet, accentless voice said behind them.

They both turned and saw a small wraith-like figure dressed in a long grey velvet coat standing in front of the delicate marble fireplace. A concealed door in the wood panelling had almost closed, and if Gideon had not heard a slight click, he might have thought Bronstein had materialised in the room by supernatural means.

Bronstein smiled, and the lines on his face converged into a thousand wrinkles, but he looked somehow ageless. Gideon had seen the same quality in the faces of old priests and those whose passions in life had been reserved for things spiritual rather than those of the flesh.

'Forgive the theatrical effect of my entrance,' he said in a high-pitched voice. 'It was for Mr Gideon's benefit. I thought he might appreciate it, coming as he does from the acting profession.'

Gideon decided to join in the spirit of the occasion and gave a slight bow. 'I am flattered, Monsieur. The world has heard of Henri Bronstein, but only Henri Bronstein has heard of James Gideon.'

Bronstein acknowledged the bow with a nod of his head. 'In these days, sir, I must know something of the people who come into my house.' Then he turned to Laszlo and became brisk and business-like. 'I understand you wish to buy some of my German pictures, Mr Vasilakis?'

' "Exchange" would be a more accurate word,' said Laszlo.

'Why do you think I would be prepared for such a proposition?'

Laszlo chose his words carefully. 'We live in turbulent times, sir. I understand that German pictures no longer give you pleasure.'

The old man pursed his lips in distaste. 'You are well informed. I try not to associate the behaviour of those in power in Berlin with the

90

paintings I have in my collection, but I am unable to be dispassionate. I wish I could be stronger-minded.' He seemed lost in thought for a minute, then looked up at Laszlo again. 'You know what I have. What are you offering in their place?'

Laszlo looked into the old man's glittering eyes, which stared without emotion into his own. 'For your Maulpertsch and Durers: three Picassos, two Braques, a Matisse and two Modiglianis. For the Holbeins: three Miros, two Dalis, two Mondrians, a Klee and a Duchamp.'

'You have reproductions or photographs of the pictures you offer?' Bronstein asked.

Laszlo tapped the leather folder under his arm. Bronstein gestured towards a table in the centre of the room, and they sat down. Laszlo spread the illustrations before the old man, who studied them carefully. Then he turned to the list of valuations Laszlo had handed to him.

'Yes,' he said finally. 'You seem to have estimated the relative values of the pictures to the nearest franc.' He paused for a moment, and then said drily, 'And I see the franc is in your favour.'

'My colleague is responsible for the valuations,' said Laszlo.

Bronstein looked at Gideon with a new interest. 'Forgive me, sir, it is often a fault of the old that we fail to remember that talent can be found in the young.' He stood up, and turned to Laszlo again. 'Subject to final inspection, I approve of the exchange.' He held out his hand and gave each of them a handshake as light as featherdown. 'Would you care to see my collection, gentlemen? There are one or two pictures I would like Mr Gideon to value. He seems to be well in touch with the present market.'

'It would be a great honour,' Laszlo said in some surprise. The Bronstein Collection was rarely seen these days, even by academics, and the owner had earned a reputation as something of a recluse in recent years.

Despite his great age, Bronstein walked with surprising swiftness. He took them through room after dazzling room, each furnished in the period of the pictures that hung on the high walls. It was as if they were visiting Greek and Roman villas, medieval churches, Renaissance palaces, the town house of a Dutch burgher, mansions of the First and Second Empires, an English country house and finally the apartment of a twentieth-century magnate. Bronstein himself fitted none of these categories, but in his curious long velvet coat he seemed equally at home in them all.

Gideon lingered for a time in the nineteenth-century French room, in front of a cluster of pictures by Degas, until Bronstein came back and stood with him.

'You like his work?' the old man asked in his high lilting voice.

Gideon nodded. 'There is a picture in London that I often visit. It is the best thing I have ever seen.'

Bronstein nodded almost in sympathy. 'Oh yes, we collectors all have one picture in our lives. For me, it is the Masaccio you saw in the third room. For normal people, it is their first unrequited love. But, for the collector, it is one special work of art.' He put a hand on Gideon's shoulder. 'Describe it to me,' he said sympathetically. Gideon began, and after a few sentences Bronstein held up a hand. *The Girl in the White Dress,'* he said. 'But it belongs to me.'

Gideon was astonished. 'Strange has displayed it in his gallery for more than a year. The story is that he won't sell it to anyone.'

'It would be most unfortunate for Mr Strange if he did,' Bronstein said drily. 'I bought it from Whitney-Ingram the day it arrived in England.'

'Why don't you keep it here?' Gideon asked.

Bronstein smiled enigmatically. 'Old men like to have their secrets, Mr Gideon. There is so little else left for us.' He took him by the arm and turned to Laszlo. 'Mr Vasilakis, may I borrow your friend for a few hours? It is seldom one meets a young person one wishes to converse with, and I think I would like to discuss the twentieth century for the rest of the afternoon.' Bronstein turned to Gideon. 'That is, if you can spare the time? I would not want to keep you if you have other plans.'

Gideon turned to Laszlo. 'I was going to meet Elizabeth for a drink, but it was just a casual arrangement. Would you keep the appointment, and ask her to telephone me on Monday?'

'Of course, my dear fellow,' said Laszlo. 'It will be a delightful duty.'

Despite the coolness of the day, Elizabeth sat at a table on the pavement outside the Café du Dôme staring into the opaque liquid in her glass. She felt tired and irritable, and her feet ached slightly. She had spent the morning shopping with her mother. The finest couturiers, milliners and designers of lingerie had laid their creations before them and they had taken whatever caught their fancy until, like a child who had sated herself in an orchard of ripe fruit, Elizabeth had insisted that they stop. Despite her promise to

92

Gideon, she had not asked her mother for permission to see him, so she had waited until Elsa had gone to rest in the Hôtel George V before taking a taxi to her rendezvous.

Laszlo watched her from the opposite side of the cobbled street while he waited for the traffic to pass. As always when he saw Elizabeth, he felt the same sensation. It was remarkably similar to the one Gideon experienced when he looked at the Degas painting. For all his beautiful manners and effortless sophistication, Laszlo was a helpless romantic with women. He could flirt, flatter and talk to them for hours, a gift very few men possessed, but anything more was impossible. It was ironic that so many women found him attractive, because he was unable to consummate a casual relationship.

In his work, Laszlo met the wives of many wealthy men, most of them beautiful, many neglected by husbands who had gone on to other conquests. It surprised them when he did not take advantage of their offers, but he always managed to keep their friendship, which in some ways was more impressive. His dark good looks belied his true nature, because his romantic illusions about a woman were destroyed the moment she made it obvious that she was prepared to be faithless to her husband.

Although ten years older than Gideon, the Hungarian had known far fewer women than his younger friend. He had remained faithful in his loveless marriage to Sylvia for two simple reasons: he had not fallen in love with any of the women who were so readily available to him; but, more importantly, he tried to live his life according to the tenets of his faith. Laszlo's Catholicism was absolute and very private.

Meeting Elizabeth on the *Mauretania* had changed all that. Despite her faults, which in many ways he could see more clearly than Gideon, he had become infatuated with her. At first he had told himself it was just her extraordinary beauty that had attracted him, because it compared so favourably with Sylvia's bland prettiness. But he soon realised that that was not all. It was some inner quality that affected him. He could sense a need, not yet fully developed, to commit herself totally. He understood that sort of commitment; he was capable of it himself.

When he approached her now, she looked up and had to shade her eyes from the sun, which had just broken through the clouds. 'Laszlo?' she asked anxiously. 'Where's Gideon?'

He sat down and put his black trilby on the seat between them. 'I'm afraid he was trapped by an important business matter and could not get away. He sent me with his apologies.'

Elizabeth pushed aside her glass of Ricard. Her eyes suddenly brimmed with tears. 'Oh, Laszlo,' she said in a voice that touched his heart, 'what could possibly be that important?'

For a moment he was nonplussed, until it occurred to him that to Elizabeth the word 'business' did not convey the same meaning that it did for others. In her world, 'business' was merely the opposite of pleasure, a term that was used to describe disagreeable duties, like the few hours her father spent talking to his lawyers once a month. It was certainly something that could be put off for more important occasions, such as a casual meeting with her.

'Believe me,' Laszlo said with conviction, 'the work he does could be vital to the rest of his life.'

Elizabeth was slightly mollified to know that it had some significance, but she would have been happier had he said it was a matter of life or death. 'What is he doing?' she asked, carefully dabbing her eyes with the snowy handkerchief he had handed her.

'He is with Henri Bronstein, who seems to have taken a great liking to him.'

Elizabeth had heard of Bronstein. Even her father spoke of him in respectful tones. In her home, rich Jews were generally referred to with contempt, but Bronstein's wealth transcended intolerance. 'Why does he want to talk to Gideon?' She had heard Bronstein discussed only in relation to banking and the manufacturing of armaments.

'Because he is one of the world's greatest collectors, and they have a woman in common.'

Elizabeth looked up quickly, and saw that he was smiling.

London, early autumn 1935

When Gideon told Anne Nettlebury how much he and Laszlo needed her, he had not realised quite how prophetic his words had been. Until they began the gallery, Laszlo had been able to carry the business about with him in his pocket. Now it fell to Anne to deal with the practicalities of their new lives. In the first week she installed telephones, found an accountant, engaged a part-time secretary and persuaded Laszlo to write down the details of the complex web of deals in which he had enmeshed the partnership. At the same time she supervised the workmen who were carrying out the renovation of the property and devised a complex cataloguing system which would enable her to evaluate the state of the business at any given time. To her own astonishment, Anne discovered she had an instinctive grasp of financial matters. The accountant, a fussy, precise man called Henry Grierson, took a positive delight in explaining the intricacies of his requirements to her.

'So often I am resented for my advice, Miss Nettlebury,' he said when they parted after their first meeting. 'People see *me* as the enemy rather than their own carelessness. But you are one of those rare individuals who are gifted with prudence.'

Anne was not sure if she should take this as a compliment or not, but to Henry Grierson it was clearly the highest praise he could bestow.

Now, a few months after she had come to the gallery, her old life at Kew seemed as distant as her childhood. Gideon had eventually given her the red sports car on permanent loan and Irene had become the envy of her classmates when she was driven to school each day. With the salaries she and her father now earned, they could afford the full-time services of Mrs Cooper, so she and her husband Tom had moved into the basement of the house. Tom tended the garden as well as working at his regular job as a fitter in the Brentford Gasworks.

But what was most important to Anne was the fact that she saw Gideon every day, although his manner seemed distant at times. He was always scrupulously polite, but some of his old bantering manner had gone. Occasionally she would notice him looking at her in such an intense way that she wondered if she were causing him displeasure.

The building they had taken a lease on had been previously occupied by a coffee merchant, and they had a great deal of work to do. Now it was the afternoon before the gallery was officially due to be opened, and Anne was the calm at the eye of the storm. Laszlo and Gideon were at lunch with Bronstein's London agent, and workmen were still fitting the doors at the rear entrance. They were making an appalling noise. Others were hanging the pictures for the opening exhibition. The wine merchants had sent cheaper champagne than the vintage specified by Laszlo. Anne looked up from her telephone call and saw the look of satisfaction Mr Temple, the building foreman, customarily wore when he had bad news to impart.

95

She replaced the receiver and prepared herself for the worst. The foreman relit the stub of cigarette he took from behind his ear and brushed the seat of the chair next to Anne's desk before he placed his dusty bottom on the black leather upholstery.

'Yes, Mr Temple?' Anne said, with barely concealed impatience.

'There's no way them doors are going to be ready by tomorrow night,' he said gloomily.

Anne thought she could detect a glimmer of triumph in his eyes. 'Why not, Mr Temple? You promised they would be ready three days ago.'

'The chippie had the flu and his mate read the drawings wrong, so they're too big.'

'Can't he cut them down to size?' Anne asked.

'Not with them brass bindings Mr Laszlo wants, he can't.'

'Mr Laszlo doesn't want them, Mr Temple, but the insurance company insist that the premises are secure. There are a lot of valuable pictures here.'

The foreman looked with contempt at a large painting by Kandinsky that hung over Anne's corner of the large room. 'Well, it's not humanly possible to get the job done, miss. You'd better start taking them down.'

Anne ignored him and called out, 'Ted', to one of the workmen hanging the pictures to Gideon's specifications. He walked over, still holding the sheet on which the positions of each picture were drawn.

'Yes, love?' he said in a Northern accent. Anne did not resent the familiarity at all. Ted Porter was a different kind of man from the other shiftless rabble Temple had brought to the job.

'They can't fit the doors at the back, Ted.'

Porter gave Temple a look of withering contempt. 'There are two million men out of work in this country,' he said with an edge to his voice. 'How come you managed to find this lot?'

'At least they're not a lot of bloody trade unionists,' Temple blustered.

Porter turned to Anne. 'Tell them to rig a tarpaulin over the gap and I'll stay here as night watchman tonight.'

'Thanks, Ted,' Anne said, relieved. 'I'll pay you extra for the time.'

'I'll pay him,' Temple said, attempting to regain authority. 'I'll add it to the bill at the end of the job.'

Anne ignored Temple and turned back to Porter. 'Ted, I've been meaning to have a word with you. How would you like to work here at the gallery on a permanent basis? We're going to need a handyman desperately.'

A broad smile of pleasure came to his face. She knew he had come south to find work; he had a family in Durham he had not seen in months. 'That would be grand,' he said gruffly.

Still addressing him, she folded her arms and turned to look at Temple while she spoke.

'Now you're employed by the gallery, Ted, will you take over the supervision of the building work?'

'It'll be a pleasure,' he said. Then he gestured with his thumb at Temple. 'Let's you and me have a word outside, bonny lad.'

Anne returned to the invitation list on her desk. A few minutes later she heard Ted Porter using a voice like a rasp-file on the workmen clustered in the rear. After a time he returned to the task of picture-hanging, and she could hear the sound of vigorous activity coming from the men he had chastised. She had been deeply impressed by the invective Porter had used. 'Were you in the army, Ted?' she called out.

He continued to work. 'I was a sergeant in the Durham Light Infantry for three years.'

The door from Bond Street opened, and Elizabeth Mueller entered. Anne got up and crossed the wide room to greet her. Elizabeth was dressed in a long charcoal-grey greatcoat that was styled like a Russian guardsman's dress uniform. Her matching pillbox hat was piped in scarlet. She led a dachshund puppy, which Anne knew had been a present from Gideon. Anne was suddenly aware of the old painter's smock she had worn to protect her frock. 'You look lovely,' she said without any trace of envy in her voice, and bent down to stroke the little dog.

'Am I allowed to look around now?' Elizabeth asked. 'Gideon forbade me to come before.'

'Of course.'

'What is that shroud outside doing, hanging over the door?' Elizabeth enquired.

'It's a surprise for Gideon,' said Anne. 'We're going to unveil the new sign when he and Laszlo get back from lunch.'

Elizabeth looked around the huge room and noticed the austere items of furniture that had been arranged with careful precision. The floor was pale polished hardwood scattered with rugs in bold geometric designs. The chairs were low, upholstered in black leather and made of stainless steel. There were standing lights fashioned from shafts of chrome with plain half-circular shades of the same material. Rows of small spotlights were set in the ceiling to illuminate each individual painting.

'What style is this decor?' Elizabeth asked. 'It's very severe.'

'Bauhaus,' Anne replied. 'It's a German design school.'

'I remember,' Elizabeth replied. 'Didn't the German government close it down?'

'That's right.'

'Why did they choose this style and these paintings?' Elizabeth gestured towards the blazing riot of abstract colour that hung on the plain white walls.

'Your father was responsible,' Anne answered.

'Papa?' Elizabeth said, puzzled. 'But he would hate these pictures.'

Anne nodded. 'Gideon and Laszlo have bought so many paintings for his collection that people began to think they were interested only in the traditional schools of Germany and England.' She nodded towards the paintings on the walls. 'That's why we decided to show modern pictures for the opening exhibition. The gallery already has one reputation. This should make it another.'

Elizabeth noticed the word 'we'. 'Do you mean that they actually consult you about what they're going to do?'

Anne laughed. 'Oh, yes, you have no idea how funny they are. Except when they're actually buying pictures, they're like little boys. They ask me about everything.'

Elizabeth raised her eyebrows and gave a tug at the puppy's lead as it strained to sniff Ted Porter's shoes.

The door opened again and Gideon entered, bringing with him a gust of cold air. He was laughing over his shoulder at something Laszlo had said. They greeted Elizabeth, and then inspected the walls, where Porter had just finished hanging the last picture.

'I hope you don't mind, Mr Gideon,' he said, 'but I changed them around slightly from your plan. I can easily put them back if you don't like it.'

Gideon glanced at the arrangement, and then shook his head. 'That's fine, Ted. Thank you.'

Anne took his arm for a moment. 'By the way, I've taken Ted on as our general handyman,' she said with a slight smile at Elizabeth, who studied Gideon and Laszlo to judge their reactions.

'Have you?' Laszlo and Gideon said in interested voices, as though the employment of staff had nothing to do with them.

They turned to the man and shook his hand. 'Congratulations,

Ted. I do hope you like it here,' said Gideon.

Laszlo laid a hand on his shoulder. 'Well done, Ted!' Then he nodded towards Anne. 'Watch out, though. You know what a slave-driver she is! She even insists that I pay income tax.'

Elizabeth found their attitude to Anne slightly disturbing. She felt like the visitor to a club where she was a welcome guest but not actually a member.

'Come outside,' said Anne. 'There's a surprise for you.'

They all went out on to the pavement, and Anne nodded to Ted. He pulled on a piece of cord, so that the sheeting which covered part of the front fell away to reveal the sign over the wide window. Lettered in gold characters on a deep green background were the words THE ARCHANGEL GALLERY, and hanging to right was Gideon's painting of the Botticelli wing.

'I thought it was going to be the Gideon Gallery,' said Elizabeth.

'If I'd wanted my name up in the West End, I'd have stayed an actor,' he replied. 'It looks wonderful, don't you think?'

Elizabeth turned to answer, but then she saw he had addressed the remark to Anne and not to her.

CHAPTER FIVE

London, summer 1936

On 11 August His Excellency Joachim Von Ribbentrop was appointed as the German ambassador to the Court of St James. A few days later he attended one of his first social engagements in London, the grand opening ceremony for Eric Mueller's Collection, celebrating the triumph of German and English art.

It was such a perfect summer evening that Gideon and Laszlo had decided to walk to the house in Belgravia. They arranged to meet at the Ritz and share a bottle of champagne in order to arrive in the proper mood.

Gideon entered the crowded bar just after six-thirty and saw that Laszlo had secured a table in the corner near the door. The Hungarian was wearing white tie and tails, but his hair was unfashionably thick and tangled. Most of the other men in the bar wore theirs closely barbered and plastered flat to their skulls. As he crossed the room, Gideon thought that Laszlo was deep in some melancholy thought, but he looked up and smiled when he noticed Gideon. He reached into the ice-bucket by the side of his chair and poured another glass for his companion. The bottle was already more than half-finished.

'Very elegant,' Laszlo said, looking him up and down. 'The Fred Astaire of Bond Street.'

'Well, at least I look as if I'm going to a dance. You look as if you're going to conduct the bloody orchestra,' Gideon replied, taking the full glass Laszlo held out to him. The bottle was now empty, and Laszlo caught a passing waiter and ordered another, which arrived almost immediately despite the crush of people.

They were not the only ones present going to Mueller's party; the Ritz Bar was the smart place to drink and was close to Belgravia, so others were doing the same. The smell of expensive scent. Virginian tobacco smoke and warm well-bathed bodies perfumed the air in the closely packed room.

'So we are both bachelors tonight,' Laszlo said cheerfully. Gideon knew that his friend was attempting to pull himself from the dark mood he had been in earlier.

He nodded. 'Under the watchful eyes of Frau Mueller, I shall be permitted to dance only twice with the object of my affection.'

Laszlo's reference to his own single status was caused by Sylvia's absence; she was visiting relatives in Switzerland, at a remote village near the border with Italy.

They drank the next glass of wine in silence until Gideon said quietly, 'Come on, what's the matter?'

Laszlo looked up and shrugged, then gave a wry smile. 'I do not particularly approve of myself at the moment.'

Gideon reached for the bottle and poured them both champagne. 'And is this disapproval reserved exclusively for yourself, or am I included in the general run of things?'

A young woman sitting inches from him at the next table turned and asked Gideon for a light. He held the flame of his lighter to her cigarette. She touched his hand with her own and looked up into his eyes as she inhaled. The gesture had been copied from the cinema screen, but the voice which thanked him was pure Home Counties, a curious mixture of harlot and Women's Institute. For a moment he considered the extent to which people were conditioned by the mannerisms of actors; no doubt the girl's grandmother had behaved like one of Oscar Wilde's heroines. He turned back to Laszlo, who was hunched over his glass, and gave another shrug. 'This fiasco we are attending tonight – the illustrated history of Anglo-German culture – it doesn't make me proud.'

'Come on, Laszlo, you're not responsible for the state of the world. We're just dealers making a living.'

'Are we?' Laszlo answered, glancing round the room that bubbled with careless cheer. 'Or are we involved in something bigger and much uglier? A part of a web, but so far from the middle we can't see a nasty big spider in the centre of it all?'

'That's just your exotic blood coming to the boil. There's a different view about what's happening in Germany, you know. Good God, the Britsh government has just signed a naval agreement with them; that means they can build battleships again. Nobody can kill you with an oil painting.'

Laszlo drank his champagne in one swallow, his head thrown

back in a movement Gideon would have used were he playing the part of a dissolute Russian. He banged the glass down on the table and smiled at his companion. 'You sound like Sylvia,' he said lightly. 'She is in complete agreement with the boys in Berlin.' He stood up. 'Come on, we don't want to miss the arrival of the new ambassador.'

Laszlo's mood improved as they walked past the great mansions lining the wide, well-swept streets. 'All those walls,' he said. 'And plenty of room for more pictures. I pray their fortunes increase and they feel the need to demonstrate it to each other.'

Eaton Square was already filled with cars when they reached Erich Mueller's house, each one depositing passengers who passed through a small crowd of sightseers held back by two rows of policemen. As Laszlo and Gideon arrived they saw His Excellency Joachim Von Ribbentrop getting out of a black Mercedes. To their surprise, he was accompanied by Anthony Strange and a young man of Gideon's build who had hair like yellow wax.

'I thought Mueller wanted nothing more to do with Mr Strange,' Laszlo said, surprise in his voice.

'I don't expect he will turn him away in such company,' Gideon said drily.

Laszlo smiled. 'Do you know Herr Goebbels' opinion of the new ambassador?' He cocked his head for a moment. 'Goebbels said: "Von Ribbentrop bought his name, he married his money, and he swindled his way into office." With such testimonials, he ought to be proud to be seen with Anthony Strange.'

A policeman close enough to overhear Laszlo's remark turned and gave them a stare of disapproval, but they pushed past him and presented their invitations to the footman at the door, who exchanged them for a programme.

They studied the contents as they shuffled across the hall in the distinguished queue of guests. The procedure for the evening was straightforward; guests were to make their way to the gallery on the top floor. When they had inspected the pictures, the assembly would descend one flight to the main reception-rooms, where supper would be served to the accompaniment of a string quartet. During supper, the gallery would be cleared and dancing would take place for the rest of the evening.

Gideon and Laszlo watched Von Ribbentrop and his party as they walked ahead of them, and a few moments later a master of ceremonies boomed out their names.

'A well-planned evening,' Laszlo said as they walked up the

staircase. 'Unless someone begins to dance to the string quartet.'

When they were announced, the Mueller family greeted them at the entrance to the ballroom. Elsa and Elizabeth looked magnificent. Sunlight streamed through the great canopy above, and was caught in the glitter of their diamonds. Elsa greeted Gideon with a humourless smile and glanced down to check how briefly his hand touched Elizabeth's.

They moved into the main body of the room, where Laszlo stopped a waiter, who gave them glasses of champagne. Anne and Nettlebury were standing in a corner at the edge of the crowd, talking to a stiff-looking grey-haired man and an equally severe woman, who glanced around the room with vague disapproval. Gideon noticed that their companion had four rows of decorations on his left breast and the cross and sash he wore matched Nettlebury's.

Nettlebury waved a greeting. 'May I introduce Colonel and Mrs Renfrew Middleton?' he said. 'Renfrew and I knew each other during the war. He's with the Foreign Office now.'

'Are you with the German section, Colonel?' Laszlo asked.

Middleton nodded. 'Four years fighting them, and seventeen making friends again.' He laughed. 'We didn't think we'd ever be going to anything like this in 1916, did we, Julian?'

'Time plays peculiar tricks, Rennie,' Nettlebury answered.

'And makes curious bedfellows,' Laszlo added. They followed his gaze to where the Mueller family stood with Anthony Strange and Von Ribbentrop.

Strange noticed their attention and raised his glass of champagne in a salute of recognition. There was enough smugness in his smile to cause Gideon a surge of irritation.

'Tell me, Colonel, how is the new ambassador settling down?'

A veil of bland discretion seemed to settle over Middleton's stern features. 'Oh, pretty well, considering he's a new boy,' he answered lightly.

'I think the man is appalling,' Mrs Middleton said crisply.

'Steady, Caroline,' Middleton warned her.

Mrs Middleton turned and changed her empty glass of champagne for a full one from a hovering waiter's tray. 'The man is like some half-trained lap-dog,' she said. 'Either licking your hand or snarling at the servants.' She turned to her husband, and her voice changed. 'What was it all for, Rennie? Both my brothers, all your cousins are dead. And now these people are in power.' She looked at

103

Gideon. 'It will be your turn next, and all for nothing.'

The gallery emptied gradually as the crowd descended to eat. Gideon stood at the back of the reception-room to listen to the music; he hadn't bothered with the buffet. During a round of applause, he felt a tug on his arm and turned to see Elizabeth standing beside him.

'Meet me in the bedroom,' she whispered. Her eyes were bright and her cheeks slightly flushed from the champagne. He nodded and, after a few minutes, glanced around to check on the whereabouts of Elsa Mueller. She was sitting at the front of the audience, flanked by Von Ribbentrop and her husband. Satisfied that he would not be noticed, he followed Elizabeth.

He found the room with difficulty; the rest of the house had changed so much that he was surprised to discover it was exactly as it had been when he had last been there with her. She was standing in the same position by the window. The room was warmer, but he sensed a different mood in Elizabeth: her smile was without humour and she folded her arms as he approached her.

'Are you having an enjoyable time?'

'Enjoyable enough,' he answered warily. She was clearly angry with him, and he could not understand the nature of his transgression.

'Is there a reason why you are ignoring me?' She turned to look out of the window again.

Gideon knew from previous experiences with Elizabeth that the conversation that would now ensue would be as barbed and barren as a wire fence. He took hold of her bare shoulders and turned her to face him. He spoke gently, knowing how difficult it could be to deal with someone whose mood had been determined by champagne. 'Your mother is watching us every minute. Didn't you notice? She could only just restrain herself from biting my hand when I touched you.'

'I don't care about her!' With a sudden movement, Elizabeth shrugged off the thin shoulder-straps of her dress. 'Make love to me now, like we did the first time.'

In the months he had been with her he had gradually learned to control the passions Elizabeth could arouse in him. He slowly shook his head. 'This ridiculous outfit takes fifteen minutes to get in and out of,' he said with regret, tapping the stiff front of his evening dress. 'In that time your mother would have organised a search party.'

The rejection jerked her back like a blow to the face. 'You coward,' she said bitterly, and, pushing past him, stalked from the room.

Gideon decided not to follow her. Instead he lit a cigarette and looked down on to the sunlit garden, where couples were strolling on the lawn. It was obviously an evening of changing moods, he reflected. First Laszlo and now Elizabeth; he wondered if there was going to be a full moon. He opened the window to throw his cigarette on to the flowerbed below and heard music; the string quartet had changed to an Ivor Novello melody being played by a dance band. Clearly the ball had begun. He paused to look around the bare little room and felt a moment of regret.

When he arrived in the ballroom, Elizabeth was being escorted on to the floor by the young man with waxen hair who had come with Anthony Strange and the German ambassador. Gideon was edging his way round the room when a voice called his name. He turned to see a tall red-haired man, who looked vaguely familiar.

'Ralph Keswick,' he said, and Gideon remembered the last time he had seen him, dressed as Sherlock Holmes on board the *Mauretania*. They shook hands, and Keswick said, 'Come and join the gentlemen of the press. We've established comfortable quarters near the bar.'

Gideon suddenly needed a large whisky, and allowed Keswick to lead the way. As they approached a noisy group, he heard Anthony Strange's voice. 'And there's Laszlo Vasilakis faking a foxtrot, as he does everything else in life.'

There was a chorus of laughter from the men and women around. 'Are you saying Vasilakis sells fake pictures?' one of the journalists asked, as they watched Laszlo glide past with Elsa Mueller in his arms.

Strange nodded. 'Certainly,' he replied loudly. He could not see Gideon, who was close enough behind him to hear the conversation quite clearly.

'He sold Erich Mueller his first fake, a Watteau, the day he met him.' Strange gestured at the walls. 'God knows what he's passed off here. I expect the Fraud Squad will be paying this place a visit before too long.'

'That's not quite what happened,' Gideon said in a voice loud enough to be heard by the semicircle of people around Strange. 'If I remember correctly, Laszlo revealed the Watteau as a fake, and *you* were the one who vouched for its authenticity.'

Strange looked over his shoulder and saw Gideon, but he had drunk enough to be unperturbed. 'Ah, Laszlo's apprentice,' he said disdainfully, and then turned back to the journalists. 'My friends, are you acquainted with this chorus boy? Now he's playing the part of Laszlo's art expert.' He placed an arm round Gideon shoulder. 'Or is it his clown?'

Gideon looked round the expectant faces. He understood the differing moods of audiences, and only blood or laughter would satisfy this one. Although he was sorely tempted, he decided it would be unwise to start punching Strange on this particular occasion.

'Stand back, gentlemen,' he said belligerently and they cleared a few feet for him. But instead of raising his fists, as they expected, Gideon executed a few elegant tap-dance steps to the rhythm of the band. Some of them applauded, and he held out his hands to the journalists. 'You see, ladies and gentlemen, what Strange says is never a complete lie, but then he's incapable of being complete about anything he says or does.'

The group clearly enjoyed the antagonism; rivalry made good copy. 'Do you think you know more about paintings than Strange?' a woman asked.

'Beyond question,' Gideon said cheerfully. 'I've learned more in eighteen months with Sir Julian Nettlebury than Mr Strange has picked up in a lifetime.'

'You're saying he doesn't know what he's talking about?' Keswick called out.

Gideon turned to him. 'Oh, he knows something,' he said innocently. 'Anthony Strange has a mind like a lazy man's navel: jammed full of fluff and a few grains of grit.'

The journalists began to laugh at the insults, and more people gathered to listen. Strange turned on Gideon, but his anger robbed him of the necessary humour.

'I've forgotten more about painting than you'll ever learn, you posturing little upstart,' he said, with such ferocity that specks of spittle sprayed from his mouth.

'I'll go half-way with your remarks,' Gideon replied, and now it was his turn to place his arm on Strange's shoulder. 'Let's put it to a test, shall we?'

Strange shrugged off Gideon's arm. 'If you dare, I'm ready.'

Laszlo had finished his dance and had come to stand at the edge of the crowd, an anxious expression on his face. Gideon paused, his timing impeccable. 'Ladies and gentlemen of the Press, I hereby issue a challenge that Anthony Strange come and identify the works of six artists at the Archangel Gallery, one week from today.' He turned to the journalists again. 'What time would be most suitable for you?'

106

'Make it three-thirty in the afternoon,' Keswick answered. 'After lunch.'

By now Gideon could see that Elizabeth had stopped dancing and was standing with her partner and Von Ribbentrop. Strange pushed his way through the crowd to join them, and the journalists pressed more whisky on Gideon.

Later, when Laszlo caught him on his own, he whispered, 'Are you sure you know what you're doing? The man is unspeakable, but he does know a good deal about the business. Are you sure you're ready to fight a duel with him?'

'I think so,' Gideon answered with a grin. 'Don't forget, the bastard left me with the choice of weapons.'

Gideon's challenge had caught the imagination of Fleet Street's news editors, and the papers gave great play to the contest that was to take place. Anne noticed a definite increase in the visitors who came to the gallery. Some were just sightseers who tended to melt away under Ted Porter's stern gaze, but others stayed and bought pictures.

Because of her upbringing she had always considered painting a serious business, an occupation that demanded long hours of thought, planning and painstaking execution to produce a piece of work that could be judged worthy of showing to the public. So it seemed extraordinary to her that people could select a painting on a caprice, as if it were a hat or a cream cake. But Anne's views on human nature in general had undergone a sea-change since she had worked at the gallery. She had not realised before that so many people were so rude or eccentric.

Elizabeth Mueller, who led a life composed mostly of spare time, had taken to calling each afternoon and insisting that they went to tea at the Ritz. After the first few visits Anne demanded that, if the practice were to continue, she would pay on alternate days, and they would visit a Lyons tea-shop on those occasions.

'People are so extraordinary,' Anne said when they had settled down with their buns and cups of tea. 'A woman came in yesterday and asked me to show her all the yellow paintings we had.'

'What did you do?' Elizabeth asked, taking quick little bites from her cake.

Anne shrugged and sipped her tea. 'I always hand those ones over to Ted Porter. He's a marvel with them. He says you can divide the customers into talkers, drinkers and leek-growers.'

'I don't understand,' said Elizabeth.

Anne explained. 'Ted says the talkers are like customers who come into pubs and never buy anyone else a pint. The drinkers are the ones who know their beer and aren't satisfied until they get what they want. He makes me serve them. And the leek-growers are there to buy something to show off to their friends. We take it in turn with them. One of us will wait until they've decided which one they like, and then the other will come up and tell the person how brilliant they are.'

Elizabeth shook her head in bafflement. 'What are leeks?'

'A sort of vegetable,' Anne told her. 'Where Ted comes from, people grow them to an enormous size, then enter them in competitions.'

Elizabeth was still confused but not interested enough to continue the line of conversation. Instead, she looked hungrily at Anne's uneaten cake until she pushed it towards her. When that was consumed, she licked the sugar from her fingers and sighed. 'I've got a terrible problem, and you're the only one I can tell,' she said in a low voice.

Sometimes Anne regretted her role as Elizabeth's confidante. She sat up straight in her chair and looked around the cavernous marble interior of the tea-shop, wishing she were seated at one of the other tables where people with less demanding companions were enjoying their moments of leisure. 'If it's anything to do with Gideon, I think I'd rather you didn't tell me,' she said firmly.

'No, it's not,' Elizabeth said, and then shook her head. 'Well, it is and it isn't.' She reached forward and touched Anne's hand. 'I've got another lover.'

'You and Gideon are finished?' Anne asked, with hope in her heart.

'No, someone else as well.'

'Does Gideon know?' Anne was ashamed to ask such intimate details about someone's personal life, but she was anxious to know the answer.

'Don't be silly! He would be furious. It's a secret, at least from Gideon.'

'Do you love both of them?' Anne wondered if such a state could be possible.

Elizabeth thought about the question. 'I'm not sure, but it's exciting to be with him. The new man, I mean.'

Anne turned her head away, her emotions and motives confused. She would never allow herself to contemplate the kind of double game Elizabeth was involved in. 'So you still love Gideon, but you want to see this other man as well?'

'Yes,' Elizabeth replied firmly. 'Honestly, Anne, you have no idea how difficult it can be, not being able to see Gideon whenever I want to. Some nights I was so lonely I would just sit in my room and cry.'

'But you don't have to cry any more,' Anne said.

The irony in her voice passed Elizabeth by. 'Not with Karl Schneider. He makes me laugh.'

'Have you made love with him too?' Anne asked.

Elizabeth shrugged. 'Only twice. It wasn't as good as with Gideon.'

'But it was better than staying at home, I suppose?'

'That's right.'

Elizabeth chattered on, but now Anne, unable to concentrate on her words, looked down at the empty plates and thought how Elizabeth always ate all the cakes on the table. When she looked up again, Elizabeth was gathering her possessions together.

'Honestly, I don't think you've really listened to a thing I've told you,' Elizabeth said, not realising how she had filled her companion with a new and deep resolve.

The day of the contest had arrived, and preparations were being made at the Archangel Gallery. Ted Porter lifted the delicate glass and tipped it at an angle, so that he could pour the newly-opened champagne against the lip of the tulip-shaped flute. He smiled as he watched the slightest layer of bubbles fizz on the surface. Doris Sherman, the gallery's part-time secretary, watched him intently, her face filled with admiration.

'There you are, pet,' Ted said, handing her the bottle. 'For the first couple of glasses it's like pouring light ales but, after that, most of the fizz goes, so you can leave them on the table and move the bottle around as if it were a pot of tea.'

'You are clever, Ted,' Doris said. 'Where on earth did you learn to do that? I thought you used to be a coal-miner.'

'I worked in a hotel for a while,' he explained with a wink. 'You pick up all sorts of things in a job like that.'

'Go on,' Doris said with an earthy chuckle. 'You'll have to tell me all about it one night.'

'Better make it soon. Me wife, is coming down to live the week after next.'

'Is she looking forward to it?' Doris asked.

Ted shrugged. 'Me daughter's dead keen, but the boy's still at school and Mabel's worried she'll miss her mother and her friends.'

'She'll be all right, Ted,' Doris said reassuringly. 'It's all rubbish about southerners being stand-offish. Blimey, round our way, everybody's like one big family.'

Ted looked at her with an appreciative smile. Doris was one of those English women who are usually found behind the bar of the best public houses. Blonde, with a little help from the hairdresser, some indeterminate age over thirty, with a round pretty face and a generous body. Talking to men in a cheerful and relaxed manner came naturally to her, as Anne had noticed when her father visited the gallery. He would always stop at her desk, and there would be laughter.

'I do like your dad,' she had said to Anne after her first conversation with Sir Julian. 'You can always tell a real gentleman.'

'How do you tell a real gentleman, Doris?' Anne had asked with genuine curiosity.

'They're the ones who treat you like a lady instead of a piece of dog dirt. It don't have anything to do with who your parents was, or where you went to school. My dad worked in the Surrey Docks all his life, but my mum said he was always a real gentleman.'

Now, as Ted had instructed, she poured the champagne into the rows of glasses set out on a long table at the end of the gallery.

'Three twenty-five. I'd better unlock the doors.' Ted buttoned the jacket of his blue serge suit.

So many members of the public had loitered in the gallery that morning, hoping to find places as spectators, that Laszlo and Gideon were worried that those with invitations would be unable to get in. Consequently, they had evacuated the premises and locked the doors for the last hour. When they opened, one of the first into the rooms was Ralph Keswick, followed by a photographer. They were greeted by Laszlo, who had emerged from the store-room in the basement.

'So what's this?' Keswick asked, indicating a row of six empty easels ranged across the centre of the gallery.

'Patience,' Laszlo replied with a smile. He handed them glasses of champagne. 'Everything will be revealed in a moment.'

The gallery quickly filled, and the wine gave a proper air of celebration to the coming event. Gideon took his own glass from Doris when he came up from the basement and stood beside Laszlo.

Keswick reached out and squeezed one of his biceps. 'How are you feeling? I hope you've been in strict training.'

Gideon smiled.

'How *are* you feeling?' Laszlo whispered when Keswick and the photographer went for more champagne. Although he too was smiling, Gideon could hear a note of anxiety.

'I wish this were a stiff whisky,' said Gideon, raising the glass in his hand, 'or even Bull's Blood.'

'Too late now,' Laszlo replied, as Anthony Strange, accompanied by the waxen-haired Schneider, pushed his way into the centre of the room.

Laszlo walked forward and held up his arms. Gradually the noise of conversation died down. 'Ladies and gentlemen, for the sake of those people who have not read a newspaper for the last week, let me explain the purpose of the events you are about to witness.' He gestured towards Strange, who was pretending to examine a picture high on the gallery wall at the back of the crowd. 'Mr Strange, a well-known dealer, has cast doubt on the integrity of the Archangel Gallery, and in particular on the knowledge of my partner, James Gideon.' He paused as a murmur of comment passed through the crowd, then held up his hands again. 'For his part, my friend has been equally severe in his criticisms of Anthony Strange.' Laszlo clasped his hands together as if in silent prayer and looked up at the spotlights in the ceiling, as though seeking divine guidance. 'Friends,' he continued, 'as dealers, the thing we prize most highly is our reputation. It is our most precious possession. Need I remind you: "Who steals my purse steals trash. But he that filches from me my good name makes me poor indeed." So this contest of skills has been arranged, and you may judge which of these two gentlemen commands the greater claim to be trusted by the public when they recommend a work of art.' He turned and pointed towards the people standing behind the easels. 'If you ladies and gentlemen would be so kind as to come to this side of the room, you will be able to see more clearly.'

'Let's get on with it,' said Strange.

Laszlo nodded. 'Mr Strange is understandably nervous, so we shall begin. The Archangel Gallery will present six pictures, which we invite Mr Strange to identify and to give an approximate date as to their execution.' He waved to the end of the room. 'Mr Porter, produce the pictures, one at a time if you please.'

The summer afternoon was sultry and, as instructed, Ted Porter had not lowered the blinds on the big window. The sun beat down on the wide expanse of glass and heated the gallery like a greenhouse, as Laszlo had intended.

Gideon, dressed in his lightest clothes, had taken the precaution of wearing a loose-fitting collar, but Strange was clearly feeling the heat. He took a large handkerchief from his pocket to mop his brow, and then a smile came to his face when he saw the picture Ted Porter had placed on the first easel. The word 'Matisse' was whispered through the crowd; it sounded like the hissing of a serpent.

Laszlo held up his hand again. 'Please, ladies and gentlemen, I beg you, remain silent when the pictures are produced.'

Anthony Strange took a gold fountain-pen from his pocket and began to write in a little leather notebook. A low murmur of conversation rippled through the room, despite Laszlo's plea. Nobody could resist giving their own assessment of the paintings. The process was repeated as Strange indicated that he was ready for the next picture. Finally, all the easels were filled.

'Are you ready?' Laszlo asked.

Strange gave a last flourish with his fountain-pen, tore the page from his notebook and handed it to the Hungarian. The murmur of voices broke into a barrage of conversation, and Laszlo had to call out again to restore silence.

'Now for the assessment. In the sequence they were displayed, a Henri Matisse still life, painted about 1910; a cubist picture by Georges Braque, about 1913; an example of André Derain in his Fauve period, about 1907; street scene by Ernst Ludwig Kirchner, about 1913; study of the Eiffel Tower by Robert Delaunay about 1911; winter scene by Pieter Brueghel the Elder, tempera on canvas, painted about 1565.'

Once again the voices swelled in the room as Gideon stepped forward. He bowed slightly, and the noise subsided. There was a slight sense of disappointment. Most of the people present were art critics, with the exception of one or two writers like Keswick. For them, the pictures chosen by the Archangel Gallery seemed obvious and easily dated. Gideon looked round the faces for a moment and saw Elizabeth, who had turned her head to listen to something Schneider said. He waited until she was looking in his direction again and then began to speak.

'Thank you for coming today, and taking part in this little ceremony,' he said in conversational tones. 'Mr Strange accuses me of being theatrical.' He smiled. 'And I must confess that, in this, he is correct. I am sure most of you will have come to the conclusion that there is a great deal of play-acting about this afternoon's entertainment. But, despite the levity, there is an underlying threat in Mr Strange's accusations that strikes at the heart of my reputation, and I must answer that slur or forfeit any right I have to your trust.' He gestured towards the pictures on the easels. 'Anthony Strange has identified these pictures as the works of great artists.' He paused, and there were comments of affirmation from the spectators. 'If his judgment is correct, they are worth a fortune to anyone, and we at the Archangel Gallery would cherish them until they took their rightful place in museums, or the homes of individuals who would treat them with the proper reverence.' He paused again, and then his voice rang out with startling ferocity. 'But if any of them were fakes, how would the Archangel Gallery treat them?' He turned, and shouted, 'Like this!'

On cue, Ted Porter threw an untipped fencing-foil the length of the gallery. It curved across the room, flashing in the sunlight that streamed through the window.

Gideon deftly caught it, and in the electrifying silence that followed, he moved with the strutting bravado he had once displayed as Romeo and quickly slashed the first five canvases to ribbons.

There was a breathless silence for at least five seconds, and then the room erupted as a shouting mob of reporters and photographers converged on the ruined pictures. Taking advantage of the hubbub, Anthony Strange hurried out of the Archangel Gallery, accompanied by Karl Schneider. Elizabeth paused for a moment, and then followed them.

Gideon stood back from the crowd, and Laszlo leaned forward to mutter, 'You didn't harm any of the frames, did you? Some of them are quite valuable.'

Later, when the interviews were over, the final photographs taken and the last well-wishers had left, Laszlo opened a bottle of champagne that had been saved for the occasion.

Doris was the first to raise her glass. 'I thought you were wonderful, Mr Gideon, when you caught that sword. I said: "Blimey, Douglas Fairbanks couldn't have done that better", honest I did!'

'Thank you,' Gideon answered. Then he glanced around. 'Didn't Elizabeth stay?'

113

'She left with that man Schneider when the photographers' bulbs started popping,' said Ted.

Like actors after a show, they all discussed the various aspects of their performance until Laszlo declared an early day. They would close up the gallery immediately. Still holding the fencing-foil, Gideon walked over to where the remains of the pictures still stood in a row, and studied them.

Laszlo and Anne came and stood on each side of him. 'Why didn't you destroy the Brueghel as well?' Laszlo asked.

Gideon smiled. 'I worked so bloody hard on that one I didn't have the heart!' he said with a sigh. Then he looked back at the ruined paintings and stopped smiling.

'You're not really very happy now, are you?' Anne asked softly.

'No.' He reached out to touch one of the shreds of canvas hanging from a frame. 'I know they were fakes,' he said after a time. 'Christ, I painted them myself. But a good fake has got something of the real painter about it, some faint residue of his talent. In a way, what I did was an insult. I won't do it again.'

Laszlo lifted the Brueghel off the easel and tucked it under his arm. 'In that case, I shall put this somewhere very safe,' he said firmly.

South of France, early summer 1937

Since the notorious competition with Strange, good fortune had smiled on the gallery. The story had been picked up from the London papers and gone around the world, altering slightly in the process, that the Archangel Gallery destroyed fake pictures if they came across them. They had been given a reputation for integrity that had begun to serve them well.

People from every conceivable country now visited them in Bond Street. They had formed an association with Piet Liebe in New York that was to their mutual advantage, and Henri Bronstein phoned Gideon at least once a week to gossip as much as to discuss pictures. He had guided an impressive stream of customers to the gallery, who were glad to accept his advice on any investment he recommended.

They had offered to pay back more than half the money that

Gideon's mother had given them, but she had refused the cash and instead asked Gideon to provide pictures for the house she and Frank had bought at Brighton when they returned from Australia.

By the end of May, exhausted but confident enough to take a vacation, they had closed down for two weeks. Gideon was glad to get away. *The Girl in the White Dress* had been removed from the window of Strange's gallery, and he missed the picture keenly.

He was now nearly twenty-four and the last touches of boyhood had long gone from his face, but he had developed the skill of talking with authority without sounding pompous, a technique helped by his dramatic training. Laszlo's coal-black hair had suddenly, in a few months, become shot with grey; oddly, it made him seem younger. He claimed to friends that it was the responsibility of the gallery, although it was Anne who really worried most.

It was the first proper day of the holiday when Gideon parked the red MG in the shade of a eucalyptus in the forecourt of Antibes station and glanced at his watch. There was plenty of time before the Blue Train was due from Paris. The morning sky was like blue enamel, and the clicking of cicadas filled the air. The scent of pines mingled with the smell of petrol and warm leather. Smoke drifted past from the cigarette of an old man dressed in faded blue work-clothes, his face the colour of walnut, who slowly plodded past carrying a long broom. He stopped to tap the bonnet of the car with a gnarled hand.

'*Très sportive,*' he muttered in admiration.

Gideon smiled back at the compliment, and the old man shrugged and walked on.

Lacing his hands behind his head, he leaned back to look up at the fragments of sky showing through the fringe of leaves. It was a time of perfect peace. He and Laszlo had arrived the day before, having driven in a leisurely fashion on the straight, empty roads that led to the south. Before they left London they had rented a small house that stood among vineyards in the hills behind the Cap d'Antibes, and now Gideon was waiting for Nettlebury and the girls to arrive. They had two weeks before they were due to return to London, and very little business to transact.

Gideon felt happier than he had for months. Part of his contentment, at least, was due to the fact that Elizabeth was in England; he would be spared the ordeal of her increasing tantrums. There was something deeply enervating in a relationship that

115

fluctuated between raw sexuality and carping recrimination. Gradually he had began to cherish the peaceful time he spent in the gallery with Anne.

The silence was broken by the sound of another car, and a Citroën pulled into the shade next to the MG. The driver, a youth in an ill-fitting dark suit, got out and strolled into the station entrance with his hands in his pockets. Then Gideon heard the train from Paris arriving.

The season would not begin until August, and only two groups were descending from the carriages when he reached the platform. Nettlebury and the girls got out of a second-class compartment – and, from the wagon-lit section, the Mueller family descended. Fussing about them like a German Shepherd dog was Karl Schneider, dressed in a white suit and wearing a straw panama hat. Gideon felt his shoulders tighten as though someone had tugged on the sinews like drawstrings.

Elizabeth shrieked with delight and rushed forward to embrace Anne, and the two families greeted each other with pleasure, as people do when they find familiar faces in exotic places. Mueller exclaimed how odd it was they had missed each other in Paris, but Gideon knew that the encounter was no surprise for Elizabeth. The Muellers said that they were staying at the Hôtel du Cap, and tentative arrangements were made to meet for dinner.

'When did you decide to come?' Nettlebury asked Erich Mueller.

'It was all Elizabeth's idea,' Elsa replied, giving Gideon a hostile glance. 'She insisted we come. I can't think why she chose the Riviera. We had intended to go to Marienbad.'

'Perhaps it was me, Mrs Mueller,' said Anne. 'I think I might have mentioned that we were hoping to manage a few weeks down here.'

Elsa turned to inspect Anne, and then noticed Irene. 'Good heavens! Is this the little girl who was with us on the *Mauretania*?' She studied her for a moment. 'Well, you've certainly grown, my dear.'

Irene blushed at the comment and hung her head. Elsa Mueller had drawn attention to the very thing she felt most sensitive about. In the last months of the summer her figure had developed to the extent that it now rivalled her sister's. In Irene's own words, she had joined the world of the mammals and she was still disturbed by her newly formed body. The driver of the Citroën, who was still transporting the luggage from the platform, had winked at her.

Anne saw her discomfort, and changed the subject. 'Surely we won't all be able to get into your car, Gideon?'

116

The driver of the Citroën began to load the mountain of the Muellers' luggage on to his roof-rack.

'Laszlo ordered a taxi,' Gideon explained. 'I'm only here to lead the way.'

Just then a dusty ramshackle vehicle, without windows and with steam streaming from its radiator cap, chugged into the forecourt and came to a hissing halt beside them.

'Taxi, Laszlo,' the driver announced in a surly voice, stepping from the driver's seat.

Anne was no longer intimidated by this type of individual. Her time at the gallery had given her a new-found authority. She spoke to him quickly in immaculate French, and his attitude changed instantly.

'Bags I go with Gideon!' Irene called out, reverting for a moment to childish ways.

When they had set off in slow procession for the house, Gideon glanced down at Irene, who was sitting hunched low in the passenger seat, her arms folded in front of her in a vain attempt to conceal her ample bosom. Although the top was down on the sports car, they drove so slowly that there was no rush of wind to disturb their conversation.

'Gideon,' she said, 'may I ask you a personal question?'

'Certainly.' He glanced into the mirror to check that the taxi was keeping up with them.

'When you were my age, did you like being a boy?'

He shook his head. 'Not much.'

'Why not?'

He eased the speed down and made an effort to relax. Elizabeth's appearance had disturbed him more than he would have expected. 'Why didn't I like being a boy?' he repeated. 'Because my parents wanted me to remain a child. It was the part they were used to seeing me play. I had other ambitions.'

'What sorts of ambitions?'

'I'd fallen in love,' he said. 'She was one of the maids in the Strand Palace hotel. All I wanted was to buy a chalk-striped suit, smoke Capstan full-strength cigarettes and take her to Lyons Corner House.'

'How did you meet her?'

'We were living in the hotel at the time. Sometimes it was hotels, sometimes boarding-houses. One summer, we lived in a huge palace in Italy where there was a monkey in the kitchen.'

Irene considered this information for a while and then spoke angrily. 'I don't ever want to be in love. It only makes you unhappy.'

'Not all the time,' he answered.

'Yes, it does. Look at you. You're in love with Elizabeth, and you're unhappy. And look how miserable Anne is.'

'Who said I was in love with Elizabeth?'

'Everybody knows you are,' she replied scornfully.

He asked his next question with a certain amount of trepidation. 'Well, what about Anne? Whom is she in love with?'

Irene looked at him to see if he were teasing her. 'You, of course, silly! Everybody knows that, too.' Her answer came as such a shock that he put his foot down hard on the accelerator and the little car suddenly shot forward, leaving a cloud of dust billowing behind. They looked back until they could see the swaying taxi emerge through the haze. When he had settled down again, Irene sank into her previous position. 'I don't know why you don't all just swap round and be done with it.'

'But who is going to love Elizabeth?'

'Oh, there are plenty of people to love Elizabeth,' Irene assured him.

The following morning Nettlebury, Gideon and the girls were sitting on the terrace of the little whitewashed house when Laszlo returned from the village with fresh bread for their breakfast. 'I telephoned the Muellers, and they would like to buy us lunch at the beach today,' he said, placing the loaves on the table. 'And guess what? There's an old friend of yours staying at the same hotel,' he said to Nettlebury.

'Really, who?' Nettlebury seemed to be more interested in the crusty bread than the social arrangements.

'Mrs Whitney-Ingram. She's there with her son and his boy. They were in Mueller's suite when I rang.'

'Abigail Whitney-Ingram,' Nettlebury said after a moment. 'Yes, I remember her. How on earth do they know the Muellers?'

'They're rich, Julian. It's a very small club,' Laszlo answered, pouring himself coffee.

'I heard the Whitney-Ingrams lost most of their money in the crash,' said Nettlebury.

Irene took a piece of the crust and, breaking it into fragments, threw it for the swallows that twisted and dived from their nest beneath the eaves.

118

'Well, it seems they've got it back,' Laszlo said, 'and now they're here on holiday.' He leaned forward and broke off another piece of bread. 'So everybody find their bathing suits. I've ordered the taxi for eleven.'

'I don't want to go bathing,' Irene said miserably. 'I hate swimming in the sea.'

'Don't worry, my dear,' Nettlebury said. 'You can stay on the beach and keep me company.'

'I hate the sand, too.' She threw more bread to the swallows.

'There no need to bother with the sand. We're in the south of France; on the Côte d'Azur they put planks down the beach.'

'They do?' Irene was unsure. 'Honestly?'

'Honestly,' said Nettlebury. 'Come and see for yourself.'

As Nettlebury had promised, an hour later Irene was walking on the warm duckboards of the hotel beach. The Mueller family and the Whitney-Ingrams had already established a suitable area close to the bar, and were spread comfortably on brightly coloured mattresses under huge parasols. The introductions had been made – with one exception.

'Here comes Charles now,' Abigail Whitney-Ingram said as her grandson emerged from the sea. His nose was peeling from too much sun, and his hair was bleached almost white. 'We've been here for weeks, and he's been bored to tears.'

'Here's someone nearer your age who can speak the same language,' Stanford said by way of introducing Irene. 'Why don't you buy her an ice-cream soda at the bar?'

Irene and Charles looked at each other as though each were a creature of a different species, then reluctantly walked away from the adults and sat down on the high stools at the counter. Charles Whitney-Ingram knew it was his responsibility to begin the conversation. By a process of deduction he eliminated baseball from his introductory remarks, but was left with a sudden void. 'Who's your favourite portrait painter?' he asked in desperation.

'I like two,' Irene replied, relief in her voice. 'Romney and Rembrandt Van Rijn.'

Thirty minutes later, Stanford looked up from his conversation to see Charles and Irene happily splashing each other in the sea. 'Well, that was a lightning romance,' he said, and everyone laughed, including Nettlebury, although the sight made him feel a little sad. He turned and glanced towards Anne, who had just emerged from

119

the sea. She pulled off a swimming-cap and shook out her long red hair. The pale wool bathing costume she wore clung to her, revealing the glories of her body. Suddenly he was reminded of a painting by Botticelli. Gideon sat close to him. He held a book in his lap, but his eyes did not leave Anne.

The next thirteen days floated past in a haze of cloudless skies and velvet nights. Most days were spent on the Carlton beach, where Charles and Irene had become inseparable. Gideon had only once managed to meet Elizabeth alone, when they had walked for the best part of the morning around the port of Antibes, holding a desultory conversation full of the usual recriminations.

It was the last afternoon of the holiday for him and Laszlo. That night they were to dine with Henri Bronstein at his villa near by and the following morning to set off for the north in the little MG. Gideon watched Schneider rubbing sun lotion into Elizabeth's shoulders for a while and then waded into the sea and swam to the raft anchored some distance from the beach. He pulled himself aboard and lay, face down, on the hot wooden surface. As his body dried, the soft lapping of the water against the edge of the raft lulled him into a half-drowsing sleep. Then the raft rocked. He opened his eyes, expecting to see Charles and Irene, but it was Elizabeth who scrambled aboard. Watching her, he noticed the paler skin of her under-arms that now contrasted with the golden suntan she had acquired. Powdered and groomed, or wet from the sea, Elizabeth was equally lovely.

He sat up and let his feet dangle. 'It was a waste of time covering you with sun-oil, wasn't it? Poor old Schneider!'

Elizabeth sat close to him on the square raft but at right angles, so that they partly had their backs to each other. She splashed her feet in the water. 'It wasn't a very good idea for me to come on this holiday, was it?' she said after a while. 'I thought we might be able to be close to each other again, but the opposite has happened.'

'Oh, I don't know. You seem to have had a good enough time.'

'What else could I do, with my mother here?' she said flatly.

'Is your mother forcing you on Schneider? I can't see the attraction myself.'

Elizabeth hung her head for a moment and then took a deep breath. 'He has a title, you know. He doesn't use it. My father says he has a brilliant career ahead of him in the new Germany.'

'Well, you'd better get back to your secretive aristocrat,' said Gideon. 'I shall look at him with new eyes in future.'

Elizabeth slipped from the raft and rested her arms on the side, with her body in the sea. 'Oh, Gideon,' she said sadly, 'you can't see anything. Your eyes are so filled with Anne Nettlebury.' Then she pushed away from the raft and struck for the shore, her long golden body moving swiftly through the dappling water.

Gideon sat for a long time, angry and bitter that he could not have everything he wanted, aware that he had forced Elizabeth away. Now he thought about what she had just said. It was true that he was drawn to her, but he was alarmed at the thought of making a commitment to Anne; with her, it would be all or nothing. He remembered his parents. Since childhood he had known that they were unfaithful to each other, yet they returned from each affair to the familiar comforts that kept them together. Is that my real nature? he wondered. Will I flit through life like a butterfly, settling for a brief time on a woman like Elizabeth, who will eventually brush me away?

While he sat thinking, Irene and Charles swam up to the raft and climbed aboard. Gideon could see from their faces that they too had their problems, and he suddenly remembered that in two days they had to face a parting. Nettlebury and Stanford Whitney-Ingram, without actually discussing the subject, had seen to it that the two young people were never left alone, so this raft had been their nearest thing to privacy: the place where they could tell each other their secrets and feelings, under the watchful eyes on the beach. Gideon looked down at Irene, and could see the echo of her sister when she lay beside him. Then he knew that he could not avoid the inevitable. He left the raft to Charles and Irene and, as Elizabeth had done, struck out with powerful strokes for the shore.

'I hope you haven't brought a sword with you,' said Henri Bronstein. Gideon turned from the Gauguin he was examining and saw that the old man was smiling. 'Yes, I know it's a fake.' He waved an arm to include all the pictures that hung on the walls. 'As are they all.' He took both Gideon's and Laszlo's arms and led them through an archway and across the tiled floor of a wide room. Gideon shivered slightly in the cold air; they were in the cellars of Bronstein's villa at the Cap d'Antibes.

'All these as well?' Laszlo asked as they moved slowly through a succession of whitewashed rooms whose walls were covered with pictures.

'Oh, yes. I committed many follies in my youth, but wealth is a

121

great comforter. Eventually I turned my mistakes into a little hobby. A pity you destroyed those pictures; I would have bought them from you.'

Gideon and Laszlo exchanged a glance, which Bronstein chose to ignore, and they climbed a staircase to re-emerge into the warm air of the ground floor, where the rooms were full of tapestries and sculpture. Unlike the house in the Avenue Foch, there was no theme or order to this part of Bronstein's treasure.

'We shall be ready in fifteen minutes,' Bronstein said to a footman dressed in white livery standing at the foot of the stairs.

They walked through a series of huge rooms out on to a wide terrace where a table lit with candles was set for dinner. Bronstein went to the balustrade and looked over at the glittering sea. There were pinpoints of light on the horizon, and the cloudless night sky was light with stars. He turned and leaned with his back to the view, to look up at the walls of the white stone villa which was flanked by giant palms.

'The Greeks were here, you know. Antibes was one of their ports,' he said thoughtfully. 'God knows why Alexander the Great wanted to conquer the East when he could have lived in France.'

Laszlo looked out at the lights on the horizon. 'The sentiments of every Frenchman I have ever known!'

'Frenchman and Jew,' Bronstein replied. 'Some of my forefathers were not so fortunate in their choice of homeland.' He turned to face them. 'And that leads me to the reason why I have invited you here tonight.' He studied each of them in turn. 'Are you aware of what is happening in Germany?'

'Yes,' Laszlo replied.

Bronstein looked at him sharply. 'I am not referring to the bluster and the comic-opera uniforms.'

'I have read Hitler's book,' Laszlo told him. 'He plans to conquer an empire in the East, and in Germany he intends to eliminate socialists, homosexuals, gypsies, mental defectives . . . and Jews.'

Bronstein nodded. 'The process has begun,' he said softly. 'The concentration camps are already full.' He placed his hands together and raised them to touch his lips. 'As you may know, I was married three times but I have no children . . . And no living relatives. But as I approach death, I feel my identity cry out with each passing day.' He smiled briefly. 'Five thousand years spent obeying a stern God leaves a deep impression. There are many foolish Jews in Germany,' he said flatly. 'People will think almost anything about

Jews – that they are dirty, evil, cunning, sly – but never that they can be foolish.' He sighed. 'If only it were so.' He slapped his hands on the balustrade. 'So I have taken it upon myself to be the friend of the foolish. I shall use my wealth and what is left of my time to get those who are trapped out of Germany.'

'How can we be of service?' Gideon asked.

Bronstein folded his arms. 'There is a certain person in a position of great power in Germany. He has many weaknesses, and one of them is his love of paintings. Like all greedy people, he is easily bribed. I intend to exchange people for pictures. It will not be easy, but I think I have a way to achieve it. The Archangel Gallery is vital to my plans.'

'How do you know you can trust us?' Laszlo asked, very seriously.

Bronstein smiled, and here in the soft light his face seemed young again. 'Because I know a great deal about you both, Mr Vasilakis, and the study of human nature was the foundation of my fortune.' He turned. 'For instance, Mr Gideon is not aware of it, but I know you are a devout Catholic and therefore you wish to be good in the eyes of God.' He turned to Gideon. 'And you are a romantic, young man, and all romantics want to be heroes, if only to themselves. It is a dangerous condition; you look for causes, for a thing to love. Romantics win revolutions, and are usually the first to be executed by those who inherit the power.' He gestured towards the table, and they sat down. 'So I am prepared to trust you both,' he continued. 'And to back my judgment, as I have always done.'

'What part do you see the Archangel Gallery playing in your plans?' Gideon asked.

Bronstein remained silent while the footman served soup to Laszlo. He shook his head when the servant paused beside him, and sipped mineral water instead, then suddenly became brisk and business-like. 'You have good German contacts through building Mueller's bizarre collection. There is a young man – you know him as Schneider. The pictures will come from me to you, and you will pass them on to him.'

The footman took away the soup-plates, and Gideon remembered something. 'By the way, the man from whom you bought *The Girl in the White Dress* is here at the Hôtel du Cap.'

Bronstein nodded. 'Stanford Whitney-Ingram? I know, he came to see me.'

'I understand he's wealthy again,' said Gideon.

'Yes,' Bronstein said casually, 'I bought his entire collection of pictures two years ago.'

123

'But I thought it was still in America,' Laszlo said in surprise.

'It suits my purposes to keep it there,' Bronstein replied. 'Whitney-Ingram has powerful friends who will be useful to my plans.'

The footman returned, but Bronstein refused the next course as well. 'By the way,' he said to Gideon, while he and Laszlo ate a delicious concoction of truffles and grouse, 'I'm sorry to tell you that I have sold the Degas you are so fond of to the person in Germany.'

CHAPTER SIX

London, early spring 1938

As it was the second day of Lent, Harriet Strange did not take milk in her morning cup of tea. While her husband Anthony ate a large piece of smoked haddock, she took one slice of toast and spread it thinly with honey. When they had first married, he had begun each day with eggs and bacon until, by chance, Harriet had mentioned that her father, the late Lord De Vierre, liked haddock for breakfast. Because that venerable gentleman stood as a yardstick for every measurement of social behaviour in Strange's life, it had been fish for breakfast ever since.

In the early months of their marriage it had touched Harriet that her husband so slavishly copied the eccentricities of her father, a man who was so removed from normal social intercourse that his odd habits were a constant source of amusement to his social peers. Then Strange's real nature began to reassert itself, and the thoughtful and happy characteristics he had carefully presented during his courtship were discarded.

The metamorphosis from porpoise to shark was completed in her eyes the day he banned her dog. Harriet was forced to banish the old red setter to the basement of their house in South Audley Street. She had pleaded with him, but Strange had threatened to put the animal down, and she realised that he was enjoying her anguish. In truth, the dog did not mind as much as Harriet; he had never cared for the presence of Strange, who had made extravagant overtures to him when he had first come to call. But Harriet felt the loss keenly. Throughout her lonely childhood she had found affection in the company of animals.

In his own way, Strange had been equally lonely in his youth, but that had been of his own choosing. Unable to form any relationship that was not to his advantage, he developed a pattern of ingratiating himself with people until he had absorbed from them those aspects of their personality that he envied and wished to emulate. Then they were abandoned in favour of the next conquest.

Strange had actually been christened Alfred Edward at a time when those names ceased to be the prerogative of kings and passed into the usage of the working classes. The only child of a monumental stonemason who practised his craft in Kensal Rise, and a mother who was a cousin of Nettlebury's father, he had won a scholarship to St Martin's School of Art in the Charing Cross Road. There he quickly realised the limits of his own talent, but also discovered that he could value the ability of others with a certain authority. On receiving his diploma, he had obtained employment with Lestrade Fine Arts, a gallery in Dover Street, and by applying his creeper-like charm had, within two years, gained sufficient promotion to be transferred to Paris. He remained there for five years, until all vestiges of Alfred Edward were eliminated from his accent and manners. On his return to London, he had mysteriously acquired sufficient capital to open his own gallery in Bond Street and begin the search for a suitable wife.

One spring morning in 1931 a short, bald-headed man with a curious long-featured face came into Strange's new premises carrying a grime-encrusted painting in an old and chipped frame. He wore a tweed suit of remarkable vintage and his shirt collar was frayed, so the assistant at the front of the showroom treated him with initial disdain. But Strange, who was near by, could sense something about the figure and came forward to take over the transaction.

'What's this worth?' the man asked with a lack of the usual pleas-antries, thrusting out the picture.

Strange felt a thrill to be treated with such arrogance and was about to react with cold, polite servitude, but instead, chameleon-like, he assumed the same careless manner as the customer and placed his hands in his pockets. 'Put it down,' he ordered, nodding to the wall.

The little man did as he was told, and they both stood back to look at the picture. Although it was thick with dirt and coated with an ancient layer of varnish that had turned the colour of treacle, Strange instantly recognised that it was a portrait by Van Dyck.

'This is a very good painting,' he said. 'How did you get it?'

'It was hanging on the wall in my house,' the little man replied.

'Well, it could be worth a lot of money.'

'Do you mean you're not sure?' the man asked.

Strange knew its value to the penny, but shook his head. 'If you want to leave it with me, I'll get a chap I know to take a look.'

126

'Right,' the little man answered. 'I'll call back later.' He started to walk away.

'You'd better leave your name and address,' Strange called after him. The man answered, but all he caught were words that sounded like: Dever, South Audley Street.

Strange was intrigued. He caught hold of his assistant's arm and instructed him to follow the visitor. 'Make sure you see where he goes,' he said.

The young man returned after a short space of time. 'He went to White's in St James's,' he said.

Strange retreated to his office and telephoned the club. It took all his considerable skill to establish that the little man was John Francis Michael Edmund, Lord De Vierre. He made several more telephone calls and, with the help of *Burke's Peerage*, learned that he was the last surviving member of an ancient family that had remained Roman Catholic despite the Reformation. There had been a son, but he had died in the influenza epidemic that followed the Great War, leaving his only remaining offspring, Lady Harriet, as the last of the De Vierres. Strange took the painting into his office and left instructions that, when De Vierre called again after lunch, he was to be told that business had taken him away for the afternoon.

That evening, a little after six, Strange paid a call on Lord De Vierre at his London residence. When the Earl received him in his faded sitting-room, Strange's darting eyes detected two paintings by Stubbs and three Canalettos. They were all coated with grime, like the Van Dyck. Lady Harriet was also present. She was a plain woman, a few years older than Strange, with the same long features and small eyes as her father, but taller and thinner, like those medieval carvings of Crusaders that decorate tombs in ancient churches.

Strange explained to De Vierre that the picture he had left with him was a Van Dyck, and of considerable value. The Earl seemed barely interested in the information.

'Do you want to sell it for me?' he asked. 'I've never cared for it myself. Too damned gloomy,' he added.

Strange said he would be happy to go ahead with the transaction, and they parted. The next few days he spent immersed in books on theology, refreshing his half-forgotten knowledge of Catholic dogma. He had been baptised in the Church of Rome, at his father's insistence, but he had always resented the visits they had made to the ugly red-brick church of his childhood. The garish plaster statues of the Virgin Mary had seemed the height of vulgarity to him, even at quite a tender age, and the predominantly working-class worshippers had depressed him.

The following Sunday he attended early morning Mass at Farm Street, and found, as he had suspected, Lady Harriet and her father among the congregation. He waited to speak to them on the pavement outside, and half an hour later was walking with Lady Harriet and the red setter in Hyde Park.

In the autumn they were married in the private chapel at Greeve, De Vierre's country house near Battle in Sussex. Due to ill-health, Strange's widowed father was unable to attend the ceremony. The only representatives from his family were Sir Julian Nettlebury and Anne, who had received an effusive letter with the invitation and had accepted with some reluctance.

The following year Lord De Vierre died, and Harriet inherited the remains of his fortune, but it was smaller than Strange had expected; as the family had declined in number, so had their wealth contracted. Greeve had to be sold to pay death duties but there was just enough money to keep the house in South Audley Street going, though not in the style that Strange would have wished. De Vierre and Harriet had been oblivious of their shabby surroundings, but Strange found the peeling paint and cracked leather chairs difficult to live with. He had to remind himself constantly that luxury was considered vulgar by some of the upper classes.

Strange finished his haddock, and Mrs Milne, their housekeeper who had come from Greeve, began to clear the table.

'Does she know what to give us for dinner tonight?' Strange asked irritably. He referred to the elderly woman as if she were an inanimate object, because Mrs Milne's deafness became more pronounced whenever he spoke to her directly.

'Asparagus soup, then roast lamb and cheese to follow,' Harriet said, nodding for Mrs Milne to take her plate.

'I've put the wine out on the side-table in the dining-room,' said Strange. 'Tell her to open the Chambertin at six o'clock. The butler from the agency will be here at seven. He'll know what to do then.'

He drummed on the table. 'Wear your blue dress,' he said finally, 'and the pearls.'

Harriet said, 'Yes, dear,' in a soothing voice.

Strange got up from the table. 'Remember that this man is a prince.'

Harriet, who was descended from a queen of Aquitaine, nodded briefly. 'I shall try to remember, Anthony,' she replied without a trace of irony. Although she had been guileless when they had first met, she had subsequently found reserves of fortitude that were necessary in any dealings with her husband.

'I've told him we live simply here, without any frills, but he may expect a certain deference. Will you curtsy when you're introduced?'

This was too much for Harriet. She also rose from the table. 'I don't think that will be necessary, Anthony,' she replied. 'German princes were very common in the Habsburg Empire, even though my family regarded them almost as equals. However, if you feel the need to bow, remember that you will not be able to present your back to him for the rest of the evening.'

A cloud of uncertainty crossed Strange's face as he studied the expressionless Norman features of his wife. Because he was without a sense of humour, he placed the most literal interpretations on any remarks she made, unaware that her only solace in life was to take gentle revenge for the cruelties he perpetrated through small acts of ridicule. She confessed these regularly, to the enjoyment of her priest. Harriet was without sin in the conventional sense; he found her transgressions a welcome relief from the more worldly exploits of his other parishioners.

When Strange had gone, Harriet let the dog out of the basement, and he circled her feet while she found his lead. Then she crouched down and hugged the creature for a long time. He sat patiently, accepting the affection with evident enjoyment until he began to strain for the door.

Sir Julian Nettlebury took the finest brush from the pot, swirled the tip in a jar of clean turpentine and wiped it dry on the cloth by his palette. Then he squeezed as much Chinese white from a fat little tube of oil paint as it would take to cover the nail of his little finger. He worked the point of the brush into the blob of paint and rolled the bristles till they were loaded with the right amount of colour.

When he was satisfied, he turned to the bottom right-hand section of the great canvas and, with infinite care, applied six tiny dots of light to the eyes of the last three figures he had painted. The work was finished. The highlights he had just applied gave the spark of life to the three savage faces he had completed during the last month. The vast picture had preoccupied him for five years. There had been brief excursions into other duties, but always he returned to this major theme. Slowly, he sat down on a stool and cleaned the

129

brush with the rag while he studied his work. There was a slight overcast to the sky, and the light that filled the studio was diffused enough to eliminate any reflection on the huge surface. He looked at the picture for a long time and then told himself it was as he had always intended it to be: his craftsmanship had triumphed.

There was a knock, and Nettlebury got up and opened the door. His housekeeper who, like everybody else, was forbidden to enter this studio, stood on the threshold. 'Perfect timing, Mrs Cooper,' he said. 'I've just finished.'

'Finished for the day, sir?'

'No. The painting is finished.' He gestured. 'Come in and tell me what you think of it.'

Mrs Cooper entered with some trepidation. She came from a background that saw sinister implications in attic rooms that were kept so private. Slowly she walked forward to stand beside him. They had known each other for many years; she had been in much demand as a model during her youth. Pictures of her hung in the homes of the wealthy and the galleries of the capital cities of the world because of one extraordinary quality she possessed: in her girlhood, she had been perfectly proportioned. Her face might have been pretty and commonplace, but her body had conformed to the artist's measure of Aphrodite.

For her own part, Maude Cooper had never been able to see what all the fuss was about. She had always considered herself too large. She had envied her younger sisters, who had been smaller and appeared less formidable to the young men who courted them. Hard times had caused her to become an artist's model, a profession that had been regarded by her neighbours in Paddington as little better than prostitution. But she had found it to be a respectable way of life, although artists had never ceased to puzzle her.

'They're a funny lot,' she had once told her mother many years before. 'When they're painting you, they treat you like a queen, telling you you're like something out of a poem and such like, but the second you get off the couch, they turn you into a bloody doormat.'

'It sounds a bit like marriage to me, dear,' Maude's mother had replied.

'Well, it's not the kind of marriage I'm going to have,' Maude had said firmly and, true to her intention, Tom Cooper had always treated her with the deepest consideration.

Now she stood next to Nettlebury, looked with him at the finished picture, and tried to think what he would like her to say. 'There's a lot of work gone into that, Sir Julian,' she said finally.

'Five years in the execution, Maude. And two planning it.'

'Do you know who's going to buy it?' she asked.

'There aren't many customers for a piece like this.'

Maude nodded her agreement. 'Well, it is a bit big, I suppose. Does it have a title?'

'It's called *The Darkness of Mankind.*'

'Well, you've caught that, all right,' she said, gazing at the vast panorama. In truth it put her in mind of a nightmare, which was part of Nettlebury's intention. The picture depicted humanity's fall from innocence, beginning with the banishment from Eden and the subsequent bestialities human beings had practised upon one another through successive ages. The execution of the work was superb, but to Maude it was like looking into Hell. Once again, the mysteries of the artist's mind baffled her. If I possessed this talent, she told herself, I would paint pretty things.

'You ought to go out and enjoy yourself, now you've finished it, Sir Julian. Living with this all these years must have got you down sometimes. Not that it isn't good, mind,' she added hastily. 'But there's a cheery side to life as well, remember. Most people need a bit of happiness every now and again, just to keep them going.'

Nettlebury considered her words. 'You're quite right, Mrs Cooper.' He suddenly sounded cheerful, and ushered her to the door. When they reached the ground floor, he walked purposefully to the telephone in the hall. The number he rang was answered instantly. 'Vera,' he said. 'It's me.'

'You caught me on the way out, Julian,' Vera Simpson replied. 'I've just put my hat on to go shopping in Kingston.'

'Well, take it off again,' Nettlebury ordered. 'I'm coming over.'

Vera Simpson sighed. 'Really, Julian, you are impossible! I haven't heard from you in days, and now you want me to drop everything the moment you ring.'

Nettlebury recognised the tone of her voice and realised that the gentlemanly pleading of excuses would bring a further rebuttal. 'Not everything, Vera,' he said quickly. 'Only one garment will be necessary for what I have in mind.'

She giggled, and he knew that her protestations were now a formality. 'The maid is here,' she said, but in warmer tones.

'Then give her your hat and tell her to go shopping in Kingston,' he suggested.

131

She thought for a moment. 'She did say she wanted to go to the cinema again this week.'

'I'll be with you in half an hour,' he said, 'with a bottle of champagne.'

'Don't bother with the champagne. There's still plenty of Colin's left in the cellar.'

Nettlebury bathed, shaved again, as he had risen early, and donned his favourite suit of lavender tweed before setting out for Vera's house, which lay five minutes away.

Vera had been a close friend of his wife and a staunch pillar of support when she died. Five years before, her husband Colin, a successful stockbroker, had left her for the daughter of one of his partners, but Vera had refused to divorce him. Instead she continued to live on in the same house and in some style, until gradually her husband's guilt evaporated and he desperately began to seek grounds based on her own infidelity. Simpson had his suspicions, but had been unable to prove that Vera was unfaithful. On two occasions she had noticed private detectives watching her movements, but a call to the local police station had sent them on their way. She and Nettlebury had drifted into an affair based more on their friendly affection for each other than on any driving passion. Their lovemaking was vigorous, mutually satisfying and devoid of jealousy. After the first year, Nettlebury had tentatively asked her to marry him, but Vera did not want to forfeit the comforts she still extracted from Simpson in exchange for life with a penniless artist.

'I like it in bed with you,' she explained. 'But I don't want to be in the kitchen while you're in the studio, scrimping to survive on your money, when I enjoy spending Colin's so much.'

Nettlebury was perfectly happy with the arrangement because he was still in love with his wife, and another woman might have wished to make changes to the home she had created. He would have found that unendurable.

As was customary, he entered Vera's house through a gate in the high-walled garden. The fruit trees were still bare and a fire of old leaves smouldered by the compost heap, so that a thin column of smoke drifted into the still, cold air. The rough grass of the lawn, uncut since autumn, lay dark green beneath his feet and snowdrops edged the turf. He felt one of those sudden surges of happiness that come at unaccountable times. He remembered Maude Cooper's words as the scent of the burning leaves wafted to him in the peaceful suburban scene.

'People need a bit of happiness,' he repeated to himself. At that moment he knew exactly what work he wanted to do next. It came to him suddenly and with great clarity. He would chronicle the men and women, the houses and gardens of the streets and footpaths that ran close to the Thames. He would paint the England he lived in, so that people in other times would know what he had known.

He entered the house by the french windows that Vera had left unlocked. The rooms were unusually warm because Simpson had installed radiators in the house. Even the hall, a part of his own home which was icy during winter, was pleasantly humid. When he reached the bedroom, he found that Vera had provided the champagne. It was on her dressing-table in a silver bucket misted by the ice inside. Vera still wore her hat; it was small with a very long feather which pointed towards the ceiling.

She smiled at him in the reflection of the looking-glass. 'Do you think I'm getting fat?'

He looked at her naked body, and shook his head. Although she was long past the first flush of youth, Vera's olive-skinned, sinewy body stirred him as it always did. Not for the first time he wondered at the sexual prowess of Simpson's mistress, that she could have tempted him away from his wife's powerful attractions. 'If I drop you on the way to the bed, you can lose two pounds,' he said and reached down with outstretched arms.

Some time later, when the feather on Vera's hat had been broken and Nettlebury was restoring his energies with a glass of champagne, he looked at the painting that hung on the wall opposite. A large landscape in an ornate frame, it depicted Highland cattle drinking at a mountain lake that appeared to be filled with molten brass. The same saffron light afflicted the surrounding mountains and sky, which was also streaked with pink and cobalt blue. He gestured at it with his half-empty glass.

'Vera, who bought that painting?' he asked.

She pushed herself up on one elbow and gazed across the room. 'Colin, of course. He doesn't have any taste at all.'

Nettlebury considered her answer and remembered his earlier resolve. 'Wouldn't you rather have a landscape of a scene you knew actually existed?'

'What do you mean?'

'Well, something around here; a place you could recognise.'

Vera lay back with her head on the pillow. 'Are you asking me if I'd like a picture of one of the local streets?'

133

'Yes, that's right.'

'Don't be silly, darling,' she said sleepily. 'Who ever heard of anyone buying oil paintings of Kew?'

Like Lady Harriet Strange, Henry Grierson was observing Lent and therefore had dispensed with his after-lunch pipe, but he was none the less a happy man. He even sang a snatch from *The Mikado* as he placed the necessary documents in his briefcase. 'I'm going to visit the Archangel Gallery, Miss Prentice,' he told his secretary, and left his dusty little office in Theobald's Road. The walk to the Underground station at Holborn did not take long, but he had to refrain from singing 'A Wandering Minstrel I' at every step.

Grierson rarely left the offices of Prescott and Campbell between the hours of nine and five-thirty; it felt like playing truant to be on the streets of London in the afternoon. He checked his watch again and saw that he was in good time for his two o'clock appointment with Anne Nettlebury.

It was the first time Grierson had visited the Archangel Gallery — Anne had always journeyed to Theobald's Road on the previous occasions they had met — so there was a pleasant feeling of anticipation when he came out of the station at Green Park.

When he reached the gallery, he stopped at the entrance to the showroom to study the large picture that dominated the window, and a little of his good humour evaporated. It was a piece of abstract art, he told himself, and that was all the information he could glean from the painting. Rectangles and swirls of dark colour surmounted each other, with occasional organic forms that might represent a primitive concept of human beings. It had obviously been executed with a great deal of care, but it conveyed nothing to him. No scale was indicated, so it could as easily be meant to be the inside of a watch or a landscape of a mountain range.

By now, all his pleasurable anticipation had vanished. The picture made him uneasy and somewhat hostile towards the artist and the gallery. Grierson considered himself a civilised man; he and his wife enjoyed music, read books and made the occasional visit to the theatre on birthdays and anniversaries. So why should abstract art always seem to mock him, as if he were some provincial numbskull, unable to cope with the offerings of a higher order of intelligence?

Anne saw him standing in front of the window, and came out. 'Good afternoon, Mr Grierson,' she said warmly. 'I see you're admiring the Marc.'

'The mark, Miss Nettlebury?'

Anne gestured at the window. 'Franz Marc. He painted the picture.'

Grierson was a scrupulously honest man even in the smallest matters. 'I'm afraid "admiring" would be an exaggeration. I was trying to work out what the devil it was supposed to be. Is it valuable?'

'It's priced at two thousand guineas in the catalogue.'

'Two thousand pounds?' Grierson repeated incredulously. 'Bless my soul! How much of that will go to the artist?'

'Nothing, I'm afraid. Franz Marc was killed during the war.'

'But he died a wealthy man, presumably?'

Anne shook her head. 'I'm afraid not. He didn't make very much money from his pictures when he was alive.'

As she led him into the gallery, they passed Gideon studying a row of pictures propped against the wall. A stocky young man of about his age stood next to him, obviously the artist. He wore a dark green tweed jacket, baggy grey corduroy trousers, a dark blue shirt and a red woollen tie. A shock of black hair contrasted with his sallow complexion, which was accentuated by the blue shadow of his chin.

He was pointing at the picture with a long bony finger. 'It's called *Blue Light*. I painted it last week in Dorset,' he said.

Grierson glanced at the young man's paintings and felt a moment of deepening depression. He could not recognise them as understandable representations of landscapes and human forms; all he saw were large shapes of pastel colour.

Gideon looked up as they passed and smiled, but Anne did not interrupt him with an introduction. Instead she stopped at Doris's desk at the far end of the showroom. 'You know each other only on the telephone,' said Anne. 'Mr Grierson, this is Doris Sherman.' They shook hands, and Anne led him on into the deeper recesses of the gallery. The contrast was immediate.

Pictures leaned against the walls of the dim, narrow corridor leading to the large store-room, which was lit by the harsh light of naked bulbs. Pictures in all varieties of shapes and sizes were stacked against the walls, but only their canvas backs showed. Some were old and stained by time, with words and hieroglyphics on ancient faded labels; others were new, the canvas white and fresh. Each bore a distinctive blue label pasted to the stretcher. Anne tapped one.

'Every time a picture is sent for exhibition, or goes to a gallery for a sale or changes hands in any way, it's registered. We all have

135

different ways of doing it. This is the Archangel Gallery marker,' she explained. 'You'd be amazed how complicated it is to keep track of where everything is. I'll show you the system I've devised in a moment.' She led him down a flight of stairs into the basement, which consisted of two large rooms, both stacked with pictures and lit in the same harsh fashion, and then on to a tiny corner office partitioned from the rest of the room. A lamp lit the cluttered desk and a silver bowl of white roses.

Grierson examined the flowers with pleasure. 'Roses in February!' he said with a smile. 'They must have come from a distant garden.'

'Gideon bought them for me. They're beautiful, aren't they?'

'They certainly are,' he agreed, and squeezed down in the chair in front of the desk.

For the next two hours they combed through the documents Grierson either produced from his briefcase or demanded from Anne. They had just finished when Doris brought them each a cup of tea. Grierson sat back and massaged the indentations his spectacles had made on the bridge of his nose. His former good humour had been restored by Anne's efficiency and soothing presence. He looked with pleasure at the heap of paperwork they had accomplished.

'Excellent, Miss Nettlebury. You seem to have everything in complete control, as usual. Mr Laszlo's propensity to barter makes things a little daunting at times, but it does seem to alleviate some of the difficulties you could have with currency regulations between here and the continent.'

Anne drank some tea before she answered. 'It's easy enough, now I've persuaded him to keep notes of what he does.'

Grierson sat back in his chair and sipped his tea. There had been a question nagging at the back of his mind and now seemed an excellent time to ask it. 'Tell me, what does Mr Gideon do, apart from bring you roses?'

'I don't follow.'

Grierson sipped some more tea. 'I can see how valuable you are to the gallery.' He gestured at the piles of papers on the desk. 'And I know from what you tell me of Mr Laszlo's escapades, but I'm unsure of Mr Gideon's duties.'

'Three main functions, I suppose,' Anne answered after a moment's consideration. 'He finds new artists and is the main salesman for the gallery, but his most important role is valuing paintings.'

'Valuing paintings? How does he do that?'

'I think I'll let him explain,' Anne replied. 'Here he is now.' Gideon entered the tiny room and shook hands. 'Mr Grierson would like to know how you price a picture,' she said.

Gideon perched on the edge of the desk and folded his arms. 'Instinct, I suppose,' he said eventually. 'Paintings don't have any intrinsic value. It's the demand individuals put on them that gives them their price.'

'That's a bit deep for me,' Grierson replied. 'Are you saying they really have no value at all?'

'In a sense, yes,' Gideon replied. The telephone buzzed, and Anne was called upstairs by Doris.

'Please go on,' said Grierson.

Gideon shrugged. 'If you cared nothing for art, what value would an oil painting have for you? There was a story recently that a man had repaired the roof of his hen-house with a picture by Sir Joshua Reynolds. He'd bought it from a junk-shop. To that man it was just a piece of waterproof canvas, and admirably suited for the use he'd put it to.'

Grierson still looked puzzled. 'I can understand masterpieces that have been around for centuries being valuable, the *Mona Lisa* and so forth. But what about that picture in the window? Who is to say that's worth two thousand guineas?'

Gideon smiled, 'People like me, and other artists, and the people who want to buy them.'

Grierson sat back, admiring the bowl of white roses. He seemed to draw comfort from the certainty of their beauty. 'So you all possess some special ability to know if a picture that ordinary people can't understand is really worth thousands of pounds,' he said finally. 'How is it you all come to the same conclusion?'

'We don't. There are huge differences of opinion about the worth of individual painters.'

Grierson was still confused. 'Is it the amount of effort an artist puts into a picture that gives it a value?'

'I know an artist who's been painting the same picture for five years. He's put an incredible amount of work into it, all his skill, feeling and knowledge. But it's worthless, because no one wants to buy it.'

'Would I be able to appreciate it?'

Gideon considered his question and thought for a moment of the disturbing subject-matter of *The Darkness of Mankind*. 'You would be able to understand it and recognise his skill, but I don't know if you would like it very much.'

Grierson began to put his papers back into his briefcase, but then stopped. 'Do you think I will ever come to like abstract paintings, Mr Gideon?'

'It's possible, Mr Grierson. It took me some time to appreciate them. And Mr Porter, our general handyman here at the gallery, has developed a wonderful eye.'

'How did that come about?' Grierson asked.

Gideon grinned. 'The truth is, he's a keen gardener, and he said it was like looking at flower-beds from a distance. If they made a nice balance, he knew the artist had something.'

'Flower-beds,' Grierson repeated, following Gideon from the basement. When they reached the showroom, he looked at the pictures with renewed interest. Suddenly one picture of bright geometric colours seemed to jump at him, and he turned to Gideon and gestured towards it. 'Using your Mr Porter's flower-bed principle, I'd say that's pretty good.'

Gideon followed his gaze. 'Well done! That happens to be a very valuable painting by Max Ernst.'

Just as Ted Porter was going to close for the night, Karl Schneider and Elizabeth came into the gallery. Gideon emerged from the store-room where he had spent the previous hour studying the work of the young artist he had interviewed earlier in the day, and found them talking to Anne. She was explaining that Laszlo was in Paris, arranging for three pictures from the Bronstein Collection to be shipped to London, and was expected home that evening.

Elizabeth held Schneider's arm, and her dachshund had circled both their legs with its leash. It seemed ironic to Gideon that he had bought the creature that bound them together. From his vantage-point across the length of the gallery, he could not help comparing Anne and Elizabeth. They both turned at his approach. He saw Elizabeth rarely these days; she still had the power to attract him, even more perhaps since he no longer had to endure the strain of her tantrums. But it was Anne who disturbed him the most.

It had been more than six months since his conversation with Irene, but he still had not been able to tell her how he felt. It was as though he were being forced to do penance for his past attitude to women; the better he got to know her, the more difficult it became. During his formative years there had been no one to teach him how to treat others and, being alone so much, he had developed a sense of self-reliance that had not widened to include much consideration

138

for other people.

Luckily his inherent character was kindly, and his considerable charm reinforced by a natural empathy for people who were less fortunate. Equals presented him with problems he was only now beginning to appreciate. Laszlo was the first real friend he had ever known and, by example, he had unconsciously taught him that real friendship implied duties and attitudes he had not previously realised.

When he saw that Laszlo was prepared to make real sacrifices for him, all the latent affection he had been unable to share with his father was concentrated on his partner, who now constituted the family he had never actually possessed. The two men were so easy in each other's company that hours could pass without the need for conversation. Yet they were still capable of laughing and plotting like schoolboys.

Laszlo's own happy childhood and his wide and deep education provided Gideon with a bedrock on which to test his own growing ideas, but he could not help him in his relationship with Anne. Because of Laszlo's unhappy marriage, there was an area of discussion neither of them could enter.

Gideon was left perforce to work out this problem alone, although in truth it was quite simple; he could not reconcile the conflicting emotions he felt about Anne. Because she was so giving in her attitude, everyone adored her, and at the same time relied upon her strength as well as the sweetness of her nature. Consequently, like everybody else, Gideon was filled with an overwhelming tenderness towards her. It was more profound than any previous feelings he had ever experienced, and he found it deeply disturbing when his other desires for her bubbled to the surface. If he succumbed to feelings of carnal lust, they would instantly be followed by shame and remorse that he could wish to subject someone so kind and warm to mere animal passion.

What he could not grasp was that Anne had her own needs for earthly pleasure, and Gideon's reticence caused equal confusion in her own thoughts. Recently, out of loneliness, she had begun to see something of a young man who had been introduced to her by Elizabeth, hoping that the relationship would prompt Gideon into some kind of decision, but so far the ploy had been unsuccessful. She still found Gideon's behaviour baffling; sometimes he would go for days not speaking, except in the most formal manner, then he would suddenly make an affectionate gesture, like the present of the white roses.

'Anne tells me that Laszlo will be back tomorrow,' Schneider said. 'That means the pictures can go in the diplomatic bag at the weekend.'

Gideon nodded. 'You know, I always used to imagine that the diplomatic bag was a small leather case sealed with wax, chained to the wrist of a courier.'

Schneider confided, 'My dear fellow, I have known grand pianos transported by that method. There have also been rumours of bodies, alive and dead, moved about the world in such a fashion.'

Elizabeth, having untangled the dog's lead, looked up at Gideon. 'Are you coming to Papa's cocktail party? We're just on our way.'

Gideon had intended to avoid the occasion, but it would now seem bad manners. 'Just for a short time.'

'And you're coming too, aren't you, darling?' she said to Anne.

'Yes, I am,' she replied firmly. 'I've even bought a new outfit.'

'Then we'll see you soon.' Elizabeth tugged at the dog's lead, and Schneider followed.

Ted Porter bolted the door behind them and went down to the basement, leaving Gideon and Anne alone.

'I didn't know you were going to Mueller's party,' he said awkwardly.

'That's because you didn't ask me, Gideon,' she said briskly. 'But if you're coming, you can drive.'

He sat at Doris's desk while Anne went downstairs to change. When she reappeared, the difference was remarkable. He was used to seeing her in a smock during the day, but now she wore an elegant suit in dark material that emphasised her fine figure, and her hair was piled beneath a smartly veiled hat. He was suddenly filled with the familiar sensation of desire for her. He was about to speak when Ted Porter emerged from the basement. Instead, they said goodnight.

'Oh, damn,' she said. 'The roof of the car is down. We'd better drive slowly.'

The reception rooms were already crowded when they arrived at Eaton Square. Elizabeth took Anne to join a group of noisy young people and Mueller drew Gideon into a circle of diplomats from the German Embassy. Colonel Middleton and his wife were there; the conversation was concerned with culture, and rather heavy going.

When there was a lull in the proceedings, Mrs Middleton leaned towards him and said in a low voice, 'I was a little unwell the last time we met, Mr Gideon. Please forgive me.'

'Not at all,' he replied, smiling at the grey-haired woman. She was drinking orange juice on this occasion.

Then she whispered, 'Mind you, I still believe every word I said.'

Gideon was suddenly addressed by one of the diplomats, who had a barrel chest beneath his evening clothes and was larded with decorations. His head was shaved almost bald, in the Prussian fashion. 'Do you approve of our policy to ban subjective art, Mr Gideon?' he asked in German.

'What is the man talking about?' Mrs Middleton asked in English.

Gideon turned to her. 'It is now official policy in Germany for the artist to produce work that will uplift the spirit of the nation.'

'Oh, like the Soviet Union,' she said in perfectly good German. 'Such a good idea to cheer people up and inspire them. I had no idea Herr Hitler and Joseph Stalin had so many ideas in common.'

The smile froze slightly on the face of the diplomat and Colonel Middleton frowned a warning at his wife.

Gideon was bored by the conversation but decided he would answer the question. 'I think there is only good art or bad art. Some of the greatest masterpieces in history were painted on commission, others were done out of compulsion. I think it is wrong to try and channel artists.'

'So you agree with Oscar Wilde,' the diplomat said, 'that there is no such thing as immoral art?'

'Not completely. A picture may be a superb piece of work, but if its use is to illustrate something bad, I think it's immoral.'

Loud laughter came from Anne's and Elizabeth's group. Gideon turned in their direction and saw that Anne was deep in conversation with the flashy-looking man she had been seeing recently. He was leaning forward, whispering something in her ear. Anne laughed at his remark, and touched his hand for a moment. Gideon wanted to go over and interrupt the intimacy, but the diplomat continued with the conversation.

'Ah, but who is to say what is a lie?'

Mrs Middleton turned to him. 'My dear man,' she said grandly, 'if you show a lot of brawny chaps enjoying themselves working down a coal-mine, that is patently a lie, don't you think?'

Everyone laughed at this remark except the barrel-chested German, and Gideon took the opportunity to leave the circle and join Anne. He discovered she had already drunk three cocktails, and was slightly tipsy. She seemed devastatingly attractive. The flashy young man was just returning with another concoction from the

141

waiter, and Gideon could see the smile of anticipation on his face. He turned quickly and nudged his arms. The man's smile turned to an expression of painful surprise, and he spilt the drinks down the lapels of his pale grey suit.

'I'm terribly sorry,' Gideon said, his voice full of remorse. 'I'm afraid I slipped.' He dabbed at one of the large dark stains with his own handkerchief. The young man backed away with a muttered excuse to Anne and hurried off towards the bathroom.

'Why did you do that?' she asked Gideon.

He could hear how much the drinks were affecting her. 'I didn't like the way he looked at you.' Gideon gave her a dangerous-looking smile.

'That's Willie Friedman. He doesn't care for girls. Not that he should bother you,' she said loudly.

Gideon glanced around. The party had already begun to thin out, and he saw that Elizabeth had noticed the exchange. He took Anne by the arm. 'Come on. I think we can go now.'

Anne did not resist, and a few minutes later she was sitting next to him in the passenger seat of the MG, which they had parked in Eaton Square. It was much colder, and neither of them wore top-coats. He was about to set off for Kew when the thought occurred to him that she might not want to arrive home until she were a little more sober. While he sat thinking what to do, the weather played a hand. The overcast sky burst into a torrential downpour and in moments they were soaked to the skin by chilling rain.

'Oh, my new suit!' Anne said in anguish.

Gideon could think of nothing else to do, so he started the car and set off in the direction of Shepherd Market. It was even colder when they got to his flat, but his cleaning lady had been that day and laid a fire in the little living-room. All he had to do was put a match to the newspaper and soon the firewood beneath the coal began to crackle. It was a comforting sound. He had given Anne a bath-towel and directed her to the bedroom. Now he stood against the mantelpiece, watching the fire begin to catch.

The room was sparsely furnished. The only pictures were old foxed engravings of cathedral towns the previous tenant had left to cover the faded wallpaper. A table and reading-lamp stood by the high-backed leather chair. There were, besides, a bookcase, a military writing-desk and, facing the fire, a faded chintz-covered sofa that was so big he often wondered how the landlord had got it

142

up the narrow staircase. Pictures were everywhere, stacked against the walls and leaning on the furniture, but in the time he had lived there, Gideon hadn't bothered to hang them. He had never seen the place as anything more than temporary accommodation; his life, so far, had not conditioned him to be a home-maker.

He had not turned on the lights, and the flames threw long shadows on the walls. When he heard the bedroom door open, he did not turn round until he heard Anne softly call his name.

She stood before him, wrapped in a raincoat she had found hanging behind the bedroom door, damp tendrils of autumn-coloured hair framing her face. Slowly she came towards him. As he turned from the fire, he felt the cold wetness of his shirt.

'Why don't you want me, Gideon?' she asked.

He opened his arms in a gesture of supplication and said, yearningly, 'Oh, Anne, I do, I do!'

She kissed his forehead, eyes and cheeks, and then their mouths came together. At first their embrace was tender and filled with gentleness, but as they began to feel the warmth of their bodies another urgency overtook them. They parted for a moment while he pulled off his clothes, and when he looked up again she had removed the raincoat. The light of the fire turned her pale skin to shades of amber.

Holding each other again, they sank on to the sofa and he kissed her swollen nipples, which were the colour of roses in the fireglow. Her figure was gloriously curved and full, but beneath her soft warm skin he could feel the firm strength of her body. Wherever they touched it was as though they melted together, causing him to swell against her, so that she could feel his hard erection against the gentle curve of her firm belly.

'Oh, Gideon, I've waited so long,' she said, her voice breaking. Then she slid her hand between them and guided him into her, circling him with her legs so that at the moment of penetration she drew towards him. She gave one sharp cry and her body contracted; then she began to thrust in time with his own rhythmic movements.

His shyness was driven away by Anne's desire. Each new confluence of their bodies brought and increased their pleasures. Both of them had lived with the imagination of this moment for so long that there was no feeling of unfamiliarity, just a perfect sensation of fulfilment. The completion was so absolute that when eventually Gideon flowed into her, her tears of happiness spilt over. Gideon kissed her salty cheeks.

There were no reservations between them now: each explored the other's body in the simple pursuit of pleasure. Anne, untutored, except for conversations with Elizabeth, was equally uninhibited, and being naturally graceful in her movements brought Gideon constantly to a state of readiness.

When he lay back, thinking the last of his energies were spent, Anne sat astride him and, with gentle insistence, coaxed his half-erection into her again. She held his shoulders and, her head thrown back, began to croon with pleasure. It was as if he had entered a softly tugging mouth and to his own surprise he grew hard once again. This time Anne rocked gently back and forth until the crooning ended with a soft moaning sigh of completion and she fell gently forward on his chest. All he could hear was the sudden gentle hiss of the dying embers of the fire and Anne's soft breathing. He could smell the musky perfume of their lovemaking and feel the mingling perspiration from both their touching bodies.

Then the room became cold again and the night air chilled them. With the tenderness of their first embrace, Gideon kissed her, and said, 'Come on, let's go to bed.'

'I knew you would ask eventually,' Anne said sleepily. She felt very happy, but more importantly she felt that his relationship with Elizabeth had finally been exorcised.

When they moved to the bedroom, Anne telephoned the house at Kew. Shivering in the half-light, she waited for someone to answer the telephone.

Eventually Irene picked it up. 'Daddy's gone out for the evening to celebrate. He's finished his big picture. I'm playing Monopoly with Mr and Mrs Cooper. When will you be home?'

'I'm staying with a friend tonight,' Anne replied. 'I'll see you tomorrow.'

'Where are you staying?' Irene asked.

'Mayfair.'

'I've got that in Monopoly. It's tremendous if people land there!'

Anne looked at Gideon, lying on the bed. He was resting on one elbow to watch her. 'Yes, darling, I know,' she replied.

It was dark and cold as Nettlebury prepared to leave Vera Simpson's house, and she insisted that he wear an overcoat her husband had left behind. Colin Simpson had been a somewhat larger man, so that the heavy cloth enveloped Nettlebury with all-embracing comfort. Vera turned up the collar for him, standing by the french windows, and

144

kissed him goodbye.

'I feel like a bloody tortoise,' Nettlebury grumbled, but he was grateful for its warmth in the night air. As he drew close to his home, he suddenly realised he did not want the day to end. The time with Vera had been as fulfilling as he could have wanted, but now he craved other stimulations. He telephoned for a taxi and informed Mrs Cooper that he was going into London to have dinner with friends. Twenty minutes later, still wrapped in the overcoat, he was heading for the Fitzroy Tavern at the corner of Charlotte Street.

Laszlo arrived home from Paris to find the mews flat in darkness. There was a note from Sylvia saying she would be in later, but no explanation for her movements. The package containing the three pictures he had brought with him had not been heavy, but its presence had been as demanding on his attention as a young child. It was with a sense of relief that he finally put it aside and considered his own comfort.

He looked around the crowded little room and contemplated the silence. The only sound was the ticking of the carriage clock and the soft creak of the boards beneath his feet. He did not find much cheer at home when Sylvia was present; but at least there was the sensation of some other living being, no matter how aloof and distant. Alone in the crowded room, he felt as if he were dead, entombed with little treasures to sustain him in an after-life.

Pausing only to scrawl 'Gone out as well' on the bottom of Sylvia's note, he replaced his hat and set off for Soho.

Elizabeth had not enjoyed the dinner at South Audley Street. Her euphoria during the earlier part of the evening had begun to evaporate when she had seen Gideon's concern for Anne at the cocktail party. By the time she and Schneider arrived at the Stranges' she was trying to conceal her feelings beneath an extravagant display of high spirits. Thinking that bright conversation might infect the others, she had kept up a stream of probing chatter, but even Schneider's usual charm seemed to have faltered.

Strange seemed equally defeated by the evening. He was in turn obsequious towards Schneider and patronising to Harriet and Elizabeth. He had even suggested that the ladies might care to withdraw so that he and Schneider could drink brandy and smoke cigars, but Elizabeth had declined with a smile and lit a cigarette. There was further desultory conversation between the men concerning a painting by Brueghel, but by this time Elizabeth was paying no attention. She had grown to hate everything about this eerie crumbling house, where even the walls seemed impregnated with dust. Even the butler who served them had smelt of mothballs. She was filled with an overwhelming desire to flee the oppressive atmosphere. As if to add a final macabre touch to the evening, there suddenly came the sound of a dog baying from the depths of the house.

'You have a dog, Strange?' Schneider asked with sudden interest.

'Oh, yes, a splendid creature. Rex.' Strange shot a glance at his impassive wife. 'But we keep him downstairs when we have guests. Not everyone cares for dogs, you know.'

'Elizabeth and I adore dogs,' Schneider said enthusiastically. 'We should be delighted if you allowed him up.'

Arrangements were made with the butler to free the setter and moments later he was padding among them. Schneider scratched the dog's ear, and looked up. 'Is it not odd how you can always tell a gentleman by his attitude to dogs?' he said to Strange.

Harriet, pretending not to hear the remark, asked Elizabeth if she would care for coffee. Elizabeth declined, pleading a sudden headache. She had noticed it was still just before ten o'clock, but she knew she could not remain in the grim house any longer.

'Rex will be pleased by an early night,' Strange said as he showed them to the door. 'We usually take him for his walk about now.'

Outside, Elizabeth gripped Schneider's arm. 'For God's sake, let's go somewhere there's a bit of life!' She and Schneider began to look for a taxi.

The Fitzroy Tavern was crowded with its usual mixture of art students, painters, poets, would-be bohemians and general riff-raff gathered in noisy confusion. As he had anticipated, Nettlebury had encountered a friend, Hammond Shelley, a painter he had known since their student days at the Slade. After a couple of drinks they had resumed an argument they had conducted off and on for nearly thirty years. It continued as they left the public house and walked down Rathbone Place. They had decided on a change of venue and were now heading for the Wheatsheaf.

Nettlebury turned just before he pushed open the door. 'I don't care what you say, Hammond,' he said belligerently. 'Cézanne ruined painting. All that bloody tosh about "the Supremacy of the Artist" and "the Personal Viewpoint". Colour on the canvas has no

146

significance unless it tells you something. All it says is, "Look at me, I'm red paint." That's about as banal a statement as it's possible to make.'

'Bollocks,' Shelley replied, following him into the crowded pub. 'You're as thick as your overcoat. Painting has more to offer people than something that looks as slick as a photograph.'

In the warmth of the long narrow room, the thick tobacco smoke stung their eyes. Laszlo was at the bar, accompanied by the young man Gideon had seen at the gallery earlier in the day.

'This is Paul Trenton,' Laszlo said, turning away again to buy them their pints of Guinness.

'What do you think painting is about?' Shelley asked Trenton, when it was established that he also was an artist.

'Beauty,' he replied with the certainty of the very drunk. 'Beauty like that,' and he pointed to Elizabeth who had just entered.

Schneider followed her. He smiled when he saw Laszlo. 'My dear fellow, I was talking about you a little while ago,' he said. Laszlo still had the attention of the barmaid, so he bought drinks for them both. Introductions were made, and Schneider drew Laszlo to one side. 'Tell me,' he said conspiratorially, 'do you still have that Brueghel at the gallery?'

'I'm afraid it's not for sale,' Laszlo said with a smile, attempting to edge back to the others, but Schneider held his arm.

'Surely everything is for sale if the price is right?'

Laszlo shrugged. 'It belongs to Gideon, not the gallery. He has told me he will never part with it.'

Schneider leaned even closer; his mouth almost touched Laszlo's ear. 'Suppose I were to tell you that the prospective purchaser was Reichsminister Goering.'

'It would still be up to Gideon. I can tell him you're interested, but I doubt very much if he will part with it. You know how some people get personally attached to certain pictures.'

'I know,' said Schneider, and Laszlo could see bands of worry-lines form across his forehead. 'But you see it is vital that I obtain this picture. The price is no object.'

'But why is this painting so important? There are other Brueghels, surely?'

Schneider took hold of Laszlo's arm again, glancing round to check that no one else was in earshot. It seemed unlikely to Laszlo that any of the Wheatsheaf's bleary customers would want to hear their conversation.

'The Reichminister is also Chief Huntsman of the Third Reich,' Schneider said in a hushed voice. 'He has built a great house called Carinhall which he wishes to contain the correct pictures. He particularly desires Brueghel hunting scenes.'

Laszlo raised an eyebrow. 'And you have assured him you can obtain this one?'

'That is so.' Schneider leaned forward and closed his eyes, so that Laszlo had to put out a hand to stop him toppling over. It wasn't until that moment that he realised that Schneider was quite drunk. Elizabeth was being crushed against the bar by Paul Trenton. Nettlebury and Hammond Shelley had renewed their interminable argument. Laszlo guided Schneider back to the group, whereupon Schneider suddenly took exception to Trenton's attention to Elizabeth.

'Would you mind removing yourself from this lady?' Schneider said, swaying aggressively in front of Trenton.

'Piss off!' Trenton retorted.

'I think you are no gentleman,' said Schneider. 'Would you care to settle this outside?'

The noise of their raised voices had carried to the other customers, who were watching the altercation with interest.

'Just a minute,' Trenton said to Elizabeth, who appeared to be enjoying the sudden conflict. 'I'll be straight back.'

The two drunks blundered out, and some of the people in the crowded bar went out to enjoy the spectacle. Trenton and Schneider returned almost immediately. Both of them appeared dishevelled, but there was no sign of damage to either of their faces.

'Perhaps their bodies are a mass of bruises,' Laszlo said drily. But Schneider and Trenton now seemed to be the deepest of friends. They embraced and swore eternal friendship before demanding that each buy the drinks to pledge their new-found brotherhood.

Elizabeth, relegated to the sidelines during this display of manly affection, was not pleased by the turn of events. 'Will you take me home?' she whispered to Laszlo.

'I would be delighted,' he whispered back.

They slipped from the public house and Laszlo quickly found a taxi. Elizabeth had also had quite a lot to drink, although she appeared to hold it better than Schneider. Once they were settled in the cab, she rested her head on Laszlo's shoulder and instantly went to sleep. He sat quite still in the darkness, thinking of all the things he would like to tell her, until the taxi stopped in Eaton Square. She woke like a cat and stepped lightly out of the cab. He paid it off.

'Thank you, Laszlo,' she said sleepily. 'It was sweet of you to bring me home.' She leaned forward and kissed him on the cheek.

He watched her go into the house, and stood for some time in the darkness. Then he set off to walk to Shepherd Market, suddenly aware of the coldness of the night.

CHAPTER SEVEN

England, late autumn 1938

On the Thursday of the last week of October, Paul Trenton had his first private view at the Archangel Gallery. It was not a major event in the art world; white wine rather than champagne was served and although the press were invited, most papers had sent their second critics. It was not considered important enough to be covered by the gossip columns. The most expensive picture, a large abstract entitled *Landscape with Figures*, was priced at one hundred and fifty guineas. The majority of the others were under fifty pounds. The exhibition was well received, and by the end of the party a satisfactory amount of red dot stickers had blossomed on the frames of the paintings, signifying that they had been sold.

Invitations had gone out to the gallery's regular customers, who tended to treat such occasions as an opportunity to see old friends as much as to examine the work of a new artist, and to those painters whom Laszlo and Gideon thought would bring the necessary ambience to the showrooms without daunting the other guests. 'Too many artists over-egg the pudding,' Laszlo had told Anne when they were preparing the invitation list. He struck out five names she had included. 'I have known disasters perpetrated by bringing a large group of them together under one roof and giving them unlimited free drink. They fight, they advise customers not to buy the pictures, they attempt to settle old scores.' He shuddered, and looked carefully at the list once again. 'This seems to thin them out sufficiently. Remember, their purpose is to act as yeast, not gunpowder.'

Henry Grierson was among the first to arrive. Before he left his office in Theobald's Road he had changed from the dark three-piece suit he wore during business hours into a sports jacket and dark wool shirt. Now he slowly paced round Trenton's paintings, holding a glass of wine and peering intently at them through his gold-rimmed spectacles. When Ted Porter pointed Paul Trenton out to him, he joined the artist, who was talking amiably to Hammond Shelley and, at the same time, glancing about him in an effort to judge the effect his work was having upon the other visitors.

'That's Julian Nettlebury's daughter over there, talking to the old couple.' Shelley pointed out Anne, who was talking to Caroline and Renfrew Middleton.

'Isn't Nettlebury here?' Trenton asked.

Shelley shook his head. 'You won't find him at this sort of exhibition, Paul. Nothing personal. He just won't look at your sort of stuff.'

Trenton shrugged. 'It takes all sorts.'

Grierson edged closer. 'I think your work is excellent,' he said quickly.

The two men looked at him in a not unfriendly fashion.

'Are you a painter?' Shelley asked.

Grierson glanced down modestly at his glass of red wine, and said, 'I do a little, mostly landscapes.'

'Which of mine do you prefer?' said Trenton.

Grierson gestured towards one particular group of pictures. 'That series: the ones in pale grey and blue. The vertical lines give me the sensation of looking through the rigging of ships in harbour.'

Shelley moved away. There was no way he could compete for Trenton's interest when someone was praising his work. He made his way through the noisy crowd and found Anne checking that there was sufficient wine for the rest of the evening. He had known her all her life and greeted her with the familiarity of an uncle. 'How's Julian? Still refusing to face up to the twentieth century?'

Anne smiled. 'You know him, Hammond. It's a pity he wouldn't come tonight.'

'Well, at least he doesn't change,' Shelley continued. 'Everything else does.'

'You have,' Anne said, 'and you're the same age.'

Shelley laughed quickly. 'I'm not a painter, Anne. Perhaps that makes me more adaptable.' He took the fresh glass she offered and sipped some of the wine.

'What do you mean? I've seen your paintings.'

Shelley raised his eyebrows and took another drink. 'Painting pictures doesn't make you an artist, any more than cooking the lunch makes you a chef.' He shook his head. 'I'm an art teacher, that's all. I'm not complaining.'

There was no self-pity in Hammond's voice, but Anne thought she could detect some traces of bitterness. 'What about Dad? Is he an artist?'

'Oh yes. He always was. Even when we were at the Slade, it was obvious he couldn't do anything else.'

'Is that the test?'

Shelley nodded. 'I think so. Talent is only part of it. Even when he was teaching, Julian was a painter.' He held his arms out wide. 'Whereas I am a teacher who paints occasionally.'

Gideon, standing close to them, had heard their conversation. 'Are there any other qualities that make an artist, Hammond?' he asked lightly.

Shelley thought for a moment. 'Bloody-mindedness perhaps? I think that helps; and the sort of determination that would let you send your mother out to scrub floors as long as you could go on doing what you wanted to do.'

'That sounds awfully selfish,' said Anne.

'No,' Shelley replied. 'But I think it's close to being neurotic. Real artists aren't like normal people.' He gestured at Trenton, who was still deep in conversation with Henry Grierson. 'Who's that talking to Paul?'

Anne followed his direction. 'Mr Grierson, our accountant.'

Shelley laughed again. 'An accountant? Christ! Paul thinks he's an artist. If you're not careful, he'll run off like Gauguin. He's already got the taste for it.'

'I think I'd better break them up,' said Anne. 'There's a short-tempered little man from one of the papers who wants to speak to Paul.'

In the event it was this introduction that caused the only trouble of the evening. Trenton began an argument about Salvador Dali with the journalist, which was about to come to blows when Ted Porter separated them. Luckily it was just after nine o'clock when the dispute took place, and most of the other guests had already left for dinner engagements.

Laszlo and Gideon could not linger to see the eventual outcome; they were booked on the sleeper service to Paris, and the train left Victoria at ten o'clock.

Anne kissed Gideon, and Ted Porter assured them that they could manage the aftermath. Reluctantly they got into the taxi and set off for the boat-train. When they had passed through the formalities of

152

embarkation, they could relax. They both laughed at the memory of Porter holding the two flailing figures apart by the collars of their coats.

'We should only deal in the work of dead artists,' Laszlo said when they were settled in the dining-car and the dark fields of Kent were rolling past.

Gideon leaned back against the head-rest of his seat and took an appreciative swallow of his large whisky and soda. 'How did he do?' he asked, referring to Paul Trenton.

Laszlo shrugged. His own drink still stood before him untouched, slopping from side to side in the glass to the rhythm of the train. 'We sold about a third tonight. Not bad.'

'Schneider bought one,' said Gideon. 'But I think he was just buttering us up. He still keeps on at me about the Brueghel.'

Laszlo did not answer, but picked up his glass and swallowed half the whisky in one draught.

'Didn't I see Sylvia there at one point?' Gideon asked.

Laszlo swallowed the other half of his drink and called to the waiter for another before he replied. 'I think she came because it is our wedding anniversary,' he said without emotion. 'She has a very peculiar sense of humour.'

Gideon contemplated the remark in silence. He had never been able to discern any emotion in Sylvia, let alone humour, however perverse. Usually any conversation concerning Sylvia would have ended at this point, but Gideon had drunk more wine at the exhibition than he had realised. 'Why did you get married?'

Laszlo smiled. 'For the usual reason. I was in love.' Gideon waited. After a time Laszlo reached out and patted his arm. 'I shall tell you the story. You deserve to know.' He looked out into the dark countryside. 'Sylvia comes from a small village in Switzerland called Zermatt. It lies beneath the Matterhorn and, although it is on the Italian border, they speak German there. Well, a curious kind of German. It sounded to me like ducks quacking. I first went there with some Irish friends to do some climbing; Sylvia was working at the hotel in which we stayed.' He paused, and looked out at the lights of some Kentish village. 'She was the most beautiful girl I had ever seen. You must agree, she is attractive.'

Gideon nodded. 'Very much so.'

'Well, in those days . . . ' Laszlo shook his head. 'She had never worn make-up; her skin, hair, everything was perfect. She did not speak English very well but she used to laugh a lot.' Gideon looked

153

up at this. 'Oh yes, she used to laugh.' Laszlo took another drink. Gideon could see that the conversation was not easy for him, but he continued, 'Those little villages are extraordinary; people were isolated in them for generation after generation. At last they bought their freedom from the aristocrats who owned them. Now they're called the bourgeoisie, and they own everything: all the shops, hotels, most of the land. In Zermatt they even have their own part of the graveyard. Sylvia's family were not descended from the bourgeoisie. In fact, they were very poor. They lived in a tiny wooden house built above the room where they kept the cows.' Laszlo laid both his hands flat on the tablecloth. 'Anyway, I became infatuated with her. When the holiday was over I went back the following month, and then again in the spring. In the summer we were married, and I brought her to London.'

He was interrupted by the steward offering him the menu. They both ordered soup, followed by fish, and Laszlo spent a long time deliberating over the wine list. When he finally came to a decision, he turned back to Gideon and said almost cheerfully, 'So now I suppose you want to know where things went wrong?' Gideon said nothing, and Laszlo looked at him with expressionless eyes. 'It was simple. Sylvia discovered that she deeply disliked the act of making love.'

The waiter returning with their soup brought the conversation to a temporary halt.

'What are your feelings towards her now?' Gideon asked when the course had been served.

Laszlo paused with a spoonful of soup close to his mouth. 'I think the expression is: Our love has withered on the vine.' He shrugged. 'We still attempt something every so often. I think Sylvia has some deep peasant superstition that, if we don't, a curse will befall her. Speaking for myself, it merely provides momentary relief rather than any feeling of fulfilment.'

Gideon felt a sense of helplessness. He tried to think of words of comfort, but nothing came to mind that would sound adequate. It seemed a terrible irony to him that his companion, whom he knew was attractive to so many women, should live without the solace of love. 'Why don't you get a divorce?' he said.

Laszlo smiled and, reached out to touch his shoulder. 'My dear fellow, you have no idea how I envy you your religion sometimes.'

'I don't really have a religion. I was christened in the Church of England.'

'Exactly. I'm afraid mine is a little more demanding.'

Gideon stared at him. 'If you believe in God, surely you can't think that He wants you to be unhappy? Life's too short for that.'

Laszlo put down his spoon. 'I think you are confusing God with the United States of America. The pursuit of happiness is not one of the primary aims of the Roman Catholic Church.'

'Well, it bloody well ought to be,' Gideon said a little testily. 'Look at your marriage. There are no children involved; just you and Sylvia. If you're not happy together, why not pack it in?'

Laszlo laughed again, but there was no humour in the sound. 'Oh, Sylvia is quite happy. In fact, she thoroughly enjoys her life. And, besides that, she is a Catholic. Divorce is out of the question.'

Gideon could think of nothing else to say. When the waiter brought their turbot, he changed the subject and they discussed their forthcoming visit to Bronstein until it was time to retire to their sleeping-berths. Later they lay in the darkness, listening to the distant muffled thuds as the sleeping-cars were loaded on to the boat at Dover. It was hot in the compartment and Gideon found it impossible to sleep. He had been wanting to ask his companion a question for some time.

'Laszlo,' he said quietly, 'have you ever known your religion to be a comfort?'

There was a long silence, and Gideon thought he must be asleep. Then Laszlo turned in the narrow berth opposite. 'When my mother was dying.'

'It helped you to get through?' said Gideon.

'No, but it helped my mother. Her faith was so absolute that she had no fear of death, only sorrow for me and my father.'

'It seems a very stern religion, to demand so much of you and offer so little in return.'

Laszlo considered the statement. 'I wouldn't say that. It holds out the hope of heaven, which is as much as anyone could ask for. Think of Henri Bronstein; his God demands obedience without the comfort of an after-life.'

'Don't Jews believe there is anything when you die?' Gideon asked.

'Not according to Bronstein. That's why the thought of a premature death is so horrendous.'

They did not speak again. Gideon lay in the close darkness, thinking how unjust life was that he could be so content while Laszlo had only his joyless relationship with Sylvia. Happiness seemed such a random matter, an arbitrary distribution of good and ill fortune. He suddenly feared for his peace of mind. But then he thought of Anne, and eventually sleep came to him.

155

Laszlo also remembered a face, Elizabeth's, laughing earlier in the evening, when she was talking to Karl Schneider. As always when he was unhappy, he turned his mind to his childhood. There had been a walnut tree in the garden of their house in Dublin. In the autumn he and his mother would gather the fallen nuts. 'It's a lucky tree,' she would tell him every year. 'Make a wish beneath it, and your dreams will come true.'

He listened for a moment to a doleful distant clanking coming from somewhere on the ship and wondered if he would ever find another walnut tree.

England, winter 1938

During the half-term holiday at the beginning of November it had rained for three days. Mrs Cooper had gone to Harrow to look after a sister who was ill. Anne had taken a few days off from the gallery and was in the kitchen at Kew, preparing for a dinner party Nettlebury was giving. She had enjoyed the last few days' housework, which in the past she had found irksome, but Irene was hanging about the table modelling a piece of the pastry into the shape of a cat in a lack-lustre fashion, emitting occasional sighs. 'I'm so bored,' she said. 'Why can't we do something?'

'I am doing something,' Anne replied. 'There's plenty of housework if you're in the mood.'

Irene flattened the pastry cat with a sudden thump of her fist and pushed it aside. 'I hate being fifteen,' she said with deep feeling.

Anne felt a momentary surge of sympathy; she too could remember the same period of her life, when childhood pursuits were yet to be replaced with more womanly pleasures. She looked at her watch. 'Why don't you take Daddy his lunch?' she suggested.

'Where is he?' Irene looked out of the kitchen window at the rain-sodden garden.

'On the tow-path at Strand-on-the-Green.' Anne took a knife and trimmed the excess pastry from the lip of the pie.

Irene wound a piece of the discarded dough round the first finger of her left hand. 'When are you and Gideon going to get married?' she asked.

'When he asks me, I suppose,' Anne replied in a matter-of-fact voice, wiping the flour from her hands.

'Is he a good lover?'

Anne pushed past her sister and opened the door of the oven. 'Make your choice,' she said firmly. 'Take Daddy his lunch or you go in here with the pie.'

'Oh, all right,' Irene said haughtily, 'but I'll have to use your bicycle. Mine's got a puncture again.' Then she suddenly cheered up. 'I'll wear my oilskins,' she said, and went off to search in her room for the clothes Nettlebury had bought her for sea-fishing on holiday in St Ives during the summer.

Fifteen minutes later she put a vacuum flask and a packet of sandwiches in the basket of Anne's bicycle and set off in the lashing rain towards the north embankment of the Thames. It was easy to find her father. There were few people about in this weather and she could see him from quite a distance, seated beneath a huge black umbrella secured to his easel by a contraption Tom Cooper had made. Nettlebury was wearing an old trench coat and a battered black trilby, but he had still managed to get fairly wet.

Irene rang the bell on the bicycle as she approached, and he looked up. 'Hello! What are you doing here?'

'I've brought you some lunch,' Irene replied when she had dismounted and propped the cycle against the rail at the edge of the water.

Nettlebury made two more swift strokes with his brush and placed it in a jar of turpentine. He took the packet from Irene and unwrapped the sandwiches.

'Bacon,' she said. 'She made enough for me too.'

Nettlebury took one and handed the packet back. He took a mouthful and gestured towards the picture on the easel with the bacon sandwich. 'What do you think?'

Irene studied the painting with a critical eye while she ate her own sandwich. 'I think it's terrific! You are clever, Daddy,' she said after a while. The picture showed the grey waters of the Thames flowing past Oliver's Island and the railway bridge that crossed the river close by. Nettlebury had perfectly caught the misty diffusion caused by the rain. It always seemed wonderful to Irene that her father could call forth those tones of grey-blue and green, and the subtle feel of earth and water, from tubes of raw paint.

They finished the sandwiches, and Nettlebury resumed his work. 'Do you want to do some sketching?' he asked. 'There's a pad in my satchel. You can sit on the paint-box and get some cover under the umbrella.'

Irene did as he suggested and they worked side by side in silence.

Then Irene asked, 'Daddy, do you think Anne and Gideon will get married?'

'It's quite possible.'

Irene considered his answer. 'Do you think they'll be happy?'

'As happy as most people are,' he replied. 'It helps that they're in love.'

'Aren't all people in love when they get married?' Irene asked, continuing to work, like her father.

'No, but some people fall in love afterwards.'

Irene sat back and studied her drawing. 'I'm not going to get married unless I'm deeply in love.'

'What will you do if you don't meet someone who comes up to your high ideals?' Nettlebury asked with a smile.

'Stay and look after you, I suppose.' She stood up and handed him the sketch-pad. 'I've finished. What do you think?'

He looked at the drawing and indicated two points of weakness. 'Take this back a bit here and strengthen the shadow on the embankment,' he said briskly. 'Apart from that, very good. Your draughtsmanship is coming along very well.'

'Good enough to get into art school?'

'When you've finished your formal education, there'll be time enough for that,' Nettlebury said in anticipation of her next question.

Irene sighed. 'Miss Newton says I'm not good for anything else, anyway.'

He chuckled. 'Is that what she tells you? They used to say that to me at Westminster.'

Irene glanced at him. 'But you always told us you were so good at school.'

He shook his head. 'Did I? Well, I may have exaggerated. Your mother was the brilliant one. She could have been anything she wanted.' As he spoke, he was carefully cleaning a brush with his paint-rag.

Irene rested her hand on his shoulder. 'Are you ever lonely, Dad?' Her voice was so close to her mother's that for a moment he found it hard to answer. 'Not in the slightest.' He leaned forward to touch the surface of the canvas with a series of tiny swift strokes with the clean brush.

'But you wouldn't mind if I stayed with you at home?' she said.

Nettlebury kept his eyes on the painting. 'Only if you learn to cook as well as your sister and Mrs Cooper!'

*

158

That evening Nettlebury lit the first fire of the winter in the living-room, in anticipation of the dinner party Anne had spent the day preparing. Gideon and Laszlo were driving together from London; Sylvia was on a trip to Brighton, buying stock for the shop.

Irene was being allowed to attend, and Anne had said she could wear one of her dresses for the occasion. 'Not that one,' she said firmly when Irene came into the bathroom.

Irene was dressed in a backless cocktail dress that revealed a good deal of her full breasts. 'I was only joking!' She took a more sedate blue frock from behind her back. 'Is it all right if I wear this?'

Anne sighed. 'I suppose so, but it is nearly new. If you spill anything on it, I'll kill you.'

Irene looked at her sister's voluptuous body and then down at her own, which was so similar. 'It's a good job we don't live in the twenties, when it was fashionable to be flat-chested! We would have had to starve ourselves.' She leaned against the washbasin while her sister languished in the tub. 'We bought some chestnuts on the way back today,' she continued. 'Shall we roast them after dinner and get everyone to play charades?'

'Only if they all want to,' Anne answered. 'Charades is the worst game in the world if you're not in the mood.'

The doorbell rang, and Irene moved to answer it. 'Gideon will want to play,' she said as she left the bathroom. 'He says it brings out the ham in him.'

When she opened the door, cold air billowed into the hall, together with the damp earthy smell of winter. Laszlo and Gideon had arrived, Laszlo carrying a crate of bottles.

'Beware of Hungarians bearing gifts!' said Gideon. Then he noticed the revealing dress, and whistled in admiration.

Irene responded flirtatiously. 'This isn't for your benefit,' she said, leading them towards the living-room. 'I'm just trying it on because I'm going somewhere much more sophisticated tomorrow night.'

When she got to the door, she decided that it might not be a good idea for her father to see the dress, so she returned to the bathroom, where Anne was towelling herself in some agitation. 'They're early,' Irene said.

'Oh, God!' Anne wailed. 'I'm nowhere near ready.'

'I don't even know why you're bothering to dress up,' said Irene. 'Good heavens, they see you every day.'

'Bull's Blood,' Nettlebury said appreciatively, examining the

159

bottles. 'It will go with the meal splendidly.'

The two visitors sat back on a large sofa by the fireplace. Nettlebury had given them both drinks and was decanting three of the bottles. After a slight hesitation, he added a fourth. Gideon was familiar with his surroundings, but after a few minutes Laszlo got up to examine the pictures on the walls and the contents of the bookcases.

'The books were my wife's,' said Nettlebury. 'She was a keen collector. We bought most of them in Paris and Rome.'

Laszlo prowled around the room with satisfaction. It was full of odd nooks and crannies, where pockets of light from a variety of lamps illuminated paintings, drawings, pieces of pottery and sculpture. The walls were painted a red earth colour and the long curtains were dark cream, edged with a Grecian design in gold. There were Turkish and Persian rugs on the woodblock floor and each item of furniture contributed to the room's solid comfort. In an alcove by the windows stood a grand piano covered with silver-framed photographs.

'So these are the suburbs,' said Laszlo. 'I had no idea it would be quite so delightful.'

The doorbell rang again and Vera Simpson was shown in by Irene, who had now changed into the blue dress. They were followed by Anne, who had recovered from her flustered state in the bathroom.

Nettlebury had been correct; the Bull's Blood was an excellent match for the steak and kidney pie.

'Absolutely delicious, darling,' Vera sighed, 'but I shall put on pounds in weight.'

When the meal was finished they returned to the living-room, but Irene would not let them rest with their glasses of port. Yielding to her pleas, they divided into teams for charades. Nettlebury and Vera began. With the lack of inhibition that the middle-aged often bring to party games, they mimed a somewhat violent, version of 'The Relief of Mafeking'. Irene and Laszlo followed and then it was Anne and Gideon's turn. They went out to prepare their piece.

Gideon could see how much Anne was enjoying herself. Despite her earlier protestations, she had entered into the spirit of the thing and was now positively girlish when they entered the kitchen. She hardly ever drank, and the few glasses of Bull's Blood with dinner had caused her to flush slightly. She brushed a wisp of hair from her cheek while she sat on the table and swung her legs. Gideon thought he had never seen her look lovelier.

In most relationships, constant proximity often brings a cooling of the passions; for Gideon, the reverse was true. Just a few days earlier

160

he had watched her speaking Italian to a prospective customer in the gallery and, hearing her use a language he could not understand, had come to that conclusion. On that occasion she had seemed aloof and deeply mature. Tonight, it was as though she were a girl of seventeen, and he felt light-headed.

'What shall we do?' she asked in an urgent, mischievous voice.

Gideon was so overcome by his feelings that he had difficulty in speaking. Anne watched him, mistaking his hesitancy for concentration.

'Will you marry me?' he finally managed to say, cursing their prosaic surroundings. He had intended to propose in a much grander and more romantic setting.

Anne looked down, deep in thought, and repeated the question, 'Will you marry me?' in a voice that told him she was considering the phrase as part of the game they were playing. Then, slowly, she raised her head.

Irene called out, 'Come on, you've been ages.'

When they returned to the living-room, now scented with roasting chestnuts, Anne held up her left hand, and Irene said, 'Four words.' Then the diamond in the engagement ring was caught by the flames of the fire.

London, New Year's Eve 1938

Irene sat at the dressing-table in her bedroom, wearing her party frock and slightly more than the amount of make-up her father deemed fitting for a girl of nearly sixteen. She was waiting for the parents of a school friend to collect her in their car so that she and Pamela Masters could attend a dance given in honour of another classmate, whose sixteenth birthday coincided with the festivities. While she waited, Irene glanced around the room, from which she had recently cleared many of the reminders of her childhood. The hamster cage had gone to a nephew of Mrs Cooper's at Harrow, and her toys were consigned to the cupboard under the stairs. She turned back to her scrapbook, where there were menus and labels from the *Mauretania*, programmes from trips to the theatre, postcards, snapshots, her swimming certificates and three photographs taken with Charles Whitney-Ingram during the summer holiday they had spent in the south of France. They both wore hats, and the hard shadows covered most of their features, but Irene

161

could still remember how he had looked. There were also the six letters he had subsequently sent her, concealed beneath the handkerchiefs in one of the drawers. The correspondence had begun in the tones of painful intimacy they had shared at Eden Roc, but had gradually declined into mundane details of life when he had returned to the familiar surroundings of his school. Nowadays, when circumstances demanded, she could manage a few tears over their enforced parting, but at the moment she did not wish to disturb her carefully applied eye shadow.

The doorbell rang, and her father called out that Mr Masters had arrived. Irene leaned towards the mirror, quickly applied a little more lipstick and hurried downstairs. Her father was talking in the hall to Mr Masters who was assuring him that he would pick the girls up later, as Irene was to stay with them at his house in Chiswick that night.

'Happy New Year, darling,' Nettlebury called after her as she hurried down the garden path towards the waiting car. Then he turned back into the hall to make a telephone call. Vera's maid answered, and assured him that Mrs Simpson had already left and should arrive at his house in moments.

'Are you ready, Anne?' he bellowed as he replaced the receiver, and was instantly answered by a calm voice behind him.

'Vera has arrived. I saw the Bentley through the living-room window.'

Nettlebury closed the front door, and they walked to the waiting car.

'I'm glad you're going to drive this monstrosity,' Vera said, changing to the passenger's seat while Anne took her place. 'It makes me feel like Sabu the Elephant Boy.'

'I'm not really used to something this big,' said Anne. 'It's a bit of a change from the MG. You'll have to give me a few minutes to acclimatise.'

'Take all the time you need,' Nettlebury said from the rear. 'I'm perfectly comfortable.'

Anne asked Vera about the unaccustomed instruments and controls and then, after a deep breath, tentatively set off in the direction of London.

'Do you remember the time we all went to Bobby Lambton's for New Year?' Vera said to Nettlebury.

'Was that the occasion Jimmy Pitman and Oscar Newheart fell into the river?'

'Yes, and the bolster burst and there were duck feathers all over the lawn,' Vera added.

'That was the year they kept playing, "My Blue Heaven",' Nettlebury said, and he began to sing, 'When whippoorwills call and evening is nigh, I hurry to my blue heaven . . .'

Vera joined in, but Anne kept her mind on driving the Bentley until they reached the restaurant where they were to meet Gideon.

Irene and her friend Pamela had arrived at the Georgian Hotel in Richmond where the dance was to take place. Pamela's parents deposited them in the ballroom and took their place with the other adults in a nearby bar, where they were to spend the evening as chaperons. The two girls had joined their other friends in an extravagant ritual of greetings caused by the cluster of youths in dinner jackets who stood at one end of the brightly-lit room.

In truth, there was little need for the adults to act as chaperons, since the boys had been recruited from a London public school, and at the ages of fifteen and sixteen were not nearly as sophisticated as the girls. They nudged each other and whispered fantastic claims of what the night held in store. The band took their places on the little stage and began to tune their instruments.

There was a moment of tension among the girls when the first waltz began, but the boys had been well schooled in the manners expected of them and no wallflowers were left to make hurried exits to the cloakroom. Irene had accepted a request to dance from a burly youth with a plaster on his nose and deep shadows under his eyes. He introduced himself and while he guided her around the floor explained that he had recently received his injuries playing rugby. Unfortunately rugby was his only topic of conversation during the two dances he had with her, and she was not sorry to see him depart. After half an hour the parents of Edith Barclay, the girl for whom the party was being held, decided to risk the effects of some weakened punch on the young people in their charge and the band increased the tempo of their repertoire.

Irene did not lack partners, but in time became bored by the paucity of the conversation she had to endure. She glanced at a clock, and wondered how her father and his party were enjoying their evening.

In fact Nettlebury and his group were not enjoying themselves very much. The restaurant had been pleasant enough, if a trifle noisy for

163

so early in the evening, but now they were wandering hesitantly through an alley behind Goodge Street.

Gideon was trying to recognise some landmark to guide them to the studio of Paul Trenton, who had invited them to a party. 'I'm pretty sure it's here somewhere,' he said, scanning the dark walls that rose each side of the cobbled yard. 'It all looks so different in daylight.'

'Your friends do live in picturesque places, darling,' said Vera. 'Why not try calling out? Perhaps someone will hear and come and rescue us.'

'It's up a flight of stairs, I know,' said Gideon.

'Maybe if we're very quiet we might hear something,' said Anne. At first there was nothing but the sound of water dripping from some guttering but then a sound of singing came closer; it was the Seven Dwarves' song from *Snow White*.

'Hey ho, hey ho, it's off to work we go . . . ' The words rang out with increasing volume, and Paul Trenton turned the corner, carrying a paraffin lamp. He seemed to have dozens of people with him, some lighting matches, others with guttering candles. Nettlebury could make out Hammond Shelley and Laszlo carrying a keg of beer between them. Everybody else had a variety of bottles.

'The bastards have cut off my electricity!' Trenton shouted above the Dwarfs' chorus. 'I've just been round to the Wheatsheaf to arrange for supplies of drink and light.'

With the aid of the hurricane lamp they found the stairway to Trenton's studio, but it was freezing cold when he ushered everyone into the gloomy interior.

'Oh, God! *La vie bohème!*' Nettlebury said to Vera as the assembled crowd began to smash beer-crates to feed the empty stove.

At the hotel in Richmond, Irene had begun to wish the evening were over. While the others seemed to be enjoying themselves with increasing abandon, she felt herself becoming more and more detached.

The parents who had stayed to chaperon had gradually become rowdier in the little bar and had eventually spilled onto the floor, demanding that the band play the Gay Gordons. They now started to perform this with drunken élan, much to the anguish of the younger generation who watched their cavorting blunders with embarrassed smiles. When he danced past her, Mr Masters reached out and swept Irene on to the floor, where she was forced to take

164

part for the rest of the performance under the ironic stares of the watching musicians.

The trumpeter, who was much younger than the rest of the band, took the instrument from his mouth and winked at her in a friendly fashion when she was allowed to rejoin her friends. Then the leader announced a break.

Still hot from her exertions, Irene found an outside balcony that overlooked the Thames. She leaned on the railing, enjoying the cold air, and then discovered she was not alone: the trumpeter had joined her. He lit a cigarette. Although he was powerfully built and smoked as if he were accustomed to it, Irene sensed that he was not much older than herself.

'Did you enjoy your dance?' he asked confidently.

'Not particularly,' she replied distantly. She was unsure of the social standing of a member of the band.

The youth laughed. 'It's always the same on these occasions. The old men have a few drinks and start chasing the girls, the wives get angry, and suddenly it's time for everyone to go home.'

'Really?' Irene said. They had started to play records inside, and the sound came out through the french windows. She thought she ought to return, but the youth's self-assurance had begun to both attract and irritate her. The record changed and Irene recognised the music: 'Just the Way You Look Tonight'.

The youth threw the remains of his cigarette into the darkness. 'This is one of my favourites. Would you like to dance?'

Irene wanted to refuse, but found herself unable to say anything, so he held her, and they began to sway together on the tiny balcony. When the record ended with a roll on the drums, he released her.

'Time to go back to work,' the trumpeter said, and she followed him back into the hall.

Edith Barclay found her after a while. 'Is it true that you were outside with Richard Cleary?' she whispered excitedly.

'Who's Richard Cleary?' Irene asked.

'The one in the band. Come on, you know, all the girls are mad about him,' said Edith.

'I only spoke to him for a minute. Where does he come from?'

'He's at William's school, but he's on a scholarship. Did he try anything?'

'We only danced to one record,' Irene said, but she could still remember the way he had held her. It had not felt like that with any of the other boys she had danced with.

Anne gripped Gideon's hand tightly as the twin engines of the Heinkel changed pitch again and the Lufthansa flight from Croydon to Berlin touched down in darkness at Templehof Airport. She could see that rain had washed the vast expanses of concrete, leaving gleaming puddles that reflected the dazzling lights from the buildings at the edge of the airfield. When they stood in the doorway, distant aircraft on other runways shimmered like mirages.

Waiting at the foot of the steps was the most beautiful car Anne had ever seen. It was open-topped, with a long bonnet and huge headlamps that protruded from the sweeping mudguards. The whole bodywork appeared to be made of steel and silver, except for the dark red leather upholstery. A Luftwaffe driver stood to attention by the driver's door. Next to him stood a relaxed and smiling Karl Schneider, dressed in a black leather motoring coat. While Schneider greeted them, the driver loaded their luggage, which had appeared almost instantly, into the boot of the car.

'One of the Reichsminister's toys,' Schneider said, in reply to Anne's admiring comments about the massive Mercedes. 'Paid for by cigarettes.'

'Cigarettes?' Gideon repeated.

Schneider nodded. 'Herr Reetsma, the biggest manufacturer in Germany, bought it for him. He also contributes to General Goering's Art Fund.'

'Why does he have an Art Fund?' Anne was sitting back in the soft upholstery, glad of the heavy motoring coat the driver had provided for her.

Schneider smiled as he slid into the seat beside the driver. 'It is well known that all the General's possessions are to be left to the nation. His palace in Berlin, where we shall go now, and Carinhall, his hunting lodge, where we shall have dinner, will eventually become part of the inheritance of the Reich.'

'Why should a cigarette manufacturer be singled out for this honour?' Gideon asked.

'Oh, he's not alone,' Schneider replied. 'Other great industrial concerns like Osram Electrics, Rheinmetall Armaments, Junkers Airplanes, C & A and Brenninkmeyer all make their contributions to the future by subscribing to the Goering Art Fund.'

The driver had finished stowing the luggage, and Gideon looked at

Schneider with surprise. 'What about customs, and so forth?'

Schneider laughed. 'Friends of General Goering are not bothered by such trivialities,' he answered, looking up at the dark sky. 'Do you think it will rain again, Max?' he asked the driver, and without waiting for a reply said 'Leipziger Platz.' The great car glided away and the wind blew into their unprotected faces.

Despite the cold, Anne enjoyed the drive through the glittering city. The tree-lined streets were filled with elegant shops and enticing restaurants and cafés. The people looked smart and prosperous; it was as a capital ought to be, she thought.

They arrived at Goering's palace to hear the roaring of a lion. The driver switched off the engine, and the throaty growl of the Mercedes gave way to the other, more primeval, sound.

'One of your host's pets,' Schneider explained. 'He likes to keep visitors on their toes with little surprises.' He instructed the servants to take a particular packing-case from Gideon's luggage to another part of the palace and the rest to their allotted rooms. 'Shall we say one hour before we meet again? The servants will bring you to me. The General sends his regrets that he can't be here to greet you.' Schneider shrugged apologetically. 'Affairs of state.'

Anne and Gideon were led through rambling marbled corridors of the massive building to connecting suites. A maid waited in attendance for Anne; it would be possible for the dress she intended to wear for the evening to be pressed. She changed into a bathrobe and explored the rooms, which were impressively decorated with antiques and Flemish tapestries. The bathroom was a heated marble cavern, and she luxuriated in a gigantic tub of scented hot water until the maid came and wrapped her in large fluffy white towels.

Gideon's valet was equally attentive. He had to restrain him from buttoning his clothes when he changed. Attentive staff then served tea and cakes from an exquisite Dresden service that made Gideon think suddenly of Sylvia.

Eventually they were escorted to a reception-room, where Schneider was waiting. 'Excellent,' he said jovially. 'We still have an hour before we leave for Carinhall. Come and see how they have hung the pictures we've purchased from the Archangel Gallery.' He led them through endless rooms of the palace, pointing out the various pictures acquired from sources other than Bronstein and the gallery.

Gideon recognised the work of many painters. Their host did not seem to have a predilection for period, style or subject matter;

167

except, perhaps, for a slight bias towards the female nude. In one room he stopped for longer than usual before a picture he recognised as a Van Eyck.

'You look puzzled,' said Schneider.

'I always thought this was in the Kaiser-Friedrich Museum,' Gideon answered. He gestured to other pictures on the same wall. 'And these.'

Schneider grinned. 'Excellent, my dear fellow, excellent! What a splendid eye you have.' He slapped Gideon on the shoulder. 'Do you know, those fools at the museum objected to handing over the paintings. Then he told them what else he would take if they didn't get them over here right away.'

Gideon thought of the man who was constantly seen on the newsreel in gaudy uniforms. He envisaged him as a fat, naughty schoolboy whose every whim was indulged, who could buy or take anything he wanted. A boy who would be prepared to play games with other children until they were in danger of winning; then he would change the rules, or repossess the bat and ball.

Schneider suddenly broke into his thoughts. 'I understand you have completed the Mueller Collection.'

Gideon returned from his reverie. 'Yes, it's been finished for some time,' he replied non-committally.

'Von Ribbentrop is a fool,' said Schneider. 'He might just as well have instructed Mueller to buy nothing but blue pictures. Not that I am against friendship with England. It would be a tragedy if we were ever to go to war with each other again. Our true enemy is to the east. Think what a fine thing it would be: England and Germany in a crusade against the Bolsheviks!'

Gideon ignored Schneider's comments. Ahead, framed by a doorway and flooded by lights shining from above, was *The Girl in the White Dress*. Smiling at him, as always, from her summer meadow.

That evening, Gideon sat at the mighty dining table in Carinhall, the palatial hunting lodge on Goering's country estate. He was beginning to feel weary of the gargantuan size of everything, and suddenly remembered how pleased he had been by the scale of Curzon Street, the day he had returned from New York.

Earlier, accompanied by other guests of the Reichsminister, they had trudged around the estate, examining the various wild animals bred for Goering's pleasure, bison, wildebeeste and bears. Their host had worn preposterous clothes that might have been designed for a pantomime: a leather jerkin, puffy-sleeved white shirt, the sort of feathered hat Gideon associated with Robin Hood, and thigh-length leather boots. He also carried a spear, which was one of the few items Gideon had seen that wasn't encrusted with precious stones.

The house itself was oppressive. Goering had explained that the design had been based on a Swedish hunting lodge, but the huge rooms and masses of carved timber reminded him of an overloaded plate, serving more to suppress the appetite than impress it.

Gideon sat throughout dinner between an elderly man, whose only topic of conversation was synthetic petroleum, and a balding prince from somewhere in the Balkans who was obsessed with big-game hunting. He could not see Anne, who was obscured by banks of flowers, but had spotted Elizabeth, who smiled distantly at him from her seat near Goering at the head of the table. After what seemed several hours, the meal was finished and the host rose to his feet. Waiters came forward to serve champagne.

'It falls upon me to make a brief but pleasurable announcement,' Goering said in a booming voice. 'I am sure all of you know my young friend Prince Reisenauer, generally called, in these revolutionary times, Karl Schneider. Someone you may not know so well, but I am sure you will come to love when you do, is Elizabeth Mueller, a delightful young girl who comes to us from America, but whose blood is as German as the waters of the Rhine. I am delighted to say that they have decided to marry, and have chosen this occasion to make the announcement. So will you all stand and drink a toast to the fortunate pair! May their future be as rich and fulfilled as that of the rest of the German people, who are blessed to live in the time of our great leader, Adolf Hitler! The toast is, the Führer, the Reich and the happy couple!'

They all stood to raise their glasses. For a moment, Elizabeth glanced at Gideon before she turned to her host.

Later, when Gideon had rejoined Anne, they stood and watched Elizabeth being surrounded by congratulating people.

'Do you think they'll be happy?' Anne asked.

'I suppose so. At least Elizabeth got what she wanted.'

Anne took a firmer grip on his arm. 'So did I.'

Gideon had been granted the use of the silver car for the duration of their visit to Berlin, so Anne, under Elizabeth's instructions, had commandeered the driver and they had gone shopping in Unter

169

den Linden. Schneider had persuaded Gideon to accompany him to the Grossdeutscher Kunst Anstellung, a huge exhibition of German art that had the official approval of Hitler, the supreme arbiter of culture in the Third Reich.

Dutifully Gideon had tramped through the halls, bored by the repetition of German glory. They were now in the sculpture hall beneath stone and bronze figures of naked Aryans. All the pieces depicted super-beings in heroic poses of defiance or demonstrating the nobility of simple toil.

'Well, what did you think of it all?' Schneider asked.

He searched for a diplomatic reply. 'Actually, some of it was very interesting.'

Schneider began to laugh. 'English is such a wonderful language! To be able to state something, and yet nothing, is truly a gift from the gods.'

'Well, there are plenty of gifts from the gods around here,' Gideon said drily. He looked up at the Nordic warrior who loomed above them.

Schneider leaned against the plinth of the statue and took a cigarette from a silver case. He carefully inserted it into a holder, lit it and held it out towards Gideon.

'Manufactured by Herr Reetsma; so a little of what I smoke will go to the freedom of the Jews.'

Gideon glanced around; the only people near by were a group of schoolchildren clutching each other in an orgy of suppressed laughter because they had seen the genitals on the statue of a naked athlete. A red-faced teacher hurried them out of the hall. The children emitted a series of explosive giggles as she scolded them.

'Well, they're in no doubt of what they feel about the Führer's choice,' Schneider said as they filed away. Their place was taken by a group of solemn Japanese, who all wore spectacles. The light gleamed from their lenses when they gazed up at the towering statues. They appeared to see no humour in the work.

Gideon was intrigued by Schneider's comments, and a little alarmed. The last few days had caused him to view the Germans in a new light. Previously he had thought of them in the accepted English way: industrious, trustworthy, stoic and arrogant. All these qualities had been discernible in his governess, and therefore he had taken them to be a true representation of the people. But now he had come to detect another thread in the national character, one that came to him as clearly as the martial music and the strutting

170

uniformed figures he had noticed everywhere; something close to hysteria. He realised that any dissent brought the real threat of violence. He looked around the sculpture hall again. No one else was present but the Japanese; the nearest other figure was a respectable-looking man in a dark suit and wire-framed spectacles, who was hovering in the next exhibition room.

'I thought you were a devoted member of the Party,' Gideon said. 'Surely you're not questioning official policy?'

Schneider laughed again. 'My dear fellow, I am first and foremost a member of the decadent aristocracy, and we have managed to survive since the time of Charlemagne by making sure we were always on the winning side. Of course I don't question Party policy. I just don't believe in it.'

'What do you believe in?'

'Insurance,' Schneider answered, 'preferably in the form of tangible assets.'

The Japanese moved on, and it was no longer necessary for Gideon to lower his voice. 'Like General Goering?'

Schneider shook his head. 'Not at all like the General. He loots and hoards like a pirate, but it is only an aspect of his sense of destiny. He actually thinks fate decreed him to be the Renaissance prince of the Third Reich.'

'So the General thinks he was selected by God for his particular role?'

'They all do. That's probably the only thing the gang around Herr Hitler have in common – the pathetic concept that they have each been chosen by some supernatural power to fulfil a divine mission. That, and their devotion to the Führer.'

'And Hitler is aware of this?' Gideon asked.

'Oh yes. He plays them off against one another like a pasha with a harem full of squabbling favourites.'

Gideon glanced at his watch. 'Shouldn't we be getting back to the hotel? Anne and Elizabeth are expecting us to take them to lunch.'

'Just a moment more,' Schneider said as the teacher returned with a worried expression on her face. She blundered into Schneider, who held out his hands to fend her off. With a flustered excuse she picked up the briefcase she had left on the plinth of a statue and retreated from the hall again. The man in the dark business suit and spectacles came and stood close to them. Schneider pointed up at the figure that had caused such mirth among the children, and said loudly, 'In a thousand years men will look at this and know the mind of the

171

Führer.' Then he strolled from the hall.

When they were clear of the building, Schneider gestured to a waiting taxi. Gideon watched the teacher organise her charges into a neat crocodile before they set off along the streets.

'Well, that should look good on my file at Gestapo headquarters,' he said as they settled in the back.

'You're being followed?' Gideon asked, turning to look out of the rear window.

'Oh yes, but it doesn't matter. It's only routine. Himmler tries to get something on Goering, and Goering's spies in the Gestapo tell us . . . It's all a game that goes round and round.' Schneider glanced casually over his shoulder and saw that the man in spectacles had also managed to get a cab. 'Good, he's still following me. I would have been a little worried if he had gone after the teacher.'

'Why?' Gideon asked.

Schneider held up a small square of folded paper. 'Because she gave me the list of Jews Bronstein wishes to exchange for his next batch of bargains.'

Gideon thought back and recalled the woman. Middle-aged, plainly dressed, her fair hair plaited neatly about her head, she had looked the epitome of German nationalism. 'She's one of Bronstein's people?' he said incredulously. 'But she looked so . . . '

'My dear fellow, what did you expect? A man in a caftan with ringlets dangling round his face?'

Gideon nudged Schneider and nodded towards the driver of the cab.

'Don't worry,' he said. 'He is one of ours.'

Gideon looked at the deep-set eyes that eyed him in the mirror, and felt he was being drawn deeper into a world of surreal make-believe. 'How can you be sure?' he asked in English. 'You say Goering has spies in the Gestapo; what's to stop Himmler having his own people in your camp?'

Schneider smiled. 'Our closest people are all Luftwaffe. They adore Hermann and detest Himmler.'

Gideon glanced into the mirror again, but this time the driver did not take his eyes from the road.

Schneider sat back with a smile, and said no more until the taxi came to a halt outside the Kaiserhof Hotel. There he dismissed the driver, and they entered the elegant, bustling lobby.

They had arranged to meet Anne and Elizabeth in the cocktail bar. Schneider said he had to make some telephone calls, so Gideon went ahead and found Elizabeth sitting alone at a table. She was drawing considerable attention from two uniformed officers sitting at the bar. For a moment he considered waiting outside in the lobby until Anne came; it had been some time since he had been alone with Elizabeth. But she saw him and waved, so he came and sat beside her.

'You seem very popular with the SS,' Gideon said, nodding towards the two officers, who averted their stares.

'They're not SS. They're Kriegsmarine officers in their dress uniforms.'

Gideon raised his eyebrows and waved for a waiter. 'Are they?' They could be postmen, for all I know. Everyone seems to have a nice uniform over here.'

After a minute, Elizabeth spoke. 'Are you still angry with me, Gideon?'

It came to him that he was, while he also realised it was simply the old remnants of his injured pride. He shook his head and ordered a whisky and soda from the waiter. 'Not any more,' he said with a smile, 'but I missed you for a long time. Then things changed.'

'You fell in love with Anne.'

'Yes.'

'I'm glad. I still want us to be friends.' She took a cigarette from the packet he had left on the table and he lit it for her, but she no longer touched his hand as she had done in the past. 'You're much better off with Anne. Mama was right about one thing: people should stick to their own kind.'

'Do you think Anne is my kind, Elizabeth?'

'Oh yes! You like each other so much and you always have so much to talk about. I used to make little lists of things to say so that you wouldn't be bored. You want to know the answer to questions I never even think or care about. Anne is like that, too.'

Gideon felt a sudden stab of shame; had he really been so insensitive towards her? He smiled. 'There were certain times when I was never bored, Lizzie.'

She lowered her eyes. 'Yes, that part was lovely,' she said softly. 'But it's not enough on its own, is it?'

He reached out and touched her hand for a moment. 'What about Karl? Is he your kind?'

She looked up again. 'Oh, yes! He's so much fun, he makes everything seem like an adventure.' There was a sad expression in her eyes. 'I laugh a lot when I'm with him, Gideon.' She reached out

173

and touched him on the temple. 'So much of your life takes place up there that you made me feel lonely when I was with you. Karl is there all the time.'

They sat in silence for a time, then, 'Where will you live?' he asked eventually.

'Here, in Berlin. I think it's wonderful. There's this incredible sense of change going on; a sort of electric feeling in the air. As if every day was special, exciting.'

'When will you get married?'

Elizabeth shrugged. 'We don't want to for some time, but I'm applying for German citizenship. Karl thinks that sort of commitment will be good for his career.'

'What exactly does Karl do?'

'Oh, all sorts of things. He's on General Goering's personal staff.'

Gideon nodded, noticing that the two officers had changed their focus of interest. Gideon and Elizabeth had spoken in English, so one of them did not bother to lower his voice when he said in German, 'I'd give a year's pay to be able to fuck her!'

Gideon followed the direction of his gaze and saw Anne coming towards him, wearing a cream silk dress. He leaned towards the sailors, and said in German, 'She doesn't just look good; you should hear her play the piano!'

CHAPTER EIGHT

It was the Monday morning following Gideon's return from Berlin when Laszlo called for him at Shepherd Market. There were decorators in most of the rooms, and the little flat glowed with fresh paint and newly-hung wallpaper. While Gideon paused to speak to the head man, Laszlo waited on the stairs, then they both descended, taking care not to brush against the wet paint.

Gideon and Anne were to be married the following Saturday, and Laszlo was taking his duties as best man seriously. With each day that passed, he became almost fatherly to Gideon.

'I still don't understand why you insist on living in that poky little flat,' he said when they reached the street. Gideon turned up his overcoat collar against the cold wind, but Laszlo ignored the weather and gestured with some emotion as they set off in the direction of Park Lane. 'You could afford a decent house now. We're rich enough.'

Gideon smiled. 'Anne likes the flat; she says she's lived all her life in the suburbs.' He turned to his companion. 'Anyway, the same applies to you; that mews house isn't exactly a palace.' He glanced up at the sky, which was the colour of gunmetal. 'Remember what you used to tell me about capital? If we put money into pictures, in the long run they will be worth much more than a house.'

'The long run,' Laszlo said gloomily. 'They're building air-raid shelters everywhere: I have grave doubts about the long run.'

Gideon shook his head. 'The Germans don't want war with us. Everyone said so in Berlin.'

They walked on in silence and then Laszlo said, 'What about the Brueghel?'

'Schneider said he loved it.'

'You were sure not to claim it was genuine?'

175

Gideon nodded. 'Just as we agreed. I told him there was no proof that it was original. Apparently Schneider's boss waved all objections aside. He is convinced he has the taste of a Medici. He insisted on making the authentication himself, just as Bronstein said he would.'

They had arrived at the bank, but paused inside the entrance to finish their conversation.

'How did Nettlebury's work go?' Gideon asked. The gallery had held an exhibition for Sir Julian while he and Anne were in Berlin.

Laszlo shrugged. 'We only sold a couple, apart from the ones you and I bought.' He leaned against a panelled wall and thrust his hands into his pockets. 'It's very sad. The man can really paint, but everyone thinks we exhibit him for sentimental reasons.'

As he spoke, the frock-coated figure of the under-manager saw them and came over.

'Mr Gideon, Mr Laszlo, how nice to see you. Mr Turner is waiting. Would you care for some coffee?'

They followed him to the manager's office, and just before they entered, Laszlo whispered, 'I'm still astonished that we are greeted with such warmth in a bank.'

'Gentlemen,' the manager said in an expansive fashion when they were seated, 'I received Mr Laszlo's letter. I take it you are here to discuss making Miss Nettlebury a partner?'

Laszlo nodded. 'It's a wedding present.'

Turner said, 'Well, I hope no one will accuse her of being a sleeping partner.' As soon as the words were spoken he flushed with embarrassment, realising the interpretation that could be put upon his unfortunate phrase. 'What I really mean is, er, I actually mean . . . '

Gideon held up a hand. 'Don't worry, Mr Turner. We shall sleep together legally on Saturday night.'

At the same moment that Gideon and Laszlo sat down before the welcoming figure of Mr Turner, a middle-aged woman got off a bus from Kilburn and walked along Bond Street to the Archangel Gallery. On previous occasions when she had been to the showroom there had always been a pleasant, reassuring calm, but today she felt an atmosphere of disorder. Ted Porter was taking down the pictures from the exhibition which had just ended, so the walls were bare and paintings were piled everywhere. The floor was littered with lengths of string, pieces of brown paper, pastepots and discarded labels.

The woman picked her way through the chaos and stood in front of Anne, who was seated at Doris's desk, deep in a complicated conversation on the telephone.

'Yes, Mr Perry, you should have sent them tomorrow . . . No, sending a day early doesn't make things easier; frankly, it's created a nightmare . . . No, if you send someone to take them away now it will only complicate things. I'm ringing to explain that if you're going to be our shipping agents in future you must stick to the schedules we agree upon. It's not as if we have a warehouse where we can store things . . . Good, I'm glad you understand now, Mr Perry. It will make things easier next time.' She covered the receiver for a moment and smiled at the visitor, whom she recognised. 'I'll just be a moment, Mrs Hawkins,' Anne said.

Mrs Hawkins nodded. As a teacher of domestic science in a secondary school for girls, she was familiar with the sort of problem now confronting Anne: ordering and storing large quantities of perishable food also had its difficulties.

Eventually the call came to an end and Anne stood up. 'I'm so sorry, Mrs Hawkins. We had a delivery of another artist's work a day early and the place is in chaos. Your picture is ready for collection; it's over here.'

She led the woman through the maze of litter and found the picture almost instantly. They both looked at it for a moment and Mrs Hawkins smiled.

'You know, it hasn't changed much at all.'

Anne looked puzzled at the remark.

'Chiswick Mall,' Mrs Hawkins said when she noticed Anne's expression, and she gestured towards the painting. 'That's just how it looks. I do wish I'd been able to meet the artist.'

'He's downstairs if you'd like a word with him.'

Mrs Hawkins turned to her. 'Really? He's actually here now? Well, that would be wonderful. If it's no trouble.'

'He'll do it for me, Mrs Hawkins,' Anne replied. 'He's my father.'

The woman looked astonished. 'I had no idea,' she called out as Anne went to the rear of the gallery. She re-emerged moments later with Nettlebury.

It was obvious how much the meeting meant to the woman; she actually blushed with pleasure when she was introduced. 'Sir Julian,' Mrs Hawkins said as she shook hands, 'this is a great pleasure. I only wish my husband were here to share it.'

Nettlebury shuffled with mild embarrassment. 'Not at all, Mrs

Hawkins. Believe me, the pleasure is all mine.'

Mrs Hawkins nodded towards the picture. 'As I was just saying to your daughter, Chiswick Mall hasn't changed much. I used to walk along there with my husband before we were married.'

Nettlebury glanced down at the painting, and smiled. 'You know, I did the same with my own wife. I'm glad we share similar memories.'

'This isn't the only painting of yours we have,' said Mrs Hawkins. 'We were given one as a wedding present; a landscape of Sussex. It was done in the autumn and there is a church in the middle distance with figures in dark clothes walking on the road in the foreground. We always used to imagine it was Sunday morning and the people had been to church.'

'Bless my soul! I haven't seen that one in nearly thirty years.'

She nodded. 'Well, it's given us enormous pleasure, Sir Julian, and I'd like to thank you from both of us.'

Anne moved away while her father continued to talk, and Ted Porter joined her. 'I'm going to have to stack all your dad's pictures against the far wall and then start hanging the new lot. If Doris can give me a hand when she gets in, I should be done by twelve o'clock.'

'Whatever you say, Ted. I shall be able to help in a little while, once I've sorted out this morning's invoices.'

She looked up and waved goodbye when Mrs Hawkins left, and Nettlebury called out to her. 'I'm just off to Sotheby's, Anne, to look at the Norwich drawings.'

Anne nodded an acknowledgment and returned to her paperwork. She was immersed for some time until she suddenly became aware of a figure standing over her. Anne looked up and saw it was Sylvia Vasilakis, bandbox fresh, with a crease of annoyance on her forehead.

'Where is my husband?' Sylvia asked without any preliminary words of greeting.

'Hello, Sylvia,' Anne replied with a smile, determined to be polite. 'He and Gideon had to go to the bank. Gideon is going on to a sale, but Laszlo said he would be back soon.'

'I shall wait here,' Sylvia said, as if she was expecting to be challenged, and sat down in the chair opposite the desk.

'Would you care for coffee?' Anne asked.

Sylvia made a face. 'I cannot drink your coffee; it tastes bad.' She glanced around with what seemed to be an air of disapproval before turning to Anne once more. 'Is there trouble at the bank?' she demanded.

178

Anne shook her head. 'On the contrary, the gallery is doing very well.'

Sylvia looked straight at her. 'I thought there might be trouble; for this last exhibition has not been a success. Rich people do not want your father's paintings; they do not sell.'

Anne strained to remain polite when she really wanted to reach out and shake the doll-like little figure before her. 'We sold about one-third of the paintings and at least half of the drawings,' she said quietly.

Sylvia gave a little sniffing sound. 'Mr Gideon bought some of them, I think, and the drawings were not priced too high. I am surprised you could afford to put on such a show, with the overheads you pay here.'

'There were two weeks to spare before we begin the German Expressionist exhibition tomorrow. The gallery didn't lose anything,' Anne said in a slightly stiffer voice. Damn it, she thought, why am I making excuses to you for my father?

Her new tone must have finally penetrated Sylvia's steel-clad skin, because she suddenly tapped on the desk. 'Please do not think I mean to be rude by these things I say. It is just that my husband tells me that when you marry Gideon they intend to make you a partner in the business.' She paused and took a cigarette from her handbag, then proceeded to blow the smoke away over her shoulder, as if she wanted nothing to do with it. 'If this is so,' she continued, 'you must understand I have my own position to consider.' She opened her handbag again and produced a carbon copy of a letter. 'It is all here in black and white.'

Anne stood up. Despite her resolution to be polite and patient with the woman, her stomach was fluttering with anger and frustration. She had to place her fingertips firmly on the desk to stop her hands from trembling, not wanting Sylvia to see how furious she had become. 'I'm afraid I know nothing about this, Sylvia,' she said, suddenly aware that Ted Porter was within earshot.

'But you must know,' Sylvia said impatiently, waving the cigarette to emphasise her remark. 'If anything were to happen to my husband I would inherit his partnership, but if you are to become part of the business, I must know where I stand. It will reduce Laszlo's share, and I have my future to think about.'

Anne folded her arms and leaned forward. 'Let me make it clear, Sylvia, that I know nothing of any plans to make me a partner in the Archangel Gallery. Neither Laszlo nor Gideon has ever mentioned

179

the matter.'

'I can understand you do not wish to discuss it with me,' Sylvia replied, as if the words Anne had just spoken were entirely without meaning. 'But I will not allow this to happen. In the circumstances, I may have to insist on a partnership for myself.' She replaced the letter in her handbag and glanced about the gallery as if trying to assess the value of the fixtures and fittings.

Anne could not stay with Sylvia a moment longer, and saw that Doris had just come in. She walked over to her, and asked, 'Can you give Ted a hand, Doris? Mrs Vasilakis is waiting for Laszlo. I've got to go out for a few minutes and get a breath of fresh air.'

Without bothering to remove her smock, Anne hurried out. She hesitated for a few moments on the pavement and then made for the Lyons tea shop in Piccadilly, where she bought a cup of tea and sat brooding over Sylvia's accusations. She had been there for some time when her father appeared and sat down opposite her.

He smiled sympathetically and thrust his hands deep into his jacket pockets. 'I gather that Sylvia has been getting you down.' He poured sugar into his own cup, which he stirred carefully before tasting the contents.

'How did you know?' Anne asked.

Nettlebury took his pipe from his pocket and began to pack the bowl. 'Ted told me when I got back. Sylvia was sitting in the gallery with a face like Medusa, so he took me downstairs and told me about your conversation.' He looked into his cup with an expression of surprise, and murmured, 'To think I once complained of American coffee.'

'I think there's something wrong with that woman, Dad,' Anne stated. 'She seemed to make the most extraordinary accusations. It was as though I had been plotting against her. Well, not just me . . . all of us.' She raised her hands in protestation and then let them fall.

Nettlebury nodded and put a match to his pipe. 'She is a singular woman,' he agreed, 'but try to understand her. It's best with people like her.'

'Why? She's so dreadful towards everybody else; why should we make an exception for her?' She had spoken louder than she had intended, so that a young couple at the next table looked up in interest.

Nettlebury took the pipe from his mouth and examined the stem. 'She is damaged in a peculiar way, I suppose. We really ought to be sorry for her.' He turned his gaze to the young couple until they

180

averted their eyes.

Anne picked up her own cup but, realising the tea was cold, replaced it in the saucer and looked at her father. 'Have you ever met anyone like her before?'

'Once or twice. I think it's a combination of two things: extreme poverty when she was young, and not having any children. In many ways she's similar to Anthony Strange.'

Anne gave a mirthless laugh. 'Perhaps they should have married each other. But why do you say they're alike?'

Nettlebury frowned. 'Poverty affects people in different ways.' He pointed a finger at her. 'You wouldn't know, young lady. And before you say anything about our having to struggle, remember that we always lived in a decent house and had enough to eat. Your mother's money saw to that. Oh, you might have known a bit of genteel poverty, but that's nothing like the real thing.' He looked into his pipe for a moment. 'Genuine poverty can tear the heart from people. It degrades and debases human beings, and they react to it in different fashions. Take Ted Porter: in his case, it gave him a sense of compassion. He'd share his last farthing with you. It made him a good man. Others . . .' He shrugged. 'It seems to eat into them like a worm. They fear it so much that they'll do anything to anyone, just so they're never poor again. It dries out their souls.' He rubbed the old brass badge on his tobacco pouch.

'What about children? How do they fit into it?' Anne asked.

Nettlebury smiled. 'Some people who don't have children never quite join the rest of us in the human race.' He shook his head. 'I don't say it goes for everyone, but in certain cases they believe they're the centre of the universe and everything that happens is directly related to them. People with children generally see that there are important things outside their own existence. They understand that life isn't a series of conspiracies directed against them.'

'Do you think that Sylvia believes we're all plotting against her, Dad?'

'Oh, yes. Just as surely as she's plotting against everybody else. Understanding her motives doesn't make her any the less dangerous. If she thinks you're a threat to her, she'll try and take some sort of action.' He patted her hand, and smiled. 'On the other hand, she's in dire danger herself; Ted and Doris were planning to take her outside and throw her under a bus for upsetting you!'

Anne looked at her father and felt her anger begin to ebb. 'It was lovely to see how much Mrs Hawkins appreciated her picture.'

181

'At least it's good to know there's someone out there who still likes my stuff.' He stood up. 'Come on, duty calls.'

When they returned to the gallery, there was a noticeable atmosphere; Ted and Doris seemed relieved when they saw that Anne's usually cheerful spirits were restored.

'Mr Laszlo came back, but Mr Gideon wasn't with him,' Doris explained. 'Mrs Vasilakis said you'd been rude to her, but then Mr Laszlo asked Ted to come and have a word with him in the office. When he heard what had really happened, he pulled Mrs Vasilakis out of the gallery. I've never seen him like that. Ted thinks the pair of them have gone off round to her shop to have it out.'

Ted Porter had been correct in his assumption. Laszlo had walked to Burlington Arcade with Sylvia, and when she had opened the shop he had drawn down the blind and locked the door. Then he stood in the gloomy interior, waiting for his wife to speak. But Sylvia, convinced that the wrong had been done to her, stood her ground and fixed Laszlo with a stare of silent defiance. On the few occasions Laszlo had been truly angry with her during their marriage, she had usually defeated him by this simple action.

Intuitively, Sylvia knew it was all a matter of letting his guilt come to her rescue. In her heart, she knew that he carried the major burden of blame for the failure of their marriage; if she remained silent, he would eventually apologise and give her what she wanted. But this time it did not seem to work.

'Why are you behaving like this?' he said quietly. 'You know Anne and Gideon are the best friends that I have.'

Sylvia lit a cigarette before she answered. 'Can't you see they are stealing the business from you? You created it, and now that woman is going to take it for herself.'

He drew a long breath and looked around the tiny shop. It was as though he were in the mews flat in Shepherd Market, so many of the items that covered every surface were familiar to him. He had to restrain himself from sweeping the clutter to the floor and grinding it beneath his feet. 'They've worked just as hard as I have to make the gallery a success.' He had to use all his self-control to keep his voice even. 'None of us could have done it without the others.'

Sylvia, who was as robust as a cheap cuckoo clock, suddenly sat down on a little velvet-covered chair. She held a hand to her forehead, then reached for her handbag and produced a small silver box from which she extracted a pill. 'Will you get me a glass of water, please?'

she said in a voice which implied a serious complaint.

In the small room, Laszlo found a water carafe on the desk. When he returned, Sylvia took the glass and swallowed the pill with a grimace.

'What's the matter?' he asked.

'I saw the doctor last week,' she replied. 'He said I have a cardiac condition.'

'Why didn't you tell me?'

She waved her hand. 'If I am careful, it is nothing. You've been busy and I did not wish to worry you, but that's why I'm concerned about the future.'

There was nowhere for Laszlo to sit in the claustrophobic little room. He leaned against a table, which began to tip towards him, so he quickly stood upright again, his hands in his pockets. 'In what way have you been thinking of the future?'

Sylvia took another sip of the water to remind him of her condition. 'Anthony Strange came to see me.' She held up her hand as he was about to speak. 'He told me that most of your business is in Germany, that the special deals you do in France are related to your major customer.'

'What else did he tell you?' Laszlo's hand slowly closed round the silver pillbox Sylvia had left on the table.

'He explained that you do all the work and the others are using you,' Sylvia said, studying her husband's face.

'So what are you suggesting?'

Sylvia gestured. 'Sell your part of the gallery before that woman marries James Gideon and dilutes the value. We can go to Germany and take all the business with us.'

'Why should I want to go to Germany?'

'Don't you see?' Sylvia said with sudden enthusiasm. 'That's where the future is going to be. This country is finished. According to Strange, Berlin is going to be the place that matters, and we shall be in the middle of it.'

Laszlo slowly shook his head. 'I can't do that, Sylvia. This is my home.'

She looked at him in bewilderment. 'Home, here, in England? What do you care for this country? You Hungarians can live anywhere.'

He turned and looked out of the darkened shop into the arcade before he answered. 'I care for this country because the people who mean most to me live here. If I have anything that resembles a

183

family, it is at the Archangel Gallery.' He looked back at his wife, and then spoke slowly. 'Living with you in Berlin would be like serving a prison sentence.'

She stood up quickly, her body stiff with hostility. 'Well, you had better get back to your family,' she said bitterly. 'I am only your wife.'

Laszlo turned again and looked at Sylvia. Then he took one of her pills and bit into it. He shook his head, then said, 'You're not my wife, Sylvia. Any more than these pills are for a heart condition.' He threw the box on the table and walked from the shop, leaving her to brood malevolently in the darkness.

Later that evening, Ted Porter saw everyone off the premises and locked up the gallery. At five minutes past six, he tucked a large package under his arm and set off at a brisk pace. It was a short walk to the Central Line station at Bond Street. He found a seat easily and sat nursing the package like a child with a favourite Christmas present. It was just before seven o'clock when he turned the corner of his street in Perivale. The evening was cold, but one of his neighbours was taking his dog for a walk. Ted exchanged a polite greeting, and thought how much warmer the encounter would have been in his home village. A group of children played beneath the light of a street lamp, his son among them. The boy waved to him when he reached his garden gate and shouted a greeting. Ted's wife Mabel was in the kitchen, and he could smell meat roasting.

'I'm home,' he called to her and went into the living-room, where he began to unwrap the package he had brought.

'Give me a hand, Ted? Mabel asked, and he left what he was doing and joined her in the kitchen. She held a large leg of pork in a roasting-tray. 'I want to pour the fat off this. Put a fork in it so it doesn't fall on the floor.' Ted did as he was asked and Mabel carefully decanted the liquid into a jug.

'Meat on a Monday? You'd think we were millionaires,' he said, sitting down at the table to read the *Evening Standard*, which it was his habit to save for this part of the day.

Mabel laughed. 'This is for the club social tomorrow night. We're having the lamb left from yesterday.'

Ted did not mind; cold lamb on a Monday was still a luxury to him. He glanced down and saw the school-books his son had left on the table. 'Our Terry called out to me in the street. He sounds a proper little Londoner these days.'

184

'Well, he is a little Londoner, if you can call Perivale London,' Mabel said. Ted nodded and looked from the kitchen window where the light revealed the parts of an air-raid shelter that had been provided by the council. 'Did you have a good day?'

Ted nodded. He could not believe how much his life had changed since he first started at the Archangel Gallery. He even found it hard to say he worked these days. The word used to mean ten hours of grinding labour that would leave him drained and numb. A day at the gallery was more like the Saturdays he used to spend pottering on his allotment. He thought of his two brothers, who still lived in the same village, and wondered how they could stay there when he had told them repeatedly how much better life was in the south of England. 'Go on, man,' one of them had said when he had been home on his last visit. 'Bloody London? You might as well ask us to go to Australia.' Those words had convinced him to give up. He knew that they would stay in the village until the day they died.

'Come and look at this,' he said to Mabel and led her into the living-room. She looked down at the sofa, where he had left the landscape Paul Trenton had given to him the previous week.

'Well, that's nice, love,' Mabel said after a while. 'What's it supposed to be? Not that I don't like it, mind.' She glanced around the walls of their living-room, which were filled with the work of other painters.

It was a slow morning in the Archangel Gallery. Laszlo had been summoned to visit Henri Bronstein the day before, and Gideon was demonstrating to his mother and father how an unscrupulous salesman would sell a picture when Doris came and stood beside him in the showroom. 'Sorry to interrupt, Mr Gideon, but it's Mr Laszlo on the telephone, calling from Paris. He says it's important.'

Gideon excused himself and went to take the call. He could barely hear Laszlo; it sounded as if someone were crushing cellophane inside the receiver. 'You're very distant,' he bellowed into the mouthpiece.

Suddenly the line cleared. 'I said: where will you be at seven o'clock tonight?' Laszlo shouted.

'Anne and I are going to have dinner with my parents and Julian. We'll be at the Connaught Hotel.' Gideon spoke the words individually, as if he were reading a telegram aloud.

'I'll see you there,' Laszlo shouted as the line faded again.

Gideon rejoined his parents, who were talking to Anne. 'It looks as if he'll be joining us for dinner this evening. We'd better re-book the table.'

'Will that dreadful wife be with him?' Gideon's mother asked.

Anne nodded. 'I think we should ask her, after all she's done in the last few days.' It was true that a remarkable change seemed to have come over Sylvia since Monday afternoon. First she had sent flowers to Anne, then a letter of apology, and finally she had called with a gift from her shop and almost begged her forgiveness. 'It does seem as if she's a new person.'

'I suspect that's Laszlo's influence,' Gideon added, then he turned to Frank, who was still looking at the pictures. 'So did you see what I was doing?'

Frank held the point of his chin between forefinger and thumb while he studied the five pictures Gideon had asked Ted Porter to bring from the store-room. 'I think so. You decided the picture you were going to sell me was the Picasso, then told Ted to bring it up first. Then you pretended it was the wrong one . . . almost as though I wasn't allowed to have it. Then you showed me all the others. Every time I asked about the Picasso, you refused to discuss it, as though you wouldn't sell it to me because it really belonged to somebody else. So all the time I wanted to talk about the forbidden picture.'

'That's right,' Gideon said. 'In the end they've managed to trick you out of the painting. Of course it only works with people who consider themselves really shrewd, the ones who aren't going to be talked into something.'

His mother turned from the pictures and spoke to Anne. 'Well, it's Friday afternoon and there are only six and a half shopping days to your wedding,' Marjorie said. She took hold of her husband's arm. 'Come along, darling, those bloody sheep are growing their little woolly coats faster than I can spend them.' Gideon's parents left the gallery, and a few minutes later Nettlebury entered.

'You look happy, Dad,' Anne said, and Gideon also noticed his self-satisfied air.

'I've just been to my tailor for the final fitting for my morning clothes,' he replied. 'Do you know, it's been fifteen years since I had a suit made, and I'm still the same measurements?'

'Laszlo will be having dinner with us this evening,' Anne said to her father.

'And Sylvia?' he asked.

'I suppose so,' Gideon answered.

Nettlebury nodded. 'I suppose it's for the best, but I hope I don't

186

have to sit next to her,' he said with feeling.

When the three of them arrived at the hotel bar that evening, Sylvia was already seated at a table. She stood up when they joined her. It was clear that she was still making an effort to be pleasant. 'Laszlo insisted that I come early and buy everybody champagne.' She linked arms with Nettlebury. 'Come and sit beside me,' she instructed him.

Gideon's parents made their entrance a few minutes later, and Marjorie blinked around the room in a short-sighted fashion. 'Is there any sign of that woman?' she asked, and then felt her husband's nudge. 'Oh, there you are, Sylvia. How nice to see you, darling,' she said when she spotted the tiny figure sitting next to Nettlebury. 'I have spent the day on hats. Tomorrow will be devoted to gloves, and I think shoes on Monday.'

'Did Laszlo tell you why he was coming home early, Sylvia?' Gideon asked when they had all been served with their drinks.

'He just said to meet him here. I thought you would know.'

'Well, we can ask him now,' said Nettlebury. 'Here he is.'

Laszlo greeted everyone with his customary care, but Anne noticed that the kiss on the cheek he gave Sylvia was no warmer than the affection he showed any other woman at the table. He glanced around the darkly-panelled room before he spoke, and saw there was no need to lower his voice. 'I am sorry to sound so dramatic, but what I have to tell you is important. It does concern us all.'

'Be as dramatic as you like, darling,' said Marjorie. 'I, for one, adore it.'

Laszlo smiled. 'It is good news but it does, I'm afraid, involve a certain sacrifice.' He turned to Gideon and Anne. 'To come straight to the point, would you see your way to postponing the wedding?'

As he was sitting next to her, Nettlebury noticed an intake of breath from Sylvia. He turned to look at Anne's face. Her eyes flickered from Gideon to Laszlo uncertainly.

'Why?' Gideon asked.

Laszlo leaned forward. 'Bronstein has offered us a fantastic opportunity. He wants us to go to New York and sell the whole of the Whitney-Ingram collection.'

Gideon put down his glass. 'To act as commission agents and actually sell it on the open market?' he asked.

Laszlo nodded.

'What does this mean?' Marjorie said in the silence that followed. 'I thought you two were always selling pictures.'

187

'We are, but not on this scale. It means a fortune for the gallery,' Gideon told her. 'The Whitney-Ingram Collection is one of the most valuable in the world.'

'Can't you go after the wedding?' Nettlebury asked. 'It's only another week.'

Laszlo looked down at his glass. 'Bronstein insists we both sail on Monday. He has no time left. His doctors have told him he's dying.'

It was the last night on board the *Queen Mary* when Laszlo and Gideon finally made an appearance in the dining-room. Although they had spent most of the journey in the comfort of a first-class stateroom, they had hardly noticed their surroundings. The days of the crossing had been spent in endless work that had caused a river of radio cables to flow between Paris, London and New York. One thing was to their advantage: the Whitney-Ingram Collection was so well known to the art world that the individual pieces needed no presentation by the Archangel Gallery. Each already had the reputation of a major work; some even came into the category of masterpieces. The major consideration of the sale was timing: if they appeared to be in too much of a hurry, it would depress the value across the entire market. Now, their preparations made, at last they had a few hours of leisure before them.

They had refused the Purser's offer to share a grander table, choosing to dine alone, but when they were seated they saw two familiar figures, Erich and Elsa Mueller, who were also without other companions. They greeted each other, and a friendly steward swiftly made arrangements for the two parties to be joined. Gideon noticed that Elsa was warmer towards him. He imagined it was because a closer relationship with her daughter was now out of the question.

'We saw your names on the passenger list,' Mueller said, 'but when you did not come to dinner we thought you must be busy. We ourselves wanted a quiet voyage.'

'I didn't see your names on the list,' said Laszlo.

Mueller shook his head. 'I'm travelling incognito.'

Gideon wondered, for a moment, why such a step was necessary. Since the plans to bring England and Germany closer had failed so abysmally, the Muellers had rather faded from the social scene in London, and they were hardly known in New York.

'What takes you to America?' Laszlo asked.

Mueller was vague about his reasons, and muttered something about legal commitments back home in Minnesota.

The rest of the evening passed pleasantly enough, and they all agreed on an early night. The following morning, Gideon stood on deck with Laszlo and watched their final approach to the Golden City.

'Does it still look as big to you?' Laszlo asked as they looked up at the mighty buildings.

'Yes,' Gideon said with a smile. 'But so do I now.'

That afternoon they visited a young Wall Street lawyer called Mr Prew, who represented Bronstein. He greeted them in his oak-panelled office on the thirty-first floor of a great granite building and, in the American tradition, got straight down to business.

'Well, gentlemen,' he said briskly, 'how much will the Whitney-Ingram Collection be worth at sale? You know that my client wants to proceed with all speed.'

Gideon took a slip of paper from his pocket. 'If we sell it by the end of the week, five and a half million dollars,' he said easily.

Mr Prew looked from one to the other. The sum impressed him. 'You seem very sure of the amount.'

Laszlo nodded, and produced a wad of cables from his briefcase. 'We already have offers amounting to that sum,' he said, placing the papers on the table.

The lawyer was young, but he was also clever. He could tell that the two men had an alternative in mind. 'What's your other proposition?' he asked.

Gideon smiled. 'Obviously Henri Bronstein has a reason for wanting short-term capital. Presumably he doesn't wish to use other money that is committed to a healthy return.' Mr Prew nodded, but said nothing. 'If you lend us the same amount for the next month,' Gideon said, 'we shall pay three points more interest than anyone else, and we shall buy the entire collection today.'

'And, of course, we'll forgo our commission,' said Laszlo. Mr Prew stood up and held out his hand. 'Gentlemen, we have a deal.'

'Won't you have to confirm with Henri Bronstein?' Laszlo asked.

The lawyer smiled, and shook his head. 'No, gentlemen. You see, I have my own cable.' He reached into his pocket and passed the slip of paper to Laszlo. It read: 'Accept their second offer. Bronstein.'

An hour later they were on their way to the Whitney-Ingram mansion in Fifth Avenue.

'I think you know Stanford's son Charles,' Mr Prew said when they

189

had dismissed the taxi and stood outside the house. 'He's here to hand things over.'

'Yes, we met when he was a boy,' Laszlo said.

The door was opened by a uniformed security guard, whom they followed inside. The interior was bare of furniture, which had gone to auction, and as in all great houses that had been stripped of their finery, there was an air of melancholy about the echoing rooms and corridors.

The security guard took them to Charles Whitney-Ingram, who was eating a sandwich in the kitchen and did not appear to be too deeply affected by the change in the family fortunes. He had altered a great deal since they had last seen him in the south of France. The gaucheness of youth had been replaced by an easy confidence, but they could still recognise some traces of the boy. When he'd finished his food, he led them through the house to the gallery.

On the staircase, he paused to ask, 'How are Sir Julian and his family? Are those daughters still as pretty as I remember?'

'Prettier,' Gideon answered drily. 'I'm going to marry one of them when we go home.'

'Congratulations! I've got one of his paintings, you know,' said Charles. 'My grandmother left it to me.'

'A landscape,' said Laszlo.

'You know it?'

'I know of it,' Laszlo answered as they reached the doors to the gallery.

'Well, there it is, gentlemen,' Charles said nonchalantly. 'Behind those doors is the pirate hoard of my grandfather Arthur. Good luck.'

'Aren't you coming in?' Laszlo said.

Charles shook his head. 'Like we say at the movie show: this is where we came in.' He left them at the doorway.

Laszlo gestured towards Mr Prew. 'After you, sir,' he said, and the lawyer opened the doors and stepped into the gallery.

This part of the mansion had lost none of its splendour. When Gideon switched on the bank of lights, the long gallery came alive again and the dancing walls of colour seemed to pulsate with life. No single individual would buy all the treasures that surrounded Gideon; soon the pictures would be scattered all over the world. Some would enter the homes of the wealthy and others grace the walls of museums. But now, and for a brief while longer, they hung as Arthur Whitney-Ingram had intended.

190

The arrangement was simple. First came frescoes of delicate Gothic figures. No artists were attributed, but the churches from which they were taken were all faithfully recorded.

Then came panels of tempera executed in the thirteenth century. Gideon began to recognise names; Cimabue, Giotto di Bondone, Duccio di Buoninsegna. Then the pictures took new forms. The primitive flat surfaces gave way to depth and a new quality of modelling: Masaccio, Fra Angelico and Filippo Lippi. The birth of the Renaissance: Messina, Bellini, Carpaccio. The pictures were overwhelming. Gideon was familiar with all of them, but until this moment he had seen only reproductions, and the originals filled him with awe. Softly he began to recite the dates Nettlebury had insisted he learn long ago.

An angel by Sandro Botticelli was so like Anne that Gideon paused before he could continue. A magnificent Giorgione and two Titians stopped him again. He felt that they were walking down the centuries, seeing the glory that remained. The achievements of princes were only words in books, Gideon told himself; but the work of artists lived for ever. He found it deeply moving that men could have created such incredible beauty.

Still they walked on until they reached the end of the gallery, where the collection ended with the modern schools beginning at the turn of the century. Mr Prew stopped beside a large Jacobean cupboard surrounded by the paintings of André Derain and Edvard Munch.

'I believe there's still some rather good sherry in here,' he said. 'Would you care for a glass?'

They both accepted and stood for a time in silence, overcome by the wonders they'd seen.

Mr Prew cleared his throat and gestured back along the gallery. 'They tell me it's pretty good,' he said to Laszlo, who nodded without speaking. 'One thing that puzzles me, is why Arthur Whitney-Ingram didn't collect any American artists. He was a great patriot, you know. The newspapers used to refer to him as Old Glory.' He turned to Laszlo again. 'Can you explain that to me, Mr Vasilakis?'

Laszlo smiled and sipped his sherry. 'That's because there aren't any important American artists, Mr Prew.'

The lawyer seemed shocked. 'Surely you're mistaken? Why, the United States is the most powerful and richest country in the world.'

Laszlo nodded. 'That's undoubtedly true, and I'm sure it's only a question of time. But, so far, America has not produced one artist of first-rank importance.'

Mr Prew continued to look puzzled. 'How can that be?'

Laszlo finished his sherry and shrugged as he placed the empty glass on the cabinet. 'Who knows? Perhaps they all went to Hollywood.'

The days passed, and as the Whitney-Ingram Collection contracted, so the fortunes of the Archangel Gallery increased. Henri Bronstein did not die, but he hovered so close to death that on his recovery he had the satisfaction of reading most of his obituaries in the world's press.

Gideon and Laszlo became famous in New York; they were written about in the newspapers and comedians told jokes about them in smart night clubs. Invitations flowed to them at the Algonquin Hotel, where they had set up their headquarters.

Towards the end of their time, Gideon became almost nostalgic for his days of poverty, which time had now gilded with happy memories. He suggested that they have dinner at the Hungarian Café and invite Vittorio Castelli, a fellow dealer from Rome, who had become a good friend in the last three weeks. That night, they all met in the bar of the Algonquin, and, accompanied by Piet Liebe, made their way to Greenwich Village. They took their places in the restaurant where Gideon had originally encountered Laszlo, and ordered the first bottle of Bull's Blood.

'This is better than El Morocco,' Gideon said as he drank the heavy wine.

'Only if one can go to El Morocco afterwards, if one chooses,' Piet Liebe answered drily.

Vittorio Castelli sipped the wine with caution. Like all true Romans, he was deeply suspicious of any kind of food and drink he had not known since childhood.

'What do you think?' Laszlo asked.

Vittorio shrugged his expensively tailored shoulders, and smiled. 'Interesting,' he said without further commitment. He turned to Gideon. 'So you have never tried to ski?' he said, continuing the conversation they had begun in the taxi. 'Then I will teach you.'

'Where will these lessons take place?' Gideon asked.

Vittorio gave one of those Italian gestures that dismiss all other considerations. 'Cervinia. There can be no other place.' He took a deeper draught of wine and placed the glass on the table before him.

192

'This is the Matterhorn, as you people call it, and here ... ' he pointed to about half-way up the glass, 'is Cervinia.'

'Is it beautiful?' Gideon asked.

'Beautiful?' Vittorio repeated. 'It is the finest resort in the world. Il Duce said so, and he should know; he ordered it to be built.'

'Does Mussolini ski?' Liebe asked.

'Il Duce does everything,' Vittorio said. 'He is the world's greatest leader, lover, poet, visionary and station-master. Nobody needs a watch any more; we just listen to the sound of trains arriving on time.'

'Don't you approve of what he has done for Italy?' Gideon asked.

Vittorio shrugged. 'As far as I am concerned, Italy can look after itself. The people are Arabs in the south and Germans in the north. I only care about Rome, and there is little he can do to her that hasn't been tried by other experts in the last two thousand years. But Rome always remains supreme.'

'Come on, my friend,' Laszlo chided him. 'Are you saying it is a greater city than London or New York?'

Vittorio laughed. 'You do not understand. Rome is the mother of all other cities, and the mother is always the most beautiful in the family.'

'If Rome is the mother, which city is the father?' Gideon asked.

'Athens, of course,' Vittorio replied without hesitation.

'Then let us drink to the mother of cities,' Laszlo said, raising his glass.

'Listen, my friends,' Vittorio said firmly, 'I know what you must do.' He turned to Gideon. 'Marry your bride in Rome. She will thank you for all eternity.' He took another gulp of wine. 'Then, afterwards, we can all go skiing in Cervinia.'

Gideon exchanged glances with Laszlo. Suddenly the idea appealed to them both. 'We shall cable our women immediately,' Laszlo said, encouraged by Vittorio's enthusiasm.

'To the mother of cities!' Vittorio said again, and the owner of the Hungarian Café stood by to refill their glasses. He always enjoyed customers who made toasts, regardless of the nation they drank to.

Rome, late March 1939

The suggestion of a wedding in Rome had been well received in England. Much to Laszlo's surprise, Sylvia had greeted the idea with the most enthusiasm. She had even taken it upon herself to make

193

most of the travel arrangements, and in some curious fashion had managed to muddle events so that she was already ensconced at the Cardinal Hotel in the Via Giulia when Gideon and Laszlo arrived in the city. They discovered from her that the others were not due for another three days.

'It is unlike Sylvia,' Laszlo said to Gideon. 'She is usually meticulous in anything she does.'

The two men had seen much of each other in the previous months; by unspoken agreement they went their own ways for the few days before the others arrived.

Rome was not how Gideon had imagined it to be. Perhaps there was too much history to be absorbed. Images were piled on top of each other like a photographic plate that had been exposed several times. Perhaps it was the weather, which still held the cold edge of winter. Harsh winds blew ancient dust through the streets and squares, spoiling the symmetry of fountain sprays. He dutifully went round the city, guidebook in hand, and studied churches, walked among ruins and gazed at legendary vistas, but the magic failed to work. All he could remember were the black-clad figures of priests and nuns, their garments blown about, each clutching a hat or headpiece against the gusting wind. Even the food, which Vittorio had assured him was greater than the poor imitations he had eaten in other countries, seemed either crude or insipid.

Late in the afternoon of the day Anne, her family and Gideon's parents were due to arrive, he was alone in the gathering darkness of St Peter's Square, having just visited the Sistine Chapel. Now he stood and tried to decide in which direction he would strike out to find a taxi. The same dark figures passed him, their clothes like the sails of a ship, and his eyes burned from the stinging grit blown against his face. Then he caught a different sound from the distant roar of traffic and the clip of shoes on the cobbles. It was his name being called, like the snatch of a song in the wind.

'Gideon, Gideon,' came through the half-darkness.

He looked around; all he could see were lamp-black clerics. But when a group of nuns drifted suddenly past, there was Anne, dressed in a pale coat, which seemed to glow in the last of the light. She took the last steps to him, and then they held each other. Her hair was blown around his face.

'How did you get here so soon?' he asked after some time.

'We caught an earlier train,' Anne said, burying her face in his shoulder. 'Oh, Gideon, I've missed you so much!'

They stood together again, and then Gideon raised his head and looked up at the majesty of St Peter's. He did not think he had ever seen anything more magnificent in his life.

He wanted to spend some time with Anne before they met the others; eventually they found a marbled ice-cream parlour that was bright with neon. They sat on iron chairs and ordered coffee, and Anne told him the things she had not mentioned in her letters.

'Sylvia's behaviour has been odd. She became very friendly and began to invite me to all sorts of places. She even took me to a party.'

'Really?' said Gideon. 'What brought about this change of heart?'

She shrugged. 'I have no idea, but she kept bringing Paul Trenton along. She even suggested, one evening, that if I wanted to have some kind of fling with him she would furnish me with an alibi.'

'Fling?' said Gideon. 'What do you mean, fling?'

'Affair, darling! She pointed out that it was disgusting the way men behaved, while women were expected to keep themselves for one person.'

'She said it was disgusting?'

Anne nodded. 'Paul Trenton said that was the key to her attitude.'

'You discussed it with him?'

'Yes, at the party. Sylvia was acting like Jean Harlow, but Paul said that when you danced with her she went rigid, like a steel girder. He doesn't think she likes men at all.'

'Perhaps she likes women?'

Anne shook her head. 'No, she's not interested in women, either.'

He smiled. 'How would you know?'

Anne looked at him and smiled, too. 'From school, darling. I know the sort of girl who prefers women.'

Gideon drank some coffee. He knew what he wanted to ask, and tried to make the question casual. 'So what about her little plot with Paul Trenton? Was he keen on the idea?'

She knew what he was thinking and reached out to take his hand. 'Paul is infatuated with himself, darling. He's all he can talk about.'

'Well, that's the way you can tell. You were all I wanted to talk about in New York.'

Anne held his hand to her cheek. 'Not always. Laszlo is in love with Elizabeth, and he never mentions her.'

'How do you know?' Gideon said with some surprise. He had imagined that he alone knew this secret. One night in New York, when they had drunk a lot together, Laszlo had told Gideon of his feelings for Elizabeth.

'I've always known,' Anne replied. 'He looks at her in the same way you used to look at me.'

Gideon thought back to the months when he had been unable to bring himself to approach her. 'Why didn't you say something, if you knew how I felt?'

'Oh, Gideon,' she replied with another laugh. 'And spend the rest of our lives with you wondering if I'd trapped you?'

The following morning they were married at All Saints, the Anglican church in the Via del Babuino. It was a charming little neo-Gothic building, with a white spire that rose above the surroundings like a beacon of dissension.

Sylvia did not come to the ceremony. Laszlo, who was best man, explained that she was unwell. Vittorio attended with his wife, Prisca, and their five daughters. Prisca was a striking blonde, as slender and elegant as a silk ribbon, and each daughter was a perfect copy of her.

Afterwards they went to the Castellis' house for the reception, which Vittorio had insisted on providing as a wedding present. When Vittorio had talked of his home, Gideon had imagined a rambling apartment full of shouting relatives. He was astonished to discover that his friend lived in a palace one of his ancestors had built at the time of the Renaissance.

They were standing in a glass-domed colonnaded hall, and Vittorio shrugged when Vera Simpson remarked on its beauty. 'Prisca's family have a nicer house,' he said, 'but they are related to Gregory the Great.' It took a little longer for Vera to discover that that particular relative had been pope in the sixth century.

'They really are the most extraordinary people,' Vera said when she was talking to Laszlo and Gideon's parents. 'They talk about ancestors who lived in the Middle Ages as if they knew them intimately.'

Marjorie nodded. 'One of the children has just been telling me of a friend of the family who crept up behind Charlemagne and put the crown on his head. It seems that's how they established the precedent of crowning Holy Roman Emperors. Did you know that one of the popes was Jewish?'

'Jewish?' Vera repeated incredulously.

Marjorie nodded again. 'Anacletus II, a member of the Pierleoni family.'

'Who is the distinguished-looking old lady who seems to be fighting back tears?' Nettlebury asked, joining them.

Laszlo looked behind him. 'That's Vittorio's mother, the Princess. She's taken a great shine to Anne because her Italian is so good.'

'Why is she upset?' said Nettlebury.

Laszlo leaned forward and whispered in his ear, 'Because of the Anglican ceremony. In the eyes of the Church, Anne isn't really married. I think she may go off soon and pray for a conversion before bedtime.'

Nettlebury laughed. 'That's one thing I like about you Catholics, you don't take yourselves seriously.'

Laszlo smiled at him a little sadly, and was about to answer when it was announced that Anne and Gideon were about to depart for their hotel. They all stood on the steps and waved as the car drove away.

Irene turned to Nettlebury. 'Oh, I wish it were me,' she said suddenly.

Nettlebury put his arms around her. 'Your day will come soon enough,' he said softly.

They stayed in Rome for five more days, and Gideon began to see the city with new eyes – Anne's eyes.

Early on the sixth day of their marriage, Vittorio assembled them all at the station for the start of their journey to Cervinia. Irene had been given a special dispensation by her father to take a holiday from school, and she chattered endlessly, and with increasing fluency, in Italian to the eldest of Vittorio's daughters. Gideon had gone to buy cigarettes at the kiosk. When he returned, he found Vittorio reassuring Nettlebury, who had grave doubts about his ability to cope with skiing.

'It is like swimming, Julian,' Vittorio said. 'You can do the easy parts or the dangerous, just as you wish.'

Gideon's parents seemed unconcerned. They simply regarded the whole business as a new part that would be mastered as all others had been.

Laszlo pointed to his wife, who had reverted to her old, sullen self. 'Sylvia can ski. Tell them how easy it is.'

She turned and regarded them all with contempt. 'Skiing is very dangerous,' she said flatly. 'Many people are killed all the time.'

Vera turned to Nettlebury, and shrugged. 'If I die, make sure my husband pays for an expensive funeral, darling.'

Vittorio decided to divert the conversation. 'Time to get on board,' he shouted, waving them on to the train. 'We are all in these carriages.'

Once on board, they arranged themselves in the dining-car. Gideon and Anne shared a table with Nettlebury, Vera and his parents; Irene paired off with the eldest of the Castelli girls. Vittorio sat with the rest of his family and Laszlo with Sylvia, who was complaining that she was unwell. Gideon noticed that she managed to eat a substantial meal despite her illness, before lying back against the headrest and going to sleep. After a time Laszlo squeezed next to Vittorio, at his invitation, and they began a game of chess with the travel set Vittorio had brought. By the time twilight came they had all begun to doze, with the exception of Irene and her companion, who continued to talk without a break.

Gideon woke with a start when the train jerked to a halt in Milan, and heard the end of a muttered conversation between Laszlo and Sylvia. It was not conducted in the friendliest of terms but they stopped when the others began to arouse themselves.

Once they had disembarked from the train, Vittorio took command again, and led the procession which was now accompanied by a quartet of porters wheeling their piles of luggage to the waiting taxis. 'I know a wonderful restaurant for dinner,' he called to them. 'I'll see you all in the lobby of the hotel at eight o'clock.'

At one minute past eight, Gideon and Anne descended the staircase of the hotel and found Vittorio counting heads. 'Only Laszlo and his wife are absent,' he said.

Gideon told him, 'Laszlo just telephoned. Sylvia is still not feeling well. They aren't coming with us.'

Vera and Nettlebury exchanged glances, but no one made any further comment. Vittorio led them a short walk to a large restaurant, where he was greeted with great affection by the staff. They were shown to a private room and food began to arrive in a steady stream. Course followed course and each was delicious. The Castellis ate with such determined gusto that Anne marvelled at the slimness of Vittorio's wife. Then she remembered Elizabeth's ability to eat huge amounts. She looked down at the great slice of creamy cake that had been forced on her by the wife of the restaurateur, and took up her fork again.

Eventually she could eat no more. She sat back with a sigh and pushed her plate away. She said to Gideon in a low voice, 'Do you think everything is all right with Laszlo and Sylvia?'

He smiled at something Vittorio called to him, but said, 'No, but I'm not going to let her spoil things for us.'

When they returned to their room in the hotel, next door to that occupied by Laszlo and Sylvia, they could hear the rise and fall of angry voices, followed by a slamming door.

Later Anne lay with her head upon his shoulder. 'Will you promise me one thing?' she said.

'What?'

'If ever in our life together I act like Sylvia, you will say the word "Milano" to me.'

'You have my word,' he answered with feeling.

The last part of their journey was by motor-bus through the Val d'Aosta, where heavy snow was falling from a lead-grey sky. Eventually, when they had been climbing for some time, the driver stopped at a small hotel built of wood in the Alpine fashion.

'We have coffee here while the driver puts chains on the wheels,' Vittorio announced.

They got out of the bus, and Gideon held Anne's hand and breathed in the cold damp air. The snow did not settle on the road; the tarred surface stretched ahead of them, black as liquorice, until it merged into the falling snow. Now that the others had gone into the little bar, the silence was absolute. Heavily laden pine trees stood each side of them in the shadowless snow and the air was filled with their scent, mingling with the drift of burning wood from the hotel. The words of a song came to Gideon's mind; without him speaking, Anne recited them aloud.

'When the valley's hushed and white with snow,' she said softly. She turned and hugged him. 'Oh, Danny boy, oh, Danny boy, I love you so.'

'Mrs Gideon, Mr Gideon,' someone called, and they saw it was one of the Castelli girls. 'Mama says, do you want coffee?'

'Yes, thank you,' Anne replied. 'We're coming now.' She put her arm through Gideon's. 'Do you know, that's the first time anyone has called me that?' she said as they walked towards the little bar.

By the time they arrived at the village, the skies had cleared and the snow-clad mountains stood above them in crystal clarity against the cloudless blue.

'Fresh snow,' Vittorio said, as they stood on the steps of the hotel. The skiing will be perfect.'

'Doesn't the Matterhorn look wonderful?' Vera said to Nettlebury.

Sylvia overheard her. 'It looks better from our side,' she said curtly.

'Your side?' Vera repeated.

'Switzerland,' Laszlo answered. 'It's just over there.'

When they had deposited the luggage with the hotel porter, Vittorio and his wife took them shopping in the narrow main street. They spent the next two hours buying a bewildering array of clothes and equipment, with the exception of Sylvia, who negotiated the purchase of a second-hand pair of skis and boots from the manager of the first shop they entered and then returned to the hotel.

Back in the street, Nettlebury turned to Vera. 'This is like being in the trenches again,' he grumbled as they slipped and stumbled across the impacted snow, clutching their awkward loads of skis, bags and boxes.

'Don't the views inspire you?' she replied.

Nettlebury shook his head and reached out to steady himself with a ski-pole. 'Frankly, no. I find this kind of scenery obvious; a bit like bananas.'

'Bananas? Why bananas?' Gideon asked.

'I've always considered them the most boring fruit,' he answered loftily. 'As an object, they lack dignity.'

'You can't say the Matterhorn looks like a banana, Dad,' Anne said, chiding him.

'I most certainly can. Look at the top.' They looked up. 'You see? The top is bent in a decidedly banana-like fashion.'

'You know, he's right,' Gideon said after a moment of studying the mountain. 'It is bent like a banana.'

'Don't pander to him. He's just grumpy because he doesn't like doing new things,' said Vera.

But when they eventually got to the nursery slopes, which consisted of a wide, gently sloping snowfield, nothing turned out as they had expected. Gideon's parents, Nettlebury, Anne and Irene found their balance almost immediately, but Vera and Gideon floundered about awkwardly, like drunken stick-insects.

After an hour or so Nettlebury started issuing instructions to Vera, who had fallen over and embedded her skis in a deep bank of snow. 'It's all a matter of one's centre of gravity. You should lean forward more and bend your knees a little.'

Vera looked up from her struggle and gave him a look of pure hatred. 'Julian, I shall break the rules of good manners that were instilled in me in childhood,' she said quietly. 'Now, will you please piss off.'

'Well, if you're going to be so unreasonable, I shall let you get on with it,' he said, and slowly glided away.

200

At the first hint of twilight, they sat on a bench at the edge of the snowfield where they had practised and wearily unstrapped their skis.

'That chap's moving fast!' Gideon said, and Anne looked up to watch a figure hurtling down the last steep stretch of mountain.

'Good Lord, it's Laszlo,' Nettlebury said when the figure got closer. 'I didn't know he could ski like that.'

As he finished the sentence, the Hungarian crossed the wide expanse of the nursery slope in a curving sweep and stopped before them in a spray of snow. 'I am buying champagne in the bar at seven o'clock,' he said cheerfully, and then quickly unwound his bindings and hurried ahead in the direction of the hotel.

'Where is Sylvia?' Anne asked Gideon as they watched his receding figure. 'I thought they went up in the cable-car together.'

'Perhaps he pushed her off the mountain,' he replied without interest, and reached down to unlace his boots.

Gideon arrived at the bar earlier than the others, and was in the mood for a drink after the day's frustrating exertions. Laszlo was already there, and clearly in high spirits. Gideon knew him well enough to realise that he had drunk more than usual.

'I have champagne on ice, but I suspect you would prefer a large whisky,' he said.

Gideon nodded. 'What are we drinking to?' he asked, when the barman set the drink before him.

'Sylvia and I are no longer married,' said Laszlo.

Gideon looked at him in bewilderment. 'How is that possible? Surely your . . . ' He did not finish the sentence.

Laszlo swallowed the last of his drink and gestured to the barman for another bottle. 'All the time we were in Rome, she was arranging for annulment. That was after I refused to end our partnership.' He laid a hand on Gideon's shoulder. 'She tried her best to stop your marriage taking place when we were in America. When that didn't work, she decided to end ours.'

'Are you sorry?' Gideon asked.

Laszlo shook his head. 'My dear fellow, I feel as if I had just been told I do not have a terminal illness.'

'Where is she now?'

'Back home in Zermatt, I suppose. I took her to the top of the

201

mountain, presented her with a cheque and she skied away in the direction of Switzerland.'

Gideon paused and drank a deep draught before he asked his next question. 'How much did you give her?'

Laszlo smiled. 'Two hundred thousand pounds.'

Gideon looked at him, and had to smile back. 'You mad bastard! That was your profit from the sale of the Whitney-Ingram Collection. Are you sure it was worth it?'

Laszlo nodded. 'Life without Sylvia is the sort of bargain that would be cheap at any price!' He turned to the window in the bar, and raised his drink in a salute towards Switzerland.

CHAPTER NINE

London, early summer 1939

It was ten past nine, and for the last fifteen minutes Mrs Cooper had carried out her usual litany of warnings to Irene that she should very soon set off for school.

Irene called back at last, 'I'm coming now.' But instead of leaving her bedroom, she turned and looked into her wardrobe mirror. There was an expression of deep satisfaction on her face, but her smile of triumph was not so much for the reflection she saw but for the knowledge that she was seeing it for the last time. She had hated the grey felt hat, dark green blazer and flat, sensible shoes for as long as she could remember, but she would never put on the uniform or make the journey again after today.

She supposed she would miss her friends, who were, in the words of her headmistress, to be 'scattered like grains of wheat into the world of adulthood'. Irene herself was ready to be scattered with all possible haste, and had bought two new dresses the previous Saturday in anticipation of the event. She took one last look at herself, pulled her blazer tight across her middle to reveal the glories of her concealed figure, turned for the door, picked up a larger bag than her customary satchel, and sang, 'Poor Butterfly' as she descended the stairs.

She was still singing when she entered the kitchen, where her father was lingering over his breakfast. Mrs Cooper looked up from the stove where she was preparing toast.

Irene took one of the slices, and said to Mrs Cooper, 'They have a machine in America called an automatic toaster. You just put the slices of bread into it and they pop up when they're done.'

'Does the machine put butter on as well?' Mrs Cooper replied. She turned round. 'Are you going to have a proper breakfast today, young lady?' Her tone of voice told Irene that she already knew the answer.

203

'Just a cup of tea, thank you,' she replied, and kissed her father on the top of his head.

He snapped his copy of *The Times* by way of a reply. 'And how are you going to spend your last day at school,' he asked, setting the newspaper aside and spreading marmalade on his toast. 'Conjugating Latin verbs, or silent prayer in the chapel?'

Irene drank some tea before she answered. 'First we go about the classrooms and cheer all the teachers we like. After that we burn our hats in the quad, next to the boiler-room. When that's done, we link arms and walk around the buildings twice while we sing the school song and give one last cheer at the Main Gate; then we're going to see the afternoon showing of *The Petrified Forest* at the Walpole Cinema in Ealing.'

'And what time can we expect you home after these fascinating rituals?' he asked.

Irene picked up a piece of his toast and took a bite. 'About six o'clock.' She kissed him again before hurrying from the house. She had arranged to meet Pamela Masters at the bus-stop and was now a few minutes late.

Nettlebury munched his toast and sat for a while looking out of the kitchen window at pink-flecked clouds in the pale blue morning sky.

'It doesn't seem possible that she's leaving school, does it?' Mrs Cooper said.

'Oh, I don't know, Maude. She just seems young. Remember, Anne was looking after us when she was Irene's age.'

Mrs Cooper placed the used crockery in the sink, and then poured herself a cup of tea. 'They grow up fast when they leave school,' she said wistfully. 'Pity, really.'

Irene had to run the last few yards, as the bus was approaching the stop, but Pamela Masters pleaded with the conductor to wait, and luckily he was in a good humour.

'Did you bring it all?' Pamela asked when they were sitting in the back seats of the upper deck.

Irene nodded, tapping the large bag on her lap. 'What about you?'

'I had to borrow a pair of my mother's shoes. I don't suppose I shall be able to walk at all; her feet are much smaller than mine.'

Irene looked down on the grey-green waters of the Thames as they crossed Kew Bridge. It was a beautiful day, but the air around them was thick with tobacco smoke. She was still breathing heavily from her run, but they did not wind down the window until they were clear of the Gas Works in Brentford, and the last lingering sulphurous smells dispersed. They were now looking down on little front gardens filled with summer flowers in South Ealing Road. The bus skirted a milk-cart, and the white-coated milkman took a marigold and placed it carefully in his buttonhole before he climbed back to the high seat behind his horse.

'I shall miss this journey,' Pamela said, sighing like a Russian heroine forced to leave her homeland.

'Well, I shan't!' Irene replied in matter-of-fact tones as they came to a halt at a request stop. 'I shall be catching the same bus here every day.' She nodded towards the large red-brick Edwardian building behind a fringe of lime trees on the opposite side of the road.

'Of course,' Pamela said as if she had temporarily forgotten. 'The West London Technical College.'

'And School of Art, Pamela,' Irene said tartly.

Her friend laughed. 'Yes, I keep forgetting: London University is such an easy title to remember.'

Irene would not let her have the last word. 'But when somebody asks you what you do, trainee laboratory assistant is much harder to say than art student, isn't it?'

'I suppose so. Anyway, lab assistant or art student – either is better than what Edith and Wendy face.'

Irene nodded. Edith Barclay and Wendy Archer were their two other closest friends, and both were beginning their training at a secretarial college in Oxford the following term.

Pamela went on, 'My mother said the place was no better than a marriage mart. The whole idea is that they meet someone eligible from the university.'

Irene considered the possibility. 'Suppose you meet someone eligible at the hospital?'

Pamela thought for a moment. 'I shall marry him and continue with my career, of course.' The bus came to a halt at the terminal in Ealing Broadway.

'Come on,' Irene said, leading the charge down the stairs. Pamela clattered after her and they stood on the pavement, laughing, as they had many times throughout their childhood.

When they approached the school, Irene kept telling herself that everything she saw or passed was being observed for the last time: the trees that lined the streets of solid Victorian villas; the stream of

205

similarly dressed girls that became a flood as they approached the high-walled grounds. She felt both sad and happy.

When they eventually passed through the gates, Pamela said, 'Do you know, I want to dance and cry at the same time.' Irene knew what she meant.

The morning assembly followed the same pattern as every year, but, as always, the words spoken and the hymns sung brought lumps to the throats and tears to the eyes of the girls who were leaving. As predicted, in her valediction the headmistress compared them to grains of wheat. They sang 'To Be a Pilgrim', said prayers, sang the school song, and then the festivities began. The ritual the girls performed remained exactly as it had in all other years, until after the hat-burning ceremony. Then there was a change. Irene and her three friends disappeared into the cloakrooms and a guard was posted on the door. Half an hour later they re-emerged and, to the astonishment of the waiting girls, they now wore make-up and had discarded their school uniforms in favour of high heels and summer frocks. In Irene's case, the transformation was even more daring, as she now possessed a pair of fully fashioned nylons that belonged to Anne.

The long sound of a collective 'Aaaah' ran through the ranks of girls standing on the wide expanse of asphalt that served as the playground. Known in the vocabulary of the school as the quad, this area was ruled by the prefects, and teachers rarely ventured there. Usually such a breach of discipline would have brought instant retribution, but until the end of the day, Irene and her friends were still the prefects who would have prescribed the punishment. It was a case of revolution by the aristocracy. For a few moments, silence fell upon the crowd, then there were waves of cheering.

Irene and her companions linked arms and led the rest of the girls in their final procession around the school. At the gate, the final farewell took place before they set off towards the Walpole Cinema. Pamela Masters was less steady than the others. As she had predicted, her mother's shoes pinched her feet dreadfully.

The sun shone down on them as they walked together through the quiet suburban streets and they laughed and chattered about the reaction to their rebellion. Ealing Common was lush with summer greenness, and they walked in the shade of horse chestnuts heavy with dense foliage. Road-menders in the Broadway called out to them as they passed. The girls held their heads high and looked straight ahead, but giggled in appreciation of the coarse compliments. Once past the church, they turned left and entered the little cinema. Irene felt almost sinful when she paid for her ticket; they had so often been told at school that attending a cinema in the afternoon was not the proper pursuit for a young lady.

Inside the thinly populated auditorium, Edith Barclay directed them where to sit in the darkness. 'On the right side,' she hissed, 'near the back row.'

They settled down after a series of shuffling bumps and giggles, and gradually their eyes became accustomed to the gloom. The newsreel had just begun, and the girls paid only scant attention to a series of images depicting marching troops and tanks moving through cities. After a few minutes, Edith passed a packet of Player's cigarettes along the line. Irene did not really want to smoke, but accepted one to go along with the spirit of the occasion.

'Do you think there's going to be a war?' Pamela said to Irene.

'My father does.'

'All the boys will go away if there is,' Pamela said in a hushed voice. 'That's what it was like in the last war, my mother told me.' She paused. 'Most of them will get killed, too.'

'Well, you'd better make the most of us while we're here, hadn't you?' a voice said close by.

Pamela turned round quickly. It was Edith's cousin William, with a collection of classmates who were also celebrating the last of their schooldays. Although they had arranged the encounter, Irene felt rather shy at the sudden proximity of the youths. She turned, and the light from the screen revealed their faces. She recognised that of the furthest from her – it was Richard Cleary, dressed in some kind of uniform. The others wore sports jackets, in the fashion of their school. There were a few minutes of whispered negotiation, and then Irene was instructed by Edith to leave a space between herself and Pamela Masters.

The boys now scrambled to take the empty seats between the girls, and Irene found she had been paired with someone who seemed vaguely familiar.

'Remember me?' he asked. 'I was the one at the dance with a broken nose.'

Irene felt her heart sink at his words. She accepted another cigarette from Edith, and waited. His arm slowly encircled her shoulder when the feature film began. He made another move, but she pushed his hand firmly away when it approached her left breast. He sighed a few times and glanced enviously along the row at the contortions of his more successful friends, then settled down reluctantly, and, like Irene, began to take an interest in the unfolding plot of the film. Before it came to an end, the youth made one more attempt to breach Irene's indifference, but his clumsily aimed kiss landed to the side of her firmly closed lips.

When they all eventually trooped out and stood blinking in the afternoon sunlight, Irene saw that Richard Cleary, with his arm round Pamela, wore Air Cadet uniform. Irene's partner moved away, trying to give the impression that he had no further interest in her. Richard Cleary and Pamela leaned against the cinema doorway, and Irene went to join them.

'I'm not getting the bus just yet,' Pamela said to Irene, and then gave a sudden wriggle. 'Excuse me for a moment,' she said to Cleary, and slipped back into the cinema. Irene watched her sudden retreat and then looked at Cleary.

'I expect she's gone into the ladies to button herself up again,' he said. He stared at Irene without smiling. 'I wish I'd sat next to you,' he said. Then, without speaking to the others, he turned and walked away. The boy with the broken nose called out his goodbyes and ran to catch him up.

When Pamela returned, she glanced around with a puzzled expression.

'He just suddenly walked away,' said Irene.

'We're going to Walpole Park,' said Edith. 'Do you want to come?' The invitation was not expected to be accepted by Irene and Pamela, who were now without partners.

Pamela shrugged. 'We might as well go home.' There was not too much regret in her voice. 'Anyway, he's going into the Air Force tomorrow.'

The two girls made the return journey to Kew in silence. When they crossed the Thames again, Irene noticed that she had laddered the stockings she had borrowed from Anne. Her mouth tasted sour from the cigarettes she had smoked, and she rather wished she was still wearing her school uniform.

London, 3 September 1939

When the Prime Minister had finished his melancholy broadcast, declaring that a state of war now existed between Great Britain and Germany, Nettlebury switched off the wireless and they all sat in

208

silence. Then Irene said, 'Does this mean that the art school won't open this term?'

Her father shook his head and gave her a reassuring smile. 'No, darling. A lot of things will go on as usual.'

'It won't be the same, though, will it?' she said softly.

'No, a lot of things will change.' He stood up and glanced at his watch. 'It's a bit early, but under the circumstances I think I'm going to have a drink.' He looked round the living-room. 'Anybody else?' Everyone accepted. When they all held a glass, he raised his own. 'Here's to better times.'

Anne looked at Gideon, and their eyes locked. He smiled. The same thought had occurred to them both. It would be hard to imagine better times than the ones they had lived through in the months since they had married.

Laszlo's settlement on Sylvia left him virtually penniless, so he had offered to dissolve the partnership and go to work for Gideon and Anne. They had refused to listen to his proposition, claiming that paying off Sylvia was a legitimate business expense on behalf of the gallery. When everything had been sorted out by a disapproving Mr Grierson, their assets came to a modest stock of pictures and little more than a hundred and twenty thousand pounds.

'We haven't got rich yet,' Laszlo said as they left Grierson's office.

Gideon put his arm round Anne while they waited for a taxi. 'I've got what I wanted,' he answered, and thought for only a moment about the Degas in Berlin.

In the first months of the war, business was brisk at the Archangel Gallery, but most of the custom came from a curious mixture of men and women who were leaving England and wanted to sell pictures. They were of all nationalities, with attitudes that varied from arrogance to furtiveness. A few bought, but in the manner of a last-minute shopping expedition at the end of a long, carefree holiday. In most instances, those who sold paintings insisted on payment in cash. The value of the gallery's stock rose dramatically, but there was a corresponding fall in the balance at the bank.

Finally, Anne had to deliver a lecture to Laszlo and Gideon about buying more bargains. 'It's quite simple,' she said as the three of them sat in the tiny office late one Friday evening at the end of November. 'If you go on in this way, we shall have to pay Ted and Doris their next week's wages by giving them the Matisse and the Braque the pair of you bought yesterday.'

'Are things really that bad?' Laszlo asked.

'Well, maybe not just yet, but they are going to be quite soon if you continue in this fashion.' She waved through the glass partition towards the store-room, which was so full of pictures that Ted Porter had arranged corridors through the stacks. Even Anne's tiny room was packed with the overflow. She sat now with paintings piled against her desk and had to take care when she pushed back her chair not to damage a Modigliani nude leaning against the wall.

She looked at their crestfallen faces, and suddenly laughed. 'Come on! It isn't that bad. Just don't buy anything else for a while.' She glanced at her watch. 'Goodness me, the man is coming to see the flat in half an hour. We'd better get a move on.' To economise, they had taken up a suggestion of Nettlebury's and moved into the house at Kew. Their advertisement in the evening papers had brought an instant response. She turned to Laszlo. 'What are you doing this evening?' Since Laszlo had returned to the status of bachelor, Anne had looked after him as she would a brother, making sure that he ate properly and did not wander into mischief.

Laszlo had accepted the role without question, and generally kept her informed of his movements. 'I'm meeting Paul Trenton for a drink later. I shan't see you until tomorrow, and then I'm coming to Kew for dinner.'

'Be a dear and bring some of our things from the flat, will you?' Anne asked.

'Of course. My taxi will be full to overflowing.'

They locked up the gallery and began their walk together in the direction of Shepherd Market. Laszlo had kept the mews house after Sylvia's departure, but he had removed the stifling bric-à-brac that had once cluttered it. He had filled the living-room with comfortable leather furniture, and it now looked like a gentlemen's club. Paul Trenton had occupied the old stable on the ground floor after he was evicted from his studio near Goodge Street. At first it had been a temporary arrangement, but with each passing week he added some extra comfort, and Laszlo enjoyed the company.

Despite their familiarity with the area, the journey was not easy in the blackout and traffic accidents were frequent, so it was with relief that Gideon and Anne arrived at the flat. A large black car was parked outside. In it, behind a slim young man in a camel-hair coat, two young women sat smoking cigarettes and watching other figures passing in the gloom.

The driver got out of the car. 'Mr Gideon?'

'I'm sorry. Did we keep you waiting?' Anne asked as the two young women also got out and accompanied them upstairs.

'Not at all,' he replied. 'We was just watching the comin's and goin's in the street.'

'Well, it's a bit cosmopolitan around here, isn't it, Mr . . . ?' Gideon said when they reached the living-room.

'Villiers is the name, Mr Gideon. Nigel Villiers,' the young man said, holding out a hand that was heavy with jewelled rings. 'And these are my sisters, Olivia and Merle.'

The two girls sat on the sofa. They had removed their coats and both wore satin evening dresses and long white gloves, and appeared to show no interest in their surroundings.

'Pleased to meet you,' they both said to Anne with quick smiles. They did not offer to shake hands.

Gideon let Anne show the young man round the rest of the flat. She took him into the bedroom. 'I'm afraid it's not very big,' she said ruefully.

'It's fine,' he said. He reached down and prodded the bed with his outstretched fingers. 'It'll do very nicely, Mrs Gideon,' Villiers said in a soothing voice. 'Me sisters like things cosy.'

'Oh, it's not for you, then?'

The young man shook his head, and smiled. 'No, no! Me and me wife have got a place over St John's Wood, but we wanted me sisters to have somewhere of their own. You know how young girls are – they like to come and go as they please.'

Anne suddenly looked concerned. 'Indeed I do. I have a young sister of my own.' She hesitated. 'You know, Mr Villiers, I feel I must say this to you . . . ' She looked around the bedroom for a moment.

Mr Villiers held up his hands, and spoke soothingly. 'Speak your mind, Mrs Gideon,' he said. 'Just spit it out; if you'll pardon the expression.'

Anne looked at one of Gideon's pictures that they had hung on the wall, and took a deep breath. 'Well, my husband and I are used to it here, and we also work in the art business, where the usual conventions aren't as important as they are to other people.'

Villiers had sat on the bed and was looking up at her expectantly. 'Go on, Mrs Gideon, get it off your chest,' he said encouragingly.

Anne had begun, but she now found it very difficult to continue. She wished that Gideon were with her instead of in the next room, where she could hear sounds of laughter. Finally she summoned up her courage. 'Well, the fact is, Mr Villiers,' she said in a rush, 'some

211

of the girls you may see on this street are . . . ' She stopped again and looked up at the ceiling, at the mouldings that had been blunted by so many applications of paint.

'Ladies of the night?' Villiers suggested finally.

Anne nodded. 'I'm afraid so. Not that some of them aren't very nice girls. And they're awfully friendly when you're polite to them.'

Villiers smiled. 'Say no more, dear lady. Me sisters are as sophisticated as you. They was over in Paris before the war broke out.' He reached inside his coat. 'Now, I'm very happy with everything, and here's a paper for you to sign making the next five years of the lease over to me.'

'Well, my husband will have to do that, Mr Villiers,' Anne explained. 'You see, the lease is in his name.'

They moved next door to the living-room, where Gideon had given the girls glasses of sherry. Anne could see that their earlier indifference had melted in the warmth of his charm. He signed Mr Villiers' document and, to their astonishment, the young man produced thick wads of five-pound notes from his pocket and laid them on the table.

'Five hundred pounds a year for five years. That's two thousand five hundred to you, sir.'

'Good God, I'd be happy with a cheque, Mr Villiers,' Gideon said, and he looked at the pile of notes in astonishment.

Villiers winked. 'Never bother with them, if I can avoid it.'

'Would you like a drink, then?' Gideon asked.

Villiers shook his head with a smile. 'No thanks, old man. Never touch it.' Then he turned to the two girls, and there was a warning note in his voice. 'Besides, it's early yet, and there's work to do.'

'Oh, you work at night, Mr Villiers. What do you do?' Anne asked.

'We're in the entertainment business, my dear.'

Anne sighed. 'I suppose business is good, what with the war. Ours is all over the place at the moment.'

Villiers nodded. 'Never been better,' he agreed. Then he turned to the girls. 'Come on, now; duty calls.'

'Oh, we forgot to give you a receipt for your money,' Anne said when they reached the door to the street.

Villiers shook his head. 'In my line of business you get to know people you can take on trust, Mrs Gideon.' Anne switched off the light on the stairs before she opened the door to the street.

'Goodnight,' he called out.

Anne could hardly make them out as they got into the car. When she returned, Gideon was finishing his glass of sherry, staring at the pile of money on the table.

'Well, he seemed decent enough, but his sisters were a bit off-hand until you cheered them up.' Anne switched on the wireless so that the soft sound of Bing Crosby filled the room. Gideon nodded. 'Do you want to go out to eat? I've hardly got any food in the house.'

'I don't mind,' he answered. 'I'm not very hungry.'

Anne went to look in her store-cupboard in the little kitchen off the living-room. 'Mrs Cooper has been stocking up on tinned food, you know. If the war lasts for ten years, Dad says we'll still be able to eat corned beef and baked beans.'

'Isn't that hoarding?' Gideon replied in a distracted voice.

Anne laughed. 'Mrs Cooper says, if the government says don't do something in wartime, it's time to do it.' Gideon began to hum to the music playing on the wireless. 'Shall we track Laszlo down?' Anne asked. 'He's almost certain to be in the Wheatsheaf.'

'Mmmm,' he replied.

Anne went to run a bath. She left the door open so she could hear the music, and after a while called out to Gideon, 'Darling, what kind of entertainment business do you think Mr Villiers is in? He looked to me like an impresario.'

Gideon came and stood in the doorway; he enjoyed watching her bathe. 'I'm sure you're right.'

'And what about the girls? They looked as if they could be dancers.'

'I doubt if they're dancers. I think they're probably members of an older profession.' He took the sponge she handed him and began to soap her back.

Suddenly Anne sat up very straight in the bath and looked round at Gideon. 'Do you mean our dear little flat is going to be a . . . ' she said slowly.

'A house of ill repute?' He nodded. 'It seems so, darling.'

'What could you have been thinking of?' Anne said, shocked.

'Actually,' he replied, 'I was thinking of going to Paris.'

It took a week for Gideon to acquire the necessary permits to make his journey, even though he received a good deal of help from Colonel Middleton at the Foreign Office. He finally set off the following Saturday morning and, after nearly three days of travelling on painfully slow trains and boats, arrived feeling distinctly grubby, as twilight was descending at the Gare du Nord.

Before he set about his business he bade a friendly farewell to the young man who had been his constant companion since leaving Victoria.

'Goodbye, Mr Peake,' he said to the worried young man struggling under the weight of two large suitcases. 'I do hope you secure your order for all those gramophone needles.'

'Me life won't be worth living if I don't, Mr Gideon,' he said in a London accent. 'It's not the Guv'nor – he's not a bad old stick – it's me wife and her mother are the ones who give me bloody hell. I'll give you some advice: never marry the boss's daughter.'

They shook hands at the taxi rank and Gideon watched him depart before he found a telephone cabin to ring Henri Bronstein. After a long delay he was connected, and felt considerable pleasure at hearing the old man's voice again.

'Forgive me for not ringing before, but I was unsure how long my journey from England would take,' Gideon explained.

'Not at all, dear boy, it is delightful to hear from you. How can I be of service to the Archangel Gallery?' Bronstein asked with his usual display of exquisite manners.

Some time later, Gideon's taxi drew to a halt in the Avenue Foch, and the driver announced he could get no closer to the address he had been given. As soon as he alighted, Gideon could see the reason for the obstruction. Six huge lorries were parked in front of Bronstein's house, and a collection of burly men were loading them with packing-cases. Because of the blackout, they were working by the light of shaded lamps. The foreman took a few moments off to put Gideon in the care of a footman, who led him through the house to Bronstein's office. It was a room Gideon had never seen before and he was a little surprised by the austere modern furniture and unadorned walls.

Bronstein got up from behind the plain metal desk where he was working, and shook hands. 'You seem surprised at my little retreat?' he said, gesturing for Gideon to sit in a plain straight-backed chair. He nodded, and the old man laughed. 'In my youth it was beautiful women that distracted me from my labours, but as I grew old it became beautiful objects. Now, if I wish to concentrate my mind, I must choose these spartan surroundings.' Bronstein took his gold watch out of the pocket of his velvet coat and glanced at the time. 'You have come straight from the station? Have you dined?'

'Not yet,' Gideon said, and he described some of the rigours of his journey.

214

The old man shook his head in sympathy, and rang for a footman. 'Mr Gideon will be staying here for the night and we shall require dinner in one hour,' he instructed. 'Please take him to his room.'

Gideon was led along one of the endless corridors, and from below he could hear the sound of humming and the noise of men moving heavy loads. When he was escorted back to Bronstein's presence for dinner, the surroundings were more in accordance with his host's usual taste. He was in a room delicately arranged with eighteenth-century furniture and lit with dozens of dancing candle-flames. Twin clocks began to chime in unison, and Bronstein rose to greet him from the small table set for the meal. Wine was served, and the host accepted a small glass.

'I suppose you are wondering about the removal men?' he said.

'Yes, I was. Are you storing the collection?'

Bronstein nodded. 'Until the end of this war. I wonder if I shall see them unpacked again.'

'Are you as gloomy as that about the outcome? Nothing much seems to be happening. There's talk that we could win quite soon.'

Bronstein held his glass up to a candle-flame. 'Yes,' he said with a sigh. 'And when I heard them say the Maginot Line was impregnable, I began to make my plans. Everything goes into Switzerland for the duration.' He took a fragment of bread from his side plate, but cast it aside. 'Ironic, to consign one's life-work to a tomb inside a mountain.'

'You think Switzerland is safe?' Gideon asked.

'For money and for objects. People can be unsafe anywhere.' Then he became brisk, in his usual fashion. 'Why do you wish to see me?'

Gideon was used to his sudden swings of mood, and was equally businesslike when he answered. 'The Archangel Gallery has a problem about available cash,' he said plainly.

Bronstein nodded. 'Too many good pictures on the market – too little money?' he asked.

'Yes. How did you know?'

'It is obvious,' Bronstein said without emotion. 'Paintings are easy to transport, but nothing is as convenient as hard currency when you are moving from country to country. There is a big demand for that particular commodity, these days.'

Bronstein took another sip of wine and put down the glass with a look of regret. He reached towards a box inlaid with silver and mother-of-pearl, which Gideon had assumed contained cigars. He

215

took out two envelopes and placed them beside Gideon's plate. One was flat, the other much thicker. 'Open them,' he instructed. 'The slim envelope contains the list of pictures I am interested in buying from the Archangel Gallery. There are also details of how I wish them to be stored in the caves at Chislehurst in Kent. The second contains one hundred thousand dollars in high-denomination banknotes.'

Gideon took the slim envelope and read through Bronstein's list.

'Agreed?' Bronstein asked when Gideon looked up.

'You've been more than generous, I would say by at least twenty thousand dollars.'

Bronstein smiled, and shook his head. 'No. There is an additional service I wish you to render, but I shall explain that to you later, if I may.'

Gideon finished eating, and Bronstein consulted his watch again, even as the twin clocks chimed ten o'clock. 'If you will excuse me, I have some work I must attend to. But if you wish to go out for the rest of the evening, please feel free to use a car I have put at your disposal.'

Although he felt tired from the journey, Gideon accepted Bronstein's offer; he did feel like a few hours on the town. He was curious to see how the city compared with war-time London, and he had found in the past that Paris was one of the few places where one could be perfectly content with one's own company. He left the house, and picked his way through the workers once more to find a Citroën parked further along the Avenue Foch. A driver awaited him. He instructed the man to take him to the Left Bank and, after a slow journey, got out in the Boulevard St Germain. At the Café Flore, the tables on the pavement were empty in the darkness, but light and noise came from beyond the doorway curtain.

He half-expected to see someone he knew inside the crowded room, but was astonished to find his mother and father at a side table. Waiters squeezed past as he leaned forward to greet them.

'Hello, darling! We thought we might find you here,' Marjorie said after they kissed.

'Mother, how on earth could you expect to find me in Paris?' He pulled up an unoccupied chair from another table.

'We saw Anne yesterday. She told us you were over here, and said that this was one of your favourite haunts.'

'But how did you get here so soon?' he asked.

'A perfectly sweet general brought us in his aeroplane,' said Marjorie. 'We arrived this afternoon.'

'Why would a general give you a lift?' Gideon had to speak in quite

216

a loud voice; the room was overcrowded and very noisy.

'We're over here to entertain the troops,' his father said. 'Building morale, that sort of stuff. I bumped into our agent in the Ivy and he said everyone is working these days. Jugglers, animal acts, conjurors, even old actors like us.'

'What are you going to give our gallant lads, Dad?' Gideon asked, but he already knew the answer.

'Oh, *Romeo and Juliet*, I suppose,' Frank said airily.

Gideon was about to comment on Shakespeare's probable popularity with the British Expeditionary Force, but instead he suddenly jumped to his feet. 'Just a minute.' He called out, 'Mr Peake!'

The ginger-haired young man with whom he had journeyed from England had entered the café and was gazing around in the noisy bustle. He turned in astonishment at the sound of his name, and then recognised Gideon. 'Well, fancy seeing you here! What a surprise, Mr Gideon.'

'Paris is that sort of city, Mr Peake. It's much smaller than London,' Gideon said, waving for a waiter. 'Look at me, I've just met my mother and father.' He introduced them.

'Pleased to meet you,' Mr Peake said, looking round the crowded café. 'Well, this is nice; and what a turn-up. It must be my lucky day!'

'Did you find the man you were looking for?' Gideon asked.

'He'd been waiting at the hotel for me since Tuesday, and he took me entire stock.'

'What, all those gramophone needles?'

'They wasn't gramophone needles, Mr Gideon. I kept telling you on the journey.' He turned to Gideon's parents. 'They was special needles for valves, the best steel you can get. The man practically went down on his knees when he saw them. He used to get his supplies from Germany.' He reached into his pocket and pulled out a handkerchief which he carefully unfolded, and there, nestling in the centre, were twelve glittering diamonds of various sizes. 'This is what he give me in exchange.'

'Are you sure they're real?' Gideon asked in amazement.

Peake did not reply. Instead, he took a diamond and scratched the side of Marjorie's brandy glass carefully.

She was impressed. 'You must tell us your entire adventure,' she instructed him, and they ordered more drink.

They sat talking until long past midnight, when Gideon's parents finally decided it was time for bed. He bade farewell to Mr Peake again, and the driver took him back to the Avenue Foch. The lorries had departed and the house seemed silent, but the chief steward was waiting for him.

'Monsieur Bronstein is in the drawing-room, sir. He asked if you would care to join him, if you are not too tired.'

Bronstein was sitting by a window looking down on Avenue Foch. He turned and nodded when Gideon entered. 'I felt a little lonely without my pictures, and there is still the service you are to render me.'

Gideon sat down in the chair opposite and tried to blink away his tiredness.

On Bronstein's instructions, Gideon had made his way across France to Switzerland. It had taken several days and devious routes, and now he was on the Geneva–Basle express. Although the train was crowded, it ran with the usual Swiss regularity, and he had managed to get a seat in a third-class compartment. He flicked through some German magazines he had purchased in Geneva, but as the train moved north, disturbing thoughts came to him and induced a feeliing of foreboding.

The smoky interior of the station at Basle seemed normal enough: travellers trudged wearily about the concourse under the burden of suitcases, mothers held the hands of sleepy children, people clutched tickets with the preoccupied look of those unsure of their correct platform. As always, there was a sprinkling of the wealthy, who conveyed the impression that no train would dare to depart without them. But then the foreboding came again when he reminded himself that a few kilometres away lay the German frontier; not the Germany of Beethoven, beer, street bands and laughing operetta, but a sulphurous war machine, ominous and threatening, like a dread left over from childhood horror stories.

In the crowded buffet, he found a table that was just being vacated. The clock above the bar showed five minutes to nine. Whoever had worked out his schedule had at least been considerate. He looked over his shoulder to where a man sweeping the floor had begun a mild argument with a scruffy individual a few tables away. Since the discussion was in Italian, he could not follow the nuances of their insults. When he turned back again, Karl Schneider was standing in front of him.

Schneider held out his hand, and after a slight hesitation, Gideon took it. 'Are we still permitted to shake hands?' Gideon said in a low

218

voice. 'After all, our countries are at war.'

Schneider sat down and straightened the lapels of his dark double-breasted suit, then took out a packet of cigarettes. Gideon was surprised to see that they were English: Capstan Full Strength. Schneider lit one and produced his cigarette-holder. 'My dear fellow, *our* countries are not at war,' he said cheerfully. 'I am a citizen of Switzerland.' He held up the brown packet. 'I don't even smoke German cigarettes now.'

'You're Swiss? But you're a German prince! You once told me you were on Goering's staff.'

'I also told you I believed in decent insurance cover,' said Schneider. 'Fortunately, my mother's family all come from Zurich.'

'So you have dual nationality?'

Schneider shook his head. 'Not at the moment, old boy. I have no desire to spend any time in field grey, which is how everyone in Germany will end up if that corporal has his way. I am now one hundred per cent Swiss.' He smiled. 'Mind you, I still perform one or two little tasks for my old employer. I understand you have something for him?'

Gideon reached inside his pocket and handed over the piece of paper, which his companion folded inside his passport and put away. 'I at least expected a hollow heel in your shoe!'

Schneider grinned. 'No one would ever be suspected of carrying secret papers in their passport. Believe me, it's much safer there.' He glanced around quickly, and then back to Gideon. 'So how are my friends in London? You know, I miss you all these days.'

But Gideon was still curious about the list he had carried from Geneva. 'Tell me, can you still get people out?'

'Sometimes,' Schneider said carefully. 'You must understand the situation. Hitler does not want war with France and England – he says so repeatedly. He just wants a free hand to attack Russia. That's why he is so accommodating towards both your countries. But his patience will not last, and then there will be no more compromises.'

Gideon looked at his watch; his train departed in fifteen minutes. 'How is Elizabeth? Are you married now?'

When Schneider lowered his eyes, Gideon sensed that something was wrong. 'We did not get married in the end. There were problems.' He took the cigarette-end from the holder and began to stub it out methodically. He did not take his eyes from the table.

'What sorts of problems?' Gideon asked, realising that Schneider was reluctant to speak on the subject.

'Did you know she became a German citizen?' Schneider asked without looking up.

'She told me that was her intention.'

'She wanted to be married in a German ceremony,' Schneider said slowly. 'It is the law now that one must prove one's Aryan ancestry.'

'So I understand.'

Schneider shrugged. 'They discovered that her maternal grandmother was Jewish. It made things a little difficult for me, I can tell you. Luckily Goering laughed and just said I'd had a narrow escape.'

'What about Elizabeth? Isn't she in danger?'

Schneider shrugged again. 'She was more of an embarrassment to the authorities. They wanted to get her out of Germany – just bundle her off to America – but you know how she can be neurotic at times. She started kicking up a fuss, going around with Jews, that sort of thing. I haven't seen her in some time.'

Gideon stood up, suddenly filled with contempt. He reached down and seized Schneider by his lapel. People at surrounding tables looked up at the disturbance, and the man with the broom hurried towards them.

'Find her, Schneider,' he snarled. 'Find her and look after her. Or, as God is my witness, I'll find *you* one day!'

The cleaner was standing three feet away with his broom held as if it were a rifle. Gideon released Schneider, and turned to him.

'This creature belongs outside with the rest of the rubbish,' he said in German, and then his train was announced over the loudspeaker.

The bright winter sun shafted through the windows of the French Pub, dividing the long room into rectangles of light and deep shadow. Laszlo stood at the crowded bar and looked back at his companions to remind himself of the drinks they'd ordered: pints of bitter for Nettlebury and Hammond Shelley, whisky for Paul Trenton and his blonde, and a Pernod for himself. He poured water into his own glass until the liquid turned opaque, then looked up at the barman.

'Sorry, no whisky left,' the man said. Laszlo had to shout over the roar of conversation from the other customers to ask Trenton what he'd like instead.

'Beer, then,' Trenton replied. When Laszlo conveyed the drinks to the party, he heard him say, 'Laszlo served me with my call-up papers today.'

'I merely handed you your mail,' Laszlo said, seeing the look of dismay on the face of the blonde. 'I played no official role in the communication.'

'Can't you say you're in a reserved occupation?' the girl asked.

Trenton laughed. 'In time of war, my lovely, being an abstract painter is about the least impressive role a member of the population can lay claim to.' He put down his beer. 'Can't you picture the scene?' He puffed out his chest and spoke in a clipped voice. 'So, Mr Trenton, you claim you play a useful part in society, and your gallant death on the battlefield would rob future generations of the fruits of your genius. What exactly do you do?'

'I'm a painter, sir.'

'Painter, painter? What sort of painter? Houses, boats?'

'No, sir. On canvas with oil paints.'

'Oh, an artist. Jolly good. So you could do pictures of Germans raping nuns, that sort of thing?'

'No, sir, that's not really my sort of work. I'm an abstract artist.'

'Abstract, abstract? What does that mean?'

'It means that my pictures don't contain the forms or colours that are found in nature, sir.'

'You mean no one can understand what you've done when you've done it?'

'Some people can, sir.'

'Foreigners, you mean? The sort of people we're fighting against?'

'No, sir, the exact opposite. The Germans have banned abstract art. Hitler says it's degenerate.'

'Does he? Hmmm, I always said that his ideas weren't all bad. Well, thank you very much, Mr Trenton. I'm going to recommend that you be posted to the First Battalion of the Royal Suicide Fusiliers. They had a fine record in the last war; none of them came back alive.'

'Thank you very much, sir.'

Laszlo, Shelley and Nettlebury laughed, but the blonde was not amused by the performance.

Trenton stared without humour along the crowded bar. At least half of the people were in uniform. 'You know, they're probably right. What in blistering hell is the point in my trying to paint anything in times like these?' he said.

Hammond Shelley shook his head. 'A lot of good work was done in the last war.' He nodded at Nettlebury. 'Julian here did some of his best stuff.'

'I'm thinking about abstract painting,' Trenton said almost dreamily. 'Perhaps a state of war is an abstract in itself.'

'Kandinsky managed to paint it rather well,' said Shelley. 'So did some of the Futurists.'

'I think you're both talking tripe,' Nettlebury said decisively. 'The world's baffling enough for people without you bastards trying to confuse them more. Particularly in wartime.'

'Are you working at the moment?' Trenton asked him.

'I just started a big picture.'

'What subject?' Hammond asked, draining his glass.

'Buy me a pint and I'll tell you,' Nettlebury said as he finished his own beer.

'Not for me,' the blonde said. 'I'm on in half an hour.' She turned to Trenton. 'Are you coming?'

'I suppose so,' he said moodily. 'Sometimes I hate fucking culture.'

They said their farewells and Laszlo turned to Nettlebury. 'What does that young lady do? I was under the impression she was a cinema usherette.'

'That's his other girl. This one plays the viola with the London Symphony Orchestra. Apparently she is absolutely brilliant,' Nettlebury replied. 'They're giving a lunch-time concert at the National Gallery. Elgar, I believe.'

Hammond Shelley returned with the drinks. 'So, tell me about this new piece of work.'

'It's called *The Ascent of Mankind*,' Nettlebury replied. 'Large canvas, big stuff.'

'How long will it take?' Hammond asked.

Nettlebury shrugged his shoulders and felt for his pipe. 'The last one I did on this scale was five years in the painting, but I learned a lot in the process. So, maybe three or four years.'

There was a short silence while they contemplated the size of the task before him. Along the bar, three soldiers began to sing 'Roll Out the Barrel'.

'Christ,' Shelley exclaimed eventually, 'the world could come to an end by then! Just how big is it going to be?'

'It will match the other picture, which is fifty feet by twelve,' Nettlebury replied evenly.

Hammond did some mental calculations. 'Six hundred square feet,' he said slowly. 'Dear God, man, you might as well make it a triptych. Then you'll know what you'll be doing until 1948.'

Nettlebury smiled. 'And what would you suggest as the third

222

section?'

'Why don't you dedicate it to Trenton and call it "The Futility of Mankind"?' Laszlo suggested. 'Then you can have a lot of abstract painters working in a vast studio and a war raging outside the window.'

They were still laughing when Gideon entered the bar; he looked exhausted. His eyes were red-rimmed with fatigue, the collar of his shirt was grimy, and his mackintosh stained and crumpled from the long journey. Laszlo could see from his worried smile that all was not well. Without being asked, Gaston, the proprietor, poured him a large whisky from below the counter.

'I thought you didn't have any whisky?' Hammond said as he paid for the drink.

'This is medicinal,' Gaston replied. 'Paul Trenton can survive on beer occasionally.'

They could see that Gideon was weary to the bone. He drank the whisky gratefully and turned to Laszlo. 'Elizabeth is in trouble,' he said quietly. 'I found out in Switzerland.'

'I thought you were in Paris,' said Laszlo.

'I was at first; but I ended up in Basle, where I met Schneider.' He loosened the collar of his grimy shirt.

'Karl Schneider?' Laszlo asked, puzzled.

Gideon nodded. 'He comes and goes. It turns out he's Swiss, not German. He didn't marry Elizabeth; he told me they discovered she was partly Jewish. It seems that marriage would have damaged his career.'

Laszlo did not speak, but gradually his face began to change and harden; it was as though the flesh were turning to stone. 'Oh God,' he said without intending profanity.

'I rang Anne,' Gideon said to Nettlebury, 'and then came straight here.' He turned to Laszlo. 'I thought we could go and see Mueller. If he's still in this country, he might have some clue to her whereabouts.'

'Doesn't Schneider know where she is?' Laszlo asked.

'He says he's lost contact with her.'

'Let's go,' Laszlo said, and they both hurried into the sunlit street.

Erich Mueller was still in London, but he had changed; he had aged twenty years. Where his portly little figure had seemed round and tight, it now sagged; the once-full flesh of his face hung pallid and

223

grey, the texture of candlewax. He was sitting in the reception-room of his house in Belgravia, with Gideon and Laszlo standing over him.

'Why didn't you try to get her out?' Laszlo asked.

Mueller raised his eyes, and Gideon could see a nerve tremble on the left side of his face. 'Don't you think we tried everything? I was there for six months until the American Embassy asked me to leave. They were having enough trouble with people who wanted to get out. I begged her to come home, but it was as if she were possessed.' He looked at each of them in turn. 'She said it was like discovering your father had gone criminally insane.' He held up a hand. 'Elizabeth seems to be making some act of atonement. She refused to leave, and she publicly embraced Judaism. She insisted it was her birthright.'

'How did this come about?' Laszlo asked. 'Why did you think your wife's parentage could remain a secret?'

Mueller shook his head. 'She did not know. It was considered something of a scandal in her family. The Nazis did not invent anti-semitism, you know! Do you remember when we met on the *Queen Mary*? We'd just returned from Germany. We knew the truth about her ancestry even then.' He stared down at the floor, and Gideon could see the pain in him.

When Laszlo spoke, it was softly. 'Do you have any money here, Erich?'

'Not in the house. I could get some in a couple of days; on Monday, when the banks open.'

'I do,' said Gideon. He unbuttoned his shirt and took from his waistband the envelope Bronstein had given him.

'Why do you want it?' Mueller asked, with a faint note of hope in his voice.

'I hold an Irish passport,' Laszlo told him. 'I can get into Germany. I'm going to find her.'

'She won't come with you,' said Mueller.

'Then I shall stay and look after her,' Laszlo announced.

'Why would you do this for us?' Elsa Mueller asked, from the doorway. They had not heard her come in.

'Because I love Elizabeth more than my life,' Laszlo said gently.

Despite his exhaustion, Gideon insisted on accompanying Laszlo on the first part of his journey. After they had called at the mews house to pack his bags, they caught a taxi to Paddington, where Laszlo bought a ticket to Fishguard. They stood on the bustling platform in the middle of the crowds shuffling past. There were uniforms everywhere. It seemed as though the whole world were on the move.

'Where will you try for?' Gideon asked.

'After Dublin?' Laszlo shrugged. 'Lisbon, Sweden? The fastest way I can find.'

There was much the two men wanted to say to each other, but the words would not come. Eventually Gideon gestured towards the train. 'You'd better get aboard. You may find a seat if you try now.'

Laszlo smiled. 'You look as if you need a seat yourself. Go home. I'm all right.'

Gideon nodded, and after a brief handshake Laszlo threw his two bags on to the train and climbed up after them. He turned to wave a final farewell.

'Give my love to Elizabeth, when you find her,' Gideon called out, and then turned and walked away.

There were no taxis to be had, and the journey by Underground to Kew was filled with changes and delays. Anne was waiting when he finally got home. Swaying with fatigue, he sat nursing a cup of tea in the living-room while she went to run him a bath.

Amongst the pile of mail on the coffee-table, one buff-coloured envelope looked more insistent than the others. He reached forward and slowly opened it. It contained his call-up papers.

CHAPTER TEN

Gideon completed his basic training as an infantryman at a windswept camp on the Yorkshire Moors. At first the army seemed a bizarre organisation. The non-commissioned officers who dominated his life were all regulars who resented the intrusion of a war on the rhythm of their previous existence as peace-time soldiers. His fellow-recruits were equally resentful at the interruption to their lives, and many of them were made sullen by the painful adaptations they all had to make. Gideon quickly realised that the key to survival was anonymity. The skills he was expected to learn came easily, but he made sure he did not perform so well that they brought him to anyone's notice. He also discovered that his educated voice made him a target for attention, so he moderated his speech patterns and learned to swear, like everybody else, with boring regularity. He made particular friends with a razor-tongued Londoner called 'Smudger' Smith, who had the physical build of a jockey.

The worst part was separation from Anne. He missed her painfully at first, and when he was at last allowed to leave camp, he would cycle the five miles to the nearest village where the vicar let him use the telephone to call home.

After basic training, he was posted to an infantry battalion stationed at a holiday camp in the south-west. It had been requisitioned for the duration of the war, and the brightly painted attractions given a coat of camouflage paint. It was there that they passed the summer and early autumn. Although Gideon was in the army, paradoxically the war seemed further away than ever. Dunkirk happened as a distant event reported in the newspapers, and the weeks that followed, when the country was supposedly in the grip of invasion fever, saw no alteration in the slow pace of his life. Anne's letters told him that business was slow at the gallery but that people were still buying pictures, and the bank was understanding.

Then the battalion was suddenly put on alert to move out of the camp. Swept by rumours of their ultimate destination, they entrained for London, where they were transferred to their new quarters, a requisitioned private school in Tottenham. Within twenty-four hours they had settled in, and Gideon was able to go home on occasional leave as more long weeks of inactivity began. He was about to go off duty one Friday evening when he was called to the Colonel's office.

As was fitting, the Colonel used the headmaster's study for his office. A few trophies and photographs still decorated the walls, but Gideon did not let his eyes wander when he stood to attention before his commanding officer.

'Stand easy,' Parker-Trouton said, looking up from the heaps of papers on his desk. 'I just wanted to let you know, Gideon, that I'm putting you forward for a War Office Selection Board on the recommendation of Captain Marwood. Do you think you're up to it?'

Gideon looked down at the fearsome figure of the Colonel. He had been wounded in the face during the last war and a scar pulled the left side of his mouth into a permanent smile, even when his mood was less than joyful. 'I really have no idea, sir.'

The Colonel looked at the sheet of paper in front of him. 'It says here that you were an actor once.'

'Yes, I was, sir.'

'Well, that should see you through,' the Colonel said with a sigh. 'If you can act as though you know what you're doing, it should give you an enormous advantage. Meanwhile, report to Room 270 in the War Office at 09.00 hours next Tuesday. Dismissed.'

Gideon snapped to attention and about-turned. In the outer office he found Captain Marwood, who smiled in an encouraging fashion. 'Has the Colonel told you?'

'Yes, sir.'

'Jolly good,' Marwood said in a friendly fashion. 'I shall look forward to having you in the Mess. Frankly, some of the other officers can be rather a bore. Nice chaps, of course, but a bit narrow.'

Gideon smiled and stood to attention. Already he felt he was in a curious kind of no-man's-land.

'Carry on, then,' Marwood said, and Gideon left the room.

He found Smudger in the school gymnasium, the part of the

building where they were billeted. Smudger sat down carefully on the edge of his bunk so that he did not disturb the neatly made bed. 'What did the old man want?' he asked in a voice that showed only mild interest.

Gideon did not tell him of the Selection Board at first; he was already having doubts about being an officer. Instead he went to his locker and took out his greatcoat. 'Not much,' he said finally.

'So when you going to be a fucking officer, then?'

'How the hell did you know?' Gideon exclaimed.

Smudger held up his hands with the palms outward. 'My friend Jack Harris, of course. Nothing goes through the Colonel's office without I hear about it. Christ, you must be a bit chuffed!'

'I don't know, Smudger,' Gideon said, buttoning up his coat. 'I'm not sure if I want to be an officer.'

Smith made a final check round the area of his cot and then turned towards the swing doors at the end of the room. 'Don't be a fucking mug, son,' he said firmly. 'It's more money, better grub and the uniform don't itch, so get in there.'

'Do you really think so?' Gideon asked as they walked towards a rendezvous with the truck across a darkened playground. They had arranged the lift in the afternoon.

'Course I do! Look, it's all right for me being a bleedin' private, but you're not cut out for it, Gidsey, old son. You make everyone uneasy with that posh accent. It's okay by me, I get on with everyone; but the boys don't like it and neither do the officers.'

They found the truck in the darkness, and after a last-minute negotiation, clambered into the back. There they made themselves comfortable on some potato sacks.

'Just remember the way you used to travel in the good old days,' Smudger said, lying back. He instantly drifted into sleep, and the lorry rumbled off along the North Circular Road towards Kew.

After a time, Gideon fell asleep as well; it was a habit he had quickly learned in the army. Suddenly he was woken by the driver shouting from his cab, 'I've got no fucking idea where I am, mate. Can you ask somebody the way?'

Gideon lifted the canvas flap at the rear of the stationary lorry. It was a black night outside, but he could smell fumes, and guessed that they were close to Brentford. He got out and stopped a woman in a headscarf who was wheeling a pushchair. She told him they were in the High Street, heading towards Isleworth.

He walked round to the cab. 'You've turned the wrong way,' he shouted up to the driver, 'but you're not far off route. Turn round and ask for Chiswick High Road at the next junction. Then it's straight on for Hammersmith Broadway. This is fine for me, thanks.' Gideon called his farewell to Smudger and set off in the direction of Nettlebury's house.

After a time he cursed himself for not staying in the lorry; it was freezing cold and pitch dark on the street. Eventually he reached the bus terminal at Kew Bridge and told himself that he was almost home.

Ealing, the same day

Hammond Shelley leaned against a cupboard in the life studio of the West London School of Art and daydreamed of a rare steak smothered in onions. In these times of shortage he thought about food in much the way as he had dwelt on women in his youth. He glanced at his watch and saw that it was five minutes to the end of the session—time for the model to change into her street clothes. 'Thank you, Miss Watkins,' he said quietly, and the woman, who had been posing for a costume life study, stood up from her chair, shrugging her shoulders to relieve them from the position she had assumed for the past two hours. Irene frowned at her drawing, and then unpinned the cartridge paper from the drawing-board on the easel.

Andrew Waller, the student working next to her, paused to glance at her work and saw that she was not pleased. He gave an encouraging smile, and said, 'You shouldn't worry. The conditions are terrible in here.' He referred to the bulbs that hung from the ceiling on long wires, giving out a weak yellowish-brown light. 'Coming for a drink?' he asked, packing away his own gear.

Irene thought for a moment. 'Yes, but I want to get something to eat first. There's nothing at home except corned beef.'

'I'll come with you,' said Andrew. He turned to a group of other students. 'We're going to the canteen. See you later in the Castle.'

They walked to their lockers in the corridor and stowed their gear. Irene slammed her door with more force than usual. She had not had a successful day, and was feeling depressed by her work and the clinging presence of Andrew. He was a nice enough boy, but he was nearly a year younger than she, and painfully infatuated with her, a condition that lent no strength to his ambitions. He had

229

attempted to disguise his obvious youth by growing a beard, but the wispy down on his chin only served to emphasise his lack of maturity.

'Costume life,' he said as they continued their journey to the canteen. 'Bloody women in kimonos. When are we going to get to the real thing?'

'Next year, Andrew,' Irene answered. 'Then you'll be able to feast your eyes on naked flesh.' He blushed and Irene knew quite well whose naked flesh he wanted to feast his eyes on. For a moment she regretted teasing him, but when they entered the dining-room, the familiar smell of boiled vegetables put the thought out of her mind. They stood in line with their trays, and a young girl in a brown overall served them with Spam fritters, greyish mashed potato and watery peas.

'No cabbage tonight, Doreen?' Andrew chided her. 'I thought I could detect its pervasive aroma. Or is it your scent again?' Doreen giggled, and gave him an extra Spam fritter. He did not have trouble with other women; it was only Irene who caused him to stumble over his words.

She turned to make for a table where people they knew were sitting, but Andrew managed to guide her away. 'Over here,' he said, indicating a space where they would be alone. But his strategy was unsuccessful: Irene was not in the mood for conversation. They ate the meal quickly and in silence. Andrew's few attempts at communication were answered with monosyllables.

'Will you come out with me tomorrow night?' he asked her, as he did every Friday.

'You know I have to stay in on Saturdays,' she replied automatically. Irene always used the excuse that her father required her to stay in and keep him company at weekends.

He stirred the scraps of Spam fritter on his plate, and gave such a deep sigh that Irene's resolve almost faltered. 'Oh, Christ, roll on the army,' he said with something like despair in his voice. 'Then I'll be killed and get it all over with.'

'Don't be silly,' she said severely. 'You mustn't say such things. Come on, you can buy me a drink in the pub.' She was sorry for her harshness towards him; if he persisted, she thought, she might give in.

They left the blacked-out building and took care crossing the darkened road to the pub. There was a happier atmosphere there than that in the grim canteen. Hammond Shelley was already at the

230

bar, a little distant from the art students in Irene's group. He was with a man in a long airforce greatcoat, whose back was to them. Shelley said hello to Irene, and the figure turned. She found herself looking into familiar eyes. Richard Cleary was darker than she remembered, and now had short black hair. The pale lines around his eyes seemed cut into his narrow face, and his complexion was wind-burned. When he smiled at her, his teeth were very white.

'I was just talking about Julian Nettlebury,' said Hammond. 'This is his daughter Irene.' He introduced the young man. 'Richard Cleary, the son of a neighbour.'

Irene realised, with a slight disappointment, that Cleary didn't remember her. She shook the hand he held out, and it was warmer than she expected. The touch made her feel awkward and shy.

'Would you care for a drink?' he asked, and then turned to Hammond. 'How about you?'

'No thanks. I've got to be off,' said Shelley. He shook hands with Cleary. 'Keep your feet dry, boy. And don't forget the party, if you feel like it later.'

The young man nodded and turned to Irene. She asked for cider, and noticed the wings on his tunic when he reached into his pocket. 'You're a pilot!' she said.

Cleary nodded. He paid for the drink and handed it to her. 'Do you know anywhere I can eat around here?' he asked. 'I'm absolutely famished.'

Irene was suddenly acutely aware of everything around her. There was a sharpness to shapes and sounds; even the yeasty smell of the pub seemed overpowering. She did not even think before she answered. 'I have some corned beef and baked beans at home. I'll cook you some if you like?'

Cleary drank his beer in one swallow. 'Lead me to it!'

As they left the saloon bar, someone had been telling a joke, and everyone in the group by the door was laughing, except for Andrew. He turned away as Irene passed.

Cleary had a motorbike outside. 'Hold tight and keep your head out of the wind,' he told her, and put on a pair of goggles and gauntlets.

He did not take the bike very fast, but Irene was freezing in the slipstream. By the time they reached Kew her legs felt numb, but no amount of cold would have altered the warmth of the feeling inside her. The house was in darkness. Irene knew that Mr and Mrs Cooper were visiting her sister, and her father had taken some

231

pictures to the gallery. A note on the hall table reminded her that he and Anne would be eating in town and late home. She and Richard stood at the foot of the staircase.

Cleary removed his goggles, greatcoat and gauntlets, and noticed that Irene was rubbing her hands to restore their circulation. He took them between his own, and held them to his warm breath. 'Better?' he asked after a few minutes.

She nodded. 'I think my father has some whisky left. Would you care for a drink?'

Cleary nodded his approval, so she took him into the living-room, where the blackout curtains had been drawn earlier in the evening. There were still the embers of a fire in the grate. While she poured him a drink, Cleary roamed about the room. He did not seem intimidated by other people's surroundings, or feel any need to break the silence. Eventually he found the gramophone, and looked through the records until he found one that he wanted.

As she handed him the drink, the melody began to play. She looked uncertainly into his eyes.

'Do you remember this?' he asked without smiling. It was the song they had danced to at Edith Barclay's birthday party.

'I thought you didn't recognise me,' Irene replied after a moment.

Cleary shook his head and took a swallow from the drink before placing it on the mantelpiece. Then he reached out and drew her towards him.

At first she thought they were going to dance again, but he kissed her, and for a moment she was about to push him away. There was no romance in his embrace, just a driving sensuality. He pushed one hand inside her blouse and grasped her breasts. Irene was hardly aware of the warmth of the room and the whisky taste of his mouth. She pressed closer. He reached down and cupped his hand beneath her skirt to brush through her pubic hair. When he encountered the sudden wetness, he thrust the first two fingers of his right hand deep into her. Irene gave a momentary shudder, and clung to him even harder.

'Do you want to?' he said softly, and held her more gently.

Irene did not want to think. The fact that they had been together only briefly, and hardly spoken, meant nothing. Since he had warmed her hands in the hall, she had known the inevitable outcome. 'Not here,' she whispered. She took his hand and led him upstairs to her bedroom.

When they had undressed, by the light of her bedside lamp she

232

could see the power in Cleary's frame. The wind-burned colour of his face and hands stopped at his throat and wrists, and the muscles of his pale body showed like the chart of an anatomy illustration. But she was not prepared for the size of him. Her knowledge of men's bodies had been gained through the study of Greek and Roman statuary, and they had not included erections.

For his part, he was equally awed by the sight of Irene; her body was far more beautiful than he had imagined. The baggy coat she had worn in the public house had not prepared him for the glories of her naked form. 'My God!' he said in a hushed voice. 'Are there any more at home like you?'

'As a matter of fact, yes,' she said as they sank side by side on the bed. 'My sister Anne and I are so alike that some people take us for twins.'

'You must invite me round one bath-night,' Cleary said, and Irene, acting instinctively, began to ease him into her. He had spoken lightly, because he was still disconcerted by her beauty. He had known plenty of girls before, but somehow Irene was different; he could not bring himself to look at her in case he lost control.

He supported himself above her on outstretched arms, while he tried to look away. His eyes were drawn to the line of her thick auburn hair where it lay on the pillow, then to her wide eyes and the hollow of her cheeks. Her lips were slightly parted and the same deep red as the swollen nipples of her rounded breasts. His resolution slipped away and he climaxed suddenly with the force of champagne bursting from a shaken bottle. Inwardly he cursed himself, but something happened that he had not experienced before because he was still looking down on Irene, in all her loveliness, and his erection had not slackened. This time, he lowered himself gently on his elbows and began to drive rhythmically into her. Irene pounded the bed on either side of her with her fists and the bedhead smashed against the wall with each clash of their bodies. Eventually Cleary's rhythmic thrusts increased in tempo, and Irene, sensing he was about to climax, raised her legs and drummed her heels on the small of his back. They both came with long moaning sighs. He waited for a moment, unable to move, and then rolled on his side. He looked up at the ceiling until his breathing returned to normal.

'It happened twice,' he said.

Irene knew what he was referring to. 'Three times for me,' she said softly.

Cleary twisted his head to look at her. 'Three times?'

'Yes,' she said, and suddenly looked worried. 'Why, is that wrong?'

He shook his head. She laid her head on his shoulder and stroked the dark hair on his chest. They lay quietly for a time and then Irene turned to him. 'May I do something?' she asked, with shyness in her voice.

'What?'

'May I look at it?' She propped herself up on one elbow. 'It's just . . . well, I've never seen one before.'

'Never?' he said in astonishment.

'Not a real one. Only in pictures, or statues. I haven't got any brothers.'

'Help yourself,' he said, and lay back with his hands behind his head.

Irene held his limp penis for a few moments, and then began to tug experimentally. The attention caused him to become erect again and she held harder against the swelling sensation.

'Isn't it wonderful?' she said in fascination. 'It reminds me of a grass-snake we caught once near St Ives. It felt the same size.'

'How old were you then?'

'About seven,' she answered, after a moment's thought.

'Your hand would have been smaller.'

'Oh, yes,' she said, squeezing him. 'This would be an enormous grass-snake!'

'Big enough for a grass-snake, small for a rattler.'

'Have you ever actually seen a rattlesnake?' Irene asked.

'Yes. We had them on the airfield where I trained in Canada. They used to kill the jack-rabbits.'

Irene tired of conversation. She gave three sharp tugs, and he rolled towards her again. Then they heard a voice calling from below. He looked at her questioningly. She raised a finger to her lips. 'It's my brother-in-law,' she said softly, and slipped from the bed to put on a dressing-gown.

Gideon was about to climb the stairs when Irene appeared on the first-floor landing. 'Hello, darling! I didn't think anyone was in the house.'

'Just me,' she replied. 'Daddy and Anne are still working at the gallery. They're going to have dinner in town later.'

'What are they doing?' he asked, and to her relief he stayed in the hall.

'Something about storing the pictures somewhere safe because of the bombing. Daddy has taken quite a lot of his work up there. He's been making trips all week. It's all being moved to Buckinghamshire on Monday.'

Gideon nodded. For some time Anne had been anxious to store the pictures in a safer place, but the cost quoted by professional companies had always been prohibitive. Recently, however, Ted Porter had discovered a farmer with a disused barn, who had agreed to let it to the gallery at a reasonable rent. The last problem, Gideon remembered, had been the difficulty of transport. Clearly Anne had finally made some arrangements.

He stood in the hall, undecided, and then looked at his watch. It was just before six o'clock. 'I think I'll go into town and find them,' he said. 'Will you be all right on your own?'

Irene nodded from the balcony. 'Don't worry about me,' she said.

The door closed behind him again and Irene returned to the bedroom.

The Archangel Gallery, the same day

'Tea!' Ted Porter called out, and handed Anne a cup from the wire basket he was using as a tray. 'There's only condensed milk, I'm afraid.'

Anne got to her feet from the pile of pictures on which she had been sticking labels. She placed her hands on her waist and stretched back for a moment, then shook her head wearily. 'I wouldn't care if it was elephant's milk right now.' She took the cup and drank the dark sweet brew gratefully. 'Well, I think we've done a fine job.'

Ted nodded agreement. They were standing in the showroom of the gallery, with pictures stacked all around them. A tabby cat Ted had brought to the gallery, to keep the mice at bay, rubbed itself against his leg. 'Mind you, they only need to load in the wrong order, and we'll be really up the creek,' he said, reaching down to scratch the tabby's ear.

Anne closed her eyes at the nightmare of such a prospect. 'Don't even think that, Ted!' she said with a shudder. She had worked out a system whereby all the pictures could be located by reference to a catalogue coded in the order in which the stacks were to be stored. 'I'm going to stand by that lorry on Monday morning and personally check the order they go on board!'

Nettlebury came up from the basement, carrying a large sheet of handmade watercolour paper. 'There's work of mine down there I

235

haven't seen in years,' he said, taking the cup of tea Ted handed him. 'By the way,' he said to Anne, 'I just found this. What do you make of it?' He handed her a sketch which had been executed in some kind of red crayon.

She glanced at it for a moment and then put down her cup of tea and held it to a stronger light. 'Good heavens, it's a Raphael!' she said, astonished.

Nettlebury took it back with a chuckle and shook his head. 'Actually, your husband did it for me as an exercise a long time ago.' He looked at the drawing again. 'Remarkable,' he said to himself. 'Quite remarkable.' Then he laid it aside on one of the stacks of paintings. 'Are you sure all these pictures will be safe in a cow-barn, Ted?'

Ted nodded. 'The barn is bang next to the main farm building, but it's between the dairy and their pigsties and hen-houses. They guard the bloody buildings with shotguns. There's so many spivs about trying to steal their stock that the pictures will have an armed guard day and night!'

'Well, I'm glad my pictures will be looked after as well as the pigs!' said Nettlebury.

Then the door of the gallery opened and two figures could be seen pushing against the black curtain. 'Shop,' a voice called out, and Lance-Corporal Paul Trenton emerged from the folds, followed by Hammond Shelley. 'We've come to take you to the party, Julian,' he announced, and they could see that he had already had a fair amount to drink. Shelley was in better order, but they had clearly been in a pub for some time.

Trenton's fears of imminent death at the hand of the enemy had been ill-founded. After basic training, he had been posted to the War Office in Whitehall, where he now served as a clerk. He had even managed to billet himself in Laszlo's old mews house, where he conducted a seemingly endless series of parties.

'I thought we were going to have dinner, Dad?' Anne said with a smile.

'We shall, we shall, but I thought we might have a few drinks at Trenton's first. I've even asked Vera to drive up so that we can go home later.'

'I asked a young friend to come along. I hope you don't mind,' said Shelley.

'Not at all. The world is welcome,' Trenton answered, and his eyes fell upon the red chalk sketch. 'Jesus! I thought that was in the King's Collection at Windsor?'

236

'He lent it to me,' said Anne. 'Now clear off, all of you. I've still got some work to do.'

The door of the gallery opened again and a blonde girl parted the curtain. She was carrying a viola case and a bottle of champagne. 'Are you coming?' she demanded in an exasperated voice.

'Just a moment,' Trenton answered.

The girl put the musical instrument down with a sigh. 'I'm going to drop this bottle in a minute! My bloody arm's about to fall off.' Always the gentleman, Nettlebury reached out and took the bottle. She nodded in recognition. 'Hello, love, nice to see you again,' she said.

'And what performance are you giving at the moment, my dear?' Nettlebury asked her.

'*Philadelphia Story*,' she answered.

Nettlebury looked puzzled. 'I don't think I'm familiar with that piece.'

'Katharine Hepburn and Cary Grant,' she told him. 'It's ever so good.'

Nettlebury, puzzled, turned to the others.

'Wrong girl, Julian,' Shelley said, coming to his rescue. 'This young lady is an usherette at the Empire.'

The girl smiled, and nudged Nettlebury in a friendly fashion. 'You confused me with Wendy. I'm Maureen,' she said with a smile, then nodded towards Trenton. 'He got her pissed in the Wheatsheaf last night and she forgot her fiddle, so I collected it for her.'

Trenton picked up Nettlebury's cup of tea and took a mouthful. 'Ugh!' He turned to the others. 'Come on, then, at least the wine's better than this.'

Nettlebury got his hat and coat and kissed his daughter.

'I'll be around to collect you later, Dad,' said Anne.

'Are you coming round for one, Ted?' Trenton asked.

Porter shook his head. 'No, thank you, lad. The wife's expecting me.'

When they'd left, Ted asked Anne, 'Do you want me to hang on and lock up?'

She looked round. 'No, bless you. It's just paperwork now, Ted. You go home.'

'See you on Monday, then. Have a good weekend,' he said, picking up his coat. The door swung closed behind him.

Anne finished her tea, which was almost cold, took up her list and made for the basement.

Richard Cleary sat at the kitchen table, and Irene put a plate of fried corned beef and baked beans in front of him. 'There's no butter, I'm afraid,' she said. 'Do you mind margarine?'

'Not at all. I'm used to it.'

She sat and watched him as he ate with enormous speed. 'You'll get indigestion at that rate!'

'We eat fast. When you get a chance of hot food, you try to get it inside you as quickly as possible.' He wiped the plate clean with a piece of bread, and then sat back and lit an American cigarette.

The scent of the tobacco seemed faintly exotic to Irene. 'May I have one?'

Cleary shook the packet towards her, the way she had seen people do in the films. The taste was sweet.

'When do you have to leave?' she asked softly.

He looked up; with her back to him, she was putting the dirty dishes in the sink. 'I'm due back at midnight.' He thought for a moment. 'Would you like to go to a party tonight?'

'Where?'

'In town. It's at the house of a friend of Hammond Shelley. He's an artist called Paul Trenton.' Then he remembered. 'Just a minute, though. I wouldn't be able to bring you home. Pity, it sounded as if it might be fun.'

Irene sat down at the table. 'If it's at Paul Trenton's, I shall probably be able to get a lift from my father. He's almost certain to be there.'

'You know Trenton?' Irene nodded. 'Do you want to go, then?' Cleary asked.

Irene reached out and touched his hand. 'If you want to.'

He looked at her. Their lovemaking had removed all traces of her make-up and she had pulled her long hair back, securing it with an elastic band. She looked so young, suddenly. His stomach gave a little lurch when he thought that he had taken no precautions earlier. Now the possibility that he could have made her pregnant caused a nagging worry. 'You know, when we were in bed,' he began. Irene held his hand. He looked down at his cigarette and then up again to watch the smoke curl towards the ceiling. 'Well, I wasn't wearing anything.'

Irene looked puzzled for a moment. Then his meaning became clear. 'A contraceptive, you mean?' He nodded. 'Oh, that's all right,' she said matter-of-factly.

238

He shifted uneasily. 'Yes, but, well . . . Things can happen if you aren't careful.'

'Don't worry,' Irene said confidently. 'My period is due in two days. The egg would have already left the ovary. I'm certain not to be fertile. I'm as regular as clockwork.'

Cleary was relieved by this information though he did not entirely understand what Irene was talking about. Before he joined the Air Force, he had studied astronomy, and therefore knew the distance between the planets. He was, however, ignorant of the most rudimentary facts about a woman's monthly cycle. None the less he was relieved by Irene's confidence, even though he found her forthright conversation unromantic.

'Put some warm clothes on. You don't want to freeze again on the motorbike.'

Irene sensed that his mood had changed, and stood up and moved close to him. Her dressing-gown cord was tied loosely, and it parted. He could see the swell of her breasts and a narrow channel of her body, down to the dark red triangle of her pubic hair. Then the scent of her came to him, a mixture of soap and muskiness. All other thoughts departed. He also stood up, and reached for her, knowing they were going to be very late for the party.

Gideon thought he saw Laszlo on the Underground station at Kew Gardens. In the darkness he could just make out a figure without an overcoat, although there was a bitterly cold wind. The outline of a black trilby hat tilted at a particular angle completed the illusion. He was about to call out, when the figure lit a cigarette, and in the briefly flaring flame he saw a stranger's face.

When it rattled in, the train was packed. He stood jammed by the crowd against the doors, and in the dim reflection of the window saw himself as another stranger. Would Laszlo recognise me now? he wondered. In uniform, with a forage cap, and the deep collar of a greatcoat turned up against the cold?

At the next stop a woman wearing a headscarf got on and recognised the middle-aged man squeezed next to him. They started talking about their respective families, and how the fortunes of war had altered their circumstances: evacuated children, grown daughters working in arms factories, sons called up, all the rewoven patterns of their lives.

Then the man produced a packet of cigarettes and found he had no matches. 'Got a light, son?' he asked, and Gideon felt for his lighter. Since he had been in the army, his new status as a private had brought him into contact with working people in a way he had never known before. In peacetime, his accent and clothes caused a barrier of reserve, but a private's uniform had bestowed upon him a new position in life that he enjoyed. The man offered the packet to him. He took a cigarette and lit both of theirs in turn.

'What mob are you in?' the man asked above the roar of the train.

'Infantry,' Gideon replied, smiling to acknowledge his thanks for the cigarette.

'I was in the Middlesex Regiment in the last lot,' the man confided. He made a stabbing motion with his cigarette to emphasise his pride in his past service.

'Was you, Ernie?' the woman said in surprise. 'So was my brother Bill. Blimey, all the years we've known each other, and I didn't know that!'

'Yes, you did, Sally,' he said, with a wink to Gideon. 'Bill and I have been telling you about it every bloody Christmas since 1922.'

Gideon smiled back, and listened as they began an amiable squabble which lasted until they both got off the train at Earl's Court. He changed trains on to the Piccadilly line at South Kensington and knew that there were just a few more stops until Green Park, but when he finally got off, a porter was walking along the platform, shouting that the sirens had sounded and an air raid had begun. For a moment Gideon considered going to the surface; then common sense told him that Anne and her father would have already taken cover. He stayed below, in the shelter of the station.

Trenton's party was attended by the crowd he usually associated with in his frequent journeys through the pubs of Fitzrovia. There were painters, poets, writers and the human detritus they brought with them – a few journalists, one or two actors; and Henry Grierson, who had blossomed in the Bohemian months since the outbreak of war. He now spent three or four evenings a week in Soho pubs and was in regular attendance at all Trenton's parties. Some of the figures in the crowded room wore uniform, but once inside the mews house, formality was suspended; other ranks mingled freely with officers.

Nettlebury, pouring himself a glass of wine, overheard part of Henry Grierson's conversation.

'Don't you think all natural form is universal?' he was saying to a young captain in a Free French uniform. 'After all, certain shapes repeat themselves in nature, whether it's in the pelvis of a woman or the rise and dip of a mountain range.'

'Which mountain range do you mean?' the Frenchman replied. 'When I talk of mountains, I think of the Alps. They are not as a woman's body. They are sharp and cruel, like the teeth of a saw.

'Perhaps I was thinking more of rolling hills,' Grierson said, making a dipping motion with his hand.

'I do not believe a mere shape is a work of art,' said the Frenchman. 'Nature herself provides enough of those.'

Grierson would not let go. 'You must admit that there's more to painting than mere craftsmanship?'

The Frenchman put down his glass so that he could gesture with both hands. 'Look, my friend,' he said in a voice that betrayed his exasperation. 'In my father's house we have two paintings by Henri Toulouse-Lautrec.' He paused. 'You have heard of him, perhaps?' Grierson nodded vigorously. The Frenchman made a chopping motion with both hands. 'One picture is of the racecourse. The colours are bright, the spectators happy, the horse is ready to race, it pulls on the reins to make the rider anxious. You understand?'

Grierson nodded. 'Go on, go on,' he urged.

'The other picture is different. It is in a brothel. The colours are garish, the men gross and lascivious, the women false in their enjoyment. They smile, but you can see that, beneath, their spirit is dead.'

'So what's your point?' Grierson asked.

The Frenchman shrugged. 'The composition of both pictures is superb. One can discuss the relationship of shape and form until your cows come home. The harmony of colours is faultless.'

'So?'

'So,' the Frenchman said. 'Great experts on the meaning of art can have endless discussions about the qualities these pictures possess . . . ' He paused again and then spoke very slowly. 'But a child can also look at them and understand their meaning.'

Nettlebury caught the captain's eye and raised his own glass in salute. It was a rare occasion when he approved of the French. As he completed the gesture, the sirens began their mournful warning.

'Sod them!' Trenton shouted in the sudden silence that fell. 'I'm staying here. There's still plenty of booze left.'

Nettlebury watched the more sober members of the party gradually drift away in search of safer surroundings. The crowd had thinned around the table where the drinks were dispensed, so he took the opportunity to pour himself another glass. He took the philosophical view that in air raids death would come only from a direct hit. He decided to see it out with Trenton, and they and the few others who remained listened, waiting, for the drone of the approaching German aircraft.

Cleary and Irene spent a further hour in her bed before getting ready to go to Trenton's party. Irene had just finished dressing warmly for the motorbike ride when there was a ring at the door. Vera Simpson had barely said hello, when the sirens began to wail.

'I thought you were with Daddy,' Irene said, following her into the house.

'I'm on my way to meet him at a party at Trenton's. I called in to take them some tins of corned beef.'

In the kitchen, she found Cleary sitting at the kitchen table. 'Oh, hello,' she said, and he introduced himself.

'We'd better go to the air-raid shelter,' Irene said, gathering the odds and ends the family usually took with them.

'Hang on,' said Vera. 'I've got some drink in the car.' She returned moments later with a large clinking shopping-bag. 'I was taking some whisky to Trenton's party,' she explained. 'We might as well have it now.'

Irene picked up the torch and they made their way to the dugout at the end of the garden. Like many people, Nettlebury had only taken rudimentary precautions when building the air-raid shelter; people knew that war would bring aerial bombardment to the cities, but expected it to be limited to the centres. No one had anticipated how widespread the night bombers would scatter their fearsome loads.

It was icy cold in the shelter. Irene lit a paraffin lamp, which revealed the narrow dugout with a curved corrugated-iron roof. The soil from the excavation had been heaped up outside and planks laid on the mud floor. There was just room for three iron cots and their straw-filled mattresses, whose musty smell mingled with the scent of damp earth. Irene had brought blankets from the house, and the two women draped them over their shoulders. Cleary was warm enough in his greatcoat.

Vera reached into Irene's basket, found the kitchen cups and poured them each a large undiluted whisky. 'I suppose this is like home from home for you, being in the Air Force?'

Cleary smiled at her words. 'I'm stationed in the country. Bomber

Command. They've only been attacking the fighters' fields so far.'

'Well, they've started on us now!' Vera replied, and then they heard the pulsating drone of the approaching aircraft.

Anne was in the basement of the gallery when she heard the first warning. There was a large shelter at the Ritz but, like her father, she was fatalistic about being hit. There was a carpenter's heavy work-bench against the front wall, and she intended to take cover beneath that when the bombing started. The bench was separated from the stacks of her father's paintings by a narrow corridor, and she was standing there looking for the tabby cat. 'Puss, puss,' she called, but the cat was off in dark recesses, hunting down the mice that scratched and squeaked in far corners of the basement.

Anne heard the anti-aircraft batteries first, crackling in the distance and gradually separating into individual detonations from the emplacements in Hyde Park. Then came the heavy droning notes of the bomber stream. She knew the incendiaries would be tumbling on to the city now, and when their fires had started, the high explosives would rain down to crack open the buildings and complete the devastation.

'Come on, cat,' she called anxiously as the thudding of the bombs began. At first it was like the sound of a giant's footsteps approaching, then she could feel the concussion of the explosions and hear the differing sounds they made. Some were like giant doors slamming, others rumbled in the distance. There were sudden frightening crashes, as though a mighty thunderstorm were raging directly above. Then Anne heard the most terrifying sound of all, a series of explosions coming closer, and she knew that a stick of bombs was falling in her direction.

'Puss, puss!' she called again, and the tabby appeared around the corner of Nettlebury's stack of paintings and padded towards her. She scooped the cat up but it was too late. The last bomb of the stick had already landed on the building behind the Archangel Gallery in Cork Street.

The fat metal casing loaded with one hundred kilograms of high explosive bored through the two-storey building and came to rest in the basement of the ladies' dress-shop that backed on to the gallery before it detonated. The cone of the blast demolished the dress-shop and the top floors of the gallery, at the same time blowing down the wall that divided the two basements. The force of the explosion hurled masonry and the mounds of pictures outwards. Anne was

243

lifted off her feet and thrown like a child's doll underneath the carpenter's bench. When the debris settled, fire from the incendiaries began to eat into the wreckage.

Gideon sat on a bench and dozed until a porter shook his shoulder and announced that the raid was over. He made his way to the surface and stood with his back to the railings of Green Park. Then he looked towards Bond Street and saw the leaping flames of the fire above the buildings on the north side of Piccadilly. He began to run towards the Archangel Gallery.

Nettlebury heard the all-clear sound to the accompaniment of cheers. Grierson and the Frenchman had continued their argument throughout the raid. They now appealed to Nettlebury to arbitrate, but he was anxious about Anne, so decided to make his way back to the gallery. When he heard where he was going, Grierson insisted on accompanying him. They left the mews together and heard the bells of fire-engines and ambulances as they made their way through the back streets of Shepherd Market.

Irene, Vera and Cleary emerged from the shelter at Kew and, standing in the garden, gazed in the direction of London. The great raging fires made the horizon glow orange and red, gradually fading to the colour of dried blood before blending into the night sky. It reminded Cleary of childhood Sunday School stories of the Apocalypse.

Firemen were already bringing the burning buildings under control when Gideon ran into Bond Street, but the Archangel Gallery had been torn out of existence. There was nothing but a ragged gap half-filled with rubble. The roadway was covered in broken glass, which reflected the fire like a carpet of rubies.

When he stopped a few yards away, his foot knocked against something. He looked down and saw it was the angel's wing sign. He stooped to pick it up, and slowly walked closer. Rescue workers were already clambering over the remains.

'Get back, mate!' a fireman told him.

'This was my place,' he said. As he faced the devastation, his stomach knotted with fear.

'This bloke owns the shop,' the fireman called out to the men climbing about the jagged heaps of rubble.

'Is there anybody on the premises?' one of the rescue workers shouted.

'I don't know,' Gideon replied. 'There could be.' He turned at the sound of crunching glass and saw Nettlebury and Grierson running towards him.

'Anne! Oh my God, Anne's still in there!' Nettlebury shouted.

Like a sleep-walker, Gideon threw the sign aside and clambered over the wreckage. He began to claw at the remains. As he worked, he prayed; the glass, brick and splintered beams cut his hands, but he was oblivious of the pain. Beside him, Nettlebury and Grierson dug with equal frenzy.

'Don't worry, mate. There's plenty of the basement intact,' a rescue worker said, gasping. The words brought no comfort. Twice Gideon's heart leaped as they uncovered shop-window dummies that had been blown by the force of the explosion into the rubble of the gallery.

'Don't die, Anne!' Gideon called out. 'Don't die!'

'Quiet,' the rescue worker hushed him. 'I can hear something.'

They stopped digging. The only sounds were the rasping of their breath and the occasional tinkling sound of glass still falling from the blasted shopfronts. Then they heard the distant mewing of the cat.

'Something is alive down there,' the rescue worker said, and he directed them to dig where Gideon told them the well of the staircase lay. Gradually an opening was revealed, and they lowered themselves into the gap. By the light of a torch they wormed like pot-holers through the jumble of wreckage towards the sound.

It seemed to take for ever. The greatest obstruction was the paintings, thrust together, until the rescue workers produced a knife and hacked a passage through. The final obstruction was a heavy beam, which they managed to move by their joint efforts. Then the wavering beam revealed Anne lying curled up, the cat in her arms.

By the light of the torch they saw that her face was as white as snow. Blood flowed from deep cuts in her shoulder and forehead. The cat jumped out of her arms and scuttled away. Gideon reached out, and as he touched her cold face, her eyes flicked open, and she smiled.

'Is that you, Gideon?' she asked quietly.

'Yes, Anne, it's me.'

'Is Daddy safe?' Her voice was weak and sleepy.

'We're all safe now,' he assured her.

'That's good. I knew you'd come for me.'

CHAPTER ELEVEN

London, midsummer 1945

It was a lovely day, so Anne decided to go out during her lunch-hour. As she walked from her office in Whitehall through St James's Park, she hardly noticed the wisps of cloud hanging high and motionless in a deep blue sky or the gentle breeze ruffling the trees. She lingered at the ponds and then made for Trafalgar Square, where she sat on a bench near St Martin-in-the-Fields to eat her sandwiches.

They were Spam again. Anne sighed, and after a few mouthfuls of the coarse bread and fatty meat, her appetite vanished. She started to feed the rest to the pigeons, but then the birds reluctantly parted, and she found a major in the Parachute Regiment standing in front of her. He carried a walking-stick and was smiling down in a familiar fashion. She crossed her hands in her lap and quickly looked away, knowing that any encouragement would bring an approach, even though she had been careful to display her wedding ring.

Then a mocking voice said, 'My darling Anne, don't say you've forgotten me after all these years?' She looked up at him again, and gradually the military trappings faded. It was Paul Trenton.

Anne stood up, and the last of the pigeons waddled away. 'Goodness, Paul, I really didn't recognise you!' She paused. 'You look so . . . so . . . '

Trenton nodded, and she realised that he seemed much older. It wasn't just that he was thinner, or had deep lines round his eyes and mouth; the youth had gone from him. He was leaning on his stick and carried a small leather-bound case in his other hand.

'Come and have a drink,' he said, making the suggestion sound like an order.

Anne glanced at her watch. She still had half an hour. 'I just have

246

time for one; then I must get back to work.'

'The war's over,' Trenton said with a smile. 'Let's celebrate a little.'

Anne was glad to see that not all his old carefree spirit had gone. 'How long is it since we've seen each other?' he asked as they walked up St Martin's Lane. Although he leaned heavily on his stick, he managed quite a fast pace.

Anne thought about his question. '1940. The night the gallery was bombed.' She looked at him again. 'You were a lance-corporal then. What happened?'

Trenton held open the saloon-bar door of the Salisbury. 'I got bored,' he answered when they were standing at the bar. 'I never could stand the idea of working in an office.' He saw two people leaving a table. 'Grab that space!' he said briskly.

When they were seated, Anne glanced at his Airborne wings. 'Did you like jumping out of aeroplanes?'

Trenton pushed a half-pint of bitter towards her before he answered. 'Jumping out was absolutely terrifying. Floating down on the parachute was rather jolly.' He drank some of his beer and lit a cigarette. 'How are you now? When I was transferred, you were still in hospital.'

'I got better,' Anne said, 'but it took about a year.'

Trenton nodded. 'How's everybody else? Julian, Irene, Gideon? Did Julian ever get on with that bloody great picture he was about to start?'

Anne smiled. 'He's still working on it. Gideon's fine; he's in Berlin now. I haven't seen him for more than a year.'

'Aren't you running the gallery any longer?' he asked.

'The gallery doesn't really exist. Many of the pictures were destroyed.'

'So where are you working?'

'At the Foreign Office. I do translations for an old friend of my father.'

Trenton sat back in his chair. 'What about Laszlo?'

Anne shook her head. 'Nothing. We don't know what happened to him or Elizabeth. Her parents went back to America eventually. I haven't heard anything of them in years.'

Trenton, having drunk his beer, stood up and winked at her. 'I'm going to have a whisky. How about you?'

Anne looked at her watch; even if she hurried, she was going to be late. Then she thought of the work she had to do, and suddenly translations of obscure Italian newspapers did not seem very important. 'Whisky with a lot of water,' she said finally.

As Trenton returned to the bar, Anne studied him. He looked very smart in his well-pressed uniform. The leather of his Sam Browne belt gleamed in the sunlight flooding through the engraved glass window. She felt drab by comparison. Although it had been altered twice, her dress was old and her shoes scuffed and shapeless. Suddenly it came to her that she was nearly thirty, and she had hardly seen Gideon in two years. Where has the time gone? she thought. Everything had been so dreary and sad for so long. She remembered what she had just told Paul: a few sentences to describe the pattern of their lives throughout the long years of the war.

Then Trenton returned, and raised his glass. 'Here's to peacetime!'

Anne sipped her drink and accepted a cigarette. 'What about you, Paul? What have you been up to?'

When Trenton grinned, he suddenly looked much younger. 'I went to see the King this morning.'

'The King?' Anne said in astonishment. 'Whatever for?'

'He wanted to give me this.' Trenton pushed the narrow leather case towards her.

Anne undid the clasp and looked down at the silver cross nestling in a bed of silk. Suddenly her heart lurched; the lost years seemed to be epitomised in the elegant, shining medal. She became aware that all the pain and sadness were in the past. No more loneliness and fear; Gideon will come home soon, safe at last. A shaft of sunlight fell on the table; the composition of the glasses and the leather case with its precious contents seemed very beautiful. Two tears of happiness welled up in her eyes and fell on to the silk lining. Anne could not remember the last time she had cried. 'Oh, Paul,' she said without looking up, 'thank God it's all over!'

When Anne left the pub, she walked back to her office with a quickened step. She knew exactly what she was going to do; and her mood matched the glorious weather. When she reached the gloomy little room she shared with Miss Frame, the supervisor of her section, she even hummed a song as she took her seat under her superior's frosty glance. Anne said nothing; instead, she reached for the telephone and rang Henry Grierson. He was delighted to hear her voice, and Anne arranged to meet him in Lyons tea-shop in Piccadilly at three.

When she had finished, Miss Frame came and stood in front of

248

her desk, her back ramrod straight and her nostrils flared for battle. 'I couldn't avoid hearing your conversation, Mrs Gideon,' the dry little woman said in a voice that had intimidated her staff for five years. 'May I remind you that personal calls are strictly forbidden. Frankly, your extraordinary behaviour astonishes me. You have returned late from luncheon without a word of apology or explanation, and now I gather you are off to keep an appointment for which no permission has been sought.

Anne listened to her words with a smile, as the woman spoke the language of inter-departmental memoranda. She took out a sixpence and handed it to her. 'This is for the telephone call, Miss Frame. It will save you instructing the paymaster to deduct it from my salary. I'm off for the rest of the day.'

Miss Frame could barely control herself at this evidence of mutiny. 'May I remind you there is a war on,' she said in a shocked voice. 'You have not done the translations from the Milan and Turin newspapers yet.'

Anne stood up and handed a bundle of cuttings to her adversary. 'The war is over, Miss Frame. We won,' she said gently. 'Goodbye.' She walked out of the cramped office with a heart as light as a feather.

She met Colonel Middleton on the stairs. 'Hello, my dear. I've something for you. Come with me.'

'I've just resigned, Colonel,' Anne said as he ushered her into his office.

'Have you? Jolly good! A lot of people will be going now.'

A few minutes later she left to keep her appointment with Henry Grierson, carrying the odorous package wrapped in brown paper that Middleton had given her.

Although she was a few minutes early, Grierson was already seated at a table near the door. 'I rang the agents,' he said. 'They're sending a chap to meet us there in twenty minutes.'

She nodded with satisfaction, and after a brief conversation they walked towards Bond Street. She felt a moment of melancholy when they stood in front of the bomb-site that had once been the Archangel Gallery. Through the chinks between the boards they could see the weed-infested rubble strewn with litter and broken glass. Heavy beams supported the raw brick walls of the deserted premises on each side, and their windows had been shuttered against the attention of vandals.

Grierson gestured towards the shop on the left. 'This would be the better location, but the lease is considerably dearer. It suffered less blast damage.' As he stared up at the building, his nose wrinkled with displeasure. 'Dear me! There really is the most dreadful smell coming from somewhere.'

Anne laughed. 'Oh, Henry, I'm afraid it's me.'

'You?' he said.

Anne held up her parcel. 'Colonel Middleton gave me a brace of pheasants. They're rather high!'

Grierson studied the parcel for a few moments. 'How would you like to join me in a little subterfuge?'

'Why, Henry,' Anne replied, 'what do you have in mind?'

Grierson looked up and down the street, then leaned forward and whispered to her.

A few minutes later they were joined by a bumptious young man with a pencil-thin moustache and too much hair-oil. Anne stayed some distance away, but close enough to pick up his patronising tones. His general attitude was so unpleasant that she had no qualms about putting Grierson's plan into action.

Eventually the agent unlocked the shop on the left, but before they entered, Grierson said he would prefer to see the other first. The young man shrugged and they strolled next door. Anne lingered and slipped into the first shop for a few moments, and then joined them.

There was a dry, dusty smell about the rooms, and the forlorn atmosphere that unoccupied buildings often have. She abandoned them after a time. In happier days, a cheerful Jewish couple selling leather goods had been their neighbours. She stood on the pavement until Grierson and the young man had finished, and then they went to examine the shop on the left. Anne remained in Bond Street until Grierson emerged again. The young man handed him some keys and walked quickly away towards Piccadilly.

Grierson watched his departure and then snorted with laughter. 'You should have seen his face!' he said. 'I pretended not to notice at first, then I asked him what the smell was. He really didn't want to linger at all. He mumbled something about drains, but I wasn't convinced. At last he settled for the sum I wanted just so that he could leave!'

Anne had a moment of conscience. 'Oh, Henry, do you think we were fair?'

'Of course we were! They're lucky to let it at all. London's full of empty property. He knew you wanted to come back here for

sentimental reasons and was prepared to charge you accordingly.'
He glanced at his watch. 'Now, can I buy you a cup of tea?'

'No, thank you. I must retrieve the pheasants, and fly. I've got to
meet someone soon.'

Ted Porter heard the harsh note of the factory siren signalling the
end of the shift and switched off his lathe. When other machines
slowly ceased their deafening whine, there was only the clatter of
tools being stored away and the loud voices of other workers. He
smeared grease on his hands and carefully began to wipe off tiny
fragments of clinging metal with a rag. While he was doing this, his
workmate grumbled, 'No bloody overtime again! We'll be back on
peacetime rates before we know it.'

'Never mind, Jack. Perhaps they'll start another war for you soon!'

In the corridor, a line of people were stamping their attendance
cards in a time-clock. Outside in the yard, other figures hurried past,
but he stood for a moment and gazed up appreciatively at the bright
blue sky before taking his cycle from the rack. By the time he
reached the main gate, he was one of the last workers to stream out
on to the narrow street that led to the Ealing Road.

He was about to mount his cycle when a voice called his name. He
turned, and saw Anne standing by the factory wall. A smile of
pleasure crossed his face when she leaned forward and kissed his
cheek. Two passing men who knew him observed her greeting with
surprise. Anne was not the sort of girl one found waiting outside
factory gates.

'Who's your fancy woman, Ted?' one of them called cheerfully.

'You wouldn't know her. She's a lady!' he replied good-naturedly.

'I'm going to start the gallery again,' Anne said.

Ted raised his eyebrows. 'I'd better ask for my cards then.'

Anne put a hand on his where it rested on the handlebars. 'I
haven't got very much money, Ted; just enough to pay you for six
months.'

He looked back along the long bleak wall of the factory and shook
his head. 'I've been in that bloody place for nearly five years,' he said
quietly, 'and every day I've remembered what things used to be like
before the war. I don't care if it's enough for six weeks – it would be
worth it.'

Anne could feel his determination. As they walked on, she began
to talk rapidly. 'The premises are the problem,' she explained.
'We've got enough pictures for a small beginning. There's Gideon's

251

collection, and Laszlo's, and we still have some that weren't destroyed by the bombing, but a lot of work has to be done to convert the shop I've taken.'

'I'd better make a start on Saturday, then.'

They stopped outside a parade of shops and talked on until Anne's bus arrived. Then she sat on the top deck as it slowly drove towards Ealing Broadway. She was more excited than she could ever remember, and when the bus reached the summit of Hanger Lane she looked across the rolling green of the park, bathed in the early evening sunlight, and felt her heart fill with happiness. This is for you, Gideon, she vowed. When you come home, there will be something real and tangible waiting; something we can build on for the rest of our lives.

London, September 1945

Hammond Shelley sat in his battered leather armchair alone in a corner by the window of the staff common room in the West London School of Art. It was the morning of enrolment day for the start of the academic year, but Shelley did not relish the prospect of a new beginning. During the war years he had begun to feel old, and even now his attention wandered from the newspaper in his hands. They were brown and speckled like autumn leaves, and the knuckles of the long bony fingers looked like old whitened stones.

He looked out of the window. From his viewpoint, he could see into the garden of the house beyond the high wooden fence of the college. It was a misty day, cold and damp; a man slowly raked leaves on the edge of a tree-lined lawn towards a smouldering bonfire. Season of mist and mellow fruitfulness, he thought. He wondered if his depression sprang from the young people he was about to encounter.

Shelley had taught art for nearly forty years, and did not consider the time well spent. His own hopes to be a painter of repute had evaporated many years before. He had sublimated his own ambitions in the thought that he might be instrumental in nursing someone of greater talent, but the generations of young people who had passed through his life had proved a disappointment. Now he was to repeat the process; a new group would be taught how to draw, paint and appreciate the mysteries of fine art. Some would drift away into other jobs, but most would gain their diplomas and go on

252

to qualify as teachers of art. Like him.

With a sigh he dragged himself out of the comfortable depths of his chair and made his way towards the hall on the ground floor where enrolment was taking place. There were long rows of prospective students waiting beneath signs directing them to the various departments. Shelley walked to the queue closest to the windows, where the line for the Art School had formed, and inspected the faces. One seemed vaguely familiar, and after a moment he realised it was Richard Cleary.

Cleary took a cigarette from the pocket of his RAF greatcoat and turned to the youth next to him. 'Do you have a light?' he asked. The boy shook his head. Shelley stepped forward and took out a box of matches. 'Thanks,' he said, leaning over the flame, and then, when he straightened up, he recognised Shelley.

'Hello, Richard!' Shelley said. 'I didn't know you were coming here.'

Cleary laughed briefly before he answered. 'Neither did I until recently!'

Shelley studied his companion. Although he himself was a shade over six feet, Cleary seemed bigger now. He stood with a straight back and martial bearing. Shelley glanced at the ill-matched group standing around in the dusty assembly hall. More than half were ex-servicemen who still wore oddments of their uniform. Like Cleary, they were taking advantage of the government's new policy of granting scholarships to those who had been recently discharged from the Forces. There were one or two youths not yet old enough to be called up, and the rest were girls who had recently left school and now seemed anxious to prove their new-found maturity by affecting an air of bored indifference to their surroundings.

'What group did you end up in?' Shelley asked, nodding at Cleary's Air Force greatcoat. It had been some years since they had seen each other.

'Pathfinders,' he answered in a deep voice.

'I thought all you lads would be on the way to Japan by now.'

Cleary's laugh seemed to rumble from his wide chest, and people turned to look at him, surprised that any joy could be found in these dreary surroundings. 'I was shot down. When I got out of the camp, they decided I could go home.'

'Where's home now?' Shelley recollected that Cleary's parents had both died some years before.

Richard shrugged. 'I shall have to sort something out, I suppose.'

Shelley continued studying him. It seemed difficult to imagine Cleary in uniform, because all traces of the youth he had last seen were gone. His thick black hair curled over the rolled collar of his heavy blue sweater, and his dark, sharply defined features now looked as though they originated on the African side of the Mediterranean. There were deep hollows beneath high cheekbones and he had a large hooked beak of a nose. His mouth was wide, and his large white teeth contrasted with the swarthy skin when he smiled. The heavy eyebrows met at a deep crease above the bridge of his nose, giving him an almost sinister look that contrasted with his pale, intensely blue eyes. His hands were large and powerful with broad, stubby fingertips. As well as his haversack, he was holding a large roughly made book covered with oilcloth.

'How long were you a prisoner of war?' Shelley asked.

Cleary reached down to scratch the knee of his corduroy-clad leg. 'Eighteen months,' he said without emotion.

'What was it like?' Shelley continued. Recent news of the concentration camps had filled the British public's minds with horror.

Cleary laughed again. 'A bit like this,' he said with a shrug. 'Without the girls, of course. Mostly waiting around in rather boring surroundings.'

Shelley looked again at the girls. There was a clear division of types, despite the rigours of five years of war. Those queuing before the sign 'Commercial Studies' wore brighter clothes and heavier make-up. Those in the line for the Art School were, like Cleary, of a more soulful appearance. Most wore no lipstick, their hair tended to be long, and their clothes were in muted colours of blues, browns, purples and greys. While the girls for Commercial Studies chattered to each other like colourful tropical birds in the pale sunlight filtering through the tall windows, the Art School contingent clutched large folders and gazed about them with the solemnity of novice nuns. Shelley waited as Cleary shuffled towards a trestle table where a grey-haired woman bowed over a list.

'Name?' she said without looking up.

'Richard Cleary.'

The woman ticked her list. 'Life One studio, first year intermediate. Two floors up, and follow the signs.'

'I'll show you the way,' Shelley offered, and Cleary nodded his thanks.

As they left the hall, Shelley noticed a girl who had been standing behind them. She was tall, with hair as dark as Cleary's, but her skin was as pale as apple blossom. She did not take her hazel-coloured eyes off Cleary as they passed.

They made their way through the college, which had been built at the turn of the century and had, by now, acquired layers of cream or dark green paint.

Cleary noticed that the lower floors, occupied by the technical schools, were dark, cool and gloomy. Their footsteps echoed on the polished stone floor, and there was a sombre studious atmosphere. Shelley pointed out that, apart from Business Studies, there were also sub-divisions of the sciences, librarianship and engineering, taught in the rambling sprawl of sooty red-brick buildings.

There was a more convivial tone to their surroundings, however, when they reached the top floor where the Art School was located. The walls were painted white, and there was a different smell. Polish and disinfectant gave way to the distinctive scent of turpentine, linseed oil and dust. In the wide area at the top of the stairwell, paintings, which Cleary assumed were done by past students, covered the walls. Most of them were stilted and formal, executed in the unmistakable fashion of the Edwardian era: landscapes of the Home Counties, still lifes and a few portraits of men and women in high collars and button blouses. A corridor facing the stairs to the left was filled with a milling crowd of newly enrolled students. They followed the signs and, half-way along the passage, entered double doors bearing the sign 'Life One'.

Inside was a large studio. Broad skylights faced the north, and tall hessian-covered screens stood against the far walls. There were easels, stacked like wood in a timber-yard, and long stained tables, piled with dusty plaster models of hands, feet, heads and parts of torsos cast long ago from antique statuary. Open doors of battered cupboards revealed dried gourds, coloured pots, lamps, glass objects and china. There was an ancient couch in the centre of the room, and Shelley, watched by the assembled students, strolled over to it, produced a blackened pipe and sat down with a studied air of indifference.

After a time, when the last arrivals had found places, he rose slowly to his feet and stuffed the pipe into the pocket of his baggy tweed jacket. Gradually the muttering conversations ceased, and he glanced around.

'My name is Shelley,' he told the students in a low and weary voice. 'Known to my friends as Hammond and to most students as Percy. You will call me Mr Shelley until we get to know each other better.' He

255

looked up towards the skylight, and then at his audience.

'Usually, the people I teach come here straight from school. That is not the case this year. Many of you have served your country in the Forces, so I expect you will have put childish things behind you. Therefore I shall treat you all as if you were adults, until I learn to the contrary.' He looked around again and nodded to himself. When he began to speak again, it was as though he were an actor tired of the same old lines. 'Until now, most of you will have been regarded as somewhat special. Even you ex-servicemen will remember that the ability to draw was regarded as an extraordinary quality, one that set you aside and made you more interesting than other people.'

Cleary understood what he meant. In his schooldays, the art-room had been a place where he could display his skills and hold discussions about painting with other boys who were keen on art. He remembered how he and his contemporaries had regarded the others with a certain amount of contempt, relishing their own self-awarded status. Even in the camp, his fellow prisoners had been impressed at his ability to draw.

Shelley looked round, and saw that his remarks had gone home, which seemed to kindle some spark of interest in his eyes. He thrust his hands deep into his pockets. 'I can hear the words now,' he said with a certain relish. 'How did you learn to do that? . . . I can't draw a straight line . . . It's a gift from God . . . We don't know where it comes from; no one else in the family can do it.' He paused. 'Sounds familiar?' The students exchanged glances: the words were familiar enough. 'Let me tell you,' he continued, 'that the ability to draw well was considered a perfectly normal accomplishment by every well-brought-up Victorian girl. That, and a reasonable competence on the piano, were matters of commonplace achievement. It is only the last forty-odd years that has seen the mystification of a skill once taken for granted by cultivated people. To be able to draw is simply a matter of technique; and, with enough diligence, something you will all be able to master in a couple of years.'

Shelley glanced at Richard Cleary, to see how he was reacting, and noticed with a slight shock the intensity of his expression.

'These skills will *not* make you artists. The ability to draw is only a beginning. Many people who can copy objects placed before them are visual illiterates, and they may never fully understand what truly makes a work of art.' He held up a hand and waved it in a sort of benediction. 'Some of you will recognise greatness in others without

256

being able to accomplish it yourselves, and you will know the bitter frustration of realising the limits of your own ability.' He paused again. 'And one or two of you may be the stuff that dreams are made of.'

The students shuffled and glanced at one another, as though seeking to recognise the greatness he referred to.

'Think of this,' Shelley continued. 'You can be taught the tricks of the trade; but no one can teach you to be an artist. That comes from within you, and in the end is nothing more than a process of self-awareness.' He took out his pipe. 'So remember what the Greeks said,' he muttered. 'Know thyself.'

As he was coming to the end of his address, another man entered the room. He now joined Shelley in the centre of the room. They looked an incongruous pair. The second man's head barely reached Shelley's shoulder, even though he stood tall, and thrust his neck out from the loose collar of his shirt in a vain attempt to gain a fraction of additional height. A three-piece brown suit hung on his emaciated frame like a limp banner draped from a flagpole. Glittering wire-framed spectacles on the bridge of his thin nose encircled watery grey eyes which moved quickly from side to side. Then he smiled suddenly to reveal large yellowish teeth, and gave a dry cough.

'This is Mr Proud,' Shelley said, and Cleary could hear the barely concealed contempt in his voice. 'The Principal of the Art School.'

'Thank you, Mr Shelley,' Proud replied in a high, cultivated voice. 'Please pay attention,' he said to the students. 'This group will be known as Life One, and for most of each day's work you will use this studio. For additional subjects such as lettering, architecture, history of art, pottery and anatomy you will go to the relevant departments on this floor and the one below. Please respect the objects stored in this studio. They took many years to acquire and the war has brought shortages to us, like it has to everyone else.' He looked at his watch. 'In a few minutes I will ask you to go along the corridor to Mr Parkinson's store-room and draw your allocated supplies. He will also issue you with keys to your lockers. I need hardly remind you that pencils and cartridge-paper are difficult to come by these days, so do not be profligate with your ration.' He then placed his hands carefully in the pockets of his well-pressed jacket and stalked from the room. His polished brogues were steel-tipped and made a curious clicking on the paint-splattered parquet, like a tap-dancer crossing a stage.

257

Cleary was struck by the difference in the two men. Although there was little hope in Shelley's voice, he had addressed them as thinking human beings, whereas Proud had used the tones of little men in authority everywhere.

Cleary was the first out of the room, and the thirteen others who now constituted 'Life One' filed after him. While they waited in a queue in the corridor, he took stock of them. The six girls were reasonably attractive, but none was as striking as the dark-haired one. Two of the group were in their early twenties and, like Cleary, obviously ex-servicemen. The last three were boys fresh from school. When Cleary lit a cigarette, the boys watched him briefly and then lit up themselves.

A fat man in his early thirties, in a grubby brown overall, was dispensing the supplies. He took the hand-rolled cigarette he was smoking from his mouth and ran stubby fingers through his heavily oiled hair. 'Students don't smoke around 'ere,' he told Cleary belligerently.

Cleary's eyes flickered over the figure. 'Stand to attention when you speak to an officer,' he said with sudden, cutting emphasis.

The fat man snapped upright as if someone had jabbed him with a bayonet. 'Sorry, sir,' he muttered contritely. 'I'm used to dealing with kids.'

'That's all right,' Cleary replied amiably. 'I could tell you were Royal Air Force.'

'Corporal fitter,' the man admitted. 'Stationed at Uxbridge.'

'When did you get your discharge?' Cleary asked in a friendly, conversational, tone.

'Six months ago, sir. I had bad legs.'

The dark-haired girl thought for a moment that the man was going to throw Cleary a salute, but they got their paper ration instead. As they walked together, Cleary turned and smiled at her.

'How did you know that man had been in the RAF?' she asked.

'I can tell things about people,' he said, without smiling.

The girl studied him; he looked like a gypsy. It was easy to believe he could read fortunes. 'What can you tell about me?'

He looked at her intently until she averted her eyes, and then shook his head. 'You're shrouded in mystery.'

'Why?' The girl's eyes flicked back to him. He noticed they were coloured green and light brown, like chips of polished stone.

He smiled. 'Virgins always are,' he said in a low voice.

The girl's pale skin flushed, and without speaking again she turned

258

and walked away.

'There's an hour before lunch,' Shelley announced in a loud voice. 'Let us fill the time with a little costume life drawing.' He turned to the same girl again. 'Would you mind very much modelling for us, my dear? What is your name, by the way?'

'Paula Tuchman,' she replied in her clear voice.

'Just make yourself comfortable here,' he said, pulling a bentwood chair from against the wall.

The rest dragged easels in a circle around her, and a deep hush fell on the studio. Eventually, when Shelley announced lunch, feet clattered and voices started to chat.

Cleary pulled his sketch from the drawing-board without unpinning it, then threw it in the waste-bin. He was about to leave, but then walked over to Paula. 'Do you fancy a beer? There's a pub over the road.'

Paula hesitated, wanting to refuse, but then nodded agreement. They left the room together, but in the corridor she found she had left her bag behind. 'Would you mind waiting a moment?' she said, and hurried back. She got her bag and was about to leave again, when, remembering Cleary's discarded sketch, she walked over to the waste-bin and picked it out. The drawing made her catch her breath. It was astonishing. The draughtsmanship was crude, but it emanated immense power; it was as though Cleary had attacked the paper. Thick black lines scored the surface, almost breaking through in some places, but the materials had become something extraordinary; the drawing was possessed with life. Paula became aware somebody else was in the room, and turned to find Shelley, who had been concealed by the easels scattered around the studio.

He walked over and looked down at the drawing. 'Impressive, isn't it?' he said casually. She nodded speechlessly. 'Don't worry,' he said, knowing how inadequate she felt about her own abilities. 'It's early days yet.'

Paula covered the drawing with a sheet of paper and placed it carefully among her own possessions. When she caught up with Cleary, they left the building and crossed the road to a pub next to a small timber-merchant's yard, and the pungent scent of freshly cut wood hit them as they were about to enter the saloon bar. Cleary stopped, and breathed deeply. Paula did the same.

'Pine,' she said. 'It's a lovely smell.'

'It reminds me of the camp,' Cleary answered. 'There was a sawmill in the woods.'

259

'It reminds me of my childhood,' Paula told him.

After he had bought two pints of watery bitter and they had sat down, Cleary asked her, 'Why childhood?'

Paula had to think what he was talking about. 'Oh, the pine! My father's a builder in Notting Hill. I was thinking of the timber in his yard. I used to go there on Saturdays when I was on holiday.' Then she continued, 'How did you know about the storeman?'

Cleary put down his glass and searched for his cigarettes. 'I knew he'd been some kind of mechanic. They never get the oil out of the little cuts in their hands. The rest was a guess.'

'Do you often make guesses like that?'

Cleary took a mouthful of beer, and smiled. 'One of the books we had in the bag was *A Study in Scarlet*. After a year, most of us knew it by heart. We started a Sherlock Holmes society. It was a joke at first, but things can become an obsession when you're a prisoner. Like planning escapes that are never going to take place.' He stood up and gestured with his empty glass to offer her another beer, but Paula shook her head. Her own drink was hardly touched. When he came back with his drink, she asked, 'Didn't you want to escape?'

Cleary smiled bleakly. 'I did nearly two tours before we were shot down. I can still remember the feeling of relief when I got out of my parachute and realised I was going to live a bit longer.'

Paula felt a slight sense of disappointment. Because she was attracted to him, she wanted to see him in a heroic light.

'Shall we try the canteen after these?' he asked.

'Fine,' Paula replied with a quick smile. When they got up she noticed that he was still nursing the book covered in oilcloth, as though it were some kind of talisman.

The canteen was full of steam and the clatter of crockery and the heat generated by lots of people. The universal smell of wartime cooking, came to them as they stood in line waiting to be served. They found a vacant table in a corner of the large room under a notice-board.

Cleary put his book carefully against the leg of his chair, then turned his attention to his food. Before Paula had swallowed her second bite, he had finished. After a few mouthfuls of the tepid, unappetising food, she had lost her desire to eat, and pushed the plate aside.

'Don't you want any more?' he asked. Paula shook her head. Cleary pulled her plate towards him and ate the remainder of her food, then sat back and took out a packet of Players. He seemed to

260

consume everything so quickly that she almost expected him to take one long draw on the cigarette and reduce it to instant ash. Then she noticed that he was staring at the cleared plates. 'We didn't get much to eat in the last year,' he said without embarrassment. 'It seems to have left me feeling permanently hungry.'

Paula nodded. 'It was the same at my boarding school; some of the girls could never get enough to eat. It had the reverse effect with me.'

'Where did you go to school?' He leaned across the table intently.

'Near Epsom.'

Cleary continued to question Paula about her schools, and she told him the story of her life. By the time he had learned that her family had lived at Holland Park, that her mother was the daughter of an estate agent and her father the son and grandson of a respectable firm of local builders and that they lived in Ladbroke Grove, the refectory was almost empty.

'What about you?' Paula asked him when he stopped asking questions. 'Where did you go to school?'

'Along the river, near Hammersmith,' he said in a distracted way and reached up to the notice-board behind her and pulled down a postcard.

'How did you become interested in art?'

Cleary placed the card on the table between the empty plates and looked up. 'At school, at first. But it became a bit of an obsession in the prison camp.' Almost as an afterthought he picked up the oilcloth-covered book and passed it to her.

It was a fascinating object. Before she opened it, Paula examined the binding; the whole thing had been crafted with enormous care from the meanest of materials. The cover was made from cardboard, sacking and oilcloth. Ring binders of rolled tin held the covers and the contents together. Inside, the leaves were mostly brown wrapping-paper. It was a sketchbook. The early drawings were mostly of heads, and even though she did not know the people, she could tell he had the gift for likeness; crude as they were, they had that lifelike quality in all of them. Once again she felt a surge of envy. After the portraits came exercises in perspective and simple still life studies.

'Where did you get the materials?' she asked.

Cleary took the book back from her. He glanced at it for a moment and then closed it and held it with both hands. He smiled, remembering. 'I used to scrounge materials from everywhere. The

261

brown paper came from Red Cross parcels. When I was given that pile of cartridge-paper this morning, it was as if someone had handed me a wad of five-pound notes!' The room was almost empty now. A woman in a brown overall was clearing away the tables. 'Where do you live?' he asked suddenly.

'At home. It's not far on the Underground.'

'I was thinking of looking for a room around here.' Cleary pushed the postcard he had taken from the notice-board towards her. Written in a careful copperplate hand were the words: 'Furnished rooms suitable for students. Ten-minute bus ride from the college.' The address was in Kew. 'Please call after 5 pm' it said in the bottom corner.

'Do you think we ought to go back?' Paula asked, returning the card to him. Cleary nodded and they slowly walked through the corridors to the Life One studio.

They passed the rest of the afternoon sketching the plaster casts scattered about the studio, and at four o'clock, when the afternoon period ended, Cleary found a workmen's café near the college. He sat there, drinking tea, until just before five. The instructions on the card were a slight exaggeration: the bus ride took longer than ten minutes. But pale sunshine had begun to break through the thin clouds by the time he reached his destination. He stood beneath the portico of the house in the Kew Road and something nagged at his mind in an irritating fashion, like the knowledge of a forgotten task to be performed. Something about the house had brought the sensation even more sharply into focus, but he could not think why.

After pressing the bell, he turned and looked at his surroundings. The trees in the Kew Road had long reached maturity, as had the rhododendrons, laburnums and magnolias in the gardens.

While he was gazing down the street, a woman dismounted from a bicycle and wheeled it along the pathway towards him. She wore a grey gabardine raincoat and her face was obscured by a wide felt hat. At the foot of the stairs to the house, she looked up, and Cleary saw she was red-headed. Something about her face nagged at his memory, too.

'Hello,' she said in surprise, leaning the cycle against the wall of the house.

Cleary felt a sense of genuine familiarity at the sound of her voice. 'I've come about the advertisement for rooms,' he said.

She nodded, and indicated that he should follow her into a vast hall. He accompanied her to the kitchen at the back of the house, and then

262

he remembered.

'Have a seat,' she said.

He took a chair at the table, which was still dominated by a large dresser filled with Staffordshire plates. She filled a kettle at the large stone sink and borrowed his matches to light the stove. Without asking if he would care to join her, she made two cups of coffee from a bottle of thick dark liquid and sat down at the table. The sunshine played against the windows and the view was a mass of grey-blues and greens.

They sat in silence for a time, and then Cleary said, 'I don't remember your name.'

Irene looked up and did not smile. 'I thought you didn't forget anything?' she replied softly.

He sat back in his chair and glanced down at the cover of his sketchbook, which he was still holding. 'It's been a long war,' he said eventually, but when he looked at her again, he saw that Irene hadn't really changed at all.

Berlin, September 1945

Gideon walked slowly along the row of soldiers who stood at attention. He looked in turn at each of their faces. None of their eyes met his own. Each youth stared directly ahead, across the parade-ground, at the walls of the barracks still pock-marked by small-arms fire from the fighting during the spring. Eventually he stopped at the end of the row and turned to the imposing figure at his side. 'Carry on, Sergeant Major,' he said quietly, and walked away.

He was making for the Officers' Mess, but he could see a figure approaching from the barracks at another angle. To those watching from a distance, the sergeant who halted before Major Gideon and snapped to attention to deliver an immaculate salute would have seemed a model example of military exactitude. If they had been closer, the conversation might have proved surprising.

'The Colonel wants you, Gidsey,' Smudger Smith said with an intimacy he used only when they were alone.

'What for?' Gideon asked, as they turned to walk in the direction of the Commanding Officer's quarters.

'Some cunt from England you've got to take on the grand tour.' Then Smudger gestured towards the replacements they could now

263

hear Sergeant-Major Heather subjecting to a series of corrosive insults. 'What are the new lot like?'

Gideon shrugged. 'The usual. Kids. I suppose they're lucky. If they'd joined us when we were in the line, they would've been dead in a few days. Two of them look as if they haven't shaved yet.'

Smudger knew that Gideon was right: the regiment had fought its way across Europe from D Day. They had taken heavy casualties at first, but after a few months it seemed to be only the replacements who were killed. The old soldiers would survive. Quite soon they stopped bothering to learn the names of the new boys. Fresh-faced youths would arrive and, within days, would be dead or carried, wounded, to the rear. The original members of the battalion seemed to go on and on until the surrender.

Smudger looked at his watch; its jewelled face had once decorated the wrist of a young German officer who now lay, long dead, in the Falaise Gap. 'I'll wait until fourteen hundred hours, so you can give him some grub, and then pick you up in the jeep outside the Officers' Mess.'

Gideon nodded. They both took it for granted that Smudger would be the driver on the forthcoming tour.

He entered the barrack block, and his boots echoed on the polished stone of the long corridor leading to the quarters of Colonel Brian Marwood. The rooms had once belonged to the Commanding Officer of the battalion of Waffen SS who had occupied the barracks, and were appointed in the style Gideon had come to classify as 'Master Race Modern': rough white walls, stags' antlers and hideous pieces of massive black-wood furniture. Marwood and another officer were both admiring the death's-head emblem executed in stainless steel that hung over the fireplace.

'It's a bloody miracle the Russians left anything,' Marwood was saying to his companion. 'They usually tore the lot out, including the lavatory bowls.' He turned and smiled at Gideon. 'Hello, Jimmy. I've got an old friend of yours here.'

When the visitor held out his hand, Gideon recognised Ralph Keswick.

'Hello, Gideon,' the journalist said with a broad smile. 'Good to see you again.'

'Well, I'm damned!' Gideon replied, and he noticed the war correspondent flashes on Keswick's uniform. 'This is a bit of a change from the West End showrooms, Ralph!'

Keswick nodded to the ribbons on Gideon's battledress blouse.

'The same goes for you.'

'They're nothing special. We all got these – those of us who lived.'

'Shall we go and have some lunch?' Marwood suggested, and he led them through the grander parts of the building. 'I want you to show Keswick around for a couple of days, Jimmy,' he said when they reached the huge doors that led to the Officers' Mess.

'Delighted,' Gideon replied. 'We can begin immediately after lunch.'

Keswick was surprised by the splendour of the room. There was a vast beamed ceiling, and the décor of rough white walls with skulls and antlers had been repeated. The tables glittered with silver, and Keswick noted that the bar was stocked with every conceivable drink, from Slivovitz to American rye. He held up his glass of malt whisky appreciatively. 'This is a lot better than we do at home, old boy!' he said with some surprise.

Gideon nodded. 'The Russians thought this was going to be in their zone, so they dumped a lot of loot here. It was a sheer accident that we managed to retain it all.'

Gradually the Mess filled with officers, and further introductions were made. Keswick accepted another whisky, and then they sat down to lunch. He was surprised by how good the food was, in addition to the excellent wines.

'The Americans help us out a bit with the rations,' Colonel Marwood explained.

'How are the Germans managing?' Keswick asked.

'They're not,' Gideon answered, and the Colonel changed the subject to ask Keswick about life in England.

At five minutes past two, he and Gideon left the Mess, and found Smudger waiting outside. He handed Gideon a holster and pistol, and Keswick noticed that the sergeant was also armed.

'Are the guns really necessary?' he asked as they climbed into the jeep.

Gideon shrugged. 'It depends on your point of view. An armed gang held up a train at Anhalt station the other day; our convoys have had shooting matches with gangs of looters recently; and there are about four murders a day in Berlin that we get to hear about. So Sergeant Smith and I tend to be a bit old-fashioned when it comes to wandering about the city.'

Gideon made a final adjustment to the holster and turned back to Keswick. 'Right, what do you want to see?'

'The city,' he answered. 'Can you show me how it works?'

Gideon thought before he answered. 'At the moment, we're in the suburbs. The fighting wasn't so bad here. I take it you came in from the West?'

'Last night,' Keswick replied.

Gideon nodded. 'Okay, Smudger, take us to the black market in the Tiergarten,' he instructed.

They left the barracks and drove for a time through handsome streets of suburban houses. Then the landscape began to change. The last stretch of the journey into the city was awesome. Keswick had seen the results of bombing in England, but this was another dimension of destruction. Sometimes the road was only a notional track through the rubble. In places, buildings appeared to be still standing, but they were only scarred and pitted façades. Everywhere Keswick looked was a universal yellowish-grey colour through which ghost-like figures moved, too dispirited even to notice the jeep pass. Keswick had to keep reminding himself that these scarecrows, dressed in flapping rags, were the citizens of Berlin, the remnants of a people once destined to rule Europe.

'How do they live?' he asked eventually.

'The hopeless die, the weak beg and the strong survive on the black market.'

The road at this point hardly existed. Smudger slowed down to a crawl. He was smoking, and flipped the remains of his cigarette into the rubble. Immediately a figure dressed in a ragged uniform darted forward and picked up the still-burning stub. Keswick looked back and saw the man take a puff and then carefully extinguish it before placing the remains in his greatcoat pocket.

'He's a "Kippensammler",' said Gideon. 'They collect those bits and remanufacture them into whole cigarettes.'

'Why?' Keswick asked.

'Cigarettes are money, now. The currency is in chaos. As soon as the fighting stopped, a group of speculators got their hands on German occupation marks that were printed for the invasion of Poland. They bought up all the gold and diamonds in Berlin before anyone realised the stuff was worthless. When people realised they couldn't trust money, they reverted to barter. Now the basic commodity is cigarettes; even the ones they make themselves.'

The jeep edged its way onto the East-West Axis, the great road that bisected the city. To Keswick, the scene unfolding before him was like something from the dark ages. The crumbling remains of once grand buildings, shorn and shattered by bombing and artillery

266

fire, poked through the heaped rubble and served as a backdrop for the milling crowds of people clad in either the rags of the vanquished or the clean uniforms of the conquering armies. Vehicles that moved by their own power were owned by the victors. Everything else – cycles, handcarts, old perambulators – was manhandled by the defeated population.

Eventually Smudger stopped the jeep on the outskirts of a great seething mob of people in the Tiergarten. It was an incredible scene. Some shouted their wares, others stood in huddled groups and conducted their business with furtive glances. As they got closer, Keswick could smell the stench from thousands of unwashed bodies.

'That's it,' said Gideon. 'The spoils of war.' He turned to Keswick. 'You can buy anything in there, including human beings.'

Keswick studied the scene for a long time. 'Is this who we were fighting? This vile mob, this rabble?'

Gideon half-turned, and an almost imperceptible glance passed between him and Smudger. 'Is this what we fought for?' was becoming a popular expression among civilians. Soldiers regarded the words with a certain amount of irony.

'They're a mixed lot in there,' Gideon said laconically. 'Not all of them are Germans; there are displaced persons, deserters, Russians, Poles, Frenchmen, British, Americans.' He smiled. 'You could say they were the cream of the scum of Europe.' He asked Keswick, 'Do you have any cigarettes with you?'

'A couple of packets,' the reporter replied, reaching into his haversack.

'Come on,' Gideon said, and climbed from the jeep. Keswick followed him to the fringes of the crowd and watched while his companion struck up a conversation with two emaciated men. They were dressed in tattered overcoats and guarding a wooden crate on which rested a little pot. Keswick recognised it as Meissen.

Gideon spoke rapidly to them in German. When one of the men replied, Keswick could see that, despite his grey features, he was much younger than he had at first supposed. Gideon broke open the packet of cigarettes and exchanged five of them for the piece of china. He walked back to Keswick and handed it to him. The little bowl was exquisite; Keswick held the fragile object as he would a bird's egg.

'Half a pound of coffee, and you could have the whole bloody set,' said Gideon. 'And the castle it came from!'

While he spoke, Gideon watched a tall figure in a tattered suit who

267

moved through the crowd and stopped to talk to an American officer. Gideon studied the man, then suddenly pushed past Keswick and made for the two figures, but before he reached them, the civilian moved away in another direction. Gideon turned to follow, but the dense crowd closed up. He looked around, almost in desperation, but in those moments the man had been swallowed up.

He turned to make his way back to the jeep and found Smudger at his side. 'Captain Whitney-Ingram wants to see you, Gidsey,' Smith said. 'He's over there with the concert party.' A tattered group of musicians had struck up and were performing rather well.

Gideon had been delighted to encounter Charles Whitney-Ingram a month before, in the course of his official duties. Charles had matured into an easy-going, dry-humoured man and was a captain in the American garrison in Berlin. Previously little more than acquaintances, they had struck up an immediate, deep friendship.

As Gideon hurried up to him, Charles turned and smiled broadly. 'I've found him! Or he found me.'

'Laszlo?'

'None other,' said Charles.

'Where did he go?' said Gideon.

Whitney-Ingram shrugged. 'Christ only knows, but we're seeing him tonight at a place called the Cotton Club.'

Keswick was silent on the ride back. Like most newcomers to Berlin, he had been deeply affected by what he had seen of the shattered city. Soon they were driving through the suburbs again. When they reached the wall skirting the regimental headquarters his eye was caught by a crudely painted slogan. 'What does that say?' he asked.

Gideon followed his pointing finger. 'Enjoy the war, the peace will be terrible,' he read. 'That's a genuine piece of graffiti.'

'Genuine?'

Gideon nodded. 'Goebbels had a department in the Ministry of Propaganda that used to go out at night and paint slogans on walls.'

'What kinds of things did they write?' Keswick asked.

Gideon shrugged. 'If you want the V-2, then work; Victory or Siberia; that sort of thing.'

Keswick shook his head. 'What sort of country would have a secret government department to deface walls?'

Gideon smiled grimly. 'Who knows? Maybe we had one as well.'

The sentry waved them through the gates and Gideon told

268

Smudger to drop them off at the Officers' Mess. Keswick went to his room to work on a story, and Gideon decided he would take a long nap before dinner.

His servant woke him at six, and when he had washed and changed, he made his way to the Mess. Keswick had been there for some time, soothing his depression with malt whisky. Later, Gideon made sure Keswick was in good company at the bar by introducing him to three of the older captains before he slipped away.

Smudger was waiting for him with the jeep and two sub-machine-guns wrapped in a grey army blanket. According to Whitney-Ingram's directions, the Cotton Club was in a part of the American sector Gideon was not familiar with, but Smudger navigated his way through the pitted streets with his usual skill. There were few landmarks left in Berlin, just a dreary uniformity about the ruins. Occasional flickering lights showed among the rubble, where people were still living in the fragments of buildings, most of them without sanitation or running water; twentieth-century cave-dwellers, Gideon thought. We must be like sabre-toothed tigers to them now.

Smudger slowed the jeep. 'I bet it's around here, Gidsey.'

Groups of troops were talking to loitering girls at the roadside, a common sight in the city. Hundreds of thousands of German women had flooded west, in advance of the Russians, and the only menfolk not in the Wehrmacht were young boys and old men. The women survived by giving themselves to the occupation troops in exchange for food. Smudger edged forward. Three privates, who were clearly drunk, were blundering along the road being held by women who called out 'Kommon, Schatzi', between shrieks of laughter.

'There's a club around here; I can smell it,' Smudger said with conviction. He stopped the jeep and leaned out towards an American private who stood in a doorway with a paper-thin blonde girl. His young features were barely distinguishable in the darkness. 'Where's the Cotton Club, mate?' he asked.

The soldier gestured with his thumb. 'Straight on, a hundred feet on the right, in the basement.' He turned back to the girl.

They found the cellar, but before Smith followed Gideon into the club he fiddled under the bonnet of the jeep to disable the engine. Theft of army transport was common; it was the way Smith had obtained the vehicle in the first place. Then he took his bundle and joined Gideon in the doorway.

269

The interior of the club was extraordinary. One end of the long room was shored up by rough beams of timber, the result of Russian artillery. A glittering ball, of the sort Smudger remembered from the dance halls of his youth, was suspended from the ceiling. Studded with tiny mirrors, it revolved slowly, throwing darting speckles of light about the crowded room. The cigarette smoke was so thick that Gideon felt for a moment that it was tangible. At the end of the cellar, near the door, was a little bandstand where four musicians, so thin that their ancient dinner-jackets hung from them like drapes over furniture, were playing a frantic version of 'Hold that Tiger'.

Waiters, carrying trays of beer and cocktails, scurried between the packed tables. Uniformed figures from each of the conquering armies sat in the gloom, but the women were all German. For the most part they looked like the kind of female Gideon had seen in nightclubs all over the world. It did not take much to imagine them, a few months ago, sitting at these same tables with officers of their own country.

The noise was stupendous, everyone shouting in their own language over the blaring instruments of the band. One shout was universal, the ever-repeated 'Mach schnell, mach schnell', urging the weaving waiters to squirm faster between the tightly jammed tables.

As Gideon and Smudger stood in the doorway, a figure approached them; like the women, he was another familiar type in the world of nightclubs. His hands massaged each other as he edged towards them with a bobbing series of bows. Gideon gave the man a packet of Players, which disappeared into the pocket of his threadbare dinner-jacket in a quick fluid movement. He was the first German Gideon had seen in a long time who was fat.

'Is Captain Crow here?' he asked, using the name by which Whitney-Ingram had told him he was known in the Cotton Club.

'This way, gentlemen,' the German said, reaching out to take Smudger's bundle. The sergeant shook his head. The man paused, and then decided not to argue. Instead he led them to the ruined part of the room, where a section was curtained off. Sitting at a small table with a bottle of American whiskey between them were Charles Whitney-Ingram and a burly master-sergeant smoking a cigar.

'This is Jack Murphy,' Charles said, gesturing towards his companion. They shook hands.

Murphy pointed to the bottle. 'Better stick to this! We brought it with us.'

270

Gideon noticed the contrast between the two sergeants. The American looked like a prosperous New York barkeeper, powerfully built, but carrying too much weight on his muscular frame, and his hand had been soft when Gideon had shaken it. Smudger, on the other hand, was just bone, sinew and muscle. Half the size of the American, Gideon knew he was twice as dangerous. A waiter scurried up with two tiny glasses. Murphy poured the drinks until surface tension caused the liquid to bulge above the rims.

'Cheers!' Smudger said, sipping his whiskey.

'Not that way, bud,' Murphy said loudly. They could hear from the slur in his voice that he had drunk most of the whiskey in the almost empty bottle. 'Like this.' He raised his own full glass and downed the drink in one gulp.

Smudger smiled and shook his head. 'Not me, old son. My mum taught me never to bolt my food.'

Murphy looked at Smudger, and his contempt showed clearly in his expression. He took the cigar from his mouth and ground it out against the wall, a crude gesture that did not impress Gideon or Smith. They exchanged a glance, and Smudger eased away from the table slightly. They could both feel the belligerence emanating from the American sergeant.

'So where's this guy?' he asked. 'I ain't got all fucking night to wait for him.'

'Take it easy,' Charles answered calmly, and turned to Gideon. 'Murphy works in the transport pool.'

The sergeant nodded. 'Murphy gets it moved,' he said with a self-satisfied smile. 'That's what the other guys say. Last week I got a grand piano back to the States for some two-bit general.' He poured another drink, and tossed it back. 'I'm the only guy who isn't jerking off in this goddam army.' He nodded twice and, leaning towards Smudger, poked him in the chest with a meaty forefinger. 'Furniture, guns, money, liquor – I can get any fucking thing home for you.'

'Is that a fact?' Smudger said, shaking his head in admiration. He had also leaned forward now so that both his hands were below the table. 'Do you think you could get a letter home to my mum? She hasn't heard from me in months.'

As Smudger had anticipated, Murphy had no sense of humour. He held his fists up to Smudger's face. 'Listen, you little limey creep, one more crack out of you, and I'll tear your fucking head off and stuff it in your asshole!'

Smudger smiled before he answered amiably, 'Can you feel something like a flea-bite just above your dick?' Murphy tried to edge away, but his chair was against the wall. 'That's an SS officer's dagger,' Smudger continued. 'Now, if you don't mend your manners soon, old son, I'm going to make you a new belly-button.'

In the pause that followed, they all listened to the sound of the band and the roar of conversation from the room.

'You're bluffing,' Murphy said finally.

It was Gideon's turn to lean forward. 'Actually, he isn't, old boy.' He lowered his voice even further, so that Murphy had to strain against the sound of the band to hear. 'I'd be nice to him,' he said confidentially. 'Our medical officer says he's a psychopath. It's because he's so small. You know how they hate big chaps.'

Murphy held up his hands. 'Listen, let's all relax. Have another drink, for Chrissakes!'

Smudger sat back and slid the dagger back into the scabbard concealed inside his battledress.

Murphy patted the cuff of his sleeve against his perspiring forehead. 'Jesus, it's hot in here! When the fuck is this guy coming?'

They sat back, and the conversation gradually ceased. The band played two more noisy numbers, and then gave way to a girl, who began to sing softly with only the piano for accompaniment, her voice as low and as melancholy as a winter's day. A hush gradually fell on the room. Gideon sat with his back to the curtain, but he knew it had been pulled to one side when fragments of light suddenly played across Murphy's and Charles's faces. Then a voice said, 'I'll draw your picture for five dollars.'

Gideon stood up and turned to face Laszlo. They stood looking at each other for a few moments, then held each other in a long embrace.

'Jesus, Joseph and Mary,' Murphy said in a shocked voice. 'These fucking guys aren't faggots, are they?'

CHAPTER TWELVE

London, September 1945

There was still some light left, although heavy grey clouds had gathered since noon, but Nettlebury decided to call it a day. The rain that had begun to fall on the great skylights interrupted his train of thought, and he had also begun to feel hungry, a sure sign that Vera was on her way. As always, he carefully rinsed his brushes in turpentine, washed them in soapy water at the sink in the corner of the attic studio, then cleaned off his palette with a paint-knife and wiped it clean with a rag. Some artists liked to build up layer after layer of dried paint on their palettes, but Nettlebury preferred to begin each day with pristine tools. Once, many years before, a teacher at the Slade had told him that painting was about the accumulation of good habits; he had reminded himself of that phrase practically every day since he had first heard it.

He took a final look at the canvas before he left the room. The light was dimmer now, through the leaden, rain-lashed sky, but it was enough for him to judge how the work was progressing. Another twelve months at least, he thought to himself, and he remembered how optimistic he had been when he had told Hammond Shelley it would take only four years.

Circumstances had changed a great deal in that time. Vera's husband had died in 1942, so she and Nettlebury were now more or less open in their relationship, but Vera still kept her own house. She worked during the day at a hospital in Barnes, and came to the Nettleburys each evening, but still insisted on returning to her own house every other night. She claimed that walking her home was good exercise for Julian.

Tom and Maude Cooper were still with them. Tom had retired from the gasworks, but he still pottered around the garden. Maude was as vigorous as ever. She had worked for a munitions factory during the war in the same shop as Ted Porter, and they had become firm friends. They had lost touch with Doris, who had moved to Hastings after the gallery had been bombed.

Nettlebury had seen their income greatly reduced, with the gallery closed and Gideon in the army, so they had found it necessary to take boarders for the last few years, mostly from the Art School, but the house had been big enough to absorb them without too much discomfort.

He arrived in the kitchen half-expecting to find Vera, but instead was confronted by a large stranger, who sat at the table drinking from a mug. Richard Cleary stood up when he entered, but Nettlebury waved him to sit down again. 'What's that you're drinking?'

'Coffee,' Cleary replied. 'At least, I think it is.'

Nettlebury grimaced. 'Oh, well, I might as well have some.' He re-lit the gas and, while he was waiting for the kettle to boil, Irene came in with a basket of apples from the garden.

'We never used to bother with these before the war,' she said. 'Now I fight the birds for them.' Then she saw her father. 'Hello! Have you met Richard Cleary?'

'We haven't actually been introduced,' Nettlebury said, and held out his hand.

'He's a new student, just enrolled today. And an old friend.'

Nettlebury looked up from the cup into which he was pouring boiling water. 'You're a bit of a late starter, aren't you?' he said. Then he glanced down at the cup again. 'Blast, I've forgotten to put the damned stuff in again.'

'Sit down,' Irene commanded. 'I'll make it for you.'

Nettlebury did as he was told, and turned and smiled questioningly at Cleary.

'I've been in the Air Force,' he said.

'Oh, yes. Ex-serviceman's grant. Good idea, that. What's your stuff like?'

Cleary shrugged, unsure how to answer.

'My father is a painter,' Irene explained. She turned to her father. 'Give him a chance, Dad! He only began today.'

'I've got this,' Cleary said, pushing the sketchbook across the table. He sat drinking his coffee while Irene's father turned the pages. More women came in, and Irene introduced them. The first was a large, handsome woman called Maude Cooper who began to prepare vegetables at the sink. The second, Vera Simpson, was more

274

glamorous; Cleary judged her to be in her late forties. She wore an expensive fur coat, but when she removed it there was a white overall underneath.

'I can't bear that ghastly coffee,' she said. 'I'm going to have a proper drink. Would you care to join me, young man?' she asked Cleary.

He accepted, and she left the kitchen, returning a few minutes later with a silver tray on which were three crystal glasses containing pink gins. Nettlebury accepted his and acknowledged her kiss on the top of his head with a slight grunt. He went on examining Cleary's sketchbook.

The last to arrive was Anne. When she bustled in, Cleary was struck immediately, as were most people, by the similarity between the two sisters. In the hall was a picture of two girls that had puzzled him. He had taken the elder to be Irene, but the style of their clothes had set it in the early thirties. Now he realised that Irene had been the younger child in the painting.

'You'll never guess what I've got,' she said to her sister.

'What?' Irene asked.

'Colonel Middleton gave me a present,' said Anne.

Nettlebury looked up. 'How is he?'

'He's in splendid form. Look what he sent you.' Anne produced a brace of pheasants from a shopping-bag. 'He shot them a couple of weeks ago. He says they've been hanging long enough to eat now.'

'I should think so, too,' said Maude. She took the birds and held them at arm's length: it was clear from her expression that she did not care for game. She hung them outside the door.

'They do pong a bit,' Irene said, 'but I'm sure they'll be delicious when they're cooked.'

'You should have seen the face of the man next to me on the Underground; I think he thought I had a dead cat in the bag. Oh, you'll never guess who I had a drink with: Paul Trenton. He's a major in the Parachute Regiment. He'd just been to the palace to receive a decoration. He sent everyone his regards.'

Cleary watched them all as they settled round the table. They appeared to accept him without question; he felt no sense of being an outsider. 'Is that the Paul Trenton who's an artist?' he asked Anne.

'That's right. Do you know him?'

Cleary nodded. 'I nearly went to a party at his house once.'

While he spoke, Irene watched him with expressionless eyes, then

275

she turned to her sister. 'You're later than usual. What have you been doing?'

Anne leaned against the dresser and folded her arms. 'Actually, I resigned. It was meeting Paul that caused it. I've decided to start the gallery again.'

'That's wonderful! Can you manage on your own?' Irene asked.

Anne nodded. 'I think so. I've already spoken to Ted Porter. He's agreed to come back.'

'Are you sure you can handle it, darling?' Nettlebury asked dubiously.

'Well,' Anne said, 'it seems your son-in-law may be home quite soon. Colonel Middleton was shooting with some friends from the War Office, and he thinks Gideon's regiment is coming up on the list to be . . . what's the word?'

'Demobbed?' Cleary suggested.

'That's right,' said Anne. She held out her hand. 'We haven't been introduced. I'm Anne Gideon.'

'Richard Cleary,' he replied. 'I'm the new lodger.'

Anne smiled. 'It's a bit chaotic here, I'm afraid. I do hope you'll be comfortable.'

'I'm sure I shall. My recent lodgings haven't been a patch on this.'

'Oh, where have you been?' Irene asked.

'Prisoner-of-war camp,' Nettlebury answered for him, and he shut the sketchbook and handed it back.

Cleary folded his hands and looked at Nettlebury with the intensity with which he had listened to Hammond Shelley earlier. 'What do you think?'

Nettlebury raised his eyebrows and drank some of his pink gin. 'I'll talk to you later, when there's a bit more privacy.'

Maude Cooper turned from the sink. 'Oh, there's a letter from Mr Gideon. It's on the mantelpiece in the living-room.'

Anne hurried away, and Irene turned to Cleary. 'I suppose you'll want to see your room before you decide if it's suitable?'

Cleary shook his head. 'No, I'm sure I'll be happy to stay here.'

'When will you want to move in?' Irene asked.

Cleary picked up the small bag at the foot of the table and prepared to follow her. 'I'm ready now.'

'Good,' said Nettlebury. 'You can stay for dinner. It'll be a pleasure to have another man at the table.'

'Come on, then,' said Irene. 'I'll show you your room.'

Maude dried her hands. 'I'll have to get out some clean linen. The bed's not made up.'

Cleary followed them from the kitchen, and Nettlebury drank the last of his pink gin.

'Do you want another?' Vera asked.

He thought for a moment. 'Yes, I rather think I do.'

'What was the young man's work like?' she asked as she took his glass.

'It depends whether he sticks at it,' Nettlebury answered.

'And if he does?'

Nettlebury drummed his fingers on the table, then looked up at Vera. 'If he does, he could turn out to be the real thing.'

Irene took Cleary to the first floor and along to a large room overlooking the back garden. The windows were big enough to flood the interior with light. An easel leaned against the wall and the bare floorboards around it were splattered with old paint. Cleary opened one of the two big cupboards built either side of a large mantelpiece, where a gas-fire was fitted. There was nothing inside except a few ancient tins of corned beef. He turned away and sat on the little bed. It felt comfortable enough.

'There are only these to sit on, I'm afraid,' Irene said, indicating two overstuffed armchairs. 'The room is a bit bare, but it's good to work in. It used to be my studio.'

'It's perfect,' said Cleary. 'Why don't you use it any more?'

Irene shrugged. 'I just haven't bothered for some time.' Cleary nodded, looking round the big room. 'This lamp works, but it needs a new bulb. There's a big sitting-room on the right as you come into the house; we all usually go in there in the evenings. There are books in there and a wireless. The room opposite is private. You're the only boarder we have at present, but do come down if you want company.'

'I've had plenty of company for the last few years.'

Irene got up from her armchair. 'I'm sorry. Perhaps you'd like to be on your own?'

Cleary got up quickly from the bed, a frown of concern on his forehead. 'Forgive me,' he said. 'That sounded very ungracious. It's just that I was surrounded twenty-four hours a day in the camp. This – a room of one's own – it's a lot more than I've been used to.' He felt in his pocket and took out a packet of cigarettes. These were English; she remembered the last one he had offered her had been American. While he held the match for her, he said, 'You know,

277

when I left that night I didn't even know the address of this house . . . '

Irene nodded, but didn't speak.

'Then I was posted to the Midlands . . . ' He shrugged.

Somehow what had happened between them before now seemed to have created a barrier. In the silence, Irene stood up to open one of the sash windows. Cleary watched the smoke from their cigarettes draw away.

'The war seemed to scatter people all over the place,' she said finally.

Cleary came over to her. He said, 'I wish I'd sat next to you in the cinema that day.'

Berlin, the same day

The band in the Cotton Club had begun to play again. Gideon sat at the table and grinned at Laszlo who, like the Americans, downed the rye whiskey Murphy poured him in one swallow. He was thinner, and the lines were etched deeper in his face, but the years had not broken him. Even his suit, which had been repaired with neat darns and patches at the elbows and pockets, had a kind of faded grandeur, like an aristocrat forced into menial labour but still proclaiming a glorious past.

There was one question Gideon hardly dared ask. 'What about Elizabeth?'

Laszlo nodded. 'She's safe.' He accepted another glass of Murphy's whiskey.

'Did you see me at the black market in the Tiergarten today?' Gideon asked.

Laszlo smiled. 'Yes, and Keswick. He's a good chap, but he does always want to write stories about everything. That's why I asked Charles to bring you here tonight.'

Charles Whitney-Ingram held up his glass. 'That's not quite correct. He said that unless I brought you here, the deal was off.'

'What deal?' Gideon asked.

Murphy leaned forward, confident enough to take part in the conversation again. He gestured towards Laszlo with his thumb. 'This guy says he knows where there's a stash of Nazi loot.' He pointed to Charles. 'And if he gets some papers to get him and his woman out of the country, we get a cut.' He sat back in his seat. 'I get

278

to handle the freight concession.' He produced another cigar, and slowly stripped off the cellophane wrapper. 'But I see we got two new partners now, so whose end does their share come from?'

'Believe me,' Laszlo said, 'according to my information, there's plenty for everyone.' He turned to Charles. 'Have you got the papers?'

Charles produced a set of documents and handed them to Laszlo.

'So let's get going,' Murphy said impatiently.

Laszlo continued examining the papers as he spoke. 'We must wait for some time. Our guide will be here at midnight.' Then he looked up. 'Thank you, Charles. These look excellent.'

Charles nodded. 'They're genuine, and that's the best that money can buy.'

'How did you get them?' Gideon asked.

Charles shrugged. 'An old school-friend.'

Smudger smiled. 'Blimey, I thought it was only England where there was an old-boy network!'

Murphy had produced another bottle of whiskey. He broke the seal and poured more drinks.

Gideon turned to Laszlo. 'How did you and Elizabeth survive?'

Laszlo took another drink, but this time sipped it more slowly. 'With difficulty. Luckily I had some friends here. The Nazi Party was always at its weakest in Berlin; they never got more than a handful of votes in this city.' He downed another shot of the whiskey and nodded when Murphy offered the bottle. Gideon could see he had not lost his capacity to handle drink over the years. Laszlo raised the glass in salute, and continued, 'Because I have an Irish passport, I was classified as a citizen of a neutral state. I did some occasional work as a translator and I dealt in the black market. A friend of mine owned some rooming-houses; we used to move all the time. Towards the end, when the bombing was really bad, the system broke down and we lived in the ruins.'

'Why didn't you go home as soon as the fighting was over?' Gideon asked.

Laszlo smiled. 'I tried, but Elizabeth is German, remember? To the Allies, she was just another citizen of the Third Reich. We couldn't get married during the war because she was classified as Jewish. We couldn't marry when the Allies took over because she was a citizen of Nazi Germany.'

'So how will the papers help?'

Laszlo tapped his pocket. 'Today, papers are everything. They are

279

proof of my annulment from Sylvia, permission to get married and, most precious of all, travel documents.'

Gideon looked at his watch. It was just before twelve. The band was now playing softer music, and a few couples were swaying on the tiny dancing area of the floor. The curtain suddenly swung back, and Gideon looked up to see another familiar figure, Karl Schneider. Time had not been as kind to him as it had been to Laszlo. As another chair was brought to their crowded table, Gideon saw that Schneider was holding his left leg awkwardly to one side. What was left of his flaxen hair lay plastered to his skull in a few greasy strands, and the ancient suit he wore hung loosely on his shrunken frame. When he smiled momentarily, he revealed an almost toothless mouth. Gideon remembered the young confident figure at the railway station years before.

As if reading his thoughts, Schneider said, 'A long way from Basel, old boy!' His voice seemed to wheeze from his thin chest.

'I thought you were going to sit out the war in Switzerland?' said Gideon.

Schneider gave another gap-toothed smile. 'I'm afraid my insurance policy expired.'

'How?'

Schneider shrugged. 'Fortunes of war. I was knocked down in Zurich by a tram.' He slapped his stiff leg. 'When I woke up, I was in prison. They had found a set of rather compromising documents on me that I was about to sell. By the time my principal had heard about it, he could do nothing. He would have been implicated himself. The Swiss were most unpleasant; they revoked my dual nationality, and I was deported.' He looked round. 'But there are always swings and roundabouts in life. In the last years of the Third Reich I was a disgraced ex-jailbird, but today, I am one of the first people to qualify as being denazified, and a trusted servant of the occupying American forces.' He took a glass of whiskey and, like Laszlo, drank it in the American fashion. 'As soon as I get my false teeth fitted, I intend to stand as mayor.' He filled his glass again. 'But I see you are anxious to get on with the business in hand.' He reached inside his shirt and produced a grimy sheet of paper, which he laid carefully on the table.

Murphy snatched it up and spread it open. 'There's no goddam names on this!' he said angrily. 'It could be anywhere.'

Schneider nodded. 'That's my latest insurance policy, old boy. I shall have to take you there.'

'Well, for Chrissakes, let's get moving,' said Murphy.

Laszlo held up a hand. 'We have one stop to make on the way.'

Murphy had two vehicles parked in the dark street: a US army lorry and an ex-German staff officer's car. They were guarded by a slight youth in American private's uniform.

'Any problems, Emerson?' Murphy asked.

'No, Sarge,' the youth replied.

'I'll take the Captain and the Kraut in the truck, with you driving. Give the keys to the Mercedes to the Limeys.'

'We shall lead first in the staff car,' said Laszlo. 'After we have made the stop, Schneider can take over.'

Smudger stowed his bundle at his feet and they set off into the night, with Laszlo in the passenger seat giving directions. They drove through the ruins for about twenty minutes, until Laszlo told Smudger to stop. Then he went to the lorry and asked Charles to join them. While Murphy and the private stayed with the lorry, the rest picked their way through a rubble-strewn bomb-site.

'You don't think they'll go on without us?' Charles said, as they stumbled in single file through the ruins.

'Don't worry,' Laszlo reassured him. 'I still have the map.' They followed him until they reached a staircase that had once been on the inside of a building. 'Stay close to the wall,' he instructed as they began to climb. Two floors up, he stopped at a dark open doorway. By the light of a torch, Gideon could see a gaping hole in front of them. He shone his torch into the bowels of the building; it smelt damp and sweet with decay. Laszlo reached up behind the door and pulled down a plank. He laid it across the gap and they edged slowly across the gaping pit into the remains of the apartment house. They were now in a corridor that was quite well preserved.

'We used to hide from the Germans,' Laszlo said. 'Now the danger comes from deserters and gangsters. We still use the blackout curtains, so they can't see our lights.'

Half-way along the corridor he took a large key from his pocket and unlocked a heavy door. 'It's me,' he called out, and Gideon and Charles followed him in. It was surprisingly comfortable, apart from the cracks in the walls.

Two figures stood in the centre of the room: a slight, shabby man dressed as a priest, and Elizabeth. Despite her waif-like slenderness and the dark rings of fatigue underneath her eyes, she was as striking as ever, but her hair was now iron grey. When she embraced Gideon, he could feel how frail she was beneath her cotton dress.

'Look, Elizabeth,' said Laszlo. 'Here is another old face from the past.'

She studied Charles for a few moments before recognition came to her. 'Charles,' she said slowly. 'I haven't seen you since you were a boy.' Then tears began to flow down her cheeks. 'Forgive me,' she said, quickly wiping them with the back of her hand. 'But I am being rude. This is our friend, Father Klaus. He too has been a fugitive.'

Elizabeth's voice had changed; there was hardly any trace of an American accent and she spoke English as though it were a foreign language. Gideon shook hands with the priest. Father Klaus nodded, and gestured for the four of them to stand in front of him. It was not until that moment that Gideon realised he was acting as Laszlo's best man.

After the brief ceremony, when Elizabeth looked round the room, Gideon could see the signs of distress in her face.

Laszlo put an arm round her shoulder. 'We're quite safe now,' he said softly.

She smiled and nodded. They bade the priest goodbye and made their way back to the others. Elizabeth accompanied them, and Gideon noticed that she was as nimble as Laszlo when they crossed the heaps of rubble.

'For Chrissakes let's go,' Murphy muttered impatiently when they reached the vehicles.

Smudger kept on the tail-lights of the lorry until they were clear of the city and into the darkened countryside. The road was surprisingly good until they swung away to the right, and it turned into a bumpy cart-track, where they stopped. The headlights of the vehicles revealed a series of concrete blockhouses surmounted by the remains of anti-aircraft guns.

Schneider made some calculations from the map and chose one of the squat little buildings. They hurried towards it over the broken ground. 'These were constructed by the Luftwaffe,' he said, 'but this one was given a little extra dimension.' He led the way into the grim concrete interior, and they splashed through a puddled floor. There was a strong smell of sewage. 'Shine the torches over here,' he said, and they focused on a series of pipes that lined the wall. One of them was a lever. Schneider consulted his document and then pulled down on one piece and a section of the wall swung away to reveal a flight of steps.

Below was another chamber, about fifteen metres square. Gideon entered first. His torch played on two small iron chests on the floor near the entrance. When he raised the beam, he saw that the rest of the room was filled with paintings. The first one his torch illuminated was *The Girl in the White Dress*. As always, she was smiling at Gideon from her summer meadow. For a few minutes he stood transfixed, until Murphy pushed past him.

'Will you look at this fucking place?' he said in wonderment. 'How the sweet Jesus did the Krauts lose the war?' He bent to pick up one of the iron chests and grunted when he felt the weight.

'Leave those until last,' Charles told him. 'Get the paintings loaded.'

'Fuck the paintings,' Murphy replied. 'Who needs them? This could be full of gold.'

Charles took him by the shoulders and spun him round. He played his torch on a picture painted in rich glowing tones of scarlet, blue and emerald green that depicted bending figures listening to Christ. 'Listen, you dumb sack of Irish shit,' he said in a voice that was barely under control, 'this was painted by Paolo Uccello before Columbus discovered America. It's worth more gold than you could carry. So get it on the fucking truck first.'

Murphy looked at the picture with renewed respect. 'Emerson,' he called, 'let's get these paintings aboard.'

Schneider, too weak to help with the loading, stood in the truck to make sure that the pictures were so arranged that they would not be damaged by the jolting lorry.

After Charles's angry words, Murphy and the private were anxious to get on with the work. Gideon went and stood with Elizabeth, who was leaning against the bonnet of the staff car. They looked towards the east, where the first pale glow of dawn was on the horizon.

'Morning soon,' she said, and took the cigarette he offered her. 'They will think you and Sergeant Smith have deserted!'

Gideon smiled, and shook his head. 'No, they don't mind us wandering off for a few days.'

He lit her cigarette and then walked back to the entrance of the pillbox just as Laszlo was emerging with one of the two iron chests. Gideon could see that it was not as heavy as the one Murphy was carrying behind him.

'Why don't you put those in the trunk of the automobile?' Charles suggested.

'This one travels in the fucking truck with me,' Murphy panted.

Charles shrugged. 'As you wish.' He lifted the boot lid so that Laszlo could deposit his load.

'Okay, let's go!' Murphy shouted, climbing into the cabin of the

283

truck with Emerson. Charles and Schneider stayed in the rear with the cargo. The engines coughed into life and they swung around and bumped towards the autobahn. They reached the main road once again as the soft dawn light was beginning to illuminate the landscape. It was going to be a lovely day.

When they had been on the deserted road for some time, Murphy lit a cigar and slapped Emerson on the shoulder. 'Don't you love this country, kid?' he said in a voice brimming with high spirits. 'I think I'll stay over here and buy the whole fucking place. It'll be great real estate when they've cleaned the crap up.'

Murphy was referring to the old battlefield they were passing through. On each side of the road, the flat featureless landscape was littered with the hulks of burned-out tanks. Most of them were Russian T34s, their turret guns pointing towards Berlin. A few German Tigers faced in the opposite direction.

'Jesus, Sarge,' Emerson said, 'the Krauts must've put up a hell of a fight! You wouldn't believe it when you see them in the streets now.'

Emerson had not taken part in the war; his unit had arrived in Europe after the surrender. But he had heard plenty of old soldiers' stories.

Murphy nodded. 'It's a good job the women don't have the same attitude.' He took a deep pull at his cigar. 'When you were in high school, I bet you never thought you'd come over here and get all the pussy you wanted for a peanut-butter sandwich!' He suddenly leaned forward, peering at the deserted road. Ahead, two battered Wehrmacht personnel carriers were parked sideways across the autobahn. 'What the fuck is this?' Murphy said, and a round of nine-millimetre ammunition punched a neat hole through the truck's windscreen and entered his skull just above the bridge of his nose. The bullet flattened when it impacted on the bone and blew away most of the back of his head, spraying blood and brains on to Emerson's shoulder. The youth reacted quickly, jamming on the brakes, and the lorry skidded to the right, on to the soft shoulder of the concrete road.

Smudger had also heard the first shot. He braked automatically and swung the staff car off to the right, on to the edge of the wide plain. Gideon saw a line of shots hit the concrete surface of the roadway and ricochet off it. Smudger brought the car to a bumping halt behind an abandoned Russian T34 tank; the blackened armour shell protected them from the guns ahead. More shots followed. Smudger reached down to the floor of the staff car and unwrapped

284

the bundle in the army blanket. It contained two Thompson sub-machine-guns and a webbing belt of magazines. He passed one of the machine-guns to Gideon. Laszlo was now lying across Elizabeth.

'Stay low! You should be safe in here,' Gideon said. Then he called to Smudger. 'Ready?'

'Ready,' Smudger replied, and they opened their respective doors and rolled out on to the rough grass by the roadside. The sound of firing came again ahead.

As Gideon lay on the cold dew-soaked grass, the familiar sensation returned to him. The Thompson sub-machine-gun smelt of steel, wood and gun oil, and a light morning breeze touched his hands.

Smudger was listening to the guns firing. 'It sounds like two M1 carbines and three automatic pistols. We outgun them, unless they've got something in reserve.' He crawled on his belly to the edge of the T34's track and cautiously peered around. 'I don't think they can see us. They've got the truck pinned down.'

'Any cover?' Gideon asked.

'Yeah, twenty yards ahead. A dead tank, then another, thirty yards further on to the right.'

'What's the ground like?' Gideon asked.

'Like a running track, Gidsey.'

There was another flurry of shots, and a round smacked against the front of the tank.

'I hope that was a random shot,' said Smudger.

'We'll soon know!' Gideon got to his feet and set his back against the tank. 'Don't give me covering fire unless they open up. I'm going now.'

Then he sprinted from cover. He ran in a straight line across killing ground, hoping the enemy would not spot him. After fifteen paces, the turf ahead kicked up from the impact of a burst of fire from one of the M1 carbines. Then he heard the distinctive rattling sound of Smudger firing the Thompson from behind. Gideon knew there was little chance of his hitting anyone; designed for street fighting at close quarters, the sub-machine-gun was not an accurate weapon at any distance, but it was a comforting sound.

The seconds seemed to last for ever before he reached the cover of another burned-out Russian tank. He waited a minute or so to recover his breath, and then edged around the heavy-wheeled tracks. From his new position he could see Charles firing with cool deliberation from the rear of the truck. Although he was only armed with a German Luger, the assailants were not attempting to flank him. There was no sign of the others.

'How are you doing for ammunition?' Gideon called out.

Charles did not turn his head but continued to fire. 'I've got about a thousand rounds!' he shouted back. 'That's what was in Murphy's iron box.'

'Can you see them?'

'Yes. Three behind the trucks in the road and one each side of the road.'

Gideon edged round and looked quickly ahead. 'I want to get Smudger up,' he shouted. 'I'll fire a long burst at the three in the centre. Concentrate your fire on the one on the right. Wait for my whistle.'

'Got you,' Charles answered steadily.

Gideon gave his recognition call to Smudger, and then leaned forward and fired an entire fifteen-round magazine at the two trucks in the road. Seconds later Smudger was beside him.

'He's doing some nice work with that poxy little pistol,' he said breathlessly, gesturing towards Charles.

Gideon nodded. 'I'm going to take the one on the right. He's only got a handgun. You and Charles move against the one on the left. When we've knocked them out, we'll pincer the three in the middle.'

'Right,' said Smudger.

'Going now!' Gideon shouted, and he started another run. When he was fifteen paces from the objective, the man firing the pistol stepped from cover to aim a shot. Gideon heard the report and brought up the Thompson and fired a short burst. The man was flung back by the force of the rounds tearing into his padded combat-jacket. He could hear Smudger and Charles firing and the staccato bark from the carbines ahead.

'I'm number one!' Smudger shouted.

Gideon understood his meaning. If they both came round the Wehrmacht trucks at the same moment, they could easily be firing at each other as well as the enemy. He began to concentrate long bursts and the three men returned their own fire, as he intended. Bullets began to ricochet off the tank he was sheltering behind. Then Smudger's and Charles's weapons opened up, and it was all over.

It was now daylight, and there was total silence. Then the birds began to sing. Gideon walked across to where the bodies lay; they wore odd scraps from the uniforms of different armies and all were young. Smudger quickly went through the pockets of one wearing an English army battledress. There were no papers; but he found one grisly object, a severed woman's finger still inside a ring set with a large emerald stone. Smudger threw it away in disgust. Then Gideon and Charles climbed into the Wehrmacht trucks and drove them off the road, while Schneider and Emerson removed Murphy's body from the cabin of the American truck.

Gideon met Charles again in the middle of the autobahn, but as they did so, the engine of the US Army vehicle burst into life. They had to leap out of its path as it roared forward, swerving past them. Gideon glimpsed a grin of toothless triumph from Schneider. Emerson, driving, was staring grimly ahead.f

'The son of a bitch!' Charles yelled, and they sprinted to the staff car.

When they got there, Smudger was examining a deflated front tyre. A stray shot had torn a long gash in the outer wall. They stood and watched helplessly as the American truck dwindled on the horizon.

Smudger changed the wheel while Laszlo and Charles examined the contents of the remaining iron box. When they saw what it contained, their spirits rose. There were three heavy, beautifully made leather body-belts and six chamois-leather pouches, each about the size of a grapefruit. Laszlo opened one of the sacks first; it was full of precious stones.

Charles gave a chuckle. 'Things are looking a little better!' He opened one of the body-belts, and whistled. They were packed with gold coins, individually wrapped in soft tissue-paper.

'Mint condition,' said Laszlo. 'Louis and Napoleons.' He looked up into Charles's face. 'Fortune has smiled on us.'

Laszlo held out one of the belts to Smudger, who took it and turned to Gideon. 'What are you doing with yours, Gidsey?' he asked.

Gideon looked at Laszlo. 'Where are you and Elizabeth heading for now?'

He shrugged. 'Hamburg. From there we will be able to get a boat to Ireland.'

'Will you take my share and Smudger's with you?'

Laszlo nodded.

Gideon thought for a moment. 'Smudger will go with you as far as Hamburg. He kept me alive a long time; you may need him.' He turned to Smudger. 'Don't worry! I'll fix your absence with the Colonel. Make sure they get on a boat safely.'

Charles was leaning against the staff car. He held two of the leather belts in each hand, as though weighing them against each other. 'What are you two going to spend your share on?' he asked thoughtfully.

Gideon and Laszlo exchanged glances. 'Open the Archangel Gallery again,' Laszlo answered for them both.

Charles considered them. 'Do you want another partner?' The two of them grinned at each other, and then nodded. 'Oh, hell! Take my share as well, then.'

In the distance they could hear the drone of approaching engines. It turned out to be an American convoy heading for Berlin. 'We can hitch a lift with those guys,' Charles said to Gideon.

'We go right at the next crossroads if we're heading for Hamburg,' Smudger said, and he started the engine of the Mercedes.

It was broad daylight by now. They made their farewells on the battlefield, and then Gideon and Charles walked to the edge of the autobahn and stopped the last lorry in the convoy. They sat in the back among boxes of powdered milk, and watched the staff car follow them until, with a wave from Smudger, it swung off towards Hamburg.

'I wonder if he'll get a good price for the stuff?' Charles said.

'The best,' Gideon replied. But his mind was not on the trinkets in the iron box; all he could think of was a girl in a summer meadow.

England, January 1946

Paula Tuchman handed Hammond Shelley her spatula and he etched three fine lines down the back of the clay figure she had worked on all afternoon. He tapped the areas he had defined.

'Trapezius, rhomboid major and latissimus dorsi,' he said. 'Remember your anatomy lessons. If you know what purpose the muscles serve, you'll see the logic in the form of the body.' He gestured towards the male model, who was standing with his back to them. 'See how the shoulders swing and pull to the right. That's what you've got to convey.'

Paula sighed, and Shelley looked at her sharply. 'Don't get discouraged,' he said quietly, so that the other students in the studio could not hear. 'If I didn't think you were worth while, I wouldn't bother with you.'

288

Paula turned and looked at him in amazement. Since the previous September, Shelley had been unrelenting in his criticism of her efforts. Sometimes it was as though she and Richard Cleary were the only people in the class to incur his displeasure. Others did mediocre work, or idled away their days, and he was courteous and mild in his rebukes; but if Cleary or she did not produce the maximum of which they were capable, he had been cutting.

Cleary seemed to be able to cope with it better. Paula thought it was because he was older, and toughened by his time in the prison camp. On three of the occasions she had been subjected to a blistering analysis of her failures by Hammond Shelley, she had gone to the cloakroom and cried. Cleary, on the other hand, just seemed to shrug it off, although he took careful heed to correct any transgression Shelley thought he had committed.

'Thank you, Mr Fisher. That's enough for today,' Shelley called out to the model.

Paula walked over to Cleary, who was covering his work with a damp towel. 'Let's have a look,' she said.

Cleary removed the cloth. It was a good piece of work, but she knew her own was better. This was not his medium; he could only manage a competent job. Paula relished working in three dimensions. It was as though her hands and mind communicated directly with the clay. Cleary came into his own when he worked on paper. She could draw well, but not with the power he could command.

'Do you want a cup of tea?' he said casually, and then walked off before she could answer. Paula was used to his behaviour by now; it was as if he had suddenly become completely indifferent to the presence of others. Paula realised it wasn't a deliberate affectation, more as if his inner thoughts blocked out other people. She covered her model and followed him to the canteen, where she found him sitting alone at a table by the window.

'Hello,' he said in a friendly way.

'You won't believe this,' Paula told him. 'Hammond Shelley paid me a compliment!' She sat down next to him and stirred her tea with a pencil from the pocket of her clay-encrusted smock.

'Why shouldn't I believe you? Shelley thinks you're very good.'

Paula put down her cup. 'How do you know?'

Cleary shrugged and took a swallow of his tea. 'Julian Nettlebury told me. He's a friend of Shelley. They were at the Slade together a thousand years ago.'

Paula put down her tea and looked at him steadily. 'When did he tell you this?' she said quietly.

Cleary thought for a moment. 'Some time before Christmas, I think. He actually said we were the best of the bunch, but he wanted to see if we were made of the right stuff.'

Paula stood up and slowly shook her head. 'You are the most infuriating person I have ever known! Didn't it occur to you to tell me before now?' She walked away from the table.

Irene passed her at the entrance to the canteen. 'What's the matter with that girl?' she said, joining Cleary. In the months he had lived at Kew, their previous relationship had faded and gradually a friendship had developed. He had begun to treat her as she imagined a brother might.

He shrugged. 'I explained why Shelley was so hard on her. It seemed to make her upset.'

Irene sat down. 'But you've known the reason for months. Have you told her only now?'

He nodded. 'What your father said was supposed to be in confidence.'

'Did you tell her that?' Irene asked.

'No, I didn't.' He showed no trace of remorse.

'Why not?' Irene asked. 'You had a perfectly good opportunity. Why be so callous?'

Cleary produced a trumpet mouthpiece and warmed it in his hands. 'I don't want to explain myself, Irene. I don't belong to other people any more. I belonged to other people for six years. I know what my motives are. If someone misinterprets my actions . . . ' He shrugged. 'Well, that's their problem, not mine.' He lifted the mouthpiece to his lips and blew one clear note, before replacing it in his pocket.

Irene smiled. 'Where's the rest of the trumpet?'

'Still at Horriston airfield, for all I know. I used to take the mouthpiece with me on operations as a lucky charm.'

'It didn't work,' said Irene. 'You still got shot down.'

He looked at her, and her own gaze became unsteady. Sometimes his presence could be disturbing, and she felt echoes of their wartime encounter.

'I shall miss living with you,' he said eventually.

Irene looked away. 'I'd hardly call it living with me,' she answered lightly. 'Half the time you're not there.' She was referring to his habit of disappearing for days on end. Nobody at the house seemed to mind, apart from Maude Cooper who found it disconcerting when he did not turn up for meals. 'We used to have a cat like that,' she once remarked to Irene.

Cleary looked down at the table and ran his finger around the rim of his cup. He pushed his cup closer to hers and nodded down at them. 'People always say they're white,' he said. 'Take a careful look. Mine has tones of blue and yours pink.'

Irene studied the crockery and saw that he was right. She looked at her watch. 'It's half-past four. Do you want me to give you a lift?'

Cleary looked up at the clock. 'Yes, if you've got time. There's a place I want to take a look at in Nightingale Road. I thought you were taking an evening class.'

'Flu has struck down the student body. Haven't you noticed?' Irene replied.

Cleary glanced around the canteen and saw that there were far fewer people than usual at this time of the day. He shook his head, and returned his attention to the cups.

Irene noted that he was capable of observing the fine difference between inanimate objects as trivial as cups, but unaware of the human beings he saw most days. 'Come on,' she said, and led the way out.

'How did you manage to get petrol?' Cleary asked when they reached Gideon's red MG. It was quite dark and very cold. Lights from the building shone on the little car.

'Ted Porter scrounged some. I wish he could get some new tyres as well!'

They climbed into the open car and drove out of the square of cindered ground at the back of the Art School. From the sculpture room two floors above, Paula Tuchman watched them until they turned out of the gates.

It was a short journey through back streets to Nightingale Road, which ran close to the common. The houses were of a similar age and as substantial as Nettlebury's. Cleary was moving from Kew because Gideon was returning home. Anne planned to turn Cleary's bedsitter into a living-room, so that they could have some sort of privacy from the rest of the family. Cleary had found an advertisement for rooms in the window of a tobacconist near the Art School and had telephoned that morning for an appointment.

Irene parked the MG outside number 22 and they walked the length of the chipped marble pathway to the sheltered entrance. Cleary rang the bell. After some time, a harassed-looking woman came to the door. She was dressed in a coat and hat and carried a shopping-bag and an umbrella.

'Mrs Lipinski?' he asked. 'My name is Richard Cleary. I rang this morning about the rooms you have to let.'

'Oh, dear,' she said in an English accent, 'I thought you were coming later. I haven't had time to clean the rooms, and I'm just going shopping.' She hesitated. 'Would you mind looking for yourselves? Only I must get to the fish-shop before they close. I'm sorry about the mess.'

'Not at all. Don't worry about us,' Cleary replied.

She reached somewhere inside the hall and produced an enormous iron key, which she handed to Irene.

'Don't worry about disturbing anything, Mrs Cleary,' she said to Irene, who did not bother to correct the mistake. 'The last tenant has vacated the premises for good, but there are still some of his things in there.' She pointed to her left. 'Past the laurels and along the passage. It's the last door before you reach the back garden. Just pop the key through the letterbox when you're done.' Rain began to patter down, and Mrs Lipinski peered anxiously at the grey sky and unfurled her umbrella.

Irene looked back at the MG. 'Damn, the hood's not working,' she said, and ran back to cover the seats with an old blanket. After the first few hesitant drops, it began to rain heavily. Irene and Cleary hurried down the narrow brick passage and unlocked the door. A staircase led down into a large basement that would have been the servants' quarters in grander days. Now it had been converted into quite a large flat. In the bathroom, covered with hideous, dark green tiles, a great geyser loomed over the ancient claw-footed tub that was stained and streaked with age. What had once been the pantry was now a narrow kitchen, furnished with a sink and a greasy gas-stove. There were cheaply made cupboards and the same green tiles on the floor. As Mrs Lipinski had mentioned, there were still items of food scattered around: tea, sugar and a mouldy loaf. Irene picked up a half-filled bottle of sour milk, poured it into the sink and let the tap run until it had washed away. The bedsitting-room was huge, with sash windows running the length of it. They looked out, at ground level, on the walled garden, where the lights revealed two pear trees on a scruffy lawn.

'Mr Lipinski doesn't appear to be much of a gardener!' Cleary commented. They turned to examine the rest of the room. Two carpets heavy with dust, a table with four high-backed chairs and a dark red sofa set in front of an old stove. Behind the sofa and against the wall was a bed covered with a large piece of old green velvet. Cushions had been scattered on it in an attempt to make it look like another sofa. The walls had been painted with a pale green wash. The whole basement smelt of damp and dust, and very faintly of gas.

'This is splendid. I'll take it,' Cleary said, lighting a cigarette.

'There's nothing wrong that about two years' cleaning couldn't put right, I suppose,' Irene said, 'but I think you're taking a chance with that cigarette. The whole place might go up.'

'Will you come and clean it for me – Mrs Cleary?' he said, sitting down on the velvet-covered bed.

Irene sat down beside him. 'She did call me that, didn't she? It was an easy mistake to make, I suppose.'

'Is that why you didn't correct her?' he asked.

'Perhaps I was trying to provoke you,' said Irene. 'I didn't think you fancied me in that way any more.'

Cleary got up, walked to the stove, opened the lid and threw in the remains of his cigarette. 'I haven't fancied anyone in that way for three years,' he said without turning round.

'What do you mean? Don't you find women attractive any longer?'

He laughed humourlessly. 'I do; the old wedding tackle doesn't.' He spoke lightly. 'Permanent brewer's droop, old girl. Hopeless case, I'm afraid.'

Irene was surprised by his choice of words; she had never heard him use this kind of slang before. She looked out of the window and saw that the rain was still falling. Cleary took off his greatcoat and laid it on the arm of the sofa. 'Do you want to tell me about it?' she asked softly.

'There's really not much to tell.' He lit another cigarette. 'Towards the end of my last tour, there was a woman I was seeing regularly in Horriston. A widow, actually; her husband had been killed before Dunkirk. We weren't in love or anything, but we liked each other. I had two bad ops, one after the other, and the old love life just went out like a candle. I wasn't the only one.' He looked down at her. 'Then, of course, there wasn't any opportunity in the prison camp.'

'Have you talked to a doctor?' Irene asked.

He nodded. 'He just said it wasn't anything to worry about. He told me to put it out of my mind and it would just happen again.'

Irene looked down at the dusty carpet. 'You know it's been a long time for me, too. Sometimes I just miss someone holding me.'

293

'I can manage that,' he said, sitting down again and putting his arm round her. She shivered for a moment; it was bitterly cold. Cleary reached out to pull his greatcoat over them and they lay back on the bed. Gradually their bodies warmed each other, and he turned his head to kiss her gently. There was no rekindling of old memories, it was as though they were meeting for the first time. At first their mouths barely brushed together, but slowly their embrace became more demanding.

Cleary unbuttoned her dress, kissed her throat and gradually the valley between her breasts. With his free hand he reached between her legs to rub the bare flesh above her stockings and worked his hand into her underwear. Then he stopped, and sat up in astonishment. 'I think something is happening,' he said quietly.

Irene wriggled beneath the greatcoat and removed her knickers. 'You'd better hurry in case it goes again.'

Cleary pulled his clothes off and quickly mounted her. She moved urgently against him, her breath coming in gasps, then, before he was ready, she climaxed in a series of shuddering sighs.

Uncertain now, Cleary was about to withdraw, but Irene pulled him back. 'Slowly,' she said, and she began to rock him to the rhythm she wanted. After a time she began to moan with enjoyment. 'Harder,' she instructed him, and then 'Faster, faster!'

Cleary did as he was told until, unable to hold back any more, he came.

Irene caught the timing and brought herself to climax again at the same moment. They lay for a time in a tangle of loose clothes, and then she said, 'Well, it seems to be working now.'

'Yes,' he said and reached for her again, but she slipped from beneath the greatcoat.

'I'm going to have a cup of tea. Do you want one?' she asked.

'There's no milk.'

'I don't mind.'

Cleary felt strangely disconcerted by their encounter. Irene had been the dominant partner this time; it was not at all how he had intended it to be.

'Why did you lie to me?' Irene called out from the other room.

'Lie to you?' he repeated warily.

'Yes,' she said. She came back into the room carrying two cups.

They sat down at the table facing one another and Irene took a sip of her tea. 'You know, ladies' cloakrooms are a terrible place for gossip. Everyone knows that you've slept with Paula Tuchman and that blonde girl with hardly any breasts.'

'She has quite adequate breasts,' he replied eventually, and gestured towards her with his cup. 'Not in your class, I grant you, but there's plenty there.'

'You haven't answered my question.'

He shrugged. 'Maybe I can't bear rejection.'

'I wouldn't have rejected you. All you had to do was ask.'

He put down his cup. 'The truth is that I fancied you again from the first day, but I was living in your house. If we had started then, I could hardly have . . . '

'Had your way with half the women in the school?' she suggested.

'Something like that.' He reached out and held her hand. 'I'd been inside for nearly two years. I didn't feel ready to settle down.'

'Well, don't worry,' Irene said briskly. 'This was the first and last time, and it was for my benefit, not yours. I don't mind being your mistress, but I'm damned if I'll be one of your bits on the side!'

He took a firmer grip on her hand. 'I don't want to give you up now. Why don't you live with me?'

Irene held her cup with both hands. 'What about Paula and the blonde girl?'

'They're girls,' he said. 'I want you. How about it?'

Irene looked at the frowsty surroundings and slowly shook her head. 'Not here. If you really mean it, you'd better move into my room at Kew.'

'Won't your father mind?'

Irene shook her head. 'If he objects, I shall insist that he marries Vera!'

As they left the basement, rain dripped on them from the laurels. The air smelt fresh, and there was a heavy scent of wet earth from the garden. Mrs Lipinski was just returning from shopping, so they handed her the key at the gate.

'It would have been fine,' Cleary said to her, 'but this young lady insists that I go and live with her.'

'Aren't you married?' Mrs Lipinski said in a shocked voice. Cleary shook his head. 'It's just as well you're not taking it then,' she said haughtily. 'My husband is very religious.'

They pulled the wet blankets off the seats and set off through the rain-washed streets in the little car.

When they were crossing Kew Bridge, Irene suddenly braked hard and scrambled from the driving seat. 'Gideon, Gideon!' she called.

Cleary watched a slim man halt in the light of a street lamp. Irene ran to him and threw herself into his arms. He dropped the case he was carrying and lifted her off her feet to hug her. Then they linked arms and walked, laughing, back to the MG.

'This is my brother-in-law, James Gideon,' she said, 'and this is Richard Cleary.' They stood by the car, ignoring the rain.

'I've heard about you,' Cleary said, shaking hands.

'And I you,' Gideon replied. 'Anne wrote to me.' He bent and touched the car. 'I'm glad she's still running.'

'Where did you get that terrible hat?' Irene asked.

Gideon removed the offending object and sent it spinning over the parapet into the Thames. Then he held out the lapel of his suit from beneath his mackintosh. 'If you thought that was bad, what about this?'

'I had one just like it,' Cleary said. 'I sold it to a man in a pub for two pounds.'

'Do you want to drive?' Irene asked, climbing on to the little ledge behind the seats.

'If I can remember how,' he answered. But he handled the sports car without difficulty.

When they arrived at the house, Anne ran down the path. 'I saw you from the living-room window!' She thew herself into his arms. 'Oh, Gideon, you're home! Thank God you're home!'

They kissed on the pavement, and a passing motorist blew his horn twice in approval. Nettlebury and Vera were waiting in the hall. They moved into the living-room and Nettlebury distributed sherry, the only drink they had in the house.

During the confusion of greetings and embraces, Irene took the opportunity to raise the subject of her new living conditions. 'Incidentally, Dad, Richard and I are going to move in together.'

'Good, good,' Nettlebury answered without much interest. 'That means that Anne and Gideon can have his room, as we planned.'

Gideon reached into his bag. 'I've brought you some presents, compliments of the United States Army. An American friend gave them to me.' He had a large bottle of gin, one of vermouth and a jar of cocktail olives.

Nettlebury clapped his hands in delight. 'Dear God, now I finally know the war is over! I can make a decent dry Martini again. Everyone over here always puts too much vermouth in it,' he fussed. 'By the way, talking of America, a letter arrived for you only today.'

Gideon took the envelope and saw that it was from Charles

Whitney-Ingram, who had been discharged a few months before him. He sat down and read:

Dear James,
   Well, here I am back in New York, and the world is ready to buy pictures. There's so much money about you wouldn't believe it. At last I know what we were fighting for – so that the guys at home could get rich. Now it's our turn, but when do we begin? Have you heard from our other partner? I hope you write soon with good news. If there is no good news, don't write. I couldn't stand the disappointment.
   Yours ever, Charles.

Gideon folded the letter away and took a dry Martini from the tray.

'To us all,' said Nettlebury.

'And to absent friends,' Gideon added, thinking about Laszlo and Elizabeth.

CHAPTER THIRTEEN

London, summer 1946

Morning light streamed through a gap in the curtains and fell across Anne's hair spread over the pillow. Life in the army had accustomed him to rising early, but Gideon could see that his wife wanted to sleep on. It's going to be a good day, he told himself. He stood at the open bedroom window and watched the paper-boy walking up the path. The weather was perfect, a light breeze and a cloudless summer sky. Anne stirred. She had pushed the bedclothes away and was lying with one arm behind her head and the other over the counterpane, so that the top half of her torso was bare. In the soft light, she still looked like a girl.

He had been astonished by how much she and Ted Porter had achieved at the gallery when she took him to see the premises. Despite the shortages of practically all building and decorating materials, they had already managed to clear one large area to make do as a showroom, and they had whitewashed the rooms and hung what pictures had been salvaged from the old stock of the gallery. With Gideon's service gratuity, they had taken the lease on the other shop that was separated from them by the bomb-site.

'When we've rebuilt the hole in the middle, this will make a wonderful flat for us,' Anne said as they stood on the upper floor. She gestured towards the wall. 'We can knock it through and have one huge area for a living-room and library, with bedrooms and everything else on the floor above.'

'It could take years to make comfortable,' Gideon said doubtfully.

'I can wait,' Anne said firmly.

He grinned and put his arms round her. 'So you want to live over the shop?'

'Over it, but not in it,' she said. 'I want us to have our own front door. There'll be no access to the flat from the gallery. This will be our home, not an extension of the business.'

Gideon leaned forward and kissed her. 'You should have been in the army. The war would have ended years ago!'

So while the work went on, they continued to live at Kew. The house was large enough to accommodate them all without getting on each other's nerves. In fact they hardly saw Irene and Cleary, who were out most evenings and weekends. Cleary had joined a jazz band formed by a group of ex-servicemen. They played mostly in pubs around London and arrived home late at night to the sound of muffled thuds, when the van owned by one of the musicians deposited them at Kew in the early hours.

Nettlebury worked each day in his studio, only vaguely aware of the people around. In the evenings he and Vera would sit in the living-room, listening to the wireless or playing the gramophone. Occasionally he would venture into Soho with Hammond Shelley and Paul Trenton who had, once again, taken up residence in Laszlo's mews house.

Gideon had seen Smudger a couple of times, but apart from one postcard, he had heard nothing of Laszlo. He was whistling as he went down to collect Nettlebury's paper from the letter-box, when the telephone rang.

It was his father, another early riser. 'I'm glad it's you, James. Your mother and I are having a celebration today. It's our wedding anniversary.'

Gideon glanced at his newspaper. 'Your wedding anniversary is in March, Dad. It's August now.'

There was a pause. 'That was the date of our first wedding. We don't celebrate that any more,' Frank replied. 'Bring everybody: Julian, Vera, Irene and that chap she lives with – Richard, isn't it?'

'That's the fellow,'

'He's a good sort,' Frank continued. 'You know we went to the same school, St Paul's.'

'I thought you told me you went to Harrow,' said Gideon.

'I went there, too,' Frank said impatiently. 'I went to St Paul's first, when your grandfather was actor-manager at the Aldwych. When he went back to touring, I was sent to Harrow. Don't forget – one o'clock at the Ivy. Be sharp.'

'Tell that to Mother,' Gideon said, referring to Marjorie's habitual lateness for anything but the curtain going up on a theatrical performance.

As he walked into the kitchen, his father's words drifted through

299

his mind. He found Nettlebury sitting at the table and gave him his newspaper, then began to sort through the odds and ends that cluttered the Welsh dresser until he found what he was looking for: the postcard that had arrived some months before. The caption read: 'St Paul's at Christmas.' The only other words, apart from his address, were 'All's well.' The card was unsigned, but he recognised Laszlo's familiar handwriting. It was the last communication he had received from him since Smudger had returned to Berlin and told him that in Hamburg Laszlo and Elizabeth had boarded a Swedish ship bound for Dublin.

Maude Cooper poured him a cup of tea and turned back to the stove.

'Who was on the telephone?' Nettlebury asked, scanning the news pages.

'My father,' Gideon replied, sitting down beside him at the table. 'He wants to take everyone out to lunch today at the Ivy. It seems to be one of their wedding anniversaries.'

Maude had made some porridge; Gideon helped himself to a bowl and sprinkled a little sugar on it.

'Really?' Nettlebury turned to the cricket scores. 'How very generous of them. I hope it doesn't put ideas into Vera's head,' he said thoughtfully. 'Women lay claim to so many special occasions: the day we met, the first time you kissed me, when we heard this song. The list grows endless over the years.'

'What list, Dad?' Anne said as she entered.

Obviously Gideon had not been as silent as he intended when he left the bedroom. He looked round. 'Can you remember the first day I kissed you?' he asked, through a mouthful of porridge.

'Don't be silly!' Anne replied. 'Of course I can.'

Nettlebury raised his eyebrows at Gideon and returned to *The Times*.

'I can remember the first time my Tom kissed me, as well,' Mrs Cooper said, banging Nettlebury's boiled egg down in front of him.

'I'm going shopping early, Maude,' Anne said, 'before the rush. What do we need?'

'Don't get anything for lunch today,' said Gideon. 'My mother and father are taking us all to the Ivy. They just rang with the invitation.'

'How lovely! Do you think we could use Vera's car? It would be so much nicer than all dressing up and then having to go on the Underground.'

'I dare say,' Nettlebury answered. 'I think she's still got some petrol left.'

'I've got a spare gallon for the MG,' Gideon added. 'We can use that, if we have to.'

'Where are Irene and Richard?' Anne asked. 'Has anybody told them about the lunch?'

'I don't think they're down yet.'

'On the contrary, they've been up for hours,' Nettlebury said. 'He's working on a portrait of Irene in the conservatory.'

'He never stops, that young man.' Mrs Cooper pushed another plate of toast to Anne, who was making out her shopping-list at the table. 'We need flour, lard, salt and baking powder,' she added.

'He's done well to get into the Royal College so soon,' said Nettlebury. 'It's probably just as well. I understand from Hammond that the Principal at the Art School was unhappy about Irene living with one of the students.' He shook his head. 'The silly fool! Fancy trying to treat a man who has fought for his country like a little boy!'

Gideon drank some tea. 'How is he coming on, Julian?'

Cleary hardly ever showed any of his work, but kept it in the room he shared with Irene. Nettlebury knew of his progress from conversations with Hammond Shelley.

'Apparently, for a student with only one year of formal study, remarkably well. But Hammond says his efforts are still outstripped by his ambition. It's common enough in the precocious. If he could add your technique to his ideas, the results would really be worth seeing. Why don't you take a look at what he's doing now?'

Gideon walked out into the garden. It was still a beautiful morning. He stood drinking the last of his tea under the apple trees and then walked into the conservatory where Cleary was working. He was oblivious of Gideon's presence, but Irene smiled without speaking. Cleary was fighting the paint and canvas for the result he wanted; it looked like a losing battle. The man worked in a frenzy; it was as though he were surrounded by an aura of energy, but so much of it was wasted. The picture fascinated Gideon; despite the crudeness and lack of coherent form, it had great power.

To Gideon, Cleary looked like a boxer as he worked, constantly poised to attack an opponent. Suddenly he came to a full stop. As if a storm had blown away, the turbulence left him. He put down his brush and began to wipe his hands clean on a rag soaked in turpentine.

'Finished?' Gideon asked.

Cleary nodded. 'That's as far as I can take it.' He took a cover and

301

draped it over the picture.

Gideon felt like an intruder. He told them about the invitation to lunch, and they thanked him and went off to make their preparations. He looked around the conservatory; it was chaotic, compared with the conditions Nettlebury worked in. Tubes of paint were scattered at random on the old table-top, some without their caps. The palette Cleary used was a large piece of hardboard, sized to prevent the oils from penetrating the surface. Great globules of colour had been squeezed on to the surface and mixed at random. Cleary had discarded the brushes he had used without cleaning them properly, so they lay around, clotted with paint.

Gideon removed the cover and studied the picture. It was heavy with muddy colour; Cleary had tried to overcome the difficulty of different tones with thicker and thicker applications of paint. He glanced at his watch, and wondered. It was just after eight-thirty; Cleary's picture was not much more than an incomplete oil sketch, but he could see exactly what the man had been trying to achieve. He made up his mind. First he replaced the caps on all the tubes of paint and arranged them in their spectrums of colour. After ordering the materials to his liking, he cleaned all the brushes and found a piece of primed hardboard approximately the size of the canvas Cleary had just worked on. He was going to use Cleary's palette, but after a moment's thought he took it to the sink and scraped it down to the bare surface. After studying the portrait, he then took quite a long while to mix the colours. Then he was ready. He looked at his watch again and saw that it was now nine-fifteen. With a fine clean brush he diluted some Prussian blue and began to sketch lightly on the surface of the board, with his old sureness.

At ten to twelve he was finished. He could hear Anne calling him to hurry and get changed. It didn't take long.

When he came downstairs again he found Cleary waiting. The two of them had been cordial enough to each other during the months they had lived in the house, but they had not developed anything close to a friendship. Now he was leaning forward and Gideon could sense his aggression.

'Julian just told me that picture in the conservatory is your work,' he said sourly.

'That's right.'

'Why did you do it?'

'Because I liked your picture. I only have a talent for copying. I don't do original work.'

It was obvious that Cleary wanted to say more, but he was reluctant to do so in the presence of the rest of the family, who had begun to assemble. The hall was suddenly full of people.

'Shall I give you a lift to the restaurant in the MG?' Gideon suggested. 'It will give the women more room in Vera's car.'

Cleary shrugged. 'That's fine by me.'

They explained the new arrangements to the others and made their way to the car. Neither spoke until they were in Cromwell Road, and then Cleary said, 'Your picture is better than mine.'

'No, it isn't. I just painted the picture you had in mind. It really wasn't my work at all.'

'You got the effect I wanted,' Cleary said as they passed the Natural History Museum.

'I know. I told you, that's the talent I have.'

After another silence, Cleary said, 'When I try to paint with that amount of control, the work just goes dead. Why didn't that happen when you copied my picture?'

Gideon stopped at the lights by Harrods. 'Why don't you ask Nettlebury? He's a better teacher than I am.'

Cleary shook his head. 'I tried, but I keep thinking my pictures will come out like his; and I don't want to paint like that. You know how I want to paint.'

Gideon nodded. Once again, they travelled in silence until he stopped the car near the Ivy, then he leaned back in his seat and offered Cleary a cigarette. 'If you like, I can show you how to achieve what you want.'

Cleary hesitated, reluctant to take up the offer. 'Why would you?' he asked intensely.

Gideon thought for a moment. 'Curiosity, I suppose. I'd like to see what you might achieve if you brought your talent under control.'

'Okay,' Cleary answered, 'I'll try it your way.'

'But you've got to promise me one thing,' Gideon added.

'What's that?' Cleary asked, suspicious.

Gideon threw his cigarette away and turned to him. 'You've got to promise to stop squeezing the bloody paint from the middle of the tube!'

Cleary smiled. 'That's what Irene says about the toothpaste.'

'Is it a deal?'

'A deal,' Cleary replied, and they shook hands.

The others had already reached the restaurant. The head waiter told Gideon that they were in the bar on the first floor. When he and

Cleary entered the little room, his father handed him a glass of champagne.

Gideon was still slightly puzzled by the occasion; he could have sworn his parents' first anniversary was in November. He was about to question his mother when he heard more footsteps on the staircase and turned to see Laszlo and Elizabeth.

They were no longer the gaunt and gold shabby figures he had last seen in Germany. Elizabeth's hair was dark and glossy again, and the deep shadows were gone from beneath her eyes. She was as elegant and smart as he could ever remember her. Laszlo was still thin, but his clothes were new and beautifully cut. It was the rest of them in the room who looked down-at-heel.

Marjorie was the first to break the silence. 'Well, that was rather a long interval,' she said, taking Elizabeth's hands. 'Now, shall we get on with the rest of the play?'

Kilburn, London, later that day

There were times when Smudger Smith wished he were back in the army; and this particular Saturday afternoon was one of them. The tiny council flat where he lived with his parents, two sisters and brother-in-law seemed filled with discordant noise that assaulted him from every direction. From the bedroom nearby came the sound of hammering as his father erected new curtain pelmets under the direction of his mother, who was whitewashing the walls. Dreadful oaths would occasionally emanate from the head of the family when the work was not going to his liking, and there was a non-stop tirade from Mrs Smith, who was highly critical of her husband's craftsmanship. The elder of his sisters, Beryl, who was married, stood a few inches from his armchair, ironing, while a wireless set on the sideboard close to his head broadcast dance-band music at full volume for the benefit of his brother-in-law, Jack Harris, who was being taught to jitterbug by his younger sister, Eileen. Their feet pounded on an area of linoleum a few feet square. From the open window came the shouts of boys playing cricket in the street. There had been times, during the war, when he had been under artillery fire and had felt more comfortable.

'Do you remember my mate Gidsey?' Smudger asked Jack Harris, more in an effort to bring the dance to an end than to start a conversation.

'What's that?' Harris shouted.

'My mate Gidsey,' Smudger replied.

'Who was he?'

Smudger turned round and reduced the sound from the wireless. 'Gideon – you remember. The one who became an officer.'

Harris thought for a moment. He had been transferred to another regiment early in the war, but finally recollected Smudger's friend. 'I remember him. Why?'

Smudger looked at his newspaper again. 'It says here that a mate of his called Henri Bronstein has died and left two hundred and fifty million pounds to help fund a new homeland for the Jews.'

The amount of money did not impress anyone in the room; it was such a huge figure that it passed beyond the reality of wealth into cosmic figures, like the distance to the sun.

'What do they want a new homeland for? Don't they like Golders Green?' Beryl said, looking up from her ironing.

'It's not just a homeland for English Jews, you daft cow,' Harris said pleasantly. 'It's a place all the Jews in the world can go to. That's what all the trouble in Palestine is about.' Harris had spent the last part of his service in the Middle East, and spoke with some authority.

'Are all the Jews the same, then?' Beryl asked with sudden interest. There was a sudden violent burst of hammering from the bedroom and no one could speak for a moment. When it stopped, Harris continued, 'Of course they are! What the hell did you think they were?'

Beryl shrugged, and continued her ironing. 'I thought they were a different lot in each country, like Catholics.'

Harris shook his head. 'No, we had a lecture from some officer when we was in Tel Aviv. It seems the Romans got pissed off with them rebelling, so they knocked shit out of them, then all the Jews buggered off to other parts of the world. Now they want to go home again, and the Arabs don't want them back.'

Eileen, his younger sister, had come to sit on the arm of Smudger's chair. She was dressed only in a petticoat and, when she leaned forward, Jack Harris could see most of her breasts, a movement that did not go unobserved by Beryl. 'Go and put some bloody clothes on,' she commanded.

'Why?' Eileen pouted. 'There's only family here.'

'He's an in-law, not your real brother,' Beryl said grumpily.

Jack Harris smiled slyly. 'In Egypt, the Gippoes marry their brothers.'

'Get away!' said Eileen. 'You're having me on!'

'Straight up! The same officer told us that the ancient Pharaohs only married their brothers and sisters. There wasn't anybody else good enough for them.'

Eileen stood up to do her sister's bidding, but before she left the room, she looked down at Smudger. 'Blimey, fancy having to marry our Stanley!' She paused. 'Mind you, the family of that girl-friend of yours would like it. Then she wouldn't be knocking around with you, would she?'

Eileen had touched a raw spot. For the last few months Smudger had been keeping company with the daughter of a local greengrocer who had a wife with social pretensions. They considered themselves several notches higher on the social scale than the Smith family, who were respectable enough because they worked, but not really suitable to keep company with their daughter, Daphne.

Smudger looked up. 'At least she doesn't go prancing about like a tart chasing a pack of Yanks!'

Eileen turned on him in fury. 'I never had to do any chasing; they was all after me!' she shouted, and her words were followed by a cry of 'Howzat!' from the boys playing cricket below.

'Is that why you learned to run backwards?' Smudger replied. 'So you could make sure none of them were getting away?'

'Well, at least I didn't go around flogging people black-market oranges at five shillings each, with me nose stuck so high people could see up me nostrils.'

'No one wants to look up your nose; it's too hairy,' Smudger said quietly.

'Shut your rotten mouth!' Eileen thundered.

The door to the bedroom burst open, and Mr Smith stood there, quivering with rage. 'For Christ's sake, stop rowing in here!' he shouted. 'It's bad enough listening to your mother moaning without you lot starting a second front.'

'He started it,' Eileen snivelled.

Smudger got up, took the newly pressed shirt from Beryl and went into the tiny bathroom to change into his best suit. Since Beryl and Jack had married and moved in with them, he no longer had his own bedroom; that had been given up to Eileen. He now slept on a Put-U-Up couch in the living-room. A few minutes later he left the flat and was passing the boys in the street playing cricket, as he had done ten years before.

Nothing changes in Kilburn, he told himself, setting off through the sunny streets towards Daphne's house. Once he would have been contented with his life, but his years in the army had broadened his outlook. Also, his relationship with Gideon had altered his perception of the world. To be sure, friendships between officers and NCOs were unusual, but Gideon had been an unusual officer; he had really only been acting the part. He was incapable of the kind of prejudice most officers showed towards their class inferiors. In front of others, Gideon and Smudger had played the charade of gentleman and servant, but in private they had always regarded each other as equals, and this relationship had changed Smudger's attitude and expectations. Gideon had taught him to think beyond the narrow confines that had previously ruled his existence, and sown seeds of discontent with his life.

After ten minutes, the block of council flats and grim mouldering old houses gave way to pleasant tree-lined streets of semi-detached houses. While he walked, Smudger thought of his plans to emigrate to Australia and make a new beginning, but he realised they were no more than day-dreams. Daphne would not agree to leave her family, and he knew now that he could not contemplate living without her.

He had met her at a dance organised by the cricket club of the factory he was working in. She was small and dark-haired, and so pretty that she had been called 'Snow White' by the other children when she was at school. 'I suppose that makes me one of the Seven Dwarves,' Smudger had said when she told him, on their first evening together, at the cinema.

Eventually he turned into a front garden and knocked on the door of the neat little house. Through the stained-glass panel he could see Daphne answering his summons. When he was in the hall, he leaned forward to kiss her and felt the same lurch in his stomach he experienced whenever he saw her.

But she pulled away. 'Mum's making tea in the kitchen,' she whispered. 'My Uncle Fred's coming today.'

Smudger made a face when her mother called out, 'Who was at the front door, Daphne?'

'It's Stanley, Mum.'

There was a pause before her mother said, 'Don't you remember, Uncle Fred's coming today?'

Daphne ushered him into the living-room and Smudger heard her exchange muttered words in the kitchen. He remained standing in the pristine room, for Daphne's mother was an inveterate plumper of cushions and he did not want to create any further work

307

for her. A marmalade-coloured cat stalked in and inspected him disdainfully before leaping nimbly on to the upright piano. It curled up in a ball among the family photographs. Smudger examined a studio portrait of Daphne, taken when she was thirteen. She had shorter hair then, but it was obvious how beautiful she was going to be. He smiled at the photograph and turned to look through the bay windows, where he could see her father edging his car into the little drive by the side of the house. Another man got out of the passenger seat. So this is the legendary Uncle Fred, Smudger thought, and watched the slight balding figure as they approached the front door.

'Oh, hello, Stanley,' Daphne's father said as he entered the room. He turned to the other man. 'This is a friend of Daphne's, Stanley Smith. Stanley, I'd like you to meet Daphne's Uncle, Fred Peake.'

Smudger shook the offered hand.

'And what do you do, Stan?'

Uncle Fred asked, sitting carelessly on the sofa, crushing cushions with thoughtless ease.

'Stan's waiting for his boat to come in – aren't you, boy?' Mr Peake said, pouring a glass of sherry from the decanter on the sideboard.

In an unguarded moment Smudger had told Daphne's parents about his share of the treasure they had found in Germany, but weeks had turned into months and there was no word from Laszlo. Now he bitterly regretted his indiscretion, for his expectations had become something of a joke with Daphne's parents. 'I work in a shoe factory,' he said, and he looked Fred Peake squarely in the face, defying him to make a slighting comment.

'What do you want to do?' Fred asked.

Smudger could see that the man was sincere. 'Start a road haulage business.'

Fred Peake nodded. 'That's a sensible idea; there's a lot of money in lorries. It's a pity you haven't got six thousand pounds, or I would have sold you mine.'

Smudger could tell that he was not being patronising.

'Why are you selling them if it's a good business?'

Peake smiled. 'Good boy. I'll tell you why. I haven't got time to run it myself any more, and it's going to pieces. You've got to watch a business all the time. People don't care a bugger if they're just working for wages.'

Mrs Peake bustled into the room and greeted her brother-in-law. There was less of a welcome when she turned to Smudger. 'Daphne tells me you're staying to tea as well, Stanley,' she said in the cool

308

tones she usually reserved for him.

'Not if I wasn't expected, Mrs Peake,' he replied.

'The place is set now.' She accepted a glass of sherry from her husband.

They moved to the table that had been prepared in the bay window overlooking the front garden, and sat down.

'That's a nice bit of ham,' Fred Peake said when his salad was presented.

His brother winked. 'Shopkeepers don't go short, Fred. We know it's not the Savoy, like you're used to, but we manage to do all right.'

'I wonder what caviar tastes like?' said Daphne.

'It's fishy,' Smudger told her.

'Have you eaten caviar, then, Stanley?' Mrs Peake asked doubtfully.

'Yes, lots of times. The Russians left a load in the barracks we were stationed in. The lads got sick of it in the end.'

'Pity you didn't bring some home with you,' Mrs Peake said. 'It would have been more use than all that gold you were supposed to have given away.'

Smudger looked down at his plate, and kept his eyes on the tiny piece of ham Mrs Peake had served him. Right now he wanted to seize the edge of the table and tip the contents over Daphne's mother. Instead, he took a firmer grip on his knife and fork and cut the meat into four small squares.

Daphne shot Smudger a glance of sympathy. Then she looked out of the window. 'There're two men getting out of a little red car and coming in here,' she said. The others followed her gaze.

'Who the hell are they?' said Daphne's father.

Fred Peake put down his napkin. 'I think I recognise one of them.' He sounded surprised.

'They're friends of mine,' Smudger said quietly. 'They must have been to the flat.'

'Well, they look like gentlemen,' Mrs Peake said, concerned. 'I'll go and let them in.'

A few moments later Laszlo and Gideon stood in the living-room. After a confusion of introductions, Gideon remembered Uncle Fred.

'Good God, Mr Peake! Did you sell those diamonds?' Gideon asked.

Fred Peake nodded. 'And it was the beginning of a lot of things,' he replied, while the rest of the family looked on in bewilderment.

Laszlo turned to Smudger. 'We did well on the deal,' he said, 'but I'm sorry you had to wait so long for your share.' He produced a thick wad of white five-pound notes from his inner pocket and handed it to Smudger.

'Is this all mine?' he said, as silence fell on the room.

'Oh, no,' Laszlo replied. 'I thought you might want to have some spending money.' He produced a cheque and handed it to Smudger, who could not speak. He handed it to Daphne, and Mrs Peake strained over her daughter's shoulder to read the amount.

'I think I'll be able to buy your haulage business after all, Fred,' Smudger said when his voice returned.

There was another silence, and then Mrs Peake said, 'Would you like some more ham, Stanley?'

England, January 1947

It was mid-morning and icy cold in the sitting-room at Kew. Anne sat at her father's desk, wearing Gideon's old army greatcoat and a pair of woollen mittens, working on a new set of books for the Archangel Gallery. The door opened, and she looked up to see Richard Cleary.

'Christ, it's freezing in here! Why don't you come and work in the conservatory, where there's an oil stove?' he said, standing over her.

Anne smiled. 'Have you any idea how noisy you are when you work? It's all grunts, groans and mutterings. I'd never get anything done!'

'Well, come and take a look. It's finished.'

Anne got up and followed him into the conservatory. Cleary ordered her to sit down in front of an easel, on which a picture was concealed by a piece of cloth. She sank gratefully into one of the old wicker chairs. She had been bending over the desk for some hours and was aware of an ache between her shoulder-blades.

'Ready?' Cleary said. Anne nodded. He pulled away the cloth, and she smiled with pleasure.

'It's lovely, Richard! They'll be delighted.'

Before her stood a new sign for the Archangel Gallery. Cleary had, once again, painted the angel's wing from the Botticelli. In recent months, under Gideon's tutelage, he had gradually gained a control that he thought he would never possess. Anne could see that the painting lacked the refinement Gideon had brought to the original, but it was, none the less, a fine piece of work.

310

Cleary stroked the edge of the board. 'A couple of coats of varnish, and it'll be ready to go up again.'

Anne looked out of the windows into the snow-clad garden. Like the rest of the country, all was frozen. The only person she knew who seemed happy with the weather was her father, who had completed *The Ascent of Mankind* and in recent weeks had set off into the surrounding suburbs to paint townscapes in their dramatic blankets of snow. Each day he wheeled a cart containing his equipment through the icy streets and returned at twilight, half-frozen, but perfectly happy.

'I think I'll put some bread out for the birds,' Anne said, and returned to hear Gideon shouting, 'Hello', from the hall.

He came into the kitchen with Laszlo and Ted Porter. Despite their heavy overcoats, they were clearly very cold – with the exception of Laszlo who, Anne noticed, had not even bothered with gloves. Gideon and Ted Porter beat their arms against their bodies and blew on their hands until Anne lit the oven so that they could warm themselves.

Gideon filled a kettle and set it on the stove. 'We saw Julian in Brentford,' he called out to Anne, who had gone to tell Cleary that he was in the house.

'How was he?' she asked, coming back into the room.

'Happy as a sandboy,' Laszlo answered. 'Or should I say snowman in this weather? We offered him a lift, but he said he was off to work on a picture of the canal.'

Anne finished making the tea. 'Bring your cups out to the conservatory. Richard has something to show you.'

They trooped after her and stood in front of the easel, which Cleary had covered again. He waited until they were all in position and then pulled away the cloth. At first he was puzzled by their silence; he had expected comments. Instead, they stood in the sharp bright reflected light from the snow-clad garden and stared at the image of the angel's wing. Then he realised that each of them was remembering his own moments from the past. It was up to him to bring them back to the present.

'How many marks out of ten?' he said, nudging Gideon, who coughed, and walked forward to examine the painting more closely.

'For execution, eight out of ten. For a kind and thoughtful gesture, full marks.'

The spell of the past was broken, and they began chattering.

'How is the old stock of pictures?' Anne asked Gideon.

311

He exchanged glances with Ted and Laszlo. They had been out to Buckinghamshire, to the barn where Ted Porter had taken the remains of the Archangel collection after the bomb-site had been cleared in 1940.

'Much as we expected. The first lorry-load we got away is fine, but the rest are mostly beyond repair. It's heartbreaking. We can save some with careful restoration; but nearly all of your father's work was intact.'

Anne stood by the window, looking out. 'I must have been in the most expensive shelter in the world,' she said.

Gideon came and stood beside her. 'It was worth every penny.' They both gazed at the bleak landscape.

'It's a hard time for birds,' she said.

'It's a hard time to be opening a gallery,' he said with a smile.

Anne rested her head on his shoulder. They watched the sparrows and starlings hungrily devouring the food she had scattered. Then the snow began to fall again.

London, the following week

Karl Schneider smiled experimentally into the foxed-looking glass of the dressing-table and reached up with a forefinger to touch one of his new false teeth. Then he leaned forward and ran the same finger along his hairline. In the last year, with the benefit of a better diet, his skin had lost its grey, lifeless texture and some of his hair had begun to grow again. In the bathroom he could hear his sister Klara singing a song that had been popular with the Wehrmacht during the Winter War of 1942. He opened the door; she was standing, quite naked, vigorously drying her hair with a threadbare towel. 'I told you to stop singing that song,' he said irritably. 'The war's over, you know.'

Klara wrapped the towel around her head, turned to the misted mirror, and began to apply her make-up. 'I remember. We lost.'

Schneider tapped the side of the bath with his walking-stick. 'We didn't lose. The Germans lost. We're Swiss.'

'I was married to a German staff officer,' she replied.

Schneider looked at her splendid body dispassionately, as he would a work of art for which he intended to find a wealthy customer. 'Well, Stalingrad was a long time ago. Now we are pleased at the outcome. Civilisation has been saved, and people will start buying pictures once again.'

Klara pushed past him and examined her meagre collection of clothes in the wardrobe. 'Will we be able to take a taxi to this place?' she asked, selecting an elegant suit that had been made in Paris some years earlier.

Her brother picked up a long rolled brown-paper package that was leaning against the wall. 'For today, we make do with the Underground. But if all goes well, it will be in taxis and fur coats once again.'

Klara nodded, and resumed her humming.

The weather was so appalling when they left the little hotel near Paddington that Karl Schneider relented and took the last pound note out of his wallet. After a few minutes' wait in the falling snow, he managed to get a taxi.

'Are you foreigners?' the driver called out as they rattled along the Bayswater Road.

'Swiss,' Schneider replied.

'I thought you might be Americans,' the driver said mournfully. 'We had a lot of Yanks here during the war. They were good tippers.'

Despite his careful hint, Schneider gave the man only sixpence when he dropped them in Bond Street. He paused for a moment to examine their reflection in the window of Anthony Strange's gallery; in his world, appearances were everything. Satisfied, they entered the showroom and found Strange in the middle of negotiating a sale. It was clear that the customer was not going to buy the painting, but merely showing off to the young woman who accompanied him.

Schneider decided to take a hand. His new false teeth, elegant suit and smart black trilby made him look quite presentable. He slid the hat forward in a quick salute to the woman. She returned his smile, and suddenly he felt confident.

'Forgive me,' he said. Then he turned to Strange. 'Anthony, I told you I wanted to buy this picture.' He bowed to the man. 'I am sorry, sir, but I have first claim on this Matisse. It was in our family collection.' He turned back to Strange. 'I have sold some of my mother's jewellery. I will buy back the picture for the price we discussed.'

Strange knew the part he was expected to play. 'I'm sorry, Karl,' he said firmly. 'Our agreement was until noon. If this gentleman now wants the picture, he must have the first choice.'

'Whatever he offers you, plus one hundred,' Schneider said dramatically.

313

Strange shook his head. 'This gallery does not conduct its business in such a fashion,' he said stiffly.

'Oh, let them have it, Lionel,' the young woman said, 'if he's sold his mother's things for it.' She spoke with a cultivated voice unlike that of the middle-aged man, who flicked a glance from Schneider to Strange and then shook his head.

'Business is business,' he said decisively. He handed Strange a card. 'Have it delivered to the Dorchester,' he instructed. As they swept from the showroom, the young woman winked at Klara, who did not care for the familiarity at all.

When they had gone, Strange said, 'I think you fooled him, but not her, Karl. Do you think you're losing your touch?'

Schneider raised his arms in an extravagant shrug.

'So what can I do for you?' Strange asked, with some condescension. Things had changed a great deal since they had last met; Schneider had even detected a note of reluctance in Strange's voice when he had telephoned to make the appointment.

'I have come to make you a proposition, Anthony,' Schneider said.

One of the other sales assistants began to approach, but Strange gestured for him to keep his distance. He did not want witnesses to the details of any deal Schneider was about to propose. 'Go on,' Strange said, watching Klara out of the corner of his eye. She had removed her coat and was examining a small Brancusi sculpture set on a plinth in the centre of the showroom.

'I have some excellent pictures in my possession,' said Schneider. 'So good, in fact, that I am willing to trade half their value for an interest in your gallery.'

Strange looked at him carefully before he answered. 'What sort of quality are we talking about?'

Schneider had rehearsed this moment in the bedroom of his Paddington hotel. 'Quality like this.' He thrust out the package. In one movement, the canvas wrapped inside the brown paper unrolled at their feet. It was the Degas of *The Girl in the White Dress*. Strange looked down at the familiar picture. Then Schneider fired his second shot. 'But forgive me,' he said. 'I did not introduce my sister, Princess Klara Reisenauer.'

At the sound of the word 'Princess', Strange's shoulders seemed to slope forward and droop in obeisance. A fawning smile came to his face and he reached out to take the hand Klara held out. It was clearly not meant to be shaken. Strange bowed forward blissfully as his lips touched royal flesh.

314

Schneider watched the scene with great satisfaction, but then his eye was caught by a figure at the window. Through the falling snow, he thought he saw a ghost from the past. It was Elizabeth, on her way to the new premises of the Archangel Gallery.

New York, summer 1947

Gideon and Charles Whitney-Ingram walked slowly in the sweltering shadows of Fifth Avenue until they reached West 44th Street, where they turned, and Gideon was glad to see the canopy of the Algonquin Hotel. Its lobby was cool and dark. They walked straight through to the restaurant. A waiter poured them glasses of iced water the moment they had taken their seats.

Gideon nodded his thanks and continued the conversation that had absorbed them since leaving the exhibition they had visited that morning.

'So Schneider is now in partnership with Anthony Strange, and *The Girl in the White Dress* is back in their window,' said Charles.

'That's right.' Although Gideon had been in New York for the past week, they had hardly seen each other. They had intended to spend the whole time together, but for the last few days Charles had been in Philadelphia, where he had been called by the death of an uncle from whom he had certain expectations. He had returned to New York that morning, and they were cramming all they could into the day. Gideon was due to leave for home that afternoon.

'Have you spoken to Schneider?' Charles asked.

Gideon nodded. 'He says he got some of the paintings, but Emerson double-crossed him and made off with the rest.'

'Emerson,' Charles said reflectively. 'You know, I can't even remember what he looked like.'

Gideon shook his head. 'Nor me. He just had one of those young soldier faces; there were thousands of them like that.'

'And we'll never know what he managed to keep for himself.' Charles shrugged. 'Oh, well. Fortunes of war. And you say Irene Nettlebury is pregnant now?'

'Irene Cleary; she got married.'

Charles thought for a moment. 'You know, I had a crush on her when we were kids. And what about Laszlo and Elizabeth?'

Gideon smiled. 'I've never seen a couple so close.'

315

'What about Elizabeth's family?' Charles asked. 'How did they take it?'

'In a curious fashion. Elizabeth's father died and left most of his money to the state of Israel, the same as Henri Bronstein. Elizabeth's mother wanted to contest the will, I think; she could never really accept that she was Jewish. But Elizabeth insisted it be carried out to the letter; that was why they were visiting St Paul's when I got the postcard from Laszlo.'

'Does Elizabeth still feel Jewish?' Charles asked, studying his menu.

'I don't think she ever really did. All her behaviour was an act of atonement. But she's found the commitment she'd always looked for in Laszlo's religion – she's a staunch Catholic now. Laszlo says converts are always the most zealous.'

Charles looked up. 'Here comes Bob Prew. We can order lunch.'

Gideon followed his glance and saw the lawyer approaching. He wore a seersucker suit, carried a heavy briefcase and appeared completely untouched by the heat outside the hotel. They shook hands warmly, and Gideon could see the years had treated him well. Robert Prew was one of those people who looked as though they had always been middle aged; a thickened waistline and a few lines on his forehead gave him the proper gravitas needed in a Wall Street lawyer.

'Sorry to keep you in the city on a Saturday, Bob,' said Charles.

The lawyer raised his eyebrows. 'My mother-in-law is visiting this weekend, and you know what she's like!' There was a wealth of information in his expression.

'Aunt Constance,' Charles said with sympathy. 'You'd better have a Martini.'

'That was my plan,' Prew answered, laying down his briefcase.

'Would you like me to put that in the cloakroom for you, sir?' the waiter asked, reappearing.

Prew shook his head and accepted the menu. They ordered, and Gideon asked for wine, while his two companions drank their cocktails and gossiped about family affairs. It always amused Gideon when Americans claimed they were a classless society. Charles Whitney-Ingram and Robert Prew were connected by marriage and distant relationships to most of the influential families on the eastern seaboard of the United States. They were part of the aristocracy that stretched from Boston down to Philadelphia, who regarded the western regions of the country as some sort of equivalent to the British Empire: a place to venture into occasionally to make money, but not part of the old country their families had ruled for so long.

When the steak Gideon had ordered arrived he was not sure he had made the right choice; in England it would still have constituted the meat ration for a family for an entire week. Prew noticed his hesitation and smiled. 'Not used to New York cuts of beefsteak, Gideon?'

'I'll get used to it again!' But he could manage only half of it. Charles and Prew also left a great deal of their food. Gideon thought how such a sight would be received at home and felt a stab of remorse, which he quickly realised was illogical. Will we ever come to a time when the British leave food on their plates again? he wondered.

Then Prew suddenly became business-like, and Gideon was reminded of Henri Bronstein and his unexpected changes of mood. The waiter cleared the table, and Prew took some documents from his briefcase. 'Okay, gentlemen,' he began, 'this is what we've worked out. All partners have invested the same capital sum, so the Archangel Gallery will be established as two independent operations in New York and London. Charles will be chairman of the American company and James Gideon, Anne Gideon and Laszlo Vasilakis will be directors and partners.' He paused, and took a sip of his Martini. 'In the United Kingdom, James Gideon will be chairman and Charles Whitney-Ingram, Laszlo Vasilakis and Anne Gideon will be partners and directors.' He drank some more Martini.

'And you think this will be the best way of setting up?' Charles asked.

Prew took off his spectacles and polished the lenses with a red spotted handkerchief. 'There are advantages and disadvantages,' he said slowly. 'At the moment, the American economy is booming and Britain is still fighting to recover from the war. Tax structures are different in each country and, I must be frank, we Americans are not too sure what the long-term implications of your present socialist government are going to be. At some time the Archangel Gallery may wish to close down altogether in Britain and base itself here in the States.'

Gideon was about to protest, but Prew held up a hand. 'I'm just doing my duty in warning you of these eventualities. Now look at the advantages.' He crossed his arms. 'Suppose the Archangel Gallery bought a real bargain in Europe. Some masterpiece for a hundred dollars, say. Well, if you were to sell it again for twenty thousand dollars, you would pay a hell of a lot of tax in Britain. But if you were to sell it to the Archangel Gallery in New York at the same bargain price, the tax paid would be in the United States, where . . .' He smiled. 'Well, shall we say the government is more understanding

317

towards the businessman. You see, having independent companies in each country will enable you to take advantage of the most profitable tax breaks each government has to offer.'

Gideon nodded. 'If you think that's the best way, then go ahead. That's if you're happy?' he said to Charles.

Charles raised his glass. 'Here's to getting rich!'

'Do you think we'll get rich?' Gideon asked Prew.

'My grandfather always said that the way to make money was to sell something cheap to all the poor people or something expensive to the rich.' He drained the last of his Martini, and stood up. 'Just make sure you get it the right way round,' he said, and shook hands to bid Gideon farewell.

After the lawyer's departure, Gideon turned to Charles. 'Those pictures we just saw,' he said, referring to the exhibition they had visited before lunch. 'Do you really think they were worth investing in?'

Charles tapped a finger on the tablecloth before he answered. 'My Uncle Humphrey has just left me fifty thousand dollars and a cottage at Newport. I'm selling the cottage, and spending the dough I raise on Jackson Pollocks.'

Gideon shrugged, and smiled. 'Easy come, easy go?'

'That's my motto!'

England, the following day

It was Sunday morning when Gideon made the journey from Heathrow into London. There was virtually no traffic in Western Avenue. His taxi passed a cycling club near the Firestone factory and he thought how different England was from the frantic bustle of America. It was the same when he got into town; a few buses but very few cars. The sun shone when he got out of the cab in Bond Street but there was none of the humidity he had experienced in New York. He and Anne were now living in a large flat over the rebuilt premises of the Archangel Gallery. They had managed to furnish the living-room, but there were still bare boards in the bedroom. He trudged wearily up the stairs. As he let himself into the entrance hall, he could hear voices coming from the living-room. Inside he found Anne entertaining Elizabeth, Laszlo and an extraordinary-looking woman who reminded Gideon of a brass-rubbing in a medieval church.

318

'This is Harriet Strange, darling,' Anne said when they greeted each other.

Gideon shook the firm hand. 'Anthony's wife?' he said cautiously.

Harriet nodded. 'We were just talking about him before you arrived.' She spoke briskly. 'He's gone off and left me for Schneider's sister.'

Gideon was a little taken aback by her directness, but there did not seem much he could add by way of comment. Instead, he accepted a drink from Anne and sat down on a sofa next to Elizabeth.

'Harriet and I have become great friends,' she explained. 'We met at the church in Farm Street.'

Harriet Strange laughed. 'Don't take that as a good omen, my dear. That's where I first encountered Anthony!' She turned to Gideon. 'How is New York, Mr Gideon?'

He was weary, but he enjoyed the whisky Anne had poured for him and he had taken a sudden liking to this curious woman. 'It seems a bit rich for us poor British,' he said. Then he went on to describe the steak he had had to leave in the Algonquin restaurant. 'We seem a bit worn out and tired at the moment; they're absolutely booming along.' He turned to Laszlo. 'I sold the pictures your friends were expecting. They send their regards, and so does Charles.'

'Did you see any American stuff?' Laszlo asked.

'Some. Charles took me to an exhibition of a man called Jackson Pollock; he's very keen on him. Have you heard of his work?'

'Vaguely,' Laszlo replied. 'What's it like?'

Gideon shrugged. 'I can't say I cared for it.' He nodded to Anne. 'I think he'd give your father a heart attack!'

'Why?' Anne asked.

Gideon put down his glass and moved his hands through the air in circular motions. 'His pictures are huge. He dribbles and flicks paint on to the canvas, and there's no discernible shape or form; it's like looking through a series of nets.'

'I can imagine how Dad would feel about that!' said Anne.

'Charles thinks he's going to be important,' Gideon said thoughtfully. 'And he's got a pretty good eye.'

'Well, we do need stock,' said Laszlo. 'But I think we'd better stick to something more reliable, at least for a few years.'

'I know where there are plenty of good pictures for sale,' Harriet Strange said, prodding Laszlo, who sat next to her on the chesterfield, to emphasise her words.

'You do, Harriet? I wish you'd tell us where.'

319

She folded her arms. 'A lot of my father's old friends are prepared to sell. They're all so hard up, and their families have been collecting for centuries.'

'What will your husband think if you help me?' said Laszlo.

Harriet smiled. 'I can only hope and pray he will be absolutely furious!'

St Ives, Cornwall, late summer 1947

'Don't move yet,' Richard Cleary said irritably.

'I've got to,' Irene replied, shifting the baby with practised ease so that the child suckled from her other breast.

Cleary made two more swift strokes to the drawing and then wrote: 'St Ives, 10th September 1947' in the corner of the sketch.

'Will you hold her for a minute? I have to go to the loo.'

Cleary took his daughter, who had begun to cry once the comfort of her mother's breast had been removed.

'Father and child,' a voice said from the open doorway of the cottage.

Cleary looked up and saw Paul Trenton, dressed in workman's blue overalls that were stained with oil paint.

'Stay like that,' Trenton said with a smile. 'It's an unusual subject. I want to commit it to memory.'

The baby suddenly hiccuped milk over Cleary's heavy fisherman's sweater. 'Oh, bollocks. For Christ's sake take her, Irene,' he said to his wife as she returned to the cramped little room.

'You're hopeless!' She took the baby. 'Why don't you go off with Paul and have a drink?'

Cleary went to the sink in the kitchen and washed the milk from his sweater. He joined Trenton in the narrow cobbled street and they walked down towards the harbour. He did not speak; it was not until they stood at the doorway of the public house with pints of bitter that he made any comment. 'Look at all that bloody scenery,' he said, draining half his drink in one long swallow.

Trenton glanced across the harbour. The sun was low in the early evening sky and the water sparkled around a sailing-boat edging towards its mooring. 'Don't you approve of the views around here?'

'I get the feeling I'm in someone else's coffin.' He drained his glass and entered the pub again, to re-emerge with two more pints.

Trenton took his and laid it at his feet; he had hardly begun his first. Cleary looked around belligerently. Trenton could see that he was tense and irritable, not the best company for a relaxing couple of hours at the end of the day.

'Why the hell do you bother to live here?' Cleary asked, waving his arm to encompass the general area. 'The sort of stuff you paint could just as easily be done in London – or Cheltenham, come to that.'

Trenton, still in a good mood, was too amiable to be drawn into the argument it was quite obvious Cleary was determined to try and bring about. He stooped down and picked up the glass at his feet. 'I tell you what,' he said in a friendly enough voice, 'I'm going inside to talk to Jack and Peter. If you feel like joining us when your mood has changed, I'll buy you another pint. Otherwise, I think it would be best for you to piss off.' Then, with a quick nod, he turned and entered the bar.

Cleary was about to follow, but changed his mind. He drained the second pint of bitter and walked away from the pub. A cold breeze came from the sea despite the clear skies, so he could feel the wet patch of shirt beneath the sweater. He strolled aimlessly away from the harbour. Everywhere the brilliant reflected light danced from white-walled buildings. The twists and turns of the roads and alleys made deep contrasts of shadow and colour, but the beauty of his surroundings only darkened his mood. Cleary felt trapped, and paradoxically abandoned. He had enjoyed the early months living with Irene; the days passed pleasantly enough, although they'd had to conceal the relationship from the headmaster of the Art School. There was no problem when he began his studies at the Royal College. But Irene's pregnancy had changed everything. Although she looked the perfect child-bearing type, things had not gone easily for her and he had begun to resent the gradual alteration of roles.

Early in their relationship she had anticipated his needs and desires, but in the last months before the birth she had become more and more demanding, and not just in the physical attention she required. As her figure grew larger, she sought constant reassurance that he still found her attractive. When she was born, Cleary was enchanted by his daughter, but gradually Irene seemed to become obsessed by her. It was as though he was an obstruction to the demands of the baby. He began to feel like an intruder in the marriage; as though his wants and needs were a tiresome duty that had to be performed before Irene could return to her true purpose, administering to the well-being of their daughter.

321

It had been Nettlebury who had noticed the strain in their relationship and suggested the holiday in St Ives. Irene had always been happy when he had taken her there on childhood holidays, but, if anything, the past two weeks had made things worse. They had rented a tiny cottage, and the even closer proximity of his wife and child had caused his present ill-temper. Usually he could sublimate his feelings by immersing himself in his work, but now each time he sought to escape, Irene and the child called him back to a world of nappies, feeds and the need for silence when the baby slept. If he went out for too long, Irene would become fretful and demand his presence, but then she would ignore him. For the past few days he had tried sketching Irene with the child, but instead of the usual calming effect work had upon him, it now only seemed to enhance his feelings of claustrophobia.

Cleary's walk had taken him from the harbour through the tight little streets to the beach on the side of the swelling promontory known as 'the island'. The wide stretch of white sand was deserted. The sunset was turning pink against the blue-green sea and sky. Seagulls, with bodies tinted crimson from the last of the sun, wheeled and squawked above. He hurled a pebble at the circling birds.

'Fuck off!' he shouted at them, and he found another pebble and ran across the soft sand. The effort of throwing the last stone caused him to lose his balance, and he fell to his knees at the water's edge. He knelt on the wet sand, sea-water lapping against his legs and hands. A long shadow was cast across him. He looked up at the outline of a dark figure, who stood against the sun that had now sunk low on the horizon.

'Hello, Richard,' the figure said. 'Throwing stones at the sunset?'

Cleary stood up and shaded his eyes. At first he did not recognise the woman who had spoken. Then he realised it was Paula Tuchman, her hair drawn back from her face and the youthful softness sharpened into more angular contours. 'Hello, Paula,' he said finally. 'What are you doing here?'

She laughed. 'This is supposed to be an artists' colony. I'm an artist – had you forgotten?'

Cleary shook his head. 'It's just the fucking seaside to me.' Then he began to pull off his clothes. When he finally stood naked before her, he gestured towards the sea. 'I'm going in. Do you want to join me?'

Paula watched him wade into the water for a few moments, and then took off her clothes.

CHAPTER FOURTEEN

England, January 1949

'Come on, Sunflower!' Gideon and Lady Guyland shouted in unison as the horses cut their way through the last few yards of frosted turf before the winning-post at Kempton Park.

'I've won again, Bertram,' Lady Guyland announced triumphantly to her husband.

'So you have, my dear,' he replied, with only the slightest hint of exasperation in his voice. Lord Guyland was a gentleman and he loved his wife deeply, but she had backed four winners and he had only managed a place on the third horse in the second race.

Gideon noticed that Lord Guyland's copy of the *Sporting Life* was becoming progressively more crumpled, as it was his habit to roll it tightly before each race and carry it under his arm like an officer's cane. When each of his selections was defeated, the only emotion he betrayed was through the whitened knuckles of his right hand, where he had taken a firmer grip on the newspaper.

Seldom had Gideon observed such a stiff upper lip. The introduction to the Guylands had been made by Harriet Strange, who had kept her word and led a string of impoverished aristocrats to the Archangel Gallery. Lord Guyland had told Gideon he wished to sell everything he possessed as they were moving from England to South Africa, where he had inherited a farm. Gideon and Anne were due to visit their house after the race meeting.

'Would you go and collect our winnings?' Lady Guyland asked, holding out her ticket to Gideon with a smile of gratitude.

Anne watched the exchange with interest. Nancy Guyland had been considered one of the most beautiful girls in England during the late thirties, when the gossip columns had related the most trivial of her exploits as a débutante. Until her pursuit by Captain the Honourable Bertie Chuter had ended in marriage at the Guards'

Chapel, it had been said no man could resist her slightest wish.

'I'll get them, Nancy,' Lord Guyland said. 'I fancy a drink, anyway. How about you, Gideon?'

Gideon would have preferred to stay and study the form for the next race, but as he was Guyland's guest it would have seemed churlish to refuse.

'Delighted,' he replied, and turned to Vera, who was sitting with Harriet Strange and Nettlebury in the corner of the box.

They looked up from the programme they were sharing and Nettlebury shook his head, gesturing at the same time with a silver flask.

'I'm still enjoying Julian's sloe gin as well,' Harriet said.

As Gideon and Lord Guyland made their way to the bookmaker in front of the grandstand, they passed through the Members' Enclosure. Guyland called out greetings to various acquaintances before he stopped to exchange brief words with an elderly couple he introduced as Edmund and Cynthia Palliser. Instead of shaking hands, Gideon leaned forward and kissed the old lady on both rouged cheeks before shaking her husband's hand.

'We're old friends,' Edmund Palliser explained to Guyland, who was obviously surprised by the warmth of their greeting. 'How are your mother and father?' the old man continued.

'They're in the West Indies at the moment, so I should imagine they're fine,' Gideon replied.

Edmund Palliser, the fifth Duke of St Kerris, looked around at the crowd bundled up against the icy weather, and nodded. 'Very sensible. I'd be there too, if Cynthia didn't insist we spend Christmas with all our bloody relatives. Do you know, somebody showed me a child yesterday morning that was nineteenth in line for the title.' He thought for a moment. 'That's about as close as I am to the throne of England, but the king doesn't have to invite me to Windsor Castle every year!' He shot a reproachful glance at his wife.

'We're just going to get a drink. Will you join us?' Gideon asked.

'Love to, but we're waiting for a chap who brought us here. Charming little fellow; you ought to meet him.'

'He only says he's charming because he's told Edmund he's going to make him a rich man,' the Duchess said.

Gideon smiled. Kerris Abbey, the home of the Duke, was considered one of the masterpieces of English Palladian architecture, and the treasures accumulated by the first three of his ancestors to hold the title were regarded with awe by the curators of the world's greatest museums.

Palliser took hold of Gideon's arm. 'You wouldn't believe it,' he said. 'There I was, without two halfpennies to rub together, and this little fellow arrives and says, "How would you like a couple more lakes at Kerris?" ' He raised his shoulder. ' "Look, old chap," I said to him, "Capability Brown dug the two you can see from the drive, and they cost seven thousand guineas each. So how much are you going to charge?" "Nothing," he says, "and if you let me dig a couple out the back, I'll pay you more than that." ' He nudged Guyland in the ribs. 'Do you know why?' Guyland shook his head. 'Gravel,' Palliser said with deep satisfaction. 'It seems that Kerris is built on masses of the stuff, and they need it for the building boom.' He paused. 'Funny to think of all those little houses built of stuff dug up from Kerris.'

Guyland stuck his rolled-up copy of the *Sporting Life* under his arm and blew on his hands. 'You'd better go and get your drink,' Palliser said. Then he pointed over Gideon's shoulder. 'No, hang on a moment and meet Mr Smith.'

They turned around to follow his gesture, and Gideon saw Smudger walking towards them. This time it was Palliser who was surprised that Gideon was already known by his acquaintance. Smudger's slight frame was as spare as ever, but his clothes, and a large cigar, spoke of his new-found prosperity.

'Blimey, Gidsey!' he exclaimed with delight. 'How are you, me old cock?'

'Can't complain, Smudger,' Gideon replied.

Guyland looked on in bewilderment. When Harriet Strange had made the arrangements for Gideon and his wife to join the party, Guyland had assumed he was spending the day with some sort of tradesman. He had been quite prepared to be civil, as he was anxious to get a good price for the pictures he wanted to sell to the Archangel Gallery, but finding Gideon's proper placing in the social stratum was becoming rather more complex as the day progressed. Harriet had been no help; she treated everyone the same, but then she considered the royal family to be no more than minor German aristocracy. Sir Julian and his daughter seemed decent enough, middle-class, types, but someone had mentioned that Gideon had been an actor and was now in partnership with a Hungarian, which really should have classified him as riff-raff. Edmund Palliser had further confused the situation by his evident friendship and intimacy with Gideon's parents, and now this Cockney character had turned up who was also a bosom pal.

'I used to be his sergeant,' Guyland heard Smudger say to Palliser.

'Which regiment?' Guyland asked, and Smudger told him. 'Oh, infantry,' Guyland replied, as if the information made all things clear to a cavalry officer.

Smudger took Cynthia Palliser's arm. 'You shouldn't be standing around here in this weather. Let's go and have a drop of brandy.'

'An excellent suggestion,' she replied, and they set off across the frozen grass with the others.

At the bar, Smudger bought drinks and then he and Gideon drifted a few feet away down the counter so they could talk in private.

'How's Daphne?' Gideon asked.

Smudger raised a thumb. 'One month to go. We're hoping for a boy this time.'

'Give her my love,' said Gideon.

'How about you and Anne? Aren't you going to have any kids?'

Gideon shook his head. 'Remember I told you she was in the building when it was bombed?' Smudger nodded. Gideon took another sip of brandy. 'Her pelvis was crushed. It healed well enough, but the doctors said it would be dangerous for her to have children.'

A look of concern crossed Smudger's face, 'Christ, Gidsey, that was bloody insensitive of me. I'm sorry I spoke.'

'That's all right. They say you don't miss what you don't have.'

Smudger changed the conversation. 'I was just mentioning you this morning, Gidsey. Talk about coincidence – me running into you like this.'

Gideon smiled. 'That's not much of a coincidence, running into you on a racecourse.'

Smudger shook his head. 'No, I don't mean that. You know Daphne's uncle, the bloke you met in Paris before the war?'

Gideon nodded. 'Ted Peake, sure.'

'Well, you're not going to believe this, but it's true as I'm standing here. Remember those paintings in the Jerry shelter.' Gideon nodded again. 'There was one you was really taken with: a big bugger, of a girl in a white dress standing in a field?'

'Yes.'

'Well, Ted Peake's gone and bought it.'

It was as if the crowded room had suddenly receded and Gideon was standing, detached, viewing the events through a thick pane of glass.

'How do you think he got his hands on it? I asked him, but he wouldn't tell me,' said Smudger.

Gideon thought for a moment. 'Remember the German with no teeth, Karl Schneider? He's back in London. I imagine he sold it to him.' He took a larger swallow from the brandy glass. 'Do you think he'd want to sell it?'

Smudger shrugged. 'I don't know; maybe. Most things Ted has are for sale at the right price.'

'Where does he live?' Gideon asked, and Smudger told him the address in north London.

Just then Palliser came up and waved a five-pound note at the barmaid. 'Same again, you chaps?' he asked. They thanked him and rejoined the others.

When Gideon returned to their box, he was so preoccupied for the rest of the meeting that Anne eventually came and took him by the arm. 'Are you all right?' she asked in a low voice.

He smiled at her. 'Absolutely fine, but we've got to make a stop on the way home.'

'Where?' she asked.

'A place called Burnt Oak.'

'It sounds delightful. Is it in the country?'

'You'll see,' he answered.

At the end of the meeting they made their farewells. Vera was driving Harriet and Nettlebury home, while Anne and Gideon were returning with Lord and Lady Guyland to have dinner at their house in St Albans and view the pictures Guyland wanted to sell.

Once they were clear of Kempton Park the traffic was thin, so they made good time to Hertfordshire. But it was quite dark when they came to the outskirts of the town. By the light of the street lamps they could see that Guyland was driving through a narrow suburban street of modest little houses. It didn't seem to Gideon to be the direction in which one would find any sort of grand home, but when the houses petered out they turned into an unmade road lined with elms and bumped along slowly to a wide farm gate. They now entered a gravelled drive which curved for a hundred yards, and then their headlights revealed one of the ugliest houses Gideon had ever seen; a Victorian, neo-Gothic monstrosity built in different strata of coloured bricks. The lines of grey, blood-red and lime yellow followed bays and battlements that rose in a spiky jaggedness

327

against the clear sky.

'Hideous, isn't it?' Guyland said when they had got out of the car and were standing beside dusty laurels flanking the doorway. 'Do you know, my grandfather pulled down a house built by Inigo Jones so that he could build this.'

When they entered the hall, Gideon could see just how single-minded Guyland's grandfather had been. The entire interior of the house was panelled in dark oak, suits of armour stood each side of the elaborately carved staircase and the walls of the long corridor that led to the hall, which served as a living-room, were lined with pre-Raphaelite paintings depicting knights errant and languid heroines.

The stone-flagged hall rose to a minstrel gallery festooned with medieval banners, and the walls were decorated with fans and circles of weapons glinting in the light cast from a copper chandelier. A modern gas fire hissed below the massive stone mantelpiece in a space large enough to burn tree-trunks. The whole house was icy cold.

Guyland took off his gloves and reached out to warm his hands at the fire. 'We can't stay in here,' he said irritably. 'Jessie!' he suddenly bellowed in a voice that caused Anne to flinch. 'So sorry, my dear,' he added contritely. 'Jessie is the name of our housekeeper.'

'Did you win?' a disembodied voice with a Scottish accent called. They saw a long thin face peering down at them from the gallery.

'Nancy did,' Guyland answered. The reply brought a sniff from the figure, who disappeared from view.

'Is dinner ready?' Lady Guyland asked.

'It'll be ruined if you're not seated in ten minutes,' the voice answered.

'What have we got?' Lady Guyland called out.

'Stew,' the voice answered from a distant part of the gallery.

'That bloody woman is impossible!' Nancy said with feeling. 'How can you ruin stew, especially hers?'

Guyland raised a warning finger to his lips. 'For God's sake, she'll hear you,' he warned.

Nancy turned to Gideon and Anne. 'She used to be his nanny, and he's terrified of her.'

Gideon adjusted his scarf and looked up at the gallery. 'Really? I was always rather fond of my nanny.'

Confusion crept into Guyland's face again. 'You had a nanny, did you?'

328

Gideon nodded. 'She used to lie about in my bedroom in her underwear, reading me novels by Colette. My mother disapproved, but my father was quite keen on her. Looking back, I think she might have been one of his girlfriends.'

'How old was she?' Nancy asked.

Gideon shrugged. 'About thirty, I suppose.'

Guyland was standing with his back to the gas fire. 'And your father knows Edmund Palliser.'

'They were at Harrow together.'

'You went to Harrow?' Guyland asked, relieved. Like the bricks of the house, he thought he had finally located Gideon's true stratum in life.

Gideon shook his head. 'No, my father went to Harrow. I didn't really go to school at all.'

Guyland gave up. 'Shall we go and have dinner?' he suggested.

The room they went to was small, and a paraffin heater had taken the chill from the air, although the fumes caused an uncomfortable stuffiness. There was no sign of Jessie, just a large tureen in the centre of the table, from which Nancy Guyland served dreadful portions of grey, watery stew. But the wine was superb.

'The only sensible thing my father did in his whole life,' Guyland explained when Gideon complimented him on it. 'He bought a cellarful of decent wine and then invested everything else in Russia.' He looked around. 'Well, at least I've sold this place.'

'To whom?' Anne asked, and held her hand over her glass when Guyland gestured with another bottle of claret.

He filled his own glass to the brim and then pushed away his plate of half-eaten stew, and Anne noticed Nancy had done the same. Now she realised how their hostess kept her slender figure.

'To a boys' prep school,' Guyland answered, while he poured more wine into his wife's glass.

'And we've sold Jessie,' Nancy said. 'She wants to stay with the property, so they've offered her a job as matron.'

'Poor little sods,' Guyland said with feeling.

'Poor little sods,' Nancy repeated, and it was apparent to Anne that they had both suddenly become very drunk.

'Excuse me for a moment,' Gideon said, leaving the room. He found the phone in an alcove under the staircase, and rang for a taxi. When he emerged, Nancy Guyland was weaving slowly towards him along the corridor.

'Just popping upstairs to lie down for a moment,' she said with a distant smile.

Gideon returned to the little dining-room and found Guyland with his head resting on the table. He resisted all attempts to wake him. Anne and Gideon exchanged glances, and then broke into explosive snorts of laughter.

'I've rung for a taxi,' he said, and then Jessie entered the room.

'I'm afraid Lord Guyland is rather tired,' Gideon said.

The thin woman gave another sniff. 'Drunk, you mean,' she said in a sharp voice. 'It's the same every night. They never eat a thing but they fill themselves with wine.' She piled the plates together after emptying the unconsumed food back into the pot before turning to Gideon again. 'Did he show you the fake Van Dyck?'

'I'm afraid I don't understand,' Gideon replied.

The woman shook her head. 'The picture in the far room. His father told me years ago it was a counterfeit; he knew a bit about art.'

'Please show it to me,' said Gideon.

They left Guyland asleep and Jessie led them to another part of the house. In the long gloomy library, hanging in an alcove above a writing-desk, was the picture Jessie had mentioned.

Gideon turned on a lamp and trained the light on the picture. He was silent for a while and then turned to Jessie. 'His father was quite right. It's not a Van Dyck, but a Van Eyck. Are there any other pictures like this around the house?'

The woman thought. 'There's a lot of stuff from the old house at the end of the wine-cellar. He says it's all rubbish. He was going to leave it for the school, if they wanted it.'

'May we see?'

Jessie got the key and led them to the basement. The wine-cellar was huge and slightly warmer than the rest of the house. Gideon rested his hand on the wall while she unlocked the door. The bricks were bone dry, as he had hoped. They passed through rows of racked bottles and reached another door which had a large key in the lock. It could not have been opened for some years and took all of Gideon's efforts before it would turn.

Beyond was a curious, undulating landscape of grey-white material that faded into the far gloom. He realised, after a moment, that it was created by a vista of ancient dust-covers. When Gideon touched the first, the fabric tore, it was so fragile with age. Beneath were a cluster of marble heads. He began to work his way slowly into the room, removing the rotting sheets. When he had covered a few yards, the air was filled with choking dust and he had uncovered a treasure trove. There were three Canalettos, paintings by Sir Joshua Reynolds, Thomas Gainsborough, Fragonard, Boucher and a whole series of the Dutch School he could not immediately recognise. Clearly somebody in the Guyland family had once had the taste of a connoisseur.

He returned to the hall, cancelled the taxi and dialled Smudger's number. The telephone was answered by Daphne. They exchanged a few pleasantries and then her husband came on the line.

'Have you got a lorry available right now?' Gideon asked.

After a few moments he said, 'Yes, I think so. I'll ask Daphne.' He came back on the line. 'Yes, there's one in the yard.'

'Can you get it to St Albans tonight?' Gideon asked. 'I'll pay the driver double time.'

'Blimey!' said Smudger. 'What you got – the Crown Jewels?'

'Something like that,' Gideon gave him the address.

An hour later a lorry was in the drive, and Smudger himself was driving. They loaded the contents of the cellar into the vehicles. There was a sense of déjà vu in the scene for Gideon. Then he remembered the lorries outside Henri Bronstein's house in the Avenue Foch, and felt a moment of sadness that he could not share this with the old man.

Jessie watched the proceedings without much interest and nodded when Gideon assured her that he would telephone Lord Guyland the following day. 'Make it after ten o'clock,' she said. 'They're not about much before that.'

Gideon said goodbye to Jessie and they set off back to town. Gideon remembered something, and asked Smudger if Ted Peake would still be up to receive visitors.

'He keeps pretty late hours. Anyway, he can only tell you to piss off.'

The lorry detoured through north London and eventually Smudger stopped in front of a semi-detached house in a neat suburban street. Somehow Gideon had expected a more lavish residence for Ted Peake, but Smudger shook his head.

'He's worth a bomb, Gidsey, but he don't believe in splashing it about. Mind you, it's comfortable inside.'

They decided it would be best if Anne and Smudger stayed in the lorry, so Gideon approached the house alone.

Ted Peake answered the door in a pair of old carpet slippers, his collar undone. In the darkness, he took a moment to recognise Gideon.

'Sorry I'm so late, Ted,' he said, 'but I'm anxious to have a word.'

Peake opened the door wide. 'Come in. I was just going to have a bite of supper. Can the wife get you anything?'

Gideon shook his head. 'That's very kind of you, but I've just had dinner.'

Peake led him into a little kitchen at the back of the house, where a formidable-looking woman in a dressing-gown was serving a plate of cheese on toast. As soon as he smelled it, Gideon remembered the wretched meal he had endured at Guyland's house and felt suddenly famished. He looked around the room and could see the shine and polish of a fanatical housewife, but it was all so ordinary; he could not imagine the Degas in such surroundings.

'Do you mind if I eat while we talk?' Peake said, and he sat down and began to devour the welsh rarebit with agonising slowness.

Gideon refused the offer of a cup of tea from Mrs Peake, and she withdrew into another room. 'I understand you've bought a certain painting,' he said after a few moments' silence. 'I wonder if you would be interested in selling it to me.'

Peake took another bite and chewed thoughtfully. 'I suppose you're prepared to offer more than I paid for it?'

Gideon nodded his agreement, but he knew now that Peake was not going to sell. All his years of dealing with people, watching the flicker of their eyes, the changing note in their voice, the posture of their bodies had taught him a language far subtler than the mere exchange of words; grammar could be imprecise, a sentence ambiguous, but there was no mistake in the message Ted Peake was signalling to him. It read: No Sale.

Finally Peake pushed his plate aside, entwined the fingers of his hands and rested them on the table. When he spoke, it was in a kindly voice. 'Let me tell you something, James . . . Can I call you James?'

'You may,' Gideon answered.

Peake looked down at his hands and laughed quietly. 'You may,' he repeated softly. 'Of course; "can I" is bad grammar, isn't it?'

Gideon shrugged. 'Forgive me. It wasn't my intention to correct you.'

'I know, my old son,' Peake answered. 'I'm just a bit sensitive. I never had any education; I left school at fourteen, you know.'

He leaned back and massaged his eyes with the thumb and forefinger of his left hand. Then he looked at Gideon again, and smiled. 'People look at you, James – they see the way you dress, even the way you comb your hair – and they recognise a gentleman.'

332

Gideon was about to protest, but Peake held up a hand. 'It's not a criticism; you behave the way a gentleman ought to. Often they don't, you know. No, James, you've got class all right. If I had a son, I'd want him to be like you.' He studied his hands. 'You see, when you go into a restaurant and ask for something, they fetch it right away. I can tell they're thinking, when they see me, who the hell are you, giving me bloody orders? Well, that's where the picture comes in. It's going to give me class.' He sat back and linked his hands behind his head. 'You see, I want it for my own personal trademark. I'm going to put it on every piece of stationery I send out, on my business and Christmas cards, in the advertisements for my companies. When people hear the name Ted Peake in future, they're going to think of that painting, not some little bloke who can't speak English properly.'

Gideon nodded. He knew human nature well enough to be sure Peake would not change his mind. 'I understand.' Then he paused. 'May I see it?'

'You may,' Peake said, and led Gideon into the living-room.

His wife was sitting at a large desk against one of the walls, working on one of the heaps of papers that littered the surface. There was a little Christmas tree in the bay window, its coloured lights in cheerful contrast to the austere business atmosphere in the rest of the room. Resting on a sofa, which was also covered with files and more scattered papers, was the Degas.

'You must be doing very well, Ted,' Gideon said with a smile.

'My business turned over three million pounds from this room last year,' Peake said with no hint of boastfulness in his voice, just a plain statement of fact.

Gideon stood by the cold grate and looked at the girl in the meadow for a few minutes more, then he thanked the Peakes and left the house. From the cab of Smudger's lorry he watched the Christmas tree twinkling in the window.

West London, summer 1949

Richard Cleary and Dixie Cavendish finished the last chorus of 'Camp Meeting Blues' together, and after the polite patter of applause died away, Dixie leaned towards the microphone and announced an interval in his curious accent, a mixture of the nasal tones of the London suburbs and the American Deep South. Cleary

333

laid his trumpet on the scarred surface of the upright piano and rubbed his mouth with the back of his hand.

'How's the lip?' Dixie asked.

'It'll do.' Cleary watched the other musicians move towards the hatch that served as a bar in the dusty hall above the Brunel pub. Dixie made a slight adjustment to the reed of his clarinet before placing the instrument on the piano top beside Cleary's trumpet.

'Come on, man, I'll buy you a beer,' he said, but Cleary shook his head.

'No thanks. I think I'll go outside and get a breath of fresh air.'

He crossed the hall, weaving his way through the rows of bentwood chairs, where bearded men in sandals and plaid shirts sat with straight-haired girls who wore little make-up. The light of the summer evening streamed through the tall windows, catching motes of dust and illuminating the illustrations on the wall, which demonstrated the mysteries of administering bandages to wounds and the art of applying tourniquets. On other nights in the week, the hall was used by the St John Ambulance Brigade, but each Friday it became, for a few hours, the Magnolia Jazz Club. The doorway was guarded by the founder of the club, and they nodded to each other as Cleary descended to the saloon bar.

Paula Tuchman was sitting at a table in the corner, nursing a half of bitter and reading a paperback. Waiting to be served, he looked around the bar to see if there was anyone who might recognise him, before he crossed the room. When he reached the table, she had set the book aside and was watching him.

'Surely there's no one here who would know you?' she said with an edge to her voice.

'What do you mean?'

Paula imitated his furtive glance in an exaggerated fashion. 'You reminded me of the character in the cartoon films, Tom the cat, looking around before he creeps up on the mouse.'

'What are you reading?' Cleary asked, deciding it would be best to change the subject.

'*Pride and Prejudice*. It's about a lot of girls trying to get husbands.'

Cleary picked it up and flipped through the pages. 'I thought it was about the conflict between Elizabeth Bennet and Mr Darcy.'

Paula shrugged. 'It all comes to the same.' She picked up her glass, but then changed her mind and put it back on the table. 'Are you finished now?'

'This is just the interval. We've got another hour to play.'

334

She sighed and looked out of the window into the garden. There were families sitting on benches and children playing in the warm evening sunshine.

'Do you want to come upstairs for a bit?' Cleary asked.

Paula turned back to him. 'You know I can't stand that stuff. Doesn't it seem absurd to you that you're just imitating a lot of old negroes in a little town in Louisiana?'

'New Orleans is a big town in Louisiana,' he replied.

'You know what I mean.'

'I don't think it's a valid point.' She could hear a warning note in his voice. 'I could just as well ask you if you thought it absurd to imitate the sculpture of a few Greek artists who lived a long time ago in a tiny Mediterranean city state.'

'Rubbish!' Paula exclaimed. 'Trying to play music in the fashion of a collection of oppressed ex-slaves is just silly. How can you possibly share their emotions?'

Cleary finished his beer. 'I suppose you're an expert on emotions?'

'I've been sleeping with you for a year,' she replied softly. 'I think that qualifies me as some kind of expert.' She got up and walked to the door.

Cleary followed, and caught her arm in the street outside. 'Where are you going?'

She shrugged him off. 'Home. I can still get a train to Paddington.'

'Stay, and come to the party afterwards,' he said without the previous anger in his voice.

She looked at him, and then shook her head. 'I'm not very good at being a camp follower,' she said, and walked away.

Cleary hesitated, uncertain whether to go after her. Then he heard Dixie calling him.

'Come on, man,' Dixie said from the doorway of the saloon bar. 'We're on again.'

Cleary went back to the hall and picked up his trumpet. As he raised it to his lips, he saw a girl in the front row smiling at him.

'Who's the number looking at us?' he asked Dixie.

Dixie followed his eyes. 'The one in the purple sweater?' he asked. Cleary nodded. 'I think she's yours for the night. Lucky sod! Why do they always go for trumpet-players?'

It was the late afternoon of a sultry Sunday in New York. Charles Whitney-Ingram stood on the sidewalk outside the Archangel Gallery as a truck approached from Lexington Avenue. The monstrous vehicle wheezed and sighed, as if some great beast were trapped inside the steel-clad body, and as it passed, he caught a glimpse of the driver before sunlight obscured the man's image. It only lasted for seconds, but when Charles saw the young man at the controls, he remembered the face of Emerson, the driver of Murphy's truck, who had escaped into obscurity with enough paintings to grace a palace. Could it have been him? Charles wondered. Then he dismissed the idea. The driver he had just seen was barely out of high school, and Emerson had looked like that four years ago. People change a lot in four years, Charles told himself, and turned to look into the gallery window.

Angela Wilmot looked back at him through the glass, her face expressing a concern to anticipate his every desire. She's a nice girl, Charles told himself, but her clinging devotion could be tiresome. Because she adored him so obviously, he was especially careful to be scrupulously kind to her on all occasions. One careless moment of indifference would cause her to withdraw to the rest-room, whence she would have to be coaxed by Raymond Quill, his other assistant.

It was a task Raymond was happy to undertake, because he was as devoted to Angela as she in turn was to Charles. He had noticed, though, that Angela did not bother to protect Raymond's feelings in any way; in fact she tended to trample on them with the contemptuous passion of a flamenco dancer.

Although everyone else was in attendance, Raymond had not come in that day. He was visiting his mother, a widow who lived in some grandeur in a massive apartment in the East Sixties with three small dogs and a collection of Chinese porcelain that the curator of the Metropolitan Museum envied. Raymond was a large young man with the body of a football player and the face of a curate. When he was nervous, which was whenever he was close to Angela, he would polish his large heavy-framed spectacles with a flapping motion of his arm, like some great bird trying to take off with only one wing. Like Charles's family, the Quills had been rich and powerful in the United States since before the revolution. It was not long by European standards, but an eternity to Angela, whose original name had been Waljeski before she won a scholarship to Columbia

University. Angela was five foot two inches tall with a voluptuous body, thick blonde hair, pale blue eyes and a rosebud mouth. The combination stopped men in the street, but to her constant chagrin seemed to have absolutely no effect upon Charles Whitney-Ingram.

Charles turned away from the window and looked once again into the deserted street. He was bored with his life and the sudden memory of the war years helped to deepen his mood. I'm thirty years old, he told himself; successful, manly of form and feature, unmarried and living in a city of beautiful women, who greatly outnumber the supply of eligible men. He looked down and saw a pack of Camels at his feet. The drawing of the exotic beast filled him with greater discontent. He kicked gently at it, and the slight effort made him aware how humid it was in the city. He walked back into the gallery and instantly felt a comforting wave of cold air that made him shiver.

'They've got it working again,' said Angela.

'So I gather,' Charles said, smiling. For the past week the air conditioning in the gallery had been out of order; the stifling heat had driven people from the showroom as effectively as a nest of vipers. Charles had claimed it was the pictures they were at present exhibiting, a collection of narrative paintings by a group of late nineteenth-century New England artists. The remark earned him wounded glances from Raymond, who had done his degree thesis on the influence of the pre-Raphaelite Brotherhood on American painting.

It had been impossible to obtain the services of an engineer all week until Angela, seizing the initiative, set off into her old neighbourhood of Queens and, through a network of family connections, tracked down the cousin of a friend's uncle who was able to undertake the work on a freelance basis, but only on Sunday.

Angela shrugged when Charles thanked her for achieving the seemingly impossible. 'Somebody always knows somebody in Queens. I'm sure you could find a stockbroker in your old neighbourhood.'

Charles had to admit that such a task would not be difficult.

'Look, they're finished,' she said, as Ernie Costello and his assistant Jack Ryan emerged from the basement carrying their tools and their coats over their arms. Their blue work-shirts were stained with patches of sweat.

Ernie held out his arms in the cool air. 'Ain't that grand?' he said, putting his tool kit down on the floor beside Angela's desk.

'Thank you, Ernie,' said Charles. 'May I offer you a beer? The refrigerator is still working.'

'A beer would be fine,' Ernie replied, and when he turned sideways to check if his companion agreed, Charles noticed a holstered revolver attached to his belt in the small of his back. He immediately looked at Ryan's waist, and saw that he was similarly armed.

Costello saw Charles's expression, and smiled. 'It's okay, we're cops,' he said quickly. 'We have to carry our guns even off duty. It's regulations.'

'Cops?' Charles repeated.

Costello nodded as he took the beer Angela handed him. 'Sure. Jack and me are due to retire in the fall. We're raising a loan on our pensions and going into the air-conditioning business.' He held up a hand. 'Don't worry; we know what we're doing. We've been going to night school at Cooper Union for the last two years.' He finished his beer and set the can down on the table. Then he slapped his large stomach. 'Right, Stanley,' he said.

'Right, Ollie,' Ryan replied.

Costello winked at Angela. 'That's what the guys at the station call us: Laurel and Hardy.'

Charles glanced from the fat little figure of Costello to his pencil-slim companion, and smiled. 'I can't think why,' he answered. He paid the men, and they thanked him and left.

'I'll just take a look around before we close the place up,' Charles said, and began a quick tour of the showroom and basement.

The gallery was located about half-way between Lexington and Fifth on 51st Street, and was much larger than the façade of the building suggested. From the original shop premises the ground floor opened up into a wide deep square that extended out into each side of the two stores flanking the window and entrance. A spiral staircase in the centre of the main showroom led to another large open area on the first floor. Charles kept his office there, overlooking the street. The original occupants of the premises, who had moved into the building in the early part of the century before efficient burglar alarms had been devised, had been a company of furriers, who had converted the huge basement into a massive fireproof safe that was eminently suitable for the storage of valuable pictures. The area was so large that Charles sub-let sections of the basement to other nearby galleries.

He switched out the lights after he had glanced round the

338

basement and pulled the great metal doors together. They moved easily on the heavy, oiled hinges, and as they settled with a dull thud, he was reminded again of the bunker where they had found the hidden loot.

When he reached the floor-level showroom again, he remembered with a twinge of guilt that Angela had also sacrificed her day off. She was waiting by her desk, looking particularly fetching in a light blue summer dress the exact shade of her eyes.

'How would you like to come to a party?' he asked in a moment of generosity that he instantly regretted.

'A party?' Angela repeated.

'Sure,' Charles replied, with a hint of testiness in his voice. He was aware that Angela knew he had intended to go on to Janice Van Duren's apartment when their business at the gallery was completed. At that moment he realised she had worn the blue dress in the hope that he would invite her.

He smiled again. 'Come on, we'll catch a cab. It's too hot to walk all the way to the Park.'

They locked the gallery and walked with deliberate slowness to Fifth Avenue, where, after a few minutes, they caught a yellow cab.

Although it was a Sunday and most people of consequence would be expected to be out of the city, an invitation from Janice Van Duren was enough to bring all but the infirm from their weekend homes. There were wealthier people in New York and others with more glamour – some were more famous and others could lay claim to greater power – but none commanded the essence of all those qualities quite so effectively as Janice Van Duren. Since she had been widowed in 1937 she had devoted her life to three charities her late husband's family had founded at the beginning of the century.

When they alighted from the taxi at the apartment house, they found Raymond Quill talking to the doorman. He blushed when he saw Angela and bade a hasty farewell to the uniformed figure.

'I wasn't expecting to see you, Angela . . . That is, I'm delighted to see you . . .' he stammered, and reached forward to push the elevator button. Charles had noticed before that Raymond was one of those people who expect to perform these little duties for the rest of the human race. If there was a door to be opened, a cab to be paid for or a coat to be held, Raymond always seemed to be first in line. It was more than manners; in Charles's view, it almost amounted to servitude.

They rose high into the building and then walked along the

mahogany and marble corridor to the high carved doors of the Van Duren apartment.

'Charlie's wife breeds Pekinese dogs,' Raymond said to Angela as they waited for the door to be answered.

'What?' she said sharply. She was already unsettled by the prospect of meeting Mrs Van Duren, and Raymond's obscure remark caused her taut nerves to jangle. For a moment she thought he was deliberately trying to disconcert her, but it was Raymond who now felt miserable.

'Charlie the doorman,' he continued. 'The guy I was just talking to. My mother has three Pekinese; he gives us tips about them.'

Then the door swung open and they were confronted by the withering stare of the butler. 'Good afternoon, Mr Whitney-Ingram, Mr Quill,' he said gravely. There was a slight hesitation as he looked down at Angela.

'Miss Wilmot is a guest of mine, Bentley,' Charles said, walking past him.

The marble hall led into a room overlooking Central Park. The room was already crowded; at first glance Charles thought he knew everyone. Prew was there in a corner, drinking a large Martini, talking to his wife and a dark thickset man Charles thought was vaguely familiar. He set off across the room with Angela clinging to his side, Raymond a step behind.

Half-way there, Mrs Van Duren suddenly confronted them. 'How nice to see you Charles, and Raymond.' She turned her penetrating stare upon Angela.

'May I present Angela Wilmot, Janice?' Charles said. 'Angela, allow me to introduce Mrs Van Duren, our hostess.'

As they shook hands, Charles pressed on to where Prew stood with the familiar figure. The man was wearing the remains of what Charles recognised as expensive Ivy League clothes. The tassels were missing from his creased loafers and the blue cotton polo shirt he wore beneath a light grey tweed jacket was frayed at the collar. His hair had not been cut for some time, and a heavy black lock fell over his forehead, but Charles could tell from the young man's self-confidence that, like himself, he belonged among these people. When Charles reached them, the man stretched out and took two Martinis from a waiter without taking his eyes off Charles's face.

'I know you,' he said. He drained the first Martini quickly and put it back on the waiter's tray, clicking his fingers. 'Dover. We were at school together.'

340

'Paul Van Duren,' Charles said, the name coming to him as the other spoke.

Van Duren nodded. 'Charles Whitney-Ingram?'

'That's right.'

'Who's the girl you brought with you, Charles?' Mary Prew asked.

They all looked back to where Janice Van Duren was talking to Angela and Raymond.

'She works with us at the gallery. Her name is Angela Wilmot.'

Paul Van Duren drained his second glass and beckoned to the waiter again. Charles could see that Janice had noticed the gesture and was frowning at her nephew's behaviour.

'She doesn't look like one of this crowd,' Van Duren said.

They could now see Janice leading Angela and Raymond through the crowd towards their corner. 'Jesus, what a great pair of tits,' Van Duren said in a low voice.

'I presume you're not referring to Raymond?' Mary Prew said drily.

'Charles,' Janice Van Duren began in a bright and deadly voice, 'Angela has just been telling us she comes from Queens. I've asked her to tell us all about it. I don't think any of our family have ever been there.'

Charles's heart went out to Angela. Despite her clinging attentions, she was a decent girl who was intelligent and ambitious enough to be tortured by Janice's snobbery. Her normally pale complexion was white as Janice turned to her again.

'And you must tell us what your real name was again. Waterjinski, was it?'

'Waljeski,' Angela said in a low voice. She was close to tears.

To the others, the line of conversation Janice had chosen seemed to be in the worst possible taste, but their own good manners froze them into silence.

Paul Van Duren, however, was an exception. 'Well I'll be damned, Janice. This calls for a drink.' He reached out and took the arm of the reluctant waiter and thrust full glasses into Angela's and Charles's hands before taking another for himself. He turned to Angela. 'Janice must be really glad you're here today.' He leaned even closer and said in a loud stage whisper, 'You see, the poor old girl isn't really one of us at all.' He shook his head slowly and the other conversations in the room died away. 'Let me tell you about our Janice,' he continued. 'My Uncle Henry was the younger brother of the family, and some said a weak-minded soul.' He put down one of

341

his glasses and tapped his temple with a forefinger. 'Anyway, during the Great War he was sent to West Virginia by my great-uncle and his eldest son, George. The family had some coal-mines there. And do you know what? That's where he met Aunt Janice.' He turned with a smile to his hostess, who was now as white as Angela. 'Of course she didn't actually work down the mines, as a lot of nasty gossips used to say. In fact her family were pretty grand; they owned the local store. They got pretty rich selling the miners soap.'

Janice Van Duren made a supreme effort to regain control. 'I think you ought to leave, Paul,' she said icily. 'We seem to have run out of gin.'

'I think we all ought to leave.' Van Duren turned to Angela and Charles. 'Would you like to come to a *real* party?'

Charles looked down at Angela and realised that their relationship had gone through a sea-change. She was looking up at Van Duren with the sort of expression that had, until now, been reserved exclusively for him. He glanced back at Janice, and nodded. 'Yes, I rather think I would.'

Back on Fifth Avenue they found another cab. Van Duren gave them an address in Greenwich Village and fell asleep instantly. When they arrived at a warehouse in a bleak and deserted street, he woke up and searched through his clothes.

'I'll pay the cab,' said Charles.

'Actually, I was looking for the key, old chap,' Van Duren said affably.

'I know this place,' Angela said after a moment. 'Robert Clinton lives here.'

'That's right,' Van Duren told her. 'I'm staying with him.'

Eventually he found the key, unlocked the door and led them up a dark staircase into a large warehouse where packing-cases were stored. They climbed another flight and emerged into a vast attic area covered in grimy industrial glass. Victorian iron pillars supported the roof; the heat created by the last of the evening's sun beating down made them gasp. There was music coming from the far end of the room and people were scattered about the echoing spaces.

'This is my part,' Van Duren said.

Charles looked around the high walls; they were covered with vast canvases painted in seemingly random slabs of bright primary colours. The pictures pulsated against his retinas. He realised, with a shock, that the effect was intentional. He could tell how carefully the

342

colours had been selected to achieve the astonishing vibrancy. 'Who did these pictures?' he asked.

'I did,' Van Duren replied. 'Good, aren't they?'

CHAPTER FIFTEEN

New York, summer 1950

The orchestra was playing 'Some Enchanted Evening' as Gideon held Elizabeth in his arms and guided her round the tiny dance-floor of the Hungarian Café. At a table on the edge of the room Laszlo leaned forward and poured champagne into Anne's glass.

'I shall be tight!' she said, but she did not take her eyes off the floor.

Laszlo refilled the glasses of Charles Whitney-Ingram and Piet Liebe, who were so engrossed in a conversation that they did not notice. Liebe was rarely in New York these days; since the Lowel Gallery had opened branches in Paris and Amsterdam, the Dutchman spent most of his time in Europe. Laszlo wondered at how little the man seemed to change. We all get older, he mused, but Piet still seems the same. Then he looked at the dance floor where Elizabeth and Gideon circled. Memories of the *Mauretania* surfaced.

He poured Bull's Blood into his own glass and said '1933' to Anne.

She turned and smiled at him. 'How did you know what I was thinking?' She shook her head. 'Oh, I don't suppose it took a mind-reader!'

They both watched for a moment. Laszlo said, 'Next time, I'll marry you!'

Anne squeezed his arm. 'Oh, it is good to see you both again. Do you realise it's been nearly two months?'

Laszlo nodded and drank his wine. As the music ended, Gideon and Elizabeth returned to the table.

'So how have they changed the place?' Elizabeth asked when they were seated.

Gideon waved his arm. 'This has all been extended. It was much

344

narrower in the old days, and the bar was over there by the door.'

Laszlo nodded. 'They've relaid the floor and taken all the smoke out, too.'

'God, yes,' said Gideon. 'You could hardly see the end of the room in the old days.'

The four of them had arranged this reunion by telegraph. Gideon and Anne had flown to New York from Italy and Laszlo and Elizabeth had been in the Middle West, visiting Elizabeth's mother.

'So how is Castelli?' Laszlo asked, refilling Gideon's and Elizabeth's glasses.

'Wonderful,' Gideon replied. 'He's exactly the same, and so is his wife. All the daughters are married now, with children of their own. We went to the palace for lunch when we were in Rome, and he sat at the head of the table with his great mane of silver hair, looking like some Renaissance prince. They were all jabbering at each other. Why does it always sound as if Italian families are fighting when they eat?'

'How's your mother?' Anne asked Elizabeth.

'She's fine. She's decided to come and live here in New York. Laszlo tried to get her to move to London, but she said this was far enough. I think she was scared by all the stories about shortages. Now she wants to donate my father's collection of pictures to the Metropolitan.'

'Will they take them?' Gideon asked.

Laszlo shrugged. 'We shall see.'

'Tell us about Italy,' Elizabeth said to Anne, referring to the Venice art festival they had just visited.

'The exhibition was astonishing,' said Anne. 'You saw that Matisse won the prize. His pictures were wonderful. Maybe it's the light there; they just seemed to glow on the walls.' She shook her head. 'Do you know, I still feel guilty when I say something like that? I expect Dad to shout "Nonsense" at me from across the room. Mind you, he would have had apoplexy if he had seen the Jackson Pollocks and the De Koonings.'

'How are things in New York?' Laszlo asked Charles, who had finished his conversation with Piet Liebe.

Charles waved a careless hand. 'We sold the Canalettos and the two Romneys. And Harriet cabled to say she has some obscure cousin who wants to dispose of a Rembrandt. Last month, we had the best quarter ever.'

Elizabeth prodded Laszlo. 'Tell them about the Norfolk pictures.'

345

'They don't want to hear about that,' Laszlo replied, but something in his tone caught Gideon's attention. He looked at Elizabeth, and she winked.

'Go on,' Gideon said casually. He leaned forward and lit a cigarette in anticipation.

Laszlo said deprecatingly. 'It was nothing, really. Just one of those things that happen.'

'Tell us,' said Anne.

'A few weeks ago,' Laszlo began. 'I decided to take Elizabeth to a sale in Ipswich one Friday and thought we could go on to Norfolk and find somewhere pleasant to spend the rest of the weekend. The sale was worth while. I bought pictures by George Vincent and James Stark, good prices. I was feeling pretty pleased with myself. We decided to stop somewhere really nice for dinner, but you know how it is on these occasions; we kept thinking we'd find somewhere better. In the end it was getting late, and we were both rather hungry, so we said the next place would be the one to stop for the night.' He paused to take a sip of his wine. 'We finally found a hotel that looked all right from the outside. It had been some sort of coaching inn, but the inside was ghastly, and the man who ran the place was equally unpleasant. He had an old crone of a mother who was like something out of Macbeth. What's more she was pretty deaf, so that he shouted at her continually. When he came out to get our bag, he saw the catalogue for the sale we'd been to and told us he'd wanted to be a dealer before his father left them the pub. After that, we couldn't get rid of him. Unfortunately, we had booked in for the night and ordered dinner while we were still at the bar. There was no one else in the place . . .'

'And no wonder!' Elizabeth interrupted.

'The bedroom was damp, and the only bathroom had a geyser that gave just a trickle of warm water. When we got to the dining-room it was deserted, but there was this most extraordinary thing: there were four pictures hanging beside our table.'

'There was nothing else,' said Elizabeth. 'Just the four pictures. And it was so dark that you could hardly see the panelling on the walls behind them.'

'You must imagine this place,' said Laszlo. 'There was no attempt to light the pictures properly, just a dim overhead lamp.'

'Shining down on a dirty tablecloth,' Elizabeth added.

'But two pictures were exceptional,' Laszlo continued. 'The others were rubbish, but what was good was truly excellent.' He paused

346

again, and Gideon replenished his glass. 'So the old witch starts to serve dinner. I must tell you, my friend, we've never experienced food like it!'

'Never,' Elizabeth confirmed with a shudder.

'Even in Berlin during the war,' said Laszlo. 'And while the old woman serves us, her dreadful son comes in, and without invitation joins us at the table. Then he tries to sell me two fake drawings which he claims are by Constable.' Laszlo sipped his wine again, and they waited.

'So,' he said finally, 'I told him I was not interested in the fake drawings, but I might want to buy two of the pictures on the wall.' He leaned forward again. 'Let me tell you about them. The two I liked were clearly by John Crome, badly framed and in need of some cleaning and restoration, but beautiful landscapes. God knows how he had got hold of them. The other two were fairly competent fakes, more Constables, in fact; but better done than the drawings.' Laszlo drew himself up. 'I begin to praise the fake Constables lavishly, but at the same time express my doubts that I can afford the asking price. Then the man says that he can't sell any of the pictures anyway, as his mother has a sentimental attachment to them. He sighs quite a lot, and then his mother serves us some coffee I can still taste to this day. Anyway, it's quite clear he's planning some sort of confidence trick when he suggests that he puts the pictures I want to buy in the boot of our car so that his mother will not see us take them out. Eventually we agree on a price for the two fake Constables, and I pay him in cash. He suggests we go back to the bar while he puts the pictures away. Then I am to suggest that we suddenly have to leave. We proceed according to plan; Elizabeth and I meet him in the car park, where he lifts the lid of the boot and shows us the pictures covered in sacking. Then the old woman comes out, and they begin to shout at each other. We drive away.'

Laszlo paused again to light a cigarette. He blew a long stream of smoke towards the ceiling and looked back at the table. 'By this time, I have decided to head for Norwich and try to book into a good hotel. When we arrive, it's after midnight and there is nothing available. We sleep the night in the car in a hotel car park, and in the morning I open the boot to examine the pictures.' He looked at Gideon. 'What do you assume I would find?' he asked plaintively.

Gideon smiled. 'That he'd given you the two dirty old Cromes, thinking that the Constables you expected to find were more valuable.'

Laszlo nodded. 'And what did I find?'

'He'd done a double switch, and given you the fakes.'

'Correct,' said Laszlo. 'I was furious! I tried to drive back and buy the two Cromes for a proper price, but, do you know, we couldn't find the place again? It just seemed to have vanished from the map.'

Piet Liebe smiled at the story. 'The whole business is changing, my friend. Hunting for bargains is a thing of the past. The big fortunes are to be found in the artist's studio today.'

Elizabeth, sitting next to the Dutchman, turned to him. 'How do you mean?'

Liebe stroked his beard. 'I was just telling Charles: museums are the key to the future. Look at the scale the young painters are doing their work; twenty, thirty feet is not exceptional. They are being encouraged by the major dealers to produce pictures that look good on the walls of museums. When they are bought by the Guggenheim or the Metropolitan, the private collectors follow. Once pictures went from the artist's studio to the private owner, then into the museum. The route has changed.'

Elizabeth glanced from Liebe to Laszlo. 'So the power of the dealer is diminishing?'

Charles interrupted. 'On the contrary, the dealer is becoming much more powerful. We're the ones who encourage painters to take a certain direction and we advise the museums on what to buy. The route's changed, but we're the ones in charge of the switches.'

Gideon reached for more Bull's Blood. As he poured, the waiter came over to him with a card on a tray, which bore the image of the Girl in the White Dress. Gideon turned, to see a familiar figure standing and waving at them. It was Ted Peake, but at first he did not recognise him. His old-style double-breasted suit and sober white shirt had been replaced by a dove-grey jacket and a flamboyant bow tie. The wispy hair had been trimmed close to his skull and he now wore a neat closely cropped beard. Gideon thought the effect was rather similar to drawings of Lenin by Soviet artists.

Gideon waved back. 'Shall we invite him over?'

'By all means,' Laszlo answered, and Gideon skirted the floor and approached his table.

'So how does the Archangel Gallery fare?' Ted Peake asked, and Gideon noticed that his voice was different. He now pitched the tone lower and spoke more slowly.

'So well that we're celebrating,' Gideon answered. 'I've come to ask if you'll join us.'

'I'd be delighted,' said Peake, 'but I wouldn't mind a visit to the boys' room first.'

'See you at the table,' Gideon said, and he returned to the others.

When Peake arrived and the conventional greetings had been dispensed with, he turned to Elizabeth. 'I understand your mother wishes to dispose of the Mueller Collection.'

Elizabeth exchanged an astonished glance with Laszlo before she replied, 'Well, yes. You could say that, I suppose.'

Peake leaned forward and spoke with the champagne glass just not touching his lips. 'Why doesn't she sell it to me?'

Gideon caught his eye, and slowly shook his head. 'I wouldn't buy it, Ted.'

Peake gestured for a waiter to bring another bottle of champagne. 'Why do you say that, James?'

Gideon shrugged and looked down at his glass. 'Superstition . . . guilt . . . a mixture of reasons.' He looked up at Laszlo. 'We built the collection, you know.'

'What difference does that make?' Peake asked.

Laszlo answered, 'It was put together for political reasons, to prove that Britain and Germany were part of the same master race.' He smiled faintly at Elizabeth. 'You know the connotations that sort of thing has these days. I'm not saying the individual pictures don't have value, but in most people's eyes the collection, as a whole, has become tainted. Even the big museums aren't keen to accept it as a gift.'

'Why do you say that, Laszlo?' Peake asked.

'Surely it's obvious? The very idea of the collection sprang from the thoughts of Hitler. When people look at it, they think of the Nazi Party.'

'You're right. I hadn't considered that,' Peake said thoughtfully.

The following evening Laszlo and Gideon stood alone in the first-floor showroom of the New York branch of the Archangel gallery. For the past forty-five minutes they had examined the exhibition of Paul Van Duren's work that filled both floors of the building. Neither had spoken. Now they stopped before the final canvas. It was twenty feet wide by ten deep, and consisted of three tones, one of muted green and another amber, on a field of red the colour of industrial undercoating.

Laszlo read the title aloud from his catalogue.

'*Walk/Don't Walk*,' he said flatly, then he shrugged and looked at Gideon with a questioning smile.

'It's a joke,' said Gideon.

'The picture?'

'No, the title. *Walk/Don't Walk* . . . It's a word-play on the colours of traffic lights.' Laszlo raised his arms in an expressive gesture of despair, and let them fall to his sides. 'You don't like them?' Gideon asked.

'I don't understand them.' Laszlo gestured at the other pictures. 'With other abstract paintings I have been able to judge them in a context; it's possible to follow a line of development, know the origins. With Mondrian, you could see him take a tree and turn it into rectangular shapes. One could follow his ideas in colour theory and proportion.' He waved at the picture again. 'With this, I am lost. These American painters, their work has no mother or father. All this says to me is: Look how big I am!'

Gideon frowned. 'We have to make up our minds before we join the others. This is an important question for the Archangel Gallery, Laszlo.'

'I know,' Laszlo replied softly, then he turned and took Gideon by the arm. 'I cannot understand these pictures. They remind me of the emperor without any clothes. I hear people praise them, but I can see nothing. The decision must be yours: whatever you decide, I will go along with.'

'Then I say we commit ourselves.'

Laszlo wasn't convinced. He looked at Gideon for some time. 'You think they are valid works of art?' he said slowly. 'Statements that will stand the test of time? Remember, if we encourage people to buy, we're committing the reputation of the gallery.'

Gideon folded his arms. 'That's a lot to pass judgement on. I can't say for absolutely certain.' He turned and smiled. 'But I do know one thing for sure . . .'

'What's that?'

Gideon took four paces forward and gently brushed the surface of the huge canvas with the palm of his hand. 'I could fake one of these.'

Laszlo looked puzzled by his words. 'My dear fellow, even I could fake a painting like this!'

Gideon smiled again and shook his head. 'No, Laszlo, you don't understand my meaning. I can only fake the real thing. If a painter's work has no substance, there's nothing there to absorb. You may hate this picture, but it is the result of deep thought and great craftsmanship. What appears to be accidental is planned, the whole thing is a total denial of paintings that look contrived, and that means it is an astonishing piece of work. It has been executed with meticulous care.' Now he spoke almost to himself. 'It must have been a hard journey for him: no reassurance; no points of reference. Imagine being able to travel so far without maps.' He stepped back and looked again at the picture, and then they walked back to the entrance.

Charles was waiting for them there, looking through the window out into 51st Street, where the lights of the city shone in the dark winter's night. He smiled as they approached. 'It's a good job I stood here. Customers were fighting to get into the joint!'

'Have you sold anything yet?' Laszlo asked.

'I'm letting a few people in tomorrow night, before the private view. The only person who's seen everything is Harold Beriac.'

'Who's he?' Gideon asked.

Charles began turning off the lights of the gallery from a master switch. 'A funny little fellow. He looks only about fourteen years old, and he's got a squeaky voice like one of the chipmunks in a Disney cartoon, but he writes stuff that is extraordinarily powerful. I know a guy, Jerry Palmer; Beriac did a piece on him for *The New York Times*. It was critical. Palmer said it was like being patted all over with powder-puffs full of razor-blades.'

'He sounds pleasant enough,' said Laszlo.

'You'll be able to judge for yourself later,' Charles added. 'He's coming this evening.'

Gideon and Laszlo returned to the hotel where Anne and Elizabeth were dressing for dinner. An hour later they arrived at Charles's apartment in the East Sixties where they were shown into a large, comfortable room overlooking the East River. The furniture had been acquired over a number of years and was a mixture of styles that Gideon knew would bring anguish to a professional decorator. The pictures were all good, and as eclectic as the furniture. He noticed that a Van Duren hung over the fireplace, flanked by two small Don Ancellos of figures at the foot of the cross.

The other guests sat in a semicircle, eating titbits of nuts, grapes and Turkish delight.

Charles stood up from the circle of chairs and made the introductions. Paul Van Duren sat beside his mother and father. They were both tall, slim Americans from old families, as was the ash-blonde girl next to them. Her name was Lydia Shaw, and the firm pressure from her handshake told of the same breeding.

351

Next to her Gideon recognised Harold Beriac from Charles's description.

The other men in the room wore dinner-jackets, but Beriac was dressed in a Hawaiian shirt and a baseball cap. When he stood, he was at least six inches shorter than Gideon, who was of average height, and his handshake was the merest touch.

'Sherry, sir?' the white-coated valet asked.

He accepted the offered glass and sat down with the others.

'Harold was just telling us why he chose this particular form of dinner-clothes,' said Charles.

Beriac gave a laugh like a little scream. 'It's all very well for you old American aristocrats to dress up like Europeans,' he said in a piping voice that contained traces of a Southern accent and the hint of a lisp. 'But we immigrants who come from peasant stock should have our own formal wear. I've chosen the leisured look of the working man.' He glanced around. 'Besides, it's much more comfortable.'

'I seem to remember a girl at Vassar called Beriac. Her family came from New Orleans,' Lydia Shaw said casually.

'My cousin Julia,' Beriac answered without looking at her.

Lydia Shaw continued, 'But I remember Julia saying that her family were French aristocrats.'

Beriac turned and smiled at her from beneath the rim of the baseball cap. 'Julia always exaggerates. The title was created by Napoleon, not the *ancien régime*.'

'Surely they wore formal dress at the court of Napoleon?' Mr Van Duren said drily. 'Perhaps you should be wearing knee breeches and a frogged velvet coat?'

Beriac gave the screaming laugh again. 'I prefer to think of myself as a new person, like your son.'

'Would you say that Paul is new, Mr Beriac?' Mrs Van Duren said, disapprovingly.

'Paul, your mother is divine,' Beriac said. Then he turned to Mrs Van Duren. 'Of course I mean "new" in the best sense, ma'am. Paul's painting is quintessentially American, like a bottle of Coca-Cola, a Joan Crawford movie or even the Atomic Bomb.' He turned to the others. 'Haven't you noticed? No one else in the world produces anything new any more, just dreary old repetitions of what they knew in the past. That's why they think we're vulgar, because they can't recognise originality, and it frightens them.'

'It frightens me,' Laszlo said with feeling.

Mr Van Duren looked towards him with some sympathy. 'And

352

me. I can't for the life of me see why anyone should want to buy one of Paul's paintings. I think billboards are more interesting.'

'Well, Father, the next time you see a billboard you like, you ought to buy it,' Paul said. 'It'll probably be worth a million dollars in fifty years' time.'

'Come, Paul! Now you're talking nonsense,' his mother said.

But Paul shook his head slowly with the deliberate motion of the very drunk. 'Billboards are the true folk art of America. They'll tell more about our culture in a thousand years' time than the entire contents of the Metropolitan Museum,' he said carefully.

Mr Van Duren turned to Laszlo again, feeling he had encountered a kindred spirit. 'Why should you think anyone would wish to buy my son's pictures, sir?'

Laszlo smiled, ever the diplomat. 'The value of any picture is only an agreement, usually between dealers such as ourselves' – he paused and gestured towards Charles and Gideon – 'and the customer.'

'What about the artist?' said Beriac.

'Oh, he has very little to do with it. I knew one painter who used to price his work by the last bill he received. If it was for his weekly groceries, the purchaser got a cheap picture. If it was for his rent, the price was considerably higher.'

'So you don't think painters are competent to handle their own affairs?' Beriac continued, and Gideon could hear the mischief in his voice.

Laszlo shrugged. 'Some are, but few wish to be bothered. Being an artist isn't a normal occupation; it rarely attracts individuals who can be bothered with the mundane things in life.'

'So . . . the value of a painter's work is entirely down to the dealers?' Beriac said in his soft lisping tones.

'And the critics, Mr Beriac,' Gideon said pleasantly.

Beriac giggled again. 'Not us, surely? What kind of influence could a little soul like me have on a painter's value?'

Gideon looked at the tiny figure with a sudden steady gaze. 'Do you have any of Paul's paintings?'

Beriac ate a piece of Turkish delight while he pretended to remember. 'Well, yes. I have three I bought when he was just beginning to paint, and then he was kind enough to give me that lovely one in aubergine and dove grey. Do you remember?' he asked Van Duren, who nodded blearily.

'Well, your opinions carry a lot of weight, Beriac,' Gideon

continued. 'If you were to write a piece for *The New York Times* which said that Paul Van Duren was one of the most important new painters in America, that would surely encourage people to buy his work, and your own paintings would increase in value. Although that wouldn't be your motive, of course.'

'*One* of the most important?' Paul said. 'I am *the* most important painter in America.' He turned to Elizabeth, who sat beside him. 'In probably the whole fucking world,' he said to her, as though she were the only person to whom he could trust this confidence.

'Shall we go in for dinner?' Charles said hurriedly.

The food was good, but no matter how much everyone tried to ignore the matter, Paul Van Duren's drunkenness came to dominate the table. He was past conversation now. He half-sprawled over his food, jabbing at each course as it was served and occasionally getting a piece of food into his mouth. Sometimes he would listen intently to a remark, or a fragment of conversation, and then would make a series of grunting noises to signify his agreement with the sentiments expressed or his disapproval.

Finally, when the coffee was served, the conversation around the table gradually ceased, and one of those curious silences containing enough pressure to affect the eardrums descended.

Paul Van Duren lifted his head, which had been slumped on his chest, and looked across at Lydia Shaw. 'Hello, Lydia,' he said with an awful clarity. 'How's Philadelphia?'

'Just fine, Paul.'

He turned to Elizabeth again. 'Lydia was the first girl who ever showed me her cunt,' he said in the confidential tone he had used earlier. 'How old were you, Lydia?'

'I was six,' Lydia replied without embarrassment.

Paul Van Duren nodded. 'Since then, I have measured all other women by that secret place,' he said in the same clear voice, 'and I have found them wanting.'

Mr Van Duren stood up, and so did his wife. 'My son may be a great artist,' he said firmly, 'but he has ceased to be a gentleman. I apologise to you all.' He turned to Charles. 'I think we'll go now. Thank you for your hospitality.' He looked down the table to Lydia. 'Do you wish to come with us?'

She shook her head. 'No, thank you.'

Paul had leaned forward and was resting his head on the table.

'I think I shall take him home,' said Beriac. 'Will someone give me a hand to get him to a cab?'

354

'He can stay in the spare room,' Charles said, but Beriac shook his head.

'Angela is waiting for him.'

'Angela?' Charles said, puzzled.

'Didn't you know?' said Beriac.

'If he's living with her, why didn't he bring her here tonight?'

Beriac giggled again. 'He didn't think his mother would approve of Angela.' He looked down at the sleeping figure. 'He may not be a gentleman, but I'm afraid he's still a bit of a snob.'

Gideon and Laszlo helped him with the comatose body, and finally Charles was left alone with Lydia Shaw. 'Shall I call you a cab?' he asked.

'A friend who's away in Europe has lent me her apartment. It's only two blocks away, and I'd prefer to walk.'

'In that case, I'll come with you,' he said.

'There really is no need,' she answered, but Charles insisted.

There was a cool breeze blowing from the East River and the melancholy boom of a tug's horn sounded in the distance as they walked through the deserted streets.

'Why did you come tonight?' Charles asked after some time.

'The Van Durens wanted me to. I thought it was obvious that I was the girl Paul should marry; our parents decided when we were children that we would make a suitable pair.' She laughed. 'It's been a constant source of astonishment to them that Paul and I haven't gone along with their plans.'

'So is there someone else?'

'Not in Philadelphia. That's why I've come to New York.'

'To find a husband?' Charles asked. They had stopped in front of an imposing apartment house.

Lydia shook her ash-blonde head as she searched in her bag for a key. 'No, plenty of men wanted to marry me. I came to New York to get laid, actually,' she said in a matter-of-fact voice. 'It's harder for me in Philadelphia if you come from a family like mine.'

'I'd be delighted to volunteer,' said Charles.

Lydia nodded. 'I thought you might. That's why I waited after the Van Durens had left.'

Charles felt a tremble of excitement as they rode in the elevator to the tiny apartment. At first he told himself he had never managed such an effortless seduction before, until it came to him that it was he who was actually being seduced. He was confident that he had encountered most types of desirable women: elegant 'career girls',

355

models, bored married women looking for a safe affair that would not jeopardise the security of their regular lives. Because he had no real desire to settle down, in recent years he had deliberately avoided that class of women he had been bred to marry, those carefully nurtured daughters of the old, wealthy families of New York who would share the same friends, keep his house and raise his children in a manner that would complement his sensibilities.

He told himself that this preference came from the brief period, after his father's death, when he had known circumstances that, to a rich man, seemed like poverty. In truth, there had always been enough money then for him to lead a perfectly comfortable existence, and like most properly brought up wealthy people he had been imbued with a deep sense of thrift. But during that time he had detected a subtle shift in attitudes among those people he had always regarded as part of his extended family. It was a change as soft and gentle as a slight summer breeze, but he had felt it none the less, and it had left him with a faint but ever-present resentment towards those who had attempted to remove their daughters from his reach. Of course their efforts had been in vain, and he had discovered to his pleasure that a warning from stern parents that Charles Whitney-Ingram was an unsuitable partner almost guaranteed a conquest. But the girls who gave themselves to him so eagerly were conditioned to marriage as effectively as one of Pavlov's dogs had been to the dinner-bell. No matter how passionate the encounter, the post-coital conversation would inevitably seem to lead to an examination of the prospects of a wedding where 'mummy and daddy would forgive all'. The course of such encounters became so inevitable that Charles gave them up altogether.

Now he was journeying towards a bedroom with exactly the class of girl he had avoided for so long. By her own admission she had been considered the perfect partner for the only son of the Van Durens, and every other aspect of her, from the choice of her clothes to the well-modulated pitch of her voice, told him that she was the class he should marry. But there was an extraordinary difference; she appeared to want him for only one thing! For the first time in his life he found himself hoping he would not prove a disappointment to a woman.

Lydia did not switch on the lights when they entered the apartment, but led him into a bedroom where the bright moon shining through the window revealed a chaos of discarded clothes. Lydia's naked body was silver in the eerie light, when he turned to

356

her after undressing. Her sprawling figure looked more like a pagan sacrifice than that of a Philadelphia débutante.

Then he learned that Lydia was certainly pagan, but that he was the 'sacrifice'. After half an hour of the most frenzied lovemaking he had ever experienced, sweat began to trickle through his eyebrows. He had to stop for a moment and turn from where they were locked on the carpet to wipe his brow on a rumpled bedsheet. While he paused, he became aware of the pain throbbing in his right hip, which he had struck violently on the floor when they had tumbled from the bed. He also realised that his elbows and knees were rubbed raw from the friction of the carpet, and he gave silent thanks for the three hours he spent each week at the athletic club. Although he had climaxed twice, Lydia had each time restored his erection with rapid manipulation of her hands and mouth; she had explored every orifice he possessed with her slender fingers and matched his physical exertions with tireless strength. There seemed to be steel springs beneath the soft skin of her slender body.

'Shall we get back on the bed?' she asked in her clear, well-bred voice.

Without answering, Charles rose to his feet, his knees trembling. Gratefully he lay back on the cool sheet and took a few deep breaths before Lydia slipped her own perspiring body on top of his own. For a moment his nose tickled as her pubic bush brushed across his face and then his mouth came in contact with her lips. For a few seconds she made fine adjustments, and Charles thought of a plump little bird settling carefully on to its nest.

'Lower, lower,' she instructed until he found her clitoris, and then with a contented sigh she took his penis between the lips that earlier in the evening Charles had thought of as prim. She set the rhythm she desired by the timing strokes he could feel from her own mouth so that it did not surprise him when Lydia achieved simultaneous orgasm for them both.

When she had finished, they lay entangled on the single bed until their bodies cooled. Then Lydia raised herself on an elbow and slowly traced his mouth with her fingers. 'Thank you,' she said softly. Charles waited for the inevitable conversation, but she said, 'I'm afraid I've got to get some sleep. I leave for home early in the morning.'

'Do you want me to go?' he asked with some surprise.

Lydia nodded. 'If it were a double bed, I'd invite you to stay, but I'm a restless sleeper, and I know we wouldn't be comfortable.'

Charles got up and found his clothes among the disorder. When he dressed, he leaned over Lydia, who was now half-asleep. He kissed her, and she nodded an acknowledgment.

'I'll ring you,' he said. 'What's your number?'

'It's in the book,' she replied, turning on her side.

He let himself out of the building and walked back to his own apartment. His raw knees and elbows chafed against his clothes and he could still taste Lydia, and smell her when he raised his hands to his face. By the time he got indoors, he wanted her again.

London, September 1950

Richard Cleary stood in the twilight, sketching the faces of women reaching out to make their purchases from a fruit and vegetable stall in Shepherd's Bush Market.

'What you doing, mister?' a young voice said from behind him.

He was used to the attention of children. Adults usually ignored him when he worked in the street, but it was common for urchins to question him without embarrassment.

'Drawing,' he answered without taking his eyes from his pad.

'Let's have a look,' the voice said, and he glanced down. There were two of them, boys, scruffy with dirt-streaked legs. But their faces were lively and filled with interest.

'Stand there and I'll draw you,' Cleary said.

The boys wriggled with laughter at the suggestion. 'What will you give us?' one asked.

'Sixpence.'

'Sixpence each?' the first boy asked.

Cleary nodded.

They stood with their arms about each other's shoulders, their faces pale blue from the lamps that hung from the stalls. Cleary worked quickly, and eventually threw them their shilling.

'Show us, mister,' they called out, and he turned the sketchbook towards them.

'Blimey, it's rotten!' one of them said. 'I could do better than that.' Then they scampered away into the crowd.

Another voice said, 'You can't get away from critics, Richard.'

Cleary turned to see Peter Quick and Trevor Wilde standing a few feet away, both of them grinning with amusement. He had hardly seen them in the past year, but in their days at the Royal College of

358

Art they had been inseparable. The other two who made up their particular group were Bernard Walton and Patric Carey. Quick and Cleary were ex-servicemen, older than the others; they had tended to lead the group – Quick, by his good nature, and Cleary because his frequent indifference to other people made him a dominant character to the immature.

Quick glanced at his watch. 'It's opening time. We're meeting Carey and Walton.'

Cleary slipped the sketchbook into his pocket and looked around.

'Are you with someone?' Wilde asked.

'I was,' Cleary replied. 'Irene was buying clothes for Bridget.' He shrugged. 'They'll be all right.'

'Shall we look for them?' Quick asked.

Cleary shook his head. 'No, they'll be okay. Come on, I'm ready for one.'

While they walked to the pub, they gossiped about their lives since the previous year. Walton, Wilde and Carey were still in their last year as students; that summer they had worked in various jobs until the autumn term started. Both Quick and Cleary were now part-time teachers, Quick at St Martin's School of Art and Cleary at Willesden Technical College, where there was an art department. Carey and Walton were waiting at the bar, but Richard bought the first round.

Irene looked for Cleary when she had completed her shopping but it had begun to drizzle, and Bridget was tired. Eventually she gave up and caught a bus to Earl's Court. Their flat was on the first floor of an Edwardian building, with spacious rooms, the largest being reserved for Cleary's studio.

Irene put Bridget to bed after her tea and began to prepare lamb stew for supper. She put the saucepan on a low gas, knowing her husband's preference for eating late, and washed some clothes. When she had finished, she turned the gas even lower under the stew and switched on the wireless, but nothing held her attention. She tried reading for a while, and then a noise below the window distracted her. It was the sound of people laughing, and it woke Bridget. Irene went to the bedroom and lay down on the bed with her. After a time they both went to sleep.

When she woke, she could tell the hour was late; there were voices coming from Cleary's studio and bursts of laughter. She opened the door; the room was full of men drinking, who called out greetings.

'Have you anything to eat?' Cleary asked. Irene nodded, and

returned to the kitchen. He turned back to the room. 'Why shouldn't we?' he said, his arms held wide.

Peter Quick looked around; there were drawings pinned to the walls, and pictures leaned everywhere. He had a chair, but the others sat on newspapers on the bare, paint-encrusted floorboards.

Trevor Wilde banged on the floor with an empty beer bottle. 'What are we going to call ourselves?' His voice was close to a shout.

'The Subjective Realists,' Carey suggested.

Peter Quick shook his head. 'I don't like that.'

'We'll find a title, and we'll get an exhibition if we handle it right,' Cleary said. 'If the worst comes to the worst, I can always ask my brother-in-law.'

In the kitchen, Irene slowly served bowls of lamb stew. Even though the flat was full of people, she felt lonely.

New York, October 1950

The moment Paul Van Duren stirred, Angela was awake. It was early, before six o'clock, she guessed, but she did not mind. Since childhood she had been used to rising before dawn. Her father had been a policeman, and she had always got up to make his breakfast when he came home from night duty.

He had liked the mornings. 'Cleanest part of the day,' he would always say, 'before people get up and fill it full of garbage.'

Paul had turned to lie on his back, looking up at the high ceiling, so Angela knew he would be ready to get up in a few minutes. She slipped from the bed and put on a bathrobe and looked round the vast space of the studio. Until recently the premises had been a warehouse used to store olive oil, but now, like five other buildings on the block, it had been converted. It was a matter of amusement to some of the more sophisticated art-lovers in the city that the Lower West Side was rapidly becoming the Montmartre of New York. Angela would have objected to the word 'converted'. When she and Paul had removed most of the junk left by the previous tenants, her brother-in-law and two of his friends rigged a shower unit and a cooking range against one of the load-bearing walls.

'It's kinda like living on a football field with a glass roof over you,' he'd said when they finished installing the equipment. Angela knew what he meant. Paul had insisted that they place the sleeping area in the recesses of the huge room, away from the windows that

360

overlooked the street, so it was at least sixty feet for Angela to walk across the concrete floor to the cooking range.

There was just enough coffee left for two cups. She set the perco-lator on the stove and looked in the massive refrigerator Max had bought for twenty dollars from a delicatessen. All it contained were three eggs, a bottle of brandy, five oranges and two bottles of champagne.

While the coffee brewed, Angela took a shower. She was one of those rare women who could be ready to face the world in under fifteen minutes, mostly because she hardly wore any make-up. She passed Paul on the way back, but they did not speak, and by the time she had put on her clothes, the coffee was ready. He had also dressed, in paint-stained sweater and jeans, but his feet were bare.

'Have you seen my sneakers?' he asked when she handed him his cup of coffee.

'There, under the bed.' She retrieved them for him. By now he was sitting on a step-ladder in front of the canvas he had been working on the previous day. It lay flat on the floor, unstretched, like the multicoloured sail of a ship.

'What do you think of it?' he asked after a few minutes' silence.

Angela shrugged. 'It's not finished.'

'How can you tell?' he asked with a smile.

'Because I don't like it yet,' she answered.

Paul nodded in agreement. 'Maybe I'm working too big.'

Angela shook her head, and then gestured towards the stack of smaller pictures leaning against a pillar. 'They work at that size because you were thinking in those proportions. Your work has grown naturally. You can't go back now.'

Paul nodded again. In the time he had lived with Angela, he had come to trust her judgment completely. She responded to pictures instinctively, like a music lover who possesses perfect pitch. He had discovered this when he had first gone with her to the Museum of Modern Art. He usually distrusted those with degrees in the theory of art, so he had been unimpressed by her doctorate, but the conversa-tion they held that day convinced him that Angela's understanding was much more than the parroting of half-remembered lectures. When he had shown her his own work, she had unerringly gone to the pictures that he felt were the most successful.

'The woman is like a truffle-hound,' he told Harold Beriac, who had questioned him on his attraction to Angela. 'You could hide a decent picture from her in a pile of crap, and she'd sniff it out.'

'And I thought you only wanted her for that sensational little body.' Beriac sighed. 'Now you tell me she's perfect.'

Angela and Paul looked down at the painting for a while longer. Then she said, 'Do you have any money? There's nothing in the ice-box except oranges and eggs.'

He pulled two crumpled ten-dollar bills from his pocket.

'You had five hundred dollars on Friday,' she said.

He shrugged. Angela knew it was pointless to remonstrate with him. For long periods he would hoard money, refusing to buy anything, pleading poverty to their friends when he was expected to buy a round of drinks. Then he would begin a reckless spending spree in the most expensive bars in the city, where he would buy champagne for any stranger who wanted to join his company. They would end only when a barman called her from wherever the latest binge finished. She or Beriac would collect him and pay for the last round he had ordered. Then he would begin to work furiously again without interruption for several weeks, before the cycle recommenced.

There was a sudden ring from the bell wired to the door on the street. Angela looked at her watch; it was still only six-thirty.

She turned to Paul; he shrugged. 'I'm not expecting anyone,' he said.

Angela went to a wire-cage service elevator in a corner of the studio and rode down to the entrance. When she opened the door, two people stood on the sidewalk. They looked unlikely visitors to the neighbourhood.

'I take it you are Miss Angela Wilmot? Allow me to introduce myself,' the man said. 'I am Anthony Strange. This is Princess Reisenauer. We hoped it might be possible to see Mr Van Duren.'

Although Angela knew who they were, she gave no indication that she recognised their names. Instead, she stood back and indicated for them to follow her. The Princess picked her way fastidiously through the trash-cans and packing-cases that littered the doorway, and entered the elevator with an expression of pained disdain.

'Have you lived here long, Miss Wilmot?' Strange asked as the elevator jerked into motion, so that the Princess reached for her companion's supporting arm. When the cage came to a juddering halt, she looked equally unhappy.

Van Duren was waiting when they alighted. 'Don't worry, it's quite safe,' he said, and held out a hand to help her from the contraption.

Klara walked past Angela and looked around. 'But this is

362

magnificent,' she said. 'Exactly the sort of place I expected you to produce such wonderful pictures from. Don't you agree, Anthony?' She turned to Strange, who was darting his head in every direction like a bird looking for morsels of food, and then produced an expansive smile.

'Let me come straight to the point, Mr Van Duren,' Strange began. 'I would like to make you an offer to join our gallery.'

Paul nodded towards Angela, and held his finger to his lips. 'It would be a breach of professional etiquette for Miss Wilmot to hear this conversation,' he said. He turned to Angela. 'You may serve us with champagne cocktails and then go.'

'I think it may be a little early . . .' Klara began, but Strange held up a hand to silence her.

'The artist knows no constraints of time,' he said loftily. 'A champagne cocktail would be excellent.'

Angela prepared the drinks, and silently departed for work.

Gideon called in at the Archangel Gallery, just as Charles was closing the premises for the night. It was the last day of the Van Duren exhibition, and a crew was waiting to remove the pictures.

'These are the papers for you to sign,' Gideon said, handing the contracts to Charles.

'What the hell are they?' Charles retorted, glancing down at the documents.

'The Mueller Collection,' said Gideon. 'The Metropolitan wouldn't take it as a gift, so Elsa Mueller commissioned us to sell it.'

'Who bought it?' Charles asked. He watched anxiously while four workmen gently lowered one of Van Duren's huge paintings to the ground.

'Edward Peake, a well-known English collector. At least, he is now.'

Charles flicked through the pages and wrote his signature rapidly in the places Gideon indicated. 'How the hell did you manage to persuade him to take all that stuff?' he asked.

'I didn't have to,' said Gideon. 'He wanted the collection. I even warned him not to buy it, but he was adamant.'

Charles put away his pen and stared at Gideon. 'Why?'

Gideon looked around at the chaos the workmen were now creating. 'Can you get away for a while?'

Charles called to Angela, 'Will you take care of things here?'

'Sure,' she replied. 'I've got nothing to go home for just yet.'

Gideon got them a cab and gave the driver directions when Charles was getting into the back. As they drove across town, Charles became curious. 'Where are we heading?'

'You'll see in a moment,' Gideon replied, and then the cab stopped. They were in Madison Square Gardens, where a picket of protestors held banners aloft bearing the legend 'Stop Nazi Exhibition'. A long queue stretched around the block, and then Charles saw the huge sign above the entrance. It read: 'HITLER'S SECRET PAINTINGS. NOW THE WORLD CAN SEE THE MONSTER'S DEPRAVED TASTE IN ART. *Children allowed in only accompanied by adults.*'

Charles was still laughing when the cab took them on towards the Algonquin.

'We should be so lucky,' said Gideon. 'They reckon ten thousand people have been there today, and it's only just opened.'

'Good God!' Charles said, suddenly sober. 'We've had that number of visitors only for the whole of the Van Duren exhibition, and Beriac gave it a rave review in *The Times*.'

'There you are,' Gideon answered. 'Ted Peake got all his publicity in the *Daily News*. Not only that, he charged a dollar a ticket.'

When they arrived at the hotel, Charles accepted Gideon's invitation to a drink in the Blue Bar, where Paul Van Duren was sitting at the counter. He was impeccably dressed and quite drunk, but he recognised them and called to the barman to serve them from his bottle of champagne.

'What kind of a day have you had?' Charles asked, when the drink was served.

'Rather splendid,' Paul replied. 'Some very pleasant people have been trying to talk me into joining their gallery.'

'Who?' Charles asked.

Paul nodded behind him, and Charles and Gideon turned to see two figures slumped in the recess by the doorway.

'How on earth did they manage to get into that state?' Charles asked.

'They've been with me,' Paul answered. He nodded towards Strange. 'You know, two years ago I tried to get to see him every day for nearly a month, but he didn't have the time. Then he turns up on my doorstep the day after the Museum of Modern Art buys two of my pictures.' He threw back his head and looked up to the ceiling. 'Jesus Christ, sometimes life is sweet.'

CHAPTER SIXTEEN

London, summer 1952

Julian Nettlebury sat in a wicker chair in the conservatory at Kew with a large sketch-pad on his knee. The piece of charcoal in his right hand moved quickly over the surface of the cartridge-paper, leaving indications of great groups of figures in a wide landscape. The words that Paul Trenton had spoken so many years before had turned out to be prophetic. Nettlebury had decided to paint a third section of his gigantic mural on the progress of mankind. The work was going well. He could see great areas of light and darkness clearly.

Then he heard Irene calling, and when she came into the conservatory, she was holding his grand-daughter by the hand. Bridget let go of her mother and hurried towards him with uncertain steps, and he forgot the pain in his back when he reached down to pick her up. Her cheek was cold as she leaned to kiss him, and her body felt firm and pliant as she squirmed in his arms. For a moment, he remembered holding his own daughters.

'Draw me a dog, Grandpa,' the child said when he had put her down and she saw his sketch-pad on the floor.

'She wants us to buy a puppy,' Irene explained. 'I keep telling her it's impossible to keep a dog in the flat.'

'If you lived here, you could have one,' he said mildly. He picked up the sketch-pad and put it on the table, out of Bridget's reach. Irene did not respond to the remark, but busied herself with the contents of a carrier bag. Since Cleary had left the Royal College they had lived in the flat, so that Nettlebury was alone in the house except for the Coopers, who still looked after him.

'I've brought wellington boots, raincoat and hat in case you want to take her to feed the fish,' Irene said. She was referring to the ponds in Kew Gardens, which were inhabited by giant carp.

'Can we go to the pet shop afterwards, Grandpa?' Bridget replied.

'Yes,' he answered. 'If you say *may* we go to the pet shop.'

Irene looked at her watch. 'I've got to fly. It took longer than I thought to get here.'

'Where are you off to?' Nettlebury asked.

Irene examined herself in the large mirror on the wall while she answered. 'I'm meeting Pamela in Swan and Edgar's. We're having lunch, and then going to a matinée.' She made a tutting sound. 'Dear me, I do look awful, and Pamela's always so smart these days.'

'Is that the Pamela who used to come here when you were children, the thin, mousy-looking girl?' Nettlebury asked.

Irene thought for a moment. 'That's her, but she's a very glamorous blonde now, Dad!' She leaned down and kissed Bridget, who had found Nettlebury's discarded stick of charcoal and was drawing a four-legged creature on the stone-flagged floor.

'It's a dog,' said Bridget.

'I know it is, darling. Now, you be good for Grandpa, and I'll be home by tea-time,' Irene said, hurrying off to keep her appointment.

'You draw a dog, Grandpa,' Bridget pleaded, and Nettlebury took up the sketch-pad and swiftly drew a Dalmatian.

Bridget took the finished drawing from him and compared it with her own efforts. 'Yours is better. Why do you draw dogs so well?'

Nettlebury smiled. 'When I was an art student, a group of us said to one of our teachers that we didn't think Landseer was a very good artist.'

'What did the teacher say?'

The occasion had taken place more than fifty years ago, but the memory was so clear that it could have happened yesterday. 'He said he would give a pound to any one of us who could paint a composition of four dogs that was equal to any of Landseer's pictures.'

'Who won?' Bridget asked.

Nettlebury shook his head. 'None of us did; the teacher said our work was awful. But it taught us how skilful Landseer really was, and it made me determined to be able to draw a dog properly.' He reached forward and tapped the sketch-pad. 'And that's why I can still draw them.'

The door to the conservatory opened again, and Vera entered.

The child ran to her and Vera picked her up, as Nettlebury had done.

'This is just cupboard-love,' said Vera. 'You know I've been to get my sweet ration, don't you?'

'What did you buy me?' Bridget asked.

Vera laughed. 'Chocolate and some sherbert lemons, the ones that make your tongue go yellow.' She looked round, and caught Nettlebury kneading the painful spot in his back once again.

'Did you see the doctor?' he asked.

Vera nodded and changed the subject. 'Are we going to the gardens?'

Nettlebury gestured towards Bridget. 'She wants to feed the fish.'

Vera smiled. 'You mean *you* want to feed the fish!'

Nettlebury agreed. 'I must confess I do like seeing those great greedy faces looming up from the water.'

They dressed Bridget in her raincoat, and left the house. Although the rain had stopped, the sharp wind stung their faces. There were not many other visitors in the Botanic Gardens. They strolled through the wet landscape and eventually threw the remains of a loaf of bread to the mud-coloured carp that rose from the depths of the ponds. Another sudden shower caused them to take cover among the tropical surroundings in the huge Palm House. Bridget wandered away, but was close enough for them to see she came to no harm.

'I love this place,' Vera said when they stopped, looking up at the heavy fronds of the exotic trees. 'Nothing ever changes here.'

Nettlebury followed her gaze, and nodded. 'Paxton designed this; it's strange how everything the Victorians did has a sense of permanence.'

'Parks and buildings,' Vera said softly. 'Bridges and pubs.'

Nettlebury nodded. 'And railways and seaside piers; it's a shame people don't last as long.' He held his arms wide apart. 'That's what I want to do in this next picture: show people what we were like.' He took her arm. 'I want people to be able to look at it in the future and say: "That's how they were, what they felt, what made them happy and sad. That was the life they led." ' He looked down at her. 'You'll understand when it's finished.'

But Vera shook her head. 'No, I'm afraid I won't see it, Julian.' Something in her voice brought him to a halt, and in that moment he read the truth in her eyes. She saw understanding come to him, and the sorrow that followed. Tears came to her, for his grief rather than out of self-pity, and she took his arm. 'I know you can't bear fuss, so I thought I'd go away. My brother's family are all in Kenya. They say the climate's lovely there.'

Nettlebury slowly put his arms round her. 'Your place is here with us. We're your family, now.' Vera nodded without speaking. He raised his hand to touch her face. 'I've never been a philanderer, you know,' he said gently. 'There have only been two women in my life.' Vera smiled, and he took out his handkerchief and brushed at her tears. He looked up at the great palm fronds against the glass roof until he could speak again. 'No man has been better loved, or loved more. Thank you.' He held her again.

Bridget, who had decided to rejoin them, turned to run back, but tripped and fell on her knees. She began to cry.

Vera picked her up and kissed the graze, then she produced the bar of chocolate. 'Come on,' she said, 'I'll show you a chocolate bean.'

When Bridget was shown the exotic tree, she looked at the curious plant and said, 'Do you know, there's an oak tree in the gardens that's been here more than two hundred years!'

'Lucky old oak tree,' Vera said, and managed to smile at Nettlebury.

It rained heavily that evening and Irene and Bridget were soaked on the walk from Earl's Court station to Nevern Square.

'One more flight of stairs,' Irene said to the sleepy child when they reached the first-floor landing. When she unlocked the door, she could hear a conversation coming from the living-room and laughter that she did not recognise. She called, 'We're home,' and started to prepare Bridget for bed. When she had bathed her daughter and read her a bedtime story, she made her way to the living-room.

'I didn't want to disturb you, so I've put Bridget to bed. Will you go in and say goodnight,' said Irene. As she spoke, a tall, very thin, figure stood up rather unsteadily from where he had been sitting in the corner of the sofa.

'Darling, this is Neville Crichton,' said Cleary. He pecked her on the cheek and left to tuck Bridget up.

The tall figure gave her hand one firm shake and then sank back on the sofa. His body seemed almost to disappear into its soft angles.

Irene sat down and looked at him. His face was long and bony, the pale flesh moulded lightly over the skull beneath. The hair that flopped over his forehead was dark but lifeless; he brushed it aside with a quick gesture.

'Are you a painter, Mr Crichton?' Irene asked.

'Good heavens, no,' he replied with a short, rattling laugh. 'I'm a journalist.'

'He's an art critic, which is much worse!' Cleary said, returning.

'Oh, really? Which newspaper?' Irene asked.

Crichton reached down and picked up his glass of whisky. 'It's just a little magazine devoted to the arts called *Forward*. I doubt if you would have heard of it.'

There was a slight tone of patronage in Crichton's voice that made Irene bridle. 'Oh yes, my father takes it,' she replied, knowing that a distinguished subscriber was often more impressive than a contributor.

'My wife's father is Sir Julian Nettlebury,' Cleary added.

Crichton raised his eyebrows. 'The First World War artist?' he asked languidly.

Irene stood up before she answered. 'He still paints, Mr Crichton,' she said, and turned to Cleary. 'Shall I make some supper? Would Mr Crichton like to stay and have something with us?'

'That's very kind, Mrs Cleary,' Crichton replied, 'but I must be at the Chelsea Arts Club later. I promised to meet Trenton.'

'I didn't know he was in town,' Cleary said, and now Irene could tell from his voice how much he had drunk that day. He turned and gently pushed her towards the kitchen. 'That's settled, then. We'll have something to eat, and then go and have a drink with Trenton.'

'Will you be joining us, Mrs Cleary?' Crichton asked. This time there was no hint of patronage, and Irene smiled, thankful for his display of good manners.

'I don't think so. I have to stay and look after Bridget.'

'Oh, come on, Irene,' Cleary urged her. 'You can ask Wendy and Jack if they wouldn't mind sitting for a couple of hours.'

Irene hesitated, and then nodded. 'Very well. A few hours more would be good; I can say I really made a day of it.' She went into the kitchen, leaving the door open so that she could listen to their conversation.

Cleary poured more whisky, and the two men settled down again.

'When did you decide to call yourselves the Cromwell Road School?' Crichton asked.

Cleary shook his head. 'We didn't. That was the *Observer*. We called ourselves "The Subjective Realists".' He gave a short laugh. 'Except for Peter Quick. He claimed he was an objective realist.'

'So geography had nothing to do with it?' Crichton said.

Cleary thought for a moment. 'I suppose it did, in a way. We had been at the Royal College together and we all live fairly close now. But the idea was that we would paint what was most familiar in our everyday lives. None of us could see the point of painting Welsh mountains or vineyards in the south of France if we were living around here. The subject-matter was to be our everyday experiences, the texture of our real lives.'

'But are your lives so unremittingly gloomy? Surely there's some lightness and gaiety? Look at all those bus queues in the rain, smoky public bars, grim bedsitters; didn't someone say it was social realism without the heroics?'

Cleary nodded. 'The *Daily Worker*, actually. Our pictures are quite popular among socialists; we're supposed to reflect the true condition of post-war Britain.'

'But you did decide to take that aspect of life for your subject-matter,' Crichton insisted.

Cleary lit a cigarette and waved the smoke from his face. 'I keep telling you that the subject-matter was determined by circumstances. Once we made the decision to reflect our everyday lives, the die was cast. We painted bleak winter scenes in this part of the city because that was the time we could afford to paint. When we were at college, we were all on grants. It was just enough money to keep us in term-time. Throughout the long summer vacation we were all working in factories so that we could survive. Painting was an activity for us that took place in the dark days of autumn and winter. As soon as we could paint in summer, the work changed. Look at Trevor Wilde's garden paintings now; they're full of colour and light. Christ, when he was doing the bus-stop pictures he'd worked all summer in the Hoover factory at Perivale.' Cleary drank some more whisky and continued, 'It's like the myth of the name, the Cromwell Road School. Bernard Walton lives in Gloucester Road, Peter Quick at Notting Hill, Trevor Wilde is in Stanhope Gardens. There's only Patric Carey who actually lives in Cromwell Road. He keeps threatening to move, but none of us will let him.'

Irene emerged from the kitchen carrying a large serving-dish. 'It's ready. Richard, will you get the knives and forks?' A few minutes later they were sitting at the table near the window overlooking Nevern Square. 'It's only corned-beef hash, I'm afraid,' she said.

Crichton breathed deeply with appreciation. 'It smells wonderful,' he said.

Cleary took a large portion and looked at Irene. 'This isn't the stuff from Kew, is it?'

'Don't be ridiculous, darling! That was given to the cat years ago,' she answered. Cleary noticed Crichton's puzzled expression and explained about the stocks of corned beef Mrs Cooper had built up for the duration of the war.

'She sounds a sensible woman,' Crichton said. 'Speaking for myself, I adore corned beef. It was the only aspect of the war years I thoroughly enjoyed.'

'What did you do in the war, Neville?' Cleary asked.

'I was in the Royal Engineers.'

'Did you get about much?' Irene asked.

Crichton shook his head. 'No, I was in London the entire time.'

'That must have been pleasant,' said Cleary. 'I spent quite a bit of mine in Germany. What was your job?'

'Bomb disposal,' Crichton answered. 'Will you pass the bread and butter, Mrs Cleary?'

'Please call me Irene,' she answered.

When the meal was finished, Irene called on their neighbours, who agreed to baby-sit, and a few minutes later Crichton, Cleary and Irene were standing in the blustery rain in Earl's Court Road, waiting for a taxi.

When they arrived at the Chelsea Arts Club, there were plenty of people they knew. Hammond Shelley, Paul Trenton and Peter Quick were sitting with Laszlo at a table near the bar. As they joined them, Crichton sat down next to Quick. 'Richard has been telling me how the Cromwell Road School was formed,' he told him.

'Has he?' Quick replied suspiciously. He was a thick-set, aggressive little man. His heavy sweater, baggy tweed jacket and corduroy trousers made him look bulkier than he actually was. He ran his stubby fingers, still stained with oil paint, through his wiry, receding hair. 'Did he also tell you that none of us knew we'd formed a school until Richard started to give interviews implying that he was our elected leader? We'd only had one piss-up at his place.'

'I don't remember your complaining when you were interviewed by the *Sunday Times*, Peter,' Cleary said easily. 'Even though no one could understand your definition of the difference between subjective and objective realism.'

'Bollocks!' Quick replied fiercely. 'Everyone knows I'm more involved with the subject-matter than the rest of you. What about that quotation from Auden you keep using?'

'So?' Cleary answered.

Quick leaned across the table. 'A tolerant, ironic eye is detached

371

and objective.'

Shelley put down his pint of beer and turned to Laszlo and Trenton. 'I don't know why they don't just call themselves the Nettlebury School, and be done with it.'

Cleary turned to him. 'What do you mean by that?'

Shelley smiled and turned to Laszlo. 'You answer.'

Laszlo shrugged. 'We were just saying earlier that Julian Nettlebury was doing the same sort of work as the Cromwell Road School in the thirties.'

Quick turned at Laszlo. 'I've only seen those fucking great battle scenes in the Imperial War Museum.'

Shelley nursed his glass of beer in his lap and turned to Cleary. 'What about the pictures he did of Kew and Brentford? Pure subjective or objective realism, I'd say.'

'What about those bloody great murals? They're more like something by William Blake – or Stanley Spencer, come to that.'

'You'd have to make your own mind up on that point,' Laszlo said. 'But most people say you're all following in a direct line from the Euston Road School. I say they should draw a line from another direction.' He added, 'Kew, possibly.'

Irene listened to their talk for a time without joining in, and noticed Paula Tuchman further along the bar. She stood drinking with two other men and took part in their conversation, but her eyes kept moving back to their table. When it came to ten o'clock, she told Cleary it was time for them to go, but he waved her away.

'You go on,' he said. 'I want to stay here awhile.'

As Irene stood up, Crichton rose from the table as well. 'May I see you home? I live quite close.'

Irene accepted and they bade the others goodnight. As they passed the bar, Irene called out 'Goodnight' to Paula.

'Who was that?' Crichton asked casually when they were standing on the pavement.

'Paula Tuchman, the sculptress.'

They did not speak again until they had caught a taxi. Once they were sitting in the warmth, Crichton said, 'Isn't she a friend of your husband?'

Irene paused for slightly longer than he expected she would. 'Yes, I think so.'

When they arrived at Nevern Square, Crichton told the driver to wait while he saw her to the door. In the darkened hall she turned, and he kissed her for a long time. She quite enjoyed the experience.

It was the first time another man had touched her since her marriage, and Crichton's unexpected taste and texture were not unpleasant.

'Why did you do that?' she asked when he released her. She could not see his face in the darkened hall, but she knew he was smiling.

'Because I could hear you ticking.'

'Ticking?'

Crichton was standing in the doorway and Irene could see his face in the light from a street lamp. 'It took me back to the war. All the most interesting bombs had the fuse burning; just like yours, Mrs Cleary. Goodnight.'

England, summer 1953

Paul Van Duren looked for a long time at one of the Holbein portraits in the picture gallery at Hampton Court and then turned to his companion. 'Did you ever see such a Tammany Hall face in your life?' he asked.

Lydia Whitney-Ingram leaned closer to the picture. 'You're right. Those close-set shifty eyes in that chubby face, the man who can fix anything.'

He shook his head. 'Jesus, he could paint! You feel you could talk to these pictures.'

They walked away, their feet echoing on the wooden floors, and eventually came out into a cobbled courtyard divided into light and deep shadows by the afternoon sun. Paul took off his blue and white striped jacket and loosened his tie. He rubbed his hand through his thick black hair and glanced up at the line of a jet aircraft's fine white condensation trail cutting across the perfectly clear blue sky.

'Shall I compare you to a summer's day? Thou art more lovely and more temperate,' he said softly. 'She must have been some girl, to beat weather like this!'

'Winters were colder in England in Shakespeare's time,' Lydia said as they strolled out of the main gates towards the river.

'Were they?' Paul asked. 'How do you know?'

'I took English literature and history in college,' Lydia replied. 'Incidentally, the quote is: "Shall I compare *thee* to a summer's day?" '

'How come it was colder then?'

Lydia shrugged. 'The climate seems to change a couple of degrees every two hundred years or so. In Roman times and in the Middle Ages there were vineyards growing here. They even made English wine. Then in Elizabethan times there were bad winters. The rivers froze, people in London held ice fairs and roasted oxen on the Thames.'

'And the bad winters killed off the vines?'

Lydia shook her head uncertainly. 'No, I think it was after one of the kings won Gascony in a war that they could import cheap wine. There was something about wood for making long-bows, too.'

Paul wasn't really interested by the history lesson, but he liked to hear Lydia talk. Although he had known her all his life, it was only since she had become Mrs Whitney-Ingram that he had begun to find her so attractive. When they saw a neat little sign giving directions to the maze, 'We've got to take a look at that,' Paul said, delighted.

A few minutes later they were walking through the tall privet hedges. As they got further in, banks of cloud began gradually to obscure the sun, so that by the time they had reached the centre, a deep gloom had descended. 'I think it's going to rain,' Lydia said.

'To hell with it!' Paul sat down on a bench and lit a cigarette. 'Do you wish you'd gone to Wimbledon with the others?'

Lydia shook her head. 'I never cared for tennis, but Charles is crazy about it.'

'So is Angela. I told her it wasn't a game for Polacks, but she got violent again.'

'I didn't know she got violent?'

Paul nodded, and flipped his cigarette away. 'It's that Slav blood, or maybe it's the religion. Look at all those Catholic Latin countries where passions run high. We Protestants are far slower to anger. They come to the boil quicker than we do.'

'What form does her anger take?' Lydia asked. He laid his jacket on the grass and rolled up the sleeve of his shirt to show her a long scar from his wrist to the elbow of his right arm. Lydia ran her fingertip along the hard white tissue. 'How did she do that?'

'With a kitchen knife. It needed thirty-seven stitches to sew me up again.'

'Why did she do it? You must have provoked her,' Lydia commented.

Paul buttoned up his sleeve and put his jacket on again before he answered. 'She found out I'd been with another woman,' he said

374

without emotion. He reached for another cigarette. 'Christ, I told her she couldn't expect me to be faithful. That's why I won't get married. She expects me to give her the same kind of commitment she gives me, but I didn't ask for that. In fact, I don't want it.'

'Don't you mind if she's unfaithful to you?'

Paul watched the smoke curling from his cigarette. 'I don't think so. I have many faults, but I don't believe jealousy is among them. How about you? Are you faithful to Charles?'

'We've only been married a year,' she replied.

Paul shook his head. 'You haven't answered my question.' As he spoke, it began to rain heavily, but it was warm, like a tropical downpour. There was no shelter, and in moments they were both wet through. The rain plastered Lydia's summer dress to her skin and ran in rivulets between her breasts. He could see the shape of her body clearly through the thin wet cotton. 'Remember when we were kids that summer on Rhode Island?' he said.

Without talking further, they stood up and began to undress. The grass beside the bench was thick and uncut where they lay down, but it could have been broken glass for all they cared. They were captivated by the opportunity, and used each other without care or tenderness. The entire encounter was without thought or consideration. All they were aware of was the warm wetness of their bodies and the parts where they entered or received each other. Like creatures in heat, the real world that surrounded them receded like a dream and the only reality was the smell, feel and texture of each other's flesh. Lydia clasped her hands behind his back and wound her legs tightly about his waist while he dug his hands into the grass and pounded in time to her grunting gasps. At the moment of climax they both gave moaning sighs, and he collapsed and let his full weight rest on her slender body. Lydia opened her eyes briefly, but the rain falling on her face made her blink them shut again. They lay with eyes closed, both feeling drained by the aftermath of their encounter. Then Lydia became aware of a curious wet object nuzzling her left ear. She turned her head away from the rain and opened her eyes to stare into the puzzled eyes of a cocker spaniel. Now that her desire was sated, she returned to reality with the shock of a train hitting the buffers. She pushed Paul aside and looked up to see a middle-aged couple in raincoats sheltering beneath an umbrella. Their faces were transfixed by shock.

'Could you possibly pass my underwear?' Lydia said, with an extraordinary degree of composure considering the circumstances.

375

Recognising her accent, the woman spoke. 'They're American,' she said in a voice filled with disgust. 'One might have known.'

The couple retreated, and Lydia and Paul dressed in the rain. As they made their way through the maze, the skies cleared, and when they emerged into the open, the sun blazed down with all its previous intensity.

At Hampton Court station, they found a taxi that would agree to take them into London. When they were still on the outskirts of Richmond and passing close to the river, Lydia began to laugh.

'Americans,' she said. 'I might have known.' He joined her laughter and then reached for her breasts, but she pushed his hand aside. 'None of that really happened, you know,' she said in a warning voice.

'Not even the cocker spaniel?'

Lydia nodded. '*Especially* the cocker spaniel. If you ever tell anyone what happened, I'll come looking for you with a knife; and it won't be your arm I'll be aiming for.'

He looked out of the window for a while and then turned back to her. 'Do you think we'll ever do it again?'

Lydia considered the question. 'Do you think we're ever going to be caught again in a rainstorm, alone in the centre of Hampton Court maze?'

'It doesn't seem likely, but on the other hand it's a fallacy to say that lightning doesn't strike twice. It frequently hits the same tree over and over again.'

When the taxi reached Brown's Hotel in Albemarle Street, Lydia was glad that Charles had not yet returned from Wimbledon. She undressed in the bedroom and examined herself in a full-length mirror. As she suspected, there were grass-stains on her buttocks. She ran a bath, and was still languishing in it when he returned.

'How was Wimbledon?' she called out.

'Superb!'

'Oh, good.'

Charles appeared at the door with a drink in his hand. 'Would you care for one of these?' he asked, holding the glass.

'Mmmm, yes, please!'

When he returned, he had her wet crumpled dress in his hand. 'What happened to you?'

Lydia took the drink from him. 'You won't believe this, but Paul and I were in the middle of the maze at Hampton Court when we were caught in this terrific downpour. Didn't it happen at Wimbledon?'

376

Charles shook his head. 'No, the storm seemed to pass us by.'

London, early autumn 1953

Anthony Strange sat at the breakfast table in his house in Holland Park Road and tried to read his *Daily Telegraph*, but the soft clicking noise of his companion's teeth as they chewed through a large plate of fried food distracted him. Strange was already dressed for the day with his usual precision, but Karl Schneider, sitting opposite, still wore pyjamas and a dressing-gown of a particularly unpleasant shade of green. His thin hair hung in greasy strands across his domed forehead and there was a stubble of fair hair in the folds of his chubby face.

From the bedroom came the sound of Klara, who now qualified as Strange's common-law wife. She was singing one of her interminable dirges about sweethearts waiting for soldiers on the Eastern Front. He drained the last of his coffee and nodded to Bessie Rawlins, the West Indian woman who kept house for them. Silently she moved forward and refilled his cup, then she turned to Schneider. He pushed his cup towards her and she poured again and left the room.

'Do you think you need new teeth?' Strange asked fastidiously.

'These are new teeth,' Schneider said, taking a deep draught of coffee. 'I only collected them yesterday.'

'Then why do they make that infernal noise?'

Schneider shrugged. 'If they are too tight, they hurt me. I have a solution which makes them stick to my gums, but I haven't had an opportunity to apply it yet. Klara was in the bathroom.'

Strange sighed and set aside his newspaper. When he left his wife Harriet to live with Klara, Strange had thought he was ascending, once more, the staircase of success: a journey that would lead to a life fit for princes. Instead, the journey had taken another direction.

Klara certainly knew how to live like a princess, but unfortunately for Strange there were no revenues from an obedient population to fund her extravagances. After several years of her regal expenditure they had been forced to leave the house she had insisted they lease in Belgravia and move to the less salubrious surroundings of Notting Hill. The previous servants had been dismissed; now they made do with the sole attentions of Bessie, whose lack of emotion when responding to his demands made him uneasy. Strange was used to thinly veiled hostility from those who worked for him; he considered it the correct relationship between master and hired hand. Bessie's total indifference was impossible to categorise.

'Have you read this piece in *Forward* by Neville Crichton?' Schneider asked, pushing the magazine across the table. Strange picked it up and noticed with distaste the grease-stains on the pages. 'Page sixteen,' Schneider said, clicking. 'It's headed "The Warts and All School".'

While Strange was reading the article, Klara came into the room. Unlike her brother, she was groomed to perfection. Bessie followed and put a bowl of grapefruit in front of her.

Klara was extravagant about everything in life except food. To Strange, it sometimes seemed she consumed nothing but small pieces of fruit and water. He finished the article and studied her face and its flawlessly applied make-up. She had never told him her age, and it was impossible to guess by looking at her. He did not even know whether she was younger or older than her brother. She had a way of deflecting awkward questions by implying that they were a form of lower-class impudence, a technique that worked to perfection. And it was pointless to ask Schneider a direct question; he lied automatically about the past.

'What do you think of it?' Schneider asked, nodding towards the magazine.

'The Cromwell Road School?' Strange replied. 'It's going to be years before they're selling for anything like real money. Mind you, if a couple of them were to die it would be worth while buying some of their stuff in.'

'I thought they were all very young,' said Klara.

Strange nodded. 'What we want is another world war. Look what it did for the price of the Vorticists when they started getting killed off!' He glanced down at the magazine again. 'Cleary is the best of them. Isn't he James Gideon's brother-in-law?'

Schneider smiled. 'Yes – and he drinks excessively. He's having an affair with Paula Tuchman; it's been going on for a couple of years.'

Strange considered the options like an insurance actuary and drummed his fingers on the table-top while he thought. Paula Tuchman's work was gaining an impressive reputation; a love-affair was always excellent material for a biography. Cleary had an obvious talent and had already completed a fair body of work that was cheap to obtain. Drinking to excess did not always ensure an early death, but it materially shortened the odds on a long life. He realised his partner was right. Richard Cleary was a good investment. He smiled back at Schneider, and raised his coffee-cup. 'He'll be at the Van Duren private view. I think we should attend.'

It seemed odd for Irene to be back in her old bedroom at the house in Kew. Because Bridget was staying the night, Mrs Cooper had retrieved all her old toys from the cupboard below the stairs, and for a moment, when Irene caught a glimpse of her daughter in the mirror in the wardrobe door, the sight of the child, with her dark red hair and fair skin, was like looking at a ghost of herself. Then the labrador barked, and Irene returned to the present. They had compromised over the dog. Nettlebury had bought the puppy to keep at Kew, so that Bridget could play with it on her frequent visits, but the creature had worked his considerable charms on Nettlebury as well, and the two had now become inseparable.

'He wants to go down to Grandpa,' said Bridget.

'That's all right,' said Irene. 'He's coming up in a moment to read you a story.'

Irene kissed her daughter goodnight and hurried downstairs, the dog barking after her retreating figure. The doorbell rang, and she knew it was her taxi. She looked into the living-room where Nettlebury was sitting with Vera. 'I'm just off, Dad. I'll be back in the morning to pick up Bridget.'

They could hear the labrador barking; Vera looked up from where she had been dozing in a chair. 'I think that the dog wants its bedtime story,' she said in a thin voice. Irene ran down the path to the waiting taxi and set off for the West End.

When she arrived in Bond Street she could feel it was going to be an exceptional evening. Chauffeur-driven cars were already depositing other guests at the door. She entered and found Ted Porter checking the list of names. 'Is it a good turn-out, Ted?' she whispered.

He winked at her. 'Best opening night since *South Pacific*!'

She took a catalogue from the table and walked into the crowd examining the pictures. That in itself was an extraordinary sight. Usually only people who had no one to talk to looked at the paintings at a private view, but tonight everyone was turned to the walls.

Irene took a glass of champagne from a passing waiter and stood in the centre of the main showroom. The atmosphere was powerful; it was like standing in an open field before the onslaught of an electrical storm. It was also clear to her that not everyone liked the pictures. She could see that the guests had polarised into those who were extravagantly impressed and those who loathed them. While she stood taking her first sip of champagne, a tall man stalked past, closely followed by his fashionably dressed wife hurrying to keep up.

'Absolute rubbish,' he muttered to her angrily. 'I can't understand what possessed them to exhibit such trash!'

'Do you think he's flung a pot of paint in the public's face?' a teasing voice said into her ear.

Irene turned to see Neville Crichton smiling down on her, and returned his smile. 'A pot of paint wouldn't go very far in one of Van Duren's paintings!' she said. 'Something more like an industrial drum would be needed.' As she spoke, a small figure emerged from behind Crichton.

'What very British badinage,' he said in a high squeaky voice. 'I do so love England. All conversation is oblique and tangential, rather as I imagine croquet to be.' He held out his hand to Irene. 'Allow me to introduce myself. I'm Harold Beriac, and you must be Anne's sister Irene. I recognise the exquisite tonal qualities of the family hair.'

As he had intended, Irene was immediately enchanted by the tiny figure. 'Are you enjoying the evening?' she asked.

Beriac nodded vigorously. 'I love tension. It's always fun to see people going through the agony of pretending to like the new.' He nodded over her shoulder, and said, 'Here come three more admirers of Van Duren. The night ahead has all sorts of possibilities.' Irene turned to follow his gaze and saw Anthony Strange, Schneider and his sister being served glasses of champagne 'Excuse me,' said Beriac. 'I must go and taunt Schneider and Strange.'

He crossed the showroom, took another glass of champagne from the waiter and smiled innocently at the new arrivals. 'Hello, my dears,' he said silkily. 'What do you think of Van Duren's latest offerings? Don't they make your mouth water?'

Anthony Strange shrugged. 'I've only had a chance to glance around, but it all looks rather repetitious to me.'

'But what gorgeous repetition,' Beriac replied. 'Wouldn't you like to have thirty per cent of it, over and over again?'

Strange and Schneider looked at the pictures like two old voluptuaries gazing at a line of chorus girls. Then Strange turned back to Beriac. 'Have you seen Richard Cleary? I understand he was due to be here this evening.'

'He's in the next room, busily ignoring his wife.'

Strange nodded an acknowledgment and left Schneider and his sister talking to Beriac. As he walked away he heard the little American say, 'Is it true that your husband was personally decorated by Adolf Hitler, Your Highness?'

Strange passed into the next room, and his eyes encountered those of his wife, who was talking to Elizabeth. For a moment a flicker of doubt crossed his mind, but he realised that Harriet was too much of a lady to cause any sort of scene.

Cleary was standing alone at the bar, drinking whisky. 'Do you mind if I join you?' Strange asked. Cleary turned slowly and tried to focus on him with bloodshot eyes. It was obvious that he had been on a drinking bout for some time. It gave Strange a thrill of pleasure that his diagnosis of Cleary's condition had been correct. He knew immediately that he was in the presence of someone who was capable of killing himself with drink. He also realised that Cleary's powerful frame would help in his own destruction; his strength and stamina would help him to go on punishing himself until one of the more vulnerable organs collapsed. Nobody had a tough liver or kidneys, Strange reminded himself with pleasure. There were no muscles in the brain cells, either. He positively beamed with pleasure. 'My name is Anthony Strange, Mr Cleary. I think you are familiar with my gallery.' The figure swayed. 'I greatly admire your work,' he continued. 'I've been meaning to ask you for some time if you would like to join Strange and Schneider?' Cleary looked at him, but Strange was unsure if his words had conveyed any meaning to the artist. 'Did you hear me, Mr Cleary?' Strange said loudly. 'I said, would you like to join Strange and Schneider?'

As he peered into the drink-slackened features, a voice spoke beside him. It was Harriet. 'I shouldn't bother the poor man any more, Anthony,' she said cheerfully.

Strange turned and was about to speak when he saw Ted Porter approaching with the look of a man about to perform an unpleasant but necessary duty. He tried to slip into the crowd, but the bodies were so closely packed together that it proved impenetrable, and he was faced by hostile stares as he attempted to thrust his way through.

Ted Porter's hand descended on his shoulder, and he turned with a weak smile. 'Excuse me, sir, but there seems to be some mistake,' Ted said in a soft voice in which was a hint of menace. 'This occasion is only for people with invitations. Your companions are waiting for you in the street.'

Strange made an effort to restore his dignity. 'You've had the

381

effrontery to put Princess Reisenauer out in the street?' he said in an outraged voice.

'What on earth is wrong with that, Anthony?' Harried said lightly. 'Isn't the street exactly the sort of place one would expect to find a woman of her sort?'

Strange shook Ted Porter's hand from his shoulder and walked out of the room with his head held just a little too high.

Paul Van Duren watched him leave before he turned back to the earnest man who had held him captive in a corner for the past five minutes. 'Do you agree that there are primordial shapes that we share as a race memory buried in the subconscious?' he was asking.

Paul looked at the man. There was such an expression of eagerness on his face, such a need to comprehend a mystery that was obviously baffling him, that he took pity. 'What's your name?'

'Henry Grierson.'

'Well, Mr Grierson,' Paul said slowly, 'I've never heard anyone put our case better. I'll tell Pollock about you as soon as I get back to New York.'

Grierson flushed with pleasure at this endorsement. Paul nodded and moved away. Suddenly he did not want to talk any more to these people, who were looking in his direction with smiles of invitation. There was a staircase at the end of the showroom; without really thinking where he was going, he descended into the gloom and found himself in a narrow corridor. He paused in the darkness, about to return to the throng above when he saw a figure move across a pool of light that shone further in the interior of the basement. He walked along and entered a large store-room crowded with pictures, where he found Laszlo pottering about in the light of a single bulb.

Laszlo looked up, and smiled with a slight embarrassment. 'I hope you don't think me rude, leaving your party. It's just that I wanted to show someone upstairs something.'

Paul could see that Laszlo had opened three enormous green-painted metal cupboards, each containing deep shelves that bore curious contents. A familiar smell filled the air. It came to him after a moment: the aftermath of a fire. When he looked into the metal depths, he could see charred wood, fragments of burned canvas and scorched cartridge-paper.

Laszlo was standing on the rungs of a step-ladder, reaching carefully into the recesses of the first cupboard. 'I think I have it here,' he said, and slowly withdrew a small picture.

'You don't like my paintings very much, do you?' Paul asked.

Laszlo descended the step-ladder before he answered. 'I think "like" or "dislike" are the wrong terms to employ. Gideon and Charles are very keen on your work. That's good enough for me.'

But it wasn't for Paul. 'Are you against all abstract painters, or just me in particular?'

Laszlo laughed. 'Young man, I was preaching the virtues of modern painting from the moment I first saw a Matisse in 1916.'

'I wouldn't consider Matisse modern,' Paul said.

Laszlo laughed again. 'He was, then. People actually used to attack his pictures. There's nobody upstairs belabouring one of your paintings with an umbrella this evening!'

'So what's wrong with my stuff?'

Laszlo shrugged. 'As I said, it's not a matter of like or dislike, right or wrong. It's more a question of personal taste. I'm aware of the might of Beethoven's talent, but my personal preference is for Mozart.'

'So you at least concede that I have the same degree of talent as Beethoven?' Paul said, but he grinned as he spoke. 'What's that you've got?'

Laszlo held out the small painting. 'It's a picture by Sir Julian Nettlebury. One of his Brentford paint sketches.'

Paul took the picture and examined it in the light of the single bulb. 'I know this man's work. Charles has a landscape by him.'

'Yes, I know,' Laszlo replied.

'What happened to this stuff?' Paul gestured towards the cupboards.

'The gallery was bombed at the beginning of the war,' Laszlo explained. 'This is the remains of our stock.'

'Can any of it be restored?'

Laszlo nodded. 'I was just thinking that we must get round to it one day.'

'Hello!' Gideon's voice called, and they turned towards the sound. The room was suddenly flooded with light as he had turned on the main bank of switches. 'You two shouldn't be hiding down here! There are patrons to be wooed and critics to be flattered.'

'We're just coming,' said Laszlo. He took the Nettlebury sketch from Paul. 'Neville Crichton wanted to see this,' he explained. 'I didn't want to carry any of the big stuff upstairs.' He gestured towards a stack of larger Nettlebury pictures that rested against the wall. Paul walked over and began to examine them.

'Come on,' said Gideon. 'Your public awaits upstairs.'

'I'd like to have a longer look at these tomorrow,' said Paul.

'You can meet the painter, if you like,' Gideon told him.

'You mean he's still alive?' Paul asked in amazement.

'Alive, and living at Kew,' Gideon answered, ushering them towards the stairs.

Paul Van Duren came out of the dream with a shock that made him gasp aloud. Although it was not particularly warm in the hotel bedroom, his torso was wet with sweat. For a moment he was unsure where he was. Then he remembered: London. He lay still for a moment and then looked at the clock beside the bed. It was just after five in the morning, but he knew he would not sleep any more.

Angela stirred as he got out of bed. 'Are you all right?' she asked.

'Sure,' he replied, and went into the bathroom. He cursed when he remembered there was no shower, only the old cast-iron tub that took forever to fill. He really wanted a shower; he wanted to feel hard, stinging needles of cold water that would exorcise the demons of the night and bring him back to the reality of the day.

'Are you sure I can't get you anything?' Angela called out.

'I'm fine,' he answered, and ran the tap in the hand-basin and splashed water on his face and over his body. It was too early to shave. He cleaned his teeth. Back in the bedroom he pulled on the clothes he had left on the chair by the window the night before. There were crumpled bank-notes in the pocket of his pants and a lot of heavy coins. Jesus, he thought, English money is heavy. You could kill someone by throwing a pocketful of change at them. He took the money and held it in his hand. He could smell the metal, and then the memory of the night before came to him in broken images, like a set of photographs taken with a flash camera. There had been a big man with them, heavy and dark, and a woman who had cried at some point. Someone had wanted to fight, but the big man had patted him down, like a woman pounding dough to make bread.

'Where did we go last night?' he said.

'A dive in a place called Soho,' Angela replied. 'Richard Cleary took us there.'

Paul made an effort to remember. 'Richard . . . Did we see him?'

Angela sat up in bed and folded her arms across her naked breasts. 'Last night you said he was your best friend. You told everyone in the place, and bought drinks to celebrate the friendship.'

'Was there any trouble?'

384

Angela nodded. 'Some guy didn't want you to buy him a drink. In fact he said you were an under-talented, obnoxious shyster, but Cleary came to your rescue.'

'He sounds a pretty articulate customer to be found in a dive!'

'It was that kind of dive,' Angela replied.

Paul went to the window and pulled back the curtain. It was a bright summer morning, and the street was completely deserted. 'I think I'll go for a walk and buy a paper,' he said.

The elderly night porter was still on duty as he crossed the lobby. Paul had a vague memory of exchanging words with him in the early hours. The desk was too close to the doorway for him to pass without any form of acknowledgment. 'Good morning,' he said neutrally.

'Good morning, sir,' the man replied pleasantly.

Paul decided to face the situation squarely. 'Was I any problem last night?'

'Not at all, sir. On the contrary, you were most generous. You insisted I accept five pounds for helping you to your room.'

Paul smiled with relief. 'Thanks! I'm grateful.'

'Any time, sir,' the man said and Van Duren stepped into Albemarle Street and breathed the fresh morning air.

It was as though he were the only person alive in the city. Pigeons strutting in the middle of Piccadilly rose in a clattering cloud when he walked among them and entered Green Park. The grass had been freshly mown; it smelt sweet and reminded him of his boyhood and his grandfather's house in Maine. He crossed the bridle path that ran alongside Constitution Hill, stepped over the low railings and crossed the road to skirt the forecourt of Buckingham Palace. The first person he saw was one of the sentries patrolling the railings facing Queen Victoria's Memorial. He muttered, 'Good morning' as he passed the impassive figure, but received no acknowledgment.

A solitary car passed him as he walked down the Mall. When the engine note died away he became aware of the birds singing in St James's Park. Gradually memories of the dream began to fade away. He walked into the Park and turned to stroll beside the lake until he came to the narrow bridge. He crossed half-way and looked down into the grey-green water at a pair of mallards paddling past. When the waters became still again, he gazed down at their smoothness and the looming shapes that began to form on the opaque surface. The same menacing sensation made his pulse begin to race and a tightness grasp his chest. He took a deep breath and looked up into the pale blue sky. Then he turned and hurried away.

He came to Green Park station again and a news-vendor was setting up for the day. Paul bought a selection of papers and crossed the road. This time there was a sprinkling of traffic and more pedestrians. When he reached the hotel, the night porter had gone off duty.

Paul returned to his room and sat down by the window to read. It didn't take him long; the stories all concerned places of which he knew nothing.

Angela began to stir, and he went over and looked down on her. She had one arm up behind her head on the pillow and the other across her upper chest, so that the hand rested under her chin. The thick eyelashes cast a light shadow on her cheeks and her rosebud mouth was slightly parted as she breathed. Her hair on the pillow was a tangled mass of gold and flax. The bedclothes were pulled down to her waist so that her heavy breasts were exposed. She was so beautiful that it seemed amazing to him that he could ever contemplate being unfaithful to her. At moments like this it did not seem possible that any other woman could match her attractions. He leaned forward and gently kissed each nipple until they hardened and Angela's eyes flicked open. He pulled off his clothes, and she opened her arms to him with a stretching sigh. Gently he entered her and moved with an easy rocking motion until, with a sigh of content, they parted and he fell asleep.

It was ten o'clock when the telephone rang, but it did not disturb him. Angela answered it. The caller was Gideon, announcing that he would be along in an hour to take them to Kew. She bathed and then refilled the tub for Paul before she woke him.

When they got downstairs, Gideon was waiting in the street with the red MG. 'I hope you don't mind a squeeze,' he said, 'but I couldn't resist bringing it out today. The weather is so perfect and I've just had it restored to its former glory.'

'I thought it was brand new,' Angela said, climbing into the little seat behind the driver.

Gideon handed her a headscarf from the glove compartment. 'I bought this during Roosevelt's first term of office. I don't think I've ever owned anything that's given me more pleasure. Hold tight,' he called out, and they set off.

When they crossed Kew Bridge, Paul looked about him in astonishment. 'Jesus, it's a village!' he said when he saw the Green.

'That's right,' Gideon answered. 'Laszlo always used to claim that this was the countryside.'

They stopped outside the house and Gideon led them to the front door. Mrs Cooper answered the bell. She was getting short-sighted now and had to peer forward to make out Gideon. 'Sir Julian is in the conservatory,' she said when she realised who it was.

Gideon led the way through the house and they found Nettlebury and Vera seated in wicker chairs. Despite the warmth of the day, Vera had a plaid rug covering her knees. Nettlebury was sketching.

It had been some time since Gideon had been to the house and he was disturbed by Vera's appearance. Whenever he had enquired on the telephone, Nettlebury had always insisted that everything was fine, so he was unprepared for how gaunt she now seemed, even though her eyes were bright. Then he remembered the saying about a failing candle.

Nettlebury was civil but uncompromising to Paul. 'I've seen reproductions of your work,' he said after the introductions. 'Why did you want to meet me? We don't seem to have anything in common.'

Paul was unperturbed by Nettlebury's remark, and Gideon could see how charming the man could be.

'I think we have certain things in common,' he answered. 'Name a painter before the Renaissance that you like.'

'Fra Angelico,' Nettlebury replied without hesitation.

Paul nodded. 'The frescos in the cells of the monastery of San Marco?' he replied. Nettlebury nodded. 'Let me tell you about the other painters you admire, Sir Julian.'

'Go on.' Nettlebury reached for his tobacco-pouch and pipe.

Paul sat down beside the old man and began. Gideon listened with astonishment as he recited the list of painters that Nettlebury had given Gideon as those who had influenced him the most when he had first come to the house for lessons many years before. It was as though Paul had read Nettlebury's pictures as one would a guide-book, and was now able to tell him the major influences upon his work.

'Turner . . .' Paul said eventually. 'You had problems with Turner.'

'Not at all.' Nettlebury leaned from his chair and knocked out his pipe on the stone-flagged floor. Gideon could see that he was enjoying making Paul wait for his verdict.

'Turner was a great genius, but painters who came after him looked at his work and said; "Ah, this is the way." They were wrong; Turner had said it all. His pictures were a final statement. By trying to push his ideas further they merely produced a meaningless parody.'

Nettlebury pointed the stem of his pipe towards the young American. 'Tell me more,' he said.

'One last guess, and then I want to see your studio,' Paul announced. He looked up at the glass roof of the conservatory, and said, 'You admire the Pre-Raphaelite Brotherhood for their application, but don't really like their work.'

This time Nettlebury chuckled. 'Very good! And quite right. Their skills were breath-taking, but oh, dear, so many of their pictures were sentimental rubbish.' He pushed himself from the chair. 'Come on,' he commanded. 'Let's see what you make of my later stuff.'

Gideon watched them depart and then sat down to talk to Vera.

CHAPTER SEVENTEEN

England, spring 1955

Gideon was in a grim mood, and it was not improved by the chaos around. The bedroom was filled with odd items of furniture and pictures from the living-room so that he had difficulty in getting into his wardrobe. Eventually he called down to Anne, who was holding a loud conversation with Harold Beriac.

'That will look divine,' the little man piped over the sound of a banging hammer.

Gideon called again, 'Have you seen my cufflinks?'

'Look in the dress shirt you took off last night!' she shouted back.

'Does he have only one pair of cufflinks?' Beriac asked wonderingly as Gideon returned to the bedroom.

Who needs more than one pair of cufflinks? Gideon thought while he searched in the linen-basket.

Beriac continued to give instructions to the workmen below and Gideon smiled at the extravagant orders. 'I want that surface to have a sheen like satin, do you understand? If the wood shines with a cheap varnish, the whole room will look like a tart's parlour.'

For the last six months Beriac had been working with Anne to redecorate the flat, and it seemed to have taken up most of her time. He had now made his permanent home in London and visited America only infrequently. Like most expatriates, he had become extravagantly devoted to his adopted land, and, with the exception of paintings, claimed all things English to be superior. His devotion to Anne was well known, and it was claimed she was the only person of whom he had never made a deprecatory remark. Together they had visited sales, commissioned fabrics and pored over sketches, until gradually the sprawling apartment seemed to sink into anarchy under his direction.

Gideon had once asked him what effect he wanted to achieve, and

Beriac had fluttered his hands. 'The entrance is impossible,' he had replied, 'so it must always remain plain and unimpressive.' Then he gestured broadly. 'But the rest will be like a wonderful oyster when it's prised open, and fitting surroundings for a magnificent pearl.'

'What's the pearl?' Gideon asked.

'Anne, of course.'

Part of Gideon's ill-temper was because he had to visit the bank. He and Laszlo had been summoned by the manager after insistent telephone calls, and they were due to meet in the Park Lane branch at ten. Eventually he was ready to leave. When Anne kissed him goodbye, he felt a small surge of resentment that his wife was not undertaking this distracting task as she had always done before the decorations and Harold Beriac had come to dominate her life.

He called in at the gallery and found Harriet Strange in the deserted showroom reading *The Times*. From her greeting, he could tell she was not happy. 'What's the matter?' he asked, forgetting for a moment the disagreeable duty he was about to fulfil.

She held up the paper. 'There's an article here about Greeve,' she said. 'Apparently they're going to pull it down.'

After a moment Gideon remembered she was referring to the house that her family had once occupied. 'Why?'

Harriet looked down at the newspaper again. 'The school is closing down and they've sold the grounds to a property developer.' She read aloud: 'One of the last candles of pre-Reformation England is about to be extinguished.'

Gideon didn't know how to comfort her. 'I must meet Laszlo,' he said. 'We'll be back soon.' He set off for Park Lane.

After a brisk walk he found his partner standing outside the Dorchester, gazing across into the Park. There was an air about him of a guilty schoolboy waiting outside the headmaster's study. 'What do you think this is all about?' Gideon asked after they had greeted each other.

Laszlo raised his hands and let them fall to his sides. In truth, neither of them had the slightest idea of the current state of the gallery's fortunes. Anne had always taken care of that aspect of the business, and whenever she attempted to interest them in their commitments they would avoid her office and plead other duties. In America, Charles was exactly the same. Raymond Quill supervised the finances; he and Anne communicated with each other in a code of figures that were as meaningless to Charles, Laszlo and Gideon as a dead language.

'I thought we were doing pretty well,' Laszlo grumbled.

Gideon had thought the same. They had never done as much business as in the past two years. The combination of Harriet's contacts and the success of Van Duren's work had given the Archangel Gallery a twofold reputation for being sound in the marketing of classical work and at the forefront of the modern schools. There had even been a suggestion by Raymond Quill that they open a branch in Paris, but Laszlo and Gideon had rejected the idea with a variety of excuses, never stating the actual reason; which was that one of them would have to move over there, and they would miss each other.

Because neither of them had children, they had become an extension of a family and the relationship had extended to the staff of the gallery. Neither Gideon nor Laszlo had any idea what salaries were paid to Harriet, Ted Porter or any of the assistants and secretaries. Occasionally Anne would make them sit down and sign cheques, which they would do with sighs of boredom. Now they were being shown into the bank manager's office and felt that they were about to undertake an examination for which they were totally unprepared.

The office had changed very little from Mr Turner's day, but the new manager was a very different man. Ian MacNeice was a tall, gloomy Scot who eyed them with wintry benevolence. There was no offer of coffee, which Gideon took as a bad sign.

MacNeice looked down at some papers and studied them in turn. 'I'm glad you could finally make time for this meeting, gentlemen,' he began. 'As you are aware, it is part of the duty of the bank to ensure that prudence is exercised in the handling of the affairs of the Archangel Gallery.' When he stopped and smiled, his manner reminded Laszlo of an executioner eyeing his victims. 'We are not here simply to act as a conduit for the movement of money; if we consider that your fortunes have reached a certain level we must point out your options to you and the courses of action we feel it would be advisable for you to take.'

Laszlo cleared his throat. 'Is it the motor-cars? The cost of petrol must be enormous,' he stated.

Some months previously, Anne had provided them both with Rolls-Royces and drivers. Although they had both enjoyed the unexpected luxury, Laszlo had secretly thought the expense excessive.

MacNeice looked puzzled by the question. 'Why should the price of petrol bother you, Mr Vasilakis? You own the garage.'

'Own the garage?' Gideon repeated. 'Are you sure?'

391

MacNeice looked at them again with something like pity. 'Do you actually know what properties the Archangel Gallery owns?'

They both shifted uncomfortably in their chairs.

'Well,' Gideon began in an uncertain voice, 'there's the premises in Bond Street and the stock of pictures . . .'

MacNeice slowly shook his head. 'And you're both unaware of your other possessions?'

They nodded their heads in unison.

MacNeice gave a barely perceptible sigh and looked down at his papers again. 'Apart from the garage in Berkeley Street, there is an apartment building in Finchley, the villa in the south of France and the two farms in Berkshire.'

Gideon and Laszlo looked at each other in bewilderment. 'How did we get into this trouble, Mr MacNeice?' Laszlo asked after a worrying pause.

'Trouble?' said MacNeice. 'What trouble? We're not here to discuss your property portfolio. It's the excessive state of your current account that is causing the bank concern.'

'Did you say excessive?' Gideon asked faintly.

MacNeice nodded vigorously. 'We would be failing in our duty if we did not point out that the money could be earning a much higher rate of interest if you placed some of it in the hands of a reliable firm of stockbrokers. We can recommend such a house, if you wish.'

'How much is involved?' Laszlo asked.

MacNeice looked at the papers again. 'A sum slightly in excess of three million pounds. It's impossible to be precise,' he added in a dry voice, 'trading, as you do, on a day-to-day basis. Luckily Mrs Gideon seems to have a firm grasp on the situation.'

A quarter of an hour later MacNeice stood at the door of his office and watched them walk away across the marble concourse of the bank. When they had nearly reached the door, James Gideon executed a little dance of joy and the tapping sound of his feet caused a few heads to turn.

'Children,' MacNeice said softly to himself. 'Two middle-aged children. Thank God for Mrs Gideon!'

When they got back to the gallery it was still empty, and Harriet sat at the same desk with the newspaper in front of her. Gideon picked it up and threw it in the air. 'Cheer up, Harriet!' he almost sang. 'We're going to buy Greeve for you.'

She looked at them both with astonishment, and then Gideon saw that Anne had entered the showroom. She was standing with her arms folded and a smile of satisfaction on her face.

Gideon leaned across the desk. 'And, what's more, we're going to hire Harold Beriac to help with the decoration. It should be finished in about twenty years.'

England, autumn 1955

Richard Cleary stood in the galley of Paula Tuchman's houseboat and made two cups of instant coffee. From a window in the flat-bottomed craft he looked across a wide expanse of puddled mud to the channel of the River Orwell, where a fully-rigged Thames barge navigated the deep water. Seagulls squawked and argued as they scavenged for food and a breeze rippled the shallows. While he waited for the water to boil, he watched Paula drawing the shape of a crouching figure on the piece of white stone on a plinth in the centre of the studio. Nettlebury would have approved; everything was in good order. He could see the work in progress quite clearly.

Two drawings were pinned to the side of the houseboat, and a clay maquette of the figure she was intending to execute: a man, powerful, muscular, curled in a foetal position.

Cleary brought over the coffee. It still surprised him that Paula worked in stone; it was such a tough medium, and she looked so fragile. But looks were deceptive. He knew she possessed an unexpected strength in that slender body. 'How do you get the stone down here?' he asked.

She pointed upwards. 'Through the hatchway. Another boat comes alongside, and they just swing it aboard on a little crane and lower it down.'

Cleary nodded. Of course. It had been a silly question. He went on watching her and then decided to take a shower.

When he emerged from the little bathroom, Paula had finished drawing and was drinking her coffee. She observed him as he dried himself, and said, 'I'd like to do a carving of you. While the muscles still have their tone.'

'Don't you think they'll last, then?'

She glanced across the muddy flats. 'Not if you go on living on whisky and cigarettes.'

'No, thanks.'

'No, thanks – to the suggestion that you pose for me?' she asked.

Cleary nodded.

'Why?'

He sat down on the bed and towelled his hair while he answered. 'Because I don't want people pointing at it some day and saying: "That was Paula Tuchman's boyfriend. She did that in her houseboat period, when she was having it off with him."'

Although he spoke lightly, there was an underlying truth that did not escape her. In the last few years her work had become well known and she was beginning to command attention abroad. All the things that still evaded Cleary. 'What would you prefer?' she asked tightly. 'A family group – the artist with wife and child?'

He could hear the bitterness in her voice. He stood up and flicked her gently with the towel. 'I'd prefer to keep our relationship on the impersonal level.'

Paula stood up as well and lifted her long white nightgown so that he could see her naked body. The pale skin was bruised in several places. 'Would you call this impersonal?' she asked.

'Christ! Did I do that? I'm sorry,' he said with sudden concern.

'That's all right.' She dropped her nightdress. 'You've got one or two wounds on your back. It comes from not seeing each other for months on end.'

He looked out of the window again and saw that the tide had turned. The mud flats were now covered with water the colour of tea. 'Why the hell do you live up here?' he asked angrily. 'You could afford to live in London.'

'I don't want to live in London,' she told him. 'I don't feel I have any individuality there.'

'That's rubbish,' he countered. 'Pure temperament. If you were in town, we could see each other all the time.'

'That's what I mean,' said Paula. Then she stood up and took his face in her hands. She felt the contours as though she had modelled them herself.

Cleary reached inside her nightdress and encircled her naked waist. He pushed his face into the crumpled material at her breast and inhaled the warm, womanly smell of her.

She ran her hands through his hair. 'If I were in London and you just popped around any time, I'd feel used, like a bucket you just emptied yourself into. As it is, you have to make an effort to come and see me. I know it isn't logical but it makes me feel worthwhile. You do understand, don't you?'

He nodded against her breasts. 'I'd better get ready to go,' he said after a moment. 'Will you run me into Ipswich?'

She looked out over the water. 'You'll have to hang on a bit longer unless you want to wade ashore. It's not deep enough for the dinghy yet.'

He reached for her again, but she slipped away. 'I'm bruised enough,' she said. 'Anyway, I want to wash as well.'

While they dressed, Paula said, 'What about the next exhibition?' She was referring to the Cromwell Road School.

'Gideon said they'll have a slot for us early next year.'

She stood over him while he packed his holdall. 'Do you mind exhibiting at the Archangel? I always got the impression you and he didn't hit it off.'

Cleary paused. 'We used to. In fact I think we could have been friends. But he knows about us, and his loyalties lie with Irene.'

'What sort of a person is he?' she asked. 'He's always polite and a bit distant when I see him.'

Cleary thought about her question. 'I don't really know. There's a secret part to him. He can draw beautifully, did you know?'

Paula shook her head. 'No, I didn't.'

'I always thought there was some kind of pun about the name "Archangel". You know, a play on Gideon and his ability to draw. I thought he might actually be taking the piss out of the people who exhibit there. Privately thinking, "I can do it better than any of you." '

'But you don't think that's the case now?'

Cleary shook his head. 'No. Laszlo told me he genuinely loves artists. It's his loyalty again. To Laszlo, Anne and Nettlebury – and me in a way, I suppose.'

Paula looked out at the deepening water. 'That what it's all about really; loyalty to someone.' Then she turned again. 'Come on, the water's deep enough now.'

England, spring 1956

Anne walked along Bond Street at a brisk pace, despite the weight of the parcel she was carrying. It was a picture wrapped in brown paper, and the heavy frame made the string cut into her hand. She paused for a moment outside Sotheby's, changed the load to her other hand and continued with the same hurrying step. When she passed the Strange and Schneider Gallery, she glanced in through the window and saw the two partners standing on either side of a Miro that was being contemplated by a prospective buyer. Anne recognised the picture; it was a fake that had been circulating among dealers for the past two years. Then she thought of the painting she carried; could it, too, be considered a fraud? It was a fine point, she realised, but she put the idea out of her head as she entered the Archangel Gallery.

Laszlo was just saying his farewells to someone on the telephone. He raised his eyebrows at Anne's parcel, and she nodded her reply. When he replaced the receiver, he asked, 'Was it worth it?'

Anne smiled. 'I think so. Where is he?'

'Downstairs,' Laszlo answered. 'Shall we go and surprise him?'

They went down to the basement, where Gideon was working with Ted Porter. They were supervising pictures for shipment, a boring task that Anne knew Gideon loathed. He looked up when they approached and waited expectantly. 'Is this going to make me happy?' he asked.

'We'll soon know.' Anne placed the parcel on a table against the bare wall and began to untie the string. She was a string-collector, and could not bear to see lengths of twine carelessly cut. 'Turn round,' she ordered, and Gideon did so. When she had propped the picture against the wall, she stood back. 'You can look now.'

Gideon faced the painting and folded his arms. He looked at it from a few feet away for some time, and then, still without speaking, moved forward and studied the surface intently. 'Beautiful,' he said finally. 'Quite beautiful.' He turned to Laszlo. 'What do you think?'

He stepped forward to scrutinise the picture with the same care. 'You are the only one I know who does work of this quality. It's fantastic! Do you remember the state it was in before?'

Gideon nodded. 'This area was all that remained.' He indicated a rough triangular shape.

Anne took a black-and-white photograph from her handbag and laid it on the table. 'This was all he had to work from,' she said. 'It was taken in . . .' She turned round for confirmation.

'December 1940,' Ted Porter said, and recited the history of the picture. 'Portrait of a card-player by Cézanne, sold to the gallery by a Mr Christopher Payne. Partially destroyed by enemy action, spring 1941.'

Gideon leaned forward to look at the picture again. He could feel the technique. This man also knew how to sublimate himself to another human being's talent; it was an eerie sensation. He remembered an expression his mother had once used when an understudy had taken over her part on a certain occasion. 'It's like someone walking on my grave,' she had said with disapproval.

396

Gideon now knew exactly what she had meant. 'This man is remarkable,' he said. 'Cézanne is one of the hardest painters to imitate. Every brush-stroke is a signature.'

'How did he manage to marry the restored part to the original?' Anne asked.

Gideon turned and grinned at them. 'He didn't. That would have been impossible with Cézanne's work at this period. The paint is too thin, almost like washes of watercolour. He repainted the whole picture.' He paused, and then said, 'I wonder what he's done with the bit left over?'

Laszlo looked at the picture with renewed interest. 'I think I would like to meet this man. Anyone who can fake a Cézanne so effectively should be a fascinating individual.'

Gideon shook his head. 'It's not really a fake, you know,' he said thoughtfully.

'But you just said that it was an entirely new painting,' Anne said, puzzled.

Gideon scratched his chin. 'Yes, but that doesn't really make it a fake, in my view. You could say that half the pictures in the great museums of the world were fakes when you consider how often they have been restored. Take *The Last Supper*. That's been altered and repainted almost since the day Leonardo da Vinci finished it, but it's still revered as a piece of work by the master.'

Anne thought about his words. 'So, if you create a picture that is in the style of Braque, you've paid a homage to the originator, but if you pass it off as the work of Braque, it's to be despised as a fake?'

'I believe that, but a lot of the world's experts would violently disagree. None the less, one day there will have to be a recognised category of paintings such as this one.'

'Why?' said Anne.

'Because your father told me so. He explained to me that painting was, in part, chemistry, and time in the end destroys everything. If we don't make copies of this quality, future generations will have only photographs to look at.' He turned to Laszlo. 'I think you're right: we ought to meet this man. Where did you find him?'

'Irene found him,' said Anne.

'Really?' said Gideon. 'How did that come about?'

'It seems he's a great jazz fan, and one night he was listening to Richard's band in a pub near Earl's Court. Richard decided to take a lot of people back to their flat, and this chap was among them. He was intrigued by Richard's paintings. He told Irene he was in a similar line of business, and gave her his card. She was here a couple of weeks ago when she heard Laszlo talking to me about getting a picture restored for you, and she produced his card. She still had it in her purse.' Anne shrugged. 'So one thing just led to another. He brought the picture back a couple of days ago, and I had it framed.'

'Do you still have his address?' Gideon asked. Anne went to her desk to find it. He glanced at it, and placed it in his top pocket. He smiled at Laszlo. 'Do you fancy a journey to the wilds of Ladbroke Grove?'

With a brush as fine as the point of a needle, Bernard Ovington traced the delicate veins of a bloodshot eye on the canvas. The picture he was working on was a large Victorian narrative painting entitled *The Return of the Prodigal*. It depicted a dissolute youth kneeling before a bearded clergyman who was laying a hand of benediction on the young man's curly head. To the right, a weeping mother and sisters embraced with joy. Sunshine from a tiny window haloed the youth's head, a symbol of redemption.

He had just completed the last scarlet line of cross-hatching, as intricate as a spider's web, when a muffled alarm-clock began to ring. 'Perfect timing,' Bernard said to the two fat brindle-coated cats who sat on the table at his elbow and now stretched themselves in anticipation of the food that the ringing alarm signified.

He unwrapped the clock from the towel and reset the alarm for five, the next time he would be called from his work. Then he carefully washed out the brush before examining his soft white hands. They were as clean of paint as the brown overall he wore to protect his shirt, waistcoat and trousers. He was a meticulous man in everything he undertook and liked his life to run with precision.

He went out to the gloomy kitchen at the back of the house to serve the meal he had prepared earlier that morning. After brewing a pot of tea, he spread three cream crackers with butter, cut a piece of cheese from the lump beneath the fly-trap, opened two cans of sardines which he emptied on to saucers and then ladled a vast portion of Lancashire hotpot into a soup-plate. When he was satisfied that it was all ready, he removed his brown overall, hung it behind the kitchen door and took the jacket of his three-piece suit from a coat-hanger. Before he took up the tray, he looked into the mirror on the wall, gave his heavy moustache a quick brush and tugged at his tightly knotted tie, which did not quite cover the brass stud in his high stiff collar.

He climbed the stairs, the two cats bounding ahead of him,

mewing greedily. When he reached the top step, his mother called, 'Is that you, Bernard?'

He sighed at the words he heard every time he climbed the staircase. 'Yes, Mother, it's only me.' The only other person who ever made the journey was Dr Maloney, who reluctantly called once a month to reassure his mother that she was in perfect health.

Mrs Ovington would then complain that if she was so fit, why did her infrequent walks to the bathroom cause her such agonising pains in the legs? The old doctor would tell her, once again, that it was because she was so fat and she took no exercise, and she would relapse into one of her sulks that lasted until the next meal Bernard provided for her.

He opened the door of her bedroom with his elbow. The two cats crossed the room and leaped on to the bed, where they circled each other, watching Bernard's approach.

'What's for lunch?' his mother asked suspiciously.

'It's Wednesday, Mother. You always have hotpot on Wednesday.'

'Has my *Picturegoer* arrived yet?' she demanded.

'You know it comes on Thursdays, Mother,' he answered gently, determined that she would not anger him. On the occasions when she did manage to penetrate his calm, his stomach would churn and boil as if red-hot lava had been released into his intestines.

He placed the tray before her, took the saucers of sardines and set them down in the alcove by the window. Then he went back down to the kitchen, where the cheese and crackers waited on the dresser. He poured a cup of tea and placed it next to the plate on the table and then went to a large wind-up gramophone. The cupboards beneath the dresser were filled with jazz records. Bernard made his selection and in moments the quavering sound of a long-dead New Orleans trumpeter filled the dark room. He sighed contentedly and bit into a piece of cheese. Then the doorbell rang.

Gideon and Laszlo stood on the doorstep, and looked around. It was as though the world had been drained of colour; everything they saw, including the sky, was in various tones of grey.

The Georgian façades of the houses, once white, were streaked and pitted with soot, and the cracked paving-stones merged into cobbled stone and patches of macadam. Ragged, dirty children played around them, their harsh accents echoing along the narrow street. The only signs of vegetation were clumps of lichen around leaking drainpipes. From the doorway of the house that faced them, a fat woman with bare mottled legs watched until the bell was answered.

'Mr Bernard Ovington?' Gideon asked. 'I am James Gideon and this is my partner Laszlo Vasilakis. We own the Archangel Gallery. May we speak to you?'

Bernard looked at them for a moment and then stood aside. 'Of course,' he replied in the soft, anxious tones of a helpful shop-keeper. 'Won't you come in?'

He led them along a dim, narrow corridor and into a long room that ran from the front of the house to a pair of floor-length windows opening on to a brick-walled yard. Gideon and Laszlo looked around with interest. Heavy wooden shutters covered the windows to the street. There were no carpets on the floor; it was a workroom, cluttered with the tools of Ovington's trade – easels, tables and a long, shallow, enamel bath that could be heated with gas jets. There were shelves containing jars of chemicals and raw unmixed colours, lamps and brushes, tracing-paper and new canvas, scrapers, cutters, scalpels and hammers, bunsen burners and neat piles of old newspapers. Despite the apparent chaos, Gideon could see that there was an absolute order to the room; he knew that Ovington could immediately put his hand on anything he required.

Stacked at one end of the room were pictures. Laszlo examined the picture on the easel. He could see the area that was being worked on, and a large expanse of raw unpainted canvas where the lower parts of the figures were just sketched in. 'A Millais,' he said. 'What happened to it?'

Bernard came and stood by the easel. 'It was partially destroyed by a fire. Luckily, it was well catalogued, so it's an easy job to restore.' He gestured towards two unmatched kitchen chairs. 'Won't you take a seat? I've just made a pot of tea. Would you care for a cup?'

While he was out of the room, Gideon examined the picture again. He could not detect where Ovington's work began; it was as though he were seeing the painting as it was when first executed by the artist.

When Bernard returned with the tea, two cats accompanied him. They jumped on to the table and sat staring at the intruders in turn.

'Can you describe the technique you're using on this picture, Mr Ovington?' Gideon asked.

'It's fairly standard,' Bernard replied softly. 'As at least a third of the original was burned away, I had to remove what was left of the painting from the canvas. First I forced melted wax through the back of the picture and floated the paint off. When the wax hardened, I could lay it down on newly stretched canvas and fix it to

400

the fresh surface. It's good that it's by Millais; the Pre-Raphaelites were such master craftsmen that there was a strong ground of gesso between the original surface of the canvas and the oil paint. The better the original preparation, the easier my job is, Mr Gideon. You wouldn't believe how sloppy some of the modern painters are! With no priming, the paint just sinks into the canvas. When that happens, I've really got a problem. I have to stick the original canvas to a new surface and then build it up until I can blend the picture at the same level, a bit like making up a wall when a chunk of the old plaster has fallen off.'

Gideon watched Bernard as he spoke and suddenly realised he was much younger than he had at first thought. The heavy moustache, the thinning hairline and the Edwardian cut of his clothes had made him seem like a relic from the turn of the century. Now he saw that he was no more than thirty, possibly less. 'Tell me, Mr Ovington,' he said, 'where did you study?'

Bernard gave a puzzled look before he answered. 'Right here, Mr Gideon. My father taught me everything I know.'

'So you never went to art school?' Laszlo said in astonishment.

Ovington shook his head. 'I left school when I was fourteen, but I'd been helping my father much longer than that. When Dad left us, I just took over the business.'

'How do you get your work?' Laszlo asked.

Bernard looked at him oddly. 'Mr Strange brings it, as he always did.'

'Anthony Strange?' Laszlo asked.

Bernard looked uncertain. 'I don't know his first name. He brings the pictures and I do them, and then he gives me the money, like always.'

Gideon gestured towards the picture on the easel. 'And how much will he give you for this one?'

Bernard smiled. 'There's at least two weeks' work in that picture. I shall probably get ten pounds.'

Gideon and Laszlo exchanged glances. 'But you must have some other kind of business, Mr Ovington? You gave my sister-in-law a card,' said Gideon.

'Your sister-in-law?' Bernard said blankly.

'Mrs Cleary.'

'The trumpeter's wife, the one with all the pictures?' Bernard asked.

'That's her,' said Gideon. 'She gave my wife your name and

401

address. She had your card.'

'That was one of Dad's old cards,' Bernard explained. 'It was still in his suit. His name was Bernard, too.'

Laszlo and Gideon exchanged glances again, and Gideon nodded.

Laszlo smiled at the young man. 'Mr Ovington, how would you like to work for us . . . for the Archangel Gallery? We'll pay you a lot more than Mr Strange.'

Bernard looked at the picture on the easel. 'How much would you pay me for this?'

'A great deal more than you're getting at the moment.' Gideon plucked a figure out of the air. 'At least a hundred pounds.'

The man did not seem impressed, and then Gideon realised that the sum was more than he could comprehend.

'Would I have to move from around here?' Bernard asked.

'Only if you wanted to,' Laszlo answered.

'I wouldn't mind. It's different now from when I was a little boy.'

England, summer 1956

Richard Cleary lay in bed and feigned sleep when he heard his daughter come into the bedroom and kiss him goodbye. He felt the gentle touch on his cheek, but he did not open his eyes until he heard the door to the flat close behind Irene and Bridget. Now there was perfect silence, but no comfort for him. It was a warm Sunday morning and the bedlinen felt like a winding cloth over his naked body. In the distance he could hear the faint peal of church bells, but the sound was more like an accusation than a comfort. In his childhood his mother had been a staunch Anglican, but it had been a long time since he had attended services; the faint tolling seemed to accuse him of yet another neglected duty.

He threw back the bedcovers and lay for a while gazing at the ceiling, which was seamed with ancient cracks. There were so many bumps and lines, patches of variable tone and discoloration that he could find shapes to fit any image that came to mind: a cinema queue he had stood in as a child, the profile of his mathematics teacher at school, the outline of a Lancaster bomber, a beckoning hand. Whose hand? Cleary knew.

He got out of bed and walked to the bathroom. The hot tap barely ran warm after Irene and Bridget had bathed. He filled the tub and lowered himself into the tepid water. All his actions were lethargic; it was as if his powerful body was drained of energy, so that each movement required an enormous effort of will-power. It was not just his physical actions; he would not let his mind dwell on anything but the superficial, the patterns on the ceiling, the warmth of his bath-water, the mild ache behind his eyes and the sour taste that was still left from last night's drinking bout. Beneath those surface preoccupations lay a deep pit of misery and despair which he did not wish to enter. He shaved by touch, and then lay perfectly still in the now cold water; the only noise was the drip from one of the taps. He managed to empty his mind by concentrating on that one regular sound, then he synchronised his breathing with the quiet rhythm until everything receded, but for the pain of his headache and the thought that now came to him. He would like to be a sea creature and swim to some far, warm ocean, where he could follow shoals of tropical fish swimming in swirling patterns and dazzling colours through the clear blue water.

There was a hammering on the door of the flat, and their neighbour Hugo shouted, 'Telephone call for you!'

Cleary climbed from the bath and wrapped himself in towels already dampened by his wife and daughter. On the landing he picked up the public phone that was used by the block of mansion flats. 'Richard Cleary,' he said.

Paula Tuchman's voice answered him in flat tones.

'Are you coming?'

Cleary hesitated. He could feel the grit and the marble floor under his bare wet feet. Outside, a child shouted a long dying note. Suddenly he felt the abyss yawn before him. 'Yes,' he answered finally. 'Pick me up at the Queen's Elm later.'

Cleary returned to the flat, now moving with the rapid certainty of someone who has made up his mind. He quickly packed a canvas bag with spare clothes, then looked around the kitchen for something on which to write a note. The only object that came to hand was an old birthday card of Bridget's, something with bunny rabbits. He folded the thin card back to expose a clean area and wrote: *Have gone away for a few days, on the move, so you can't contact me. Don't worry, see you soon. Richard.* When he slammed the door of the flat behind him, the card fell from the dresser and fluttered to the floor.

He did not go direct to the Queen's Elm, but made a diversion to a newsagent's. While he waited for the man behind the counter to serve him, he picked up a bar of milk chocolate. The only craving that still remained from his time in the prison camp was for sweet things. He bought two papers. Outside the shop, he ate chocolate with slow deliberation, reading a review of the latest exhibition at the Archangel Gallery. They were no better than the daily papers had been.

The first he turned to was by Harold Beriac, headed: 'The Road to Nowhere'. He began to read:

When artists come together and bestow upon themselves a title, they usually believe they are undertaking some epic journey of discovery. I am sure that when the group who call themselves 'The Cromwell Road School' first met at the Royal College of Art they saw themselves embarking on an odyssey as heroic as that of Ulysses. So how have our intrepid youths fared? Did they find truth and earn glory? I fear not. Instead they have come perilously close to another art form – 'The Road Film'.

Those of us familiar with the work of Paramount Studios will recollect with affection the films starring Bob Hope, Bing Crosby and the delectable Miss Dorothy Lamour. Although the plots were flimsy (if indeed one could claim there was any discernible plot at all), they usually conformed to the following pattern. Our two feckless heroes would be stranded in some remote part of the world, looking for a way to return home. Mr Hope, cautious, timid and easily led, would be persuaded to undertake various dangerous tasks by Mr Crosby, the more worldly of the pair. Miss Lamour would appear and inform them of a treasure that existed in some fabled place and whilst simultaneously competing for Miss Lamour's favours, our engaging heroes would set off to seek wealth and glory despite the intervention of various villains, who also wished to obtain the treasure. Subsequently, Mr Crosby would sing some pleasant melodies. Mr Hope would amuse us with the difficulties he encountered whilst fighting the villains, and Miss Lamour would remain decorative and undecided as to which of our two heroes she would choose, until the final reel, when it would always be Mr Crosby.

For the purposes of the analogy one has to accept the casting of the following roles: Mr Richard Cleary plays Bing Crosby, the Muse plays Miss Dorothy Lamour and the rest of the Cromwell Road School play Bob Hope. The mainstream of modern painting is the villain. Let us now continue with the plot. Mr Cleary, along with the other young men of the Cromwell Road School, is stranded, without inspiration, at the Royal College of Art. The Muse appears to Mr Cleary and whispers to him that there is an alternative to the challenge of Abstract Expressionism – a sort of urban naïve painting. All they have to do is follow him, and glory awaits them. So they set off on the Road to

Nowhere, Trevor Wilde, Bernard Warton, Peter Quick and Patric Carey each following Richard Cleary, yet each pursuing an individual style that roams through the spectrum of British painting, encompassed by Walter Sickert and Julian Nettlebury.

It is as if the twentieth century does not exist for them, and because they cannot meet the intellectual responsibilities of the modern world, they have marched sideways in time, down a safe, cosy byway lined with rose-covered cottages. It's an easy walk, but it isn't one of the paths of glory, and it does nothing for the growing reputation of British painting. Richard Cleary and his companions should remember that the Cromwell Road merely leads to Hammersmith.

Cleary did not bother to look at the other newspaper. He folded them both carefully and thrust them into the side pocket of his holdall before setting off for the Queen's Elm. When he arrived he found Peter Quick and Trevor Wild standing outside, both holding pints of beer, a little distant from the other people they knew who were taking advantage of the warm sunshine. As always, when he saw the two men together, he thought fate had mismatched their names. Trevor Wilde was cadaverously thin, with the jerky nervous movements of a startled animal. Even now he gave the impression that he was about to dart away from the wall he was leaning against and take cover in one of the nearby gardens. Peter Quick, however, truly deserved the name 'Wilde'; it was though he were in a permanent state of rage with life. Every movement he made seemed to emanate aggression and his face wore a fixed scowl, even in repose.

Trevor Wilde bought Cleary a pint of beer and they stood in gloomy silence. All three had enrolled at the Royal College of Art on the same day; they had long exhausted their capacity for small talk. In fact their relationship was more like that of a large family of grumbling relatives. Outsiders could take their squabbles as signs of distaste for each other, but when outsiders criticised any one of them they would come to each other's defence with a tribal ferocity. Now, as they leaned against the wall of the Queen's Elm, to a casual observer they would have appeared barely acquainted, but in truth they were as united as a square of British infantry.

'Has he turned up yet?' Cleary asked, in a mild, inquisitive voice.

'No,' Trevor Wilde replied. 'But those sniggering pricks are waiting for him.'

Cleary glanced up casually and saw three men clustered round two pretty girls who wore the black-stockinged uniform of art students. Those three had studied sculpture at the Royal College at the same time as Cleary and his companions. All had the reputations of being bar-room brawlers. One of them said something, and the others exploded with raucous laughter, glancing towards Cleary's group. He noted their attention and then entered the crowded bar to buy another round. Inside, near the door, he encountered Hammond Shelley and Laszlo.

'Hello, we'll come out and join you,' said Laszlo.

Cleary shook his head. 'I wouldn't if I were you. We're poor company this morning.'

'Beriac's article?' Laszlo asked.

Cleary shrugged and leaned against the wall. Then he smiled. 'The critics kicked us to pieces, Laszlo. Anyone would have thought we'd spent our lives illustrating chocolate boxes and women's magazines, judging from the crap they wrote about us.'

Shelley shook his head in sympathy. 'At least you're honest enough to say that it hurts.'

Cleary nodded and passed on to the bar. When he carried the three glasses outside, he found Paula Tuchman standing with the others.

'Are you ready?' she asked impatiently.

'I'll just be a little while longer,' Cleary answered, holding up his full glass of beer. 'Would you care for a drink?'

Paula shook her head. 'We've got a long drive ahead of us.'

'I know,' he said. 'But there's still something I have to do.'

Paula paused. 'In that case, I will have a drink,' she said. 'Don't worry. I'll get it myself.' She entered the bar just as a taxi pulled to a halt in the Fulham Road and three giggling figures descended. They were all quite drunk. Cleary knew the signs of a group who had continued through the night.

The two youths with Beriac stood swaying at the kerb while their leader paid off the cab. One, wearing a well-cut crumpled suit, paused to light a cigarette for his companion, who had to brush long limp hair away from the flame of the offered lighter. Beriac turned and linked arms with them both and they all stumbled across the wide pavement towards the group of sculptors.

'Ready?' Cleary said quietly.

Trevor Wilde and Peter Quick nodded, and all three walked forward holding their full glasses. Paula emerged from the saloon bar just in time to see three pints of beer hit Beriac like a wave breaking over the prow of a ship. Enough of the liquid had escaped

406

the target to extinguish the cigarettes of his companions. Some of the beer had also splashed the three sculptors, who moved forward with obviously aggressive intentions. But Cleary dropped his empty glass, and it shattered on the wet paving. His early lethargy had left him; he looked a fearsome figure.

Although the three sculptors were known to enjoy a fight, they all recognised the primeval aggression of someone prepared to kill, and that was the clear message Cleary was signalling. His body strained forward, and his face was transformed into a frightening mask of hatred.

Beriac slipped on the beer and fell, still clutching the arms of his two companions, and all three wallowed together in the beer and broken glass from Cleary's pint pot.

Paula quickly crossed the pavement and took Cleary's arm, then placed herself between him and the three sculptors. 'Richard, Richard,' she said in a softly urgent voice, gazing up into his terrible face. Slowly he looked down at her and the fog of dark rage began to lift from him. 'Come away,' she said, pleading. 'Come away now.'

Gradually the rigid muscles of his face relaxed and he allowed her to tug him towards her canvas-roofed jeep. He took his seat without protest.

'I have a bag,' he said distantly.

Paula found it resting against the wall of the pub, picked it up and tossed it into the rear of the jeep. The gears made a grinding sound as she slammed them into first and the little vehicle lurched away from the milling crowd outside the Queen's Elm.

'We appear to have missed something,' Shelley said to Laszlo as they emerged from the saloon. 'What happened?' he asked Trevor Wilde.

'We just bought Beriac a drink,' he said cheerfully, gesturing towards the dripping man.

'A pint of beer in the face of a critic,' Shelley mused. 'I wonder if Ruskin would have approved?'

Laszlo shrugged. 'As long as it doesn't start to take place in galleries, I really don't mind,' he said with a smile, glancing towards an approaching figure. 'Here comes the fellow I was telling you about,' he said to Shelley.

'He looks like an ironmonger I remember from my boyhood,' Shelley said. 'Quite a remarkable moustache.'

Laszlo nodded. 'He is an extraordinary young man. I cannot decide if he has an intelligence that matches his talent or if he is just simple-minded.' He nodded when Bernard Ovington stood in front of them. 'Good morning, Bernard. Would you care for a drink?'

Bernard gave the question deep consideration. 'Perhaps a half of Guinness,' he said eventually.

'My shout,' Shelley said, taking Laszlo's empty glass.

'Are you sure you don't mind working on Sunday mornings, Bernard?' Laszlo asked.

Bernard shook his head with a slight smile and brushed the broad sweep of his moustache with a quick gesture. 'Not at all, Mr Vasilakis. Sunday is the day my mother's sister comes to visit. It gives me the opportunity to get out of the house.' He glanced at the crowd around them. 'I usually go to a pub in Isleworth where they have a jazz band.' When Shelley returned with his half-pint, he drank it in one long draught, brushing the creamy foam from his moustache with the same quick gesture. He placed the empty glass on the pavement, and Laszlo and Shelley exchanged a glance.

'Would you care for the other half, Mr Ovington?' Shelley asked.

Bernard shook his head. 'No, thank you. I have delicate bowels. A half of Guinness acts as an excellent laxative. More, and I become a prisoner of the lavatory.'

Shelley covered the lower part of his face with a bony hand for a moment. 'Well, I certainly wouldn't want to be responsible for *that*.'

Bernard smiled again. 'Yes, it's worked, as always. I shall just be a moment.' And he entered the pub in search of the necessary facilities.

Laszlo turned to Shelley. 'You see what I mean?'

'He seems to know his own mind, or at least some other part of his anatomy.'

Laszlo nodded thoughtfully. 'I'm always a little wary of people who are such experts on their bodily functions.' It seems to be so totally self-centred.'

Laszlo finished his drink as Bernard returned. They said goodbye to Shelley and made for Laszlo's car, which was parked a little way along the Fulham Road. Bernard sat stiffly in the passenger seat and crossed his arms. 'Do you drink much on Sunday mornings, Mr Vasilakis?' he asked.

'Only six or seven pints,' Laszlo replied innocently, and roared away from the kerbside under the nose of a bus.

Bernard stretched out his arms and gripped the dashboard for the entire journey to Bond Street.

Laszlo parked in the empty street and they walked to the

Archangel Gallery. As he led his companion through the showroom, he noticed that Bernard did not bother to glance at any of the pictures. It surprised him, as there were some impressive paintings displayed. But suddenly it was clear to him that Ovington had no intrinsic interest in art. The pictures that would have drawn the admiration of a collector were of no more concern to him than wallpaper.

When they reached the old lockers in the basement, Laszlo found the keys and handed them to Bernard. 'Just browse through in your own time,' he said. 'I'll be in the office. Give me a call if you need anything.'

Bernard nodded. 'A glass of water would be welcome.'

When Laszlo returned with the water, Bernard was immersed in the contents of the first cabinet, some of which he had spread on a large table. He took the glass of water without comment and continued to study the pile of sketchbooks, loose drawings and canvases in various states of damage. A large stiff-backed exercise book lay open among the disorder.

Laszlo glanced at the pages and noticed Julian Nettlebury's handwriting.

'Are you familiar with Nettlebury's work?' he asked.

Bernard nodded without looking up. 'Oh yes,' he replied softly. 'A wonderful craftsman, it will be a pleasure to work on his paintings.'

Laszlo paused. 'I think we would prefer it if you gave some of the other pictures more priority,' he said, but Bernard did not seem to hear him. Laszlo drifted away back to the office and left him still poring over the material on the table-top.

Had he lingered a few minutes longer, he would have heard Ovington mutter, 'Brueghel, Brueghel, and so nicely done.'

Kew, the same day

Neville Crichton stood beneath the pagoda in Kew Gardens and watched Irene walk towards him with her head down and her hands plunged deep into the pockets of her raincoat. He knew for certain, before she reached him, that the affair was over. Her slow pace and the hunch of her body told him everything she was going to say. When she reached him she smiled. He smiled back. It was the greeting friends give to each other at funerals: sad, sympathetic and without humour.

He glanced furtively at his watch. It was twelve forty-five. Swiftly he rearranged his plans for the rest of the day. He had intended to take her for a quick drink and then to a friend's vacant flat on Richmond Hill. Past experience had taught him that Irene could manage only a few hours in his company before guilt drove her back to household duties or the care of her daughter. This would be shorter, he told himself. Ten minutes of silence and five minutes of stilted conversation, then it would all be over. He was resigned to the inevitable, but he still felt a stab of regret at the sight of her pale skin and dark red hair.

Crichton's first love affair some years before had ended badly, in pain and humiliation for him. Since then he had avoided anything more than superficial commitments. It sometimes surprised him how many women were satisfied with the same arrangement. But he had never been sure with Irene Cleary.

Most times, in the hasty encounters of their affair, she had seemed detached, despite the vigour of their lovemaking. But on a few occasions there had been a warmth and sweetness he found disconcerting. These moments were much more difficult to deal with than the simple release of animal attraction. He did not enjoy the sudden feeling of loneliness that would afflict him until he could regain a firm lock on his emotions.

He kissed her quickly, and they turned in silence and began to stroll towards the Palm House. Sunday morning was a busy time at the Botanic Gardens. There were young couples who had arrived by bicycle, with sandwiches and thermos flasks in haversacks, and families with picnic baskets accompanied by bored children who could not see the point of looking at exotic plants. A few elderly couples walked at the same slow pace as Irene and Crichton, but with more enjoyment than the silent couple.

Eventually Irene spoke. 'I'm afraid I've got to change our plans,' she said with sudden firmness. Crichton did not answer. They walked on before she spoke again, but with less assertion. 'It's Bridget – she's not very well. I can only leave her with my father for a few minutes.' Crichton still did not reply.

Irene suddenly stopped and looked up at him, the line of her jaw set firm. There was sadness in her eyes, but no sign of tears. 'That's not true,' she said.

Crichton stood with his hands in his pockets. He had already ended the relationship in his own mind. He was now waiting for Irene to catch up with him.

410

She sensed his attitude, and the hurt in her eyes turned to anger. 'I'm trying to tell you it's over,' she said.

Crichton nodded, but now there was an empty feeling in the pit of his stomach that he had not expected. For a moment he glanced at the symmetry of her features and then turned away and took out a pack of cigarettes. He cupped his hands over the match and was surprised to find them tremble.

Irene's voice grew softer. 'Do you want to marry me?' she asked. 'Live with me, day in and day out? Will you take responsibility for my child?'

Crichton drew on the cigarette; a breeze blew the smoke away. Irene had held something out to him, something warm and embracing, but it felt as if he was being smothered.

'If you say yes,' she said, 'you will have all of me – everything I have. Everything I am.'

The words were spoken in a matter-of-fact voice, but Crichton knew the commitment that lay behind them. He wanted to reach out to her, but could not take what was offered. Part of him was too damaged to respond. He dropped the cigarette and stood motionless, without answering.

Irene looked at him, and then her expression changed again, as if she understood. She turned and walked away. At first her pace was brisk, but as the distance increased she slowed down.

When she reached her father's house, Nettlebury was in the conservatory. He stood at the easel, drawing bold lines with a stick of charcoal on an Imperial sheet of cartridge-paper. Irene liked to watch him work; it was the only constant factor she could remember throughout her life. Through the window she could see Bridget playing happily in the garden beneath the trees. Nettlebury stopped to consider his progress and Irene came and laid her head on his shoulder. He glanced down at her head, and felt a moment of sadness. Vera had been gone for some time.

'Why can't people be happy, Dad?' she said.

He put his arm round her waist and followed her gaze into the garden where the child played. He took some time to answer. 'Because nothing lasts,' he said gently. 'Grief or joy – it all passes. Only work lasts, girl. Try and find something to do with your life.'

411

CHAPTER EIGHTEEN

New York, summer 1957

Charles Whitney-Ingram paid the cab-driver at the entrance to Flanagan's Bar. The night air was like steam and he could feel a prickle of sweat where the damp shirt clung to the small of his back.

Inside, business was slow. There was a sprinkle of customers at the long mahogany counter that ran the length of the room and a few groups of people in the booths to the right. At the far end, next to the john, was a glowing jukebox. A Charlie Parker solo cut through the smoke-filled room and the air conditioning was turned up full blast so that his perspiring body gave an involuntary shudder at the impact of the cold air. He paused half-way down the bar and saw Paul Van Duren in a booth with three other men. Charles slid into a seat with a nod to the other occupants.

'Charles Whitney-Ingram,' Paul said. 'This is Al Davis, he's a press agent. The other two are Pete Moyle and Mick Grady.'

Al Davis stuck his hand out first. He was thin with dark receding hair and a prominent Adam's apple that bobbed above a bright blue bow tie. His chalk-striped suit looked several sizes too large. Charles could tell the two Irishmen were cops; Grady was florid with drinkers' veins on his cheeks and bulbous nose, while Moyle was younger and fitter, heavily built with dark curly hair, a broken nose and a wide smile.

Paul leaned forward and said to Charles, 'Have you brought the money?'

Charles glanced at the other men at the table. 'I could only get three.'

'Three?' Paul said angrily. 'I asked for five thousand!'

'Christ!' said Charles. 'You only rang me at seven o'clock this evening. Haven't you ever heard of banking hours? I had twenty-seven dollars on me. It took me two hours to get this for you.'

412

He took out a wad of notes and pushed them across the table to Paul, who picked up the bundle and carelessly thrust it into his jacket pocket. Then he turned to Al Davis. 'So what time is the game?'

Davis looked at an old-fashioned pocket watch. 'In exactly thirty-two minutes,' he said briskly.

'Will they accept IOUs?' Paul asked.

Davis nodded. 'If they're redeemed in twenty-four hours. That's the rule of the game.'

Charles looked round the table. 'What kind of game is this?' he asked. The other men remained silent. 'I'm his agent.' He nodded towards Paul. 'That's a bit like being his mother.'

Davis shrugged. 'It's a poker game I've organised for a client who's flown in from Hollywood.'

'Go on,' said Charles.

Davis shrugged again. 'This client is a big number in show business. He loves poker, but he likes a safe environment. A few years ago he played in Detroit and some bad guys held up the game. Since then, he likes to be protected.' He nodded towards Grady and Moyle. 'These two gentlemen are devoting their professional services to making sure all is on the up and up. The game will take place in the room of a respectable hotel and if there is any foul play or interruption, Mr Grady or Mr Moyle will shoot the offenders full of holes with the police specials they have concealed about their bodies.' Davis smiled.

Charles looked round the bar. The place was filling up.

Davis said, 'Time to go.' They all stood. 'Do you want to play in the game?' he asked Charles.

Charles shook his head. 'Thanks, but no.'

While they stood paying the check there came a sudden crash of thunder, and everyone turned towards the window to see sheets of rain lashing down.

'Shit!' said Moyle. 'The automobile is parked a block away.'

Charles watched the others walk to the doorway, then found a gap at the bar. He caught the barman's eye and ordered a beer. When it came, he asked, 'Can you call me a cab from here?'

The barman looked towards the windows, and shrugged. 'It could take a long time in this storm.'

'That's fine by me.'

Charles took a mouthful of beer. 'I'm in no hurry.'

The barman smiled. 'I'd have taken you for a married man.'

Charles looked down at his beer and said, 'It's a modern marriage. She's the bachelor.'

Detective Grady blinked awake and realised that his neck ached where it had rested on the leather arm of the sofa. The hotel room was in darkness, except for a pool of light over the blanket-covered table where the poker game was taking place, and the air smelled metallic from the throbbing air conditioner. Four men still played at the table. Moyle sat close to them, with his chair slightly drawn back, watching but not taking part. With a sigh, Grady eased his feet into his shoes and straightened up. There was a pain in his side where his holstered revolver had dug into him while he slept. After stretching a few times, he walked to the window.

They were on the seventh floor of the hotel, and the rain still fell in torrents on Lexington Avenue. He lit a cigarette. His mouth tasted sour. He took a ginger ale from the drinks trolley and swilled it around in his mouth before he swallowed. The only sound in the room came from the air conditioner and the snap of cards being dealt. The amount of chips and scrawled notes in front of the players told him how the game had progressed.

Al Davis had a moderate pile of chips, which he fingered constantly. Harry White, the film producer he represented, had a larger pile. A powerfully built man, he was chewing on a large cigar. His silk shirt was unbuttoned to the waist and thick black hair sprouted over his undershirt. Next to him, Paul slumped over the table, slowly picked up the five cards he had been given and studied them with some difficulty.

The dapper, smiling figure who had dealt laid down the pack and picked up his own hand. 'Five card draw, gentlemen,' he said with a foreign accent. 'A pair of jacks or better to open the pot.'

Harry White threw a red chip in the middle. 'I'll open for fifty,' he said.

'I fold,' Davis said, and tossed his cards on the table.

'Make it a hundred,' Paul said, pushing in his own chips.

Grady and Moyle exchanged glances, and Grady lifted his shoulders in a slight shrug.

The dapper figure examined his cards carefully and then tossed two chips in the pot. 'I'm in,' he said.

Harry White pushed in another fifty-dollar chip and threw down his discards. 'I'll take three.' The dealer slowly placed the cards in front of him.

'I'll take four cards,' said Paul.

'Four cards?' Harry White was incredulous.

'Yeah,' Paul said, his head nodding with slow, drunken deliberation.

'How the fuck can you make a fifty-dollar raise when the best you have is an ace?' White asked in an exasperated voice.

'It's my lucky ace,' Paul replied.

'Dealer takes one card,' the dapper figure said. 'Opener to bet.'

Harry White looked at his cards. 'I check,' he muttered.

'Four hundred,' Paul said, and put in the chips.

Harry White shrugged angrily and turned to Davis. 'Who the fuck plays poker like this? He could have anything.'

'Four hundred, and raise one thousand,' the dealer said.

Harry White threw down his cards and crossed his arms.

'Are you out?' the dealer asked politely.

'Yeah, I'm out,' White said angrily. 'I must have been fucking crazy to be in in the first place.' He turned to Davis, who winced at his expression. 'Next time I want a game organised in New York, I'll fly someone in from Loony Tunes.'

The dealer looked at Paul. 'Your thousand, and up five thousand, Mr Van Duren.'

There was a pause while Paul looked at his small pile of chips left. 'Your five, raise you ten,' he said.

The dealer wrote an IOU and passed it to Paul, who took the offered pen and scrawled his signature. 'I'll call you,' he said.

Paul flipped over his cards. 'Three aces,' he said with a lop-sided grin.

The dealer turned his own cards. 'Four threes,' Davis said softly. 'Jesus Christ!'

The dealer slowly stacked his chips and made a pile of the IOUs in front of him. 'That's fifty-seven thousand dollars you owe me, Mr Van Duren,' he said quietly.

Paul said nothing; he just gazed at the table before him.

'Would you like a solution to your problems?' the dealer asked. Paul nodded without looking up, and the dealer took a stiff folded sheet of paper from his pocket. 'If you sign this contract, I shall destroy these IOUs and consider them an advance fee.' He turned to the others. 'Perhaps Mr Davis and Mr White would be kind enough to witness the document?'

Paul took the pen again, signed, and passed it to the other men.

White took a fresh cigar from the drinks trolley. When he had lit it, he blew a thin stream of smoke towards the ceiling. 'Any time you feel like going into the movie business, give me a call, Mr Schneider,' he said respectfully, and another crash of thunder echoed above Manhattan Island.

London, December 1957

It was just after nine o'clock on Christmas morning when Irene opened the door to the house at Kew. Her sister Anne pecked her quickly on the cheek and hurried into the hall. 'God, let me get warm. I'm absolutely freezing!' she said, going into the living-room where a fire was already burning. Anne stood with her back to it and sighed with pleasure. 'Where is everyone?'

'They're still in bed,' said Irene. 'Bridget was up at about five-thirty opening all her presents. She went back to sleep again about half an hour ago.' She watched her sister turn and stretch her hands out towards the flames. 'Why are you so cold?'

Anne grinned up at her. 'Actually, it's my own fault. I bought Gideon one of those old RAF leather flying jackets as a Christmas present, and he insisted on driving here in the MG with the roof down. I swear he thought he was flying a Spitfire!'

Irene laughed. 'That's what you get for marrying an ex-actor!'

Gideon entered the room laden with carrier bags. Irene gave him a kiss and stroked his leather jacket. 'Very dashing! You should grow a handlebar moustache.'

He dumped his parcels on the sofa, and Anne glanced down at them. 'Where's the Hamley's bag?' she asked.

Gideon shrugged, 'These were the only ones in the car.'

Anne held up her hands in dismay. 'We've left Bridget's present in the bedroom. Oh, Gideon, I've been promising her something special all week!'

They stood looking at each other for a moment, and then Gideon nodded. 'All right, I'll go back for it.'

Irene shook her head. 'Really, don't bother, she already has enough toys.'

Gideon turned up the fur collar of his flying jacket. 'Nonsense! I can manage another quick trip, there's nothing on the roads.' He turned to Anne. 'Mind you, there'll be no flying this afternoon. I intend to make some savage dry Martinis before lunch.'

Anne moved from the fire and kissed him. 'You are a darling. I

416

can't even blame you, it's my fault. You'll find the bag at the bottom of my wardrobe.'

Gideon gave a casual salute, and departed.

'There's some tea in the pot. Do you fancy a cup?' Irene asked when they had put the presents Anne had brought under the Christmas tree.

'Mmmm, yes, I do,' Anne replied, and they went into the kitchen.

'How's Dad?' Anne asked when they were sitting at the table.

'Slower,' said Irene. 'But he's still working.'

After a silence, Anne said, 'How are you and Richard?'

Irene glanced away. 'The same,' she said eventually. 'He's only here for Christmas because of Bridget.' She got up to stand at the sink. Anne could see she had been preparing vegetables and had been interrupted by their arrival. Irene took up a knife again to peel potatoes. 'I don't think he wants to marry her, you know,' she said suddenly. 'I think he'd really like to live with us both like some eastern potentate, with me as his number one wife and Paula Tuchman as his concubine!'

Anne said, 'Why do you put up with it?'

'Sometimes I still love him, other times I hate the bastard.' She paused. 'Occasionally I feel complete indifference. I suppose if the balance tips completely, I'll leave him.'

Anne walked over to her sister, who still faced the sink, put her arms round her and gave her a gentle hug. Irene continued to peel potatoes. From somewhere above came the sudden sound of a trumpet. It was Cleary, playing 'Oh Come All Ye Faithful'.

'That's for Bridget,' said Irene. 'He's been playing carols all week for her.' She didn't speak for a moment, and Anne knew that she was crying. 'I wish she didn't love him so much.'

Anne could think of nothing to say, but stood listening to the music.

Less than half an hour later, Gideon climbed the staircase to the flat above the Archangel Gallery, and on opening the door, heard the telephone. When he lifted the receiver, a female voice said, 'Good morning. May I speak to Mr James Gideon?'

'I'm Gideon.'

'Will you hold the line, please?' the voice said. 'I have Sir Edward Peake to speak to you.'

After a long pause, a familiar voice said, 'Gideon? Ted Peake here.'

'What's all this "Sir Edward" stuff, Ted?' Gideon asked.

There was a chuckle at the other end of the line. 'That's not officially announced yet. My secretary is a little premature.'

'Congratulations.' Gideon's eyes strayed to the mantelpiece where Anne had displayed the Christmas cards they had received. He found Ted's without difficulty. As always, it was a reproduction of *The Girl in the White Dress*.

'Can you come and see me?' Peake asked. 'I've got a nice piece of business I want to put your way.'

'When would suit you?' Gideon asked.

'Well, now,' Peake answered with surprise in his voice.

Gideon smiled. 'Ted, it's Christmas morning!'

'That's all right. I'm near St Paul's. There's no traffic about. I promise I won't keep you long. I'll even send my driver for you.' As Gideon paused, he urged, 'One drink. That's as long as it'll take.'

Gideon considered for a moment and then gave in. 'Okay, but I'll drive myself.' He glanced at his watch. It was just nine-thirty. 'Give me the address.'

He took another look at the Christmas cards. A hand-made one showed Hammond Shelley in a kangaroo's pouch raising a glass. For the past six months he had lived in Australia with his sister's family. Next to Hammond's card was one from Harriet, an engraving of Greeve. Laszlo and Gideon had given it to her as a 'grace and favour' house on the understanding that eventually it would revert to the Archangel estate. It was also a magnificent setting in which to show their traditional paintings, and very popular with American buyers.

He drove through the deserted city streets to the stumpy glass tower Ted Peake had described rose to meet him from the craters of weed-infested bomb-sites all around the cathedral. A uniformed figure was waiting to unlock the glass doors of the building. With echoing foot-steps, they crossed the marble entrance hall to a wide concourse where a row of lifts stood with open doors. Although the vast glass-encased area was empty, Gideon felt that the presence of people would not improve the cold, featureless area. In New York, shops, shoeshine boys, tobacco kiosks and newstands gave life and character to the entrances of buildings, unlike this bleak and forbidding place.

Gideon headed for one of the lifts, but the uniformed figure shook his head.

'No, sir, not these. This way, please.' He led Gideon to a separate, smaller lift to one side, and inserted a key in the lock in place of a button. The doors slid open to reveal an oak-panelled interior. Gideon found the little space claustrophobic and was unprepared for the sudden lurching speed. The man smiled at his surprise. 'Fastest lifts in London, sir,' he said, and they slowed suddenly, like a fairground ride coming to a halt. The lift had stopped inside what appeared to be a pink marble box. At the far end stood two polished doors embellished with glittering brass. It was as if they had come to the front door of a giant's castle. The doorman stepped back into the lift, and Gideon was left alone.

'The doors are open, Gideon. Come in,' a disembodied voice announced and when he pushed, they swung apart at the gentlest touch. Ted Peake was waiting in the centre of a room the size of a tennis court. The far wall was glass. They faced south-east, towards St Paul's and the Thames. The room was almost devoid of furniture, except for two long black leather sofas at the far end, and a blackwood desk. Hanging behind it, *The Girl in the White Dress* was the only picture in the room.

Peake was heavier than the last time Gideon had seen him, but the tailor who had crafted his dark grey suit had almost concealed the extra pounds. He held out his hand as Gideon approached, and said, 'Dixon, bring the champagne.'

'Who have you got working for you?' Gideon asked, taking Peake's hand. 'Poltergeists?'

Peake laughed. 'Poltergeists are mischievous spirits, Gideon. All mine are perfectly well behaved!'

Out of nowhere a grave figure materialised bearing a silver tray. They took the drinks and Peake raised his to Gideon. They clinked glasses.

'Merry Christmas,' Peake said, and then he laughed. 'A bloody long way from Burnt Oak, isn't it?' He made a circular motion with his glass to include his surroundings. 'Come and sit here.' He led Gideon to one of the soft leather sofas. 'How's Anne and the family?' he asked.

Gideon nodded. 'All well.'

'And Laszlo and his wife?'

Gideon nodded again, and looked at his watch. 'In an hour I should be having a drink with them. They're coming to Nettlebury's for Christmas lunch.'

'Are they?' said Peake. 'I was hoping I could get you to join me at Claridge's.'

Gideon shook his head. 'Thanks for the offer, but I'm committed.'

Peake looked away for a moment. 'You know my first wife died, don't you?'

Gideon sipped his champagne. 'I had heard. I'm sorry, Ted.' There was a silence, and he shifted his weight. The leather beneath him gave a squeaking sound.

Peake looked down with a sudden frown of annoyance. 'Bleeding stuff,' he said in his old accent. 'Every time you move, it sounds as if you're farting.' Gideon gave an explosive chuckle. 'Don't laugh,' he said ruefully. 'I had a cabinet minister there yesterday. You'd have thought he'd eaten nothing but baked beans for a week.'

'So why do you want to see me so urgently?' Gideon asked.

Peake leaned forward. 'I'm flying to New York tomorrow morning, after that San Francisco, then to Hong Kong and Sydney. I'll be away for . . .' He shrugged, 'maybe two months.' He stood up suddenly. 'Come and look at this.' He walked over to the desk beneath the painting.

The surface was covered with blueprints and architect's drawings. At first Gideon thought he was looking at the plans of a factory, but after a few minutes he realised it was a house. There was also a heavy leather-bound book on the desk.

'Have you heard of Capability Brown?' Peake asked.

'Yes.'

Peake grinned again. 'Of course you have!' He flipped open the book. 'I've bought this property. He landscaped the grounds. There's a bloody great Georgian house there; it's just a shell now. I'm pulling it down and putting this house up in its place.' Gideon waited for him to continue. Peake stood up straight and crossed his arms. 'I want you and Laszlo to sell the Mueller Collection and buy all modern stuff for the house.'

Gideon looked down at the plans. 'When will it be finished?'

'11th May 1959,' Peake replied without hesitation. 'The grounds will be restored by the end of August.'

'Well, we can start then,' said Gideon.

Peake shook his head. 'No,' he said in a firm voice. 'I want to move in on 20th May, and I want the whole bloody place finished by then, right down to the lavatory paper.'

Gideon drank some champagne. There was an echo from the past that he could not at first identify, then he remembered: Mueller. It was as though Mueller was urging him to complete his original collection again. What is it that causes such men to be in so great a hurry with life? Gideon wondered. This curious need to devour pleasure like a glutton trying to consume a feast by cramming all the courses into his mouth at the same time.

420

'Well, what do you think?' Peake's voice was impatient, and Gideon thought he could detect a note of anxiety.

'I suppose it could be done . . .' he said reluctantly, and looked up. The frown vanished from Peake's face, to be replaced by a sudden smile. 'You don't approve, do you?'

'Not really. It's a bit like getting books by the yard for a library. Usually collectors want to share the pleasure of buying pictures.' Gideon sipped his champagne. 'I suppose we should be flattered that you have so much faith in us.'

Peake held up his hands. 'There is someone I want you to consult,' he said. 'My new wife.' He said, without raising his voice, 'Darling, will you join us?'

A concealed door in the pale wood panelling clicked open and a woman in a green Chinese silk dressing-gown entered the room. Her blonde hair was tousled and she wore no make-up, but she was extraordinarily beautiful. She looked to him like the illustration of a princess in a child's fairy-tale book.

'Gideon,' Peake said with a voice full of pride, 'I'd like to introduce Gloria.'

'Pleased to meet you.'

'How do you do?' Gideon answered gravely. He looked at the flawless complexion and the slim hand she offered, and calculated she could not be more than twenty.

'It's Gloria's birthday today,' said Peake, reading his thoughts. 'Tell him how old you are, darling.'

The girl smiled suddenly. 'I'm nineteen. Getting to be a right old lady, eh, Ted?'

Peake put his arm round her waist. 'There's one other thing. I want a portrait painted of her. One I can recognise, something that does her justice.'

'Do you have someone in mind?' Gideon asked.

'Sir Julian Nettlebury,' Gloria answered without hesitation. Gideon looked so surprised that she laughed. 'Did you see that, Ted?' she said in an amused voice. 'Blimey, his eyebrows nearly fell off!'

He felt a moment of embarrassment. 'I'm sorry,' he said with a certain amount of confusion, 'I didn't mean to appear patronising. But tell me, why do you want Nettlebury to paint you?'

Lady Peake thrust her hands deep into her dressing-gown pockets. 'Because I think he's great.' Then she shrugged. 'Vanity, I suppose.' Gideon continued to look surprised, and she laughed again. 'It's for him, really,' she said, nodding towards Peake. 'He says he wants a picture he can recognise, and Julian Nettlebury can do that better than anybody. Ted wanted Annigoni to paint me, but I thought his picture of the Queen was bloody awful.' She smiled again. 'I'm studying history at London University. You thought I was in the chorus line at the Windmill, didn't you?'

'You're more than beautiful enough to be, Lady Peake,' Gideon said with a slight bow.

'Blimey,' she said, glancing towards Ted. 'You're right, he's got enough charm.'

'How did you two meet?' Gideon asked.

They exchanged glances. 'In my dad's office,' Gloria answered. Gideon looked puzzled. 'He's a funeral director,' she went on. 'He buried Ted's wife.'

This macabre piece of information caused a sudden blight on the cheerful atmosphere. An idea occurred to Gideon. 'Did you say you were having lunch at Claridge's today?'

Peake nodded. 'Just the two of us. If you can't come.'

'Why don't you come to Kew? Laszlo will be there,' he turned to Gloria, 'and you can meet Julian Nettlebury.'

They exchanged glances again. 'Are you sure we wouldn't be intruding?' Peake asked.

Gideon shook his head. 'Of course not. We have masses of everything. The turkey is the size of a barrage balloon!'

'What's a barrage balloon?' Gloria asked innocently.

Ted made a gesture with his hands. 'They used to float over London during the war to stop . . .'

Gloria punched him lightly in the ribs. 'I'm only kidding, soppy! I'm not that young. We used to see them in Bethnal Green, you know.'

Peake turned away. 'Right, I'm going to cancel the table at Claridge's. You show Gideon to the lift.'

In the pink marble hall, Gloria was about to insert the key in the lock when she looked at Gideon. 'Do you think I ought to change my accent, learn to talk posh?' she asked with sudden intimacy. Gideon knew how serious the question was. He looked around the hall, but she knew what was on his mind. 'It's all right. I switched off the system. Ted can't hear. Go on.'

Gideon paused, then spoke carefully. 'I was brought up to be an actor. My parents were on the stage. Practically the first thing they taught me was that we live in a world where appearances and impressions are vital.' He smiled at her. 'What kind of impression do you want to make, Gloria?'

She had been staring down at her bare feet on the marble floor, and now looked up. 'I want Ted to be proud of me. I don't want to let him down.'

Gideon nodded. 'Then be an actress. Everybody is in life. It's just that most people aren't aware of it. Learn the tricks and you'll be glad you did.'

She inserted the key in the lock and then reached up on tip-toe and kissed him gently on the cheek. 'Thanks,' she said. 'I won't forget. See you later.

Gideon smiled as he descended in the lift. He had found her impromptu gesture strangely touching.

London, July 1958

It was a fine summer evening when Neville Crichton climbed the staircase of the Royal Academy for the Summer Exhibition private view. He took a glass of wine from a waitress and nodded towards two other critics who stood in the first showroom. There was something reassuring about the people crowding the galleries: débutantes with their parents, eligible young men, painters, gifted or talentless, people who wanted to see the pictures and some who had come to exhibit themselves. A cabinet minister stood talking loudly to a famous actress, and a younger group of painters lingered by the long table that served as a bar, drinking their way steadily through rows of wine glasses. Crichton had collected a programme. He flicked through it, found where Sir Julian Nettlebury's three pictures were on display and made his way towards them. He liked the aroma of the great rooms, expensive perfume mingled with turpentine and linseed oil.

'Strange how this room smells like a cricket pavilion,' a vacuous young man was saying to a plump, perspiring girl as he squeezed past. The flowers in the girl's straw hat tickled his face briefly.

When he came to the section where Nettlebury's pictures hung, there was a large crowd before the life-sized portrait of Lady Peake. It was understandable why it drew so much attention. The picture showed two images of her, both naked. A knee rested on a chair, while she looked into her reflection in a long mirror. The effect was

423

extraordinarily erotic because of the bold direct look Nettlebury had caught.

Harold Beriac was in the front rank of spectators. He looked up when Crichton squeezed in beside him. 'A piece of barber's shop pornography?' he said. 'It's a pity I can't write that, but it would break Anne's heart.'

'Don't you approve?' Crichton asked.

'My dear,' Beriac said with a shudder, 'surely painting is about the application of paint, not sex.'

Crichton gazed at the picture. Beyond question it was full of sexuality, but that was because of the subject-matter. By God, he knows how to paint flesh, he thought. It was as though he could reach out and touch the pale skin. He knew how the delicate shoulder would feel.

'Well, what do you think?' Beriac asked with curiosity.

'I think: Lucky old Sir Edward Peake!' Crichton replied, and then whispered, 'I may not know much about art, but I know a good fuck when I see one.'

'Well, it's all lost on me, dear,' Beriac replied. 'I can judge it only from an aesthetic point of view, and it fails lamentably on those grounds.'

Crichton nudged him in a conspiratorial manner. 'Suppose we'd all misjudged Nettlebury? What if his quality of realism became fashionable again, and we were suddenly accused of being blind fools?'

A flicker of uncertainty crossed Beriac's face, but then he gave his curious laugh and pushed his way through the crowd, calling out as he departed, 'I'm like the boy in the cartoon. I know it's spinach, and I say to hell with it.'

After Crichton had finished looking at the picture of Lady Peake, he turned his attention to the real reason he had sought out Nettlebury's work. It was a portrait of Irene in a summer dress, sitting in a wicker chair in the conservatory at Kew. Nettlebury can paint flesh, he thought once again; he had seen Irene in similar light before. He contemplated buying the picture, but as he looked at it he felt the same ache he had experienced that day in Kew Gardens.

He moved away and a few minutes later Laszlo and Elizabeth stood on the same spot. They looked for a time in silence and Elizabeth thought how curious it was that pictures changed when they were displayed in different surroundings. She had seen the portrait at Kew and in the basement of the Archangel Gallery, but it was different here, in the environment of this gallery. Somehow the nakedness was more provocative. She recognised the expression Nettlebury had captured; she remembered how it had been to feel like Gloria Peake. She smiled. Then she looked at the hands in the picture and at her own, and they reminded her of the years that had passed.

'What are you smiling at?' Laszlo asked suddenly.

'I'm thinking of supper.'

Laszlo nodded, but Elizabeth knew he was troubled by other thoughts. 'Do you want to leave now?' he asked.

'We'll be much too early for the table,' she objected.

Laszlo glanced around at the crowd that surrounded them. 'It's a lovely evening. Shall we walk to the French Pub and have one drink before we go to the restaurant?'

'I wouldn't mind. My feet ache from standing. A walk will do them good.'

At the exit they found Gideon and Anne at the head of the staircase. He was talking to an Archangel Gallery customer. Laszlo did not want to become engaged in the conversation; the man Gideon was listening to was a notorious bore, and he was not in the mood for his droning opinions on the state of British painting. He gave a quick gesture to Anne that they were departing and made a walking motion with two fingers. Anne nodded her understanding, and Laszlo slipped past with Elizabeth.

They crossed the courtyard and turned left into Piccadilly, walking at an easy pace without speaking. Elizabeth looked at their reflections in the showroom and shop windows; a middle-aged couple, she thought. Well-preserved, well-dressed, but decidedly middle-aged. She did not really mind. She had no desire to return to the turmoil of her younger years, to be a captive of her emotions; that roller-coaster of elation and depression held no appeal for her. She linked arms with Laszlo, who squeezed hers in an absent-minded fashion.

'What's the matter?' she asked lightly when they reached Swan and Edgar.

Laszlo glanced up at the statue of Eros for a moment. 'I don't want to go to America,' he said mildly.

Elizabeth was surprised by his words. For some weeks he and Gideon had planned to go to New York. Charles had made preparations for them to view pictures for the collection planned for Ted Peake's new mansion. Not until they were in Shaftesbury Avenue did she ask, 'Why?'

425

Laszlo stopped outside the Apollo Theatre. 'I suppose it was when we got the proofs for the catalogue of Tony Flagg's exhibition,' he said.

Elizabeth had to think for a moment. Then she remembered: Tony Flagg was an abstract Expressionist painter. She had paid little attention to his vast pictures executed in earth colours with broad swathes of pink and scarlet cutting through thick paint. They reminded her of photographs showing the surface of another planet.

Laszlo took her arm again as they walked on. He was ready to speak now, and he began to emphasise his words with chopping gestures of his free hand. 'I remember reading the words, and trying to relate them to the pictures.' He paused to recall some of the phrases. ' "The rich ambiguity of the surface, sudden exciting splashes of colour that only serve momentarily to conceal the deeply felt melancholy of the artist's underlying intention." ' He gestured again. ' "Viewpoints of a landscape seen from above, as though the horizon were the centre of the earth. Ravishing tonal values that echo on the retina of the eye like the sunsets we remember from childhood." He shook his head. 'I do not mind if someone writes nonsense about a painter, provided I have a personal understanding of the pictures, but Flagg . . .'

Elizabeth interjected. 'Are you saying you don't like his work?'

' "Like" is not the right word,' he answered. 'I was completely baffled by his pictures. Even when I was selling them to people, I felt like a cheap confidence trickster.'

Elizabeth squeezed his arm. 'Surely you are used to selling pictures you don't like?'

Laszlo smiled. 'Many times. But it's not the same thing. Personally I am not fond of Leger's later work, but I can appreciate what he was doing. Flagg's paintings mean nothing to me. I can see no sunsets from my childhood, no ravishing tonal values. Just large rectangles of thick oil paint. If his work produces any emotion in me, I can only truthfully say that it is one of mild irritation.'

'But you do like some modern painters,' Elizabeth continued, glancing up to see that they had stopped outside the French Pub.

'Oh yes,' Laszlo said, nodding vigorously. He tried to find the proper analogy. 'I suppose it's rather like musical instruments. I can hear every note on a clarinet, but I'm damned if I can hear the sound of a dog whistle.'

426

'Do you think Gideon can really hear the note, or is he deceiving himself?'

'Oh, Gideon can hear the note,' Laszlo said mildly. 'I'm sure he actually likes Tony Flagg's work; but for me it's meaningless. I really don't want to go to America and take place in a charade of pretending to admire pictures I find irritating or boring.'

'Then don't go,' Elizabeth said firmly. 'There's too little of life to waste it.'

As she spoke, the door of the French Pub opened and Paula Tuchman brushed past. It was clear from her manner that she was upset, and she did not recognise or notice either of them. Inside, Laszlo and Elizabeth found Richard Cleary standing near the door.

'You two look as if you need a drink,' Cleary said. It was obvious that he was sober, but Elizabeth was aware of three long half-healed scratches on his left cheek, and he had the rough, unkempt look that some men acquire when they are without the care of a woman.

'How are you, Richard?' Elizabeth asked.

It was obvious that he was in the bitterest of moods. He fumbled in his pockets and produced cigarettes, accepted a light from Laszlo and then drank a substantial amount of whisky in one gulp. He put the glass down on a ledge and looked from one to the other. 'Actually, I'm in a fucking terrible state,' he announced quietly. 'What I'd really like to do is go down to the docks and get on the next boat leaving for anywhere.'

Laszlo could see that he meant it. The man's nerves were frayed, the flesh around his eyes was puffy and the tic of a trembling muscle jumped in his right cheek.

Cleary looked at Laszlo, and spoke as if Elizabeth were not present. 'Don't ever think of taking a mistress, old man,' he said in a voice that was supposed to be good-humoured. 'You get half the pleasure of a wife and twice the trouble.'

Elizabeth raised her eyebrows to her husband, and indicated with a tilt of her head that she was joining some friends further along the bar.

'Things are difficult, are they?' Laszlo asked when he had bought Cleary another drink. Cleary nodded. 'Do you want to talk about it?'

This time Cleary shook his head. 'No, I bloody well don't! That's all I do, talk about it. First to Irene, then I talk about the same subject to Paula.' He paused and rested both elbows on a narrow ledge. 'They both say the same things to me, and I give the same answers.' He lit a cigarette from the stub of the first. 'What do you think I ought to do?'

Laszlo drank some of his Pernod and smiled briefly at Elizabeth further along the bar before he answered. 'Perhaps you should get away for a time. Tell me, would you like a free ticket to America for a couple of weeks?'

New York, summer 1958

Gideon waved his hands to show that he was ready and then peered through the viewfinder of the movie camera. Charles and Lydia walked towards him arm in arm, laughing. When they stopped, Charles pointed with his free hand and Gideon panned the camera up to the sign of the Archangel Gallery and zoomed in on the sign of the angel's wing. When he lowered the camera, Charles and Lydia were no longer standing quite so close. He remembered the sounds of their argument that morning when he had lain in the bedroom next to theirs in their apartment.

Gideon normally avoided staying with friends when he was in a foreign city. No matter how close the affection of the hosts, there always came a time when he felt like an intruder, or he wished to pursue some activity of his own that clashed with their plans. But Charles had insisted, and against his better judgment, Gideon had complied. After a few days it had become clear that the marriage was in difficulties. Charles and Lydia were civil to each other when he was around, but it was as though he caused the connection; the moment he moved away from them, they began to grate upon each other. He had brought the movie camera to give himself some kind of excuse to separate himself. He was beginning to find their company as stifling as the heatwave that had descended upon Manhattan with his arrival ten days before.

Two youths passed Charles and Lydia and suddenly stood in front of him. They wore jeans and black nylon jackets with tigers embroidered on the left breast. Both were olive-skinned with long oiled hair. One had the face of a matinée idol, but his companion's was disfigured by pock-marks.

'Hey, man, take our pictures,' the good-looking one called out in a voice heavily laced with Spanish overtones. The two cavorted for a moment and then passed on laughing. He turned to watch them go and saw the words 'Bad Cats' emblazoned on the backs of their jackets.

Despite his many visits, Gideon still felt like a stranger in New

428

York. It was a city that changed faster than any other he knew. Of course there were constant factors – certain landmarks and aspects of the weather – but fashions altered with bewildering speed, and the ethnic mixture of the city changed with each new wave of immigration. It amused him when New Yorkers talked of their great melting-pot of American culture. He did not see a melting-pot at all. Irish, Negroes, Jews, Chinese, Italians and now Hispanic immigrants had thrust their way into the bursting city, and simply carved out their own ghetto. Gideon was reminded of a drink he had once seen a barman pour: the bands of liquor rested on each other within the glass without mixing.

Charles held the door open, and he entered the gallery. 'What happened to Lydia?' he asked when he stood in the cool lobby.

'She got a cab while you were watching those Spanish kids,' Charles explained. He turned to a severe-looking girl who sat at the reception desk. 'Anything happen while we've been away, Irma?'

'Some of the pictures have arrived,' she said, 'and the two guys who bought them said the Rothkos would be here by five o'clock. Mrs Todd rang. Her husband adores the two Picasso prints, so we can go ahead and present the cheque.' She paused.

'Anything else?' Charles asked.

Irma turned to Gideon, 'Richard Cleary came in with Paul Van Duren. He borrowed three hundred dollars and said you would give it to me.'

Gideon reached into his pocket and gave Irma the money.

'With Van Duren, you say?' Charles asked.

'Irma nodded. 'He left this note.' She passed it to him. 'Is there anything else I can do?' she asked.

Charles shook his head, but Gideon held out the camera. 'There is something,' he said. 'You know the shop along the street where I bought this?' She nodded. 'Will you pop along there when you have a moment and ask them to take out the film and load a new one for me? I'm still nervous about doing it on my own.'

Irma smiled. She loved Gideon's accent and seemed to melt whenever he spoke to her. 'Sure I'll pop along,' she said. 'God, I thought people only said that in P.G. Wodehouse books!'

He smiled his thanks and followed Charles into the showroom, where they stopped before the recently delivered pictures.

'Well, here we are,' Charles said. 'Thirty-five feet of De Kooning. Do you think that'll make Sir Edward Peake happy?'

'Not really. I don't think he likes modern paintings at all. He's really

429

happiest in his flat in Pont Street with the portrait of Gloria.'

Charles glanced down at his note from Paul. 'We're invited to a party tonight in honour of Richard Cleary.' He looked up. 'You wouldn't think those two would have anything in common, would you?'

Gideon shrugged. 'Paul always got on well with Julian Nettlebury. You know painters, most of them are crazy. Who can follow the logic of someone who locks themself up alone all day? Nettlebury used to say they were all barking mad.' He paused. 'I thought Paul hadn't been painting recently. I heard gossip that he had some kind of block.'

Charles nodded. 'There was a piece about him recently in *The New York Times*. He's moved out to a farm near Bridgehampton on Long Island. He's got a beautiful studio there, in a converted barn. The place belonged to a photographer who put in a glass roof, but apparently he hasn't painted anything.'

'What time does the party start?' Charles handed the letter to Gideon. 'Good God!' he exclaimed. 'It began yesterday!'

Charles nodded. 'The two of them probably came into the city to raise money for more booze.'

'Shall we go and take a look?' said Gideon.

Charles grinned. 'Why not? It'll probably take us back to our days in Berlin.'

As they left the showroom, Irma met them on the sidewalk and presented Gideon with his camera while Charles hailed a cab.

Paul and Cleary lay in the long rough grass beneath the fruit trees surrounding Paul's studio. From the farmhouse came sounds of music, laughter and the sudden splinter of broken glass. Cleary picked up a brownstone jug and took a swallow from the contents. 'What's this stuff called?' he asked.

'Applejack,' Paul replied, taking it from him and raising it to his mouth.

'It tastes like horse-piss,' Cleary said in the slow tones of the pedantically drunk.

'How do you know what horse-piss tastes like?' Paul propped himself up on one elbow and passed the jug back to Cleary.

Cleary tapped his temple with two fingers. 'Imagination. The most vital element in the repertoire of the artist.'

'Now that's horse-piss,' Paul said confidentially. 'Look at your paintings. Just a lot of tricks to make paint look like reality. That's not imagination – just a cheap conjuring trick.'

'Bollocks!' said Cleary. He took another pull from the jug. 'Anyone can produce that crap you call painting. If you make anything big enough, people will be impressed. Look at the Pyramids; the ignorant bastards have been admiring them for a thousand years because of their size. Make one the size of a cigarette packet, and no one would give it a second glance. Anyway, your stuff's just splashes of pigment. How can you tell when one of your paintings is finished?'

'There's a sense of when it's going right, and when it's finished. You must get that.'

Cleary nodded. 'That's understandable when you're creating a recognisable image.' He shook his head. 'But all you're saying is, Look! This is paint.'

'No, I'm not. I'm saying – This canvas, this paint, this wall it hangs on says something to me.'

'That's right. It says: I'm a heap of horse-piss.'

Paul laughed. 'You can't have a heap of horse-piss. You mean a heap of crap.'

Cleary thought for a time. 'Do you actually enjoy painting?'

Paul shook his head. 'When a piece starts to work, it's good. The rest of the time it's a fucking nightmare.'

Cleary climbed slowly to his feet. 'Show me,' he said.

'What do you mean?'

'Show me how you do it, your kind of painting,' said Cleary.

Paul lay back and blinked at the clear blue sky. Then he also got to his feet. 'All right.'

He and Cleary pulled open the doors of the barn. The glass roof had created a choking heat inside. Propped against one of the walls was a roll of white duck canvas. Paul laid it on the floor and unrolled about twenty feet. Then he took a large pair of shears and cut away the remaining roll. Ranged along the walls were cans of decorator's paint. He took a tool from a shelf and began to prise open some of the cans. Meanwhile, Cleary drank from the applejack jug. Finally Paul took a large brush and began to flick yellow paint on the canvas at his feet from the can under his arm.

Gideon and Charles arrived when the last of the setting sun was beating down on the glass roof of the studio. From the house, the sound of revelry still echoed over the nearby fields. Gideon saw the open doors of the barn, and waved for Charles to follow. They stood together and watched Paul and Cleary, now both stripped to the

431

waist, simultaneously splash and flick paint on the canvas at their feet.

CHAPTER NINETEEN

New York, spring 1959

When Anthony Strange lay back in the barber's chair he caught a glimpse of the slowly revolving fan above his head before a white-coated figure wrapped the hot towel around his face and obscured his vision. The blades of the fan brought a disagreeable reminder that he was catching an aeroplane in a few hours. Despite the introduction of jet engines, Strange still thought of aircraft as possessing propellors. He also thought of them as the most unpleasant form of travel ever devised. Ships were fine, there were lifeboats; women and children could always be elbowed aside. Aircraft were hatefully egalitarian. When they went down, passengers of all classes and physical strengths were condemned to the same fate.

If greed had not been the deciding factor, he would have made his journey to Los Angeles by trans-continental train. While he considered the disagreeable prospect, he felt the barber's strong fingers kneading the muscles of his face through the hot towel. When it was removed, bay rum was patted into his cheeks, there was a light dusting of face-powder and a few more flicks of the comb. Then the barber worked the mechanism of the chair with his feet so that Strange slowly rose with the majestic grace of old-time cinema organists and faced himself in the mirror.

The barber, a master of flattery, slowly shook his head so that his pendulous dewlaps quivered. 'I don't know how you do it, Mr Strange,' he said mournfully. 'I've been cutting your hair on and off for thirty years, and you don't look a day older.'

'Age is a state of mind, Joe,' Strange said as the barber brushed the shoulders of his dark suit.

'I'll remember that, Mr Strange,' he answered as he took the twenty-dollar bill.

Strange nodded his farewell, and walked out onto Fifth Avenue. The weather was perfect, a cool, bright day of cloudless skies with a light breeze that blew the fumes of traffic away from the sidewalks. He enjoyed his stroll to the Waldorf Astoria, where he was to meet Klara and her brother for luncheon. They were both at the table when he arrived. Klara was sipping iced water, but Schneider was half-way through his first Martini.

Strange remembered that he would be flying soon, and decided to join him. 'Aren't you sorry you're not coming with us?' he asked jovially. The visit to the barber's shop had put him in a good mood, despite the unpleasant prospect of a long flight.

Schneider took a sip of his Martini and extracted the olive. 'There are too many Jews in Hollywood,' he said. He gestured towards Klara. 'It's all right for her – people think she's some kind of Marlene Dietrich. I speak, and they start thinking of the Waffen SS.'

Strange did not answer because the waiter had brought his Martini. When the figure departed, he made a sweeping motion with his hand. 'What about New York? It's full of Jews.'

Schneider shrugged. 'It's different here. They're not in charge. I hope you enjoy your flight. The weather report says that there are electrical storms in the Middle West.'

Strange's good humour evaporated. For the rest of the meal he drank two more Martinis, but could hardly eat his chicken salad.

'Remember we're having dinner when we arrive,' Klara warned him when he ordered a fourth drink.

Strange waved her objections away. 'Did you bring all the documents with you?' he asked Schneider.

'Yes.' Schneider reached down and patted the briefcase resting against his chair. Strange nodded unsteadily, and Schneider gave his sister an anxious glance.

'Don't worry,' she said calmly. 'I know how to deal with it.' She glanced at her watch. 'It is time to go? Is the taxi ordered?' she asked her brother.

'Ordered, and the luggage ready,' he replied.

'Then let's go,' Strange said, and rose uncertainly to his feet.

Once the aircraft had lifted off, Strange was violently ill. Klara instructed the air hostess to provide a large glass of tomato juice, to which she added two powerful sleeping pills. When Strange emerged from his drugged sleep, they were approaching Los Angeles airport.

Klara looked with distaste at the figure of Al Davis, who introduced himself as they stood waiting for their luggage.

'Hi,' he said in a friendly voice. 'You must be Mr and Mrs Strange.'

Klara found his pink safari jacket and scarlet trousers unpleasing. 'This is my husband, Anthony Strange. I am Princess Klara Reisenauer.'

'Nice to know you, Princess,' Davis said cheerfully. 'Let's get your bags. I got the Rolls outside.' The huge car was white as milk and open to the bright sunlight. 'Welcome to Hollywood,' Davis said as they drove away from the airport down an avenue lined with palm trees. He steered the car with one hand and glanced constantly at the sidewalk, which seemed to be peopled with an extraordinary number of pretty girls. 'We've booked you into the Beverly Hills Hotel. Harry White wants to meet you in the polo lounge for drinks at six o'clock. We thought we'd have dinner at seven in the hotel. Harry guessed you wouldn't want too much hassle this evening, what with the journey and everything. The appointment in the morning is at ten o'clock. Does that suit you folks?' he asked with good humour.

He glanced in the rear-view mirror for affirmation, and received a frozen nod from Klara.

When he dropped them at the canopied entrance to the hotel, Strange and Klara registered and were taken into the grounds and led along pathways through lush green lawns to one of the bungalows scattered around the main building.

Strange collapsed at once with a groan on one of the beds, but Klara immediately telephoned for the services of valet, maid and porter.

Just before six, a restored Strange, in blazer and white flannels, escorted Klara to the polo lounge. Al Davis was seated with Harry White, who was wearing a jacket made from material that looked like the fuzzy interference on a television screen. He was talking to three swarthy middle-aged men at the next table. They all laughed a lot and spoke in an accent she could barely understand.

While they talked, it struck Klara that she was the oldest woman in the room, a situation she did not relish. Although the men wore expensive clothes, they were not attractive. Most of them were overweight, squat and had peasant features. The women, however, were youthful, glamorous and obviously eager to please their hosts.

After a moment Harry White turned to her and held out his hand. 'Princess,' he said. 'And you must be Tony Strange.'

'Anthony Strange,' said Klara.

'Anthony,' White repeated without embarrassment. 'I like that; it's

435

got class.' He turned back to Klara. 'And you're right on time.'

Klara waited until she was seated before she replied. 'It was the way I was brought up, Mr White. My father taught us we had an obligation to others to be gracious. Unpunctuality is so crude, don't you think?'

White smiled. 'What do I know? All I can remember was my old man telling me time was money.'

They sat at the table for an hour sipping champagne, while various people approached White, like supplicants applying to royalty for a favour. Sometimes he was friendly, occasionally effusive, and on two occasions coldly dismissive. Klara could see that in the kingdom of Hollywood, Harry White was the aristocrat, with all the privileges and obligations that rank entailed. Eventually he suggested that they have dinner. It was a mixture of fruit and salad that tasted ice cold and quite flavourless to Strange, who was still feeling delicate from the excesses of the day.

'How's your brother?' White asked when they were served large cups of weak coffee. 'He's one hell of a poker player.'

'He's fine,' Klara replied.

A waiter came and whispered in White's ear. 'Uh-oh,' he said. 'My car's here. Gotta go. Listen,' he said, suddenly serious, leaning forward to add emphasis to his words, 'you're seeing Jack Stapoulas tomorrow morning. He's one of the biggest men in this town. Don't try and bullshit him. I made the introduction, so I feel responsible, okay?'

He rose to his feet and his eyes swept over both of them. 'Good night, Princess, thanks,' he said, and strode off through the tables to the door, looking neither left nor right.

At eleven o'clock the following morning, Strange and Klara sat out by the swimming-pool at Jack Stapoulas's Beverly Hills mansion. They had waited for an hour, without shade, in the blazing sun. Strange's damp shirt clung to his body, which still ached with a severe hangover, and he was bored almost to distraction by the mindless stream of conversation Al Davis had kept up since they had arrived. Klara was in better condition; she wore a wide-brimmed hat that protected her from the sun.

Finally, at the sound of a voice issuing commands, they turned towards the house and watched an entourage approach. The first figure was a white-jacketed Mexican servant bearing a large pool umbrella aloft as though he were protecting some oriental potentate from the sun. The man in the shade of the umbrella wore only a brief swimming costume. His body glistened the colour of polished mahogany. A secretary of extraordinary beauty, with a notebook and pen, was also clad in a two-piece bathing costume. She was followed by a young man in a lightweight tropical suit with a large briefcase. Another Mexican servant brought up the rear bearing a telephone, which he plugged into a socket by the sun-bed next to Strange's chair. In moments the umbrella was arranged and Jack Stapoulas, the mahogany-coloured figure, lay in the shade studying Strange and Klara silently.

Although he was in excellent physical condition, the man was not young. Deep lines ran down each side of a prominent, beaky nose. Almost immediately the telephone rang and Stapoulas picked it up himself, even though other hands darted forward. When he began to speak, it was in Greek. After a muttered farewell, he put the phone down on the table. The secretary leaned forward and placed it quickly in its cradle. The reclining figure looked back at Strange, Klara and Davis.

'Get lost,' he said to Davis in an emotionless voice. Davis got up without protest and walked towards the house. Stapoulas looked at the thin gold watch that hung from his wrist on an expanding bracelet. 'Say what you've got to say,' he said in the same flat tone he had used to dismiss Davis. 'You've got twenty minutes.'

Strange unzipped his briefcase and took out a wad of papers. 'This is my offer, Mr Stapoulas,' he began confidently. 'The Strange and Schneider gallery control the world-famous painter Paul Van Duren . . .'

'I know that. You won him in a poker game. Harry White told me,' Stapoulas interjected.

Strange nodded and continued, 'Van Duren's work is in most of the important galleries in the world. I have a list here of their locations.' Stapoulas clicked his fingers in the direction of the young man in the lightweight suit, who took the paper from Strange and began to check the names against a list of his own. 'In addition, I have all the names of private individuals who have works by Van Duren in their possession.'

One of the white-coated waiters reappeared pushing a trolley laden with drinks. When it came to his turn, Strange requested a glass of iced mineral water, which he drank gratefully. He sat up straighter when he was refreshed. 'Mr Stapoulas, do you know the single greatest factor that increases the value of an established painter's work?' he asked.

The Greek looked at him. 'You tell me.'

'The death of the artist,' Strange replied.

There was a pause, and the reclining figure glanced around at his entourage. 'So what are you going to do?' he asked. 'Have the guy hit?'

Strange shook his head with a gentle laugh. 'There's no need. Van Duren's already doing the job for us.'

'Go on,' Stapoulas said, and Strange could now detect a slight edge of interest in his voice.

He drained the last of the water and placed the glass at his feet. 'Van Duren hasn't painted a picture for over a year, and he's drinking two bottles of hard liquor every day. Three, when he can manage it.' His host remained silent. Strange leaned forward, and there was genuine enthusiasm in his voice. 'The Strange and Schneider gallery has in its possession two hundred and seventy-eight pictures by Van Duren. They are the only ones that exist outside private collections, museums and galleries.'

The young man in the lightweight suit whispered something in Stapoulas's ear. He nodded, and turned back to Strange. 'What about the pictures in Van Duren's own private collection?' he asked in a light, menacing voice.

Strange smiled and glanced at his own watch. 'You must have contacts in Manhattan. *The New York Times* will be on the streets by now. Ring and ask if there are any news items about Paul Van Duren.'

The Greek nodded to the young man, who immediately began to make the call. While he was occupied, Stapoulas looked at Klara, who had remained silent throughout the business that had been conducted. 'I didn't realise you two were married. My information was that Mrs Strange was a Catholic, and wouldn't give him a divorce.'

Klara looked at him with haughty loathing. 'We arranged a Mexican divorce some time ago.'

Stapoulas shook his head. 'A Mexican divorce? The Pope don't give a shit about those.'

Klara crossed her legs and looked away. 'The opinion of the Pope is of supreme indifference to me, Mr Stapoulas,' she replied.

Strange was about to join in the exchange when the young man hung up the receiver. Stapoulas looked at him with interest. 'There's a piece on page one of *The New York Times*, sir. It seems there was a fire at Paul Van Duren's Long Island studio yesterday afternoon.

438

The building was gutted. Apparently a Mr Schneider helped Van Duren from the flames. Schneider is quoted as saying that the loss to the world of art is of indescribable magnitude. Van Duren is in a clinic in Manhattan.'

Stapoulas nodded, and suddenly there was a very ugly expression on his face. 'Get on to New York later,' he said bitterly. 'They knew I had a deal going through with this guy's work. I want someone to suffer for not giving us a call.'

'Yes, sir,' the young man muttered, making a note on a yellow-lined legal pad.

When Stapoulas looked at Strange again, the ugly expression had vanished. There was a discernible look of admiration on his face. 'Where do we go from here?' he asked in a friendly manner.

Strange shrugged. He was completely relaxed now. 'You buy six paintings for two million dollars. It will make headline news. From then on, our gallery will guarantee an annual increase in value of a hundred per cent on each picture.'

'How can you do that?'

Strange clipped his briefcase shut before he answered. 'If any Van Duren painting comes on the market in the next two years, my gallery will buy it. As soon as word gets round that we are buying in Van Duren's work, prices will be inflated. Meanwhile, we won't sell any of the pictures we possess. In two years' time we will hold an exhibition. It will probably be posthumous by then. We shall sell only three pictures at that time. You may sell three of yours at the same exhibition if you wish.'

There was a pause while the Greek considered. 'How do you know this is going to work?'

Strange stood up and walked to the drinks trolley, where he poured himself a large whisky, adding ice cubes. Klara could see that her husband had triumphed.

'It's worked for the past fifty years. Why should it stop now?' Strange raised the glass in a salute.

Stapoulas nodded, and pointed to the young man in the tropical suit. 'Go to the house and tell them we've got extra guests for lunch,' he said. Then he got up and linked arms with Strange. 'You know, Anthony, I think I've just turned into an art lover.'

439

Although Irene held a paperback open on her lap, her thoughts were elsewhere. Then Bridget, sitting in the next seat, nudged her suddenly. Irene looked at her daughter, who was dressed in the uniform of her old school, and leaned to catch her whispered words.

'Mummy,' she said, 'are they art students?'

Irene followed her gaze to the youths clustered by the doors at the centre of the carriage of the District Line train.

The two girls had long straight hair. They wore little make-up, but their eyes were emphasised by dark lines and they dressed in sombre clothes in earth colours and purples. Each wore thick stockings. The three boys with them wore buff-coloured duffle coats, college scarves, enormous sweaters and trousers so narrow that Irene wondered for a moment how they had managed to get into them. Their hair was thick and arranged in a style copied from the statues of ancient Romans. Only one had a beard, which straggled from his chin like wispy down. Piled about them were portfolios, guitars and a variety of baggage.

She nodded to her daughter as the train slowed to a stop at Ealing Broadway. 'Yes, darling,' she replied with a smile.

Irene glanced around as they followed; she had always enjoyed the bustle of the station. There were platforms for Underground trains and a mainline service to Paddington. For her, the most attractive element was the Victorian character of the surroundings: decorated cast-iron pillars, the scalloped edges on the eaves of the roofs, the solid brass-trimmed doorways, and the dark paintwork that always brought memories of her childhood.

When they had climbed the stairs from the platform, Irene paused in the arcade of shops that led to the Broadway. 'I'll meet you here at half-past four, so don't dawdle,' she instructed Bridget. Then she leaned down and kissed her.

When they parted, Irene waved again and crossed the road. It was a hot day. Bright sunlight dazzled her until she walked in the shade of shop blinds over the pavements. At St Mary's Road, she slowed her pace. The horse-chestnut trees on the green were still heavy with foliage and cast cool shadows. She passed the Red Lion and suddenly remembered a warm evening during the last days of the war when she and Hammond Shelley had stood on the pavement drinking their halves of bitter.

Ahead walked the group of students she had seen on the train.

She guessed by their self-assurance that they would be the second or third year, just about seventeen or eighteen, and then, with a slight shock, she thought, I'm thirty-six! I feel about the same age as them; but they would see me as a woman of their mothers' generation. But everything seemed the same – the trees, the houses, the shops, the long brick walls.

Then she reached the forecourt of the West London Technical College. Instead of the dark red-brick façade she remembered from her childhood, a new building curved towards her. A shallow flight of steps led to a pillared entrance faced with glass. Irene entered the revolving door, and paused before she walked across the wide concourse to the reception desk. A smart, middle-aged woman with carefully permed white hair looked up as she approached.

The woman studied Irene's face with dawning recognition and said, 'Is it Irene Nettlebury?'

It took a few moments for Irene to realise who the woman was. 'Molly!' she replied. 'Molly Redding.'

She rose and took Irene's hands. 'How lovely to see you, dear. How long has it been?'

Irene thought before she answered. 'Twelve years, Molly. It's been twelve years!'

'Bless my soul, how time flies,' said Molly. 'And you haven't changed at all!' She paused and patted her hair, which was tinted with lavender. 'Not like me,' she added. 'I certainly look my age!'

Irene thought suddenly of the war years; she could remember Molly in the arms of an Air Force sergeant at a dance they had held for the victory celebrations. She had been slim then, with long dark hair. Irene's mind flicked back to the students she had followed from the Broadway. It isn't how old you feel, she told herself, it's how old you look.

Molly continued, 'You had a little girl, didn't you?'

'Yes, her name's Bridget. She started at senior school today.'

'And what are you up to now?' Molly asked.

Irene raised the palm of her hand to the ceiling and said, 'I'm back here. I've been accepted for a teaching job again.'

'Well, that's lovely,' Molly said with feeling. Then she looked around. 'What do you think of the new building? I've been out here on reception since Mr Thomas retired. I prefer it to being a secretary.'

'It's nice, but I shall miss the old place,' said Irene. 'Well, I'd better report for work. Where do I go?'

'Take that lift on your left. The third floor, and the first door on

441

your right. That's the Art School secretary.'

Irene followed her instructions and a few minutes later was shown into the Principal's office. He was a shambling figure with a fringe of white hair round a smooth bald head. His face was ruddy pink, and unlined, like a baby's. When he smiled, Irene noticed his blue eyes. 'I'm Alistair Duncan. I knew your father,' he said in a Lowland Scottish accent.

'Yes, he remembers you well,' Irene said with a smile.

Duncan flipped open a brown file. 'And you ceased to be a member of staff here in 1946,' he said almost to himself. 'Tell me, why did you decide to return to teaching, Mrs Cleary?'

Irene sat on the edge of the chair before the desk and looked down at her hands folded in her lap. 'My daughter began senior school today, so she no longer requires my full-time attention.' She paused and looked up at him again. 'And quite frankly, Mr Duncan, recently I've felt that I've been wasting my life. I'm a trained teacher, and I'd like to put that training to some use.'

Duncan smiled again. 'In that case, you'd better get on with it,' he answered, glancing at his watch. 'In five minutes your class will be in room 204 on the floor below this. Instructing a group of the first-year general students into the mysteries of costume life.' He got up and walked to the door with her. 'By the way,' he said as she was about to leave, 'how's your father? I was one of his students, you know. He must be getting on.'

'He's frail, but he's still working.'

Duncan nodded. 'Yes. Painting isn't a job you retire from.'

A group of young people stood waiting outside room 204. Irene opened the door and ushered them into a large, airy room with a polished parquet floor. There were chairs against the walls and stacks of half-imperial drawing-boards. For a moment she thought nostalgically of the dusty, shabby studios of the old building they had inhabited when she was a student. It had just occurred to her that they did not have a model when she heard a loud knock on the door. A slender figure stood in the doorway, whom she took to be somewhere in his thirties. He wore a dark-blue velvet jacket, tight black trousers and a floppy bow tie. His long hair framed a narrow face with accentuated cheekbones.

'Am I right in assuming this is Mrs Cleary's class for costume life?' he asked in a deep, dramatic voice.

Irene nodded, and the figure slowly crossed the room like a

442

prince inspecting his subjects. He suddenly held out a hand, and she wondered whether she was expected to curtsy. But then he smiled, and she saw that he was much younger than she had assumed.

'Clive Hamilton,' he said quietly. 'I'm ready for the engagement.'

Irene also noticed on closer inspection that the splendid clothes were older. The patent leather shoes were cracked, and the cuffs of the white shirt frayed. She smiled. 'Will you stand, Mr Hamilton, or would you prefer to sit?'

Hamilton glanced round the studio and saw an article of furniture half-concealed behind a hessian screen. 'Perhaps, if we used the chaise-longue, I could recline,' he said.

This time she laughed aloud. 'Why not ask some of these young men to help you move it?'

When the couch was placed in the centre of the room, Hamilton turned to Irene again. 'Would you care for something like the death of Chatterton, or a less studied pose?'

'Just sit comfortably on the couch, Mr Hamilton.'

He leaned back and crossed his legs with one arm draped along the back of the arm-rest.

While the class settled down, Irene sat and read for a time. After half an hour, she started to move quietly about the room. As she expected, the work was of varying quality, and she had to remind herself not to concentrate on those with the most obvious talent.

They all look so young, she thought. Hardly any older than Bridget. She recalled the classes she had taken years before: art students had seemed like adults then, grown men and women. Then she remembered that she had not called the register the Principal's secretary had provided, and decided to do that at the end of the session. More time passed as she moved among the working students. She sat down beside one girl and made a small sketch in the corner of her drawing to demonstrate the proportions of Hamilton's legs. Gradually she became absorbed in her own work, and then noticed that Hamilton had stifled a yawn and was glancing pointedly at his watch. Instantly she realised she had not paused for a break.

'Rest period,' she called out.

During the interval, she consulted her timetable for the rest of the week, and Hamilton lay back and closed his eyes. When fifteen minutes had passed, she walked over to the reclining figure. His breathing was light and regular. She reached out and touched his shoulder. He opened his eyes and it was obvious, for a moment, that he could not recollect his whereabouts. Now he seemed very young

443

and vulnerable. Then he smiled at her and assumed his previous self-mocking attitude.

'Forgive me,' he said, moving effortlessly back into the exact pose he had adopted all morning.

In the second half of the session Irene kept a closer watch on the time and she called the register early. Then she told the class that they had a history of art lesson in the lecture theatre during the afternoon, followed by an anatomy class, which would be supervised by another member of staff. The students filed from the room, and Hamilton rose from the chaise-longue. When he was on his feet, he swayed for a moment and sat down again. Irene noticed his unsteadiness and looked at him with concern.

He tried to smile. 'Bit light-headed, I'm afraid,' he said dismissively. 'All this sitting about, I expect.'

Irene guessed what was the matter. 'Would you have lunch with me?' she asked.

Hamilton pursed his lips and then smiled again. 'That's very decent of you. I'll return the compliment when I receive my fee.'

'It's only the college refectory,' said Irene. 'We won't be dining at the Ritz.'

'I'm sure it will be fine,' Hamilton replied.

'By the way,' Irene said when they had left the studio and were walking along the corridor, 'do you know where the refectory is in this building?'

Hamilton opened a pair of swing doors for her. 'Actually, it's not in this building at all,' he explained. 'We go across a sort of bridge into the part of the original Art School that still survives.'

Irene followed him. When they reached the furthest part of the new building they passed down a short length of corridor.

For Irene it was like entering the past; everything was the same, the cream paintwork, the polished stone floor, the long frosted glass partitions of the classrooms and studios. Even the same smell of polish and disinfectant took her back, and memories flooded her mind as they descended the staircase.

When they sat down eventually, Irene recognised it as the table next to the one she and Cleary had shared on his first day at the college. She had taken only a bun and a cup of tea, but Hamilton had a loaded tray. Although he was obviously famished, he managed to keep his table manners. Irene, watching him, suddenly felt very sad. The time she had spent with Cleary came back to her as fresh and raw as an open wound.

444

Hamilton looked up and caught her expression. 'Gone, all are gone, all the old familiar faces,' he said.

'I'm sorry?' said Irene.

'It's a poem,' he explained. 'You were remembering something from the past.'

'How did you know?'

He laughed. 'I'm an actor. It's my job to recognise emotions. You looked like this.'

Now it was Irene's turn to laugh. He was miming an expression of remembrance perfectly. It made her own nostalgia seem slightly ridiculous. 'Why did you become an actor?' Irene was determined to change the subject.

Hamilton shrugged, and accepted a cigarette. 'My father wanted me to be a gentleman, so he sent me to a public school of such dismal lack of distinction that, even to this day, I can't remember its name. It was located on the mud-flats of Norfolk and ruled over by an ancient clergyman of bitter moral rectitude. One day an old touring actor came to give us readings of Shakespeare and Dickens. I was overwhelmed. After the performance, I went to the chapel and prayed that I could become an actor; my prayers were answered.' He gestured with his cigarette. 'There, that's the story of my life.'

Irene smiled. 'Don't you want to know about mine?'

He sat back and stared at the ceiling. 'You are the daughter of Sir Julian Nettlebury, the painter. You taught here during the war until you married an ex-RAF pilot who was a student, called Richard Cleary. You have a daughter of eleven years of age.'

Irene gazed at him in astonishment. 'Good heavens,' she exclaimed. 'Are you a mind-reader?'

Hamilton shook his head. 'Just a friend of Molly Redding. I followed you to her desk this morning. She told me all about you.'

They looked at each other for a few moments, and Irene suddenly felt herself blush. She knew Hamilton was attracted to her, and she also felt a corresponding interest. At the same time she was acutely aware that it would not work.

There was a sudden burst of laughter from the next table. Irene turned to see the cause of their mirth and recognised the students Bridget had pointed out on the train. She looked back at the young man in front of her. He must be fifteen years younger than me, she thought. How cruel time can be.

'You've got a free period this afternoon,' Hamilton said quietly. 'Would you like to spend it with me?'

445

Irene smiled, and shook her head. 'I've got some work to do in the library.'

'Oh, take some time off,' he urged. 'A break does everyone a bit of good.'

She shook her head again. 'I won't forget the meal,' he answered. 'Thank you again.' Then he got up and walked out. As Irene watched him, she noticed that three of the girls at a nearby table watched him, too.

Later that evening, Bridget hurried the last few yards ahead of her mother and waited at the entrance of the Archangel Gallery. Ted Porter peered short-sightedly at them before he made out Irene's features.

'Hello, Mr Porter,' Bridget said.

He looked down and smiled. 'Good Lord! What a big girl you've got to be. And in school uniform, too.'

'I'm changing in a minute,' said Bridget. 'Mummy and I are going out on a treat.'

'Well, you both deserve it, pet.'

'Who's here, Ted?' Irene asked.

'Just Mr Laszlo. He's downstairs. Your sister will be back in about twenty minutes; she's gone for a cup of tea with Mr Laszlo's wife.'

Irene went to phone her father, and Bridget made her way to the basement. She found Laszlo sitting in the centre of the largest room. He was surrounded with paintings which he viewed with evident pleasure. Bridget was very quiet, and Laszlo did not hear her approach. She stood behind him and looked at the picture he was studying. It was a landscape of an English meadow, and the different plants, trees, flowers and bushes were painted in extraordinary detail. She noticed that each of the other paintings was executed with the same detail and technique.

'Who did these, Uncle Laszlo?' she asked.

He glanced at her, and then back at the picture. She stood close to him, and he encircled her waist to give her an absent-minded hug. 'Peter Quick.'

'He was one of the Cromwell Road School, wasn't he?' Laszlo nodded. 'Uncle Laszlo,' she said after a moment, 'do you think Daddy is a very good painter?'

Laszlo said seriously, 'Yes, I do. A very good painter.'

Bridget pointed to the picture Laszlo was studying. 'Better than Peter Quick?'

446

'Yes, although I like Peter Quick's work very much.' He leaned forward. 'Look at this: you can see the honeysuckle and the dog-roses.' He gestured. 'Those are bramble flowers, and those bluebells, and that's a peacock butterfly.'

Bridget looked amazed. 'I thought you never went into the countryside. How do you know all the names?'

Laszlo smiled. 'A friend of mine is a botanist. I asked him if he could identify all the plants for me, and I remembered them.'

Bridget nodded. 'So you can go into the countryside by just sitting here?'

'That's right.'

When she returned to the upper galleries, Bridget found her mother talking with her Aunt Anne. 'I'm coming to the cinema too,' Anne said, 'but I'm going to be a little while, so we'll take a taxi.'

Bridget went to her aunt's flat above the gallery to change out of her uniform into a dress. Then she wandered around for a time, seeking the paintings in the collection that had been drawn by her father. Later, when she sat in the tip-up seat of the black cab, she looked out of the window, while her mother talked to her aunt. She knew that if she kept quiet long enough they would forget her presence and talk with more intimacy.

'Where is he now?' Anne asked, and Bridget knew she was referring to her father.

Irene shrugged. 'He doesn't bother to tell me.'

'It's just as well he's a good painter,' Bridget said suddenly.

The two women looked at her in surprise. 'What do you mean, darling?' her mother asked.

Bridget shrugged. 'Two of the girls at school said he was a bad father – that's all,' she said in a matter-of-fact voice.

West Coast of Scotland, spring 1959

Horizontal sheets of rain lashed against the cracked glass enclosing the cabin of the tiny coaster as it battled through the grey, turbulent seat. Inside the cramped cabin, Richard Cleary held on to the chart table and took the mug of dark tea handed to him by the rough-haired boy who emerged from below. The captain took another mug, keeping one hand on the wheel, and continued to peer through the rain-streaked glass. Then he kicked a locker with his boot. 'There's a bottle in there,' he said.

447

Cleary reached down and found the whisky. The captain held out his tea, and Cleary added generous measures to both their mugs. 'How long now?' he asked.

'An hour, maybe more. It's hard to judge in this weather.'

'How will you spot it in this storm?' Cleary asked.

The captain puffed on his blackened pipe and filled the stuffy cabin with more of the evil-smelling smoke. 'We won't. This weather will pass soon. It'll be clear by the time we reach the island.' He glanced at Cleary. 'You don't doubt my word?'

'I was a flyer once. I know how fast a warm front can move,' said Cleary.

The captain laughed. 'I was in frigates. I thought you RAF boys only flew when the weather was good.'

For a moment, Cleary remembered German fighters swarming through a clear night sky, and shook his head. 'No, sometimes we liked a bit of cloud.'

As the captain had predicted, the rain blew itself out and patches of blue slowly emerged through the overcast. The grey, slabby sea gradually calmed and changed colour to a deep white-flecked green.

He altered direction by several degrees, and a small dark smudge appeared on the horizon. 'That's Conway ahead,' he said.

Cleary scratched his chin. He had been travelling for nearly three days and had not had an opportunity to shave or change the heavy fisherman's sweater he wore beneath his greatcoat. 'It must be a hard life up here,' he said.

The man took the pipe from his mouth. 'What kind of work do you do?'

'I'm a painter.'

'That's a good steady job,' he said, and Cleary realised he had assumed he decorated houses.

'Not that kind of painter,' said Cleary. 'I'm an artist. I paint pictures.'

'Is that so?' he said with interest. 'I don't see many pictures.'

Cleary looked at the great sea around him and the changing cloud formations. 'You see enough,' he said after a moment.

Eventually the little boat came alongside a stone jetty, and Cleary found his canvas bag.

'Conway,' said the captain. 'Population, seven people and a thousand sheep.' When they stood on the jetty, he pointed to a track that led away from the tiny cluster of white-painted buildings.

448

'Twenty minutes' walk along the path, and you'll find the house you're looking for.' He gestured with his pipe. 'I'm putting up with my sister until eight o'clock tomorrow morning. If you stay after that, you'll be here until the middle of next month.' He handed over a bundle of letters. 'Don't forget the mail.'

Cleary followed his directions and set off along the steeply-rising path. When he reached the peak of the hill, he could see that he was on the highest point of the island. It was a treeless landscape of gentle rolling hills and strange outcroppings of grey rock. Sheep browsed in distant scattered clumps and sea birds wheeled and called. The track curved away to a solitary grey-roofed, white-painted house with a single large outbuilding. As he came closer, he could make out a figure standing in the doorway. It was Paula. She wore a long blue smock encrusted with modelling clay, and leaned against the frame of the doorway with her arms crossed. She did not speak until he stood before her.

'I could see it was you from a long way off,' she said.

'Did you get my letter?' he asked. When she shook her head, he felt in his coat pocket and produced the bundle of mail. He flipped through them and found his own. 'Personal delivery!'

She took the letter, and studied him. 'You look awful. The heater is on; you can take a bath.' She turned for him to follow her into the kitchen.

The walls were painted white, and there was a wide fireplace where a peat fire burned. A window looked out on the west side of the island, where it sloped down to the sea. A wooden staircase led to the upper floor. Paula took him to the bathroom, where he shaved while he waited for an iron tub to fill. There was a man's shaving tackle on the shelf below the mirror: soap, shaving-brush and an old-fashioned open razor.

After he had soaked in the hot water for a time, he dried himself with the large rough towels Paula had provided and changed his clothes. When he went down to the kitchen, she was seated at the table. He sat down opposite.

'You're living with someone?' he asked.

Paula held up her left hand. He had not noticed the wedding ring earlier because her hands were still covered in dried modelling clay. 'Where did you meet him?'

'Here, on the island.' She nodded over her shoulders. 'He converted the barn into my studio.'

'A working man,' Cleary said with a smile.

449

Paula shook her head. 'Not originally. He was in the RAF, like you. After the war he wanted to live somewhere quiet.'

'Where is he now?'

'Building sheep-pens down at the village.'

'The village?' Cleary asked.

Paula smiled for the first time. 'We call those buildings down at the jetty the village.'

He looked round the room. 'Do you have anything to drink?'

Paula went to the cupboard, returning with a tumbler and half a bottle of malt whisky. She poured a large measure and ran a little water from the tap into the glass. 'Tom told me a little water brings out the flavour.'

Cleary drank half the measure before he answered. 'I don't drink it for the flavour.' He looked around the room again. 'Tom, that's his name, is it?'

'Tom Griffin.'

'Griffin? That's Welsh, isn't it?'

'He isn't a Scot; he just came here because he wanted some peace.'

'Some peace,' he said, almost to himself. He poured another drink. When he sat back in the chair, he half raised the tumbler. 'I brought you the London papers with the reviews of your exhibition.'

'Did you?' she replied with interest.

'Yes,' he said, and she could hear resentment in his voice. 'They could be described as rave reviews. You are compared with Elizabeth Frink, Henry Moore, Jacob Epstein and Brancusi. They left out Michelangelo. I suppose they couldn't spell his name.' Paula said nothing. 'Doesn't it mean anything to you?'

She shook her head. 'Oh, the money will come in useful, but no; the reviews don't mean anything to me any more.'

After a while, Cleary asked, 'May I see what work you're doing now?'

She got up without speaking, and he followed her from the house to the outbuilding. It was a good studio, full of light from the enlarged windows. There were rough white walls and a stone floor. Several stands were placed around the room; each held a piece of work, tall, elongated abstract shapes that echoed animal and human forms.

Paula stroked one of the pieces. 'I don't do any carving here.' She smiled again. 'It's a bit difficult to import great slabs of stone.'

He moved among the pieces for a while. 'They're bloody marvellous! Beautiful work. You deserve what they wrote,' he told her.

'Thank you,' she replied without emotion.

450

He gestured towards one of the pieces. 'How do you go from this to bronze?'

'I ship them to a foundry in Whitechapel. They scale them up and cast them. I go down for the final touches.'

Cleary ran his hand over one of the smooth surfaces. 'Don't you worry about damage?'

Paula shook her head. 'Tom makes the frames; he's a good carpenter.' She looked through the window towards the sun, low on the horizon. 'He'll be home soon.'

'I'm home now,' a voice said behind them, and Cleary turned to see the figure in the doorway. Tom Griffin was of medium height, thick-set with dark brown hair. 'You must be Richard Cleary,' he said.

Cleary took his hand, and felt the rough calloused texture of the palm. 'I've been drinking your whisky.'

Griffin smiled. 'There's more in the house!'

After a time, Paula could see that Cleary and Griffin liked each other. When they had eaten an evening meal they sat before the fire and drank whisky. After a while, Paula went to bed and left them alone.

'Where did you catch it?' Cleary asked quietly.

Griffin touched the livid scar down one side of his face. 'We caught fire over the Ruhr. I was lucky. Only two of us got out. I was bloody glad to end up in the bag.'

'So was I,' said Cleary. 'Funny, no one believes you when you say that. They think you're being modest.'

'Modest?' Griffin repeated. 'Christ, I was just shit-scared every time I went up!' They sat in the flickering light in silence, until Griffin said, 'How is your work? Paula says you're very good.'

Cleary took a mouthful of malt whisky. 'I'm a moderately successful painter. That means I barely keep body and soul together.' He paused. 'Mind you, I'm not so sure about soul.'

'What about your marriage?'

Cleary shook his head. 'That's over.' He looked up. 'She finally stopped loving me . . . I used it all up,' he said slowly.

They were silent again, and then Griffin said, 'Why did you come here?'

Cleary held his hands out towards the fire without looking at Griffin. 'I came to say I was sorry.' Then he picked up his glass. 'I've hurt too many people. I used not to feel guilty, but I do now.'

Griffin poured most of the remaining whisky into Cleary's glass.

451

'Paula is fine,' he said. 'You can stay with us for a while, if you like. It might do you some good.'

Cleary raised his drink. 'Thanks, but I'll move on in the morning.'

'Suit yourself.' Griffin climbed to his feet slowly, and stretched. 'Well, I'm off. You know where your room is.'

Cleary nodded. He raised the glass again in farewell and then sat before the flickering fire, looking for memories in the changing shapes of the flames.

CHAPTER TWENTY

London, early summer 1960

Gideon turned the MG off the Uxbridge Road into a wide avenue of red-brick Victorian houses trimmed with white stone. The journey from town had been quicker than he had expected; it was just after three-thirty, and all was quiet in the suburbs of west London. Warm sunshine drenched the flower-filled gardens either side of the road. Following Anne's instructions, he turned right again and saw the long high brick wall of her school. When he reached the wrought-iron gates at the entrance, he stopped and parked the car underneath a lime tree and switched off the engine. All was silent.

Suddenly he remembered parking beneath the eucalyptus trees in the forecourt of Antibes station. He tried to recall the year; it must have been 1936, he told himself. Why did I think of that moment? he wondered. Was it the heat of the day, the sudden silence? He recalled the old man who had spoken to him and complimented him on the car. He would be long dead now. Things change. Then he looked at the MG's wooden dashboard and touched the polished surface with his fingertips. Perhaps some things remained the same; this car was as it had looked when he first bought it. Once, however, little sports cars had been a common sight; now they were venerated by collectors. It was the same with paintings. A portrait commissioned by a wealthy Dutch merchant, depicting his wife going about her everyday tasks, would have had a different meaning to those who looked at it three hundred years ago. They would have seen a familiar figure, in commonplace surroundings, wearing clothes they recognised and in relation to objects and rooms that were part of their lives. Now such a picture would hang on the wall of a museum and be judged by the reputation of the painter.

He got out of the MG, lit a cigarette and leaned against the tree. After a few minutes, a trickle of girls began to come through the

453

gates. Younger ones came first; some hurried ahead and others dawdled in chattering pairs. He peered anxiously in their direction; it was difficult to distinguish between them.

In the end it was Bridget who approached him; she broke away from a group and seemed rather embarrassed by his presence. Her friends stopped to watch. 'Hello, Gideon,' she said in a voice loud enough for them to hear. He smiled in their direction and gave a half-bow before he turned to her. She whispered, 'Drive away quickly. I told them you were my boyfriend.' Then she grinned, took off her hat and climbed quickly into the passenger seat. Gideon was about to comply with her request when the group of giggling schoolgirls parted to make way for a grey-haired lady.

'Hello, Bridget,' she said in an authoritative voice. Then she confronted Gideon. 'My name is Miss Crawford. I am headmistress of this school.' It was clear that her power and domain extended beyond its walls.

Gideon held out his hand. 'How do you do? My name is James Gideon; I am Bridget's uncle. My sister-in-law asked me to collect her today.'

Miss Crawford nodded at the explanation. 'I see. I hope you didn't mind my approaching you in this fashion. It's just that I saw you from the window, and we do get some peculiar types of men in the vicinity.'

Gideon smiled. 'I do understand. I shall tell Bridget's mother of your vigilance.' He got into the driver's seat and saw that Bridget had put her hat on again.

When they reached the junction with the Uxbridge Road, she said, 'I wasn't expecting you, Gideon. I thought Mummy would be waiting for me.'

'She had made other arrangements. Your grandfather is much worse. She and your Aunt Anne are at the hospital.'

Bridget nodded, and Gideon glanced at her before he turned the car into the main road. She had taken her hat off once again. But for the red hair, she did not look at all like a Nettlebury. Her skin was pale olive, like her father's, he thought. Without her uniform, it would have been impossible to guess her age. She was one of those girls who go from girlhood to maturity instantly; there had been no period of transition.

She became aware that he was studying her. 'The King Edward VII Hospital for Officers and Gentlemen,' she said. 'It seems an odd place for Grandpa to be . . .'

Dying, Gideon thought, but she doesn't want to say the word. 'I believe he has two portraits hanging there. He was an important war artist, you know.'

Bridget thought for a moment. 'War artist,' she repeated. 'It's a curious title, isn't it? You don't get war choreographers or war musicians. Why did they choose to rope in artists to dignify war?'

Gideon thought he could detect another influence behind her words. 'There's plenty of great literature on the subject,' he said easily. 'And you could say the 1812 Overture was about a battle.'

That silenced her for a few minutes. 'Well, there won't be any artists next time, just plenty of charcoal.' It sounded as though she were reciting something she had learned by heart. When she spoke again, it was in less certain terms. 'What great literature do you think has been written about war?'

Gideon considered this while they waited at the traffic lights at Shepherd's Bush. '*The Iliad, Henry V, War and Peace* and *All Quiet on the Western Front*.'

He pulled away from the lights and they were nearly at Notting Hill before Bridget said, 'Anyone else?'

Gideon thought again. 'There were the war poets,' he answered. 'I suppose in a way they were war artists, too.'

Bridget was obviously interested. 'Who were the war poets?' Somehow she sounded younger with each question.

'They were from the Great War,' he said. 'Wilfred Owen, Siegfried Sassoon, Robert Graves, Isaac Rosenberg.'

'Robert Graves?' she said quickly. 'The man who wrote *I Claudius*?'

Gideon nodded, keeping his eye on the road. 'Have you read it?' He remembered certain passages that might be considered a bit strong for a girl of fourteen.

'Oh yes! A boy I met on the Aldermaston march lent me a copy.'

'I didn't know you went on the march,' he said.

Bridget shrugged. 'Well, not all of the march. Mummy wouldn't let me. We had to join on the last day.'

The traffic grew thicker as they came close to Marble Arch, and finally they slowed to a halt in a long tail-back. Gideon leaned back and looked down at her again. 'What do you want to do, Bridget?' he asked. 'When you leave school, I mean.'

'Go to art school, I suppose, like the rest of the family.'

'Can you draw?'

Bridget reached down and took a sketchbook from her briefcase. She flipped open a page and showed him an ink and wash portrait. It was of a film actor, and there was no denying the skill and assurance of the work. 'It's not for me,' she said quickly. 'I do them for the girls at school. They buy them.'

'What do you charge?' Gideon asked with a grin.

'Seven and six for a film star, ten bob if it's the photograph of a boyfriend. They're harder. Most of the snapshots they give me to work from are rotten.'

This time Gideon laughed. 'Well, you certainly sound like an artist; most of them complain about commissioned work. If you ever feel you need an agent, you'd better come and see me.'

The traffic cleared, and Gideon turned off Park Lane into the back doubles of Mayfair. He parked the car and they walked to the gallery. Outside, Bridget asked, 'Did Mummy bring my other clothes?'

Gideon nodded. 'Your suitcase is in the spare bedroom in the flat.'

'I'll go up and change, then,' Bridget said.

Gideon unlocked the door for her and realized that they had not talked about Julian at all.

She paused, as if reading his mind, and said, 'Do you think I should go and see Grandpa?'

Gideon shook his head. 'He's unconscious, darling. I'll ring later. If your mother thinks it's a good idea, I'll take you there.'

Bridget smiled her thanks and climbed the stairs. She always enjoyed visiting Gideon's and Anne's home. The narrow staircase, plain white walls and dark carpet appeared modest and did not prepare people for the scale of the flat beyond the door at the top of the staircase. She let herself in with the latchkey and entered a vast room that extended over and either side of the Archangel Gallery below. Victorian decorated cast-iron pillars had replaced the load-bearing walls. At the far end, to the left, a great spiral staircase led to the floor above where there were bedrooms, a dining-room, the kitchen and Gideon's study. Set each side of the staircase were rows of bookcases forming the library. Bridget reached for the bank of switches and turned them all on. Because the sash windows were only of a moderate size, the room did not really come to life until it was flooded by lights. Now concealed spotlamps bathed the living area, giving shape and form to the furniture Anne had collected, and the pictures that filled the walls blazed with colour. To the right, at the opposite end from the library, a large sofa and a collection of comfortable armchairs were grouped round a delicately carved white marble fireplace.

Bridget had never previously been in the room on her own; most visits had been for family occasions. Now she began to walk slowly round, studying pictures and objects she had not had time to notice before. Everything struck a deep note of pleasure within her.

She could draw well, but she also possessed a rarer quality: an inherent response to beauty. Colour, form and proportion affected her strongly; she felt them like a physical force and could be moved to joy or sadness by any work that artists and craftsmen had lavished their gifts upon. Such an endowment had its defects; she was distressed by ugliness, and the juxtaposition of ill-matched colours caused her similar distress.

She already knew what she wanted to do in life; her upbringing had made her familiar with art galleries and museums since early childhood. She knew Florence and Paris as other girls of her age knew seaside towns. Some people drew spiritual solace from cathedrals; Bridget found the same fulfilment in the great galleries of Europe.

She continued to wander the length of the great room until she reached the bookcases. Then she remembered Gideon's words about the war poets. The books were classified by subject matter, and after a few moments' search, she found the poetry section. Eventually she selected a book and, taking it with her, climbed the spiral staircase and found her bedroom.

The housekeeper who looked after Gideon and Anne had unpacked her clothes and put them away in the dresser and wardrobe. She had also left a brief note on the bed. The handwriting was bold and simple, like a child's:

Dear Bridget,
   If you are hungry, there are some chicken sandwiches in the fridge.
   But don't eat too much. I think your uncle is taking you out for a meal.
   This is my afternoon off. I will be in at nine o'clock,
                                  Tessa.

Bridget put the book down and went into the bathroom. In the years she and Irene had lived with her grandfather, she had suffered the bathroom there under protest. The cold marble floor and bleak tiled walls made visits a question of discipline. The room she now stood in was designed for pleasure. There were thick carpets, big rough-textured towels hung on heated rails, potted plants stood on stands and pictures decorated the walls. In the mahogany cupboards were cut-glass bottles of bath crystals.

457

Bridget ran a scented bath and stayed in it until the water cooled. Then she dressed and sat reading poetry in her bedroom until Gideon called her from below. She descended the spiral staircase and found him with another man. When he turned, she realised it was her father.

It had been years since she had seen him last, and he had changed. She always remembered him as a bear-like man, but he was much thinner now, and his hair was shot with grey. His swarthy complexion was paler and there were dark shadows under his eyes.

'Hello, Bridget,' he said in the same deep voice.

'Hello,' she replied calmly, but her emotions were in turmoil. One instinct told her to run and embrace him, as she had when she was a child; another inner voice told her to be cold and reserved, to punish him for the neglect he had shown.

'You've grown up,' he said a little sadly. 'You look just like your Great-Aunt Beattie.'

'I didn't know her,' Bridget replied.

Cleary nodded. 'She was my mother's sister, the beauty of the family.'

Gideon looked at her. 'I've asked your father to come to dinner with us.' It was almost a question.

'As you wish,' she replied, almost in a whisper.

They stood awkwardly for a few moments, and then Cleary noticed one of the paintings on the wall. 'Good God!' he exclaimed. 'I haven't seen that since the day Peter Quick finished painting it.'

The picture showed a woman in the back yard of a working-class house. She was operating an old-fashioned mangle and a young girl was taking a blue-grey dress from between the rollers.

'Peter had three goes at that dress,' said Cleary. 'It was red at first, then green. This was the final colour.'

Bridget's curiosity overcame her reserve. 'Why did he change the colours?'

Cleary stood before the picture and gestured again. 'It was the child's face,' he explained. 'Peter wanted it to reflect the colour of the dress. The first time, he said it made the girl look like a Red Indian. The second time he said she looked too bilious. This version makes the face pale, and the grey-green gives her that drained look he wanted.' He looked round. 'Do you have any of my stuff here?' he asked.

Gideon nodded. 'Quite a lot.' He waved to the far end of the room, and the three of them walked over together.

It was nearly ten o'clock, but there was still enough light in Nettlebury's room for his two daughters to observe his sleeping face. His frail arms lay on the coverlet, each hand so pale and thin that the sinews and veins stood out like ridges on the paper-white flesh. There was no sound except for his shallow, rasping breath. Irene and Anne sat silently, waiting for the inevitable: the last ritual women perform for men. As the darkness finally closed on the figure in the bed, the doctor came into the little room. He was young, burly beneath his white coat, and wore a large spotted bow tie. He swung the table-lamp away from Sir Julian before he switched on the light. 'Any change?' he asked in a voice with a faint Welsh accent.

They both shook their heads. 'Nothing,' Anne said in a tired voice.

The doctor stood back with his hands thrust into his coat pockets. 'Matron told me he did the two portraits at the end of the landing. I've never bothered to read the name until now.' Anne smiled. 'When did he retire?' he asked.

Irene looked up. 'He finished a painting four days ago.'

'Good Lord! That's marvellous.' He paused. 'I'm afraid I'm not up on these things. Was he very famous?'

Anne looked at her father's head on the pillow. 'He was once, but that was many years ago. He hasn't sold a painting for a long time.'

'Are his pictures expensive? It's just that I'd like to buy one . . . if I could afford it.'

Irene shook her head. 'We'll give you one.'

The doctor was embarrassed. 'Oh, no,' he protested. 'I couldn't accept something so valuable.'

Anne smiled at him sadly. 'Nobody wants to buy his pictures, Doctor. They have value only to us, and we'd like you to have one.'

Before he answered, he crossed the room and shut the window. It had suddenly become cooler with the darkness. 'In that case, I would be honoured to accept.' With a smile of thanks, he left the room.

There was silence, and then a curious sound: Nettlebury was laughing.

'Dad?' said Anne. They clutched his hands. 'The value comes when you're working,' he said faintly. 'It doesn't matter when it's done.' He paused, and then spoke in a clear firm voice. 'There was a fourth part: *The Folly of Mankind*.' He laughed again. 'A great final

459

picture of people making fools of themselves.' He gazed intently at the ceiling. 'I can see it quite plainly.' Then he closed his eyes again, and the life went out of him.

Gideon sat with Bridget and her father in L'Escargot, at a table downstairs. Bridget had been given the best seat so that she could look round the room, but since they had left the flat they had continued to talk about painting and she had been interested only in her father. Be cause she now seemed so mature, Gideon noticed, Cleary was talking to his daughter as he would to an adult, with none of the half-patronising tone parents often adopt with their children. But then, he thought, Cleary was not typical of most parents. He watched Bridget sit enraptured, listening to her father describe the effect he had experienced when he first saw the Velasquez's and Goyas in the Prado.

How unfair life is, Gideon thought. Cleary had treated Bridget and his wife with indifference for years, and now, in one short evening, his daughter hero-worshipped him. The waiter hovered to take their order, but Gideon shook his head. It was going to be some time before they were ready to order food.

New York, evening the same day

Angela Wilmot sat in Flanagan's Bar, waiting for Peter Moyle. She had begun to see the detective because she was one of those women drawn to the weaknesses in men. Moyle was big and easy-going, with a deep voice and an assured manner that others generally took as an indication of a strong character, but Angela saw how he really was the first time she came into Flanagan's. Instinctively she realised that the easy-going style was actually the mark of an indecisive mind, and the bluff hearty figure who slapped shoulders and bought strangers drinks was really a man who feared people's opinions of him.

When Angela had first met Paul Van Duren, she had felt the same need, and had responded as some women would to an abandoned dog. Despite his erratic moods, and his sudden swings of temperament from fierce affection to cool indifference, she knew he needed her. Angela was a safe island he could return to. But two years earlier, Paul had changed. The general pattern of his behaviour did not alter; if anything, it intensified. But one day she realised that he did not need her any more.

460

It had happened in the early hours of the morning when he returned to the New York studio. Angela had expected him to be drunk, but he sat in a chair in the darkness and chain-smoked. Eventually she got up and made some coffee. When she put a cup in his hands, he looked up at her.

'I can't get rid of it any more,' he said in an ordinary voice. She imagined he was referring to something commonplace. If he had been drunk, she would have ignored the remark.

'You can't get rid of what?' she asked.

Paul put the coffee cup down. His eyes seemed slightly out of focus. He shrugged. 'For years, since I was a kid, I've been frightened.'

'I don't understand.'

He looked away into the darkened recesses of the studio.

'Something I see . . . Now I see it all the time.'

She tried to speak in a comforting voice. 'What made you see it before?'

He waved a hand. 'Anything smooth.' He looked at her, and saw she was still confused. 'Walls,' he said. 'Water, a clear blue sky. An empty canvas.'

'How can you be frightened of them?' she said nervously. He was more disturbing in this mood than when he was violent.

'I begin to see this shape,' he said slowly. 'It has no form. Sometimes it seems solid, massive, threatening, then it's like an open crater. As if I were being pulled into nothingness.' He stopped, drank some coffee, and began again. 'It started when I was a boy. I was looking into a grey overcast sky, and it was there.' He stopped and they sat in silence for a long time.

'How did you deal with it?' Angela asked eventually.

Paul leaned forward, hunched in his chair. 'I filled my head with images. It worked when I was in control. Sometimes when I slept I dreamed of it. I would wake up, and if it was completely dark, it would still be there.'

'And now you say it's with you all the time?'

He nodded. 'Just recently I've been seeing it constantly, like a mass at the centre of my vision.'

Angela desperately sought something comforting to say. 'This shape, this void,' she said in a soothing voice, 'have you ever tried to paint it?'

There was a long silence, and then Paul said in a weary, contemptuous voice, 'You poor, stupid, bitch. You've no idea what I've been talking about, have you?'

461

The sentence was delivered so distantly that she became aware that he had no further need of her. No matter what horror his dreadful vision filled him with, he would not come to her for refuge again.

From force of habit they stayed together for some months. Then, one night when she was alone, a friend called from Philadelphia to say that he had to speak to Paul urgently. She tried certain numbers, and Charles Whitney-Ingram suggested Flanagan's Bar. She rang, but he would not take the call. By the time she got there he had gone, but Peter Moyle bought her a drink instead.

Later in the evening Moyle suggested they might have dinner together. Nothing happened; he had drunk so much by the time he paid the bill that Angela just got them a cab and dropped him at his apartment. The following night he telephoned.

'How did you get my number?' she asked.

Moyle laughed. 'I'm a cop, remember? That's what we do, find out about people.'

'So what did you find out about me?'

Moyle paused. 'That you're a smart lady, and you don't have any prejudice about cops.'

It was Angela's turn to laugh. 'Not in my family!'

Moyle asked her out again, and she accepted. It felt good to be needed once more. Of course Moyle was married, so their affair could only develop so far. She had never raised the question of a divorce, but Moyle did constantly. He swore that nothing could mean more to him than for them to be able to live together, but his wife was a devout Catholic.

Angela saw her once, one Saturday morning in Macy's department store. She spotted Moyle first and was about to greet him when he signalled with his eyes to a fair-haired, handsome woman and two young boys. Angela passed him as if they were strangers. She and Paul continued to live together, but now their relationship was like people who shared a railway carriage, polite and indifferent. Their sex life ceased completely. But Moyle was bitterly jealous; he would question her incessantly. She knew he did not believe her assurances that nothing happened between her and Paul. He wanted her to take an apartment on her own, even though she insisted she could not afford it.

Since she had left the Archangel Gallery, there had been another curious shift in the pattern of her life. Like many women who mould their existence to suit their men, she had, unconsciously, altered her

462

class and social status. When she was with Paul she had been the companion of an artist, her conversation and speech patterns reflecting his values and expectations. Moyle was a simple, uncultivated man, so Angela changed herself to put him at ease and become more acceptable to his friends. Her accent reverted to the one she had used in childhood and, when she got another job, it was as a saleswoman in a furnishing store. She went bowling now, and the movies she saw reflected Moyle's taste, which had also become hers.

Now she sat talking casually to Pat Rourke, one of the other detectives from the precinct. 'Pete's late,' she said.

'He won't be long,' Rourke replied. 'They're busting a bookie joint.' He looked down at a noisy group by the jukebox. 'They're celebrating Clancy's engagement. Let's go join them.'

Angela picked up her drink and followed him down the bar. After a few moments she was dancing with Terry Clancy, the young detective for whom the party was being given.

Peter Moyle lay face down on the tenement landing. The floor smelt of urine, but at that moment he had other things on his mind. Eighteen inches above his head, bullets from two semi-automatic handguns chipped plaster from the decaying walls. It had been a lousy day. That morning he'd scraped a taxi on Third Avenue. He'd only had the car back from a paint job for two days, and now the off-side door was smeared with yellow streaks. In the afternoon he'd been in court and the case had gone badly; in fact the judge had been scornful of his testimony. He had barely escaped without a reprimand. Now he was lying on a stinking floor while two drugged-up spics used him as target practice. It was supposed to have been a simple bust, but when he kicked down the door, bullets had come at him like a hailstorm. His partner, Grady, had moved out of the arch of fire, and Moyle had fallen back down the flight of stairs to where he now lay.

They must have an arsenal, he thought. They'd been shooting at him for what felt like five minutes. Christ, he thought, just a few years ago all they would have been armed with would have been a couple of Saturday-night specials. These two seemed to have as much fire-power as the Marine Corps. Six more shots thudded into the wall, then he heard a shout from below.

'Police!' a voice called out. 'Who's up there?'

Moyle rolled over. 'Detective Moyle,' he shouted back. 'I'm pinned down.'

463

'Hang on,' the voice replied. 'We're coming in with gas.'

Moyle stayed on the floor until he heard feet coming up behind him on the staircase. There were two blasts of a shotgun and then the curious popping sound of a gas-grenade-launcher. One of the tear-gas shells bounced off the doorjamb and landed next to him so that he inhaled a lungful before he rolled back to bounce down the staircase. He climbed painfully to his feet and stumbled out of the building. He pushed through the group of spectators crowded round the stoop and leaned gratefully against a squad car. Tears streamed from his eyes; it was as if someone had emptied a pepper-pot into them. His throat and lungs were burning as if he had swallowed liquid fire.

Grady came out of the building after a few minutes. Behind them, the uniformed cop led away two skinny boys with their hands cuffed behind their backs. Grady came and leaned against the car. He took out a cigarette and took two long drags. 'Jesus!' he said finally. He turned to Moyle. 'What do you think? Do you want me to drive you home? I can take care of the paperwork.'

Moyle shook his head and wiped his burning eyes with the cuff of his jacket. 'No,' he said after a moment. 'I've got a date with Angela.'

Grady shrugged and held out his hand. 'Give me the keys to the car. I'll drive.'

Schneider and Strange sat in a booth near the door in Flanagan's. For the past three hours they had accompanied Paul round a series of bars where he had become progressively drunker, but he had still not given them the information they so dearly wanted. Now he had left the booth to go to the toilet, Schneider spoke quietly. 'I do not see how anyone in his condition could possibly still be painting,' he said in a bad-tempered voice.

Strange looked at his partner with distaste. 'It helps to be an alcoholic to do the kind of paintings he produces,' he said waspishly.

Schneider waved dismissively. 'You still have to be able to stand up. I tell you, I'm sure he hasn't painted anything in years.'

Strange leaned forward. 'Then why does he have paint on his clothes?'

Schneider shrugged. 'Perhaps they're old clothes,' he suggested.

Strange raised his eyes to the ceiling as if he were seeking solace. 'He has paint on his hands, as well. I tell you, he is working again. We must get hold of anything he has produced. It could ruin the market.'

When Paul came out of the men's room, he noticed Angela dancing near the jukebox with Rourke. The sight of her in another man's arms did not bother him, but he wanted to talk to her, and their paths had not crossed for a couple of days.

While he waited by the jukebox, Peter Moyle entered the crowded bar. His eyes still burned, and his suit smelled of the tenement floor. Now he was in a foul mood. There were three cops he knew standing near the entrance. 'Have you seen Angela?' he asked.

One of them laughed. 'Sure, she's having a swell time with some guy down there.' He nodded to the densely crowded end of the bar. 'He's probably humping her by now.' One of the others nodded. 'If you can't see her straight away, she'll be in one of the booths giving him a blow job.'

Moyle pushed his way through the crowd in a blind rage of jealousy. The music had stopped, and Angela was laughing at something Rourke said. She turned away from him and saw Paul standing close to her. A man pushed past him, and Paul lurched forward and blundered into her in a clumsy embrace. Moyle broke through the edge of the crowd and saw him with his arms around Angela. The day was too much for him. He drew his thirty-eight calibre revolver and shot Paul Van Duren twice through the body.

Philadelphia, early summer 1960

Paul Van Duren's mother sat in her bedroom by the open window. It was still early evening, and the room was filled with fragrant scent from the garden below. Birds sang, and a feeling of peace pervaded the room. She had spent the last hour preparing for the funeral of her son, which was to be held the following morning. All day the telephone had rung and the house had been besieged by reporters. Finally Walter Pierce, the family lawyer, had read a statement to them and asked them to leave.

Mrs Van Duren had a photograph album on her lap; she was slowly turning the pages, looking at pictures of Paul in his childhood. She remembered the boy well. The man had become a stranger to her, but that did not blunt her grief. The pain of his death was like a physical numbness now. At first she had not been able to accept the news; it was unnatural for a child to die before his parents. Her husband had coped with the information by locking himself in his study, leaving her to arrange the transport of the body home from New York. He had also told her to invite whom she thought appropriate to the funeral. She had hoped it would be quiet and dignified. Only now, under the worst possible circumstances, was she beginning to realise just how famous her son had become.

There was a gentle knock on the door, and the housekeeper entered. 'Excuse me, ma'am,' she said in a soft Irish brogue, 'Bunnington asked me to come up. He doesn't want to leave the door; there are still some reporters hanging about.'

Mrs Van Duren lifted her eyes from a photograph of her son grinning at the camera, clasping a fish he had caught on holiday in the Bahamas just after the war. 'What is it, Kathleen?' she asked.

The Irishwoman came over to her. 'There's a lady downstairs. She says she's Princess Ryson.' Kathleen had difficulty with pronunciation.

'What does she want?' Mrs Van Duren suspected she was another person from a newspaper.

'She wouldn't say, ma'am.'

Mrs Van Duren closed the book. 'A princess? Do you think she is genuine?' she asked.

Kathleen nodded. It took a true servant to recognise a genuine aristocrat. She was in no doubt.

'Show her into the drawing-room,' Mrs Van Duren said. Then she remembered that it was filled with flowers from the garden which were still to be delivered to the church. 'No, put her in my study. I'll be down directly.'

Kathleen left the bedroom and returned downstairs to the hall, where Klara was examining a portrait of one of the family ancestors. Bunnington, the butler, stood in the doorway like a graven image depicting servitude, ready to repel any unwanted callers.

'Mrs Van Duren will be down directly, ma'am,' she said to Klara. 'Would you care to follow me?' She ushered her into one of the rooms that led from the circular hall. 'This is Mrs Van Duren's study,' she explained as Klara gazed around the little room, which contained a Second Empire desk, bookcases and two easy chairs. Klara nodded, and Kathleen withdrew.

Klara could hardly believe her luck. As soon as the door closed, she went to the desk and opened an address book. She flipped through the pages and found what she was looking for after a few moments: the address of Paul's studio, which he had been so careful to keep from Strange. Quickly she copied the information into a notebook and sat down in one of the chairs.

A minute or so later the door opened and Mrs Van Duren entered. Klara stood up. The women were the same height, and each realised at once that they were dealing with equals in social standing. It often surprised Klara that these Americans had managed, in a few generations, to translate themselves from working farmers into a fair approximation of European aristocrats.

'My name is Klara Reisenauer, Mrs Van Duren,' she began. 'I was a friend of your son. Please forgive me for intruding at such a difficult time, but I thought such a visit tomorrow would be inappropriate.'

Mrs Van Duren nodded, and said nothing. Klara opened her handbag and produced a slim silver cigarette lighter. Mrs Van Duren recognised the object at once; it had been a birthday present from her husband in 1937. She had not seen it for years.

'Paul gave me this some time ago,' Klara continued. 'When I read the inscription, I realised it might have some special value to you. As I was coming to the funeral, I thought I would take the opportunity of returning it to its rightful owner.'

Mrs Van Duren took the heavy little object. 'That's very thoughtful of you,' she said after a moment.

Klara held out her hand again. 'I won't take any more of your time, but I would like to offer you my condolences, and those of my husband, Anthony Strange. Personal commitments prevent him from being here, but he did want me to say how sad he was at the terrible loss of Paul.'

Mrs Van Duren nodded, and walked to the door with Klara to bid her goodbye. When she had gone, she looked down at the lighter. Vaguely she remembered her son talking about a man called Strange, but as she recalled, it had been in terms of contempt. Oh, well, she thought; even she had to admit that Paul had been a difficult boy to get on with.

Klara had kept a taxi waiting outside the Van Duren mansion. When she left the house, four photographers took pictures of her, and she gave a brief interview to a reporter from New York who was covering the event for a society page. Then she told the driver to take her to the Colonial Inn. Every room at the hotel was booked, including the Presidential Suite. Journalists, being creatures who find security in a herd, had decided to make the Colonial Inn their headquarters. The waiters who provided room service were happy, as the press tend to be good tippers, but the girls on the switchboard

467

were frantic; they were used to the modest demands of a more stately clientèle, and the constant requests for long-distance calls were more than they could cope with. When Klara reached her room, it took some time for her call to New York to get through, but finally she was connected with her husband.

'I've got it,' she said without preliminaries and read the information to him from her notebook.

Strange and Schneider sat each side of an old-fashioned partner's desk in the New York offices of their gallery. When Strange had replaced the receiver, he tore the note from the memo pad and held it up in triumph. 'Let's go and find Benny Fisk,' he said. The drive to New Jersey did not take them long, and at Fisk's house his wife directed them to a nearby bar.

Strange entered the premises alone and found Benny seated at the bar with two cronies, watching a basket-ball game on television. All three men were thick-set and wore plaid working shirts. They left the game reluctantly and walked through to the back where a large truck was parked.

'What does this usually transport?' Strange asked.

'Furniture,' Benny answered. 'Ain't that right, Ernie?' he called out to one of the other men.

'Right,' his companion replied.

'And do you realise the keys to this warehouse we're going to are lost? Will you be able to get in?'

Benny laughed. 'Max can get in anywhere. Can't you, Max?' he said, slapping the other man on his shoulder.

'Right,' he replied. 'Anywhere.'

Benny laughed again. 'Mind you, Max can't get out of anywhere. He was locked in his last apartment for two years.'

Strange ignored the laborious joke and returned to Schneider, who was waiting in the car. In less than an hour they were back in New York, driving through empty streets lined with warehouses on the Lower West Side. After some difficulty, Schneider found the address and a few moments later Max was opening the lock with the aid of a long slender metal object.

Strange and Schneider entered the premises first. When they turned on the lights, they saw it was a large, well-lit studio. Stacked against the wall were row upon row of pictures. Spread on the floor was a large expanse of canvas that Paul had obviously been working on recently. Schneider squatted down and pressed against the surface of a thick swirl of chrome-yellow paint. The surface yielded,

468

and he saw by the bright overhead lights that he had left a clean impression of fingerprints in the soft paint. He stood up quickly and stamped on the surface so that the wet paint beneath broke through and smeared the edge of his shoe.

Strange began to direct the men as to which pictures to load on the truck.

'Aren't we going to take them all?' Schneider asked.

Strange looked at him with contempt. 'Did you ever rob a bird's nest when you were a boy?' he asked. Schneider nodded. 'Well, didn't you leave some eggs in the nest?'

Schneider shook his head. 'I always used to take them all,' he answered, puzzled.

Strange looked at him with distaste. 'That's because you weren't brought up in England. Remember, his family knew he had this studio. They're bound to send somebody to look it over. If we leave a few pictures, it will make a good story. Can't you see the newspapers? *"Secret hoard of murdered artist worth a fortune."* ' Schneider nodded. 'Van Duren's work will revert to his parents. He doesn't have any heirs. If we suggest some names to form a board of trustees, we'll still be in control of the market.'

Schneider nodded happily and watched the three men lifting a vast canvas under the careful direction of Strange. 'You know, this is going to be a lucky night for us,' he said. 'The last time I did anything like this was in 1945.'

Benny Fisk looked at the last picture Strange had indicated for removal. Then he shook his head in bewilderment. 'Who'd want to steal anything like this?' he said to Max. 'If they was mine, I'd pay for someone to take them away and drop them in the East River.'

Max nodded. 'I'm glad I ain't rich. Think of having to have this shit on your walls!'

The bar of the Colonial Inn was so crowded that Charles Whitney-Ingram had to search for minutes before he spotted Bruce Timpson, an old college friend working for a New York television company. Eventually Timpson stood up and waved for him to join the group he was with at the bar. Introductions were made, but Charles forgot the names instantly.

'How's Lydia?' Timpson asked.

'She's with her parents,' Charles answered. 'We're staying there.'

Timpson nodded. 'I forgot. This is her home town, isn't it?' He paused. 'How are things going with you and Lydia? Carole told me

469

things were a little cool between you.'

Charles took the glass of bourbon Timpson handed him, and nodded. 'Up and down, Bruce, up and down.'

Timpson shrugged. 'You heard Carole and I are getting divorced?'

'Yes,' Charles replied. 'I'm sorry.'

'Don't be. I couldn't be happier.' Timpson took a swallow of his drink. 'You know, people like us used not to get divorced. I think I'm the first in our family.' He looked around. 'Look at this circus! All for a guy who painted pictures nobody could understand.' Then he smiled. 'But I forgot. You can understand them, can't you?'

Charles waved to the busy barman with his empty glass. 'They're not for understanding, Bruce,' he said a little wearily. 'They're for appreciating. Nobody understands the Rocky Mountains or the Pacific Ocean. Paul Van Duren's paintings weren't supposed to be a story in a book you could read and follow the plot.'

Timpson shrugged. 'But they're not about anything, are they?'

Charles wasn't in the mood for this conversation. 'Yes, they are, Bruce. They're about themselves, that's all.'

Timpson laughed. 'Just think,' he said, waving at the bar again. 'Television, newsreels, radio, wire services, reporters and photo-graphers from all over the United States and the world. Just to cover the death of a man who painted pictures nobody could understand.' He raised his eyebrows and smiled again. 'That is, except for a handful of dealers, critics and collectors. No wonder "The Emperor's New Clothes" is such an all-time favourite fairy story.'

London, the same day

Richard Cleary waited for a taxi at Richmond station and glanced up at the overcast sky; he could smell the weather changing. The first drops came when he opened the cab door. The driver knew the way, and it did not take long. When they pulled up before the soot-stained church, Gideon was standing in the porch. It was raining quite hard.

The church was practically empty. A small group of people Cleary could not identify sat with shoulders bowed in the right-hand pews before the altar. He walked down the aisle and sat in a half-filled row. Now he could see who was there: Laszlo and Elizabeth, Gideon and Anne, Bridget and Irene. As the clergyman came to the altar,

470

there was the sound of footsteps and he glanced up to see the familiar figure of Peter Quick. Cleary had not seen him for some time. They nodded briefly to each other, and then the service began.

Cleary could not concentrate on the clergyman's droning voice; the words conveyed nothing to him. They seemed to hang in the damp air of the cold church like the meaningless babble of a distant conversation. He looked at the coffin for a moment, but could not connect the brass-trimmed wooden box with Nettlebury. One of the stained-glass windows depicted St George among British troops. He guessed it was some kind of memorial to the Great War. In a niche cut into a pillar stood a small statue of the Virgin Mary. It was like a plaster doll. Suddenly he thought of Paula Tuchman's work. He wondered how one of her pieces would look in the alcove. Then he glanced to his side and saw Bridget watching him. He smiled at her. When Irene turned to look at him, her face bore no expression at all.

An organ started playing, and the tiny congregation rose. The hymn, 'To Be A Pilgrim', he had known all his life. His daughter moved closer to him and held out her hymnbook. He looked down, even though he knew the words, and gradually, to his surprise, he felt tears on his cheeks.

After the service he squeezed into one of the cars with Laszlo and Elizabeth. The rain was still falling heavily, but he shared an umbrella with Peter Quick when they stood at the graveside. The clergyman continued his meaningless recital.

All Cleary could concentrate on was the composition of the dark-clad group opposite as they watched the coffin lowered into the raw, wet earth. Finally it was over, and they trudged back to the cars.

'Will you go with Irene and Bridget?' Gideon asked.

Cleary nodded. He squeezed into the back seat of the vehicle and sat next to his daughter. Nothing was said when they drew away, but after some time Irene turned to him.

'I'm surprised you came,' she said.

Cleary looked out of the window at the wet street where a group of people huddled in the rain at a bus stop. For a moment he wished he were with them. 'I liked your father very much,' he said without turning his head. 'He taught me a great deal.'

'And little good it did you,' Irene answered. 'You might just as well have got into the grave with him.' She began to cry. Bridget reached out for her.

When they reached the house at Kew, the others went in, but Cleary stood on the pavement.

471

'Are you coming in?' Gideon asked.

'I don't think so. Perhaps I shouldn't have come.'

Gideon shook his head. 'You did the right thing. Bridget will always remember you were there.'

Cleary nodded. 'Say goodbye to everyone, will you?' He set off for Kew station. Irene's words kept coming back to him. He thought of the sad, empty church and the handful of people at the graveside. And all the years Nettlebury had worked. For what? A lifetime of paintings nobody wanted. He reached the ticket office of the station and stood for a moment at the window. Suddenly he did not know where he wanted to go.

CHAPTER TWENTY-ONE

London, early autumn 1962

Elizabeth crossed the living-room of their flat in Charing Cross Road and raised the sash window. It was a bright day with small clouds moving slowly across a hard, pale sky. She shivered in the cold air and listened as Big Ben began to strike the hour: seven o'clock. The roar of London's traffic had not yet begun. A solitary policeman walked slowly across Trafalgar Square. A great cloud of pigeons rose before him and whirled, clattering into the air, to circle above St Martin-in-the-Fields before settling by the fountains once again.

Elizabeth loved living in London. When they had become rich again, she had eventually persuaded Laszlo to leave the whole of the mews house in Shepherd Market to Paul Trenton, but neither of them had wanted the problems of a larger home. Their years in Berlin had given them a preference for modest surroundings, at least in terms of space. Both liked to be within calling distance of each other. The flat on the edge of Trafalgar Square suited them admirably. When they wished to entertain on the grand scale there was always Greeve, which Harriet had restored to its former glories. Lately, however, Elizabeth had felt another calling, and today she had decided to do something about it.

In the kitchen, she set about making coffee. When they had first lived together, it was the only thing she and Laszlo disagreed about. Elizabeth preferred it the way it was served in America, weak and watery, as Laszlo described it. Gradually he had converted her to the method he had been taught in Italy. She shook the beans into the grinder and, for a moment, remembered how rarely they had tasted coffee in the war years. The Christmas of 1943 came to mind as the aromatic scent filled the room. The couple who were hiding them had a son who was serving aboard a U-boat. He had come home on leave with two pounds of coffee beans he had brought from South

473

America, and they had drunk the first of the precious brew on Christmas Day after a meal of sausage and tinned sauerkraut.

She took the coffee into the study and found Laszlo reading the newspaper. 'I didn't hear you get that,' she said.

Laszlo gazed at her over the top of his spectacles. 'I can still move with cat-like grace when I want to,' he replied drily.

Elizabeth kissed him. 'I'm glad we're awake early. We should catch the eight o'clock train easily.'

When Laszlo was in the bath, Anne rang. Elizabeth could hear him singing 'I Love Paris', imitating Maurice Chevalier.

'You've got him to go?' Anne asked.

'Yes,' Elizabeth said, looking up at the painting that hung above the telephone. It was a winter landscape by Peter Quick that Laszlo was particularly fond of. 'He thinks I want some of the furniture. Actually most of it is lovely, but I want more than that.' The sound of the Chevalier imitation ended and Elizabeth said, 'I'll ring you later, when we get back.'

At ten to eight, well-wrapped against the cold, Elizabeth and Laszlo strolled to Charing Cross station and bought tickets for Little Fenton. The journey took just over an hour. Laszlo was absorbed by a book the entire time; the countryside of Kent passed by without his giving it a momentary glance.

'We're here,' Elizabeth said eventually.

He looked out of the window at the little Victorian station. 'I hope there's a taxi,' he said when they stood on the platform.

'There's no need. It's only a few minutes' walk.'

Laszlo glanced across the track as the train pulled out. 'Fields?' he said with surprise.

'What did you expect? The Sahara desert?'

Laszlo shook his head and followed her through the booking office into the station forecourt. They stopped for a moment and Elizabeth gestured at the narrow road, lined with hedgerows and elm trees, which curved away from the station. To the left was a dairy farm. Cows grazed in the distant meadows; they looked like lead toys to Laszlo. At a narrow point in the triangle between the road and the railway line was a wood.

'What kind of trees are they?' Elizabeth asked as they strolled in the direction of the village.

Laszlo looked at the autumn colours of the foliage before he replied, 'Oak, ash, beech. That one is a hornbeam. People often think they're beech trees; you can see how similar they are.'

474

Elizabeth followed his pointing finger. 'How many times have you seen a hornbeam?'

Laszlo smiled. 'I think this is the first time, outside paintings,' he replied.

The wood ended at a village pond fringed with rushes. There was a wide green edged with horse-chestnut trees and a Norman church next to a barn with a beautiful tiled roof.

'That's the building I told you about,' Elizabeth said.

They stopped, and Laszlo saw how the village rose behind the church to give a foreshortened effect to the landscape. Something stirred in his memory, like the echo of a half-remembered snatch of song.

'That's a tithe-barn,' he said, studying the half-familiar landscape. 'Tithes were a tenth of the produce of the farms. They gave them to support the clergy. That's where the produce was stored.'

Elizabeth smiled and shook her head. 'How do you know so much about the countryside?' she said, chiding him.

'It's amazing what you can pick up from books. I can even tell pigs from sheep!'

When they turned into the main street of the village, he asked, 'How did you and Anne find this place? It's a bit off the beaten track.'

Elizabeth stopped and looked into the window of a butcher's shop. 'Anne and Irene spent a summer holiday here when they were children. She wanted to see if it had changed. Apparently it hasn't at all.' Then she nudged him in the ribs. 'Remember those sausages you liked so much last Saturday? This is where I bought them.'

Laszlo looked at the sausages and then glanced at his watch. It was nine-fifteen. 'Well, you'd better buy some more when they're open.'

They walked on up the steep, cobbled hill and paused to look at a small rose-brick Georgian house that stood on the brow behind low iron railings, framed by two beech trees. They turned to look back down the village street. There were more people about now. A horse-drawn drayman's cart was unloading kegs of beer at the public house half-way up the hill and a greengrocer was opening his shop.

Then Laszlo looked at the notice on the gate.

'Oh, dear,' Elizabeth said. 'I must have read it wrong. I thought the sale began at nine-thirty.'

Laszlo shook his head. 'How unlike you,' he said with a smile.

Elizabeth shrugged. 'It's a lovely day. We could go on walking for a bit.' She pointed to a gap between two of the red-brick cottages. 'That leads down to the edge of the woods. It's very pretty.'

475

Laszlo still felt the echoing sense of a half-remembered thought. They walked between the high banks of the narrow lane and emerged next to the wall of the Georgian house. He looked down from the high ground, and the sensation overwhelmed him. There was something so familiar about the view, yet it still would not come to him. Then two geese came honking at them from one of the cottage gardens and he suddenly saw them against the background of a holly bush. He turned his head slightly, and the bush was just where it should be. This was the point where Peter Quick had painted his winter landscape.

Laszlo studied the view for some time, then he turned to Elizabeth with a smile. 'How much is it?' he asked.

'What?' she replied innocently.

'The house. I ought to know when I'm being sold something!'

Elizabeth smiled with relief and began to talk quickly. 'There's a reserve of fifteen thousand pounds for the house and contents. It's a listed property; it was built for one of Nelson's captains. His family still lived in it until two months ago. Peter Quick showed me an article about it in *Country Life* when he was in the gallery last week.'

Laszlo nodded. 'We'd better go and take a closer look.' They walked back to the front of the property and he read the name over the door: 'Trafalgar House,' he said softly. 'This is too much of a coincidence.'

Elizabeth took his arm. 'Maybe some things are meant to be,' she said happily.

'I'll tell you if it was meant to be when the bidding goes over twenty thousand!'

Just then a man in a dark suit emerged from a car and unlocked the gates. 'Good morning,' he said cheerfully. 'My name is Garfield. I'm the auctioneer. We're still a bit early, but you can take a look, if you like.'

Laszlo thanked the man and they walked around the side of the building so that Elizabeth could show him the gardens. At the front there were beech trees, laurels and small lawns each side of a gravel path that led to the pillared doorway. A red-brick wall curved round the brow of the hill at the back of the house. There were more lawns, fruit trees and a box hedge screening a vegetable garden. Dominating everything was a tall walnut tree. Elizabeth stooped to pick up one of the fallen nuts, still half-encased in its outer flesh shell.

'Don't touch that!' Laszlo said urgently, and she straightened up

476

with a puzzled expression. He took a handkerchief from his pocket and picked it up. After he had removed the outer case, he broke open the still wet shell and gave half the nut to Elizabeth and ate half himself. Then he showed her the dark brown stain on the white handkerchief.

'Walnut juice. There's no way you can get it off your hands.'

Elizabeth smiled. 'I suppose you read that in a book as well?'

Laszlo shook his head. 'If you want to make a wish,' he said, 'now's the time to do it.'

Elizabeth did as she was instructed and they walked to the entrance. They were still the first. They found Mr Garfield and an assistant setting up his lectern in one of the drawing-rooms, which was quite bare except for some empty display-cases.

Mr Garfield could see the curiosity on Laszlo's face. 'The last member of the family, Mr Gerald, was a bachelor who devoted himself to his collection of antiquarian statues and drawings,' he explained. 'He left the contents of this room as a bequest to the Ashmolean Museum.'

Laszlo nodded, and he and Elizabeth continued to explore. They encountered other people now, and nodded to each other in a polite fashion as they moved about the rooms. He liked the little house; most of the furniture had been made when it was new and crafted for the rooms it occupied. Everything was in pleasing proportion, nothing grand, just good serviceable pieces, lovingly cared for by generations of occupants.

One item did puzzle him. It was in the bedroom that he assumed the last owner of the house had used. The room bore the signs of a bachelor's habitation: plain wooden furniture, brass lamps and an old leather armchair near the fireplace. There were bookshelves, a set of steel engravings of the ruins of ancient Rome and a very old photograph of a group of young men in an Oxford quadrangle. In these surroundings a large piece of eighteenth-century French furniture in the bay window, half obscuring the view from the rear of the house, was an oddity. The piece was florid. Heavily inlaid with marquetry and gilded in parts, it was both a desk and a storage cabinet.

Laszlo opened some of the drawers; they were all empty. 'See if the door locks,' he said quietly to Elizabeth. She crossed the room and turned a key. He looked at the surface of the marquetry on the writing area for a moment and said, 'Do you have any face-powder with you?' Intrigued, Elizabeth handed him her compact. He

477

sprinkled some powder on the surface and blew gently, to distribute a thin layer across the whole area.

Elizabeth could see that the powder had settled in fine lines between sections of the marquetry. He spread both hands and pressed with his fingertips on the four sections of inlaid wood. There was a click, and the surface of the desk rose to reveal a shallow concealed panel. Inside were five large sheets of paper, separated by tissue, and a letter. He looked through them quickly and closed the panel. He wiped the surface with the walnut-stained handkerchief and winked at Elizabeth. They unlocked the door and walked downstairs again.

The room that had housed the antiquarian collection was almost full now. Laszlo saw a couple of antique dealers, three other couples who were clearly home-buyers and a few people who had just come along for something to do. Garfield began the bidding, and Laszlo joined in when it reached £17,500. An antiques dealer in a sheepskin coat took him to £19,000, then dropped out. Laszlo bought the house and the contents for £19,100. When they had completed the formalities, Garfield shook hands and handed them a bunch of keys.

'Let's go and buy some sausages,' Laszlo said to Elizabeth and they walked out into the cold October air.

Now that they were going to live in the village, he looked at the main street with new eyes. He could see why Elizabeth had fallen in love with the place. There was a variety of houses on each side of the cobbled street. All lay in the line of buildings, but some had narrow front gardens, others forecourts. There were shops and a variety of façades: cottages, double-fronted houses with white porticoes and iron balconies. Lanes led off on both sides of the street.

The public house, called The Victory, was open now; through an archway they could see a cobbled yard and stables. They opened the door and were greeted by the scent of wood logs burning in a wide inglenook fireplace. The floor was covered with large stone flags. A young man in shirtsleeves greeted them in a country accent. 'Come for the sale, have you?' he asked in a friendly fashion.

'We bought the house,' Laszlo said.

The young man smiled and held out his hand. 'I'm Bob Doggert. If you're going to be neighbours, I'd better buy you the first drink.'

'My name is Laszlo Vasilakis, and this is my wife Elizabeth.'

Bob Doggert laughed. 'My Lord, that's a mouthful!' He called out, 'Daphne, come out here a moment.'

A young woman answered his summons, looking sturdily built

478

with a fresh face and dark hair. Elizabeth guessed she was from a farming family. 'This is Mr and Mrs Vasi . . . Vasser . . . Blessed if I can pronounce the name. What was it again, sir?'

'Laszlo Vasilakis and Elizabeth.'

'I take it you'll be Elizabeth,' the young woman said in the same friendly tones as her husband.

'They've bought Trafalgar House,' Bob told his wife.

Daphne Doggert nodded. 'Did Mr Garfield mention my sister?' she asked.

Laszlo and Elizabeth exchanged glances. 'No, I'm afraid not,' Laszlo answered. 'What was he supposed to say?'

Now it was the Doggerts' turn to look at each other. Daphne sighed in exasperation. 'My sister Ruth looked after the house for old Mr Gerald. She went in every day for the last fifteen years. And her eldest boy, my nephew Martin, he's looked after the garden and done all the odd jobs.' She paused and shrugged. 'Mr Garfield said he'd put a word in for them with the new owners. No guarantee like, just a recommendation.'

Elizabeth nodded sympathetically. 'I'm sure it just slipped his mind. Perhaps we could meet them while we're here?'

'What time are you leaving?' Bob Doggert asked.

Laszlo looked at his watch. 'In about an hour and a half. We thought we'd do some shopping and catch a later train back to town.'

'We could fetch them in an hour,' Daphne said.

Laszlo nodded, and ordered another drink. 'Is there anywhere we can get some lunch?'

'You can get lunch right here,' Daphne answered. 'We started a dining-room in the spring.'

'That's right,' Bob added. 'We started when the boys in the barn began to eat us out of bread and cheese.'

'The barn?' Elizabeth asked.

Bob nodded. 'Last year two young lads bought the tithe barn from the church. They set up a business down there.'

'What are they doing?' Laszlo asked.

'Writing software programmes for computers,' Bob told him.

'What on earth is that?' Elizabeth asked.

'Blessed if I know! But it doesn't get them very dirty. They don't wear overalls to work. Mind you, they do work long hours. Some of them come in here before closing time for a pint. They're a nice crowd, but nobody can understand a word they say when they talk about their work.'

'You can't tell it's a business from the outside,' said Elizabeth.

Bob nodded. 'That was one of the conditions of the sale. They couldn't alter the appearance of the building and they have to park their cars the other side of Fenton Wood, so you can't see them from any part of the village.'

Laszlo and Elizabeth finished their drinks and set off on their shopping expedition. They bought sausages, and fruit from the greengrocer. There was also a small arts and crafts shop run by a rather grand old lady in tweeds. She sold hand-thrown pots and art supplies.

Laszlo bought two half-Imperial sheets of art board and Elizabeth selected a pot she liked. Then they walked back to Trafalgar House and made for the bedroom.

Laszlo sprang the concealed drawer in the cabinet and took out the drawings he had discovered earlier. He placed them carefully between the two sheets of board, sealed them together with sticky tape, and put the letter in the inside pocket of his jacket.

When they walked back to the saloon bar of The Victory, Bob Doggert waved to them from the end of the counter. Ruth and Martin were waiting to be introduced. Their family name was Colter; Elizabeth could see the resemblance to Daphne. She liked the look of them at once.

'I do hope you will go on looking after Trafalgar House for us,' she said.

The woman gave a smile of relief to her sister, who nodded encouragement.

'How often would you want me to come?' she asked.

Elizabeth thought for a moment. 'Well, we shall only come down at weekends. Friday or Saturday nights, probably.'

'Oh, so you won't be here every day?' Mrs Colter said with a hint of worry in her voice.

Elizabeth understood her concern immediately. 'How much did the previous owner pay you, Mrs Colter?' she asked quietly.

'Mr Gerald gave me six pounds a week, and Martin got three pounds for looking after the gardens.'

Elizabeth nodded again. 'Well, if you can keep the house in the same way you always have, I'll pay you ten pounds a week. And Martin can have five pounds for looking after the gardens.'

Mrs Colter beamed at her son, who put down his pint. 'One thing, sir,' he said to Laszlo. 'The vegetable garden produces a lot of stuff and Mr Gerald used to let me keep some of the extra.'

Laszlo shrugged. 'Just go on doing what you did before,' he said.

'When do you want me to start, Mrs . . . er . . . Mrs . . . ?'

Elizabeth laughed. 'Vasilakis,' she repeated. 'Right away. In fact, we'd better leave the keys with you.'

'That's all right, Mrs Vasilakis,' Mrs Colter said, managing the name quite well. 'I've still got a set.'

A moment later, two young men came to the bar and ordered pints of bitter. 'What's for lunch, Daphne?' the taller of them asked.

'Egg and bacon pie,' she replied.

Bob Doggart drew the beer they'd ordered and nodded to the two men. 'New neighbours for you . . .' he said, 'Mr Vasilakis and his wife. They've bought Trafalgar House. This is Roger Brantree and Clive Chilton. They run the barn.'

Elizabeth and Laszlo shook hands with the young men. Brantree was the taller of the two; he wore a dark suit and looked a great deal smarter than Clive Chilton, who was short and tubby with a shock of wiry brown hair, and spectacles that had been repaired with tape. His hands, when he took them from his sports jacket, were surprisingly delicate.

When Daphne announced that the food was ready, they went into the dining-room. Laszlo and Elizabeth shared a table with the two men.

'That's a lovely house you've bought,' Chilton said. 'My wife and I had a look at it, but she wanted something more modern. How much did you pay?' Laszlo told him. Chilton whistled. 'That's more than I could have gone to. I hope it's worth it!'

Laszlo smiled. 'I think so,' he said, and took a mouthful of egg and bacon pie.

New York State, early October 1962

It was so cold in the duck hide that Gideon decided to drink the last of the brandy. He emptied the silver flask into the plastic cup and topped it up with coffee. As he raised it to his mouth, Charles Whitney-Ingram's gun barked twice and Frank Cooper called out, 'Good shot!' The two Irish setters plunged into the cold water of the lake and swam out to retrieve the ducks that had fallen nearby.

'That's it for the day,' Cooper said.

Charles laid aside his shotgun and blew on his hands. 'Is there any brandy left?' he asked.

481

Gideon handed him the last of the drink he had just mixed and plunged his hands deep into the pockets of his thick hunting jacket.

'My God!' Charles said with enthusiasm. 'Will you look at that sunrise!'

Gideon glanced towards the horizon. 'If someone presented you with a picture painted in those colours, you'd laugh him out of the gallery,' he said grumpily. The early morning sky was now a garish mixture of orange, vermilion, yellow and pale blue-green.

'God's allowed to be corny,' Charles replied. 'Anyway, it was your idea to come up here.'

'I just said let's get out of New York,' Gideon retorted. 'I didn't say anything about satisfying the killer instinct.'

'Come on,' Charles said with good humour, 'when did you last have so much fun?'

Gideon tried to remember. 'December 1944, during the Battle of the Bulge. It was the last time I was as cold as this, too.'

Cooper, who had brought the rowing-boat to their hide, heard the answer. 'Were you in the Battle of the Bulge?' he asked. Gideon nodded. 'Well, what do you know? I was in Bastogne with the 101st Airborne.' He thought for a moment. 'You know something? You're right. It was more fun shooting Krauts.'

They climbed into the boat and Gideon sat facing the two Irish setters as Cooper rowed them to the landing jetty across the lake.

Gideon looked up at the hotel in appreciation. Although it was modelled on a Ruritanian hunting-lodge, it had hot baths, warm beds, and he could smell the scent of frying bacon.

'I'm just going to wash my hands in the men's room,' said Charles. 'I'll shower and shave after breakfast.' He turned to their companion. 'Are you coming in for a cup of coffee, Frank?'

Cooper shook his head. 'No, thanks. I've got to open the store and get the kids up for school.' He opened the door of his pick-up truck and the two dogs jumped in. 'See you later,' he called out.

The washroom was close to the door of the hotel. Charles filled a basin and washed his face and hands. While he was drying his cheeks with a paper towel, he looked at his reflection in the mirror, and said, 'You know Lydia's left me?' in a flat voice.

Gideon continued washing his hands. 'I thought something like that had happened,' he answered. Charles lit a cigarette and inhaled deeply. 'Are you going to get a divorce, Charles?'

Charles shrugged. 'I don't know. The guy she's moved in with is married. I suppose it could happen eventually.'

'Do you still love her?' Gideon wished he could think of something more original to say.

Charles ran the tap on the burning end of the cigarette and dropped it in the waste-basket before he answered. 'I don't know if I ever loved her in the usual meaning of the word,' he said mildly. 'She's not like most other women I've met.' He slapped his hand against one of the toilet doors. 'You know the way some guys are? The ones who can never give up chasing women?' Gideon nodded. 'She's like that. A lot of fun when she's around, but there's always another blonde or redhead she wants to try for.' He paused. 'She used to tell me about them. Funny. It seems fine when a guy does it.'

Gideon couldn't think of anything to say as he followed him into the lobby. When they passed the reception desk, the clerk called out, 'Mr Gideon, Mr Whitney-Ingram, there's a gentleman looking for you.'

They stopped. 'What kind of gentleman?' Charles asked.

The young man put down his ballpoint pen. 'He's about sixty, with grey hair and conservative clothes. He wears a vest with a fraternity symbol on the watch-chain, and he's about five-ten and 180 pounds. Speaks well. I'd guess he was a lawyer.'

'Did he mention his name?' Gideon asked.

The clerk looked down at his pad. 'Walter Pierce.'

'Where is he now?' Charles asked.

The clerk picked up his pen again and pointed across the lobby. 'In the coffee-shop.'

Charles turned to Gideon while they headed for the door. 'That's what you get from a generation brought up on detective shows. Television has changed this country.'

Walter Pierce looked up when the two men entered the room. The only person there, he was sitting at a table near the window. There was a cup of coffee before him, a pack of Camels and a lighter. They had been arranged neatly, square with the paper coaster. 'You must be James Gideon,' he said without smiling. 'And you, Charles Whitney-Ingram.'

They sat down opposite him. 'How can you tell?' Charles asked.

Pierce nodded towards Gideon. 'Your friend has an English haircut,' he replied, and now he smiled. 'Gentlemen, I need your help.'

Before he could say anything else, the waitress arrived and filled their water glasses. Charles ordered breakfast. Gideon settled for coffee.

483

'I'm a lawyer,' Pierce began, 'representing the Van Duren family. I understand Paul Van Duren was a client of yours once?'

'We sold his pictures until he moved to the Strange and Schneider gallery,' Charles answered.

Pierce frowned slightly. 'Didn't he have a contract with you?' Charles shook his head. 'Why not?'

Charles shrugged. 'We're an art gallery, not a movie studio. If people don't want to deal with us, that's fine. The policy has always worked in the past.'

Pierce's face cleared. 'So it's not true that you lost Van Duren's contract in a poker game?'

'That's an old story people like to tell,' Charles explained. 'The truth is, he lost himself in the game.'

Pierce sighed. 'Well, that's a pity. It would have been quite illegal, and I could have settled this whole business easily.'

The waitress brought their order, and Gideon asked, 'What business, Mr Pierce?'

The lawyer lit a cigarette before he answered. 'The Van Duren family don't know a lot about art. In fact, I can go so far as to say that they haven't bought a picture since before the Civil War. Paul was a complete mystery to them, but they're kind of proud of his reputation now. When he died, he didn't leave a will and all his estate reverted to the family. The contract that Strange and Schneider had with him was a poor document; it stated only that they could sell the paintings he supplied to them. It was okay if they actually had possession of the pictures, but until that point they still belonged to Paul.'

Gideon nodded. He could see immediately what Pierce was getting at. 'So what happened to the pictures that were in his studio?'

Pierce waved his cigarette. 'They came into the possession of the family, and the family didn't have a contract with Strange and Schneider.'

'Go on,' Charles said between mouthfuls of egg.

Pierce sighed again. 'I checked on the reputation of Schneider and Strange after the family had taken their advice about appointing a board of trustees to administer the disposal of the pictures.' He shrugged. 'You understand, the family were proud of Paul's reputation, but they didn't want to have the paintings around the house. They were hoping they'd go to museums where they wouldn't actually have to visit them. Preferably in other countries, in fact.'

484

Charles smiled grimly and pushed his empty plate away. 'So what happened?'

'A very peculiar thing,' said Pierce. 'The trustees started selling the pictures, but they were only getting peanuts for them, and they were all going to private collectors.' He held out his empty coffee-cup to the waitress, and she brought him more. He took a sip and added some sugar. 'Now, the Van Duren family don't know a damn thing about art, but they know an awful lot about money. That's why they set me on the business.'

Gideon nodded. 'So Strange and Schneider have got to the trustees and are buying the pictures in at nominal rates?'

'I understand from the people I've been talking to that if they get them all, they'll be able to rig the market,' said Pierce.

Charles took a cigarette. 'That's right, Mr Pierce.'

Pierce shook his head. 'Well, they've picked on the wrong people this time. The Van Durens have gone to the Supreme Court of New York to invalidate their contract. Strange and Schneider were greedy gentlemen, and now they must suffer.' He spoke the last sentence with a certain relish.

'This has been a long trip just to tell us that,' said Gideon.

The lawyer sat back in his chair, and smiled. 'There's more. The family want the Archangel Gallery to act as agents for the estate. It's quite extensive. We've put a court order on the pictures they still have in their possession. We can't do a damn thing about the ones they've already sold, or the ones they own personally, but in about two years' time the pictures that are frozen will be available. Are you interested?'

Gideon and Charles nodded in unison. 'We'd be delighted, Mr Pierce,' said Gideon. 'And you can assure the Van Duren family that in two years the price of Paul's work will amaze them.'

Pierce smiled, and sat back. 'Good! You know there are no real hard feelings towards these two guys. After all, it's only what the Van Durens did with half the coal mines in West Virginia a hundred and fifty years ago. Perhaps that was their problem: they were just old-fashioned.' He stood up. 'I'll be in touch.' After he had walked out, they began to laugh.

When Gideon eventually returned to his room, he was shaving when Anne woke up.

'Did you shoot any duck?' she called out.

'I didn't,' he answered with a certain amount of satisfaction, 'but a very nice man called Walter Pierce got two for me.'

485

Anne and Gideon returned to London on an overnight flight the following day. When they reached the flat, she went to bed, but Gideon, although disorientated by the flight and tired, could not sleep. Eventually he dressed and went down to the gallery. Graham Todd, a young graduate who had just joined the gallery, gave him a message asking him to meet Laszlo at one o'clock in Prunier's restaurant, if he could make it. It was already half-past, but he decided to go. It was only a few minutes' walk away in St James's Street.

When he entered the restaurant, Laszlo was at a table with Piet Liebe. The old Dutchman was devouring a vast platter of oysters. Gideon noted the quality of the champagne in the ice-bucket and realised that Laszlo was seeking a favour.

'My dear Gideon,' Liebe said in his faultless English, 'I can recommend these fellows.' Gideon shook his head and ordered a grilled Dover sole. 'Just back from America, eh?' Liebe said, sliding another oyster down his throat. 'You're probably too full of protein. All that red meat they eat. You should have settled for a salad.'

Gideon smiled. 'How are you, Piet? The people of Amsterdam will feel their savings are safe with you out of the country!'

Liebe sat back and sipped a little champagne. 'I have never been better,' he said, brushing his little spade-shaped beard with the back of his hand.

Gideon noticed the speckle of liver spots. No one knew what age the Dutchman was; Laszlo said he could remember him coming to his father's shop when he was a boy, and he had seemed old even then.

'Let me show you what I have acquired today,' Liebe said, and took a carrier-bag from beneath the table and passed it to Gideon. Inside were three oil paintings that had been removed from their stretchers and rolled and secured with elastic bands. 'I bought them this morning. Aren't they beautiful?'

Gideon examined the pictures. They were exquisite. He recognised the work of a nineteenth-century German painter called Wilhelm Leibl.

'These will be with me in my house tonight,' Liebe said with contentment, taking another swallow of champagne.

Gideon raised his eyebrows. 'Are you just going to walk through customs with them?'

'Certainly. It says in my passport that I am an artist. Our names are similar enough; if I am stopped, I shall merely say I painted them myself.' He turned to Laszlo. 'I was about to tell you about Adolph Block's widow.'

Laszlo nodded. 'Go on.'

'You know Block's collection; very eclectic?' said Liebe. Laszlo nodded again. 'He loved only his parrot as much as that collection. You remember the wife who was always sunning herself in the south of France?' Laszlo smiled. 'Well, when Block died, a curious thing happened to her. She began to worship his memory. His collection became an obsession with her and she turned it into a sort of shrine to him. She kept his parrot in the room on an iron stand; it had a chain so that it could fly about a bit.' The waiter poured more champagne, then he continued. 'Block had a Dada piece he was very proud of. It consisted of a small metal gallows and, hanging from it on a piece of string, a bratwurst sausage. It was titled *Retribution*. One night the widow went out to dinner, and when she got home, a calamitous thing had happened.' He paused, relishing the story. 'The parrot had eaten half the sausage and died. Of course the woman was distraught. She sent the bird to a taxidermist and then she rang me. I hurried around to her apartment and examined the damage. She pleaded with me to find a solution, so I recommended that she get in touch with Willi Swann.'

Laszlo and Gideon nodded. Willi Swann was a famous picture restorer with an international reputation.

'So what happened?' Laszlo asked.

Liebe brushed his beard again. 'I ran into him last week and asked him what he had done. Willi said he'd told her it would be a difficult job. Then he kept the piece for a month in his studio before he bought another sausage from the butcher and gave it a coat of varnish. He charged her 1,000 marks for the job.' While they laughed, he squeezed from the table. 'I must answer the call of nature,' he said.

'Why are you seeing the old rogue?' Gideon asked when he was out of earshot.

Laszlo took an envelope from his pocket and handed it to Gideon. There was no address, merely the words, 'To whom it may concern.'

Gideon took a single sheet of paper out of the envelope. The writing was in a fine copperplate hand and the date in the top right-hand corner was 15th August 1959. The letter said:

My name is Gerald Thornton. I have lived a long and extremely pleasant life, but I suspect it will come to an end quite soon.

If you have been able to find this letter and the contents of the compartment, you must have some intelligence, so I am sure you will have deduced that I had a reason for concealing the drawings. Quite simply, they are all stolen property.

The bulk of my collection has gone to the Ashmolean, but it would cause fearful embarrassment to present them with objects of such contention. The first three belonged to a Russian grand duke whose other treasures were confiscated by the Bolsheviks. The fourth was at one time supposedly in the collection of J.P. Morgan, a most unpleasant man. I once had luncheon with him and can bear witness to his character. The last, which I only recently acquired, is a mystery. Perhaps you may solve it.

There was no signature. Gideon folded the letter away and handed it back to Laszlo. Before he could ask any question, Liebe returned, and they continued the meal. When it was finished the Dutchman wiped his mouth carefully with his napkin and said, 'Now I shall sing for my supper.'

Laszlo reached down and produced a slim leather portfolio. Liebe took it on his lap and untied the ribbon. Inside were the five drawings Laszlo had found in the desk.

'My God!' Liebe said in a hushed voice. He slowly leafed through the sheets, only touching the edges with his fingertips. When he had finished, he tied the tape and handed the portfolio back to Laszlo. 'I think I deserve a decent brandy after that,' he said. 'You shouldn't shock an old man so!'

'Well?' Laszlo asked finally.

Liebe nodded. 'The two red chalk drawings are by Michelangelo. The pen and ink studies are definitely Rembrandts. The Raphael drawing is a fake.'

'Are you sure?' Laszlo asked.

'Quite sure,' said Liebe. 'Although it could easily be sold as the genuine article.' Laszlo nodded. 'Where did you get them?' the Dutchman asked.

Laszlo winked at him. 'A friend left them to me in his will.'

'If you want a buyer, I can arrange it,' said Liebe. 'And I could get full market value for them.'

Laszlo shook his head. 'No thank you, Piet. I already have a good home for them.'

Liebe looked at his watch. 'In that case, I must be off. I'm having dinner in Amsterdam tonight.'

488

They saw him into a taxi and walked up St James's Street towards the gallery. Gideon had not spoken. 'I wonder if he's right about the Raphael,' Laszlo said. 'You know how devious Piet can be.'

'It's definitely a fake,' Gideon replied thoughtfully.

'How can you be so sure? It's not your period.'

Gideon turned to him with a smile. 'That one is,' he replied as they reached Piccadilly. 'As a matter of fact, I drew it.'

Gideon and Laszlo did not go on to the gallery, but went to Gideon's flat and sat facing each other in the armchairs on either side of the fireplace. Gideon took the portfolio from Laszlo and examined it once more.

'You're quite sure?' Laszlo asked.

Gideon nodded. 'I remember Julian Nettlebury asking me to do it. He wrote the instructions; they were very precise. "Prepare a cartoon that Raphael might have drawn for a study of Plato and Aristotle for his picture, *The School of Athens*." This was the work I did.'

Laszlo thought for a time. 'Just how much did you do for Nettlebury?' he asked.

'Dozens of drawings and paintings. He used to make me work bloody hard!'

Laszlo took the sketch from Gideon and put it back in the portfolio. 'And what happened to them all?' he asked.

Gideon scratched his chin. 'They all stayed at Kew. Julian would have either destroyed them or filed them away. You remember how meticulous he was. He despised artists who worked in disorder. Richard Cleary used to call him the civil servant.'

Laszlo tapped his hand on the arm of the chair. 'We must find them all. It's vital!'

Gideon rose and stood with his hands in his pockets, leaning against the fireplace. 'Why? It all happened years ago. The only one we ever sold was the Brueghel, and we never claimed it was an original, even then.'

Laszlo frowned. 'The whole foundation of the Archangel Gallery is based on our reputation for honesty. People still remember you as the man who destroyed fakes. Think what would happen if they knew you possessed the skills that you do. No one would trust a painting we sold them!'

Gideon could see the logic in his argument. 'What shall we do?'

Laszlo took the Raphael sketch from the portfolio without speaking. He placed it in the empty grate and put a match to it. The

489

thick, hand-made paper caught after a moment, and the image remained when the fire had consumed it. He crumbled the curled sheet to dust. 'We must destroy everything we can find,' he announced. Then he got up and leaned against the fireplace. 'What about those cupboards downstairs in the basement?'

Gideon shrugged. 'We never really paid much attention to Julian's work. Remember, we told Ovington to concentrate on the other stuff.'

'Let's go downstairs and check them now,' Laszlo urged.

Below, in the gallery, business was brisk. Laszlo's practised eye could tell that two of the assistants were closing sales. Anne was on the telephone when they passed her office. She had clearly got over her jet-lag.

When they reached the basement, Gideon found the keys and opened the first metal locker. Inside were rows of files. The second contained stationery, and the third was empty. While they were still gazing at the contents in a perplexed fashion, Anne joined them.

'Looking for envelopes?' she asked.

Gideon turned to her. 'What happened to all the stuff that was in here?'

Anne looked at them both, and sighed. 'I told you ages ago. Bernard Ovington took everything that could be restored back to his studio.'

'What about your father's work?' Laszlo asked.

Anne shut the doors to the cupboard. 'We sent it back to Kew years ago. Irene wanted it.'

Gideon glanced at his watch. 'What time will she be home?'

Anne could sense their concern. 'What's the matter?'

'Something has come up,' Gideon answered.

Anne thought for a moment. 'She won't be going home tonight, she's promised to take Bridget to the theatre.'

'Can we ring her now?' Gideon asked.

'I'll see if I can get her.' When she got through, Gideon took the receiver.

'Sorry to bother you at work,' he said.

Irene laughed. 'Teaching teenagers the history of art isn't work, it's drudgery! I was glad of the interruption.'

'Irene,' Gideon said intensely, 'may we come over this evening and look through Julian's collection? I must find something urgently.'

There was a pause. 'Oh, darling,' she replied, 'I can't be there this evening. I've promised Bridget a night out. She's looking forward to it.'

490

'That's all right. Anne has a key. We can look ourselves.'

There was another pause. 'You'll never find anything without me,' she said. 'The collection is all over the house. Can't you come in the morning? I'm free until noon.'

Gideon thought for a moment. 'No, that's impossible. Laszlo and I are on the early flight to Berlin. We can't get out of it.'

Irene thought again. 'How about late tonight? I promised to take her to supper.'

'Where are you going?' he asked.

'Luigi's.'

'What if we joined you there?' Gideon suggested. 'I'll fix the table.'

'Fine,' Irene replied. 'Better make it for ten-thirty. You'll feel awful in the morning after such a late night.'

Gideon replaced the receiver and saw Anne's expression. 'We have a bit of a problem,' he said. 'You'd better sit down.'

Anne did as he suggested. 'Is this a story with a beginning. We're in the middle at the moment.' Then he began to tell her about the find at Trafalgar House.

'So, you see,' Gideon said finally, 'the reputation of the Archangel Gallery is of paramount importance. We've been appointed as trustees to the Van Duren estate because we're pure as the driven snow. Now a drawing turns up that I faked. If that news got out, people wouldn't come to our gallery to buy a reproduction of Constable's *Hay Wain*.'

'But you didn't fake a Raphael,' Anne said. 'They were just exercises for Dad.'

Laszlo shook his head. 'No one would believe that.'

'So what are we going to do?' Anne asked.

Gideon drummed his fingers on the corner of the desk. 'There's only one thing we can do. Track down as much as we can, and destroy it.'

'Who do you think sold the Raphael sketch?' she asked.

Gideon shrugged. 'Everything passed backwards and forwards between here and the house at Kew.' He nodded towards the basement. 'Part of the work was down there for years.' He held up his hands. 'The one thing we do know for certain is that the drawing was bought by Gerald Thornton in 1959. It could have been around for years before that.' Suddenly he felt a wave of tiredness. The jet-lag was getting to him. 'I think I'll sleep for a few hours. It could be a long night.'

Anne nodded sympathetically. 'I'll be up to see if you want

anything in a little while.'

He was cold when he climbed the stairs to the flat, and numb with weariness. When did I last felt so tired? Gideon thought. It must have been when I was in the army. He took his clothes off at the bedside and let them fall to the floor. As he pulled the coverlet over himself, he remembered Frank Cooper saying, 'I was in the Battle of the Bulge.' Life was simple then, he thought. Just life or death. How complicated the pieces in the middle could be. Then he went to sleep.

Bridget felt a surge of affection for her mother as they walked along the Aldwych towards the theatre that evening. It was caused by the admiring glance a young man gave them both as they strolled along the wide wet pavement. Bridget was happy. London seemed exciting; she loved the crowds and the roar of traffic.

She took Irene's arm, and said, 'My friend Allyson Woodcraft didn't believe you were my mother. She thought you looked like my sister.'

Irene laughed. 'Maybe it wasn't a compliment to me *but* an insult to you?'

'Rubbish!' Bridget said. 'All my friends think you look ever so young.' She gazed up at the lights over the theatre. '*The City Boys*,' she said aloud. 'It really is supposed to be marvellous. All my friends have seen it. I do hope you like it, Mum.'

Irene laughed again. 'Well, if I'm young enough to be taken for your sister, maybe I'll be young enough to enjoy it.'

Bridget thought about her comment. 'You know it's about people my age?' she said.

'Yes, darling. It's about three boys who come to London for a good time and spend the whole day in a coffee bar in Soho. I do read the newspapers, you know.'

They had stopped outside the theatre and Bridget was studying the photographs of the youths in the production. Irene smiled as she remembered herself at the same age. She and Pamela had seen *Wuthering Heights* three times.

'Laurence Olivier,' she said. 'Now there was a heart-throb!'

Bridget glanced around in sudden embarrassment. 'Mum,' she said quietly, 'for God's sake act your age!'

'We'd better go in,' Irene replied, 'before I break down completely and tell you about Rudolph Valentino.'

Despite Bridget's misgivings, Irene did enjoy the play. It was funny and at times moving. She could see why the three young actors had become heroic figures among Bridget's contemporaries. When it was over, they walked with the crowd through the foyer. Bridget talked non-stop until they reached the pavement, and Irene waited until there was a pause. 'Shall we go back-stage?' she asked innocently.

Bridget laughed. 'Fat chance!'

But Irene produced a letter from her handbag. 'I think this might get us in,' she said confidently, and led her mystified daughter to the rear of the theatre. There were clusters of girls and a few boys waiting in the alley, but she showed the note to the doorman and he directed her to a dressing-room.

Bridget looked about her as they made their way through the narrow corridors. Irene found the door she was looking for, knocked twice, and a clipped voice called out, 'Enter.'

When they opened the door, Clive Hamilton was standing in front of a mirror surrounded by light-bulbs. His slicked-back hair was sharply parted and he wore a silk dressing-gown. One limp hand held a long cigarette holder. 'Darling!' he said in the same voice, taking Irene's hand. 'This is all too divine.'

Bridget gazed at him with astonishment. How could this preposterous person be the youthful figure who had so recently enchanted her?

Hamilton and Irene began to laugh, then he covered his head with a towel and rubbed his wet hair. When his face was revealed once again, it resembled the character he had portrayed in the play. 'Forgive my childish joke,' he said to Bridget, 'but your mother and I haven't seen each other for some time. I was just playing a trick on her.'

Irene jabbed him in the ribs with a forefinger. 'Passing yourself off as a teenager is trick enough for me!' she said.

'I'm not thirty yet, madam,' he assured her. Then he looked at Bridget. 'We met on the steps of the West London School of Art.'

'I didn't know you were famous then,' she said.

Hamilton laughed. 'Neither did I!' Then he smiled at Irene. 'But your mother did. Every time I used to ring her and moan about my career, she used to tell me to pull myself together and remember I was destined for stardom.' He gave them glasses of rather warm white wine in odd glasses.

While he finished dressing, Irene explained that there would be more people at supper.

'And you say this brother-in-law of yours insists on paying?' said

493

Hamilton. 'Splendid. If he's a patron of the arts, I'll let myself go.'
When they left the dressing-room, he remembered something.
'Would you like to meet Brian Longman and David Hunter?' he
asked Bridget. She nodded blissfully.

They stopped at another door through which came sounds of
noisy conversation. Hamilton knocked, and opened the door
slightly. Cigarette-smoke poured out of the room, which seemed to
be packed with young girls who looked Bridget up and down in a
predatory fashion. It was impossible to enter. Longman and Hunter
looked over the wall of hostile female faces.

'Two friends of mine,' Hamilton called out. 'Irene and Bridget
Cleary.'

The two young men waved; they could not get near enough to
shake hands.

'Would you like to come in for a drink?' Longman shouted, but
there was no way through that wall of bodies.

'No, thanks,' Hamilton replied. 'We're off. Some other time.'

The walk to Luigi's took only a few minutes. The usual scent of
freshly-ground coffee greeted them as they entered, and a chorus of
Italian voices wished them good evening.

Gideon dreamed he was lying face down, scrabbling at the
snow-scrubbed ground. There was no cover, just the raw frozen
earth. The enemy fire came closer every second. He looked for
Smudger, but instead he found Laszlo lying beside him. I brought
you here, he thought. I'm going to get you killed as well.

Then Anne gently shook him. 'Come on, darling,' she said. 'Time
to get up.'

He blinked at the ceiling and then swung his feet to the floor. He
was still dazed with sleep. 'What time is it?'

'Just before ten,' Anne told him. 'I almost let you sleep on, but you
were grinding your teeth, so I thought I'd better wake you.'

Gideon rubbed his face. 'I'm glad you did.'

It didn't take him long to dress, as Anne had laid out his clothes,
and within half an hour they were with the others in the restaurant.

Laszlo and Elizabeth had already arrived. Hamilton was
entertaining them all with a story about the rehearsals for the play.
It was a pleasant meal; Hamilton did most of the talking and was
very funny. Just after midnight, he bade them goodnight as they all
left.

They caught a taxi and dropped Elizabeth off at Trafalgar Square, then the rest headed for Kew, with Bridget still chattering about the evening. She was eventually persuaded to go to bed, and Irene went through the house, turning on all the lights.

'Most of the period you're talking about is stored in the attic studio,' she said when Gideon had explained what they were seeking. 'The rest is split into two sections in the last two bedrooms on the second floor.'

It had been many years since Gideon had been above the ground floor of the house, where Nettlebury's pictures filled all of the available wall space, so he was not prepared for the effect on the floors above. Irene had hung as much as she could.

At first he and Laszlo just wandered from room to room, looking at the pictures. The effect was astonishingly powerful. The collection was so many things, a visual diary of a part of England and the people who lived there. The streets of the suburbs in different seasons. The subtle changes different light brought to the Thames. A whole series on the Botanic Gardens that Gideon had never seen. In the upper rooms were plan-chests full of drawings and sketchbooks.

Gideon realised now why Irene had hesitated when he had said he would pop over and take a look. The sheer volume of work was overwhelming. She must have worked for years just to assemble it so comprehensively.

At last they narrowed the search down to six large plan-chests. After an hour's sorting, they had a pile of Gideon's work in front of them. There were fifteen paintings, none of them on stretchers, and twenty-seven sketches he could identify.

He shook his head. 'I did more. A lot more.' He turned to Irene. 'Would he have thrown any of the stuff away?'

She shook her head. 'No, he kept everything. Look.' She opened a nearby chest, took out a small sketchbook and flipped through the pages. 'This was the sketchbook he took on honeymoon with him. He kept everything.'

Gideon looked down at a drawing of her mother, and then Irene closed the book and replaced it in the drawer. He leaned against one of the chests and looked up at the walls, at a series of water-colours of Hammersmith Bridge through the changing seasons.

Laszlo examined them as well. He was the first to speak. 'Where now?'

'When we get back from Berlin, I'll try to make a list of what I can remember,' said Gideon.

'What about Dad's diaries?' Irene said. 'Would they be a help?'

'I didn't know he kept a diary,' said Anne.

Irene nodded. 'They were a secret. I don't think he wanted us to read about his love-life when we were children.'

She led them to a small room on the first floor and unlocked the door. It contained a small brass-bound desk with an old-fashioned typewriter and a collection of wooden filing cabinets. It was the only room in the house where the walls were bare.

'He used to type?' Laszlo asked.

Anne nodded. 'He always said that when he wrote by hand, he was distracted by the shape of the words he was creating.'

One of the filing cabinets was full of diaries, leather-covered and ring-bound. Each page was carefully dated. Irene sorted through them until she reached the thirties.

'Why don't you all go downstairs for a drink?' Gideon suggested. 'I can manage this on my own.'

'I'll bring you one up,' said Anne. 'What would you care for?'

'A cup of tea would be splendid,' he replied, and began to flip through the pages. It was an extraordinary sensation when he came to the entries concerning himself; he found it rather moving, like looking at snapshots he had no previous knowledge of. When Anne returned, she found him still absorbed.

'It's all here,' he said. 'Every picture he made me study, every exercise I had to do. Everything.' He laid the book aside. 'I wonder what else he kept?' He opened another of the filing cabinets and flipped at random through the files. When he found one labelled 'Van Duren', he saw that the two men had carried on quite a lengthy correspondence. Everything was in sequence, according to the dates of Van Duren's handwritten letters. Interspaced were carbon copies of Nettlebury's replies. Gideon did not bother to read them, he'd done enough for one day.

'I think I'll go down now,' he said, feeling suddenly sad. 'I can make out a complete list when I get back from Berlin.'

'I'll turn the lights off up here,' said Anne. Gideon nodded and left the room.

Anne waited until he had gone and then picked up the last diary he had been reading. A ribbon still marked the page. She read it for some time and then closed it and went downstairs to join the others. They were sitting in the kitchen and Laszlo was telling them stories about Piet Liebe.

Anne came and stood behind Gideon and put her arms round his

496

neck. 'There's no need to make out that list,' she said when Laszlo had finished. 'I can do it just as easily.'

Gideon reached up and touched her hand with his own. 'You know, I'm going to buy in all your father's work we can get our hands on. Some day, people will realise what a bloody genius he really was!'

CHAPTER TWENTY-TWO

England, winter 1963

The snow that had been falling steadily for the past three days had stopped. Although the sullen sky signalled only a brief pause, Laszlo took the opportunity to compare his Peter Quick painting with the actual view of Little Fenton from the brow of the hill. He stood now at the very point Quick had chosen and looked down at the village. The light was different in the picture. There, the sky was clear and the hard blue had accentuated the few colours he had used so sparingly against the snow. The sky today was leaden, so that the dark shapes of the houses and trees below were the only contrast in the white landscape, luminous in the last light of the afternoon. But Laszlo could see that the composition was the same, even if Quick had extended Fenton Wood to halve the actual proportion of the village green. He nodded with pleasure and turned and trudged back towards Trafalgar House.

The wind blew steadily against him and drifted snow against the hedgerow to his left. Even so, it almost came to the top of his wellington boots, and just before he reached the house, it began to fall heavily again. He was reminded of stories he had read in his boyhood of men in the Klondike, dying of exposure a few yards from the safety of their cabins.

When he shut the door, the warmth of the kitchen enveloped him and he inhaled deeply; Elizabeth was cooking, and the scent of roast pork filled the room. He stamped his feet on the mat to clear his boots and then put on a pair of slippers.

'How did it look?' Elizabeth asked, without glancing up from the vegetables she was chopping.

'Pleasant,' Laszlo replied, 'but not as good as the painting. You can't see the railway line now; it's just a shallow indentation. The snow has drifted into the cutting.'

She nodded, and stirred a simmering pot.

Since they had bought the house, Elizabeth had become a devoted cook and Laszlo had begun to put on weight. Now he had to be careful of what he ate in town, so that he could do justice to her efforts at the weekends. He leaned over her shoulder and inhaled again. 'It smells delicious,' he said. 'What is it?'

Elizabeth added some more seasoning. 'Just a little Hungarian dish like your mother used to make.'

'My mother was Irish. The only thing she knew how to cook was boiled potatoes.'

Elizabeth pushed him away. 'Go and see to the fire. I think you'll have to bring some more logs up from the cellar.'

'You're enjoying this, aren't you?'

'I hope we're stuck here for a month. Imagine how awful London must be in this weather.'

Laszlo went off to tend the fire and to see whether the telephone was working. A few minutes later he was talking to Gideon. 'The lines have been out of action all day, and the trains aren't running.'

'I know,' Gideon answered. 'We heard it on the news. Anne was worried that we mightn't get through to you.'

'Oh, we're fine,' said Laszlo. 'In fact, Elizabeth is enjoying every minute of it.'

'What about you?'

Laszlo sighed. 'I know how Napoleon must have felt on the retreat from Moscow! Imagine a lot of frozen water causing so much frustration.' He ran his fingers through his hair. 'How's everything going?'

'Absolutely fine,' Gideon replied soothingly. 'We shut the gallery this afternoon, and we're well ahead. There's only the back showroom to hang now. By some extraordinary piece of good luck the catalogue turned up this morning. It looks marvellous.'

'I wish I were there.'

'Why?' Gideon said with a mirthless laugh. 'You don't think anyone's going to come, do you? If anyone turns up, it'll be a bloody miracle. It's just another piece of Richard Cleary's abominable luck. They decide to do a television programme on him and we mount a major retrospective exhibition. Then we get the worst snow in twenty years. The only good thing is that Cleary isn't around to blame us for it all!'

'I could have been there with you worrying and being miserable, all the same,' Laszlo replied.

Gideon laughed again. 'Well, be miserable at Little Fenton.'

Laszlo became serious. 'Some people don't seem to have any luck in life, do they?'

Gideon paused. 'It does look like that sometimes. You know, I used to play cards in the army, and I could never seem to win. Smudger used to say I got all my luck in other ways. I wonder if he was right.'

They said goodbye, and Laszlo hung up and poked at the fire so savagely that a shower of sparks rushed up the chimney.

'Why are you so angry?' Elizabeth had entered the room and seen his attack on the logs. 'You were the one who taught me to be calm in face of the inevitable.'

Laszlo let the poker drop so that it clattered into the fireplace. 'I was young then. I'm sixty now.'

Elizabeth put her arms round him. 'Well, you look just fine to me. I've no complaints.'

'Look at me,' he said. 'Do you realise I'm wearing carpet slippers? That's a clear indication of old age.'

Elizabeth laid her head on his shoulder. 'I've got some more bad news.'

'Tell me.'

'You know I said we were going to have pommes Lyonnaise with the pork?'

'Yes?'

'We haven't any potatoes,' Elizabeth said in a mock tragic voice.

Laszlo thought for a moment, then went upstairs to the landing and looked from the window over the portico. When he came downstairs again, he was brisk and business-like. 'There's hardly any snow on the pavements, and there are no cars on the hill. Get your hat and coat.'

'Where are we going?' Elizabeth asked.

'There's something I'm going to bring up from the cellar,' he answered, and a few minutes later he emerged with a toboggan.

'Oh, no!' said Elizabeth.

'The journey down the hill is going to be easy.'

'But how will we get back?' she asked.

Laszlo shrugged. 'Perhaps our luck will change.'

A few minutes later, wearing heavy coats against the cold wind and the snow, they sat on the sledge at the top of the hill.

'How do you stop?' Elizabeth asked.

'There are no brakes. When I say so, stick your feet into the snow.'

He pushed off and the toboggan began to gain momentum. They slid down the hill with increasing speed. Then, ahead of them, Laszlo saw the lights of a car turn into Hill Street. He put out his feet and shouted to Elizabeth. The toboggan swerved to the side and they were both thrown into the snow by the roadside. They rolled for a few feet and lay in the cold fluffy drift, laughing helplessly.

The Land-Rover that had caused them to crash had stopped, and the driver got down and peered anxiously at them. It was Clive Chilton.

'Good God, it's you two!' he said in astonishment. 'I thought it was a couple of kids.'

Laszlo and Elizabeth got to their feet, still weak with laughter. 'We just popped out to do some shopping,' Elizabeth said eventually. Then she looked into the open door of the car. 'Oh, hello, Marion. How are you?' she said when she saw Chilton's wife.

'Awful,' Marion replied. She was five months' pregnant, and already enormous.

'Our central heating has packed up,' Chilton explained. 'The house is like an icebox. We were just on our way to see if they could put us up at The Victory.'

Laszlo looked at the Land-Rover. There were chains on the wheels. 'Will this get to the top of the hill?' he asked.

'You could get to the top of Mount Everest in this.'

Laszlo held his hand out to Elizabeth. 'Our luck *has* changed,' he said, and then he slapped Chilton on the shoulder. 'You come and stay with us,' he said. 'We've got roast pork for dinner. But there's a television programme you've got to watch this evening.'

Kew, the same day

The bus took ages, but Irene rather enjoyed the journey; she liked the effect snow brought to familiar surroundings. Even the dreariest view looked fresh and original. Most changes in the seasons came slowly, but snow was dramatic, almost theatrical. Probably that was why it brought so many memories of childhood. She stepped from the bus and carefully picked her way across the icy pavement. The hall was cold when she entered the house, but the kitchen was warm. Bridget was there, seated at the big table, doing her homework.

'How did you get home?' Irene asked.

'They gave us the afternoon off.' Bridget marked the place in her

501

textbook, and looked up. 'Aunt Anne phoned. She said, will you ring her as soon as you get home?'

Irene kept her coat on and went to the telephone in the hall.

'What's it like out there?' Anne asked when they were connected.

'Very cold, very beautiful, very difficult to get about,' Irene answered.

'Yes, it's the same in town. I do hope it melts quickly. I hate it when it gets all filthy and frozen and hangs about for weeks.'

'Do you think many people will come tomorrow?' Irene asked.

'I don't know, darling,' Anne replied after a pause. 'It's pretty difficult to get about.'

'Poor Bridget,' said Irene. 'She was so looking forward to the exhibition. It will be a great disappointment to her.'

'Oh, the reason I wanted to talk to you . . .' Anne continued. 'The papers have been ringing all afternoon. I take it you don't want me to give them your number?'

'Yes . . . I mean no. I don't want them to ring here.'

'They keep asking the same question,' said Anne. 'Where is Richard Cleary now?'

Irene sighed. 'Well, there's no point in talking to them. I really don't have the faintest idea where he is.'

'Are you going to watch tonight?' Anne asked.

'I suppose so.' Irene shivered. The hall was painfully cold.

'See you tomorrow, then,' Anne said, and they hung up.

When Irene got back to the kitchen, Bridget was closing her books.

'What do you want to eat?' Irene asked.

'Not much. I had something earlier.'

'I'm just going to have soup and toast,' said Irene.

Bridget nodded. 'That will be fine by me.'

When Irene had prepared the food, she and Bridget ate in silence for a time. It was dark now, but the kitchen was filled with the afterglow that snow brings. Irene looked into the garden as she put the bowls in the sink and could see the bare fruit trees quite clearly.

'I must put some bread out for the birds,' she said quietly. She could feel that her daughter wanted to talk, so she sat down at the table again and folded her hands.

Bridget looked up and said, 'Do you still love Dad?'

The question took Irene by surprise. She tried to think of a proper answer, but none came. 'Why do you ask?'

Bridget shrugged, and in the movement suddenly looked very

much like her father. 'I just wondered how you decided how to live your life.'

Irene smiled, and answered without reflection. 'I didn't decide how to live my life. It just happened.' As she spoke, she realised how weak her answer sounded. Oh, God, she thought, how can I explain the meaning of life to her, when I don't understand it myself? But she saw the intensity of Bridget's expression and knew that some kind of explanation was important. She tried to remember the things her father had told her during her adolescence. She leaned forward and cupped her chin in her hands.

'Your grandfather always used to say that the first thing you must come to terms with is the fact that life isn't fair,' she said slowly.

Bridget looked up. 'In what way?'

Irene thought for a moment longer. 'He said it was cruel and silly for anyone to claim that we were all born equal, when it was obvious that brains, beauty, strength and common-sense were dished out in a whole variety of proportions.'

'Did he believe in predestination?' Bridget asked.

'I don't think it was as grand as that. He was just trying to comfort me when I said it wasn't fair that your grandmother had died.'

'But surely you can decide about certain things in your life?' said Bridget. 'Otherwise it's just a hopeless mess.'

Irene was taken aback. The phrase 'a hopeless mess' seemed a pretty good description of life occasionally. But she tried again. 'I think he was trying to tell me that you can control some aspects of your existence, but quite a lot of what happens to you is in the hands of other people. No matter how much you may love someone, you can't make them love you in return if the desire just isn't there.'

Bridget looked down at the table. 'So you can go on loving someone hopelessly for years, like Yeats did?'

Irene shook her head. 'It can happen, but I think that's unusual. You've heard the old saying, "Time heals"?' Bridget nodded. 'Well, I know that's true. You can love someone so much and then lose them, and you think your heart will break. But after a time you start to forget, and then one day you remember them again and there's no pain at all, just a slight feeling of surprise that they could ever have hurt you so much.'

Bridget stood up and glanced at the clock. 'I'll go and light the fire in the other room. The programme will be starting soon.'

Irene nodded. 'I'll be straight in.'

She wiped the dishes and put them away and then followed

Bridget into a small room at the back of the house where they spent most evenings. It was furnished with a sofa and two armchairs, and the old gas fire hissed and popped, but it heated the room and cast a warm light on the pictures that covered the walls.

She switched on the television set just as a woman wearing an evening dress was announcing the programme. The sound of a Bach prelude was followed by the title 'British Painters', which dissolved into the figure of Neville Crichton standing at a lectern in a pool of light. He gave a shy smile into the camera, and said, 'Good evening.'

According to the newspapers, women all over Britain were at this moment swooning or showering their television screens with kisses. During the past two months, Neville Crichton had become that most peculiar of phenomena, a television personality. His gaunt features, wavy hair, heavily framed spectacles and bow tie were now as familiar to the general public as any film star, cabinet minister or member of the royal family. People sought his opinions on subjects as diverse as the existence of God or the proper wine to drink with a meal. He made frequent guest appearances on the radio and television programmes, and it was rumoured that he made huge amounts of money opening supermarkets and petrol stations. A Sunday newspaper was serialising his life story.

His sudden fame had taken all who knew him by surprise, including Crichton. When he had been contracted to make a series of half-hour programmes on modern British artists, the budget had been small. There had been a considerable body of opinion at the BBC that a man showing paintings in black and white, attempting to describe their colourful qualities to the public, was doomed to a tiny viewing audience.

But television had worked its strange alchemy on Neville Crichton. His voice projected a pleasing resonance and the camera lens turned a reasonably presentable man into a figure of god-like feature and proportion. And since the programmes had begun, galleries all over the United Kingdom had registered greater attendances, the sale of art books had soared and the value of the artists he portrayed had increased noticeably.

As she watched, Irene found it difficult to relate the man on the screen to the one she had known so well.

Crichton frowned, and folded his arms before speaking.

Until now, I have concentrated on British artists who are well known to the public. But tonight, in the last of this present series, I wish to

504

bring to your attention the work of a man who may, one day, rank with the greatest painters these Islands have ever produced. He is, at the moment, languishing in relative obscurity. But his work is well known to critics, as is the work of his particular contemporaries, the Cromwell Road School. His name is Richard Cleary, and it is my contention that he has been despised and dismissed for so long because he has chosen to pursue a style of painting and a choice of subject matter that has not been fashionable in recent times.

He paused, and an early picture of Cleary's appeared on the screen. Crichton's voice continued:

> Richard Cleary is a figurative painter, that is to say, an artist whose work and subject-matter can be understood by the public as well as the relatively few people who have made a lifelong study of art. Of course, there have been other modern British figurative painters who have been successful, but Richard Cleary and some of the other members of the Cromwell Road School made a fatal error in their work. They chose to depict a type of painting that is as old as art itself, the Narrative Style. In other words, they painted pictures that told a story, like the early Christian painters whose work depicted incidents from the Bible, or, in more recent times, the Pre-Raphaelite Brotherhood of the late nineteenth century. For this cardinal sin, Richard Cleary has suffered grievously. For, in this day and age, received wisdom states that painting should only be about painting.

Crichton went on to describe the qualities of Cleary's pictures, the use of colour and the development of his technique, and people throughout the country sat engrossed before their screens, with a rising sense of injustice that the work of someone they could comprehend should be so ignored by the arbiters of taste and fashion.

Wales, the same day

The snow had stopped, but a hard and bitter wind blew from the east, causing drifts against the mountainside and moaning down the valley in the lee of the Black Mountains. Richard Cleary crouched against the wooden side of the tractor trailer and looked up into the sky. It was filled with stars that glittered like chips of broken glass. He closed his eyes. His hands were thrust deep into the pockets of his greatcoat, and a long woollen scarf was wound round his ears and the lower part of his face. Despite the thick socks he wore inside his boots, his feet were frozen. The jolting of the trailer against the roar of the tractor engine reminded him of the Lancaster bomber he had flown so long ago.

The tractor stopped again, and Morgan Jones shouted, 'Drop the last two here and we'll bugger off home.'

Cleary leaned forward and threw the bales of hay out of the back of the trailer, then crouched down again and sheltered from the wind as Morgan turned the tractor and headed for the farm. Further down the valley, Cleary could see the lights of the village.

When they eventually reached the yard, Morgan stopped at one of the out-buildings and they pulled open the big wooden doors to drive the tractor under cover. 'Best get that bugger safe for the night. Machines aren't like sheep. They'll die after a night in the snow, same as people.' He stopped for a moment and looked up at the mountain-side. Patches of bare rock and grass showed darkly against the broad swathes of snow. 'It's too bloody cold to stick much. It's blowing away like washing powder. Mind you, there'll be some bad drifts in places. That's where we'll loose sheep . . . Stupid creatures! They're daft as women,' he said bitterly as they trudged the last few yards to the house.

They entered the warm kitchen and found it deserted. From the sound coming from the room next door they could tell that Iris, Morgan's wife, and their daughter were watching television.

'What's to eat?' Morgan called out. 'We're starving!'

'Tea's in the pot, and there's stew on the stove,' Iris called back. 'I'm watching my programme.'

They washed their hands at the sink and Cleary hacked thick slices of bread from a loaf while Morgan served them both large plates of lamb stew. When they sat down to eat, he looked at his plate in disgust.

'More bloody sheep,' he said in a voice full of loathing.

Neither had removed their greatcoats; despite the warmth of the kitchen, the cold was still deep in their bones. When they finished eating they sat at the table, too numb with weariness to make a move.

After a few minutes, Iris came in to pour another cup of tea. 'Oh, he's lovely!'

'Who?' Morgan asked.

'Neville Crichton. He's just been talking about a chap with the same name as you, Rich.'

Cleary looked up at Iris without much interest. 'What did he say about him?'

506

Iris thought for a moment. 'He said, Richard Cleary was the unknown genius of British painting, and some day our leading critics would hang their heads in shame because of the neglect they had shown his work over the years.'

Cleary nodded. 'I've heard tell critics are like a lot of sheep,' he said wearily.

London, the following day

Gideon sat by the fire in the living-room of the flat. He knew it was late in the morning, but he was enjoying those moments of guilty lingering. Then Anne came in with a cup of tea and the morning newspaper. When she pulled back the curtains, he saw that the light had changed. A shaft of bright sunshine shone through the window and there was the distant rumble of traffic. He smiled at her and drank his tea.

'What time is it?' he asked.

'Just after nine-thirty. I've only just put the telephones on. I had them switched through to the gallery.' She sat in the chair opposite and glanced at the paper. 'Good heavens! There's an article on the front page of *The Times* about Crichton's television programme.'

'What does it say?' Gideon asked.

Anne studied the article for a few moments. 'It seems that the BBC's switchboard was jammed with calls from people saying they were angry that he had been neglected by the art establishment. They're comparing him with Van Gogh.'

Gideon took the paper and began to read. 'That's because they don't know Richard Cleary,' he said ruefully. 'He's more likely to cut off someone else's ear than his own.'

When the telephone rang, it was Graham Todd. 'Things are getting a little difficult down here, Gideon,' he said. The words were not delivered in his usual languid voice.

'What's the matter?'

'Well, the telephone hasn't stopped ringing, for a start; every newspaper wants to speak to you or Laszlo. And the crowd is getting bigger by the minute.'

'What crowd?'

Todd did not answer, but exclaimed, 'Oh, my God! There's a child trying to pick paint off one of the canvases. I must go. Look out of the window, old boy!' He hung up.

Gideon shook his head in astonishment. 'That's the first time I've heard Toddy flapping!'

He walked to the window and looked down; the sight below was extraordinary. Two policemen were controlling a crowd that stretched along Bond Street. There were press photographers, and a van was parked in the road with a television cameraman on the roof. Most of the snow from the night before had melted, but there was thick slush at the kerbside where the police were insisting the crowd waited.

Gideon dressed quickly and hurried downstairs. When he tried to enter the gallery, a police sergeant barred his way.

'You'll have to wait your turn like everyone else, sir,' he said in a voice that was half-threatening and half-polite.

'I am one of the owners of this establishment, Sergeant,' he said stiffly.

'Oh, are you, sir?' The sergeant's voice changed to one of nagging complaint. 'I wish you'd given us some warning of all this.' He waved around him. 'It practically adds up to a disturbance of the peace.'

Gideon shrugged his apology. 'In more than thirty years, I have never seen such a crowd at this gallery. Believe me, I had no idea this was going to happen.'

Just then, Laszlo pushed through the mass of people. 'This is incredible, just incredible!'

'It's called the power of television,' Gideon answered as they edged their way into the premises.

Graham Todd had done a good job under the siege conditions that had been thrust upon him. The entire staff had been mobilised, including the secretaries, and were now busy moving the crowd through the gallery. He gestured for Gideon and Laszlo to follow him to one of the offices. It was piled with catalogues for the exhibition.

'What are they doing in here?' Laszlo asked.

'I had them brought in,' Todd answered. Laszlo looked puzzled. Todd gestured towards the people outside. 'They started gathering before we opened the doors,' he explained, and slapped one of the piles of catalogues. 'These tell you what you could buy a Richard Cleary picture for yesterday. If we sell them at this value, every dealer in London will clear out the gallery, and next week they'll be selling them at treble the price.'

No one spoke for a time and then Gideon turned to his partner.

508

Laszlo raised his shoulders in a slow expansive shrug, then he turned to smile at Todd. 'Graham, I am extremely glad you didn't go into your father's bank!'

Gideon flipped open one of the catalogues. 'What are you telling those people who want to buy pictures?'

Todd suddenly looked more relaxed, and slid his hands into his jacket pockets. 'I've told everyone to say that this is a preview. The private view is tonight, and we don't begin to sell the pictures until tomorrow.'

Gideon and Laszlo exchanged glances again, then Gideon turned to Todd. 'You've done well, Toddy. Not just for the Archangel Gallery, but for Richard and his family. You deserve a present.'

Todd grinned. 'I've already chosen the picture I want,' he said as he opened the door. 'Oh, by the way, there's a list on the desk of the people who rang from the newspapers. I told them you would call back.'

Gideon picked it up, glanced at it for a moment and then tore it in half. He handed one piece to Laszlo.

'I'll stay here,' said Laszlo.

Gideon nodded. 'I'll use the room in the basement.' It was nearly two hours later when he returned to the office.

Laszlo was still on the phone. 'I can assure you it is *not* a publicity gimmick,' he said testily. 'Richard Cleary has not been contactable for the past year or so. His daughter received a card on her birthday with a Welsh postmark, but he could be anywhere . . .' He paused and raised his eyebrows at Gideon. 'My dear fellow, the reason the world has not known that a famous artist vanished over a year ago is because until last night he was not a famous artist. Nobody gave a damn about him. Don't take my word for it, ask your art critic . . . Your paper doesn't have an art critic? It doesn't surprise me.' He hung up and raised his eyes to the ceiling. 'What a suspicious press we have in this country! Half of them think we've spirited Cleary away as a publicity stunt.'

'It was the same with my lot,' said Gideon.

Anne came in, carrying Gideon's movie camera. 'I've been filming the scenes outside for Irene and Bridget,' she said. 'It really is quite wonderful. I even saw Strange and Schneider in the crowd. They actually skulked when they saw me point this at them!' She put down the camera and hugged Gideon. 'Oh, I'm so pleased for Irene. It must have been hard for her over the years.' She looked at her husband. 'I know you've bought some of Dad's pictures from her,

509

but she had the worry of bringing up Bridget on her own, and that big house to look after. Now she'll have a lot less to worry about.'

'How did you know I'd bought pictures from her?' Gideon asked.

Anne kissed him on the chin. 'You have no secrets from me, O master!'

Gideon frowned. 'She wouldn't take the full value, you know. She always claimed half the picture was yours, so she would take only half the money.'

Graham Todd came into the room again. 'It's a nightmare out there! A religious maniac just got in and told us we were all worshipping godless images.'

Gideon laughed. 'How did you cope with that one, Toddy?'

He shrugged. 'I called for the police, of course. Luckily it only took fifteen seconds for them to arrive. The constable knew him quite well, he called him George. It seems he pops into the Ritz quite often. The madman, that is, not the police constable.'

'Any other problems?' Gideon asked.

'There's a situation developing that I think should be dealt with at the highest level. A fearsome little old lady has brought all her life savings. She insists that we sell her every picture in the exhibition.'

Gideon looked at Laszlo. 'I think he's telling us we should take part in the battle outside.'

Laszlo nodded. 'We've shirked our duty long enough.'

'Wait for me,' Anne said, picking up the camera.

Wales, the same day

The snow still clung to the Black Mountains when they left the farm, but the thaw had begun by the time Morgan drove Richard Cleary into Abergavenny. When he had parked his van, the two men stood awkwardly together, then Morgan stuck out his hand.

'Well, good luck. Have you got your money?' Cleary patted the trouser pocket where he had seven hundred and fifty pounds. 'Look after that. You've earned it!' The Welshman smiled suddenly. 'You look a bloody sight better than you did a year ago, I can tell you.'

Cleary nodded. 'I feel better, too.'

Morgan smiled again, and Cleary raised an arm in a half-salute and walked away. There was more than an hour before his train departed, and he wondered how to spend the time. Then he caught sight of his reflection in a shop window and it came as a shock to see how rough he looked. On the farm, his appearance had not mattered. The shapeless, ill-matched clothes and heavy boots were serviceable enough there, but in the city he felt like a tramp.

He set off at a brisker pace and found a barber's shop. He waited until the first chair was available and then faced a pale young man with elaborate hair of his own.

'What style do you want it?' the youth said disdainfully.

For a moment, Cleary toyed with the options: Impressionist, Fauve, Vorticist, Cubist. Cubist hair might be interesting, he thought, but instead he said, 'Short all over.'

'You want a mod haircut?' the youth asked.

Cleary nodded, not really understanding the question, and looked at his face in the mirror. He remembered Morgan's words, and decided that he did look better. The flesh of his face had lost the puffy, sallow look of a year ago. His complexion was dark and wind-burned now, the whites of his eyes sharper and his cheekbones better defined.

As the youth clipped away at his long hair until it was close to his skull, Cleary began to take an interest in his face again. For a long time he had not looked at himself properly; now he felt he could be gazing at another man's features.

The youth stepped back and examined his work with a critical eye and nodded his own satisfaction. 'Well, the haircut looks good. Mind you, it doesn't really go with those clothes.'

Cleary handed him a ten-shilling note. 'Where can I get a suit?' he asked.

'Try Phillip's, four doors along on the right,' he answered.

By the time Cleary boarded the London train, no one would have recognised him in the Black Mountains.

London, the same day

From her vantage-point at the corner of the bar, Pandora Gray surveyed her domain. It was early evening and the members and their guests were packed into the long narrow room that constituted the premises of Pandora's Club. The temperature had risen, like bread in an oven, after four steady hours of afternoon drinking. Now a heavy pall of cigarette smoke thickened the humid air, occasionally stirred by the violent gestures of one of the groups jammed into the bar.

511

Pandora, a heavily-built woman with powerful arms and elaborately-coiffeured purple hair, sat opposite one of her regulars, a florid-faced man in a pin-striped suit. She was chain-smoking, and offering the odd monosyllabic comment to the mournful monologue he had kept up since he had first entered the bar after a hard morning in the city.

Carl Frazer loosened the collar of his button-down shirt and brushed the long, light-brown hair from his perspiring brow. He was a slim, hollow-cheeked young man with a narrow face that looked melancholy in repose. He had leaned against the far end of the counter and tried to attract the attention of a sulky barman for at least five minutes when Pandora noticed his plight and summoned him.

'Come here, darling,' she ordered with an imperious wave of her arm. Frazer obeyed, and as he approached, Pandora said, 'Make some fucking space here,' to a pair of actors standing next to the pin-striped man. The two actors shifted without rancour and Frazer squeezed into the space.

'Who brought you here, darling?' Pandora asked in a deep nasal voice.

Frazer gestured to a corner by the window overlooking Dean Street, where a group sat on bar stools. 'Mr Beriac.'

She looked him up and down again. 'Oh, you're a painter, are you, darling? I thought you might be a poet. Most of the young men who looked like you were killed on the Somme.' She looked into his face again and said, 'You're not queer, are you, darling?' Frazer smiled and shook his head. Pandora nodded. 'That's why Daisy here is ignoring you.' She turned to the barman. 'Come on, you petulant little poof! Give this fucking lad some service.' When she heard his order, she said, 'So Harold Beriac is on gin, is he? That's bad news. He always climbs on his broomstick after a skinful of Gordon's. You'd better watch out.'

Frazer nodded his thanks to the woman and began to ferry the drinks to his group. In truth, he did not know them at all. They had begun to gather in the French Pub during lunchtime. Originally he had been with Peter Quick, and then other people had joined them. The crowd had grown and decreased until closing time. By then Quick had departed, but Frazer had nowhere special to go and had been subsequently drawn along by the group when someone suggested they move on to Pandora's Club.

From then on the day had passed like a flickering picture book.

Frazer had been raised in a hard-drinking Scottish family and was used to men who could manage a bottle of whisky a session, so the amounts consumed by these men did not seem unnatural. He was also used to the alteration in mood brought on by alcohol. He recognised that Harold Beriac was a man of variable emotions, and he sensed that a change was about to take place.

Frazer had spent a curious afternoon; two of the men in the group were the painters he admired most in Britain. He would have liked to talk to them about their work, but earlier they had succumbed to the whisky and for the past two hours they had sat on their stools, their heads nodding occasionally when they were asked if they wanted anything more to drink. All the talking had been done by Harold Beriac and a grey-faced man called Colin, whose hair grew from his face and chin like winter bracken.

Colin seemed to be designing a book that Harold Beriac had written, or was about to begin. It was impossible to decide which, because Beriac would sometimes use the past tense, as though the book was completed, and then suddenly explain how well he would write it when he got down to it. Alternatively, he would compliment the man called Colin on his genius as a designer, then threaten him with dreadful punishments if he did not deliver his finest efforts. Then the conversation would start again and cover exactly the same ground. Frazer began to feel very bored. He looked at the two great men sitting in silence beside him and decided he would go after the next drink.

But fate intervened; one of the great painters raised his arm suddenly, as if to ask a question in a schoolroom, and the effort made him topple sideways on his stool so that he collided gently with his companion. Very slowly at first, the pair collapsed against others until five people lay in a tangle of thrashing bodies and bar stools on the grimy, odorous carpet.

'Time to go,' Beriac said with a giggle, plucking at Frazer's sleeve.

While Colin leaned down and attempted to free the bodies on the floor, they slipped from the club. A few minutes later they stood in the narrow Soho street. Beriac stepped over the heaped slushy snow at the kerbside and hailed a taxi. 'The Archangel Gallery, Bond Street,' he told the driver, and then settled back in the seat. 'What did you think of Britain's two greatest painters, dear?' he asked Fraser mis-chievously. The little man seemed to be bubbling with good humour.

'I didn't really have a chance to speak to them,' Frazer replied carefully.

Beriac touched him lightly on the knee. 'Well, you didn't miss anything, dear. One of them is interested only in horse-racing and the other in sex. The pair of them are pissed out of their brains all the time, anyway, so any kind of conversation tends to be a bit of a bore.' He bubbled on maliciously until they reached the gallery, and Frazer saw that it was packed with people.

'He's with me,' Beriac said to the attendant at the door, but the moment they entered he was absorbed into the crowd.

Frazer was left alone, holding a glass of white wine. For a time he could still hear Beriac's high-pitched comments above the other voices until they gradually receded into the distance. After a few moments, he decided it was a relief not to have to listen to him any longer. He drank half the wine and tried to look at the paintings, but the gallery was so packed that it was almost impossible to get close to the walls. There did not seem any point in trying to penetrate deeper into the long showroom. He did not know any of the people, and he had heard enough of Beriac's opinions for one day. He turned to go, and felt a sudden pain on the back of his left hand, like the sting of a wasp.

'I'm terribly sorry,' a voice said, and he looked up at the concerned face of a young woman who held the remains of a cigarette.

'That's okay,' he replied, smiling his reassurance because the girl seemed so disturbed by the accident. 'It really doesn't hurt at all.'

'You seem to have spilt your drink; let me fill your glass,' she said.

Frazer laughed. 'I spilt it down my throat, but I will have another if you'll stay and talk to me.'

The girl looked down, and he realised she was younger than he had at first supposed. But when she looked up again there was a boldness in her expression and a cast to her features that caused a sudden quickening in his heartbeat.

Since his boyhood, Frazer had had an image of a girl in his mind that had never left him. In the part of Glasgow where he lived as a child, there was an ice-cream parlour owned by Italians. They had been a short, thick-set family with heavy, coarse features, but one year, when he was thirteen, a cousin had come from Italy to stay for the entire summer. She had served behind the counter, and he had found her so beautiful that he had gone to the shop whenever he could just to look at her. Sometimes, when he had no money, he would stand outside and gaze through the window just to see her smile. His passion was not carnal; his heart went out to her beauty.

The coal-black hair that fell about her flawless oval face and the thick eyelashes shaded her dark eyes. She laughed often, showing small white teeth; sometimes she would poke her tongue out when she saw him standing at the window. He thought everything about her was perfect: the slight down on her arms, the swell of her breasts, her long slim hands. Late in the summer, when she was speaking better English, she asked him his name. He told her Carl.

She nodded. 'Carlo. It's a nice name.' That was all she ever said to him; the following day she left for home. He never saw her again, but her image had stayed in his mind ever since.

The girl now standing before him seemed almost identical, but for her dark red hair.

'I'll get you another drink,' she said.

Frazer looked around at the crush of people. 'You'll need a lot of influence!'

The red-headed girl, as if prompted by his own memory, poked her tongue out at him. 'I happen to have a lot of influence. I'll pull rank.' She did not have to go far; a waiter snaked out of the crowd and Frazer replaced his empty glass.

'Do you work here?' he asked.

The girl shook her head. 'I'm an art student. What do you do?'

'I'm a painter.'

The girl nodded. 'What do you think of these pictures?'

Frazer gazed around for a moment, then he shrugged. 'Not much. They're not really my kind of thing. What do you think of them?'

When Bridget answered, there was a certain amount of frostiness in her voice. 'I suppose I'm prejudiced,' she replied. 'My father painted them.'

Deeper in the showroom, where the crowd was thickest, Harold Beriac stood facing Neville Crichton. 'Surely you're wearing the wrong sort of clothes for this occasion, Neville,' the little man said in a piercing voice.

Crichton looked down at the curious figure; he was almost a foot taller than Beriac. 'I don't follow, Harold,' he answered in a friendly fashion.

Beriac gestured towards Crichton's tweed suit with a brushing motion. 'You ought to be wearing a top hat and a red tail-coat. After all, you're the ringmaster responsible for this ridiculous circus.'

'I didn't paint the pictures,' Crichton said mildly.

But the little American was not to be placated. 'You don't think

515

these flabby examples of a dead imagination can be called painting, do you?'

Crichton smiled. 'You saw my programme, Harold. You know what I think of his work.'

Beriac stood even closer and poked Crichton in the chest. Most of the people nearby were now straining to listen to the exchange, and the little man was aware of his audience.

'How could you possibly claim that Paul Van Duren and Richard Cleary affected each other's work?' Beriac said, his voice becoming shrill with emphasis. 'On what grounds can you make such a ridiculous statement?'

Crichton kept his temper. 'Because Van Duren told me so, Harold.'

'Told you, told you?' Beriac shouted. 'How, through a spiritualist? What evidence do you have?' He gestured round the room. 'You only have to look at this trash to know such a claim is impossible. Van Duren was one of the great painters of the twentieth century. This man is just another dead hand that has stifled art for centuries.'

Sir Edward and Lady Peake had been on the fringe of the argument, talking to Gideon, until Beriac's voice rose above everyone else's. Ted Peake raised his eyebrows. 'That settles it,' he said. 'If that little bastard doesn't like Cleary's paintings, I'm going to buy as many as I can get my hands on.'

'Shush,' Lady Peake said, squeezing his arm. 'I want to hear this.'

They watched as Crichton grasped Beriac's shoulder. His knuckles whitened, and Beriac began to squirm. 'Let me say this plainly, Harold, and without indulging in the purple language you see fit to use. Paul Van Duren himself told me that he had been influenced by certain British painters. I have my notes of the conversations, and I will explain every claim I have made in the book I am writing about Van Duren.'

Beriac's face drained of colour. One moment it had flushed pink, now it seemed to take on an oily, greenish hue. 'You're writing a book on Paul Van Duren?' he squeaked. Crichton nodded. 'But you know I'm writing one,' he said, as if accusing Crichton of some foul act.

Crichton shrugged. 'You've been talking about writing a book on Paul Van Duren for the past five years,' he said in the tone of voice one would use to placate a spoilt child. 'My publishers commissioned me last Thursday. They didn't seem to think your rather whimsical project posed any sort of a threat.'

516

Beriac totally lost control. He began to drum on Crichton's chest with his tiny fists. 'You can't, you can't!' he sobbed in frustration. 'If you make any lies up about Van Duren, I'll ruin you!' he shouted. Then he turned and pushed his way out of the gallery.

Frazer and Bridget watched his departure. 'Is that the man you spent the afternoon with?' she asked.

'Harold Beriac. He's a famous critic.'

'Yes, I know.' Bridget smiled. 'What were you just saying?'

Frazer saw a gap in the crowd and took the opportunity to place his empty glass on the corner of a table. 'I said, would you care to have dinner with me?'

Bridget looked at him with a half-smile. 'I thought you'd been drinking all afternoon.'

Frazer brushed the hair from his forehead and held out his hand to show how steady it was. 'I come from Glasgow,' he said quickly so that she had to lean towards him to catch his words. 'All my family are alcoholics. I don't like being drunk.'

Bridget looked at his hand. 'I'll ask my mother.'

Irene, who had been watching her daughter's conversation, was not happy when Bridget told her of Carl Frazer's invitation. 'You promised to have dinner with your uncle and Anne,' she said. 'It would be very rude to cancel because you've had a better offer.'

Bridget was about to protest, but she saw her mother's expression and shrugged, resigned.

Anne joined her sister as she watched Bridget go to tell Frazer the news. 'Why don't you come and have supper with us, too?' she said.

Irene said, 'I feel a bit tired. I think I'll just get the tube home.'

Anne took her by the arm. 'You can afford a taxi now, you know.'

'Can I?' Irene gave an ironic laugh. 'I think it's too late for me ever to think of myself as rich.' She held out a hand when she saw her sister's reaction to the remark. 'Oh, darling,' she said quickly, 'I didn't mean to imply anything about you and Gideon. Both of you have always been wonderful.'

She looked around. The crowd was beginning to thin out. When she spoke again, Anne could hear her bitterness. 'All these years these people have ignored his work, and I don't think they really looked at it tonight.' She turned to her sister again. 'I'm off, then. Say goodnight to Gideon. I can see he's still busy.'

Anne saw that Gideon and Laszlo were talking to Neville Crichton.

'It was a splendid irony that Harold should be so upset at an

517

exhibition of Richard Cleary's work,' Laszlo said. 'I particularly enjoyed his threat to ruin you!'

Crichton tugged at an earlobe. 'I'm not so sure. The little weasel is not entirely without influence, and he did know Paul Van Duren pretty well at one point in his life.'

Gideon asked, 'Do you have any kind of corroboration for the conversations you had with Van Duren?' Crichton shook his head. Gideon stuck his hands in his pockets, and smiled. 'Seldom is it possible to return a favour with such alacrity!'

'What do you mean?' Crichton asked.

Gideon stopped a waiter and handed Crichton a glass of wine before he took one himself. 'Let me tell you about some letters my sister-in-law has in her possession.'

Crichton caught Irene as she was putting on her coat. They talked for some time and then he realised the gallery was almost empty. He glanced at his watch. 'Oh, God, I must go,' he said apologetically. 'I'm late for supper. Can I drop you anywhere?' Irene shook her head, and he hurried away.

When she did leave the gallery, a figure standing in a doorway on the opposite side of the road stepped into the light, and she checked her stride. Then she crossed and came face to face with Richard Cleary. 'Why didn't you come in?'

Cleary shrugged. 'A bit melodramatic, don't you think?'

'You missed Bridget,' Irene said, and as she spoke, it began to snow again.

'I saw her leave with Anne and Gideon,' he said. 'It was you I wanted to speak to.' Irene shivered against the cold. Cleary turned up the collar of his new overcoat. 'Can we go somewhere and have a drink?'

'Where do you suggest?' Irene asked.

Cleary nodded down the street. 'The Ritz Bar is close enough.'

They walked together without speaking and crossed Piccadilly. The snow was thicker now; Irene could see it was settling on the pavement.

At the bar, Cleary turned to Irene when the barman asked what they wanted.

'I shall have a champagne cocktail,' she said firmly.,

'Ginger ale for me,' said Cleary. Irene looked at him in surprise. 'I haven't drunk anything for over a year.'

'Why? Did it suddenly stop being fun?'

Cleary shook his head. 'It was never fun.'

'What made you do it, then?' Irene asked, sipping her cocktail.

'It blunted things. When they were sharp, they could be painful.'

Irene looked at him without compassion. 'That's called real life, Richard. It's supposed to be sharp. It wouldn't work if we all went around blunting reality.' She put down her glass. 'So what stopped you eventually?'

He shrugged. 'Drinking started hurting more than real life.'

'Did you see a doctor?' she asked.

'More than a year ago.'

Irene pushed the glass aside. 'What did he say?' Somehow she knew what the answer would be.

'He said I had a couple of years, maybe a bit more,' he answered without emotion.

Irene reached into her handbag and produced a cigarette. She blew the smoke away and stared at the far end of the room. 'What do you want from us?' she asked.

Cleary looked into the mirror behind the bar. 'I want to come home.'

There was a silence between them for some time, then she said, 'You don't have a home, Richard. You used to live in a flat in Earl's Court. Someone else has it now.'

'You know what I'm saying. I want to come and live with you and Bridget.'

Irene shook her head. 'You mean you want to come and die with us. That's different. If you come now, Bridget will see you every day, an experience she didn't have for most of her childhood. Naturally she will grow to love you more and more. She already hero-worships you, but as an abstraction, someone who doesn't live in the same world that she does. When you die, she will mourn you. But can you imagine the grief she will suffer if you become a reality in her life?'

Cleary looked down at his hands. They were calloused and seared from his work on the farm. 'So you think I shouldn't see her at all?'

'I can't stop you seeing her, that's up to you. But I think it would be selfish to fill a part of her life and then take it away again.' Irene stubbed out her cigarette and stood up. 'Thank you for the drink,' she said. 'I must go now.'

When Irene had gone, the barman took away the empty glasses. 'Anything else, sir?' he asked.

Cleary nodded. 'Yes, bring me a very large whisky, and ring reception to tell them I wish to stay the night.'

CHAPTER TWENTY-THREE

Gibraltar, early summer 1963

Carl Frazer stood at the airport bar and took a mouthful of the harsh Spanish brandy. He lit the last of his cheap cigarettes and inhaled the tobacco so deeply that the heat seared his mouth. He glanced at his wrist and saw a white band of flesh where his watch had been. Then he remembered that he had exchanged it the previous day, and now he had nothing worth stealing.

When he had left London some months before, it had been in the middle of a harsh winter and he was so loaded with baggage that he'd struggled under the weight of his possessions. Gradually, on his long journey through Europe, he had shed nearly everything. Two suitcases had been entrusted to a young couple he had met in Nice. They were on their honeymoon and had come from a cruise ship to the cheap waterside restaurant where he was eating. Frazer had helped them with the menu and at the end of the evening they had offered to take his cases back to London. Since then he had travelled light; now the last of his money was gone, exchanged for an air-ticket home. He drank the last of his brandy and looked down at his boots; they were high in the instep and shaped so that his feet looked like narrow little coffins. He had bartered his own shoes and watch for them with a drunken guitar-player the night before. At the time both of them had been deeply satisfied with the exchange, but Frazer now wondered if the gypsy was pleased with his side of the bargain; it was difficult to swagger in sandals. For a few moments he looked again at the tooled leather and then at his cheap, worn, workman's clothes. He was dressed in a costume that was unremarkable in his present surroundings but would cut a rather exotic figure in London. The thought was put from his mind by the announcement that his flight was ready for boarding, and he made for the gate.

When the aircraft had reached sufficient height, the 'No Smoking' sign flicked off and the young man sitting next to Frazer lit a cigarette. The scent of the Virginia tobacco seemed stale to him after the more acrid brands he had grown used to in recent months.

The young man sensed Frazer's interest and asked, 'Does my smoking bother you?'

'Not in the least,' he replied. 'It's just been a while since I tried an English cigarette. I wondered what they still tasted like.'

The young man offered him the packet, and he took one. Frazer thanked him. 'You've been in Gibraltar for some time?' he asked.

'Just a day. I came in only to catch the flight.'

'Same here,' the young man said. 'I was in North Africa. Strange place, Gibraltar. I was there for a bit when I was in the army. Can't say I cared for it greatly.'

Frazer said, 'I missed National Service.'

'Lucky chap,' the young man replied. 'Frightful waste of time. At least in my life it was.'

'What do you do?' Frazer asked.

'I sell paintings.'

Frazer nodded. 'I paint pictures. How's business?'

The young man laughed, and held out his hand. 'My name's Graham Todd.'

'Carl Frazer.' They shook hands. 'Why were you in North Africa?'

Todd stubbed out his cigarette before he answered. 'I wanted to see why Matisse liked it so much.' Frazer nodded. 'What have you been doing?'

Frazer said, 'I won a travelling scholarship at the Royal College. Enough money for three months' grand tour. I stretched it to six.'

'Has it been worth it?' Todd asked, offering Frazer another cigarette.

This one did not taste so stale. 'Yes,' he replied. 'I'd hardly been out of the country until now. It sounds silly, but I hadn't realised that the south of France really was the colour of those Cézanne landscapes.' He gestured. 'Light changes everything. Not just colour and form, but attitudes, people's existence. No wonder they used to worship the sun.'

Todd and Frazer talked on throughout the flight, and parted at Heathrow, where Todd headed for Buckinghamshire and Frazer caught the bus to the Cromwell Road terminal.

The weather in London was mild with patchy clouds in a bright sky, but the slight breeze felt cold; he had grown accustomed to the heat of southern Spain. Frazer decided to walk home, but by the time he descended Campden Hill, his feet ached in the high-heeled boots. He felt like a scruffy intruder as he hobbled past the handsome red-brick houses that stood back from the tree-lined road. Once he had crossed Holland Park Avenue, the seedier surroundings made him feel less conspicuous. Finally he reached his own front door, between two dusty shops in Princedale Road.

It was Sunday, and the street was deserted. He looked up and down the litter-strewn roadway and cracked pavements, then remembered, for a moment, the villages of Italy and Spain. By this time of day people would have finished their siesta and would be on the streets again. The British remained secure inside the drabness of their homes.

When he opened the door, the dark corridor, the length of the two flanking shops, was dank and smelt musty. Beyond another door a collection of small rooms led into a brick-walled area with a tin roof. It had been a garage before he had taken the premises. He had painted every surface white, including the tin roof and concrete floor, which he had covered with odd pieces of old carpet. Long strips of neon lights gave off a hard glare. On the table was a welcome sight: a loaf of bread, tea, some eggs, a bottle of milk, a large parcel and a pile of mail. There was also a note from the wife of the owner of the hardware shop next door. Frazer had written to her the previous week asking her to lay in the provisions. She had also brought in his laundered bedding, which was in the parcel.

Frazer spent the next few hours in quiet domesticity. He made up the iron cot in a corner of the garage. The honeymoon couple he'd met in Nice had been as good as their word; they had delivered the suitcases to the hardware shop as promised. He took his dirty washing to a laundrette near Ladbroke Grove, and then pressed the clean clothes and the crumpled suits. By the time he had finished ironing, the water was hot in the heater, and he showered and dressed in warmer clothes.

Then he looked at the paintings he'd left behind. It was as though he were seeing the work of somebody else; they seemed remote, like schoolbooks from his childhood, written in a hand he could only vaguely recollect as his own. He found the newspaper he had bought at London airport and began to read, but he could not concentrate. Reported events in Britain seemed far outside his area of concern.

He laid the paper aside and opened a large tin trunk; inside was his equipment, the brushes cleaned and rolled inside cloth.

522

Everything was in good order. The tubes of paint yielded to the pressure of his thumbs, the pigments were still pliant enough to use. He lifted out the large tin of white primer and weighed it in his hands. Then he nodded to himself and put the paint-pot on the table, which was still scattered with bundles of letters he had yet to read, prised open the lid and stirred the contents with a stick.

Then he took four large pictures from among those stacked against the wall. They were painted on hardboard, the images flat and almost smooth to the touch, but he worked on each with glass paper before he was satisfied. He applied white primer, and when the first coat covered the pictures he sat and looked at the surfaces again. The hard-edged, geometric shapes beneath the primer showed like ghosts. Another coat tomorrow, and the board would be ready to use again. He cleaned the brush and sat at the table, still studying the white surfaces with their pale haunted images. Then he saw the faces again, jumbled and interchanged, overlying one another against the surfaces of the half-obliterated pictures until he could not differentiate which memory separated into the original.

It had begun one sultry day when he had stood in front of a painting in Toledo and studied the face of the Virgin Mary in El Greco's painting of the Holy Family. The picture had taken his breath away. This was no moon-faced Madonna gazing with adoration at some fleshy infant. The face was of a lovely girl, innocent and sensual, the features aristocratic but without arrogance. It was the face he had seen in an ice-cream parlour in Glasgow when he was a boy and, again, six months ago in the Archangel Gallery.

Frazer concentrated on the images for a few moments longer, and then turned his attention to the letters. Most of them were circulars, but four were worth reading: he recognised the handwriting on three of them. The first was his brother's, the second from his old art teacher, the third from a friend at the Royal College. The fourth was postmarked W.5, and the italic characters told him that it was from someone who had studied at an art school.

He read the letter, which was from Bridget Cleary, and then hurried out into Princedale Road. A few minutes' walk took him to the pub. There was only one other customer, a morose figure in a cloth cap sipping a pint of beer as if it were a necessary but unpleasant medicine.

Frazer stood at the counter and drummed his fingers impatiently. Fairly soon there came a curious, irregular step on the staircase and a cadaverous figure appeared. Frazer observed the skull-like face, limp grey hair and pale watery eyes, and was reminded of his own immortality.

'So,' the figure said, 'we haven't seen you in some time.' There was a hint of disapproval in the landlord's voice; he might have been a headmaster chastising an idle schoolboy.

'I've been away for a few months, Bill,' Frazer said. 'Will you cash me a cheque for a fiver, give me twenty Players, a pint of bitter and some change for the telephone?'

The landlord thought about the request, then said, 'I suppose something could be arranged.'

The transaction completed, Frazer took the pint of beer to the phone in the corner of the bar and dialled the number in the letter he'd brought with him. Irene answered at the third ring.

'May I speak to Bridget, please?' he asked.

After a slight pause, Irene said, 'Who shall I say is calling?'

'My name is Carl Frazer.' There was a silence so long that he thought they must have been disconnected, then he heard Bridget's voice on the line. 'I've just got your letter,' he said. 'I've been away for six months.'

There was another pause, and then she laughed. 'Oh dear! And I thought you were playing hard to get. Where have you been?'

Frazer managed to light a cigarette. 'France, Italy and Spain. I thought about you a lot.'

'That's very flattering, after such a brief meeting.' There was a confidence in Bridget's voice that made him hesitant.

'I'd like to see you again. Can we meet?'

'When?' she asked.

'How about tonight?' He fumbled with the cellophane on his cigarette packet.

'Sorry,' Bridget said abruptly. 'That's impossible.'

There was another long silence, and then she said something in such a quiet voice that he could not hear her words. There was a click, and he realised she had hung up.

When Frazer returned to the bar, there were more customers now, but they were all as depressing as the man in the cloth cap. He finished his pint and left. After a few minutes' walk, he was again in Holland Park Road, and on a sudden impulse hailed a taxi. When he paid the fare in Redcliffe Gardens, he wasn't even sure Peter Quick and his wife would be home, but Valerie answered the bell and she was glad to see him.

'What beautiful boots, Carl,' she said in her breathless voice. 'I wish Peter cared more about his clothes. A man came to repair the cupboards in the kitchen last week and he thought Peter was an odd-job man.'

'Where is he?' Frazer asked as he followed her into the flat.

Val waved a hand towards one of the doors in the corridor.

He went in and found Quick sprawled on the sofa drinking wine to the sound of Mozart. He poured Carl a glass. 'So, how was the Grand Tour?' Quick asked, lighting a cigar. 'Did you learn anything?'

Frazer smiled a little ruefully and nodded his head. 'When I saw my stuff again today, it looked a load of crap.'

Quick slowly shook his head. 'Don't confuse self-debasement with humility!'

Frazer laughed. 'Don't worry, I still think I've got talent. It's just I've got to manifest it in a more positive manner.'

Quick sat back and looked at his cigar. 'Christ, that was an ugly sentence. Have you been mixing with Americans?'

'I haven't been mixing with anybody.'

'No love life?' Quick asked.

'There is a girl,' Frazer said slowly, 'but I hardly know her. I met her the day you introduced me to Harold Beriac in the French Pub.'

'Who is she?' Quick asked.

Frazer looked around and found a painting by Richard Cleary in an alcove. He pointed to it. 'His daughter, Bridget Cleary.'

'Richard's daughter?' Quick said with surprise. 'Jesus, you're in love with the Heiress!'

'Heiress?' Frazer repeated, puzzled.

Quick nodded. 'Didn't you know? Where the hell have you been, man?'

'France, Italy and Spain. Don't you remember?'

'Didn't you read any papers?'

Frazer shook his head. 'Not since last Christmas. Why?'

Quick leaned forward. 'Where did you say you met the girl?'

Frazer was beginning to feel slightly queasy. 'At the private view of Richard Cleary's exhibition.'

'Don't you know what a great success it was?' Peter asked.

'I noticed there was a good turn-out,' he answered carefully, 'but I left for France the following day. I didn't see any of the critics.'

'Critics be buggered,' Quick said. 'There was practically a people's uprising! Cleary's probably now the most acclaimed painter Britain's had since Turner.' He raised his arms. 'Christ, even *I'm* popular now! All of the Cromwell Road School are.'

Frazer took another mouthful of wine, hoping it would settle his stomach. 'Oh, come,' he said, gesturing around the room. 'Look at all this; you've been successful for years.'

'That was all Val's money. The boys' father paid for them to go to Rugby, not me. Why the hell do you think I was teaching all those years?'

'So, she's rich now, is she?'

Quick tapped him on the arm. 'You've only heard the half of it. Her grandfather, Sir Julian Nettlebury, is about to rival Lazarus in the resurrection stakes!'

Frazer looked at him with eyes that were slightly out of focus. 'Go on.'

Quick relit his cigar before he continued. 'Neville Crichton made a television programme on Richard. He said that Paul Van Duren had been influenced by certain British painters, namely Sir Julian Nettlebury and Richard Cleary. Well, you can imagine the effect this had on the art historians! It was like someone claiming Prokofiev had been influenced by Vera Lynn. Harold Beriac poured piss on the whole idea. He wrote articles everywhere. Christ, he even had a letter in *The Times*.' Quick paused for a moment with obvious enjoyment.

'What happened then?' Frazer urged him.

'A couple of things happened, actually,' Quick continued. 'First, the Tate bought ten of Nettlebury's early works from a private collection in Germany. Then Crichton dropped his bombshell on Beriac. It seems that Nettlebury had been corresponding with Van Duren for years, and Crichton had got his hands on all the letters. They confirmed everything Crichton claimed Van Duren had told him: colour theory, proportion, form, mass. The only thing they disagreed about was what a fucking painting should actually look like.' Quick glanced up as Val brought in two mugs of coffee. 'Would you like some more wine?' he asked.

Frazer nodded. 'That would be fine.'

Quick got another bottle. 'Crichton's writing a book about it all,' he said when he sat down again. 'His publishers are rushing it out in the autumn.' He laughed suddenly. 'You know, it's rather funny, the idea of somebody rushing to publish a book about art.' He banged the table. 'Stop the presses,' he shouted. 'We've got a hot story about Leonardo da Vinci!' He sat back in his chair and drew on the cigar again. 'To get back to the main event, Crichton wrote a long article

for the *Observer* and included a lot of the letters between Nettlebury
and Van Duren. What with all the fuss, and the Tate buying the
Nettleburys anyway, the upshot is that there's going to be a major
retrospective exhibition of the life works of Sir Julian Nettlebury at
the Tate in the autumn. Crichton's book is probably going to be a
best-seller and those few people who own examples of Nettlebury's
work will be grinning like Cheshire cats!' He poured more wine.
'Bridget Cleary, the final descendant of both Richard Cleary and Sir
Julian Nettlebury, will be the potential owner of riches beyond the
dreams of avarice, and Harold Beriac will probably commit suicide.'

As these words were spoken, Frazer slowly leaned his head back
and closed his eyes.

Quick looked at him, and said, 'I think I'd better ring for a taxi,
old boy.'

'That wine got better as it got older,' Frazer muttered before he
went to sleep.

London, the following day

The first thing Frazer became aware of was a gentle, pattering
sound like the tapping of thousands of tiny hammers. Slowly he
opened his eyes and the blazing strips of neon light seared his vision.
He was lying on his bed, naked except for the Spanish boots, which
he had been unable to remove the night before. When he started to
alter his position, it was as if his whole body, from the crown of his
head to the throbbing feet, was being attacked with red-hot pincers.
The inside of his mouth was a dusty furnace, and his stomach
suddenly twitched as if a giant hand had plucked at his intestines.
When he reached up to run his hands through his hair, it felt like
rubbing splinters of broken glass into his scalp.

With infinite care he rose from the bare mattress and found the
bedclothes. After spreading them on the iron cot, he swallowed half
the bottle of milk on the table, then he switched off the lights, eased
off the boots and crawled back into bed.

The drumming on the tin roof increased and he realised it was
raining heavily. Pale light came through the grimy window. It did
not look as if it was going to be one of those days that made the heart
sing, but at least the clean sheets were cool on his burning body. For
a moment he thought wistfully of the glorious mornings in southern
Europe, and closed his eyes. But sleep would not come. He turned

on his side and looked at the sheets of hardboard he had primed the day before. Gradually the three faces came into his mind again. He gave a long groaning sigh and looked up at the tin roof, rattling with the heavy rain.

A sudden sharp ring on his bell made him flinch. With a curse he got out of bed again, wrapped a towel round his middle and hobbled barefoot along the passage to the door. When he opened it, Bridget stood there, her hair plastered by the rain, holding the collar of her mackintosh closed at the throat. He could see a sketchbook under her arm.

'Well, are you going to let me in,' she asked impatiently, 'or shall I write for another appointment?'

Frazer stood back so that she could enter and led her down the passage. When they reached the studio, she looked about her with interest. 'What *was* this place?' she said. 'It looks too uncomfortable to have been a stable.'

He sat down on the bed, feeling at a distinct disadvantage. In his imagination, their next encounter had not taken place with his clutching at a towel like a customer in a Turkish bath. 'Actually, it was a garage,' he said rather formally.

Bridget nodded. 'A garage,' she repeated doubtfully. 'My Uncle Gideon knew an artist who lived in a garage. His name was Paul Trenton. But that was in Mayfair.'

'I'm sorry my garage is in such an undesirable neighbourhood.'

Bridget stroked the bed. 'Clean sheets. I'm glad.' Then she smiled. 'Do you have another towel?' she asked, not wanting to move. He nodded towards the pile of clean linen. Bridget took one, and began to dry her hair. After a few minutes she said, 'That will have to do.'

She folded the towel neatly over the back of a chair and began to undress. Frazer watched her actions with wonderment, unsure whether he was experiencing reality or not. Finally she stood before him, quite naked apart from a pair of blue-and-white shoes.

'What do you want?' he asked weakly, then realised it was rather a stupid question, considering the circumstances.

'To lose my virginity, of course,' she replied briskly. As soon as she spoke, Frazer felt himself lose the erection that had been growing for the last few minutes. She lay down on the narrow bed beside him, and said, 'Now you'll have to show me the rest.'

'Don't you know anything?' he asked.

Bridget turned and nestled in the crook of his arm. 'I've read some books,' she said. Then she glanced down. 'Shouldn't you be stiff now?'

528

Frazer was still disoriented. In his daydreams he had visualised a period of adjustment, some time getting to know each other – walks in the park, visits to the museums, drinks in riverside pubs, culminating in a consummation so blissful it was still obscured by a rosy haze. This confrontation was like a starving man being presented with the raw material for a banquet and no equipment with which to light the fire. 'The first thing we do is indulge in foreplay,' he suggested.

'How does that begin?' she asked.

Frazer thought for a moment. 'How about making a cup of tea?'

Bridget glanced at his face; his eyes were still fixed on the tin roof. She got up with a sigh and began to potter about the gas stove, searching for the necessary equipment.

While she did this, Frazer watched her. The pale light from the solitary little window caught the edge of her figure and defined the form so beautifully that he could appreciate every curve and line of her graceful body. It was an image so powerful that he knew it would be etched in his memory for ever. Then she turned, and he saw the firmness of her breasts and flat line of her belly, and when she walked towards him with a cup of tea, his arousal was complete.

'I can see you're ready now,' she said softly. She set the tea aside, and he held out his arms.

'I think I'd like to kiss you first,' he said, but as he drew her closer, she seemed to be overcome with shyness. When their mouths brushed together, she began to tremble and he felt a sudden ache of affection. He ran his fingers through her still damp hair, and she made a soft noise of pleasure. Now he was trembling, but his hunger for her was overwhelming. 'Are you quite sure?' he whispered.

'I was sure six months ago,' she said softly.

England, early summer 1964

Graham Todd edged his car closer to the lorry, changed down and accelerated past it into the empty road. The satisfying roar of the Aston Martin's engine brought an accompanying surge of happiness as he contemplated his lot. It had stopped raining half an hour before and the countryside was bathed in sunshine. His new car was everything he had anticipated, and so was Peggy Gorton, the girl beside him. She had been introduced to him at a sale at Sotheby's nearly two weeks before by a fashion photographer called Ryder.

529

'Here's the bird for you, my son,' the photographer had said with irritating self-confidence. 'Legs Gorton.'

It was easy to see why she was called 'Legs', although the rest of her anatomy was equally impressive. She turned when Ryder mentioned her name, and he said, 'Listen, Legs, this is a mate of mine who wants to give you one.' He winked at them both and pushed off into the crowd, leaving Todd to smile weakly into a lovely face wearing an expression of disdain. He knew he had to move fast.

'Please don't judge me by Ryder's comment,' he said quickly.

Peggy Gorton paused. 'Why? Wasn't he telling the truth?'

Todd could tell he was still in with a chance, although one of her shoulders was still pointing away from him. 'I wouldn't wish to spoil our relationship with a lie,' he said, 'so I must say yes. In mitigation, I have to tell you that Ryder was reading my mind, not repeating my words.'

He watched as she turned to face him squarely and her sudden laugh filled him with relief. It was the sort of laugh he had known throughout his life. He had heard it at hunt balls, dinner parties, point-to-points and agricultural shows. It reassured him instantly that Peggy Gorton came from the same drawer as himself, and one that was at the very top of the cabinet.

The reason for his relief had been simple. The moment they had looked at each other, Graham Todd decided that he wanted her, and he had always relied on his impulses. The possibility that she had come from a class other than his own would have created a certain amount of difficulty, but fate or nature had arranged the meeting well.

Peggy looked at Todd's elegant velvet dinner-jacket and asked, 'Are you in the fashion business?'

Todd gestured round the room, which was now crowded with people. 'No, I'm a picture-dealer.'

'Are you buying or selling?'

'Neither.' He pointed to a large abstract on the wall. 'Although I did sell that picture once.'

She studied the mutual oblongs of green and red that seemed to shimmer together. 'Is it valuable?'

Todd said solemnly, 'The most valuable here tonight. It's by Mark Rothko.'

'I've never heard of him; but then I haven't heard of any of these artists.'

'Aren't you interested in pictures?'

She smiled. 'Not this sort. We didn't have anything like this at home.'

'Why did you come?'

She glanced around. 'Ryder brought me. He was rather vague. I thought it was going to be an exhibition of photographs. I didn't think he was going to buy a painting.'

Todd smiled. 'I doubt if even Ryder could afford one of these.'

She looked doubtful at his remark. 'He's quite rich, you know.'

Todd slipped his hand into the pocket of his jacket and produced a silver cigarette-case. 'The cheapest picture will fetch more than one hundred thousand.'

She looked impressed, but not overwhelmed by his assessment. 'So Ryder was just being flash?'

'Just being flash,' he repeated, noting how her speech patterns fluctuated between boarding-school and Bethnal Green. The new Eliza Doolittles, he thought, this time cultivating their Cockney accents.

She glanced round again. 'I thought they served drinks at private views.'

Todd shook his head. 'This isn't a private view; it's a sale.'

She looked puzzled. 'Isn't this a gallery?'

'No, Sotheby's and Christie's are auction houses.'

'I don't follow.'

Todd tried to judge whether she was really interested or just making conversation. She was so beautiful, he decided, it was worth the effort even if she didn't understand a word. 'I work for the Archangel Gallery,' he began. 'We just buy and sell paintings. We manage artists as well. Auction houses handle all sorts of stuff – furniture, pottery, silver, tapestries, objets d'art – as well as paintings. They work on a commission basis. If someone wants to put something up for auction, either to dealers or the general public, they come here and the house takes a percentage of the sale.'

Peggy looked around at the smart crowd dressed in evening clothes, and laughed. 'This lot don't look like the general public,' she whispered.

'This occasion is special,' he agreed. 'They hold them only a few times a year for grand pictures. They have other sales in the daytime that anyone can go to. This is by invitation.'

'Are all these people dealers?'

As she spoke, they could see movement around the lectern at the end of the room, and Todd gestured her to a seat in one of the rows of gilded chairs. 'No,' he replied. 'Some are collectors.'

531

The first picture to be auctioned was a large, almost plain, canvas divided by three narrow bands of primary colour.

'I think I'll stick to our Van Dycks and Canalettos,' she muttered as the bidding began. 'I prefer some things to be traditional.'

Todd looked at her again. So do I, he thought.

Two weeks passed, and by the standards of the time Todd's courtship had been a long one. The days of flowers, phone calls and drinks were about to culminate in a splendid night of consummation at the Grand Hotel, Brighton. All that separated him from the moment was a single pleasant task he had to perform for Gideon that afternoon in Lewes.

Peggy was doing the crossword puzzle in her newspaper. He glanced at her, and saw that she was frowning with concentration. She scratched her nose with the end of her pen.

'What's the clue?' he asked.

Peggy rapped the elegant wooden dashboard twice before she answered. 'Two words, three and four characters: Cheese is the calibre of this man.'

Todd thought for a moment. 'Ben Gunn.'

'It doesn't fit.'

'Two n's in Gunn,' he told her.

'How did you know that?' she asked, inking in the words.

'*Treasure Island.* Ben Gunn was the pirate abandoned by the others. He asks Jim Hawkins if he's got a bit of cheese.'

'You were just lucky,' she said.

'Ask me another,' he challenged.

Peggy studied the newspaper again. 'Five letters. Bigger style of trans-alpine transport. First letter, J.'

'Jumbo,' he said instantly.

She nodded, and stretched her long body. It was a distracting thing to do while he was driving. 'Do you think my breasts are too big?' she asked dispassionately.

'How many letters?'

Peggy threw the newspaper on the back seat. 'It's not a clue, silly! I'm asking you a proper question.'

Todd shook his head firmly and kept his eyes on the road before him. 'No, I most certainly do not.'

Peggy sighed. 'They've cost me a fortune, you know. If they hadn't been so big I would have been in Ethiopia right now doing a swimwear job.' He changed down again to pass a dawdling Morris Oxford as she continued her lamentations. 'I don't know why people call me "Legs". "Tits" would be more suitable with these two huge udders dangling in front of people's faces. I look like an advertisement for one of those awful Italian movies.' She thought for a few more moments. 'Ryder always says he wants to pump me up. I could be "La Pumpa".'

'And have you ever let him?' he asked lightly, but Peggy knew how much he actually cared about her answer.

'Most certainly not! I believe this current idea of rushing around fucking everyone you like the look of is extremely short-sighted.'

Todd kept his eyes on the road. 'Is that a moral judgment? Or are you speaking pragmatically?'

'I don't understand.'

Todd managed to light a cigarette before he answered. 'Do you object to people screwing around on ethical grounds, or do you think it has practical drawbacks, such as the spreading of disease, the lowering of self-regard or the limiting of ultimate marital prospects?'

Peggy thought for a moment. 'Both, I suppose. From a pragmatic point of view, my Great-Aunt Dorothy says it just doesn't work. She told me everyone was frightfully sophisticated in Edwardian times, having affairs all over the place and pretending no one was noticing. But the most incredible pressures built up between people, and every now and again someone would either go mad or shoot themselves.' She looked out of the window. 'When I get married, I don't want my husband to look at every man I introduce him to, and think, was he one of the boys who banged my wife in her carefree days?' They exchanged a glance, and she smiled briefly. 'Has that spoilt your plans for the weekend?'

Todd smiled. He was trying very hard not to show the sense of relief he was feeling. Peggy was still worried about the way the conversation was going. 'Anyway,' she said, 'none of this has any bearing on the fortune my tits have cost me.'

'Why don't you look on the positive side and think of the vast amount of money that could be yours because of them?'

Peggy shook her head. 'No, thank you. My family think posing for *Vogue* is one step from the gutter! If I flashed these into the camera, a little corner of Wiltshire would die. I couldn't do it to them.'

'I wasn't thinking of that. I actually meant that you could always marry me.'

Peggy looked at him; she could tell nothing from the serious profile. 'But you haven't got lots of money, darling. Everyone knows you're a younger son. Surely it all goes to Perry?'

He grinned. 'No, I'm a younger step-brother. My own father died when I was nine.'

'So you've got your own money?' Peggy asked with interest. Unlike the middle classes, she did not find discussing the subject of wealth vulgar.

He nodded, and slapped the steering wheel. 'You don't think I could afford this from my salary at the Archangel Gallery, do you?'

She shrugged. 'I thought there was a lot of money in selling paintings.'

'There is, but not for assistants. I shan't make any of the real stuff until I become a partner or start my own gallery.'

Peggy was silent for a while, and then she said, 'If you're already rich, why do you bother to work?'

He laughed. 'Well, actually, I enjoy it. I'm really doing what your father does.'

'What do you mean?'

He thought carefully for a moment. 'Well, I already have all the money anyone could want.'

Peggy shot him another glance. 'Are you that rich?'

'Oh, yes. So now I just enjoy myself.'

'How can you compare yourself with my father? He works non-stop on the estate . . .'

'Doing what?' he interrupted.

'Visiting the tenants, looking after the game. He's on two committees, and he's a magistrate.' She paused. 'You're right: he does enjoy himself . . . He's the same as Perry; they actually like farm animals and fields full of crops.'

He nodded 'I enjoy paintings, I love the country at weekends, but on a wet Wednesday in November I'd rather be in Bond Street.'

'And where are we going now?' she asked.

They had arrived at a crossroads, and Todd had stopped the Aston Martin. 'To the estate of the late Francis Leslie Holton, if I can find it.' He consulted various documents and then produced a map from the glove compartment. While he was searching, Peggy had got out of the car and was standing under a vast elm on the corner. She felt very happy that she wasn't in Ethiopia.

'Found it!' Todd called out eventually.

She took her seat again, and before they drew away, she took hold of his arm. 'Let's not go to Brighton. Let's go to Wiltshire instead and tell my parents.'

'Tell them what?' he asked innocently.

534

Peggy punched him. 'That you've offered to marry me, you wretched man!'

The prospects for the weekend were not at all what he had planned, but he realised that his own questions had taken him to this point. 'All right,' he said after a moment. 'But you'll have to ring the Grand Hotel and cancel the booking.'

'Won't you want to ring your parents as well?' she asked.

'They're sailing in Bermuda. I'll see if I can get in touch from Wiltshire.'

She squeezed his arm again. 'What a perfect day!' she said as they pulled on to the road.

It was just after two-thirty when they stopped in the wide gravel forecourt of Holton Manor. The house was large and ugly, built of yellow brick and half covered in dusty ivy.

'I bet they're going to turn it into an old folks' home,' said Peggy. 'It's just the sort of place that would make people miserable.'

In the entrance hall, Todd found the man in charge of proceedings talking to a rather tense secretary, who turned to them. 'If you've come to buy pictures, I'm afraid you're a teeny bit early. Mr Braithwaite has decided they will now be auctioned at the end of the sale,' the woman said in a breathless voice that implied that the two of them could accept the situation or clear off.

Her use of the word 'teeny' had already set Peggy's teeth on edge, but Todd saw the desperation in her strained manner. He realised that she was under pressure, and decided that charm would achieve more than argument.

'That must have caused you a great deal of difficulty,' he said sympathetically.

'Oh, we can cope,' she said, her inflection rising. 'The difficult we do immediately, the impossible takes a little time.'

'Quite so,' Todd continued in the same soothing tones. He noticed that Mr Braithwaite had taken the opportunity to slip away. 'Talking of the impossible, I don't suppose there's a telephone anywhere my fiancée could use?'

Peggy shot an amused look in his direction at the first use he had made of the term.

'Up the stairs to the landing and the first room on your left,' the secretary said.

Peggy followed her directions and Todd went on, 'You must have had a terrible day.' He knew now that she was one of those people who

535

could not handle any changes in a pre-ordained plan.

'Just when I had everything organised beautifully,' she said, and he thought for a moment she was going to cry. 'All the picture-dealers are here. I told customers who were interested in the furniture not to bother to come until at least four-thirty. What will they think of me now?'

'What caused the change of plans?' Todd asked.

'Mr Braithwaite,' she said, in a voice filled with loathing. 'Just because some London dealer rang up and said he couldn't be here until later, he's thrown all the arrangements into chaos.'

'What dealer is coming from London?' Todd asked. He produced a packet of cigarettes and offered her one.

'Mr Schneider of Strange and Schneider,' she replied, accepting the cigarette. 'And he's interested in only one of the lots.'

'Really?' Todd answered. He blew smoke away from the woman. 'Which one is that?'

'Number 14,' she said. 'The Holbein drawings.'

'Well, I mustn't keep you,' said Todd. 'Here come some more customers.'

With a nod he made his way further into the house and found the room where lot 14 was on display. It consisted of three separate drawings, which he recognised as preliminary sketches for a painting called *Portrait of Erasmus of Rotterdam*. The first was a study for the face, the two others of the hands. Todd studied them for a few minutes, but the light was bad and they were in a showcase in a dark corner. He went back and found the secretary. 'It's me again,' he said. 'The impossible man, with another request.'

'What is it?' It was clear that she rather enjoyed performing simple tasks that she could achieve without difficulty.

'The Holbein drawings. I wonder if I might look at them in a natural light?'

She took out a large bunch of keys, and he followed her to the showcase. There was a momentary confusion over the keys before she unlocked it. Todd examined the drawings by the strong light from the window. After a few minutes he smiled his thanks and was replacing them in the showcase, when Peggy returned.

'All done?' he asked.

She nodded. 'The Grand is cancelled, and my parents are expecting us for dinner.'

'Bit short notice. I hope they don't mind,' he said.

Peggy shook her head. 'Mummy guessed.'

536

'What was her reaction?'

'Tears and laughter.'

Todd glanced at the Holbein drawings again and wrote something in a notebook. 'Let's go outside and get some fresh air,' he said, but when they reached the hall he took her by the arm. 'Show me where the telephone is.'

Peggy led him to the room that had once been a study but now contained only a chair, a telephone and a frayed Persian carpet. When he got through to the Archangel Gallery, Peggy could hear the urgency in his voice.

'Ralph,' he said to one of the assistants,' I must speak to Gideon or Laszlo.' It was Laszlo who came to the phone. 'The Holbein drawings that Gideon told me to buy,' he said. 'I'm pretty sure they're fakes, and Schneider is coming here as well. Do you want me to let them have them?'

'Just a moment,' said Laszlo. 'I'll put you on to Gideon.'

'Hello, Toddy,' Gideon said after a brief pause. 'What makes you think the drawings are fakes?'

Todd spoke slowly. 'They look good; but there's something wrong with the paper, and one of the sketches is definitely odd.'

'Explain.'

'It's a drawing of the hands. The pen has supposedly written some Latin on a parchment.'

'Go on,' Gideon urged.

'Well, in the actual portrait of Erasmus, he's using his right hand. In this sketch it's the left. The inscription reads: *Mens sibi conscia recti.* The hand has almost finished the word "Ovid" – but Ovid didn't write that; I'm pretty sure it was Virgil. Don't you see? It's some kind of pun about being right- and left-handed. The Latin means: "A mind conscious of the right".'

Gideon flexed his own right hand before he spoke. 'Listen very carefully, Toddy. I want you to buy those drawings no matter the cost. Understand?'

'I understand what I'm to do, but I don't understand why,' he replied.

'I'll explain it all later. Just make sure you get the pictures. There could be a junior partnership in it for you.' He was about to hang up, when he remembered something. 'You say the hand hasn't quite written out "Ovid"?'

'That's right,' said Todd. 'Just the first three letters.'

Gideon put down the receiver and turned to Laszlo. 'Toddy has solved the puzzle. It's Ovington who's been selling my work.'

'Ovington?' Laszlo said incredulously.

'Oh, yes,' said Gideon. 'He's added an extra hand to the drawing I did – and a message.' He wrote the words down and then repeated them. 'A mind conscious of the right. I wonder what he's getting at?' he said softly.

CHAPTER TWENTY-FOUR

London, summer 1964

After a blazing argument with her daughter, Irene rushed out of the house and into the garden, to the place by the tall brick wall where she had always gone as a child in times of trouble. Her breathing was heavy and her hands trembled, but gradually the anger subsided.

It had been a long time since she had been to this corner; years, she suddenly thought. The man who came to tend the garden for her had begun to make changes. There were shrubs planted in front of the pampas grass that grew around the old summerhouse. Soon they would alter the view from the kitchen completely. He had already cut down two of the fruit trees, claiming they were too far gone to save.

Suddenly she wanted it just as it had been when she was a girl. She would tell him the next time he came. Everything had to be exactly the same. There were old photographs in the album, taken some time in the thirties; she would give him those and make sure it was restored to the original.

Gradually her breathing returned to normal and she walked back into the house. Everything was strange; the walls were quite bare. Her father's pictures were still away on loan.

The exhibition at the Tate had been an extraordinary success. It had gone to Paris and Frankfurt, then to Glasgow and Manchester. Two more weeks, and the pictures will be home and everything will be the same again, Irene told herself. But she knew nothing would.

Slowly she climbed the stairs to the bedroom where Bridget was packing. The door stood open. She watched her daughter take clothes from the wardrobe and place them neatly in the suitcase on the bed. Bridget looked up, but did not pause in her task.

Irene decided she would try one more time. 'Won't you just stay tonight and talk it over?'

Bridget shook her head and continued packing her possessions with great care.

'We've already talked it over endlessly. We always end up in the same place. You hate Frazer, and I love him. That's all there is to it.'

'But you're throwing your life away!' Irene said despairingly.

'That's what we all do, Mother,' Bridget answered in a calm voice from which all passion had gone. 'It just depends in which direction we throw it. You think I'm going off to ruin my life, and I think I'm going to live with the man I love.'

Irene came into the room and stood on the other side of the bed. 'You're going to live in a garage, in a slum,' she said, trying very hard to keep the anger out of her voice. 'Dear God! You could go wherever you want, now. Paris, Rome, New York . . .'

Bridget folded a sweater over her arm. 'You had nothing when you started.'

Irene shook her head. 'I had less than nothing; I had your father. I thought his selfishness made him interesting and his dedication to painting romantic, a commitment like a religious belief.'

'What about Grandfather?' Bridget asked. 'Wasn't he dedicated?'

'He was, but he had room in his life for other people. Richard Cleary's world was himself. You could either cling on or fall off. It didn't matter either way to him.'

Bridget closed the final suitcase. 'Carl isn't like that. I know.'

'You don't know anything,' Irene answered, but Bridget could hear that the fight had gone out of her voice.

'Look, Mother,' she said kindly, 'I'm only going to Notting Hill, for God's sake. That's not the end of the earth!'

Irene spoke without emotion. 'When you're sitting there with a baby in your arms, it will seem like it.'

Bridget shook her head again, as though her mother were the child who would not see reason. 'I have no intention of having a baby for many years to come.'

Irene looked down at the bed. 'You can't always plan these things.'

'Yes, you can, Mum. That's exactly what you can do. It doesn't have to be down to the man to make those decisions, you know.'

'How can you be so cold-blooded about everything?'

Bridget shook her head almost in despair. 'I'm not being cold-blooded, just sensible. Carl and I love each other now, but I know it may not last. Perhaps you're right; in six months or a year things may have changed. No harm will be done. I'll come home.'

Irene spoke slowly. 'Suppose you've given everything to him and he walks out on you? You could be so much in love with him by then that it will break your heart.'

'No, it won't, Mother,' Bridget replied. Irene could see the resolve in her face. 'I remember what happened to you, and I wouldn't put up with that.'

Irene could see she was telling the truth and she suddenly remembered Bridget was Cleary's child as well as her own. She stood with her head bowed.

Bridget walked from the room and hurried from the house into the street, where Frazer was waiting for her with Peter Quick's old Riley.

'How was it?' he asked as they drove away.

'Terrible.' There was so much feeling in her words that he did not press her.

Irene walked slowly through the house when Bridget had gone, remembering the pictures that had hung in the pale patches. Then she found it was opening time; I ought to be able to track Richard Cleary down, she told herself.

At first she intended to go by Underground, but then remembered that she could afford a taxi. It was two-fifteen by the time she reached Soho, and she told the driver to wait while she went from public house to public house. Eventually she found a group, in the French Pub, who told her that he had just left for Pandora's. She paid off the taxi and climbed the narrow stairs to the first floor to the old familiar surroundings. It still smells the same, she thought: bodies, cigarette smoke and the yeasty scent of spilt beer.

Cleary was there, sitting alone at the bar, his head hanging over his glass. At first she thought he might be asleep; his eyes were closed, and the cigarette that burned between his fingers had a long drooping ash. A fringe of white hair fell over his lined forehead. The flesh seemed to have shrunk from his face, and his once-broad shoulders were now frail and wasted beneath the thin material of his lightweight jacket. Despite his neglected body, the clothes he wore were expensive. It was clear he was determined to face death drunk and well dressed.

He looked up suddenly with a jerk of his head when she sat down on the stool next to him. When he spoke, the words came from deep within his meagre frame. It sounded to her like a medium speaking with the voice of a dead man.

'What do you want, Irene?' he asked. 'It can't be money. Would you care for a drink?'

She shook her head. 'I've come to speak to you about our daughter,' she answered in a low voice. 'Can you still take things in?'

Cleary sat straighter on the stool and ground out the cigarette. 'Oh, yes,' he replied with a nod of his head. 'Fifty per cent of me is still operational. Mind you, the bottom half packed in some time ago.' He reached into his pocket with slow deliberation and took out another cigarette. His hands trembled, but she could not feel any pity for him, only a slight anger at the waste. 'What about Bridget? I saw her last week with some young Scottish prick who claimed he was a painter.'

'That's what I've come to talk to you about. Bridget has gone to live with him. I want you to talk to her.'

Cleary lit the cigarette and inhaled deeply. His body was racked by a sudden spasm of coughing. 'What do you want me to say to her?' he asked eventually.

She glanced around before answering. 'I want you to tell her that she's ruining her life.'

'Is she?' Cleary asked slowly. 'Well, that's no surprise, considering her parents. I would have thought she was only bowing to the inevitable.'

Irene looked at him impatiently. 'You're the one who set the example. But she still listens to you, God knows why! Now I'm asking you to point out to her that she can choose to live her life another way.'

He turned his head slowly to look at her. 'I see, Irene,' he said flatly. 'So I'm the bad example, and you're the one she's supposed to follow.' He pointed towards the mirror behind the bar. 'Take a look in that: there's two dead people standing here. I chose to drink myself to death, but you've just decided to wither away.' He drew on his cigarette and turned to her again. 'Remember those pieces of fruit in the Still Life room? They looked alive, but when you picked them up they were as light as dust. Nothing inside them; they'd just dried up. Well, that's you.' He shook his head. 'If she's chosen to go off with that young fool, so be it. He talks a lot of piss about painting, but at least he's alive. She won't be locked up in a shrine like some nun worshipping at the tomb of her father.' He held up his glass to the barman.

Irene did not want to hear any more. She left the club and walked slowly down Greek Street towards Shaftesbury Avenue. For a moment she thought of visiting Anne, but dismissed the idea. Instead, she got a taxi and asked the driver to take her home. He sucked his teeth in disapproval at her request.

'Kew? Blimey, love, that's going to cost you double fare,' he moaned.

542

Suddenly the rage rose in her, and she shouted through the partition, 'I don't care if it costs a thousand bloody pounds, just take me there right now!'

The driver shrugged his shoulders and put the cab into gear.

When they got to Cromwell Road, the past came back, and she felt as if her heart would break. At Earl's Court, she began to cry, and the taxi-driver gave her troubled glances in his rear-view mirror for the rest of the journey.

London, spring 1965

Gideon was waiting at the barrier when Charles Whitney-Ingram stepped out of the crowd on to the concourse at Heathrow.

'No luggage?' Gideon asked as they walked towards the chauffeur-driven car.

Charles shook his head and held up a small bag. 'I'll tell you about that in a minute,' he said, following Gideon into the rear of the Rolls-Royce. 'This is pretty fancy! New?'

Gideon nodded and gestured for Gibson, the driver, to go on. He leaned back and smiled. 'If you want to see how vulgar it really is, take a look at this.' He lowered a panel to reveal a cocktail cabinet.

'What the hell!' Charles said. 'It's still night time in New York. Give me a large brandy.' When they had settled back with their drinks, he told Gideon why he had no luggage. 'I was walking in Central Park last Sunday when I had to stop because a child was standing in my path. A little boy about so big.' He held out a hand to denote the size. 'Then his mother reached out to grab him, and said, "Come on, let the old gentleman pass." ' Charles shrugged. 'I called her a mother, but she only looked about sixteen. Her words really got to me. When I reached my apartment I took a look at myself in the mirror and, Judas Priest, I did look like an old man! I had this goddamn homburg on because it was such a cold day, and an overcoat. I've had to wear spectacles for about a year, and suddenly I'm standing there and I saw my father in the looking-glass staring back at me. So I thought, this is it. When I get to London I'm going to buy an entirely new wardrobe.' He leaned towards Gideon. 'What do you think of these?' he asked, pulling down one of his lower eyelids.

'What am I supposed to look at?'

'Contact lenses,' Charles said triumphantly. 'You see, you couldn't spot them!'

543

'I thought that was the idea,' Gideon replied. 'Do they hurt?'

'Like hell at first, but I'm getting used to them. Jesus, Gideon, I'm a long way from fifty.' He raised his drink in a salute. 'So how are things? Are Laszlo and Elizabeth well? And Anne?'

Gideon opened the car window a fraction before he answered. 'Laszlo and Elizabeth are fine. Anne has been a bit sad the last few days. Nettlebury's old housekeeper, Maude Cooper, has finally gone into retirement. We bought her a cottage in Devon.'

Charles clicked his fingers. 'Talking about old retainers, did I tell you what's happened to Raymond Quill?' Gideon shook his head. 'You're not going to believe this. He married Angela Wilmot.'

'Angela?' Gideon said. 'Van Duren's girlfriend?'

'The very one.'

'How did his family cope with that?' Gideon asked. He remembered that they were rather stuffy, and Angela had received a good deal of ugly publicity at the time of Moyle's trial.

Charles drank his brandy. 'Raymond's mother died and left him all the money, so he didn't really care about the rest of them. Angela moved away from New York to Chicago. She got a job with a branch of the Lowel Gallery. Anyway, Raymond just went there and stood outside her apartment. At first she ignored him, but you know how cold it is in winter. He almost died of exposure. After about three days she took him in. They got married two weeks ago.'

'Well, here's to them!' Gideon raised his glass.

Charles glanced out of the window of the car. 'Where are we going?'

'Buckinghamshire; you've been requested for a special authentication,' Gideon replied. 'Then back into town. Unless you want a rest? I know how tiring overnight flights can be.'

'No, I slept like a baby on the plane. In fact, that's all the sleep I may bother with while I'm here. If London is the Swinging City, I'm her man!'

Gideon smiled. 'Well, I'm older than you, so I'm going to take a nap. Gibson will tell you when we're nearly there.' He lay back in the soft leather upholstery and closed his eyes.

Some time later, Gibson woke him, and he saw that Charles was also fast asleep. 'Come on, wonder-boy, we're there,' Gideon said as they drove through high gates into a landscaped park.

The walls of the building were constructed of some white, impervious material that looked as if it would deflect the blast of a nuclear bomb. There were elongated black-framed windows set into the façade and the frontage was broken by bays and towers, some rounded and others square.

Charles thought it looked like a vast modern chess-set that had been leaned against a lavatory wall. 'The architect of this place must have been an escaped Nazi war criminal,' he said.

'What makes you say that?' Gideon asked.

'Hitler was against the Bauhaus. This guy was out to prove he was right.'

'It's not so bad inside,' said Gideon. 'Come on.'

But Charles found the interior just as soulless, despite the pictures that hung everywhere. The floor was covered in a substance similar to a motor-tyre. He tapped his foot experimentally, and a voice from above said, 'It's a form of nylon. The engineers who laid it claimed it would last longer than the Pyramids.'

Charles looked up and, from a balcony in the well that rose through the centre of the house, they could see Lady Peake gazing down. She descended the wide metal staircase and shook hands with Gideon.

'This is my partner from New York, Charles Whitney-Ingram,' Gideon explained.

'I'm delighted to meet you,' she said. 'I take it you don't care for my house?'

'I suppose it takes some getting used to,' Charles answered diplomatically.

Lady Peake laughed, and her breasts shook inside her loose silk shirt.

Charles was impressed; word had reached New York that women were wearing extraordinary clothes in London. He gave a speculative glance at Lady Peake's white stockings and short skirt. Her face was framed by short hair that looked as though it had been shaped with a scalpel.

'I suppose it's all right,' she said, 'but I hate it now.' She glanced around. 'I insisted my husband build it like this. I'm afraid we knocked down a Georgian house to make this hideous monstrosity come true.'

Gideon, listening to her, noted that each vowel was as true as a church bell. Lady Peake had certainly got one thing right: her voice would earn full marks from the most fastidious elocution teacher now.

'I must say one thing in its favour, though,' she continued. 'It does show the pictures to great advantage. I suppose one could claim it's

545

the only thing of any merit about the entire place. Would you care to see the rest of the folly?'

Charles and Gideon nodded, and she led them from room to room. Her claim was no exaggeration. The pictures were well displayed against the tall white walls; the stark contrasting tones of the surroundings made a perfect, if rather antiseptic, backdrop for the dazzling paintings in the collection.

'If you would like to come up to the first floor, gentlemen, I'll show you the reason I asked you to come here today,' she said, and they climbed the spiral staircase.

The first floor was one huge showroom that ran the entire length of the building, devoted to Van Duren's work.

Lady Peake gestured towards the far end of the gallery. 'Just last week my husband acquired four more paintings by Van Duren in the United States. As they didn't come from the Archangel Gallery, I wanted you to authenticate them,' she explained as they walked, with hardly the sound of a footstep, across the strange black floor.

For Charles more than Gideon it was a journey through the past. Some of the pictures were like old friends, others no more than casual acquaintances, but each represented a period in his life.

When they reached the far end of the room, Lady Peake said, 'I'd like a cigarette. Would anyone else care for anything?' She pressed a button, and a few minutes later a woman in a maid's uniform emerged. 'Bring some tea and cigarettes to the roof, Yvette.' The dark little woman nodded, and disappeared. Then Lady Peake gestured towards four pictures that were grouped together.

Charles nodded when he looked at them. 'Yes, Lady Peake,' he said at once, 'that's definitely the work of Paul Van Duren. And you have them placed in correct sequence. The paintings are called *Manhattan Transfer*. These are two of the "A-train series".'

'You're absolutely sure?' she asked.

Charles nodded. 'Beyond question. I visited his studio quite often when he was working on them.'

She sighed, and smiled with relief. 'I'm delighted,' she said quickly. 'I trust my husband's judgment in everything, except buying pictures. When he came back from America and told me he had a bargain, my heart didn't exactly leap for joy.'

Gideon and Charles exchanged glances. Then Charles turned to her. 'These pictures belonged to Jack Stapoulas, didn't they?'

'That's right. It was a private sale, but originally they came from Anthony Strange. You can understand now, I think, why I was

546

doubtful about their authenticity.'

Charles nodded, and she turned and led them away from the paintings. 'Let's go up to the roof. I'm sure you'll be ready for some tea now.'

The word 'roof' was a misnomer. In fact they found themselves in a vast conservatory, dense with tropical plants, where brightly coloured birds flashed between the vines, chattering and whistling in the heat. Gideon stood and looked over the English countryside, which was just beginning to show the first signs of green in the budding trees. 'This part of the house works,' he said.

Lady Peake nodded. 'Whole sections of this roof lift off if the temperature outside reaches a certain level. They used the same equipment that raises the landing gear in a jet liner.'

'The house must have cost a fortune,' said Gideon.

'Pity nobody likes it,' she said ruefully, 'Still, Ted thinks he's found a solution to the problem.'

'He has? What's that?'

She smiled mysteriously. 'You'll have to give me a lift into town to find the answer to that.'

'I shall be delighted,' Gideon answered.

'Just give me a few minutes, and I'll be ready,' she said.

When they had finished their tea, Charles and Gideon were escorted to the car by Yvette. They found Gibson, the driver, looking up at the building with a thoughtful expression. He came to attention when he saw them and opened the rear door of the Rolls-Royce, but Gideon did not enter.

'What's your opinion of this place, Gibson?' he asked.

'Bit like my mum's new block of flats, sir.'

'Does she like the flats?'

The young man shrugged. 'She don't mind because she's on the ground floor. But the ones on the top moan like hell.'

'What do you think of them?' Charles asked.

'About the flats, sir? I think some will keep them nice and some will turn them into pigsties, same as they have with everywhere else they've lived.'

'I take it you're not a socialist, Gibson?' said Charles.

The young man shook his head. 'No, sir, I am not. It's all right for the bloke who built this place, I know he's Labour. But he can afford to be; he's rich, and it's all right if you're just sitting around waiting for a handout like half of them living in my mum's flats. For us in the middle, who work for a living, socialism's a bloody liberty.'

547

Lady Peake emerged, and Gibson hurried to open the car door again. When they were all seated, Gideon operated the glass partition to seal them from the driver.

'My God,' Charles said in an awed voice, 'that fellow should get a job on Wall Street. He'd feel very much at home.'

Gideon chuckled. 'That, my friend, is the authentic voice of Conservative Britain. No wonder the ruling classes feel safe in their beds at night, with people like Gibson on guard!'

'Perhaps that's what you should turn him into, a guard for the gallery. I'm sure he'd like a savage dog for company,' said Charles.

Gideon shook his head. 'No, he doesn't like the gallery at all. When he's there, he just keeps asking the secretaries the price of the pictures and then saying: "That much just for a load of tripe?" It's having rather a depressing effect on them.'

The journey into London took some time, but eventually they reached the Peake building, where they were greeted with a great deal of deference by a pair of uniformed commissionaires. Lady Peake looked at her watch as they ascended in the private lift. 'Ten minutes to go. We timed that nicely,' she said, and winked at them. She still had not told them the reason why she had insisted they accompany her.

When they arrived at the executive suite, they found a long baize-covered table in the corridor, where two smiling secretaries were handing information packs to groups of men arriving by the public lifts. Gideon realised that a press conference was imminent. He was going to take one of the folders, but Lady Peake hurried them up a narrow staircase into the office where Peake sat at his desk speaking on the telephone. Behind him hung *The Girl In The White Dress*, and Gideon studied it until Peake hung up.

'Take a good gander, my old son. I'm afraid it's going away on holiday for a while.'

Gideon glanced at him in surprise. 'Really, Ted? If you're not going to keep it on the wall, why not sell it to me?'

Peake stood up and put his arm round Gideon's shoulder. 'Now, you know if I was ever going to let it go, I'd sell it to you, James. But I can't part with it, you know she's my lucky mascot.'

'What are you going to do with it?' Gideon asked.

'It's going to Switzerland, with some of my other stuff. To a nice bomb-proof bank vault under Zurich airport.'

Gideon was about to ask him more when an aide entered the room. He coughed discreetly and announced that the gentlemen of the press were ready.

'Can't keep them fellows waiting,' Peake said, and he ushered everyone towards the conference room where the reporters waited.

When they entered, a waiter offered Gideon a tray full of drinks. Gideon took a whisky. He was feeling more than a little depressed by Peake's news. He and Charles stood to the side of the room while the aide spoke into a microphone.

'Gentlemen, please be silent for Lord Peake.'

Peake stood up and walked to the microphone. The mumbled chatter and the odd clink of reporters' glasses faded into silence.

'Lord Peake,' he repeated. 'Where else could a man like me achieve something like that except in the Britain of today?' He gestured towards the long window that ran the length of the room. 'When I started developing this part of London, there was nothing around St Paul's but bomb-sites. Well, look at her now.' The men in the room stared through the window at the dreary panorama of box-like buildings surrounding them. Peake boomed on, 'And I'm glad to say that I am responsible for much of what you see before you today.' He paused again. 'When I first came here I was just plain Ted Peake, but Britain being what it is, our dear Queen saw fit to ennoble me, first with a knighthood and then with a peerage.' He smiled. 'Now, most fellows, when they get made a baron, say they only took it for their wives. But I'll own up and say I took it because I earned it, and I took it for all the people in my companies who helped to put me where I am today. I like to think it is for them as well as for me.' He paused, as if expecting tumultuous applause, but there were only a few enthusiastic claps from his employees.

'Yes, gentlemen,' Peake continued, 'I have given the city of London a great deal of my life, but now the time has come for me to seek new pastures.' He took a sip of water, and now there was a murmur of interest from the journalists. He smiled slightly. 'I've called you here today to announce that I have sold Peake Industries to an American conglomerate called the Rainbow Group. I know what you're asking,' he said in a jocular fashion. 'What's Lord Ted going to do next? Well, I'll tell you. I'm going to go on earning money for this country of ours, but I'm going to do it abroad for a while. I'm going to fund a new entertainment division with the Rainbow Group; fifty per cent American and fifty per cent British, just like the partnership we formed in the darkest days of the war.' This time there was a louder chatter and he held up his hands. 'Some of the more cynical among you may ask if I'm leaving Britain

549

for good. Oh yes, I can read it in your faces. "Old Lord Ted has made his pile," you're saying to yourselves. "And now he's buggering off to some tax haven." Well, let me tell you, nothing is further from the truth. In fact I'm leaving something behind I value much more than money, and it's going to the nation. My art collection.' There was another loud rippling mutter of comment. 'The collection is world famous' – he shook his head – 'but I can't take all the credit for that. My wife, Lady Peake, must be first in line there, and also my old friends from the Archangel Gallery, Mr James Gideon and his equally distinguished American partner Mr Charles Whitney-Ingram.' Peake gestured towards them. 'They have helped me to assemble this magnificent collection, and I'm sure they will verify my claims for it. The mansion I built to house the collection and the paintings themselves are my gift to Great Britain. I hope future generations will come to see them. Who knows, some little lad might decide that anything Lord Ted Peake could do, he could do better, and he might go out, roll up his sleeves and build the sort of empire I have.' Once again he held up his arms. 'Now, are there any questions?'

The first one was directed at Gideon. 'Can you tell me, sir, what value you put upon the Peake Collection?' the reporter asked.

Gideon shrugged, and looked at Charles. 'It's very hard to say, off-hand,' he replied. 'The value of paintings alters all the time.

Another man stood up. 'But they rarely go down in value, do they, sir?'

Gideon smiled. 'Very rarely, I'm glad to say.'

'So how much would you hazard? More than a million, less than two million?'

Gideon shook his head. 'Oh, no. The Peake Collection is worth easily in excess of ten million pounds.'

There was a sudden silence, and then the journalists stood up and began to move towards the door.

Ted Peake watched the exodus with a satisfied smile. Not one of the reporters had asked him a question. He shook Gideon's hand as they were leaving. 'Take care, James,' he said. 'I'll be seeing you soon.'

When they had left the building, Charles yawned. 'I shouldn't have taken that drink.'

'Where are you staying?' Gideon asked.

'The Ritz.' Charles stifled another yawn.

'We'd better get home. Anne is preparing an early dinner. Laszlo and Elizabeth will be there, too.'

They paused on the pavement by the car, and Charles said, 'How's

Anne's sister these days?' He thought for a moment. 'You know, we haven't seen each other since we were kids.'

'She's fine, just fine,' Gideon replied, opening the car door.

When they reached the flat in Bond Street, Gideon left it to Laszlo to give Charles a drink and went to find his wife. Anne was stirring a pot on the stove when he found her in the kitchen.

'Where's Irene? I thought she was coming,' he asked.

Anne held up her hands. 'She rang half an hour ago and said she couldn't make it.'

'Is she ill?'

'I don't think so,' she replied. 'Did you tell Charles she was coming?'

'I thought it better not to. Plainly I made the right decision.' When he got back to the others, Charles was describing the events of the day.

Laszlo turned to Gideon as he opened a bottle of champagne. 'What do you think Ted is up to?' he asked.

Gideon brought the bottle over and poured drinks. 'I don't know yet, but it was obvious that we were meant to be part of the show. You should have seen them all run when I told them what the collection was worth!'

Charles got up and began to walk slowly round the room, studying the pictures. 'This must be worth a king's ransom now,' he said in front of a landscape by Julian Nettlebury. He drank some of his champagne. 'It doesn't look a damned bit like a Van Duren to me,' he said with a smile.

The following morning Charles was shown to a table in the dining-room at the Ritz. He did not really want breakfast, but he had been awake for a couple of hours and had grown bored in his bedroom. *The Times* had been read from cover to cover, and he had started to make notes for a book he had been considering writing for the past year, but his mind was in a butterfly state. He decided on some coffee before he set off to shop for clothes. When he was seated by the windows looking on to Green Park, he heard laughter coming from a family at the next table who were watching the father performing a trick with his napkin.

Their merriment suddenly made Charles feel very lonely. He glanced at the family, hoping they would not think he was staring, but they were too occupied with each other to notice. He guessed that the father would be about his own age, perhaps a bit younger.

551

His wife was attractive, with a slender figure of which she took good care. She had ordered grapefruit. The others – the father, a boy and a girl – ate bacon and scrambled eggs. They were clearly British, because they spoke in low voices. Charles had noticed that American children had become much more strident in recent years, and these reminded him of the way he and his friends had been taught to behave. How can a nation change the habits of its children so quickly, he wondered, in just one generation? The waiter poured his coffee and he drank it in an absent-minded fashion.

It had crossed his mind the night before, when they were sitting at dinner, that there was no second generation for the Archangel Gallery. Who will inherit it all? he wondered. For his own part, there were some distant cousins he never saw.

Then he thought of Anne's sister again, remembering that she had married Richard Cleary. He had seen Cleary in New York several times, but never Irene. Vaguely he recalled that he'd had a schoolboy crush on her one summer before the war. He could still remember the ache he had endured when they had parted. He smiled at the recollection, and then wondered why. The memory was not a particularly happy one. In fact, he thought, it had all been damned painful. Suddenly he could see her face quite clearly, the pale skin dusted with freckles and the deep red hair. He knew she still lived in Nettlebury's house, which was some kind of museum now.

He finished his coffee and made his way to the reception desk. The clerk on duty was helpful and well informed. 'Can you tell me the address of the Sir Julian Nettlebury museum?' Charles asked.

'It's not a museum, sir, it's a private collection and can only be viewed by apppointment,' the clerk answered.

'You sound as if you've said that before,' Charles replied.

The young man smiled. 'It was the *Reader's Digest* article, sir. Since that appeared, they've been coming from all over the world. And it's a convenient trip, you see, the house being opposite Kew Gardens.'

Charles nodded. 'I want you to do three things for me,' he said. 'Write down the address, get me a map of Greater London and hire me a car.'

'Will that be self-drive or chauffeur-driven, sir?' the clerk asked.

Charles thought for a moment and then said, 'I'll drive. I'd like it here for twelve o'clock.'

'Certainly, sir. But I must warn you, there are strict rules at the Nettlebury house. No one is allowed in without an appointment.'

'Thanks, but don't worry,' said Charles. 'I'm an old friend of the family.' He thanked the clerk again and walked out into the street.

There was a cool breeze, and the sky was filled with dark pewter-coloured clouds, but he now felt quite cheerful. One of his first purchases in Jermyn Street was a military-style mackintosh. It was just as well, because the rain was falling quite heavily when he drove the hired car along the Kew road some hours later. He turned off to the left and found a place to park.

The hat he had chosen to go with the raincoat was a brown fedora. The man in the tiny shop where he'd bought it had assured him it was called a trilby. 'Gentlemen wear them to go horse-racing, sir,' he'd said.

'Is it okay if I just walk about the streets in it?' Charles had asked.

'Oh yes, sir,' he replied. 'After all, you're wearing a trench-coat, and I'm sure you don't intend to kill anyone.'

They had both laughed at that and Charles had worn the hat from the shop. Now he wished he had bought an umbrella as well.

When he arrived at the address, he found the garden path crowded with Japanese in transparent plastic raincoats, festooned with cameras. They jostled on the short flight of steps and thrust handfuls of money towards Irene, who was trying to explain to them that the house was not open to the public. Watching her, he realised his memory had not played tricks after all; she seemed just as attractive. Maybe it was the red hair.

Charles listened to the jabbering figures; one of them was talking German. He shouted loudly in the same language and they all turned to face him. He issued staccato orders and suddenly the figures shrank back from the doorway and retreated down the path.

'If you speak English, I'm very grateful,' Irene called through the driving rain at Charles's dim figure, 'but the house is closed to the public.'

He stepped forward and took off his hat. 'Hello, Irene,' he said, suddenly shy. 'Don't you remember me?'

She gazed into his face with a blank expression for a moment before she recognised him. 'Charles? Is it really you?' He nodded. 'Oh, do come in,' she urged him, and he stepped into the hall. 'Let me take your coat. You look drenched!' He shrugged off the wet trench-coat. 'What did you tell those Japanese that made them dash off so quickly? I'd been trying to get rid of them for ages.'

Charles rescued his cigarettes from the pocket before he handed her the wet coat. 'I told them the house was a restricted area on

553

grounds of health because of typhoid,' he answered.

She began to laugh. 'Oh, what a wonderful idea! I must put up notices saying that in all languages.'

He gave her his hat, and she hung the clothes in a closet. 'Do you know how many years it's been since we last saw each other?' he asked when she turned back to him.

'I'm afraid I do,' she said. 'It was 1936.'

They stood looking at each other in the pale light that filtered through the small window over the door. Finally Charles said, 'My God, I had a crush on you! Why the hell haven't we seen each other until now?'

Irene shrugged, and smiled. 'If wishes were horses, then beggars would ride.'

'My grandmother used to say that.'

Irene nodded. 'Yes, I know. You told me. In France when we were children. It took me ages to work out what it meant.'

Charles looked round the hall and saw the family portraits Nettlebury had painted of Irene and her sister. 'It sure makes sense to me now,' he said, then he turned to her again. 'I'm sorry to drop in on you like this. Have I come at a bad time?'

Irene shook her head. 'No, I was just dealing with some correspondence. Most of my life is taken up with letters now, and visits from young art historians. Dad would have been amused to know how many people would rely on his work to get their degrees.' Then she remembered something. 'Good heavens, I've got a saucepan on the stove! Why don't you come through?' He followed slowly as she hurried to the kitchen. 'It's soup,' she said. 'Would you care for some? I don't usually have a big meal in the middle of the day.'

He smiled. 'Well, yes, that would be fine. Actually, I was going to ask you out to lunch.'

Irene smiled back. 'Well, that was sweet of you, but this is ready now. It's only pea and ham; is that all right?'

'Pea and ham will be fine,' he replied. 'Is there anything I can do?'

'Just sit down. Oh, and get some napkins from the left-hand drawer in the dresser, will you? I don't want you to spill anything on that splendid waistcoat.'

'I bought it this morning,' he said. 'What do you think?'

'Very dashing,' she answered, ladling the thick soup into bowls.

'I bought a lot of clothes this morning. I'd decided it was time to get rid of my old stuff. I was going to try for a new image; younger, more aggressive.'

'What happened?' Irene asked.

Charles dipped his spoon into the thick smoky soup, and laughed. 'I ended up buying the kind of stuff I usually buy.' Then he lifted the napkin. 'Except for this. I did think it was kind of sharp.'

Irene nodded. 'So we beat on, boats against the current,' she said.

Charles finished the sentence. 'Borne back ceaselessly into the past.' He set his spoon aside. 'I didn't think anyone read Scott Fitzgerald these days.'

'Oh, he had a big revival over here a few years ago. My daughter was a devoted fan.'

'Where is she now?' Charles asked.

Irene got up and put the dishes in the sink. 'She doesn't live here any more,' she said, with her back to him.

He decided to change the subject. He looked around; the whole room reminded him of an illustration from an ancient copy of the *Saturday Evening Post*. The sink was stone and big enough to wash a dog in. 'I guess you don't throw things away over here,' he said eventually.

'What do you mean?'

He gestured round the room. 'This place; it's wonderful. Everything is so old-fashioned.'

She nodded. 'I wanted to keep it the same. I grew up in this house.'

He thought for a moment. 'It's good to be able to have somewhere to return to.'

Irene's laugh was ironic. 'I suppose I never went away,' she said.

'But you did get married to Richard Cleary?'

'Yes, but we're divorced now.'

Charles lit a cigarette and then remembered to offer the packet to Irene. She accepted and sat down beside him again.

'You were married, I seem to recall.'

He nodded. 'We got divorced as well. Nobody stays married any more.'

'Except my sister; they go on and on for ever.'

Charles looked at the framed drawings on the wall by the dresser; they showed Irene and Anne as children sitting at a table with schoolbooks open before them.

'Do you know, for a long time I wanted to marry you,' he said, turning back to her. 'I used to lie in my dormitory at night in the

555

freezing New England winter, thinking about you.'

She studied his face, searching for the boy beneath the man. There are still traces, she thought, but his eyes are sadder.

As if reading her mind, he said, 'You've hardly changed at all.'

Irene waved smoke away from her face and slowly shook her head. 'You're deceived by the light in here.' She gestured to the window streaked with rain. 'All this dimness is good for a girl's complexion. You should come out into the conservatory and count the lines.'

But he could see that she was pleased by the compliment.

'Would you mind showing me the collection?' he asked.

'Have you the time?'

Charles shrugged. 'I'm on vacation. I've got all the time in the world.'

For the rest of the afternoon Irene escorted Charles round the house. They began in the attic studio, where the three great murals were displayed, and then slowly descended through the house and Nettlebury's life. He pored over the plan chests of drawings and turned the pages of endless sketchbooks, saw room after room of pictures and followed the infinite variety of the man's vision. Eventually they stood together in the conservatory and watched the rain falling on to the garden.

'And this is where Gideon came for lessons,' he said.

Irene nodded. 'And Richard Cleary.'

Charles stood with his hands in his pockets, looking into the garden. 'This place is extraordinary,' he said. 'A work of art composed of works of art.' He turned to her. 'Has anyone written a book about it yet?'

'Neville Crichton refers to it a lot in his book on Paul Van Duren. That's where the *Reader's Digest* article came from. The collection is catalogued, of course. I did that.'

Charles rested a palm on the cold glass, then turned his head and smiled at her. 'Have dinner with me tonight?'

Irene hesitated. 'Oh, I don't know. Going into town is a difficult business.'

'We don't have to go into town. Isn't there somewhere out here along the river that you know?'

She thought for a moment. 'There was a place at Maidenhead. I haven't been there in years. I can't even remember its name.'

'Fine,' he said decisively. 'We'll just get in the car and go.'

'It's going to take me a long time to get ready,' she said slowly.

556

'No problem,' he replied. 'I told you, I've got all the time in the world.'

Later, in the early evening, they drove west, following the turns in the Thames. The rain on the windscreen blurred the lights on the road to Maidenhead. Eventually Irene said, 'I think this is the place,' and Charles turned into a car park where the trees were strung with fairy lights.

'Aren't you sure?' he asked.

Irene shook her head. 'Everything was so different after the war; buildings were always in darkness.' They walked to the entrance, and it was hard to tell at first if it was a public house or a hotel, but Charles liked the atmosphere immediately. They had drinks in the bar, and then a waiter led them into the dining-room. There was even a little dance floor with a band playing.

'I hope you don't mind, sir,' the head waiter said, holding out Irene's chair. 'There's an anniversary party at the big table.'

'That's all right,' Charles replied. 'It's our anniversary, too.'

'Really, sir?' he said. 'How many years?'

'Twenty-nine.' Charles's voice was serious.

'I can hardly believe it, madam,' the waiter said, equally seriously. 'You must have been a child bride.'

'I was,' Irene answered, entering into the spirit of things, 'but I'm making up for it now.'

When they had ordered their meal, the people celebrating took their seats at the long table. The party was clearly in honour of a middle-aged couple, whose sons and daughters surrounded them. The men wore dinner-jackets and the women party frocks. They were Thames Valley people, the sort Irene had known all her life. She knew that the boys would have gone to schools along the river and met their wives at regattas and tennis-club dances. They were a happy gathering and their good spirits spilt out into the rest of the room. The band played softly throughout the meal and Charles told Irene about his life since they had last met.

'You don't sound as if you bear your wife any ill-will,' she said eventually.

He shook his head and drank some of the coffee, which had been served to them in tiny cups. 'I knew what I was getting into,' he said. 'Lydia never made any attempt to disguise the sort of person she was. I'm just glad we didn't have any children.'

Irene thought for a moment about Bridget. Then the waiter appeared at their table, bearing a bottle of champagne.

557

'Forgive me, sir, but the people at the next table asked me to invite you to have a drink with them, as it's your anniversary as well.'

Irene and Charles turned to smile at the group and raised their glasses. 'Tell them we would be honoured,' Charles said, and when their glasses were filled, they returned the salute.

Then the band began to play 'Always', and they could tell from the applause at the table that it was a special song for the middle-aged couple. After they had danced alone for a few minutes, the young people joined in.

'Shall we?' Charles said, and he led Irene on to the little floor. 'Congratulations,' he said as they circled the celebrating couple.

'And to you also,' the man answered. 'We seem to have been lucky in our choices.'

Charles nodded, and lowered his head to smell Irene's hair. He felt as though his whole mind and body were suffused with a sense of well-being. 'Are we just drunk, or are we dancing rather well together?' he said to her.

'I used to love dancing,' she answered.

He thought for a moment. 'I can't say I cared for it much until now.'

He bought the people at the next table more champagne. Then, when the band played the last number, he circled the floor with Irene in his arms once again. When the music stopped, they held each other for a moment longer before separating.

After he had paid the bill, there were handshakes with the other family and then they made their way to the car park. The rain had stopped and the sky was clear now.

'I wonder what time they turn the lights off,' Irene said, looking up at the glowing colours in the trees above their heads.

'Perhaps they're some kind of beacon, like the lighthouse at Alexandria,' Charles suggested. 'The fairy lights of Maidenhead has a certain ring to it.'

Instead of going straight to the car, he took her hand and they crossed the wet empty road to stand and look down on to the dark waters of the Thames. They said nothing for a time, watching the dancing columns of lights reflected on the slowly moving surface.

'My father loved this river,' Irene said eventually. 'He didn't care for the sea, but he said you could always trust the Thames. Is the Mississippi like this?'

He shook his head. 'That's a big rough river. It rips up trees and tears the bank away. Sometimes it's as wide as the sea.'

'It's strange how you expect all the rivers in the world to be like the one you know.'

Charles was still watching the dancing lights. 'I want to come home with you,' he said. Irene did not reply. 'I'm not a kid any more. I'm not looking for a new sensation. I haven't had a good time like this in quite a while. I want it to go on.'

Irene took his hand. 'Don't you think you'd better kiss me first?' she said gently.

CHAPTER TWENTY-FIVE

London, one week later

Anne smiled when Elizabeth reached out towards the last piece of chocolate cake on the plate. She saw Anne's expression, and hesitated. 'Would you like this?' she asked.

Anne shook her head. 'You have it.'

Elizabeth took the cake. 'You know, I was always the greedy one when we were young. Then, in Berlin during the war, when we had nothing, I used to dream about all the things I'd taken for granted: soap, clothes, food. I swore that if those days ever returned I'd be more generous.'

'Did you keep your vow?'

Elizabeth thought about the question. 'I hope so. I try to think of Laszlo first, so I suppose that's something.'

Anne looked around the Palm Court of the Ritz and thought of the times she and Elizabeth had once had in Lyons teashops. 'At least you don't have to worry about your figure,' she said.

Elizabeth nodded and looked for her handbag. 'Must we go now?'

'Afraid so,' Anne replied. 'I must get back. Laszlo and Gideon are seeing someone in Bristol today and Toddy is in Paris, so I'm minding the shop.'

'Why have they gone to Bristol?' Elizabeth asked, putting three pounds on the table and nodding to the hovering waiter.

Anne lowered her voice to say, 'It's to do with that man Ovington. Remember? Another of Gideon's drawings turned up in a sale, and they think they are nearer to tracking him down.'

'Tracking him down?' Elizabeth repeated. 'It sounds like a detective story!'

'I suppose it is, in a way. But no one can work out the motive for the crime.'

'Isn't it greed? It usually is.'

560

Anne shook her head. 'I don't think so. You must remember what an incredibly modest little chap Ovington was. He didn't appear to have any ambitions at all, as far as they can gather. It seems that Gideon must have offended him in some way. All the people who bought the drawings got them at bargain prices.'

'Well, I hope they solve it soon,' said Elizabeth. 'I hate mysteries. The *Marie Celeste* has infuriated me ever since I was first told about it.' She pulled on her gloves and leaned forward to kiss Anne. 'I'm going home now. Don't work too hard.'

Elizabeth set off along Piccadilly, and Anne walked slowly back to the gallery, still thinking of the missing Ovington. On her desk there was a message scrawled on the memo pad: 'Please ring your niece.' When she got through, Bridget sounded worried.

'Do you know where Mummy is?' she asked. 'I've been ringing the house for the past three days, and that silly woman who works for her keeps saying she's gone away. She makes it sound as if she's been murdered.'

'I shouldn't worry, darling. She'll be back this afternoon,' Anne said quickly.

'So you do know where she is?' Bridget persisted.

'Well, not exactly. She's on a boat somewhere on the river,' Anne replied.

'On a boat? On her own?'

'No, darling. Actually she's with a man,' Anne said as lightly as she could.

'What man?' Bridget sounded as though she were a policeman interrogating a difficult witness.

'His name is Charles Whitney-Ingram. He's the American partner in the Archangel Gallery, as a matter of fact.'

'Why have they gone on a boat together?' Bridget asked, mystified.

'I suppose they fancied a holiday,' Anne said. 'Your mother does work very hard at that house. I imagine a bit of a break will do her the world of good.'

'You say she's coming home today?' Bridget said frostily.

'That was the arrangement,' Anne said blithely.

'I shall go to the house and wait for her,' Bridget said, making it sound as if she were quoting from the Old Testament.

'Don't be too hard on her, darling,' Anne said. 'Remember, you're only middle-aged once.'

Bridget put down the telephone and looked across the room at Frazer, who was painting.

Although the canvas he worked on was huge, his face was only inches from the surface, and he was using a sable brush that delivered a line as fine as a cotton thread.

'I've found my mother,' said Bridget.

'Good,' he replied, preoccupied.

She got up from the bed and walked over to stand behind him. The picture depicted the front of an old-fashioned cinema, built in the style of a Moroccan palace. The word 'Regal' was emblazoned, as if in neon lights, above a black-and-white portrait of Humphrey Bogart and Ingrid Bergman. Frazer had painted it with such skill that it was hard, at first, not to take it for an actual photograph. With a grunt he finished the last eyelash on Bergman's face, then leaned back and raised his shoulders from the cramped position he had assumed for the last hour.

'What do you think?' he asked.

Bridget looked at the picture for a while. 'I think it's finished.'

'Thank Christ for that!' He sounded grateful. 'You're a harder taskmaster than Peter Quick.'

'I didn't know he was a slave-driver,' she said, winding her arms round his neck.

He reached up and touched her arms. 'Oh, yes,' he said, continuing to study the picture. "Work, work, work," he used to shout at us. "Draw, draw, draw. Learn your alphabet first, and then you can start on the poetry." '

'Well, you certainly can draw.' Bridget stood up. 'I'm going to take the car. Is that all right?'

'It's yours. Do what you want with it.'

'Oh, come on, Carl,' she said, pleading. 'Just because I bought it with Dad's money.'

He shrugged. 'I'm sorry. What time will you be back?'

'I'm not sure. Why?'

He gestured towards the painting. 'Peter and Val are coming around to see this. I said we'd go out for a Chinese meal afterwards.'

'That's fine,' she said, 'but I don't want to be late. I've got work in the morning.'

'Okay. A one-bottle evening.'

'One bottle each, you mean!' she said and kissed him goodbye.

When he heard the front door slam, he walked over to the bed where she had been sitting and picked up the sketchbook that had been on her lap for most of the afternoon. He flipped through the pages and looked at the sketches she had done of him crouched over the picture. They were very good. He closed the book and laid it beside him on the bed. 'Jesus, the competition is stiff around here!' he said softly to himself. Then he stood up again and looked at the five other huge pictures that leaned, unframed, against the whitewashed wall. They were all on the theme of cinemas; the faces of legendary movie stars dominated the surroundings. Sometimes, in his moments of self-doubt, Frazer thought they could be living in the store-room of an old cinema.

Are these paintings really valid? he wondered. Or are they just the meaningless doodles Richard Cleary described them as, when he had last blundered in on a visit. Maybe Cleary is right, Frazer thought; perhaps he was confusing the effort he had put into their execution with the value of a proper picture. He shook his head. 'Fuck Cleary!' he said aloud. 'I could paint his kind of picture with a paintbrush stuck up my arse.'

Bridget drove the black Volkswagen towards Kew in the same determined mood as on the day she had left home. In the first few weeks away from her mother they had kept a frigid silence, but eventually Anne had breached the hostility by taking them both to lunch. They had subsequently discovered that they could get along quite well, providing the subject of Carl Frazer was never raised. Gradually they had fallen into the habit of talking on the telephone every other day. Then there was this sudden silence from Irene, and now Bridget was anxious to get to the bottom of it.

When she got to Kew, Mrs Riley, the Irishwoman who helped her mother with the housework, was using the vacuum cleaner in the living-room. She had not heard the key in the door and so she looked up and clutched her breast in shock when she saw Bridget's glowering figure.

'When are you expecting my mother?' Bridget demanded.

Flustered, Mrs Riley looked at the clock. 'Any minute now, I should think.' Bridget turned on her heel. 'Can I get you anything?' she called out after the retreating figure.

'No, thank you. I know where everything is.' But Bridget couldn't find the tea-caddy in its usual place and the sugar was in a different pot. When she finally raised the cup to her lips, she heard the front door open and Irene call out a greeting to Mrs Riley.

Bridget composed her features into a study of indifference, which her mother failed to notice. Bridget had never seen her like this before; it was as though she were another person. Irene's hair was pulled back in coiled plaits, and her face was flushed from the cold weather. She wore a loose grey top, jeans and some kind of expensive tennis shoes. Good God! Bridget thought. My mother in jeans!

Irene was laughing over her shoulder at something the man following her had said. He was tall and rather good-looking. He also wore jeans, a fisherman's sweater and a trench-coat. Both of them carried carrier bags full of groceries. 'Darling!' Irene said with pleasure, leaning forward to kiss the presented cheek. 'Oh, you're lovely and warm. I'm freezing. Charles has an open-top car.' She turned suddenly, 'Oh, I'm sorry; you haven't met each other, have you?'

'How do you do?' Bridget said frostily when Charles reached out a cold hand.

Sensing the atmosphere, he decided to leave them alone. 'Excuse me for a minute. I've got to go and get some cigarettes,' he said, closing the door behind him.

'Is there another cup in the pot?' Irene asked. She found a mug and poured herself some tea. 'Well, what do you think of him?' she asked, sitting down opposite her daughter.

Bridget shrugged. 'I don't know. I've only just met him.' Then she looked at her mother harder, and said, 'What's happened to you? I've never seen you like this before.'

Irene clasped both hands round her mug, and sighed. 'Oh, darling, it's called sex.'

'Mother, don't be disgusting!' Bridget said, shocked.

Irene raised her eyebrows. 'I hardly think you're in a position to chastise me about my morals.'

'I didn't mean it was disgusting. It's just well, just . . . undignified at your age.'

Irene nodded. 'I can understand your attitude,' she said slowly, 'but I don't intend to apologise to you. And I still think you were too young when you chose to go and live with a man.' Bridget was about to speak, but Irene held up her hand. 'I know, what's done is done. You thought you were ready, and I didn't. There's no right or wrong in that sort of situation. It's not a game.' She put down her tea and looked at her daughter. 'The only things that matter are happiness and contentment. I haven't scored many of those for a long time and I was frightened you'd do the same as me.' She leaned forward, and Bridget could see just how happy she was. 'Charles and I are going to get married. There's no purpose in long engagements at our age.' She reached out and held her daughter's hand. 'And we're going to live in New York.'

Bridget looked up, suddenly frightened. It was as if a bleak wind had suddenly blown through the house. She was quite prepared to leave home, but the thought that her home might leave her was an eventuality she had never considered.

'What about this house? Who will look after it?'

Irene sat up. 'Yes, well, we've talked about that. As you've decided to go on living with Carl, we thought the pair of you could move in here. The conservatory is still a wonderful studio, and the house should be lived in.'

'Carl won't accept charity,' Bridget said.

Irene smiled. 'Won't he? Then he's a very peculiar artist. Believe me, if he can go on working without worrying where the next meal is coming from, he'll accept.'

Bridget sat and thought for a while; it seemed a great deal to assimilate suddenly. She had always expected that, no matter what else happened, Irene would remain here. It was as though the captain of a ship were walking away from the bridge in the middle of a storm, calling for one of the passengers to come and take the wheel.

'Do you think you could manage?' Irene asked.

Bridget finished her tea before she answered. 'I shall have to, won't I, if you're running away to New York?'

The doorbell rang, and Irene went to let Charles in. They did not return immediately. Bridget was starting to realise that her life was changing. Going to live with Carl Frazer hadn't seemed so important, but her mother's news was of enormous consequence. She looked at the old, familiar surroundings and thought about the past. So many people had gone. Her grandfather, Maude Cooper, her father – and now her mother was leaving as well. Childhood is finally over, she thought.

When Irene and Charles returned to the kitchen, Bridget was on her feet. She turned to look at them. 'Carl and I are going out for a Chinese meal this evening with some friends,' she said. 'I wonder if you would like to come too?' And this time she smiled at Charles.

London, winter 1966

Schneider sat in the comforting fug of the half-empty cinema, nodding with pleasure. He had seen the film three times before, but

565

he still enjoyed the moment when Edward G. Robinson beat Steve McQueen at poker. Most of all he liked the look of discomfort on the younger man's face as he contemplated the cards that had defeated him. At the end of the film he hobbled from the cinema. It was a colder winter than any he could remember. When he stood for a moment on the pavement, a harsh wind blew grit and litter along the gutter and the ground felt like ice under the thin soles of his hand-made shoes. At first he thought of going home to his flat in Bloomsbury, then decided that he needed company and a couple of large brandies. It wasn't too far to Dean Street and the comfort of the Black Sheep Club.

The wind blew into his face as he walked along Shaftesbury Avenue. Ahead, he could see a group of young people skylarking on the pavement. The youths wore no overcoats, despite the freezing night air. They were throwing a girl's handbag to each other; the girl was laughing as she ran from one to the other. Schneider hated the young, their brashness and the noise they made, their outlandish clothes and the certainty of their opinions. He had stopped watching television because it seemed infested with them. Now they were everywhere on the streets. Hitler was wrong, he thought as he caught up with the cavorting fools; it wasn't the Jews who were the enemy, it was the young. Nevertheless he moved through them with a set smile, muttering, 'Excuse me, excuse me.'

When he eventually reached the staircase that led to the Black Sheep Club, he gave a sigh of relief; there would be no children in here. The door swung open in answer to his kick and he glanced about with pleasure. The decor of the club had stayed the same as long as Schneider could remember. The walls were painted matt black, but the carpet still showed a vague shadowy design of entwined flowers, despite being encrusted with generations of grime. There was a fringe of tables against the walls, and various rickety, unmatched chairs. Each table bore a small lamp with pink shades that shone dimly on tablecloths marked with ancient stains. The blinds at the shrouded windows were the original blackout curtains from the war years; Schneider had never seen them drawn. The bar extended almost the full length of the room, save for the small space allowed for the entrance, where a large fire-extinguisher leaned in the corner. Behind the bar, on the first row of shelves, stood a collection of seaside mementoes that vied with each other in their hideousness: strange dogs in glazed chalk, clocks decorated with shells, miniature lighthouses and novelty barometers.

566

The club was surprisingly crowded; there were even customers sitting at the table where three dreadful hostesses plied their trade. Schneider was lucky to find a stool at the bar. When he asked for a brandy, as was the custom of the club for old customers, the barmaid produced a bottle of cognac and passed it to him.

He glanced around, but did not recognise any other members. Then he noticed a familiar figure standing on the outskirts of the group of younger people.

Schneider never forgot an individual. Because of the sort of life he had led, he kept those he had wronged firmly in the forefront of his mind, lest a chance encounter should lead to embarrassment. Quickly he sorted through his memories and came to the conclusion this man would not bear him any ill-will.

'Mr Ovington,' he called out with good humour. 'Allow me to buy you a drink.'

Bernard Ovington turned and blinked in his direction, brushing his large moustache with the back of his hand. 'Oh, hello,' he said after a moment, and took a couple of steps towards him.

'What will you have?' Schneider asked.

'That's very kind of you,' Bernard replied. 'A half of Guinness, please. Then I must be off home.'

'A half of the black stuff,' Schneider ordered, watching the man swallow the contents of his glass.

'Just popping upstairs,' Bernard said. He put down his glass and left.

When Schneider's Guinness was placed on the counter, with a sudden impulse he poured a huge measure of brandy into the foaming top. Then he took the drinks and put them on a vacant table.

As Bernard returned to the bar, Schneider beckoned him over. 'So how are you keeping now?' he asked, raising his glass in a salute. 'Still in the picture-restoring business?'

Bernard shook his head. 'Oh, no. I gave that up years ago. I work for television now.'

'Television?' Schneider asked incredulously.

Ovington nodded. 'At Wembley studios. I've got a little flat over a shop there. Nothing fancy, but it's nice and cosy for me and my mother.'

'What do you actually do?' Schneider asked.

'I paint scenery.'

'And what brings you to the Black Sheep Club?'

567

Bernard looked about him. 'I came with some chaps in the Magnolia Jazz Band.' Then he took out a large pocket watch. 'Good Lord, is it eleven o'clock already? How time flies! I'd better get a move on or I shall miss my train to Wembley Park.' He picked up his Guinness and swallowed it in a short series of gulps. He was about to rise, but Schneider held out a hand to restrain him.

'Don't go just yet; there's plenty of time for your train. Tell me about your work in television.'

Bernard looked at his watch again. 'Well, I suppose I do have a few minutes more,' he said, and let out a loud hiccup. 'My word,' he said, 'I've never done that before!'

'You need another drink,' Schneider said decisively.

'Do you know, I believe I do!'

Schneider waved to the bar and ordered another Guinness.

By the time he had finished the next drink, Bernard was speaking with a dull clockwork monotony. He described his work at the television studio in such minute detail that Schneider began to feel so bored that he had to change the subject. 'Tell me about your work for the Archangel Gallery,' he said. 'Were there any really interesting jobs you did for them?' Bernard considered the question for so long that Schneider thought that if he leaned close enough he would actually hear wheels and cogs turning in the man's head.

'I did do some nice jobs for the Archangel,' he said finally. 'And they paid me a lot better than your gallery, Mr Schneider, if you don't mind me saying so.'

Schneider shrugged and smirked. 'We had such huge overheads,' he muttered.

'But then my life changed,' Bernard said slowly. 'I became a Christian Comrade.'

'A Christian Comrade?' Schneider repeated. 'What's that?'

Bernard leaned forward and tapped the table-top with a forefinger to emphasise his words. 'It's an association that combines the teachings of Jesus Christ with those of Karl Marx,' he said, his voice becoming gradually indistinct.

'I thought the two ideas were incompatible? Surely Marx said that religion was the opium of the masses?'

'I can't explain it. I'm not clever with words. But when I heard my first sermon I knew I had to give up restoring pictures for the rich and do something for the people.'

'So you went into television?' said Schneider.

'That's right.' Bernard stared into his empty glass. 'I wouldn't mind

568

another one of those.'

But Schneider was bored with him now and tired of buying all the drinks. 'You'd better go, or you'll miss your train.'

Then Bernard remembered something else. 'One odd thing about the Archangel Gallery . . . I could never understand why Mr Gideon didn't do the restoring himself.'

'You think he was capable of it?'

Bernard nodded. 'Oh yes! He was as good as me. The Brueghel he painted must have been lovely, if I'm any judge of that kind of work.'

Schneider sat forward. 'Did you say he painted a Brueghel?' Bernard nodded. 'How do you know it was any good? he asked.

'I saw all the preparatory work; the cartoons and paint sketches,' Bernard told him. 'As I told you, it was beautiful. If his other work was anything to go by, the Brueghel must have been perfect.'

'But you didn't see the actual picture?' Schneider asked searchingly.

'No, but I can tell you what it's like.' Bernard began to give a detailed description.

Before he was half-way through, Schneider recognised it as one of the pictures the young GI in Berlin had taken as his share of the loot. Excitement bubbled inside him and memories began to whirl in his brain like the patterns in a kaleidoscope. Barely-remembered conversations with Strange about a fake Watteau, the pictures destroyed in the gallery; suddenly it all fell into place when it became clear that Gideon could fake pictures. An idea came into his mind, half-formed but full of potential. 'This painting,' he said carefully. 'Do you think you could draw it?'

'Of course I could. I can draw anything I've ever seen.' Schneider stood up. 'Where are we going?' Bernard asked.

'Back to my place,' said Schneider. 'I don't want you to come to any harm, and it's a dangerous journey to Wembley at this time of night.'

New York, early spring 1967

At first, Irene had worried that she might be homesick, but now she frequently felt guilty at how little she missed her old surroundings. She loved America, and particularly New York. She had only a few memories from her childhood visit, but they remained as sharp and

569

clear as the illustrations she could remember from her childhood books: Grand Central Station, the automat, the top of the Chrysler buiding all returned like the faces of old friends.

It was morning now, and she had been married for two months. She was standing by the window, looking down on Central Park. Through the happiness came a small, stabbing doubt; it can't last, it can't last, she thought. 'Yes, it will!' she said out loud, and Charles, still in his pyjamas, looked up from the letters in his hand as he walked into the bedroom.

'What will?' he asked.

'It will be another perfect day,' she answered.

'Just don't use them all up at once! Keep a couple for Thanksgiving and Christmas.' He extracted a large package and handed it to her. 'Special delivery from London, ma'am. Any tip for the mail-man?' Irene gave him a kiss. 'Huh, I can get kisses anywhere! How about something a little more exotic?

She thrust one knee forward so that her body tilted into a seductive pose and opened her bath-robe. Charles set aside his bundle of letters and carried her to the bed.

Irene looked down at her naked body. 'Oh, look at my saggy breasts,' she sighed. 'How can you fancy an old broad like me?'

Charles pushed up on his arms. 'Gee, you mean you're not twenty-one any more? Does this mean I get to send you back?'

Now Irene reached up and seized hold of him. 'If you value these, sir, you'll curb that jesting tongue,' she said, pulling his head down to kiss him.

Later, when they had showered, Irene sat on the bed and opened her package. There was a reel of film and a letter from Anne. 'Listen to this,' she said and read aloud:

Dearest Irene,

Enclosed is the film of your wedding. I don't suppose you remember much of it, considering all the champagne you drank. Poor old Charles, I bet he didn't know he was getting a dipsomaniac for a bride!

Everything here is wonderful, except for the weather, which is pretty foul. We had dinner at Kew last week with Bridget and Carl. Did you know there was a piece in the *Sunday Times* colour supplement about him and some other of the Pop Painters? I enclose a cutting. God knows what Dad would have made of it all. I must confess their work looks to me a bit like those old enamel signs you used to see on railway stations and the front of shops. I said that to Toddy, and he told me that was the idea.

Give that husband of yours a kiss.

Love from us all,
Anne

Charles picked up the reel of film. 'Would you like me to rig up the projector?'

'Have you got time?'

'Sure,' he replied, making for the living-room.

When the telephone rang, Irene picked up the receiver. 'Is that Mrs Whitney-Ingram?' an English voice asked.

'Speaking.'

'Hello, my dear,' the voice continued. 'I don't know if you remember me? Ted Peake. We met a few times at the Archangel Gallery.'

'Oh, yes, Lord Peake. I remember you well.'

'Congratulations on your marriage,' he continued. 'And please call me Ted.'

'How can I help you, Ted?'

There was a chuckle, and Peake said, 'Actually, it's the other way round. I've got a little bit of news your brother-in-law might like to know.'

'Yes?'

'There's a man called Ovington – Bernard Ovington. Got that?' Peake asked. He spelt out the name. Irene made a note on the pad by the bed. 'Strange and Schneider have contacted him. They seem to think it will give them some sort of hold over Gideon. I don't know any more detail than that, but it may make sense to him.'

Irene wrote it all down. 'Thank you for calling, Ted,' she said, 'but why don't you tell Gideon yourself?'

'Can't be done, love. I'm at Kennedy airport now. I only heard this a few minutes ago and I don't know when I'll be able to call the UK. Must go now. Tell James I owed him this one.'

Irene hung up and made a careful note of everything before she joined Charles in the living-room.

'Are you ready?' he asked.

'Okay,' she replied, but all the time the film flickered on the screen her mind kept turning to the conversation with Peake.

'Well, that was a big hit,' Charles said as the film finished. 'What was the name of that place again?'

571

'Caxton Hall,' she replied, distracted. 'Darling, have you ever heard of a man named Ovington?'

Charles shook his head. 'Why?'

'That was a call about him from Lord Peake, with a message for Gideon.'

Charles looked up. 'Lord Peake? I want to talk to Gideon about him. Let's put a call through now.'

They rang the overseas operator, and after a few minutes Gideon was on the line. Charles handed Irene the telephone.

'Gideon,' she said, 'I've just had a call from Ted Peake. He was phoning from the airport, but he wanted me to give you a message. He said that Strange and Schneider have got hold of a man called Ovington . . . That's right, Ovington. Lord Peake seemed to think they will be able to get to you through him in some way. Does this make sense? Oh good, it's very confusing to me. Give my love to everyone. Hang on, Charles wants to speak to you.' She handed the phone to her husband.

'Hi, Gideon! Everything okay?' They chatted on, and then Charles said, 'By the way, this fellow Peake. Remember when we visited his house, the one he was giving to the nation? Do you recall the Van Durens Lady Peake asked me to authenticate? You do? Well, I saw Bob Treacher yesterday, and he told me he'd seen one of those pictures in Texas last week. That's right, one of the Manhattan sequence. I just thought I'd let you know.' He was about to hang up when Irene gestured to the receiver. 'Hang on; Irene wants another word.'

'I forgot to say, Gideon,' she said quickly. 'Ted Peake said he owed you this one.'

Gideon sat and thought for a while when he put down the phone, then he walked out into the showroom. Toddy was talking to an old customer; they were discussing a set of Matisse prints spread out on the table. Gideon knew the man would not buy them; he was on his way to his club and had really popped in for a chat. Anne was arranging for the delivery of a picture to a customer in Spain. There were problems with the import licence, and she was barely holding on to her good humour. He stopped beside her.

'It's a lovely day. How would you like a trip into the country?' he asked.

'It's a dreadful day!' Anne replied.

'In that case, it will look better in the country.' He turned to

Anne's secretary. 'Lucy, will you please ring the mews and ask Gibson to bring my car to the front right away? We're going out of town.'

'Of course, Mr Gideon,' the girl said with a dimpled smile, hurrying away.

'Of course, Mr Gideon,' Anne repeated when the girl was out of earshot. 'I'd fire the hussy if her typing wasn't so good.'

'Anne,' he said in a shocked voice, 'she's only a child!'

'She has the mind and a body of a home-wrecker!'

'Go and get your coat, or I'll take Lucy in your place!' he said.

A few minutes later, after he'd given the driver directions, he pressed the button that closed the rear of the car.

'Don't you feel awful doing that?' Anne asked. 'Poor Gibson, it certainly puts him in his place.'

Gideon shook his head and glanced out at the soft rain drifting down on Piccadilly.

'Certainly not. Gibson prefers it. He would feel deeply uncomfortable if I treated him as an equal.'

'Stuff and nonsense!' she said firmly. 'You're just quoting *The Admirable Crichton*. That's the trouble with you actors, you get all your ideas from the plays you were in.' She pressed the button, and the partition slid down. 'Mr Gibson,' she said, 'would you prefer this window open or shut?'

'Shut, madam, please. Unless you have any instructions for me.'

Anne sat back and shrugged. 'Perhaps he saw the play, too,' she said. 'Where is this place you're taking me to?' Gideon told her. 'Is that the house Ted gave to the nation?'

'That's right,' he replied. 'Peake Manor. There's been some trouble with the building for quite a while; that's why the Ministry hasn't taken it over. Something to do with the conservatory on the roof. Apparently the lake kept flooding over and pouring water into the well of the building.'

'There's a lake on the roof?'

Gideon shrugged. 'More of a large pond, really.'

Anne sat back. 'Oh, I'm getting so old, darling. I like everything old-fashioned now.' She gestured towards the cabinet. 'For God's sake, give me a gin and tonic!' Gideon gave her the drink and took a large whisky for himself.

His prediction had been right; the countryside did look better than the town. Rain and mist drifted across the landscape, changing the mundane into something much more attractive and mysterious.

When they stopped at the entrance of Peake Manor, a workman in blue overalls opened the gates. At the front door, a worried-looking man in spectacles opened it and peered out at the Rolls-Royce.

'I'm afraid the collection isn't yet open to the public,' he said officiously.

'I am the Collector of the Pictures,' Gideon boomed at him.

The combination of the Rolls-Royce and Gideon's imperious manner was too much. The man in spectacles stood back and allowed them to enter.

'I do like the title, "Collector of the Pictures",' Anne whispered. 'You should have it printed on the stationery! It sounds like "Master of the Rolls" or "Lord Chamberlain".'

Gideon stopped abruptly in the hall, and said, 'There's something odd going on here.' He led her to the conservatory at the top of the house, and they slowly descended floor by floor. When they reached the place where the Van Durens had been hung, Gideon began to laugh.

Anne was puzzled; the walls were sparsely covered with indifferent mid-nineteenth-century landscapes. 'What is all this stuff?' she asked. 'I thought it was meant to be one of England's greatest modern collections?'

Gideon shook his head and lowered his voice. 'Ted's pulled a fast one, and he used Charles and me to do it.'

'Explain.'

He spoke quietly, because the man in spectacles was hovering at the far end of the gallery. 'Ted got Charles and me to the house on the pretext of valuing some of Van Duren's work, so we would see the pictures that were hanging here then. Then he made sure we were at the press conference when he announced his plans to sell the Peake Corporation to the Rainbow Group.' He paused. 'Are you getting this?' he whispered.

Anne was staring at a painting of a rather large stag gazing out of a heather-clad mountain landscape. 'I think so. Go on,' she whispered back.

'Ted obviously didn't want any difficult questions at the press conference, so he created a diversion by announcing that he was donating this place to the nation. He even got me to give an off-the-cuff valuation of the pictures. I thought he meant the modern work, but he's obviously shipped all the good stuff out. The papers lapped it up: "Multi-Million Collection from Lord Ted". What he didn't make clear was that he was leaving his other pictures from the house in Pont Street. The really valuable pictures have all gone abroad.'

'So Ted used you in a confidence trick?' Anne said. 'I don't think that was very decent!'

Gideon shook his head. 'No one has been hurt, and the investors in the Peake Corporation have made money from the takeover.'

'What about you?' Anne asked.

Gideon smiled. 'I shall just say the Peake Collection of modern paintings is worth every penny I valued it at. That's true.'

They walked slowly through the rest of the house, still shadowed by the man in spectacles and another figure they were aware of but never actually saw. Eventually they stood outside the curious building and looked up at its bleak exterior and then across the tranquil landscaped grounds and gardens.

'What an extraordinary place!' Anne said. 'What could have possessed them to build it?'

Gideon shrugged. 'I think Gloria Peake was actually trying to create something stunning and new. It just didn't come off. Who knows, in a couple of hundred years it will probably be part of the heritage of Britain. Protection societies will be founded to prevent anyone pulling it down.'

'I suppose you're right. At least the gardens are lovely.'

They strolled around a while longer in the gently falling rain before making their way back to the Rolls-Royce.

When they got to the car, Gibson was emerging from the entrance. He apologised for not being at his station as he opened the door.

'Where have you been? Looking at the pictures?' Gideon asked.

'As a matter of fact I have, sir.'

Gideon was intrigued. 'What did you think of them?'

'I thought they were excellent, sir,' Gibson replied in a clipped voice. 'Much better than the paintings at the gallery, if you don't mind my saying so, sir.'

Gideon and Anne could think of nothing to say. They sat in the back of the Rolls-Royce for a long time in total silence and then gradually began to laugh as they rolled through the misty landscape back to London.

Fort Worth, Texas, spring 1967

The telephone rang, and Frank Palmer glanced at the clock on the

575

wall of his office. It was early for business calls. The voice that spoke was smooth as butter. 'Good morning,' it said. 'My name is Karl Schneider. May I speak to Frank Palmer?'

'I'm Palmer,' he replied. 'How can I help you?'

Schneider laughed. 'Perhaps we can help each other, Mr Palmer. I have a job that may be of interest to you. Can we meet for a drink?'

Palmer took the cold cigar from his mouth. 'Well, you'll have to tell me a little more before I decide to meet you, Mr Schneider,' he said, reaching for his lighter.

'I'm trying to trace a friend, an ex GI,' Schneider continued.

Palmer blew some smoke away. 'Why do you need a detective? Have you tried the telephone book?'

'I've tried everything, Mr Palmer – but I know he used to live in your part of the country.'

'Where do you want to meet?'

'Shall we say, the bar of the Madison Hotel at twelve o'clock?'

'See you at twelve o'clock, Mr Schneider.'

It was five minutes after noon when he entered the bar and saw Schneider right away, sitting on a stool; he was the only solitary man.

'Shall we go to a table?' said Schneider. 'It will be easier to hold a conversation.' He bought drinks, and they carried them across the room.

When they were seated, Palmer took a notebook from his bulging pocket. 'Okay, when you're ready.'

Schneider leaned forward and spoke confidentially. 'The man I want to trace is called Otis P. Emerson. He wasn't a fighting soldier; he was in your Transport Corps.'

'A truck-driver?' Palmer asked, not taking his eyes from the notebook.

'That's correct,' Schneider said with a smile. 'But he always wanted to work on a ranch.'

'Anything else?' Schneider shook his head. Palmer closed the notebook. 'This may take a while, Mr Schneider. Will you be here in the hotel?' Schneider nodded.

It took two days for Palmer to find out what had happened to Otis P. Emerson. Unable to afford the ranch he had set his heart on, the young man had settled for the next favourite profession of the cowboy: he had become a bank robber. Palmer found the cuttings on him in the library of the *Forth Worth Examiner*. The last job he had pulled had gone awry and a customer was shot. That led to a sentence of ten years. He had been released the previous summer. Palmer went to see the parole officer.

'You're too late,' the man told him. 'Otis died last month of a heart attack.'

'Did he have any next of kin?' Palmer asked.

'Sure,' the parole officer said. 'He married a widow who owned a gas station. It's a fair haul out of town.'

Palmer offer to drive him, but Schneider decided he would make the journey alone. After nearly two hours, he found the gas station on the highway in the middle of a pale-brown plain that stretched to the featureless horizon. The air was like molten glass when he stepped out of the car. Nothing moving but the shimmering haze on the distant surface of the road. There was a diner attached to the gas station. When he entered, he saw a woman sitting alone behind the counter watching television. The air was cool, but it smelt of stale cooking.

'Can I get you something?' the woman asked in a broad accent.

'Are you Mrs Otis P. Emerson?' he asked.

The woman looked at him coldly. 'Mister, I ain't responsible for any of his debts,' she said warily.

'So you are Mrs Emerson?'

She nodded in a resigned fashion. 'Sure.'

'I'm an old friend of your husband,' he said sympathetically. 'What happened to him?'

She leaned on the counter, and spoke without emotion. 'He told me he had big plans, but all he did was sit here and eat hamburgers until he put on twenty pounds. Then he dropped dead.'

Schneider stepped forward. 'Did he ever mention any paintings, Mrs Emerson?'

'Sure,' she replied quickly. 'That's about all he ever talked about: the paintings he sold for two thousand bucks after the war.'

'Sold?'

She nodded. 'Yeah, all except one. It was of some guys in Europe walking around in the snow. He said he was going to sell it to a company that prints Christmas cards in Dallas, but he never got round to doing it. I was going to take it into Forth Worth tomorrow and see if I could sell the damn thing myself.'

'May I see it?' Schneider asked.

She went to a room behind the counter and returned a few minutes later with an unframed canvas. Schneider was still smiling when he wrote her a cheque for five hundred dollars.

CHAPTER TWENTY-SIX

Miami, summer 1967

Throughout the long journey from the North, Irene had thought about the reason for their trip. Bridget and Frazer had decided to get married, and when she had written with the news to Clive Hamilton, he had suggested it should take place on his yacht, which he had been sailing in the Gulf of Mexico.

'Now there's a sight you don't see very often in America,' Charles Whitney-Ingram said, and Irene looked up from the map spread out on her bare knees. He took one hand from the wheel and gestured at a group of black youths passing a soccer ball to each other with effortless elegance as they swept towards a goal-mouth. Irene watched them with interest; she was more taken by the changing compositions they formed against the unfamiliar landscape than their athletic skill. Everything was wide and flat, so that the dark, running figures moved across four bands of colour: the bright-green tropical grass, a thinner strip of white sand, and then the sea, the colour of sapphire beneath a powder-blue sky.

'What do you mean?' she asked.

'A game of soccer; those kids must be from Cuba.'

Irene looked down at the map and measured the distance they had travelled from New York by the span of her hand, then altered the position on the map. 'Do you realise that if we'd gone due west instead of south, we'd be in Omaha, Nebraska, by now?'

'And if we'd gone east, we'd be in the middle of the Atlantic!'

'Don't laugh at me,' Irene said. 'I thought that was pretty interesting.'

For the last five days they had driven south from New York, stopping where Irene chose. Now they were due to pick up Carl and Bridget at Miami airport.

'How are we doing for time?' Charles asked.

'We're fine if we don't have any problems finding the airport,' she said.

'That should be easy. It'll be near the ocean.'

'How do you know?' Irene chided him. 'You told me you hadn't been down here since you were a boy. I don't suppose they had an airport then.'

Charles shook his head. 'Everything is near the ocean in Miami. If you go far from the beach you end up in the Everglades, and the alligators eat you.'

Irene turned her face up to the blazing sun. 'What an extraordinary country this is! Alligators at one end and polar bears at the other.'

'There aren't any polar bears in the States,' Charles said. 'Only grizzlies.'

'What about Alaska?'

Charles dug her in the ribs. 'Just because you've got the map, smartass! Anyway, Alaska doesn't count. It's outside the land-mass of the United States.'

'Rubbish, man! It's all North America to us English.'

'I know,' Charles said with a shrug. 'And if the British had gone south instead of west, there would be Mounties singing on Miami beach.'

Irene laughed and turned her face again towards the blazing sun.

They found the airport without difficulty, and the flight was on time. Bridget hardly recognised her mother when she and Frazer came through the barrier; it was Charles she spotted first.

'Look at you!' she said as they embraced. 'I've never seen you this colour. How did you get so brown? And look at all those freckles!'

Irene held up her arms. 'Five days in an open-top car! The weather has been lovely all the way from New York.'

'Where did you stop?' Bridget asked as Irene led them towards the car park.

'Oh, everywhere. But my favourite place was Charleston. I've wanted to go there since I was a girl.'

'Why?' Bridget asked. She could not imagine what would attract her mother to a town she had hardly heard of.

Irene smiled. 'Because Rhett Butler came from there. My friend Pamela and I used to imagine we would find the streets full of men who looked just like Clark Gable.'

'And were there?' Bridget asked.

'No,' Charles said, catching up with the conversation. 'Just a lot of kids who looked like Mick Jagger.'

When they reached the car, Frazer was impressed. 'A Thunderbird!' he said admiringly.

'My favourite automobile,' Charles assured him. 'Do you want to drive?'

'May I?' Frazer was like a child with an expensive toy. Charles handed him the keys. 'Are you positive you should, Carl?' Bridget asked 'They drive on the other side of the road over here.'

Frazer slid behind the wheel. 'They do in France, as well. You didn't mind my driving there.'

'That's different,' Bridget replied.

'I know it's different,' Frazer parried. 'The road signs are in French.'

Irene and Charles exchanged amused glances. 'Well, you certainly sound as if you're married,' Irene said, getting into the rear seat.

Bridget was frowning up at the sun. 'You'd better put some cream on,' she told Frazer. 'You know how you burn.'

He took the tube and smoothed cream on his exposed skin without comment.

Charles consulted the map and then folded it away. 'Okay. We go this way,' he said, indicating the direction. 'They said the boat was moored at Coral Gables.'

When they reached their destination, they found that *Apollo* wasn't the biggest yacht moored in the harbour, but she drew an appreciative whistle from Charles, who regarded her with the same degree of awe that Frazer had shown for the Thunderbird. 'I thought she'd be a gin-palace,' he said in a low voice. 'This looks like something out of Joseph Conrad!'

'Welcome to *Bounty*!' a thin man with dark receding hair called down from the deck. 'Captain Bligh, says, would you take your shoes off? The crew have just swabbed down.'

'Does he mean it?' Bridget asked.

Frazer nodded, pointing at her high heels. 'Those would punch a hole in the deck.'

When they had removed their footwear, they walked up the gang-plank and shook hands.

'Hi,' the man said. 'I'm Clive's manager, Al Davis. He's on the quarterdeck finishing his work-out.'

Beyond him they could see a powerfully built, squat man in a training suit, crouching next to an almost naked figure performing press-ups.

'Ninety-six, ninety-seven, ninety-eight, ninety-nine, one hundred. Okay, that's it!' the squat man shouted, and Clive Hamilton got to his feet and came towards them.

He had changed a great deal since he had modelled at the West London School of Art. His once slender figure was now well muscled, and when he smiled, his perfectly-capped teeth glowed a luminous white against his deep tan. The squat man followed him, draping a towel over his shoulders.

Hamilton greeted them warmly and then introduced his companion. 'This is Henry Willis, my trainer.'

Charles looked at him and said, 'Cobra Willis, the Fastest Left in the West?'

Willis smiled, and flexed his left arm. 'You remember, huh?' he said in a broad Brooklyn accent.

Charles nodded. 'I saw you fight Kid Riley in, when, 1947?'

'1948.'

'The fight went the distance,' Charles continued, 'and you won on points.'

Willis nodded. 'The Kid was Irish; he had a head like the Blarney Stone. Only guy I couldn't knock out.'

'They got you wrong on that day!' Charles continued. 'They all said you were a one-punch man.'

Willis waved deprecatingly with his legendary left hand. 'Sport-writers, what do they know?' he growled. 'After I outpointed Riley, they said I was the best combination puncher since Sampson.' He turned to Hamilton. 'Hey, boss, you didn't say any fight fans were coming! I was expecting a bunch of fairies with paintbrushes.'

'Carl used to box,' Bridget said defensively.

Willis looked at Frazer doubtfully. 'Where was that?'

'Glasgow. When I was at school,' Frazer answered.

'I fought a guy from Glasgow. Jimmie Campbell.' Willis pointed to his misshapen nose. 'He butted me in the head twice and broke this.'

Frazer smiled. 'It's called "the Glasgow nod". We do it up there instead of shaking hands.'

Willis turned to Hamilton again. 'Hey! These guys are all right. Shall I go and fix for everybody to have a drink?'

'Okay,' Hamilton replied as two other men materialised behind him wearing matching blue t-shirts. 'These are Paulie and José. They'll show you to your cabins.' He looked up at the sun. 'Let's eat out here tonight.'

581

They were shown to their cabins and Bridget set about unpacking the luggage.

When Frazer had showered and changed into a pair of jeans and a sports shirt, he went back up on deck. Al Davis was leaning against the rail looking at the other boats moored to the jetty.

'Hi,' he said easily. 'I prefer this view to the sea.'

'Don't you like water?' Frazer asked.

'Nicely frozen and covered in Scotch, I like it,' he replied. 'Heavily salted and deep enough to drown in?' He shrugged. 'I'd rather look at all this floating money.'

They were silent for a while, and then Frazer said, 'Is all this really his?'

Davis smiled. 'Sure is, kid!' He dropped his cigarette into the water. 'One hit movie, and he's richer than a lot of the old-timers were after a lifetime in the business.' The old boxer looked at him. 'Say, are you the guy who painted those pictures he bought?' Frazer nodded. 'I like them. I could recognise the people. Jesus, I even saw the movies. You don't do that stuff that looks like bowls of coloured spaghetti?'

'No,' said Frazer, 'I don't do that stuff.'

Davis lit another cigarette. 'You know what I mean?'

'Abstract Expressionism?' Frazer guessed.

'That's it.' He nodded. 'I used to work for a guy who collected it: Joe Stapoulas. I never could understand why. I mean, if you've got a spare million bucks, why not spend it on a good time? There's enough nightmares in life without hanging them on the wall.'

Frazer looked around the boat again. 'Is that what he earned from *The Rivals* – a million dollars?'

Davis shook his head. 'Much more, and it's still coming in.' He inhaled deeply. 'Mind you, they ain't so sure of his latest one. A lot of people won't want to see a movie about a singing highwayman.'

'But I read it was going to be a big hit?'

Davis aimed carefully and tried to drop his cigarette on the butt of the previous one. 'That's called publicity, kid. They're not going to say it's a pile of horseshit, now, are they?' He glanced around. 'The word on the coast is that it's as bad as *The Kissing Bandit*.'

'What was *The Kissing Bandit*?' Frazer asked.

'Exactly,' Davis replied. 'And Frank Sinatra starred in that.'

A crew member approached them. 'They're serving drinks in the stateroom, gentlemen,' he said with a Spanish accent.

'Okay, José,' Davis replied. 'We're coming.'

582

In the stateroom, everyone else was assembled, drinking champagne. Frazer looked round with a deep feeling of happiness. The room was hung with his series of Hollywood pictures, each one set into a panel and perfectly lit.

'To the star of the show,' Hamilton said, raising his glass.

'Thank you,' Frazer answered, and leaned forward to receive a kiss from Bridget. 'It's wonderful! I wasn't expecting this at all.'

'I only did it to increase the value of the boat,' Hamilton said. 'Come and see what I've got in the next room.'

He opened a set of doors to another large cabin, furnished in green leather and brass-trimmed mahogany. The only painting in the room was *The Girl in the White Dress*.

Charles walked up to it. 'How on earth did you get hold of this?' he asked.

Hamilton smiled. 'It was a present from Jack Stapoulas. He knew I'd begun to collect paintings, and he asked if there was anything I wanted. I said I'd like a really good Impressionist. When he gave me this, there was a note with it: "Ask, and it shall be given".' He added, with a grin, 'Of course, it came off my fee for *The Rivals*.'

'What do you think he'll give you for your next picture?' Davis asked.

Hamilton shrugged. 'Who knows? I'm playing a boxer; probably Madison Square Garden.' They laughed. Then he turned to Davis. 'Shouldn't everyone be here by now?'

Davis smiled reassuringly. 'Relax! They telephoned. There's another hour to go before they arrive.' He gestured to the others. 'Anyone would think he was the one getting married!'

As he spoke, a voice called, 'Hello' and a large, breathless lady wearing a white suit and a hat trimmed with flowers entered the cabin. She glanced around and saw Davis.

'Are the couple here?' she asked anxiously. Al waved towards Bridget and Frazer with his champagne glass. 'Thank God!' she replied. 'I'm Maggie McGuire from the studio publicity department. We've had to bring the ceremony forward. ABC television want it for their evening news, and they have to send it down the line earlier than we anticipated. How long will it take you to get ready, darling?'

Bridget shot Irene a look of sudden panic. 'How long have I got?' she said nervously.

'About thirty-four seconds, darling. There are shoeless photographers swarming all over the decks already.' Maggie turned to Hamilton. 'There are a couple of British reporters here, too, who say

583

they know you.'

Clive nodded. 'I'd better go up and give them a drink.'

Maggie beamed at them all. 'Isn't it a pity the captain couldn't marry them? Apparently it's not legal.'

'Except in the movies,' Davis said, putting down his empty glass.

Irene looked at Bridget and Carl uncertainly. 'Oh, darlings', she said. 'You don't think it's all a bit too vulgar, do you? I didn't know it was going to be quite such a circus!'

Bridget handed her glass to José and turned to Irene. 'Are you mad, Mother?' she said firmly. 'Personally, I think it's all quite wonderful.'

Maggie McGuire was delighted with the way the ceremony went. A band had been hired to play by the quayside, and when the clergyman pronounced Bridget and Carl man and wife, the boats around sounded their foghorns in salutation. Al Davis and Maggie McGuire ushered the last guests ashore just after nine o'clock, and an hour later the original party sat down to dinner.

'It's a strange wedding breakfast, darling,' Irene said as they were finishing.

'It's been wonderful,' said Bridget. 'I'd like to propose a toast of thanks to Clive.'

They raised their glasses to him. Then Willis got up. 'Come on, champ,' he said. 'If you want to look like a fighter in your next movie, you've got to get your shut-eye.'

The group started to break up. Davis drove Maggie to her hotel and Charles was taken below to examine Willis's scrapbook. Bridget said she wanted to thank the crew.

Eventually Irene found herself alone with her new son-in-law. They sat awkwardly for a while and then she said, 'You will look after her for me, won't you?'

Frazer smiled and looked her in the eye. 'You've got it wrong, Irene,' he said slowly. 'She looks after me.' He let out a long breath and sipped some of his wine. 'I honestly don't think I could live without her now.'

Although he spoke the words without emotion, Irene could tell how much he meant them. 'I really don't know you at all, do I?' she said.

Frazer shrugged. 'There isn't much to know. My family aren't very nice people; that's why none of them is here today. Bridget is the only person who's ever loved me in my life. I don't ever want to lose that.'

584

'How on earth did you choose to become a painter?'

Frazer laughed. 'It chose me. When I went to school, someone stuck a paintbrush in my hand one day, and I haven't been able to let go since.'

Irene nodded. 'Does it bother you that Bridget is going to be rich?'

Fraser pushed his glass aside.. In the silence they could hear the sound of water lapping against the side of the boat. 'Have you ever been poor?' he asked finally.

'Once or twice.'

Fraser shook his head impatiently. 'I'm not talking about having to decide what size eggs to buy. I mean, have you ever lived in dirt and squalor, where your clothes stank and you could feel vermin on you?'

'No, I've never been as poor as that.'

He smiled gently at her again. 'No, Irene, having a rich wife will never bother me.'

She got up and kissed the top of his head. 'Goodnight,' she said. 'Sweet dreams.'

A few minutes later Bridget came back and sat down next to him. She took his glass of wine and drank a little of it.

'Happy?' he asked her.

She threaded an arm through his and leaned her head against his shoulder. 'It would have been perfect if Dad had been here,' she said wistfully. 'It was a bit like one of my birthdays.'

London, autumn 1967

A morning train drew into Charing Cross station and the last of the rush-hour crowd hurried towards the barrier. Elizabeth started to get up, but Laszlo held out a restraining hand.

'There's no need to go so fast,' he said.

She looked at him in surprise. 'You're the one who's always dashing for a taxi,' she said. 'You've been ten paces faster than me all our lives.'

'Well, I'm not rushing today,' he said with a smile. 'In fact, I'm taking the morning off.'

'Well, don't get under my feet,' Elizabeth said cheerfully. 'We're spring-cleaning today.'

At the station entrance Laszlo looked up at the overcast sky and turned up his coat collar against the wind blowing in from the west. 'Spring-cleaning in November? That's a little premature, isn't it?'

Elizabeth put an arm through his and they walked past the south side of St Martin-in-the-Fields, where children were playing in the yard behind the church. 'I shall be working in my study this morning,' he said. 'So no vacuum-cleaners in there.'

'As you wish,' Elizabeth replied. 'If you're happy to live among all that dust, who am I to dissuade you?'

Laszlo was as good as his word. As soon as they reached the flat, he went to his study and shut the door. It's a big room for one man, he often thought, but there was no other purpose they could put it to. He sat at the desk and looked at the pictures around him. They were all connected with his life.

His favourite was a crayon sketch of Gideon and himself drawn in Juan-les-Pins in 1949. They had been sitting in a pavement café and the artist had sketched them together. Afterwards, he and Gideon had tossed a coin for it. Laszlo had won, and the old man had been so amused by Gideon's crestfallen expression that he had quickly drawn another. There was also a life-sized portrait over the fireplace, which Nettlebury had painted in the early fifties. Laszlo could remember the suit he had worn for the sitting; it had always been a favourite.

Suddenly he realised how cold it was; the central heating had not been switched on during the weekend, and the house was chilly. He thought about making a fire, but decided that work would take his mind from the cold.

When Elizabeth bought him his coffee at ten-thirty, she found him immersed in papers spread out on the top of the desk. 'Are you warm enough in here?' she asked, when he wrapped his hands round the cup.

'I'll be through in a minute. Then I'm going out.'

'Where to?' Elizabeth asked, running an experimental finger along a bookshelf and grimacing at the dust.

'To see Richard Cleary. Apparently he's in the London Clinic.'

'May we come in here when you go out?' she asked.

Laszlo nodded. 'But don't try to tidy any papers!'

'Yes, sir, anything you say, sir,' she replied, saluting.

When he had finished his coffee, Laszlo put on his overcoat and left the house. After a few minutes he caught a taxi outside the National Portrait Gallery and directed the driver to Harley Street. There, instead of going straight to the London Clinic, he told the driver to stop half-way down. He paid him off, watched him drive away, and then climbed the steps of an imposing private house. Inside, the receptionist looked up at him enquiringly.

He smiled. 'I don't have an appointment, but Dr Turner is a friend of mine. Do you think it would be possible to see him this morning?'

'I'll see, sir. Whom shall I say is calling?' she asked. He gave his name.

'Oh, yes, Mr Vasilakis,' she said with a broad smile. 'We've talked on the telephone many times.'

'Indeed we have,' he said.

'Won't you take a seat, sir?' she said. 'I'll be as quick as possible.'

Laszlo sat in a corner and read a copy of *Country Life* for a while, and then a door opened and the portly figure of George Turner emerged.

'I've got someone in there for the next few minutes, but then I'll be free,' he said in a low voice. He winked and re-entered his consulting-room.

He was as good as his word. Five minutes later Laszlo glanced up and saw a familiar figure sweep out without noticing him. Then he was ushered into the room, where Turner sat smoking.

He stubbed out the cigarette with a shudder. 'Dreadful habit!' he said with a shrug. 'Now, what's up with you?'

Laszlo described how tired he'd felt in recent months. Turner examined him thoroughly, and then told him to get dressed again.

'It's my heart, isn't it?' Laszlo asked.

Turner shook his head with a wry smile. 'No, old boy, it's called age.' He nodded towards the door. 'The last customer was the one with heart trouble.'

'Ted Peake?' Laszlo said with surprise.

A frown of annoyance crossed Turner's face. 'You know him?'

'Yes.'

'In that case, I shouldn't have said anything. Forget it, will you?'

'Of course.'

Turner folded his hands. 'You're suffering from stress. When you get to your age you're supposed to start taking it easy, otherwise it can develop into something else . . . For a start, you can try to get a decent walk every day, but, most important, you're going to have to give up worrying. That's an indulgence you can no longer afford.'

Laszlo smiled. 'How can I give up the habit of a lifetime?'

Turner put his fingertips together. 'Well, when you get up in the morning, think of Elizabeth weeping by your graveside. Then make a list of all the things you were going to worry about that day. Don't just think about them, write them down. Read through the list and ask yourself, "Which of these are worth dying for?" That's what I do.'

'You?'

Turner nodded. 'I know, I know – I smoke, and I'm three stones overweight. But I don't worry, and it works for me.'

When Laszlo said goodbye and left the surgery, it was still cold. He crossed the road and walked towards the London Clinic. In Cleary's room, he found Peter Quick and Val, who were about to leave. Cleary stood by the window dressed in a bathrobe, looking so frail that Laszlo thought the draught from the open door would blow him over. He was holding a large drink, and a cigarette smouldered between his fingers.

Val kissed him on the cheek before she collected her bag. 'We'll see you on Thursday,' she said.

Cleary shook his head. 'Don't plan so far ahead,' he said in his deep voice.

'Bollocks!' Quick said gruffly. 'You're going to outlive us all.'

When they had gone, Cleary pointed to the bottle of whisky on the table by the bed. 'Have a drink,' he said.

Laszlo shrugged, remembering Turner's words about not worrying, and poured himself a large one.

Cleary sat down slowly and carefully arranged himself in the chair. Each movement was made with a deliberation that was almost theatrical. 'So what's wrong with you?' he asked.

'What do you mean?' Laszlo said. He drank some of the whisky.

Cleary nodded to the window. 'I saw you coming out of one of the consulting-rooms across the road, and you were wearing an expression like a bloodhound in mourning when you came in here. Most people who visit me put on a cheerful face and keep up a string of inane comments about how much I'm improving.' He gestured across the room. 'You look as if you want to get into that bed instead of me. What did he say you've got?'

Laszlo shrugged. 'Just stress.'

Cleary laughed. 'I've got a bad heart and a bad liver and a bad case of stress. It's just like a bloody agent to have a third of what I've got!'

To Laszlo's astonishment, he realised that, in his own grim way, Cleary was attempting to cheer him up. He suddenly found the man's

588

efforts deeply moving. 'How are you feeling now?' he asked.

Cleary shook his head. 'I'm not feeling anything at all. They give me drugs that make me numb. I'm like one of those prehistoric monsters that took hours for pain to register on their central nervous system. If you kicked me up the arse now, I wouldn't feel it until about nine o'clock tonight.'

Laszlo laughed and shook his head. Cleary looked at him. 'You believe in God, don't you?'

Laszlo looked up. 'We have to. My religion insists on it.'

Cleary was silent for a moment. 'Do you still go to church?' he asked eventually.

Laszlo smiled again. 'They insist on that as well.'

'Say a prayer for me next time you're there,' Cleary said, and finished his drink.

Laszlo was surprised. 'Do you believe in the existence of God?'

Cleary got up slowly and walked towards the table, where he poured himself another drink. He held up the bottle, but Laszlo shook his head. He said, 'Oh yes, I don't doubt it for a moment.'

'You surprise me,' Laszlo said. 'I always thought of you as a convinced atheist. Why are you so sure?'

Cleary took out another cigarette and lit it from the stub of the one he still held. 'It's the only explanation for beauty that's ever made any sense to me.' He gave a long, racking cough, and held out his hand when Laszlo stood up to help. Gradually the attack subsided, and Cleary continued, 'The rationalists win all the other arguments hands down, but they've never been able to convince me that music, poetry or painting are just a kind of mental masturbation.'

'So you think you were doing God's work?' said Laszlo.

'No, I was doing my own work. I believed in the existence of God; I didn't say I trusted the bastard. That's where you lot went wrong.' He drank deeply and then put down the glass. 'I asked you to come here because I want you to do me one last favour.' He took some papers from a drawer. 'I want you to be one of the executors of my will.'

Laszlo looked at him bleakly. 'Are you sure I'm the best person?'

Cleary waved a hand dismissively. 'You'll last a lot longer than me,' he said, and he laughed again, but the laughter led to another bout of coughing. When it stopped, he passed the papers to Laszlo. 'Don't worry about my body,' he said. 'I've left it to the doctors. They're rather keen to look inside. According to them, I should have died years ago. They're interested to see what kept me going.' He waved a hand. 'Everything is quite simple. The whole estate goes to Bridget, except for the pictures Paula Tuchman has. She keeps them until she dies, then they go to Bridget as well. That's all there is to it.'

'Where's Bridget now?' Laszlo asked. 'Don't you want to see her?'

'She's in California with that boy who paints road-signs. If she's happy, I don't want to disturb her . . . You know, Irene always used to say I was selfish, that I only cared about myself. When I wanted to get to know Bridget, she said it was too late; the more I saw her the more it would hurt her in the end. Well, I don't want that to happen. No tearful deathbed scenes.' He got up again and shuffled over to the window. 'What's it like out?'

'Bloody cold, and it looks as if it might rain.'

Cleary turned and smiled. 'I'd like to sleep now. I'm thinking of having a night on the town later.'

Laszlo laughed, and got to his feet. 'I'll look in later in the week. At least you can get a decent drink here. Pubs are so crowded these days.'

Cleary watched him go and then lay down on the bed. His eyes drifted to the window. As Laszlo had predicted, it soon began to rain. He got up and pressed a bell for a nurse. It took some time and a great deal of unpleasantness, but he finally persuaded them that he meant to discharge himself from the hospital. He dressed carefully. Then he opened the suitcase he had brought with him, studied the contents and took out three photographs. One was of his aircrew during the war; the second was a snapshot taken in 1946 on the steps of the Art School. Both Paula and Irene were in the picture. He stood between them, but apart. The third, of Bridget's wedding, was in colour. It seemed unreal. He put them in his inside pocket. Feeling about inside the lining of the case, he took out an old metal object tarnished with age, the trumpet mouthpiece. He weighed it in his hand and wondered what his life would have been had he become a musician. He smiled. There really hadn't been a choice. Whatever forces had fashioned him, they had not intended music to be anything but a passing pleasure: rather like the people I've known, he thought wryly. Leaving the suitcase on the bed, he stopped a passing taxi outside the clinic.

'Where do you want to go, mate?' the driver asked.

'Drop me in Cromwell Road,' he told him. 'Near the Royal College of Art.'

590

The traffic was slow because of the rain, but eventually Cleary paid off the cab and stood on the pavement. There were few other pedestrians. He began to walk slowly, whilie the rain soaked his overcoat and the cold began to seep through his body. The rain blurred his vision as he turned into Earl's Court Road. The lights above the shops were just smears of garish colour. Each step was a terrible effort now. As he began to fall, he felt no other sensation but the memory of his aircraft dropping from the sky.

Two young men nearby hurried forward as he collapsed. Half-way across the pavement, his hand opened and the trumpet mouthpiece rolled away into the rain-filled gutter.

New York, winter 1968

Charles looked out of his bedroom window on to the darkness of Central Park while he fashioned his black evening tie into a bow. It was one of his little vanities that he could perform the task without the use of a looking-glass. 'Well, I'm ready,' he said to Irene.

Still in her bathrobe, she was sitting at her dressing-table. 'This is the first movie premiére I've ever attended, and you don't have false eyelashes to contend with,' she said, peering into the mirror.

'I prefer that natural, unmade-up look you had before I married you,' he said.

Irene smiled. 'I've got red hair, pale skin and freckles. That's the hardest face in the world to give a natural, unmade-up look.'

Charles took a brush and gave his hair a couple of sweeps. Then he put on his jacket and left the bedroom. The maid was arranging glasses on the sideboard in the living-room.

'Shall I open the champagne now, sir?' she asked. The front-door bell rang.

'No, I'll do that, Mary,' he said. 'You get the door.'

The cork on the first bottle popped as Clive Hamilton and Al Davis came in, accompanied by a striking blonde girl and Maggie McGuire.

'That's my signature tune you're playing,' Davis said. 'Don't give my boy any, he's still in training.' He took the blonde girl by the arm and brought her forward. 'Ingrid Svenson, Charles Whitney-Ingram.'

'Hi,' she said. 'Are you in the movie business?'

Charles handed her a glass of champagne and shook his head. 'No. I *sell* pictures, though.' He gestured at the walls. 'This kind.'

She looked around. 'Do you know Jack Stapoulas? He owns a lot of paintings. He just bought one today.'

Charles nodded. 'I know. I read about it in *The New York Times*.'

'It was a Van Duren,' she said. 'He paid a record price for it.'

Charles handed a glass of champagne to Clive Hamilton, who looked preoccupied. 'I have two Van Durens at the other end of the room. Would you care to see them?' he said.

The girl looked at him with interest. 'Are they worth as much as Jack paid for his?'

Charles nodded. 'I think so.'

'In that case, I'd love to,' she answered.

They walked away from the others, and she examined the paintings for a few minutes, then shook her head and sighed with a troubled expression.

Charles watched her. The tall body was beautifully proportioned and her face was as innocent as a child's. In repose it was conventionally pretty, but then an expression of pleasure or doubt transformed it into something much more interesting. 'What's the matter?' he asked.

'Jack paid one hundred thousand dollars for one of these?' Charles nodded. 'How could he tell if it was a fake?' she said.

Charles laughed. 'That's where people like me come in. It's my job to guarantee that a painting is genuine.'

'How do you do that?'

'Well, in the case of the painting Mr Stapoulas bought today, it would be easy. I actually saw Paul Van Duren working on the picture one afternoon a few years ago.'

He could tell from her look that she was impressed. Paul Van Duren's name was now in the American pantheon of famous people, along with movie stars and baseball players.

'You knew him?' she said quickly. 'What was he like?'

Charles began to tell her of their association, and was still engrossed when Irene emerged from the bedroom.

'Who is the naked woman with Charles?' she asked, greeting Hamilton and Davis. The men looked down the long room at Ingrid's backless white dress.

'She's co-starring with me in *The Temptations of Saint Anthony*,' Hamilton replied.

'Ingrid Svenson, the child with the face of Garbo,' Davis added.

'Is she all the temptations, or just one of them?' Irene asked.

'She's a pain in the neck,' Hamilton said gloomily. 'But I love her.' He seemed to make an effort to change his mood. 'At least I'm supposed to. We're promoting my next movie. Ingrid,' he called, 'Come and say hello to your hostess.'

Charles and the girl rejoined them and Irene noticed Hamilton take her hand.

'Did you learn anything about painting?' Davis asked. From his voice, he might have been asking a child what she had done at school that day.

Ingrid smiled sweetly at Irene. When she spoke, her voice was deeper; the breathless American accent she had used earlier had gone.

'You know, Mrs Whitney-Ingram, I speak three languages quite well and I have a degree in humanities from Stockholm University, but everyone in Hollywood seems to think that I have the mental age of a twelve-year-old child.'

'That's because you've been playing the part since you got here,' Davis said. 'If you want people to treat you like an adult, you'd better stop the Shirley Temple routine.' He spoke more sharply than Irene thought necessary, and she smiled at Ingrid to reassure her.

Irene enjoyed the evening, for the most part. The ride to the cinema with the star, the cheering crowds and flashing cameras were exactly as she had imagined the scene. There was a reception before they took their seats, and she recognised a lot of the famous people. Each of them appeared to be having a wonderful time. They were loud in their conversation and laughed a great deal. The ordinary people at the reception, among whom she counted herself, seemed more subdued. After a time she felt a tap on her shoulder and turned to face Ted Peake, who looked splendid in a red velvet dinner-jacket. Charles was talking to a man with a sad expression. When she tugged Charles's sleeve to gain his attention, she noticed Anthony Strange and Schneider in another group.

'You remember Ted Peake, don't you, darling?' she said.

'Yes, of course,' Charles said, glancing round. 'You're on your own tonight, are you, Ted?' he asked.

Peake nodded. 'Gloria's popped over to London to see a few things. Pity, she would have enjoyed it here tonight. How's old Gideon and Laszlo? Blimey, they must be worth a fortune these days, with the way the Cromwell Road School shot up!'

Charles nodded. 'It's only because nobody else would buy them, you know. It really is success by default.' He hesitated, and then said, 'Tell me, why did you sell the Degas Gideon always wanted to

593

somebody else?'

Ted Peake shook his head. 'I felt really bad about that, but I was faced with a dilemma. When I went into partnership with Jack Stapoulas . . . ' He saw Charles's surprised expression, and stopped. 'Didn't you know about that?' Charles shook his head.

'Oh, yes,' Peake continued. 'You know Jack controls the Rainbow Group?'

'I must confess my ignorance on these matters,' Charles said.

'Well,' Peake said, 'there I was, in partnership with Stapoulas, and he says to me he wants that picture more than anything else. I've always made it a rule in life that partners come first; after all, if you can't trust your partner, who can you trust? Gloria always used to say, "Ted, you think more of your partners than you do of me!" ' He shrugged. 'I ask you, what else could I do?' He looked over Irene's shoulder and waved. 'Excuse me,' he said. 'There's somebody I just have to speak to.'

Charles watched him go with a thoughtful frown. 'You know,' he said to Irene, 'Gideon tried everything to get that picture from Ted Peake. Pity he never thought of going into partnership with him.'

'Did you talk to Clive about it?' Irene asked.

Charles nodded. 'He told me he couldn't let it go just then as it was a sort of present from Jack Stapoulas. It would look like a slap in the face. But he said that as soon as it was decently possible, he'd sell it to me.'

'Oh, that's splendid news,' Irene said. 'It would mean so much to Gideon.'

Then an usher announced that it was time for everyone to take their seats.

Jack Stapoulas stood at the door of the dress circle, accompanied by two aides. He smiled constantly as he reached out to shake every hand and mutter, 'Enjoy the movie.' When the last of the guests had filed past he turned and strode quickly away, so that the two men with him had to break into a trot to catch up. Without looking at either of them, he said, 'Get Strange and Schneider to come and see me at the party.'

Both men attempted to make a note as they tried to match his long stride, and the younger one ventured a question. 'Aren't you going to watch the movie, sir?'

'No. I made the piece of shit,' he replied. 'That gives me some rights.'

Irene tried to enjoy the film, but eventually had to admit that it was terrible nonsense. There was a half-hearted attempt to get the audience to applaud at the end, but it quickly petered out.

Afterwards there was the party in Stapoulas's suite at the Sherry Netherland hotel. The ride there in the studio limousine was difficult. Clive Hamilton sat in morose silence, looking out of the window, while Al Davis attempted to make cheerful conversation, mostly about the way New York had changed. No one mentioned the movie. It was as though the event they had just attended had not taken place at all.

'This is awful,' Irene whispered as they crossed the lobby of the hotel. 'Poor Clive! I don't know what to say to him.'

'Nothing is best,' Charles replied. 'We'll leave as soon as we can.'

The atmosphere in the suite was better than Irene had anticipated. Few of the guests were in the movie business and discussion was general. Nobody seemed to want to talk about *The Singing Highwayman*. After a time she noticed that their host was not with them. It seemed odd behaviour to her, but Davis explained that there was probably another room where two or three of the really important guests were now assembled.

'There's always an inner sanctum,' he said. 'In the old days in Hollywood, Howard Hughes used to take people into the john to talk to them.'

As he spoke, Irene watched one of the two aides approach Strange and Schneider, and they followed him from the party.

Jack Stapoulas was sitting in a high-backed chair, the only source of light a standard lamp behind his head. He gestured at the two chairs drawn up before him. 'Take a seat,' he said. 'What did you think of the movie?'

'Interesting,' Anthony Strange answered.

'I liked it,' Schneider said, almost enthusiastically.

'It's going to lose a great deal of money,' Stapoulas said softly, 'and that presents you with a problem.'

'Us?' Strange was wary.

'Yes, gentlemen. You,' the Greek replied. 'Let me explain to you some of the realities of the business I'm in.' He paused and took a sip from the glass of brandy on the table by his side. 'The movie industry is based entirely on success these days. The good old times

595

when the big studios were completely in control and could take a loss are gone. Everything is done by independents, who have to put the deals together, raise the money and take the flak.'

'Why are you telling us this?' said Strange. His voice was nervous.

Stapoulas raised his hand. 'Hear me out,' he said. 'Now, let me give you an example of what actually happens. I took a kid called Clive Hamilton and gave him his big break. I made him a star in a movie called *The Rivals*. Everyone thought I was crazy; a musical set in England, with all the men dressed up like fags and the women like Christmas trees? "You must be out of your mind!" they said.' He paused, and sipped more brandy. 'Well, *The Rivals* made more money than *The Sound of Music*, and suddenly I'm a genius. Everybody wants to back the next movie I make. This time it's going to be about a singing highwayman: same period, same star. We got some hot-shots from Broadway to write the songs; I tell you, it was the best talent we could get together. You saw the result tonight.' He stopped and gave a long sigh. 'Now this brings us to your problem. At this moment in time, we have Clive Hamilton's latest block-buster in production: *The Temptations of Saint Anthony*. It's a modern movie, set in New York, about a kid who wants to be a priest but because of circumstance has to become a boxer. It's almost finished, but it's run over time so we need another injection of capital to wrap it up. Now, how can I go to anyone and ask them for money when they read the kind of reviews *The Singing Highwayman* is going to get tomorrow?'

Strange could see the juggernaut rumbling towards him, and made a feeble effort to side-step. 'Perhaps they will like this film?'

'No way,' Stapoulas answered. 'The movie bombed, gentlemen. That's why I want you to give me two million dollars to complete *The Temptations of Saint Anthony*.'

'Two million dollars?' Schneider repeated. His voice broke with emotion.

'That should do it,' the Greek said with a smile.

Strange stood up. 'I'm sorry, Jack,' he said regretfully. 'We'd love to help you. But we can't raise that kind of money.'

'Yes, you can.' His voice sounded like a knife being drawn from a scabbard. 'Because, if you don't, I shall have to tell certain people about the paintings you've sold around Hollywood for the last ten years. You two have unloaded more fakes than a ten-dollar hooker turns tricks. Some of the people out there aren't as nice as me. They would be tempted to call up friends from Sicily.'

Schneider knew when to throw in a losing hand, and when the

deal was done, Stapoulas smiled again. 'Now, is there any favour I can do for you?' he asked expansively.

Strange thought. 'Yes,' he said slowly. 'The painting you gave Clive Hamilton.'

'The Degas?' Stapoulas said.

Strange nodded. '*The Girl in the White Dress*. Give it to me.'

The Greek didn't hesitate. 'It's yours,' he said. 'Hamilton's had it long enough.' Then, with the same smile, 'Is there anything else?'

Strange paused again. He had just paid two million dollars for a painting and was feeling light-headed. 'Tell me, Jack,' he said earnestly. 'You're a rich man. Why don't you pay for the completion of the movie?'

Stapoulas laughed. 'Gentlemen, gentlemen! No sane person puts their own money into movies!'

CHAPTER TWENTY-SEVEN

London, spring 1968

Anthony Strange stood in the office of their gallery in Bond Street, listening to Schneider. When he had finished, Strange sat down slowly behind the partner's desk. 'Nothing? No sign of him at all?'

Schneider shook his head. 'I'm afraid not. He seems to have vanished completely. I went to the flat in Wembley, but there was no sign of him or his mother. The neighbours said they'd gone away. They wouldn't say where to.' He stood up. 'I'm sorry.'

Strange banged the desk slowly. 'Damn, damn, damn!' he repeated.

Klara was talking in the outer office to Strange's secretary, who had her coat on and was ready to go home. They walked to the door, and Klara looked in at the two men. Then she turned to the secretary. 'You may go. They will not need you until tomorrow.'

Klara's brother was slumped on the sofa. Strange was leaning over the desk, biting the knuckles of his right hand, looking out of the window with a preoccupied expression. Neither of them noticed her. She opened the drinks cabinet and poured two large measures of vodka. She then took a small plastic container from her handbag and shook out four little pills. 'Take these,' she instructed the men.

They swallowed the pills and vodka like sleep-walkers, and the combination of amphetamine and alcohol jolted their nervous systems awake. Strange reacted like a limp puppet with his strings taken up again; he jerked away from the wall and began to pace up and down. Schneider finished his vodka and took another large measure.

'Let me review the situation,' Strange said confidently. 'We have experienced the most catastrophic year in the history of the Strange and Schneider Gallery.' He began to count out on his fingers: '*The Temptations of Saint Anthony* has been a total commercial failure.'

598

'But a great critical success,' Schneider interrupted.

Strange looked at him with distaste. 'The critics will not give us back our two million dollars. The Greek has made that abundantly clear.' He held up his hand again and counted off the next finger. 'We decided to put all the resources we possessed into the new gallery in Paris. Then the bank refused to extend our credit.'

This time Klara interrupted. 'So we do not have the necessary finance to stock the premises with paintings.'

Schneider took another mouthful of vodka. 'And now that little bastard, Ovington, has run out on us. Before he could paint the pictures we required.'

Strange continued, 'The bank still refuses to extend our credit.'

Schneider poured another vodka. 'Let's take what we have left and go to South America,' he said. 'We still have friends there.'

Strange banged his fist down so hard on the desk that his full glass of vodka slopped over. 'I don't intend to spend the rest of my life in some imitation bierkeller eating knackwurst and reminiscing about the good old days,' he said. He stood back. 'Not when we have James Gideon's Breughel in the safe downstairs.'

Schneider licked some of the vodka from his hand. 'Ovington left us all the proof we need that Gideon painted that picture.'

Strange nodded. 'The solution to our problem is easy,' he said. 'It lies in the Archangel Gallery.'

In another part of Bond Street, in the flat over the gallery, Anne, Irene, Elizabeth and Peggy Todd sat looking at an old photograph of Schneider in an album of Anne's. Their husbands stood in a group by the mantelpiece.

'Good heavens! Here's a picture of me with Charles when we were children,' Irene exclaimed. 'Charles!' she called, 'Come and look at this.'

The men finished their conversation and came over. 'By God, I was handsome then!' Charles said, then he glanced at his watch. 'We're due at the Haymarket in thirty minutes.'

As he spoke, Bridget and Carl Frazer descended the spiral staircase.

'Shall we go?' Gideon called out. 'The cars are waiting.'

On the way to the theatre, Irene clutched Charles's arm as they turned into Piccadilly Circus. 'Oh, dear, I do hope it doesn't turn out to be like that dreadful night in New York,' she said.

Charles patted her hand reassuringly; he did not say that the same thought was in his own mind. They were attending the first night of a new production of *Hamlet*, starring Clive Hamilton and Ingrid Svenson. It had been produced and directed by a brilliant young man, who had chosen them for the parts after he had seen *The Temptations of Saint Anthony*.

The next day they were due to leave for the villa in the south of France, leaving the gallery in the hands of Graham Todd. The decision to go had been taken suddenly by Gideon and Laszlo, and Elizabeth and Anne had spent the last week making hasty arrangements.

They took their seats expectantly, and when the curtain rose, five great grey blocks of rough-hewn material, suspended above the dimly-lit stage, slowly began to revolve and form the shape of the battlements of Elsinore. The production was a triumph. Hamilton played the part with startling vigour, leaping about the stage with power and grace. His months of training with Cobra Willis had served him well. One highlight of the evening came during Ingrid Svenson's performance as Ophelia. In her final scene, her splendid body was naked but for a few wisps of gauze; it caused an audible intake of breath from the audience.

Afterwards, Irene and Charles went back-stage with Anne and Gideon while the others went on to the party. The four managed to pass through the crowded corridor into Hamilton's room, where they discovered, to their surprise, that they had been preceded by Jack Stapoulas, accompanied by Anthony Strange. Al Davis was pouring drinks.

'This is going to make a great movie, baby,' the Greek enthused. He took a glass from Davis and waved it at Ingrid. 'And we'll make sure your part is bigger, Ingrid. That death scene came too early. We can fix that.'

More people crowded into the room, and Gideon found himself close to Anthony Strange. 'I saw you outside our gallery today, admiring the Miro in the window,' Strange said. 'You should come in and have a better look.'

'I understand that's all you have these days, Strange. Paris must be a grave worry for you.'

'But I still have something that will interest you,' Strange said with a sudden smile. 'You didn't know I had your favourite Degas again, did you?'

Gideon looked into his eyes, trying to decipher the truth. 'I thought Hamilton still had it.'

600

Strange continued to smile. 'No, I have been fortunate again.'

'Would you be interested in selling?' Gideon asked.

Strange shrugged. 'Anything is possible.' He moved slightly as more people squeezed into the little room. 'But this is hardly the place to talk. Unfortunately, I'm going to the south of France tomorrow.'

Gideon raised his eyebrows. 'So are we. Perhaps we can meet while we're there?'

Strange smiled again and edged away into the crowd. 'I'll give you a ring,' he said, and turned to talk to Stapoulas.

Eventually the crowd left the dressing-room and made their way to the party at the Savoy. The others, who had gone ahead, had already secured a large table.

When they had eaten, Anne called across the table to Laszlo, 'You'll never guess who we saw at the theatre!' Laszlo shook his head and made a mime show of not being able to hear. 'Anthony Strange in Clive Hamilton's dressing-room,' she said more loudly.

Laszlo got up from beside Elizabeth and came over. 'You saw Strange?' he said.

Gideon nodded. 'He wants to do some kind of deal.'

'I don't like it.'

'He's never worried you in the past,' said Gideon. 'Why should this be any different?'

Laszlo shrugged. 'He's lost so much – the Paris business. The story is that they're broke. I don't like dealing with desperate people.'

Gideon laughed. 'He's not a tiger, you know. Strange will never be more than a rat.'

Laszlo stood up. 'Rats are notoriously dangerous when they are cornered!' He tried a half-hearted smile, and patted Gideon on the shoulder.

Clive Hamilton and Ingrid arrived at the table. 'Did you enjoy it?' Clive asked. They could see how joyful he was, and expressed their congratulations. 'Make sure the party goes on late. I intend to dance till dawn!' He sat down next to Gideon, 'I'm sorry about Strange being in the dressing-room,' he said. 'Jack brought him. I know you can't stand the man. I'm sorry about the Degas, too. I didn't want to sell it, you know. Stapoulas made me.'

Gideon smiled. 'Don't worry. It may work out, anyway. Strange said he might want to do a deal.'

Hamilton stood up while the group around the table thanked him and said their farewells. Laszlo was the last to do so.

'Gideon tells me he's negotiating with Strange. Is peace breaking out between your noble households?' Hamilton asked.

Laszlo shrugged and looked at Gideon thoughtfully. 'A glooming peace this morning with it brings. The sun for sorrow will not show its head.'

Ingrid joined Hamilton in time to hear Laszlo's parting remark, and turned to him. 'Why was Laszlo quoting *Romeo and Juliet?*'

Hamilton shrugged. 'People always quote Shakespeare. It's because he said everything anyone ever wanted to say.'

The following morning, Irene packed their bags in the bedroom she had slept in the night before Bridget was born. It was early, but Charles had already gone with Gideon to get petrol for the Rolls-Royce. A solitary motorbike passed on the Kew Road, heading for Richmond, then there was silence. She glanced out of the window and saw how the sunlight caught the tops of the trees. There were patches of fine white cloud against the pale blue sky. The leaves of a copper beech moved in the breeze, changing colour from purple to fire-red. She tried to remember how the morning had been twenty years ago, but her thoughts stayed stubbornly in the present. She paused when she had closed the last case, and smiled with contentment, then descended through the silent house to the kitchen.

After she had made tea she reached for the milk jug, and the day of Bridget's birth came back to her as clear and sharp as the reflection in a polished mirror. There had been no milk for their morning tea. She could remember her father grumbling as if he were in the room now, and it had been raining. Vera had said it was cold weather for June.

Taking her tea, Irene walked outside and stood beneath one of the apple trees. The new saplings the gardener had planted the previous year were strong; she could tell they were going to thrive. There was movement inside the conservatory; she could make out a figure, but the light shining on the glass obscured the person's identity. For a few moments she imagined it was her father, then the figure moved again and she saw it was Frazer, standing before an easel. He saw her, and raised a hand in greeting as she walked to the door. 'What are you doing?' she asked.

'A present for Bridget. I was hoping to have it finished before we went away, but it's taken longer than I expected.'

The picture on the easel was a portrait of Irene's daughter

602

standing in front of a Coca-Cola sign. The colours were harsh and vivid, with deep shadows caused by a hard Californian sunlight. The painting seemed very foreign in their present surroundings, but she liked it; it had strength and vitality.

'Do you think she'll like it?' Carl asked.

'I'm sure she will. But if she doesn't, I'll have it!'

Carl laughed. 'That's praise indeed from the daughter of Sir Julian Nettlebury!'

Irene smiled. She had begun to form a deep affection for her son-in-law. 'Do you want a cup of tea?'

'Yes, please,' he answered and returned to work.

By the time Irene reached the kitchen, Anne was there. 'Thank God the weather is fine,' she said. 'I had nightmares of it pelting with rain all day. It should be a lovely drive.'

Irene took the cup of tea to Carl, and then returned to her sister.

'You were up early,' said Anne.

Irene sat down at the table with another cup of tea. 'It's living in New York. Everyone gets up early there.'

Anne smiled. 'Do you remember how you used to hate getting up to go to school?'

'Bridget was the same.' Irene glanced at the clock. 'She still is. I think we'd better get a move on. Laszlo and Elizabeth are due in an hour.'

Carl came in with his empty cup. 'Is there anything I can do?'

'Yes. Make sure Bridget's ready by nine-thirty!' Irene answered.

Mrs Riley, the housekeeper, arrived a few minutes later. 'The eggs are boiling for the sandwiches,' Irene told her. 'Everything else is packed in the hampers. We're leaving at ten.' Mrs Riley nodded; she had gone over the arrangements several times.

Laszlo sat in his study, looking down at the sheet of paper. He was supposed to write down anything that worried him. All he had written was the name Anthony Strange. The door was half-open, and Elizabeth came in. Casually he screwed up the paper and threw it in the waste-paper basket.

'Are you sure you want to drive today?' she asked. 'You look very tired, darling.'

Laszlo smiled. 'Of course I do. Can you think of anything more relaxing than a trip to France?'

'Sitting back while I take the wheel.'

'This is what I get for marrying a young wife,' he sighed. 'All my friends warned me that it wouldn't last.'

'All the same,' she said, 'I'm going to drive tomorrow.' Then she looked at the picture propped against his desk. It was one of Peter Quick's rural paintings. 'This is lovely. It reminds me of Little Fenton.'

'Would you rather be going there than the south of France?' Laszlo asked.

'No, but it will be lovely to come home to.'

When the car was loaded with luggage, they set off for Kew, where they joined up with the others and drove down to Dover in convoy. The weather stayed perfect and the crossing was calm. After a picnic lunch in the late afternoon, the only two who felt energetic enough to stretch their legs were Gideon and Frazer. They strolled down a country lane into a village. The place was deserted. They stopped at a war memorial and looked up at the weeping angel, enjoying the heat and the mellow peace of the place.

Then Gideon said, 'Are you going to settle in Kew again now?'

Frazer ran his fingertips over the names engraved in the stone. 'I think so. We've spent enough time in America.'

'Does moving back to England bother you?' Gideon asked.

'I've got the sun out of my system now. I think I'd like to work over here for a while.'

'Would you like the Archangel Gallery to handle your work?' Gideon asked carefully.

Frazer looked up at a group of starlings wheeling overhead. 'Join the family business, you mean?' He thrust his hands in his pockets. 'Do you really think I'm any good?'

'Why do you ask?'

Frazer shrugged, and looked away. 'Richard Cleary hated my work. He never missed an opportunity to tell me it was a load of rubbish!'

Gideon smiled. 'I shouldn't worry about what Richard said. He was a brilliant painter, but his artistic judgment wasn't infallible.'

'You didn't answer my question.'

Gideon folded his arms. 'Don't worry, I know you're good.'

'*How* do you know?' Frazer pressed him.

Gideon tipped his straw hat further over his forehead. 'Because I've been buying and selling pictures for thirty-five years. Don't think I'm offering you charity. The reputation of the Archangel Gallery means more to me than that.'

Frazer smiled. 'In that case, I'll sign the contract.'

604

Gideon held out his hand. 'This is the only contract we bother with.'

They stopped at a hotel south of Paris in the late evening, and arrived at the villa late on the evening of the following day, both cars within ten minutes of each other. Elizabeth noticed the red MG parked in the driveway, where Gideon had arranged for it to be delivered. The housekeeper had prepared supper on the terrace, as the weather was exceptionally fine for late April. When the others had gone to bed, Gideon, Laszlo and Charles lingered over their brandies.

'So you're going to sup with the devil,' Charles said, when Laszlo reminded them of Strange's offer to discuss the sale of *The Girl in the White Dress*.

Gideon nodded. 'I think our spoons are long enough.'

Charles saw Laszlo's doubtful expression. 'You don't seem so sure?' he said.

Laszlo stood up slowly and leaned against the balustrade. A lizard scuttled across the white wall and stopped as if turned to stone. He watched the motionless creature while he collected his thoughts. 'There's something wrong with the man,' he said eventually. 'He's a force for evil. I think we should have nothing to do with him.'

Charles held up his brandy glass against the light of the candles, and spoke easily. 'I didn't mean my reference to the devil to be taken literally!'

Gideon and Laszlo said nothing, and Charles realised it had become a difficult subject for them. He got to his feet. 'Well, I'm off to bed. I'm going into Antibes in the morning to run errands for Irene. Would anyone care to come with me?'

Gideon declined, but Laszlo decided he would enjoy the drive in the MG.

When Charles had gone off, they sat in silence for a time. Then Gideon poured more brandy. 'He can't hurt us,' he said.

But Laszlo shook his head, and the movement made the lizard vanish. 'How can we be sure? Who knows what Ovington has given him, or what evidence Strange now has? He'll ruin your reputation if he can. The very fact that he agreed to talk fills me with suspicion.'

'You used not to fear him like this,' said Gideon. He hadn't realised just how deeply Laszlo felt.

The older man shivered slightly. It had grown cooler on the terrace. 'Once, I thought he was just a crooked dealer.' He held up his hands. 'God knows there are a lot of them in the business! But Harriet told me some things about him that changed my mind. Apparently the man enjoys inflicting pain.'

Gideon sipped his brandy. 'Are you saying he used to beat her?'

'No, something worse. He was married before Harriet, you know.'

Gideon looked up in surprise. 'I had no idea.'

'Yes, in Paris when he was a young man, to a widow who had some money. It seems that she went mad and drowned herself. But, according to Harriet, Strange would boast how he caused her to become insane. He hinted that he was responsible for her death.'

Gideon looked into his glass. 'We're not defenceless women,' he said after a time. 'He wouldn't try anything with us.'

Laszlo leaned across the table and gripped his arm. 'Evil people enjoy their vices. They're as important to them as food and drink.'

'I dare say, but we have some advantages. We know he needs money, and we do have another little surprise for him.'

Laszlo sighed. He knew his companion was determined to go ahead with the deal, and all he could do now was to remain on guard. 'He needs pictures as well. If we're going to fight him, let's use his greed.'

They sat drinking for a time, then Laszlo slapped the table. 'How long is it since we visited the cellars?'

Gideon looked up at the star-filled sky, then drained the last of his brandy. 'By God, what great crooks we could have been!' he said with a slow smile.

The following morning Laszlo and Charles set off for Antibes. The weather was fresh and the air scented with pine as Charles negotiated the MG along the narrow winding road that ran along the coast. Eventually they skirted the harbour and entered the little town. Charles parked the car and went off to do his marketing, while Laszlo sat in a café reading a paper. He had half-intended to visit the market, but decided it was more comfortable where he sat.

Charles returned when he was on his second cup of coffee. He laid down his various packages and ordered a beer. 'Do you fancy a look round the port?' he asked after a few minutes.

Laszlo had no interest in nautical matters, but he knew of Charles's enthusiasm. They walked out of the town gate and strolled towards the lines of boats moored in the harbour. After ten minutes' inspection Laszlo noticed that the weather had begun to change and there was a smell of rain in the air. He was about to suggest they head back to the car, when Charles suddenly exclaimed, 'Good God, *Apollo!*'

Laszlo followed his gesture and saw that he was pointing to a beautiful ocean-going yacht.

'I wonder who's aboard,' said Charles.

When he hailed the boat, the familiar figures of Ted and Gloria Peake came up from below. They greeted them with affection, and Laszlo noticed that Ted Peake was a good deal thinner, while both of them were deeply tanned. Peake seemed to glow with health; it was hard to remember what Turner had told him of his heart condition.

As soon as Charles and Laszlo were on board, the rain began. Gloria ushered them below and they sat in the salon where Frazer's pictures still hung.

'We've just brought her over from America,' Peake explained. 'I've always wanted to cross the Atlantic in a yacht.'

'I didn't know you were a sailor, Ted,' Laszlo said, accepting a glass of beer from Gloria.

'I wasn't until now.' He laughed. 'I learned a lot on the voyage.'

'How long have you been here?' Charles asked.

'Oh, a few days,' Peake answered carelessly. 'The crew are taking a holiday. There's only me and Gloria on board.'

Laszlo was aware of a familiar scent. 'Has someone been painting?'

Peake laughed again. 'That was me! I always wanted to have a crack at that, too.'

'Will you show us your efforts?' Charles asked.

Peake shook his head. 'They were bloody terrible. I threw them overboard. You know why we're here, don't you?'

'Tell us,' said Laszlo.

'To deliver *The Girl in the White Dress* to Anthony Strange. When I hired the boat from Clive Hamilton, I offered to do the job as well, if it didn't mean landing in Britain.'

'The painting is on board?' Laszlo asked.

'Strange collected it this morning. You were lucky to catch us. We were thinking of setting off for Portofino this afternoon. You know Smudger Smith lives there now?'

Laszlo nodded. 'I'd heard he'd retired.'

'It's a beautiful house,' Gloria said, 'on the cliffs above the town. I've never been able to get Ted to go there before.'

Peake shrugged. 'I suppose I've put too many things off.' He touched Gloria's arm. 'Still, I'm trying to make up for it now.' They talked on until the rain stopped, and then Ted Peake saw them to

607

the jetty.

'Incidentally,' Charles asked as they were departing, 'whatever happened to the Mueller Collection?'

Peake frowned. 'Oh, Hitler's pictures, you mean? I sold them to a Jap years ago.' He smiled nostalgically. 'I made a lot of money out of them, one way and another.'

Charles laughed as they made their way back to the car. 'It's a good job Peake didn't go in for picture-dealing! None of us would have survived.'

When they got back to the villa, they found Gideon reading on the terrace. 'Strange called. He's coming over tonight,' he told them.

Laszlo described their encounter with Ted Peake.

'How did he look?' Gideon asked.

Laszlo thought about the question. 'Well, but I got the impression he was ticking things off a list. Crossing the Atlantic in a boat, going to stay in a villa by the Mediterranean; he even tried his hand at painting.' He looked down towards the glittering sea, then he glanced up. 'Perhaps I'm reading too much into his actions.'

Gideon stood beside him. 'I wonder how he felt about giving up the Degas a second time?'

Charles shaded his eyes against the slanting sunlight. 'It didn't seem to bother him, but he always was good at hiding his emotions.'

They stood in silence until Anne joined them, dressed in a bathing costume. 'All the others are down at the pool. Are you joining us?'

'I think so,' Gideon replied. Then he turned to Laszlo and Charles. 'By the way, have you heard the news? There's some sort of trouble in Paris. The students were rioting in the Latin Quarter last night.'

It was almost ten o'clock that evening when Anthony Strange, accompanied by Klara, drove from Antibes towards the villa at the Cap. Strange was in such an excellent mood that he did not need any of Klara's stimulants to maintain his elation.

'Do you think Gideon's looking forward to this as much as you are?' Klara asked.

Strange nodded. 'He thinks I'm coming to negotiate the sale of the Degas. His mood will alter when I tell him about the Brueghel.'

'Are you actually going to sell it to them?'

'The Brueghel, yes. There's an art to blackmail. People will only be pushed so far.'

'But you won't have anything to hold over Gideon if you let it go,' said Klara.

Strange tapped her leg. 'I shall still have the Degas. That will always eat away at him.'

They drove through the gates and parked the car in the forecourt. Klara looked up at the façade of the house.

'This used to be the Villa Bronstein,' Strange said, ringing the bell. 'Anne Gideon bought it for a song years ago.'

The door was answered by a housekeeper, who led them along a corridor. At one point, through an open door, they saw a dinner party taking place on the long terrace. Strange smiled grimly when he heard the laughter.

The housekeeper ushered them into a large reception-room where tall uncurtained windows overlooked the sea. It was comfortably furnished, but the pictures on the walls made Strange's throat constrict with excitement. Each was by an Impressionist, and there was hardly a space between them. Like a beggar at a feast, he recognised the Monets, Pissarros, Van Goghs, Gauguins, Manets and Lautrecs.

There were double doors, half-open, leading to another room of similar proportions. 'Look in here,' Klara called softly, and she pushed the doors wider. Here were the modern masters of the early part of the century – Picasso, Cézanne, Matisse, Rouault, Kirchner, Delaunay, Fresnaye, Chagall.

After a silence, Strange turned to Klara with glittering eyes. 'I think our problems are solved,' he whispered.

They heard laughter in the corridor, and Charles, Laszlo and Gideon came in. They appeared to be in high spirits, and none of them took seats.

Gideon approached Strange and came to the point directly. 'Are you prepared to sell me *The Girl in the White Dress*?'

When Strange slowly shook his head, Laszlo exchanged glances with Charles. 'I think you may wish to look at this,' Strange said, taking an envelope from his pocket.

Gideon weighed it in his hand and then turned to a table, where he spread out the contents. Laszlo and Charles gathered round and studied a set of photographs.

'I think you will agree,' Strange said silkily, 'that those are incontrovertible evidence that you forged the Brueghel. I have everything: your preliminary sketches, notes from Nettlebury and the finished work. I shouldn't bother to deny it.'

609

At last Gideon looked up. 'And what are you asking for this material?'

An almost dreamy expression came into Strange's eyes. 'What is it worth?' he asked softly. 'After all, it is the entire reputation of the Archangel Gallery we are talking about.' His words did not seem to be having the effect on Gideon he had expected. 'What kind of offer are you prepared to make?' he asked, suddenly suspicious.

Gideon put his hands in his pockets. 'You'd better hear what I have to say before you become too ambitious, Strange. Do you remember a picture you sold to an American gentleman called Vito Betaluchi?' Strange looked uneasily at Klara. Vito Betaluchi was also known by another name – 'the Meatman' – a title he had earned in his youth that was supposed to refer to his method of disposing with his opponents.

'I sold Vito Betaluchi one painting. It was called *Homage to Charlie Parker*,' Strange said quickly, 'and was absolutely genuine.'

Gideon nodded. 'I know it's genuine, but suppose I were to tell you that I could have that picture removed from Mr Betaluchi's collection, with all the attendant publicity that would entail, and demand fifty per cent of its market value?'

Strange's eyes flicked round the room. 'You're bluffing!' he said, but a note of uncertainty had entered his voice.

'No, I'm not, Strange,' Gideon said flatly. 'Look at this.' He nodded to Charles, who had moved to a small cinema projector against one of the walls. Strange had barely noticed it.

The lights were dimmed, and Strange and Klara watched a short silent film. It showed two figures, Van Duren and Richard Cleary, in the fading light of a Long Island afternoon. Both, stripped to the waist, were painting the same canvas with equal gusto. The picture was undoubtedly *Homage to Charlie Parker*.

When the film was finished, Charles turned on the lights again, and Gideon smiled sympathetically at Strange. 'Certainly the law would uphold your proof that I painted the Brueghel. But it would also support the claim by Richard Cleary's estate that they owned half the picture you sold to Betaluchi.' He paused. 'And Mr Betaluchi and his friends have unpleasant ways of settling scores.'

Strange felt a powerful pressure about the heart, as though two great hands were squeezing the contents of his chest cavity. The bile rose in his throat and his hands began to tremble. He wanted to throw himself at Gideon and tear at his face with his hands. Instead, he forced a giddy smile and clenched one hand with another.

It was Klara who broke the silence. 'Why don't you do a deal?' she

610

said. 'You both have ways to ruin each other.'

An hour later Strange and Klara were in the car returning to Antibes. They drove without speaking, and Strange's mood was no longer euphoric.

'You got more than I expected,' Klara said eventually, but Strange did not answer.

When he stopped the car outside the apartment, he gripped the wheel, and said, 'They underestimate me. They'll learn!'

Inside, he took a mixture of pills and vodka and then put a call through to Paris. Schneider answered. 'Listen carefully,' said Strange. 'The plan has altered.'

'Things are bad here,' said Schneider. 'Have you seen the news?'

'Don't interrupt!' Strange answered. 'I want you to write all this down. Bring the Brueghel and all the evidence to the Café Boune in Rue Colbert at exactly eleven o'clock tomorrow night.'

'What's happened?'

'Things have changed,' Strange told him. 'They have something on us. Just do as I say. Bring the Brueghel and the pistol that's in the third drawer of the filing cabinet in the office.'

'Must I?' Schneider said doubtfully. 'There are riots here; it's dangerous to go out.'

'Do as I say,' Strange said, in a voice full of menace. 'Let the police worry about the students.'

'Are you going to give him the evidence?' Schneider asked.

'What do you think? Just be there.'

When Strange and Klara had departed, Charles, Laszlo and Gideon rejoined the others on the terrace.

'How did it work out?' Frazer asked.

'We're leaving for Paris in two hours,' said Gideon.

'All of us?' Elizabeth asked.

Laszlo shook his head. 'Strange is picking us up in a lorry. Just Gideon and me.'

'What did you settle for?' Anne asked.

Gideon smiled. 'We get the Degas and the Brueghel. Strange gets half the pictures in the house, and the film of Richard Cleary and Van Duren painting *Homage to Charlie Parker*.'

'I thought he'd want more,' said Elizabeth.

Laszlo smiled. 'We drove a hard bargain.'

'Will he leave the Degas here?' Anne asked.

611

Gideon shook his head. 'We exchange everything in Paris tomorrow night.'

At two in the morning, Strange returned with the lorry. The Degas was already crated in the back. The men loaded the pictures that had been agreed on, and by three they were heading for Avignon on the first stage of their journey to Paris. They were to take it in turns to drive.

In the beginning there was a strained mood in the cabin, but gradually the numbing monotony of the drive caused all three of them to take refuge in their private thoughts. They stopped for petrol and a brief meal at a workmen's café shortly after dawn.

It was late evening when they reached the outskirts of Paris and were halted by a long traffic jam, caused by a police road-block. Only essential traffic was being allowed into the city. After an angry exchange conducted by Strange, which culminated in a handful of money being thrust into the hands of the senior policeman, they were allowed to continue.

Everything seemed normal enough at first, although the roads were more deserted than usual, but slowly they saw more and more police. As they approached the Cimetière de Montparnasse, the roads were choked with riot vans and prison vehicles. Charabancs full of gendarmes and state security police were parked at the roadside; the bored young men watched them pass with little interest. Then they began to smell burning, and the air was filled with drifting smoke. A few moments later they saw the ruined husks of cars. The streets here were strewn with rubble and broken glass, and ahead they could see the glow of fires in the sky. There were only armed police on the streets and hardly any civilian cars.

'This looks bad,' said Laszlo. It was the first any of them had spoken since the argument at the road-block. 'I don't think the Café Boune will be open,' he added.

'Schneider will be there, nevertheless,' said Strange.

By now they had turned into the familiar surroundings of the Boulevard St-Germain, but nothing was the same. Cafés, cinemas and restaurants were shuttered. Most of the shops were in darkness. Burned-out vehicles were lit by the street lamps and the harsh glare from the headlights of police vans. And there was a new scent; sweet and acrid, it drifted through the open windows of the lorry and reminded Gideon of peardrops he had eaten as a boy. Then their eyes began to sting and burn.

612

'Tear-gas,' said Strange.

As they drove slowly forward, a group of police marched by in long leather overcoats, carrying long batons. Strange, who was driving, made a move to enter the Rue Colbert, but it was blocked by a company of security police with plastic riot-shields. An officer held up a hand and came to the door. Just then a shower of cobblestones rained through the air and bounced off the shields of the police. One managed to penetrate the defences, and the figure who was struck in the face was quickly dragged away by his companions.

'I wouldn't go down there,' said the officer. 'There's a group of students holed up.'

'Bastards!' Strange said with feeling. 'Look, we've got to, officer. We have a valuable load here and we must get it off the streets.'

'Show me,' said the officer.

Strange slid from the seat and opened the rear doors. Satisfied that there were no weapons or reinforcements for the students in the Rue Colbert, the officer held a hurried conference with a colleague. 'Okay,' he said finally. 'You can go down there, but drive slowly.'

Laszlo looked at Gideon. 'They're going to use us for cover.'

Gideon nodded. 'They don't want to use a police vehicle. The street's too narrow. Too easy to ambush.'

'Are you scared?' Strange said impatiently.

'Just as long as you understand the danger,' Gideon pointed out.

'Right!' the police officer called out. 'If I bang on the side, stop.'

Strange edged forward into the pitch-dark of the narrow curving street. The lorry's headlights cut through the blackness for a moment and then, after a few yards, there were two splintering crashes and the lights were extinguished.

Now they were aware of darting figures each side of the lorry. Suddenly there were shouts and the sounds of clashes behind. They could just make out the shapes of the police retreating into the Boulevard St-Germain, silhouetted by the light in the main thoroughfare. Strange shone his powerful torch ahead, through the window. The wavering beam picked out the doorway of the Café Boune and the crouching figure of Schneider. But there were other scuttling figures around. Strange seemed unaware of the danger. He stopped the lorry and climbed down from the cabin.

'We'd better get out of this,' Gideon said, and he and Laszlo also got down into the street.

Gradually their eyes became accustomed to the gloom, and they

613

saw that Strange had reached Schneider. He took something from the crouching figure and turned to Laszlo and Gideon. He was about to speak, when a dark figure with a handkerchief tied across his face took him by the arm.

'Well done, comrade,' a youthful voice said, pitched high with excitement. 'We need the lorry for the barricade.' A girl was climbing into the cabin.

Gideon took Laszlo's arm and guided him to the other side of the street. Strange pulled himself away from the youth and hurried forward to the girl in the cabin, who was searching for the ignition keys. Other figures grouped round the vehicle, and shouts came from the entrance near the boulevard: 'They're coming! They're attacking!' There was the sound of running feet, and people began to jostle past Gideon and Laszlo.

Strange had walked swiftly back to the driver's door. 'Get down!' he shouted, but the girl ignored him. He looked back to where three youths were syphoning petrol from the tank into wine bottles. 'Get away! All of you!' he screamed, waving something at the girl.

'We need this, comrade,' the young voice said again angrily.

Strange thrust his arm forward, and there was the report of a pistol. Then he reached out and pulled the body of the young girl from the cabin.

The youths syphoning petrol looked up in confusion, and the running voices called, 'They're coming! They're coming!'

Gideon could feel panic sweeping about them in the confined space.

'Get away!' Strange screamed at the youths at the petrol tank, and he raised the pistol and fired twice. One of the boys fell. Strange pulled himself into the cabin and scrabbled for the keys.

Gideon was about to move forward, but Laszlo held his arm. The lorry coughed into life again, and one of the youths holding a bottle full of petrol calmly stuffed a strip of material into its neck. He put a match to it as the lorry lurched forward, and with a long overarm motion lobbed the Molotov cocktail. It was a lucky shot. It hit one of the lorry's supporting struts and exploded in a bright sheet of flame. The sudden inferno forced Strange to swerve against a wall, trapping him in the cabin.

By now the flames had reached the paintings. Canvas, oil paint and gilded wood burned hungrily. They could still hear Strange screaming when the petrol tank caught.

'My God! My God!' a voice called out beside them. It was

614

Schneider, carrying a bulky package. Gideon grabbed it and threw it on the flames. Schneider stared at them, panic in his face, then scuttled away towards the advancing police.

EPILOGUE

It was a Friday evening; the Archangel Gallery would shortly close
for the week. Gideon stood at the window of the flat and looked
down at the crowds hurrying home. He was in a reflective mood.
Sometimes the memory of Paris returned, and he was filled with
sadness, but he told himself not to be sentimental, to consider the
advantages that had come from the destruction of the lorry. It did
not always work. It was a form of grief, Laszlo said; gradually time
would heal the wound. But his thoughts still returned to the smiling
girl in the meadow and the night of her destruction.

Laszlo had led them away from the police in the Rue Colbert. It
seemed almost second nature to him to escape danger; Gideon
wondered how many times he had managed similar journeys during
his days in Berlin. Eventually they had made their way back to the
south of France, but Gideon was a sadder man. He had begun to feel
older in the last few weeks. The girls who worked in the gallery said
that he smiled less than he used to.

As he looked down now, a shooting brake stopped, and someone
went into the gallery, but it was impossible to identify him. A late
shopper, he imagined, wanting something for a wedding
anniversary or a birthday. Then he saw something being unloaded
from the car, but he took no interest. He crossed the room and
poured himself a drink. Sitting down in an armchair near the
fireplace, he picked up a book he had been reading the night before.

After a few minutes, Anne came in. 'Guess who's downstairs?' she
said, smiling. 'Smudger.'

'Really? Why didn't you ask him up?'

'He said he'd rather stay in the gallery,' Anne explained. 'He
wants to buy a present for his wife.'

Gideon put the book aside. 'Well, I'd better pop down and see
him.'

Smudger was the only customer on the premises, and most of the staff had left. He looked up and winked when he saw Gideon approaching. 'How about a discount on this one?' He gestured towards a large Van Duren that dominated the wall.

Gideon waved to a soft leather armchair, and they sat down and gossiped about family matters until the last of the staff had gone home.

Smudger looked around. 'So tell me what really happened in Paris,' he said. 'Did all them paintings go up in smoke?'

'Only one of any value.'

'Go on!' said Smudger. 'I heard it was a big collection. Impressionists and everything.'

Gideon shook his head. 'They were all fakes, except for *The Girl in the White Dress*.'

'Fakes?' Smudger repeated.

'Henri Bronstein collected them. He'd had them bricked up in the corner of the cellar in 1940. During the war, the place was taken over by Germans as a convalescent home for wounded officers. They never found them.'

'Go on!' Smudger said again.

Gideon smiled. 'When we discovered Anne had bought the place, Laszlo and I excavated the collection again.'

'And you hung 'em on the walls?'

'Terrible place for art robberies, the south of France! We decided we'd be safer with them than the real article.'

Smudger sat back and laughed. 'So they was all fakes?'

'Everything but the Degas,' Gideon said ruefully.

Smudger tapped him on the knee. 'I got a bit of a surprise for you, son.' Gideon waited expectantly as his friend lit a cigarette. 'Did you hear Ted Peake died?' he said eventually. Gideon nodded. 'Bad heart,' Smudger said. 'He came to my place for a holiday. That's where it happened.'

'So I heard.'

'Funny bloke, Ted. Hated income tax, but said he believed in paying his dues.' Smudger puffed away for a moment. 'Did you ever know a bloke called Ovington?'

'Oh, yes,' Gideon replied. 'Very well.'

Smudger looked up at the ceiling. 'Well, Ted had the dead needle with Anthony Strange. It seems he and a bloke called Jack Stapoulas pulled a nasty trick on him over some paintings. Ted found out that this bloke called Ovington was highly prized by Strange, so Ted nicked him. It seems Ovington did a little job for Peake before he died.' Gideon looked at him with a sudden lurch of hope in his heart. Smudger grinned, and stood up. 'That's right,' he said. 'Well, I must be off. Go and take a look downstairs.'

Anne, who had returned to the gallery, watched Gideon walk through the showroom. The lights led him to the basement. She waited for a long time and then followed him down the stairs, where he was seated on a stool in the centre of the big room. Before him was *The Girl in the White Dress*. She came and stood beside him. Without taking his eyes off the picture, he reached out for her hand. 'Not bad for an eighty-year-old, is she?' he said softly.

'Very beautiful. Now you've got everything you ever wanted.'

Gideon shook his head and smiled at her. 'No, I'll never have everything,' he said in the same quiet voice. He gestured towards the picture. 'What he had, I'll never have.' He stood up. 'I can see any other picture in the world and know just how the artist felt when he painted it. But this one . . . ' He shrugged. 'It's different.' He touched the surface lightly with his fingertips. 'For one moment in time, he saw this vision and he created something perfect.' He smiled sadly. 'When he made this, he flew like an angel.' Then he turned to Anne again. 'All I could do was flutter on the ground. I only had one wing.'

'Is that what you wanted?' she asked. 'To be up there with the angels?'

'Just for a moment. Most of the time I like it down here.' He said, and then he encircled her with his arms.